Trouble at Wild River

Adventures of the Northwoods

1. *The Disappearing Stranger*
2. *The Hidden Message*
3. *The Creeping Shadows*
4. *The Vanishing Footprints*
5. *Trouble at Wild River*
6. *The Mysterious Hideaway*
7. *Grandpa's Stolen Treasure*
8. *The Runaway Clown*
9. *Mystery of the Missing Map*

TROUBLE AT WILD RIVER

Lois Walfrid Johnson

BETHANY HOUSE PUBLISHERS
MINNEAPOLIS, MINNESOTA 55438

Big Gust Anderson, Gust Berglund, Walfrid and Edla Johnson, John Peterson, Steven and Edith Powell, and Charles and Hannah Saunders lived in the Grantsburg/St. Croix River area during the early 1900s. Except for the location of the maple trees tapped, Katherine Cloud is based on the historic Katherine Cloud who lived on the Trade River. All other characters in this book are fictitious. Any resemblance to persons living or dead is coincidental. The geographic locations are accurate with the exception of Sand Creek, which is fictitious.

Cover illustration by Andrea Jorgenson.

Copyright © 1991
Lois Walfrid Johnson
All Rights Reserved

Published by Bethany House Publishers
A Ministry of Bethany Fellowship, Inc.
6820 Auto Club Road, Minneapolis, Minnesota 55438

Printed in the United States of America

Library of Congress Cataloging-in-Publication Data

Johnson, Lois Walfrid.
    Trouble at Wild River / Lois W. Johnson.
        p. cm. — (The Adventures of the northwoods ; bk. 5)
    Summary: In 1907 in Wisconsin, Kate and her friends discover a timber swindler while visiting their Indian friend Joe and suspect that Kate's uncle, newly arrived from Sweden, may be involved.

    [1. Swedish Americans—Fiction. 2. Logging—Fiction. 3. Wisconsin—Fiction. 4. Uncles—Fiction. 5. Indians of North America—Fiction. 6. Christian life—Fiction. 7. Mystery and detective stories.] I. Title. II. Series: Johnson, Lois Walfrid. Adventures of the northwoods ; bk. 5.
PZ7.J63255Tr 1991
[Fic]—dc20   91–26802
ISBN 1–55661–144–7   CIP
                                                                        AC

To Jeff and Cynthia
Daniel and Justin

with my love and appreciation
for the way you are.

LOIS WALFRID JOHNSON is the bestselling author of more than twenty books. These include *You're Worth More Than You Think!* and other Gold Medallion winners in the LET'S-TALK-ABOUT-IT STORIES FOR KIDS series about making choices. Novels in the ADVENTURES OF THE NORTHWOODS series have received awards from Excellence in Media, the Wisconsin State Historical Society, and the Council for Wisconsin Writers.

Lois has a great interest in historical mystery novels, as you may be able to tell! She and her husband, Roy, are the parents of a blended family and live in rural Wisconsin.

In the time in which this book was set the Native Americans in the St. Croix Band of northwest Wisconsin were called Chippewa. In recent years many are once again using the name of Ojibwa (Oh-JIB-wah).

Contents

1. Mysterious Noises 11
2. The Timber Swindler 17
3. Kate Decides 23
4. Surprise for Mama 31
5. Papa's Warning 37
6. Growing Evidence 45
7. The Stranger 53
8. Sand Creek 63
9. Lonely Meeting 71
10. More Trouble 77
11. The Wild River 85
12. Another Warning 93
13. Fight for Life 99
14. Which Way Now? 107
15. Caught Between! 115
16. The Black Hat 121
17. Moonlit Terror 129
18. Close Call 137
19. One Step Forward 143
20. New Beginning 149

1

Mysterious Noises

*I*n the glow of the lantern Katherine O'Connell's deep blue eyes sparkled. As she brushed aside the black hair escaping her braid, she looked ahead. Wildfire, the mare, trotted easily over the patches of snow, pulling the farm wagon in which Kate rode.

Far above, a lopsided moon lit the sky. On that cloudless March night the stars shone brightly, seeming just beyond the treetops. Sitting between her stepbrother Anders and her friend Erik Lundgren, Kate felt warm and safe.

Then, as Anders turned Wildfire onto a trail through the woods, an owl hooted. From off in the distance the call came— each note a lonesome cry. Kate shivered, but not from cold.

As the mare stretched out her legs, long shadows fell across the path. Like pointing fingers, pine branches reached toward the wagon, almost touching Kate.

Soon the call came again. *Whoo, whoo, whoo, whoo—whoo, whoo, whoo, whoo-ah!*

"That's not an owl," said Erik in the quiet that followed.

"It isn't?" asked Kate. "Then what is it?"

"Someone signaling." The lantern Erik held cast a flickering light on his wavy brown hair. But certainty filled his eyes. "Shhhhh!"

Anders reined in the mare, and the hooting seemed closer this time.

"It's a barred owl," Anders said as the call faded away.

"No, it's not." Erik sounded sure of himself. "It's someone talking through the woods."

Anders laughed. "I thought Kate was the one with a big imagination."

"She is," said Erik. "This isn't imagination. It's real."

"Yah, sure," Anders told him. "You betcha." He flicked the reins across Wildfire's back, and the mare stepped out.

But Kate felt curious. "Erik, how do you know? Why do you think it's not an owl?"

"I can't explain it," he answered. "I just hear the difference."

As Wildfire trotted on, Kate stared into the darkness, hoping to catch a glimpse of a large owl. Yet she knew Erik was seldom wrong. His ability in music helped him recognize other sounds as well.

"If it's not an owl, what is it?" Kate asked.

"You mean *who* is it," said Anders. "*Who* is creeping around in the depths of night? *Who* is ready to snatch you from this wagon?"

"Oh, Anders!" Since coming to northwest Wisconsin, Kate had fought against her fear of the nighttime woods. Yet she didn't want to admit that fear to this stepbrother who was also thirteen. Like Erik, Anders was six feet tall and broad-shouldered from farm work.

Pretending she wasn't afraid, Kate gazed up into branches still without leaves from winter. No large owl flew from tree to tree.

In that March of 1907, the northwest Wisconsin days had been warm. Yet the nights dropped below freezing, providing perfect weather for a strong flow of sap from the sugar maples. For two weeks farmers and their families had worked hard, collecting the thin sap and boiling it down.

Dark came early to these woods, and Kate felt concerned that she'd miss what she wanted to see. "You're sure Joe's grandmother will still be making syrup?" Kate looked forward to meeting the Chippewa family.

"Yup," Anders told her. "He said his grandma would work late. She'll be finishing up for the day."

Joe's grandparents owned a farm on Trade River. Anders and Erik had known the Indian boy for some time, but Kate was new to the area. A year before, her mother had married Anders' father, and Mama and Kate moved from Minneapolis to Windy Hill Farm.

"Why does the Cloud family use trees near here?" Kate asked.

"They don't have sugar maples on their own land," Erik told her. "Usually they tap trees closer to home. This year Mrs. Cloud asked a farmer near Big Wood Lake if she could use his maples. When she gets done, she'll give him syrup and candy."

A grin crossed her brother's face. "You know, Kate, you can help Joe with all the work. That is, if you can keep up to him."

By now Kate knew Anders well enough to see through most of his teasing. Still she was curious. "What does he do?"

"Gathers wood to keep the fire going. Collects pails filled with sap. Brings 'em in to the fire."

"It's hard work," said Erik. "Joe's brothers help too. They start when the sap begins running in the morning and keep on till it slows down at night."

As Anders turned the mare into the ruts of yet another trail, Kate asked, "Where are you going?"

Anders flicked the reins. "Taking a shortcut along the lake."

"With all the warm weather, it might be mucky in there," Erik warned.

Anders acted as if he didn't hear. Before long, the trees on either side of the path thinned out.

Again Wildfire slowed her pace and stepped gingerly. Suddenly she sank knee-deep into mud.

Nervously the mare tossed her head. Anders clucked to her.

"You're all right," Anders called, his voice soothing. "C'mon, girl. Giddyup!"

Wildfire turned her ears to the sound of his voice and lunged into the harness. The wagon jerked forward as the wheels churned through the mud.

As they moved more and more slowly, Kate grew impatient. "We'll be too late!" she said to Anders.

Her tall, blond brother paid no attention. At last they came to an open area with no trees. Here and there patches of snow remained on the ice of Big Wood Lake.

A large black heap loomed up in the darkness. Soon Kate saw more dark shapes along the shore. As they drew closer, she realized what they were—great piles of neatly stacked logs.

During the winter, farmers around the lake worked hard, cutting trees on their land. By selling the logs to a large company, the men earned money they needed for their families.

"When the ice goes out, the farmers will open the dam," Erik said. He pointed into the darkness. "The logs will go out of Big Wood Lake, through the dam, and down the Wood River to the St. Croix."*

Kate knew that the St. Croix River marked the border between Wisconsin and Minnesota. Once there, the logs floated downstream to sawmills at Stillwater, Minnesota.

Just then Anders stopped the mare, turned his head, and listened.

Quickly Erik blew out the flame of the lantern. "Shhhhh!" he warned.

Anders slipped to the ground and slogged forward in the mud. Standing by Wildfire's head, he laid his hand on her neck.

A moment later Kate heard what she'd missed before. From a short distance away came a strange sound. What was it?

When Erik dropped down, she knew he'd heard the same thing. Kate followed him, leaping over the mud in the track to walk on firmer ground near the trees.

Soon she caught up to her brother. He stood still, as though

---

*The river that divides Minnesota and Wisconsin is pronounced "Saint *Kroy*."

listening. When Wildfire moved restlessly, Anders laid his fingers across the mare's muzzle.

In the stillness Kate heard the mysterious noise again.

Wildfire stomped her foot. Anders quieted her, then led her off the path. In the light of the moon Kate saw him tie the mare's lead rope to a tree. Lowering her head, Wildfire began eating the brown grass that reached through the little snow that remained.

When Anders returned to them, Erik took the lead. By now Kate felt curious. What was going on? Why were the boys being so careful? She felt afraid to speak, even in a whisper.

Erik reached the first pile of logs and waited until Kate and Anders caught up. Though the boys were six feet tall, the logs towered above them. From somewhere beyond, the sound came clearly.

Then Erik moved on, a shadow darker than those around him. As Kate and Anders followed, the soft ground deadened their footsteps. When they reached the next pile of logs, they again stopped to listen.

This time Kate recognized the sound of sawing wood. But why would anyone work in the dark? What was he trying to hide?

Pushing aside her uneasiness, Kate followed Erik to the third pile of logs. This one was smaller. In spite of her short height, Kate looked over it.

Not far away, a lantern sat on the ground. The light of its flame reflected on a nearby saw.

A man dressed in dark clothes crouched close to still another pile of logs. He worked quickly, filling a gunnysack with slices of wood from the ground.

When the sack bulged, the man closed and tied it. Then he picked up a tool with a wooden handle. *What is it?* Kate wondered. *An ax?*

As the man moved closer to the lantern, Kate had a better look at the tool he was using. It seemed different from an ax— more like a small sledgehammer.

Taking a stand near the end of the logs, he swung the hammer. In the crisp night air, iron thudded against wood. Again and again the man swung, striking the end of one log after another.

After a time he straightened up. Turning his head, he seemed to listen. In that instant Wildfire whinnied.

The man leaped over to the lantern and blew out the flame. In the darkness running footsteps were heard. Then all was quiet.

Kate blinked, struggling to see beyond the small flame that danced before her eyes. Anders darted forward, and she followed.

Erik took one way, Kate another, and Anders a third, searching as quickly as they could without a light. Yet they found no dark shape kneeling down, trying to hide within the shelter of the logs. Whoever had been there was gone.

Then Kate heard a noise farther off. "Over there!" she called.

As she ran in that direction, she rounded a great pile of logs. One log stuck out farther than the others and caught her in the chest. Kate's arms flew up, and she fell backward into the darkness of night.

2

The Timber Swindler

*T*he next instant Kate landed hard. *I can't breathe*, she thought. *I can't catch my breath.*

For what seemed an eternity she lay still, too stunned to move. Then Erik called, "Kate, where are you?"

She heard his voice, but could not respond.

Erik kneeled down, close to her head. "What happened? Are you hurt?"

But Kate couldn't answer.

"Knocked the wind out of her," Anders said.

Kate groaned and finally drew a long, ragged breath. From a short distance away she heard a quick movement. Was the man escaping?

Then Kate felt the dampness of the ground on which she lay. The cold crept through her long stockings and dress.

Turning her head, she opened her eyes. In the light of the moon she saw how scared Erik and Anders looked.

Erik helped her sit up.

"What were you doing?" demanded Anders. "Don't you know that's a good way to get hurt?"

Kate flinched at the sound of her brother's voice. It made no difference that he always talked that way when he was upset. Listening to him, Kate felt even worse.

"I got hurt all right," she muttered when she could speak.

"I mean *really* hurt," Anders grumbled. "What were you thinking, running after that man? What if he decided to go after *you*?"

She hadn't been thinking, Kate knew that. She just wanted to make sure the man didn't get away. Yet she didn't care to admit her mistake to Anders.

Slowly she stood up. Bending over, she tried to brush the dirt off her coat and long stockings.

As she wavered, Erik caught her hand. "Be quiet, Anders," he said. "She knows it was a dumb move."

"Dumb, was it?" Kate was returning to normal. She dropped Erik's hand, wanting no more of his help.

Anders hurried to the wagon and returned with the farm lantern. Erik lit it again, and the two boys searched the area. After studying the ends of the logs, they walked in a circle, holding out the light.

Soon the lantern bobbed away. Kate started to follow, then realized she still felt shaken from the jarring she'd taken.

As the light disappeared, Kate trembled. Were the boys finding footprints in the soft ground? She didn't like being all alone. What if the man came back?

When the minutes stretched long, Kate returned to the wagon and climbed up to the high spring seat. Looking about, she gazed up at the night sky and the lopsided moon. Right now she'd welcome an owl with its large feathery body passing between the tall trees.

A cold wind blew from the lake, and she huddled beneath a blanket. From somewhere behind, a branch snapped. Kate jumped.

She twisted around, and the glow of a lantern pierced the darkness. Two dark shapes separated from the trees. When Anders and Erik stepped out, Kate felt relieved.

"We followed quite a ways," Erik told her. "But we lost him when the ground got firm."

The two boys climbed into the wagon, and Anders clucked to Wildfire. As they started off once more, he looked down at Kate. "Because of you, that man got away."

"Because of *me*!" Kate exclaimed. Sitting up, she flipped her long braid over her shoulder. "Because of Wildfire, you mean. She whinnied."

"If you hadn't landed flat on your face, we could have kept up with him," Anders said.

It was true, Kate knew, and she probably felt sorrier than anyone. Already she felt better and as curious as usual. "What was that man doing?"

"Stealing logs," Anders growled.

"Stealing logs? How do you know?"

"Remember the sawing we heard?" Erik asked. "The man was cutting thin slices off the end of each log. Looked like he had a gunnysack—"

"For picking up the slices," Kate said. Until now, she hadn't understood all that was happening. She knew only that whatever the man was doing, it had to be wrong. He was trying too hard to keep it a secret.

"Why did he hit the logs with a sledgehammer?" she asked.

"It wasn't a sledge." Anders urged Wildfire ahead. Here the trail was firmer, and the mare moved faster.

"It's a smaller hammer," said Erik. "It's smaller and lighter and called a stamp hammer. On both sides of the iron head there's a raised design that makes a mark."

"Like the brand ranchers use on cattle?"

"Sort of. But ranchers use a hot iron to mark an animal's hide. Loggers pound their mark on the end of a log."

As the boys talked, Kate learned that every farmer who sent logs down the river, as well as every logging company, had their own special mark. In the light of the lantern she saw Erik's eyes.

"Loggers get paid according to how many logs come in with their mark," he explained.

"So the man is a timber swindler," Kate said slowly. "He pretends something that isn't his belongs to him."

Erik nodded. "And the farmers who work hard cutting down

trees won't get paid for their logs. It's the same as stealing money from them."

Kate breathed deeply, and knew she was back to normal. At the same time, just thinking about the swindler made her afraid. What would he try to do next?

Before long, Erik leaped down from the wagon to open a gate. In the pasture through which they passed, the woods thinned out. A fire glowed in the darkness.

As they drew closer, Kate saw four upright poles at the corners of the fire. Between them stretched other poles that crossed above the flames. From this framework a number of chains hung down. One held a huge iron kettle. Other chains held smaller kettles and pails.

An Indian woman wearing a long dress stirred the contents of the largest kettle. When Anders stopped Wildfire, a slender youth of about fourteen came forward.

"Joe, meet Kate," Anders said.

In the light of the lantern the boy grinned. With black hair and dancing black eyes, he looked athletic and strong.

"C'mon with us," Anders told him. As Wildfire trotted through the pasture into the farmyard, Joe ran next to the wagon.

At the hitching rail Kate climbed down and started for the house. Erik stayed close by and made sure she felt all right.

When Anders knocked, young children opened the door and went to find their father.

"Come in," the man said. "We're just having coffee."

In the warm kitchen, Kate saw another man and two women at the round table. As they looked her way, they stopped talking.

Then Kate saw beyond them. A tall man stood along the wall. His head reached more than a foot above the doorway.

"Big Gust!" Kate exclaimed. She was surprised to see the seven-foot, six-inch-tall Swede. "I forgot that your sister lives near here."

As marshall in the nearby village of Grantsburg, Big Gust had helped Kate and Anders solve a mystery more than once. Now a welcome grin lit the giant's face.

"*God dag, god dag,*" he said. It sounded like "Good dog," but Kate knew it was the Swedish hello.

Then Big Gust glanced beyond her to the boys, and his smile faded. Quickly he moved around the table. "What's wrong?" he asked.

For the first time Kate realized how she looked. Small pieces of wood clung to her coat. Here and there smudges of dirt darkened the cloth, as well as her stockings and dress. She stepped back, wishing she could hide.

But Big Gust was already following the boys outside. As Kate joined them, Anders spoke quickly, telling the marshall what had happened.

Big Gust wasted no time. His deep voice rumbled as he said, "Just a minute." When he returned from the house, he wore his coat and brought the two men. The marshall towered over both of them.

Kate and the boys hurried toward Wildfire. As Kate climbed up and sat down on the high seat, Anders spoke sharply. "You're not going with us."

"Yes, I am," answered Kate.

"No, you're not," said her brother.

Then Erik came alongside, and Kate turned to him. "I can go, can't I?"

Erik shook his head. "It's not safe."

Kate couldn't believe what she was hearing. "I was in on the beginning. Why can't I go now?"

Anders climbed up beside her. "This is just for men."

"For men!" Kate sputtered. "You and Erik aren't men!"

"Yah, but we are!" Raising one arm, Anders flexed his muscles.

"We're in a hurry, Kate," said Erik as he waited for her to get down.

Kate glanced toward Joe, who stood a short way off. She felt embarrassed at being treated like a baby. "Why can't I go?" she asked her brother.

"Because you might get hurt again." Erik looked at her steadily.

Knowing that she had no choice, Kate climbed down. She started for the house with her back stiff and straight. Yet when she heard Anders cluck to Wildfire, her curiosity proved too much.

Kate looked around to see the spirited black horse take the lead. Another wagon with Big Gust and the two men followed.

Then Joe bounded across the yard. His feet were swift and light and skimmed the patches of snow. As Anders entered the trail into the woods, the boy caught up and ran alongside.

He runs as swift as a deer, Kate thought as she watched Joe. Already she understood why Anders and Erik liked him.

Then the wagons disappeared from sight. Again Kate longed to be with them, to see what was happening. Had the timber swindler returned to the logs? Or was he, even now, hiding somewhere among the trees?

3

Kate Decides

*T*rying to push aside her disappointment, Kate followed the trail the wagons had taken out of the farmyard. With each step she wondered where the swindler was now. Then she wondered about the men and boys. *Are they headed into danger?*

Walking quickly through the pasture, Kate soon saw flames leaping upward in the darkness. In spite of everything that had happened, she felt excited about watching Joe's family make syrup.

When she reached the fire, she found children of all sizes gathered around Joe's grandmother. Eagerly they waited for the syrup to boil down into candy.

As Kate watched, Mrs. Cloud took smaller pails from chains hanging above the sides of the fire. From these she poured sap into the large black kettle hanging over the center.

Erik had told Kate it took more than thirty pails of sap—perhaps even forty—to make one pail of syrup. But that was all she knew.

"How do you get sap from the trees?" Kate asked Mrs. Cloud.

The grandmother looked her way without speaking. Yet Kate felt sure that she heard.

Kate opened her mouth to speak again and just as quickly closed it. As though it were yesterday, she remembered her first day at Spirit Lake School. She'd been the only one unable to speak Swedish. Now she wondered, *Does Mrs. Cloud speak a language I don't understand?* Kate wished she knew the words to use.

"I'm Katherine O'Connell," she said finally.

Mrs. Cloud pointed to herself. "Katherine."

Kate felt confused. "Katherine O'Connell," she repeated, pointing to her own self.

The grandmother broke into a smile. "Katherine Cloud," she said.

"Really?" Kate asked. "*You're* Katherine too?"

Her eyes sparkling with laughter, Mrs. Cloud nodded.

Just then a boy of nine or ten brought in wood for the fire. A younger boy carried pails filled with sap. As Kate watched, he emptied the sap into a large stock tank.

Mrs. Cloud spoke to the older of the two boys, using another language. When the grandmother finished speaking, the boy turned to Kate.

"Mamana speaks Chippewa," he said in English.

"*Mamana?*" Kate asked. It was a new word for her.

"It means *my mother*," he explained. "Our mother calls our grandmother that, and so do we. What do you want?"

Again Kate wished she knew the language. She felt grateful someone could translate. "I want to know how she makes maple syrup and candy."

Turning back to Mamana, he spoke rapidly. When Mrs. Cloud glanced toward the woods, the boy gave Kate a couple of pails and took one for himself. Carrying a farm lantern, he headed for the trees.

"Who are you?" Kate asked, as she followed him.

"I'm Peter," he said. Though shorter than Kate, he seemed taller because of the way he carried himself.

Soon they reached the sugar maples. Holding out the lantern, Peter explained how they cut a diagonal slit in each tree from which they collected sap. They inserted a small narrow trough just below the newly made opening.

The sap had stopped dripping for the night, but Kate saw a clear thin liquid in the birchbark container below the wooden trough.

Peter explained that not everyone tapped trees in this way. Some families pushed out the soft center of a sumac branch to use a tube instead of a trough.

The boy went from tree to tree. Each time he found a full container, he poured the sap into one of the pails they carried.

"You're Joe's brother?" Kate asked, as they started back to the others.

When Peter nodded, his eyes glowed with pride. "Joe runs miles without stopping."

"Miles?" asked Kate, curious how far Joe could go.

"Many, many miles," Peter said. "He runs faster than anyone I know."

Kate was sure that Peter's pride was more than a young boy bragging about his older brother. "Are you a good runner too?" she asked.

"Not as fast as Joe," Peter answered. "But I will be."

For the rest of the way, he told her everything he knew about his big brother. As she listened to Peter, Kate wondered what had happened to Joe and Erik and Anders. Why were they taking so long?

When Kate and Peter reached the fire, they emptied the sap they carried into the large stock tank. Then they joined the children gathered around Mrs. Cloud.

Before long the grandmother strained the syrup she had cooked down and filled several large containers. Using a long paddle, she continued stirring the contents of the biggest kettle. When the syrup thickened even more, the moment the children had been waiting for arrived.

With a wooden ladle, Mrs. Cloud poured some of the thick syrup into small containers. She poured other syrup into a clean patch of snow. Soon the snow hardened the syrup into candy.

The minute it was cool enough to eat, Peter gave Kate a piece. As her mouth closed around the maple candy, she wondered if she had ever tasted anything so delicious.

When she finished eating, Kate walked over to the woman who still worked by the fire. "Mrs. Cloud," she said. "Mrs. *Katherine* Cloud."

A glint of laughter lit the grandmother's eyes.

"The candy is very good," said Kate, and she was sure Mamana understood.

By the time the wagons returned, it was late. "We'll post a watch every night," Kate heard one of the men say to Big Gust.

"Hop in!" Anders told Kate.

"What happened?" she asked, as they headed back over the trail.

"Nothing." Anders sounded tired and discouraged.

"What do you mean?"

"We stopped quite a ways off and left the horses. But there must have been a bear around—"

"A bear?" When Kate lived in Minneapolis her friend Sarah Livingston told her there would be bears in these woods. Ever since moving to northwest Wisconsin, Kate had expected to see one.

"Whatever it was, it spooked the horses," Anders said. "One of the men stayed with them, but right after we left, Wildfire started thrashing around. She snorted and made all kinds of noises. I ran back to her, but it was too late."

"Too late for what?"

Anders sighed. "If the timber swindler came back, he sure wasn't around when we got there. He had plenty of time to clean up anything we missed."

"Whoever the man is, he's mighty tricky," said Erik. "And dangerous."

"Did the owl hoot again?" Kate asked.

"Yup," Erik told her. "But this time it was real."

"Oh, Erik! Are you sure you can tell the difference?"

"I'm sure," Erik said quietly. "Even Anders agreed with me."

When they pulled into the Windy Hill farmyard, the boys worked together to unhitch Wildfire.

As Anders headed toward the barn, Kate spoke softly, hoping

he wouldn't hear. "I'm sorry, Erik. I'm sorry that the swindler got away because of me."

"That's all right," he said. "Any one of us could have fallen." Anders turned back. "We could have, but we didn't."

A surge of anger rushed through Kate. Flipping her long braid over her shoulder, she hurried off. By the time she reached the kitchen door, she'd made up her mind. From now on, she'd do her best not to be left out of anything. From now on, she'd prove to Anders she could keep up with him or any other boy.

At breakfast the next morning Kate and Anders told the Nordstrom family about the timber swindler. As they sat around the kitchen table, they spoke in English. Yet five-year-old Tina, who had not yet learned English in school, seemed to understand. With white-blond hair wisping around her face, she looked from Kate to Anders, her blue eyes wide.

Nine-year-old Lars listened to every word without speaking. As usual, a tuft of red hair stood up at the back of his head. Beneath his freckles, he still looked pale from his bout with pneumonia.

Except for a question now and then, Mama remained silent. Even this early in the day, she had combed her golden hair upward, piling it on top of her head.

Mama's pretty, thought Kate. Her mother moved slowly these days. Beneath Mama's large apron and the blue dress that matched her eyes, the baby she expected had grown large.

As Anders talked, Kate watched her mother. Though it had been just a year ago, it seemed a long time since she and Mama lived in Minneapolis. It was even longer since Daddy O'Connell died in a construction accident. But Kate remembered those days well. She remembered how often she woke up to hear Mama crying in the night.

Now whenever Mama looked at Papa Nordstrom, her eyes seemed to glow. Even her smile looked soft.

When Anders finished talking, Papa had the most questions.

With a frown on his bearded face, he asked Anders to go back over the details.

"You actually saw the man cut off an end from each log?"

"We couldn't see that, but we heard it," Anders said. "We watched him put thin slices of wood into a sack. We think he stirred the dirt around, because we couldn't find sawdust."

"And there was a new mark on the end of the logs?"

"You betcha," said Anders. "When we went back, Big Gust and the other men checked the mark. None of the farmers who log around there use the one we saw."

"Well, I suppose the first thing to do is to warn the mill people at Stillwater. Find out who registered the false end mark."

"Big Gust said the same thing. He'll talk to Charlie Saunders."

"The county sheriff?" asked Mama.

Anders nodded. "Charlie will talk to someone at the mill. But Big Gust knew it might not do a bit of good. The swindler probably gave a false name. And now he knows we've seen what he's doing. If he's smart, he'll change the mark he uses."

Papa sighed. "Farmers are going to lose a lot of money if the thief isn't caught—money they really need. What's more, I don't like having a timber swindler wandering around the woods."

"We'll stay close to the house, Carl," Mama quickly assured him. "And before long the little one will come."

Papa smiled, and the frown on his face disappeared. "Yah. Soon we'll have another Nordstrom."

Tina looked at Mama and spoke quickly in Swedish. Kate understood Tina's question: "Do you think it'll be a boy or a girl?"

Mama's gentle smile erased the tired lines around her eyes. "We'll take whatever God gives us. And we'll be thankful."

"Are you hoping for a girl?" Lars asked Kate.

"For sure," she answered. "No more brothers!"

But Anders broke in. "No more *sisters*, you mean!"

"No more *brothers*!" Kate insisted. "Lars is fine, but you're—" She stopped, trying to think of a name she could say in front of Mama and Papa.

Mama held up her hands. "Stop it! Stop it! We'll be grateful if we have a healthy normal baby. That's what you should want too."

Anders pushed his chair away from the table. "Don't want any more dumb girls."

"Anders." Papa spoke sternly. "I don't want to hear you talk about a dumb girl again. And I want you to show respect for your mother."

The tall blond boy closed his mouth. But when Papa stood up to take the Bible from the shelf, Anders tipped back in his chair. Behind his father's back, he smirked at Kate.

Kate turned her head and pretended she didn't see. But she felt last night's rush of anger. As Papa read the chapter for that day, her thoughts leaped far away. It wasn't hard to remember what she'd decided.

I'll show Anders, she promised herself. *Whatever he tries, I'll do better. I'll prove a girl can do anything as well as a boy.*

A moment later Papa closed the Bible, and Kate realized she hadn't heard a word he read.

When Papa finished praying, Mama stayed in her chair instead of starting to work as she usually did. "I wonder," she said quietly, looking at Papa. "I wonder if I've really forgiven my little brother. It still hurts so much when I remember what he did."

As though it were yesterday, Kate thought back to January and the letter Mama had received from Sweden. For days she had walked around, looking sad.

"My little brother Ben," Mama said now. "He did something he never should have done."

Tears welled up in her eyes. Impatiently she brushed them away. "Stealing from a shopkeeper. Running off, no one knows where. Such a black spot on our good family name."

Mama sighed. Placing both hands on the table, she lifted herself from her chair.

As Mama walked over to the cookstove, Kate watched her heavy steps. Until the past few months Kate had never seen her mother look awkward. Any day now the baby would be born.

Thinking about it, Kate felt uneasy. Out here in the country, far away from doctors, it was sometimes hard to get help. If possible, Erik's mother would come. As a midwife, she often helped women have babies. But what if she didn't get here in time?

As Kate washed breakfast dishes, she tried to push aside her uneasiness. Yet one thought kept going around in her mind. *What if something goes wrong?*

4

Surprise for Mama

As soon as Kate finished the dishes, she went outside to pump fresh water and carry it to the chickens.

When Anders found her near the barn, he pushed back his cap and grinned. "Papa says I'm not supposed to call you a dumb girl. So I won't. I'll just treat you like one."

Kate gasped. "I don't have words to describe you," she sputtered.

Anders laughed. "Well, I can tell you what to say—about yourself, I mean."

Throwing back her shoulders, Kate lifted her chin. *How can I possibly get even?* she wondered. With her head high, she stalked to the house.

At lunchtime she glared at Anders, but refused to speak to him. Every time he spoke, Kate looked down at her plate. When the family finished eating and only she and Mama were left, Kate tried to escape.

Her mother's voice called her back. "Kate!"

Slowly Kate turned.

"Don't go out the door without forgiving the one who hurt you."

"Oh, Mama! Anders is always looking for ways to be mean! I don't *want* to forgive him."

"If you don't, it'll hurt you even more than it does him."

Kate groaned. "How can I possibly forgive him?"

A smile lit Mama's face. "You choose to forgive."

A lump the size of a walnut tightened Kate's throat. "It's all right for you," she said. The words spilled out before she could call them back. "You don't have to live with your brother every day."

"You don't think it costs me anything? To forgive my brother, I mean?" Mama's voice was still quiet, but sparks lit her eyes.

As Kate escaped down the trail to Spirit Lake School, her mother's words seemed to follow her. The more Kate thought about Anders, the more upset she became. "Dumb boy!" she said aloud.

The next moment she caught her breath. She had called Anders the very name he called her! It almost struck her funny.

Almost, but not quite. "That's what he deserves to be called!" Kate's angry voice shouted into the wind. She wasn't going to forgive him. Not until *he* changed.

Choose to forgive? Kate scoffed at the idea. But she couldn't push aside the awful way she felt.

Later that afternoon Kate walked the long trail to the main road and the mailbox. She found just one letter—an envelope addressed to Mrs. Ingrid Lindblom O'Connell Nordstrom. Someone certainly knew all of Mama's names.

The letter was written in a script that looked as though its writer lived in Sweden. But there was no return address. And the postmark read, "Duluth, Minnesota."

Kate hurried home with the letter. She found Mama sitting with Anders and Papa at the kitchen table.

Mama looked at the postmark, then turned the letter over in her hands. "Who can it be?" she asked.

"Well, maybe you should open it," Papa said gently. "I think you'll find out."

Mama laughed. "Yah, Carl, you might be right."

As Papa emptied his coffee into a saucer, Mama poured another cup for herself. Then she slit the envelope open with a knife and pulled out the single sheet of paper.

Mama glanced down at the signature. Her smile disappeared. "It's Ben," she said, and her voice trembled. "My little brother Bernhard."

Kate bit her lip. She remembered how many times Mama had been upset because of Ben. As far as her mother knew, no one had heard from him since he ran away.

As Mama read the letter, her lips moved, but no sound escaped. When she looked up, tears stood in her eyes. Quickly she brushed them away.

Mama shook her head, as though not believing what she'd seen. "I must read it to you."

As Mama read aloud, she translated into English for Kate.

Dear Sister Ingrid:

You may be surprised to hear from your youngest brother. I admit I am afraid to write to you. However, you may know the worst about me already.

Eight months ago I stole money from a shopkeeper in our hometown. I had the America fever and ran away. I went over the mountains to Norway. There I bought a ticket and took a ship to New York.

While on the ship I suffered a terrible sickness. I nearly died, but I came to myself. I was ashamed of the bad thing I did. When I reached America, I found a job on the docks. I earned the money to repay the shopkeeper and set that right.

I am deeply sorry I disgraced our family name. I have asked God's forgiveness, and now I ask yours. Can you find it in your heart to forgive me?

I am now working in Duluth, Minnesota, and have learned that you live not too far distant. I want to see you, but am afraid you do not want to see me.

People tell me I can cross the St. Croix River at Tennessee Flats near Grantsburg. I will come to the top of the hill on the Minnesota side of the river. I will be there at sundown, 28 March 1907. If you are there to meet me, I will know you want to see me. If you are not there, I will go away and never trouble you again.

Your youngest brother,
Bernhard

This time as Mama looked up, she smiled through her tears. "My little brother! Of course, I want to see him!"

Papa's eyes looked thoughtful. "What's the postmark on the letter?"

Mama turned the envelope over. "February 20th."

"That's over a month ago!" exclaimed Papa. "How can a letter take so long to come from Duluth?"

"And today is March 26th!" Suddenly Mama returned to earth. "March 28th is only two days away. We need to get ready!"

Papa shook his head. "A woman who could have a baby at any moment should travel all the way to the St. Croix River?"

"My little brother will be waiting for me," answered Mama. "He'll think I do not care. He'll go away, never to return again."

"Yah, that is true," Papa said, stroking his long brown beard. "But you shall not be there. What if your time comes while you are on the road?"

"I'll go instead of Mama," Kate said quickly. "Anders and I can meet Ben."

Anders grinned. "We'll take Wildfire. If we start early tomorrow, it'll be easy to reach Tennessee Flats by sundown the next day."

"Yah, it might work," said Papa slowly. "Then I can stay with Mama. I'll be here if the baby comes."

"Good! Then it's all settled!" exclaimed Anders. "We'll get ready right away." He started toward the door.

"Just a minute, Anders." Mama's voice called him back. "You can go. But I want you to ask Erik if he can go with you. Kate will stay here."

"Stay *here*?" Kate jumped up so fast that her chair tipped over. She couldn't believe Mama's words.

"Certainly." Mama's voice sounded as though her mind were made up. "I don't want you running around with a timber swindler hiding in the bushes."

"Oh, Mama!" Kate wailed. She looked toward Anders, hoping for his support.

But no responding grin lit his face. Instead, a strange expression darkened his blue eyes.

An awful thought crossed Kate's mind. What if—

From across the room Anders looked at Kate. Their gaze met. Was he wondering the same thing?

Slowly Kate picked up her chair and sat down. As Mama poured Papa another cup of coffee, Kate tried to think things through.

She decided to try again. "Mama, what if something goes wrong?"

"That's what I'm afraid of." Mama's voice sounded brisk.

Kate bit her tongue. She had certainly found a bad way to start. On her next try she was more careful. "Mama, you know I'm good at figuring things out—if there's a mystery or something."

Mama nodded. "Yah." She couldn't deny that.

"If something goes wrong, I can help Anders decide what to do."

Anders made a choking sound.

Kate glared at him. "Maybe I can think of something he wouldn't."

When Mama did not speak, Kate rushed on. "It's really important that we get there in time. If we miss your little brother, even by fifteen minutes, you'll never hear from him again."

"Yah." Again the tears welled up in Mama's eyes. "How awful it would be for him to think that. To think I do not have it in my heart to forgive him."

Kate nodded. "It would wreck Ben's whole life. So I'll help Anders find him."

Anders cleared his throat, but Kate refused to look at him.

Mama sat quietly, thinking about it. "You're right, Kate, two heads are better than one."

Kate sighed with relief.

But Mama wasn't finished. "Anders, you go over and talk to Erik."

Mama turned back to Kate. "If Erik can go, it should be his head and not yours."

"Oh, Mama!" Kate wailed again.

But her mother's mind was made up, and Kate knew it wouldn't do a bit of good to say more. As Anders headed out the door, she pulled on her coat and followed him.

"I want to go with you," Kate said when safely away from the house. "Tell Erik I want to meet Mama's little brother."

Anders pushed back his thatch of blond hair. "Remember, Kate. Mama's little brother is now eighteen years old."

Again Kate felt uneasy. She remembered the strange expression she'd seen on Anders' face. "Are you thinking what I'm thinking?" she asked.

Her brother shrugged. "Well, depends." The look in his eyes told Kate Anders was more concerned than he sounded.

He started for the barn, then stopped and came back. "Are you wondering if Mama's brother has already crossed the river?"

5

Papa's Warning

Kate felt as if a cold March wind had struck her. That's what she was wondering, all right. Even though she and Anders were alone, she spoke softly. "Anders, do you suppose Ben is the timber swindler?"

"I don't know," he said. "Can you remember anything to give us a clue?"

"How the swindler looked, you mean?"

"Yup." For once Anders sounded serious. "It was pretty dark," he said.

"I think he was tall," answered Kate. "And thin. Not heavy around the middle."

"That's what I thought too." Anders squinted into the morning sunlight instead of looking at Kate. "You know what that means."

"I'm afraid so." Kate spoke in a low voice, as if even the nearby bushes could hear. "Some older men stay thin. But some look more—more—heavyset."

"Broad through the shoulders," said Anders. "And thick through the middle."

Kate giggled, but the laughter died on her lips. "The swindler was thin through the waist, wasn't he?"

"But strong in the shoulders," said Anders. "So he could be most any age."

"I think there's something we need to know." Kate spoke slowly. "If we find out that Ben is the swindler, would Mama—" She stopped, hating to even ask the question.

Anders finished for her. "Would Mama want us to bring him home?"

Looking as if he disliked the idea as much as Kate, Anders walked back with her to the kitchen. When he opened the door, Mama and Papa were still at the table. They looked startled, as though they had suddenly stopped talking.

Anders joined them at the table. "Mama, do you have any idea what your brother looks like now?"

Mama glanced at Papa before she answered. "The most recent picture was taken—" Mama stopped to think. "Probably six years ago."

"It's in the trunk?" Kate headed for the dining room.

"On the right side," Mama called after her. "Near the bottom."

Mama had brought this trunk from Sweden at the age of seventeen. On the flat top stood a photograph. Picking it up, Kate studied the faces. She knew the story of the picture well.

Mama's parents sat in the center, surrounded by Mama's five sisters and two brothers. The youngest sister held a framed photograph of Mama.

"So I could still be part of the family," Mama often explained. Soon after coming to America, she'd had the photo taken and sent to her family.

Now Mama's youngest brother interested Kate most—little Bernhard. Two and a half years old at the time his sister arrived in America, he looked blond and chubby and happy.

Kate stared at Ben's round boyish face. How could a boy like that steal from a shopkeeper?

Setting the family photo aside, Kate opened the trunk and searched for the more recent picture of Ben. It was far down, beneath blankets and towels. *Bernhard Lindblom*, it said on the back, along with the date, *1901*.

Ben was still blond, but now he had stretched up. Ben's grin reminded Kate of Anders.

When Kate brought the picture to her mother, Mama gazed at the face without speaking. "Yah, Ben's tall," she said at last. "Like my Papa."

"And thin," said Anders, looking over Mama's shoulder.

"And thin." Mama bit her lip, as though it hurt to look at her brother.

"He's starting to get broad shoulders," Papa said.

"Yah, from the farm work," Mama answered. "Always there was more work than money. The farm was too small for a big family. Papa and Mama worked night and day, but it wasn't enough."

Then Kate noticed something she hadn't seen in the earlier picture. "Ben has a scar on his chin."

Mama looked closer. "You're right, Kate. Something must have happened to him between the two pictures."

As Mama set the picture down, Anders turned to Kate. "You ask," he said.

"No, you." Kate dreaded the idea.

"It's *your* job." Anders sounded unwilling to give in.

"It's *yours*," Kate answered.

Anders shook his head. "She's *your* mother."

Mama looked from one to the other. Her eyes flashed. "And I hope I'm *your* mother, too, Anders. Even though I'm the second one."

Anders flushed, and Mama turned back to Kate. "Now tell me. Just what are you and Anders talking about?"

Kate cleared her throat. "About Ben, Mama." But she couldn't go on.

"Ahhhh!" A light entered Mama's eyes. "Are you wondering if he's the timber swindler?"

Kate felt the warmth of embarrassment creep into her face.

Mama nodded, as if she had her answer. "Carl and I just talked about it." Mama glanced toward Papa, as though needing his support. "We wondered if Ben has already crossed to this side of the St. Croix River."

Mama bit her lip. In her eyes there was something even greater than hurt. Was it worry? Or more? To Kate it seemed as if her mother's heart were being squeezed. Unable to bear the pain in Mama's eyes, Kate looked away.

For long minutes no one spoke. In the stillness Kate heard the tick of the clock in the dining room. Then a piece of wood dropped in the cookstove.

"I want to believe," Mama said at last. She wiped her hand across her eyes.

After a moment she went on. "No, it's more than that. I *do* believe Ben meant what he said in the letter."

Mama drew a deep breath. "When Ben says he's sorry, I have to believe he means it. I have to believe he's changed, unless he shows me he hasn't."

When Mama spoke again, her voice sounded stronger. "Whatever Ben did in Sweden, it's over. It's over because I forgive him."

Grasping the edge of the table, Mama pulled herself up. As she walked from the room, her back was straight, but her shoulders trembled.

When Anders returned from talking to Erik, Kate heard the good news. Mr. Lundgren and Erik's older brother were gone, so Erik needed to stay home to do chores.

Mama gave permission for Kate to go with Anders, but a troubled look shadowed her blue eyes. "Anders, there's something you have to promise me," she said.

"Sure, Mama. What is it?" His lopsided grin told Kate that he knew what was coming.

"I want you to promise that you'll take good care of your sister."

Anders lifted his right hand and did his best to put on a straight face. "I solemnly swear, Mama. I'm very good at taking care of Kate."

"I want you to do more than that," Papa added. "I want you to promise that no matter what happens, the two of you stay together."

Anders' smirk disappeared. "Yes, Papa," he said solemnly.

Mr. Nordstrom turned to Kate. "You promise?"

"I promise." Kate looked at Papa because she refused to look at Anders.

When Kate hurried to her room, she felt excited. She had gotten what she wanted, after all. She could go to meet Ben. And there was something more. *I'll prove to Anders I can keep up with anything he needs to do.*

As Kate packed her other dress and a warm sweater, she looked forward to going to Grantsburg. The Nordstrom family traveled the eleven long miles only when there was a real need.

What will it be like? Kate wondered, as she thought about going five miles beyond the village. Kate had been to the St. Croix River only once—when coming to live at Windy Hill Farm.

Now Kate wished that Erik were going along. It was always fun being with him. Yet something else bothered Kate much more.

During the late afternoon, she and Mama worked together, preparing supper. For a time the two of them were alone. Kate cracked butternuts and watched for her chance. Finally she asked, "Mama?"

"Yah?"

Kate looked at a nutshell instead of her mother. "What if the baby comes while I'm gone?"

A smile lit Mama's eyes. "Then I'll have a little one for you when you get back."

"That's not what I mean." Kate tried to choose her words carefully. "What will happen when the baby is born?"

Mama looked surprised. "Why, you know. Papa will go for Erik's mother. She's a good midwife and has promised to help me."

Again Kate hesitated. "I know Mrs. Lundgren is a good midwife, but—" Kate stopped, then went on. "What if—" Once more, words failed her.

Mama sat down next to Kate. "What if something goes wrong? Is that what you're asking?"

Unable to look into Mama's eyes, Kate nodded.

Mama reached out, putting her hand on Kate's arm. When she spoke her voice was gentle. "You're right, Kate, sometimes things go wrong. Out here in the country, I'm far from help. I know that."

"I'm afraid, Mama," Kate whispered.

"Afraid that something will happen to me, yah?"

"Yah." The word sounded strange, coming from Kate. "If something goes wrong, would having a baby be worth it?"

"I believe God wants me to have this new life," Mama said. "I need to trust that He'll take care of me."

Mama took Kate's hand. "Here, Kate. Feel the baby's foot."

At one side there was an extra bulge in Mama's large stomach. As Kate touched that place, she felt a small kick.

Kate laughed, but her mother looked serious. "That's what it's like," Mama said. "That's what it's like to know a little heart beats beneath my ribs."

Mama patted her stomach. "In the whole world there's no other baby who will be exactly like this one. I'm the only person who can give this little one life."

That evening Papa sat down at the kitchen table to help Anders and Kate plan their trip.

"You'll have terrible mud for at least part of the way," Papa said. "But you've got two good days to travel. When you get to Grantsburg, go to Walfrid Johnson's and ask if you can stay overnight."

As he finished sharpening a pencil, Papa put down his knife. "If you get up early the next morning, you should have more than enough time to find Ben."

Papa started drawing a map. "There's no bridge over the Wood River between Grantsburg and the St. Croix."

Papa drew a jiggly line showing the Wood River as it flowed through the north side of the village.

"That means you have to cross on the bridge in Grantsburg. Then go north until you turn left here."

Papa drew another line. "If you follow this road, you'll find a bridge across Sand Creek. Someone cut down two big trees and laid them from bank to bank. Small poles cross the trees. They're enough so that Wildfire's hoofs won't go through."

"Won't the creek be frozen?" Kate asked.

"Aw, Kate," said Anders. "Every one knows that if a crick flows fast, it won't freeze in winter." He tipped his head slightly, as though trying to say something without words.

Kate looked beyond Anders to the wood cookstove. Mama stood there, baking cookies for them to take along. She seemed to be listening.

Papa extended a line across the creek. "Keep on this road. Then take a right and a left. You're going west, then north, then west again."

Anders nodded, and Papa began writing. "You'll come to the Berglund farm. Near his house take the trail into the woods, and you'll end up at Tennessee Flats."

"Tennessee Flats?" asked Kate.

"The first settler in that area was a man named Isaac Tennessee."

Kate leaned forward to study the map.

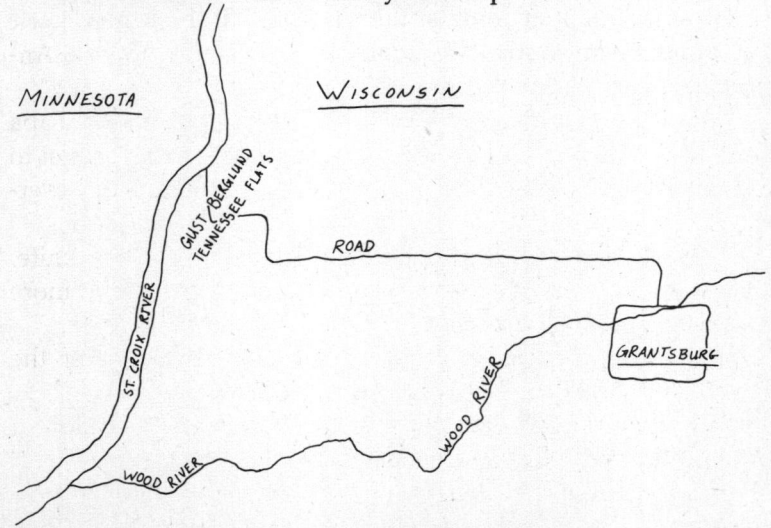

Papa pointed to an area near the St. Croix River. "In the early days people traveled up the Wisconsin side of the river and forded it there."

"What do you mean?" Kate asked. In spite of her desire to make the trip, she was starting to wonder about all that could happen.

"They crossed it," Papa explained. "There's no bridge there, but the river is wide and shallow. In summer there are ferries at other places along the St. Croix. But people used to walk over at Tennessee Flats, or take a team of horses. They stayed on the west side of the river to go to Duluth."

Anders tipped back in his chair, as though sure that he knew the way. "So we cross the river at Tennessee Flats."

As Mama walked into the dining room, Papa lowered his voice. "I hope so."

"What do you mean, you hope so?" asked Kate, her voice just as quiet.

Papa sighed and ran his fingers through his beard. "If the river is still frozen, you'll have no trouble crossing over. If not—"

Anders nodded as his gaze met his father's.

"If not what?" Kate whispered.

"I don't want your mother to worry," said Papa. "She's got enough on her mind right now."

He looked first at Anders, then at Kate. "If the ice has gone out, you'll be in trouble. Big trouble."

6

Growing Evidence

The next morning Kate awoke with a feeling of excitement in her bones. As she went outside, the sun peeked over the horizon.

Already Anders had backed Wildfire between the shafts of the wagon. The mare's black coat and white socks shone in the early light.

The farm wagon looked like an oblong box with the large wooden wheels in back bigger than those in front. Kate climbed up into the wagon bed.

Anders handed her Mama's two baskets of food. Kate knew what they contained—enough of her mother's good brown bread to last for four days, apples from the barrel in the root cellar, carrot sticks, and oatmeal cookies. Mama had made certain they'd eat well.

Carefully Kate covered the food with a heavy horse blanket. She could only hope that if it rained, the blanket would keep the sandwiches and cookies dry.

Anders handed up a wooden box with extra clothes for each of them, as well as more blankets made from the hides of animals. A tool box came next, as well as a hatchet, ax, shovel, and bucket.

"Why do you need all this stuff?" Kate asked.

Anders shrugged. "Well, you never know."

As they finished loading the wagon, Lars started across the yard.

"Bye, Lars," Kate called. Then she jumped down. Her nine-year-old brother had gotten up early just to see them off.

With a coat pulled over his nightshirt, Lars wore boots too big for him. Though the morning sunlight showed the whiteness of his face, Kate felt grateful for his growing strength. She couldn't take that for granted. Not anymore.

"You're a good brother, Lars," she said quietly when Anders went to the other side of the wagon.

Lars flushed. "Yah, sure." He sounded like Anders. Yet his eyes shone, as though Kate's words meant something to him.

Thinking about the pneumonia he'd had, she wanted to say more. With all her heart she wanted to tell him, "I'm glad you're alive. I'm glad you're *you*." But the words stuck in her throat.

Instead she said, "When I get back, we'll read another book together. All right?"

"Sure thing!" Lars answered. His wide grin warmed Kate.

As she turned away, Lars spoke softly, as if he, too, felt afraid Anders would hear. "You're a good sister, Kate."

Her throat tightened. This from the brother who once put a dead mouse in her bed?

"Thanks, Lars," she whispered.

A moment later Tina flung herself at Kate. The little girl rattled a string of words too fast for Kate to catch the Swedish. Yet she understood Tina's hug.

As Tina let go, Kate saw Mama in the kitchen doorway. Her golden blond hair shone in the morning sunlight. Seeing her, Kate felt torn between going and staying.

What if the baby comes while I'm gone? she wondered. *What if Papa needs help, and I'm not here?*

Then Mama hurried forward. Halfway across the yard, she and Kate met. Her mother's arms went around Kate.

"It's important that you go," Mama said softly. "It's important that we're a family for Ben."

For a moment Mama stroked Kate's long black hair. "My job is to have the baby," she said. "It's your job to find my little brother."

Tears welled up in Kate's eyes, and she could not speak. *Strange!* she thought. So often Mama seemed to know what she was thinking.

Her mother followed Kate back to the wagon. Anders' dog lay near the front wheel.

"Are you going to take Lutfisk?" Mama asked. Anders had named the dog after the dried cod that Swedes soak in lye and eat at Christmas.

At the sound of his name, Lutfisk sat up, as though snapping to attention. With brown, black, and white hair, he had tan markings on his face. He tipped his head to one side.

"Well, I don't know," Kate answered. "I'd hate to have him run off and get lost."

"Lutfisk might come in handy," Mama said.

The dog's ears perked up as if he listened in on the conversation.

"Sure, Kate," Anders broke in. "Handy dandy Lutfisk, that's him."

Lutfisk tilted his head the other way. His bright eyes seemed to cling to every word.

"You better take him, Anders," said Mama. "He can protect Kate."

"Protect *me*?" asked Kate.

"From that man who's running around the woods," Mama answered.

Anders pounded his chest. "*I*, her trusty brother, will protect Kate."

Kate glared at him, then remembered. Her mother could still change her mind about letting her go.

"Good idea, Mama." Kate's voice sounded as sweet as she could make it. "We'll take Lutfisk."

"C'mon, boy!" Anders called. "You can go with us!"

Lutfisk leaped to his feet and barked. His tail wagged so fast Kate wondered if it would fall off.

"Did you see that?" Anders asked proudly. "That shows you how much he understands."

As Anders held Wildfire still, the family gathered around the wagon.

"I want to remind you of God's promise," Papa said, looking first at Anders, then at Kate.

Recalling Papa's warning of the night before, Kate stood straighter.

"Joshua needed to cross the Jordan River when it was at flood stage," Papa went on. "God told him, 'Have I not commanded thee? Be strong and of a good courage; be not afraid, neither be thou dismayed: for the Lord thy God is with thee whithersoever thou goest.'"

Again Papa looked long at Kate and Anders, as though wanting to be sure they caught what he was saying. Then he bowed his head.

"We thank thee, Heavenly Father," Papa prayed. "We thank thee that thou wilt be with Kate and Anders when we cannot. We ask thee to give them courage, wisdom, and protection."

For a moment he paused, then said, "Ah-men."

"Ah-men," echoed the others.

Mama cleared her throat, and Papa clapped Anders on the shoulder. "Don't forget your promise to us. Stay together, no matter what happens."

Anders and Kate climbed up and sat down on the high spring seat.

Papa stepped back from the wheels. "Do you have the map?"

Anders patted his shirt pocket and nodded.

Kate started to wave. Instead, a question spilled out. "If the baby comes while we're gone, what are you going to name her?"

Mama looked at Papa. "We're still talking about it. Both of us want to name the baby after someone special."

"Hmmmm," said Anders. "Well, that could be me."

Kate laughed. "I can't believe you said that. Sometimes your—your—" She thought for a moment. "What's the word? Arrogance. Your arrogance amazes me."

Anders winked at Papa, then offered Kate his lopsided grin. "That so?"

"Besides, it's going to be a girl," said Kate. "Can you imagine a girl named Anders?"

Lars snickered. Tina jumped up and down, clapping her hands. Kate wondered if the little girl knew English well enough to understand the joke.

Anders flushed, but refused to give up. "Well, if that awful event occurs, how about something *like* Anders? Andrea, Annabelle, Annie."

This time even Mama laughed. "We'll give it some thought," she said, as though trying to be serious.

Anders turned to Wildfire. "Giddyup!" he called. The high-spirited mare pranced out of the farmyard with Lutfisk running alongside.

Twisting around, Kate waved to Lars and Tina, Papa, and Mama. Then the barn blocked her view.

Tall trees lined both sides of the trail they took to the main road. Here in the woods patches of snow had escaped the sunlight. The iron rim around each wooden wheel left a deep track.

When Kate and Anders reached the main road, they found even deeper ruts cut by passing wagons. Because of below-freezing temperatures the night before, the ground was still firm. Though the wagon bumped up and down, they made good time. Yet Kate knew that as soon as the sun warmed the roads, the dirt would turn to mud.

At first Anders took the way they normally drove to town. Lutfisk ran back of the wagon, now and then disappearing into the bushes. Then Anders turned onto a road Kate hadn't seen before. Before long, the road became a trail.

For some time they traveled without seeing anything but trees. "Where are we?" asked Kate as her uneasiness grew.

"Near the Wood River," Anders told her in a low voice.

A few minutes later he stopped Wildfire, and he and Kate climbed down. "Be quiet," he warned. He snapped a lead rope onto the mare's halter and tied the rope to a tree.

Soon the woods thinned out, and they came to great stacks

of logs. Stopping at the first pile, Anders studied the ends of the logs. He pointed to the sawed edge. "Looks all right to me. They're a bit weathered."

But then he and Kate walked around to the other end, the side away from the trail. Here the ends of the logs were newly sawed and marked.

Anders traced the mark with his finger. "Remember this," he said. "Don't forget even one line."

Turning away, he checked the other piles of wood near the river. In each case, someone had tampered with the logs.

Kate felt uneasy. "There's something I don't understand." She, too, spoke softly, as if someone might hear. "Wouldn't the farmers notice that someone tampered with their logs?"

"Maybe. Maybe not," Anders said. "Look at the ground."

Kate saw what he meant. Whatever sawdust there had been, it was now mixed into the dirt.

"And there's something else. When the men open the dam between Big Wood Lake and Wood River, they want to catch the rush of water. They don't lift the logs into the river one by one. It'd be too much work."

Anders led Kate to the river side of a pile of logs. "See how the logs are set on skids?"

The skids were timbers that slanted down toward the river. Anders pointed to a key piece of wood at the front of the logs.

"When it's time to send the logs downstream, a man stands at each end of the pile. They knock out that piece with a sledgehammer. They've got to be mighty good jumpers."

"What do you mean?" asked Kate.

"It's dangerous work. The logs tumble into the river. But if one of them goes crossways or gets out of line—"

"It hits the man?" Kate asked.

"It could. Whoever sends the logs into the water gets paid extra. But some of them never collect."

As Kate's uneasiness grew, she glanced around. For some reason the woods seemed darker. Then she looked up between the branches. Murky clouds covered the sun.

"Where do you think the timber swindler is now?" Kate whispered.

"I don't know. Could be most anywhere, I guess." He grinned. "Even looking at us from behind a bush."

Kate didn't think her brother's teasing was funny. "Let's go," she said.

She and Anders hurried back to the wagon. When they climbed up to the high spring seat, Wildfire seemed eager to leave the trees behind.

As they reached the main road, the rain began. Kate doubled the blankets covering the food.

"This will take care of any leftover snow," Anders said.

At first a cold drizzle filled the deep ruts in the road. Then the dampness seeped through the heavy blanket Kate pulled over her coat.

Soon Lutfisk leaped into the back of the wagon and crept forward to where Kate and Anders sat. As the rain increased, the ruts in the road softened and the mud grew deeper. The wagon wheels lurched down, in and out of potholes.

The cold rain entered Kate's bones. "How much farther?" she asked finally.

"Three or four miles," Anders told her.

A moment later the rain moved like a wall of water against them. Kate pulled a blanket over her head until only her eyes showed.

As the rain pelted them, Wildfire plodded on. Muddy water splattered up around the wagon. Kate's teeth chattered.

Anders looked down at her. "Your teeth rattling in your head, Kate?"

In spite of her misery, Kate giggled. It seemed only a moment since that muddy March day a year before. On that terrible trip, she and Mama had come from Minneapolis. In mud like this, Anders had asked the same question.

After a long stretch of potholes, the rain eased, then stopped. Kate pulled out sandwiches. Soon they finished the apples and carrots. But it was all right, Kate told herself. Plenty of cookies and bread remained.

Before long, they came to a partly cleared field dotted with large stumps. The ground was less chewed up, and Anders directed Wildfire off the road. As he guided the mare between the stumps, the wagon jolted up and down. Even so, they made better time.

Then the field ended. Trees and underbrush blocked the way. Anders directed Wildfire back to the road.

Once again they lurched through deep ruts. As a front wheel dropped into a hole, Wildfire strained forward, then stopped.

"Giddyup!" Anders called. "C'mon, girl! Move out."

Wildfire's beautiful black coat was brown with mud. As far ahead as Kate could see, the road looked bottomless.

"Giddyup!" Anders urged the horse again.

This time the wagon moved, and Kate was glad she was riding instead of walking.

Yet as they came out of the hole, she glanced down.

"Oh, Anders!" she exclaimed. "Look at the wheel!"

7

The Stranger

As Kate stared, the iron rim circling the outer edge of the wheel wobbled. From side to side it moved. Then the rim separated from the wood underneath.

Quickly Anders turned Wildfire to the side of the road. But trees grew close to the trail, offering no place to go.

The rim slipped crossways at a right angle to the wheel. "It's coming off!" Kate warned.

Anders tugged the reins and managed to stop the wagon before the rim fell to the ground.

Kate sighed with relief. But she knew their trouble was only beginning.

Anders moaned. "Always thought rims came off wheels in dry weather. 'Course these awful roads don't help."

He ran his fingers through his thatch of blond hair. "Come to think of it, an old-timer told me it can happen any time of year. Especially in spring, when a wagon hasn't been used all winter."

"So what do we do?" asked Kate.

"Get the wheel to a blacksmith."

"A blacksmith?" Kate stared at the mud surrounding the

wagon. If she climbed down, that oozing brown water would go over the top of her boots.

"A blacksmith," Anders said again.

"Can you tell me how we get to a blacksmith?"

"Nope," said Anders. "The closest one is at least three miles away. But if I use the wheel without the rim, I'll wreck it. And that's big money."

He stared down at the mud, then at the long stretch of road. From the look on his face, Anders didn't like the idea of walking any better than Kate. In either direction there was no one in sight.

"I've got a pliers," Anders said after some thought. "And some other tools, but—" Again he looked at the mud around them.

"There's only one thing to do," he said finally. Crawling behind the seat, Anders found the pliers, then slipped over the side of the wagon.

With his first step he sank deep in mud. With his next step the mud oozed over the top of his boots. With every step after that, the mud sucked at his boots and splattered his clothes.

"You better stay there," he called as he reached firmer ground. Boots and pants brown with mud, he stood at the edge of the road.

"Stay here!" exclaimed Kate. "What choice do I have?"

Then she caught her brother's grin. At least he was the one getting dirty.

As Anders stretched out his long legs, Lutfisk stood up in the back of the wagon. With one look at Anders, the dog jumped off the end. When he landed, the mud sprayed up, covering him.

Kate groaned, but Anders laughed. "C'mon, boy!" he called, and the dog went to him.

Anders stayed along the trees, and Lutfisk followed close on his heels. Before many minutes passed, they became two small dots, far ahead. Then they disappeared.

As time grew long, Kate looked at the woods. The trees seemed to move closer by the minute. In spite of the mud, she wished she had gone with Anders.

Then a breeze stirred the bushes.

"I refuse to be afraid," Kate said aloud. Yet she couldn't help but think about the timber swindler. What if he were nearby? What if he suddenly appeared? There was no place to go. Except through mud, that is.

Then against the horizon a small dot appeared, then another. Was that Anders and Lutfisk?

As Kate watched, the dots grew larger. Soon she could see her brother and the dog.

When Anders reached the wagon, he held up a long piece of wire.

"Where'd you get it?" Kate asked as he pushed the rim back over the wood.

"Found a barbed-wire fence," said Anders. Wrapping the wire around the rim, he passed it between the spokes of the wheel.

"You cut a barbed-wire fence?" asked Kate. "The cattle will get out!"

"Nope. Barbed wire has a double strand. I cut the wire without barbs and unwound it. I'll buy new wire in town and fix the fence when we come back."

Carefully Anders wound the wire until it held the rim against the wooden circle of the wheel. At last he threw the pliers into the tool box and climbed up to the seat.

Mud covered his overalls well past his knees. As he sat down, Kate moved as far away as possible.

Lutfisk barked, wanting to get up. But the dog was so dirty Kate wouldn't let him near the wagon.

When they reached Grantsburg's main street, Anders turned right toward Walfrid Johnson's. The family lived on the second floor of a large frame building. Beneath, on the ground floor, was Mr. Johnson's blacksmith shop. Anders stopped Wildfire close to the large open door.

As Kate climbed down from the wagon, she felt glad to be on solid ground again. When Mr. Johnson came outside, Anders explained what had happened.

Taking a jack, the blacksmith raised the heavy wagon and

slipped off the wheel. When he rolled it into the shop, Kate saw a tall thin boy standing along the wall.

"Stretch!" she exclaimed.

The boy turned and grinned. But somehow he seemed to have changed.

"How're you doing?" Kate asked.

More than a month before, Stretch had been badly hurt at the Trade Lake Creamery. When he was unloading ice, a large chunk crashed down the ramp, smashing his hand against another block of ice.

"Just came in on the train from Minneapolis," he said.

"You saw a doctor there?" Anders asked.

Stretch nodded. "For the second time. Mr. Swenson took me right after the accident." Since Christmas Stretch had lived at Swenson's farm with Josie's parents and her eight brothers and sisters.

Kate remembered her fright on the day of the accident. The buttermaker had rushed Stretch to the doctor. He had sent Stretch to another doctor in Minneapolis.

Now Kate noticed that the tall thin boy held his injured hand behind his back. "Are you having trouble?" she asked. "Is that why you went back to Minneapolis?"

Again Stretch nodded. He seemed quieter, without his usual swagger.

"What did the doctor say?" Anders asked.

Stretch shrugged. "To give it time."

Kate still wondered what was wrong. Although Stretch and Anders didn't always get along, Stretch usually liked talking with her. Usually he had plenty to say.

Today Kate felt like a dentist with a tooth—pulling information out of him. "Are your fingers all right?" she asked.

"Well, sorta," Stretch answered. "The breaks are healing." Just the same, he kept his hand behind his back.

"What are you afraid to tell us?" Kate asked.

A shadow flickered across Stretch's face. He pulled back.

Anders stepped forward. "Hey, we're friends, Stretch, remember?"

Kate was surprised. Not long ago there'd been bad feelings between the two boys.

For a moment Stretch met Anders' gaze. Stretch was the first to look away.

"Friends?" he asked. His laugh sounded hard and brittle. "What good will that do?"

"What do you mean?" asked Kate. Then she remembered Stretch's dream. Was that why he stood in this shop, watching Walfrid Johnson work?

The tall boy's eyes looked dark with pain. "I ain't sure if I can ever be a blacksmith. I ain't sure if I can ever have my own shop."

Slowly, as though it were the last thing he wanted to do, Stretch withdrew his hand from behind his back. He held it out for Kate and Anders to see.

Kate winced. Stretch's thumb and one of his fingers looked almost normal. But the other three fingers curled back toward the palm of his hand.

"Doc says I hurt the tendons," Stretch said without looking at Anders or Kate.

Swallowing hard, Kate stole a glance at her own hands. She thought about how she liked to play the organ. And how much she needed her hands to play.

"Is it permanent?" asked Anders when Kate could not speak. "Maybe it needs more time, like Doc says."

"Don't know yet," said Stretch. "I can't do nuthin' with it." Again he put his hand behind his back.

Again Kate swallowed, trying to push aside the lump in her throat. She wished she knew what to say. All she could think of was "I'm sorry." But Stretch seemed to understand.

When Anders finished talking to Walfrid Johnson, he went around to the pump. There he washed off Wildfire and Lutfisk and the worst of the mud on himself. Then he and Kate climbed the outside stairs.

Halfway up, Kate stopped. "Did Papa give you money?" she asked.

"Yup," said Anders. "But not enough for fixing a wheel and

getting barbed wire, and paying to stay overnight. I'll do the talking."

"Oh, you will?" asked Kate, wondering how he'd handle this.

At the top of the stairs a short woman answered the door. When she heard what Anders wanted, she said, "Come in, come in. We'd like to have you stay with us."

Then she explained. "During the school year, we rent one room to girls from the country. They go to high school in Grantsburg. Kate, you can sleep in their room."

Mrs. Johnson opened the door wider. "We use the other bedroom for our family," she went on. "But Anders, you're welcome to the floor in the dining room."

Anders nodded and looked glad to use the floor. "But your husband is fixing our wagon, and we're almost out of money. Can Kate help you in the kitchen—with the meal and washing dishes?"

Kate stared at him. No wonder Anders wanted to do the talking.

"Certainly, certainly," said Mrs. Johnson.

Anders grinned. "Good. I'll take care of some things in town and be back in time for supper."

When Anders started down the stairs, Kate hurried after him. "Me too," she called to Mrs. Johnson. "I'll be back in time to help."

As soon as Mrs. Johnson could no longer hear, Kate exploded. "Anders, you are the meanest big brother I've ever had!"

"The *only* big brother, you mean," Anders said calmly.

"I wanted to look around town."

"That's what we're doing right now." Anders led her to the fire hall, where they found Big Gust.

The village marshall listened carefully to their story of the damaged logs they'd spotted earlier in the day. Big Gust then said, "I want you to tell Charlie Saunders." The county sheriff owned a harness shop and livery stable near the railroad tracks.

As they walked down the hill with the tall marshall, Anders

turned to Kate. "Once the sheriff ordered four hundred wild horses from out West."

Big Gust's deep laugh rumbled. "When the village board heard about it, they quickly passed an ordinance. Made it against the law to break horses on village streets."

"Kate, you should see Charlie's wife," Anders went on. "She shoots like Annie Oakley. Now that's something you haven't tried."

"Maybe *she'll* be sheriff someday," said Kate.

When Anders laughed, Kate insisted. "She'd be the first woman sheriff in all of Wisconsin!"

When they entered the harness shop and stable, Kate looked around. In addition to selling horses, Mr. Saunders rented them out. He also sold blankets, robes, whips, curry combs, and brushes.

As Anders told the sheriff about the logs along the river, Charlie stroked his handlebar mustache.

"Will you draw the end mark for me?" he asked.

Using the paper he gave her, Kate put down the design she had seen.

Anders agreed that she had it right. "We thought the mark could stand for Wood River or wild river."

"Hmmmm," said Charlie. "The swindler's using a different log mark this time. I wonder how many marks he has registered? Any idea who the man could be?"

For an instant Kate hesitated. Unwilling to speak of their

concern about Ben, she glanced at Anders. He seemed to feel the same way.

"He's tall," said Kate after a moment. "Strong shoulders, thin through the middle. It was dark when we saw him, but his hat looked black."

"Could be a lot of people," said the sheriff. "But I'll see what I can do."

When they left the livery stable, Anders led Kate toward the Antler's Hotel. "Something there I want you to see," he said.

The minute Kate entered the lobby, she knew what her brother meant. Along one wall stood a tall upright piano. Kate forgot all the mud and cold of the day. She even forgot how upset she'd been with Anders.

"Can I play it?" she asked him.

"Ask him." Anders tipped his head toward a man behind the counter.

When he gave permission, Kate sat down on the three-legged stool. Finding it far too low, she stood up and twirled it higher, then settled herself again.

The ivory keys were new and white against the black. It would be different than playing her reed organ, Kate knew. Yet with all her heart she wanted to try. Reaching out an uncertain hand, she sounded one note.

Anders laughed. "You can do better than that."

Kate felt a hot flush creep into her face. She wished that just once her brother would leave her alone.

What can I play? she wondered. With no music it had to be something she knew from memory. Or something she could play by ear.

Then Kate knew. A Swedish folk song, "Children of the Heavenly Father." With all that had gone wrong that day, she needed the promise of God's care.

Placing her hands above the keyboard, Kate started to play. At first the notes sounded choppy and uneven. Then Kate found the pedal and figured out how to use it. Before long, the melody sang.

She couldn't count the times she'd played the song before,

yet now it meant something new. She and Anders were far from home, off on their own. Here, where Mama and Papa couldn't help them, there was someone who could—their heavenly Father.

Kate played the song through, then started over. After several more times, she felt good inside, even peaceful.

When at last she stood up, Kate thought Anders had disappeared. Instead, he waited near the door.

As the two of them left the hotel, she glanced down the street. Ahead of them, a man with a clean-shaven face leaned against a building.

Anders started toward him, and the man straightened up. From his tall height he looked down. His icy blue gaze met Kate's.

Without thinking, she stopped in the middle of the boardwalk. Anders kept going.

Kate blinked, but the man did not. Beneath a black hat and bushy eyebrows, his stare seemed fixed in place.

8

Sand Creek

*K*ate looked away, then back. Deep furrows lined the stranger's face. His cold eyes seemed dark, even evil.

Kate tried to hurry past him, but her feet felt weighed down, leaden.

Halfway down the block, she glanced around. Even at this distance, the man watched her. A chill slid down Kate's spine.

Anders called to her. "C'mon, Kate! What's keeping you?"

Feeling as if she'd wakened from a nightmare, Kate flipped her long braid over her shoulder. It seemed forever before she caught up to her brother.

"Let's get going," she whispered. Forcing herself not to run, she walked as quickly as possible.

"What's the matter?" Anders asked when they were a full block away. "You're white as a ghost!"

Kate tried to laugh, but the sound died on her lips. "I feel like I've seen a ghost. Did you notice the man back there?"

"The one against the wall?"

Kate nodded. "I know him. I don't know where. But he knows me."

She trembled. "Did you see him stare? When I looked at him, he wouldn't look away. He just kept staring."

A strand of hair blew into Kate's eyes. When she reached up to push it aside, her hand shook.

But Anders grinned. "Oh, Kate, you're just making things up."

"Making things up? How can you say such a thing? You saw the man. Didn't you see the way he stared at me?"

"Nah. He's just watching two good-looking Swedish kids walk down the street."

Kate tried to ignore her scared feelings. "One good-looking Swedish boy and a beautiful Swedish-*Irish* girl," she said. "Don't forget the Irish part of me!"

But her attempt to shrug aside her fear didn't work. Her memory of the stranger's cold eyes was too frightening.

"Anders, I can't remember where I've seen that man. But somehow I know him. He scares me."

"Aw, Kate! I've told you before. You've got too much imagination."

"No, I don't!" Kate was certain about her feelings. "Whoever that man is, he's trouble."

In spite of her best effort to stop, she still trembled. She wished she could forget the icy look in the man's eyes.

Together Kate and Anders continued down the street. When they reached the blacksmith shop, they found Big Gust talking to Walfrid Johnson. Often the marshall ate meals with the Johnson family.

"*God dag!*" the gentle giant greeted them. "So we see you again. And you had a problem with a wheel. Well, it's about ready now."

As Kate and Anders watched, the blacksmith rolled the wheel outside. When he tried to place it on the wagon, the axle slid off the jack.

Mr. Johnson jumped back out of harm's way. But the axle lay on the ground.

The blacksmith took up the jack. Before he could put it in place, Big Gust stepped forward. Bending down, he picked up the heavy wagon as if it were a match stick. Holding it steady, he waited until Mr. Johnson slipped the wheel into position.

When they left the shop, Anders and Kate followed Big Gust and the blacksmith up the outside stairs and into the dining room.

"I hope we aren't too many for you," Kate said politely when they all gathered around the table.

"Nonsense! Nonsense!" Mrs. Johnson threw up her hands. "Where there's room in the heart, there's room in the home."

After Kate did the dishes, she and Anders took another walk down Grantsburg's main street. This time Big Gust was lighting the carbide streetlamps.

"We should tell him about that man this afternoon," said Kate.

But Anders laughed at her. "You can't report someone just because he looks at you the wrong way."

Leaving the main street behind, they walked up the hill to the large red-brick jail. Nearby stood the county courthouse, and next to that, the small wooden jail that was no longer used.

When they walked back downtown again, Big Gust was gone. Kate looked around, wondering if she'd spot the staring stranger. One part of her wanted to see him again. Another part felt afraid that she would.

When she and Anders returned to the Johnson home, the sun had slipped below the horizon. Electricity had come on. In the dining room one bulb hung down at the end of a wire.

"We have over 600 lights in the village now," Mrs. Johnson told them proudly.

The electricity would stay on until midnight. Then the lights would blink as a signal that they were about to go off.

Kate looked at the bright bulb hanging from the ceiling. A long string dangled from the socket that held the bulb. When Kate pulled the string, the light went off. When she pulled it again, the light went on.

"Can you imagine what it would be like, having electricity all the time?" Kate asked. On the farm she'd grown used to facing the sun to see what she was doing. At night she turned toward a kerosene lamp.

For once Anders didn't laugh. His eyes looked thoughtful. "Maybe someday we'll use electricity for everything. If the lines come our way, I'll figure out how to string a wire. We could have lights in the barn."

Kate giggled. "Do you think the cows would like it?"

But Anders was serious. "Can you imagine what it would be like having a machine for milking cows?"

Kate shook her head. "No, I can't." It was hard enough for her to milk cows by hand. Even with all her imagination, she couldn't think how to use electricity.

But Anders could. "Maybe I ought to be an inventor," he said. "I'd think up newfangled things."

"To help you get out of work," Kate teased.

Anders grinned. "Yah, sure, to get out of work." But as he pulled the light off, then on, he had a faraway look.

To Kate it seemed he was seeing down through the years. More than once he'd figured out a way to do things—things she couldn't dream of doing.

Her brother's grin disappeared. "If I become an inventor, I won't leave the farm. I want to stay, no matter what. I want to live there all my life."

The sky was overcast when Kate came out of the Johnson house the next morning. Standing at the top of the stairs, she studied the clouds. What if it rained again? She wanted to see new places, but didn't look forward to another cold day.

When Kate reached the bottom of the steps, Anders set the baskets of food inside the wagon. Next came a wooden box with their extra clothes. Kate covered everything with heavy horse blankets, then sat down on the high spring seat.

Anders finished harnessing Wildfire and climbed up beside her. He flicked the reins, and whistled for Lutfisk. The dog raced around the corner of the house.

Stepping high, the black mare pranced down the dirt street. Near the Antler's Hotel, Anders turned north past the mill pond. Soon Wildfire crossed the bridge over the Wood River. Farther on, Anders directed her west toward Tennessee Flats.

Before long, the sun broke through the clouds, warming Kate's back. "At least we won't have to sit in wet clothes all day," she said as they came over a rise in the road.

"Don't talk too soon," her brother warned. A worried frown creased his forehead.

Then Kate saw what he meant. At the bottom of the hill, water covered the road.

Anders shook his head, as though unable to believe what he saw.

"This is Sand Creek?" Kate asked. Both upstream and down, trees and bushes stood in water. The dirt road disappeared into what looked like a large lake.

Pulling up Wildfire, Anders studied the situation. "Must be all that rain we had yesterday. Plus the snow melting real fast. I bet it's never been this high before!"

Kate's stomach tightened. The swiftly moving water hid whatever tree trunks and poles served as a bridge. Or had they been washed out? It was impossible to tell.

Some distance beyond the swollen creek, the road reappeared, partway up the hill.

Finally Anders pointed. "That must be the center of the crick. The water moves fastest there. If we drive straight out—"

He dropped his hand, lining up the closest part of the road with the road that emerged on the far side. "If we drive straight through, we should find the bridge."

"If?" Kate asked. "It's a long way across. And that water looks deep!"

"It is," he answered. "If I miss the bridge, we're in trouble. Like Papa says, big trouble."

Kate stared at the swirling water, as though it were an enemy. Then she realized it really was an enemy—one that could keep them from reaching Ben on time.

After another long look at the water, Anders clucked to Wildfire. As the mare stepped out, Anders guided her in a straight line toward the road on the far side.

Soon Wildfire's feet splashed in shallow water. Before long, the creek rose to her knees. The mare paused and looked around.

Anders flicked the reins, and Wildfire kept on. She walked carefully, feeling her way. The water surrounded the wheel hubs, reaching upward to the wagon bed.

Suddenly Wildfire froze, as though unwilling to take another step.

"Anders!" Kate warned.

"I know," he said. "But we can't go back."

He clucked to the mare. "Go on, girl!"

Wildfire turned her ears to the sound of his voice. But as she struggled forward, she stumbled.

"Must have stepped in a washout," Anders muttered, his voice tense. "Keep moving, girl!" He slapped the reins. "C'mon!"

The water lapped at the mare's belly. As though testing her footing, she stretched out one leg, then another.

In the next moment, Wildfire found better ground, but Anders pulled off his coat.

Kate looked down. In spite of the high wheels, water pushed against the boards of the wagon bed. A strong current swirled around them.

"Go on, Wildfire," Anders called. "Go on, girl!"

He handed the reins to Kate. "If the water gets any deeper, she can't swim. Not with the wagon. Not against this current."

"The wagon will pull her down?" Kate couldn't imagine anything worse than watching the mare drown.

Anders pulled off his boots and dropped them on the seat. Then he took the reins again.

The water of the main channel swept strong and cold against the mare's chest. In the next instant she wavered.

Kate clutched the seat. "Has the bridge washed out? Or did we miss it?"

Anders didn't answer. Whatever they had done, Wildfire had lost her footing. Thrashing in the water, she fought the stream. Instead of moving forward, she slipped sideways.

In the next instant Anders threw the reins at Kate and jumped off the wagon. As water sprayed up, he vanished into the creek.

Kate waited, her gaze on the spot where her brother went

down. The water was deep here. Too deep. Had Anders hit his head, jumping in?

Fighting against fear, Kate started to pray.

Then Anders surfaced. Treading water, he tossed his head to get the hair out of his eyes. But the current washed against him, carrying him downstream.

Once again Anders disappeared.

9

Lonely Meeting

*K*ate's hands clenched the reins. Her brother was a good swimmer. But could he handle the strong current, weighed down by clothes? Could he survive the ice-cold water?

As Kate stared at the place where Anders went down, panic overwhelmed her. Where was he?

Again Kate prayed. "Help him, Jesus. Help him!"

A moment later, her brother's blond head appeared above the water. As though he'd received extra strength, Anders fought the current, trying to reach his horse.

A short distance away, the mare thrashed in the water. Her eyes rolled in terror. As the wagon slipped sideways, it pulled Wildfire down.

Kate had all she could do to hold on. Then she saw Anders swimming toward the horse.

He reached for her bridle, but the mare's legs thrashed. Anders was forced to back off.

A moment later Wildfire found solid footing. Anders grabbed her bridle. Leaning into the harness, the mare surged ahead. Her large body rose from the swollen creek.

Leading Wildfire, Anders staggered up the sloping bank. Water streamed out the back of the wagon.

"We made it!" cried Kate. But her brother barely turned his head. He looked too tired to stand.

Hanging on to the bridle, Anders stumbled along the side of the creek. When he reached the dirt road, he started up the slope, then stopped the mare.

Wrapping his arms around Wildfire's neck, he hugged her. "Good girl!" Then Anders collapsed on the ground.

Suddenly Kate remembered Lutfisk. As she jumped down from the wagon, she saw the dog swimming across the creek. When he came up out of the water, he shook his body and sprayed Kate. Finding Anders, he licked his master's face.

Here the soil was sandy, the patch of earth dry. Anders lay there, too exhausted to move. His face looked gray white, his lips blue with cold.

Kate gave him his coat, and he sat up long enough to peel off his wet shirt. In the brisk morning air, he trembled, unable to stop his shivering. His hair dripped water.

Kate pulled off her own coat. "Rub your head," she said, then hurried to the wagon.

There she found every blanket wet. Quickly she searched the wooden box. When she discovered dry clothes for Anders, she felt she'd received a miracle.

As Kate gave him the clothes, he said, "We've got to rub down Wildfire."

"First you need a fire," Kate answered. "Where are the matches?"

"In the tool box." Anders spoke through chattering teeth.

Kate found the matches dry and safe inside a watertight tin. She had never built a fire outside, only within stoves. Now there was no choice.

Trees lined both sides of the road. As Kate headed into them, she moved quickly, searching for kindling.

The undergrowth was still wet from yesterday's rain. In protected places Kate managed to find the small sticks and dry leaves she needed. She carried them to Anders and found he'd pulled on dry clothes.

Kate hurried back to the woods for larger branches. When she returned a second time, Anders sat with knees pulled up, his arms trembling.

"Anders! Stand up!" Kate said. "Stamp your feet! Get moving!"

When he obeyed, Kate guessed how terrible he felt. Her six-foot brother bossed her around so often that it seemed strange telling him what to do. Even stranger to have him obey.

When Anders sat down again, he pulled Kate's coat over his wet head, but continued to shake.

On a patch of dirt a safe distance from the trees, Kate mounded the kindling she'd found. Lighting a match, she held it against the leaves and twigs. The small flame flickered, then went out.

Again Kate lit a match. Again the wind caught the flame before it took hold.

A third time Kate tried. A third time the wind blew out the match.

With each unsuccessful attempt Kate's panic increased. At last she sat back and stared at the small metal box. Only three matches left. She couldn't afford to lose even one more.

She looked at Anders sitting with a coat over his head. "Help me!" she wanted to cry out. But a nagging thought bothered her. Like a small voice it came. *Remember? You were going to keep up to Anders. You were going to do anything he could do.* Now Kate wasn't so sure.

Just then Anders pulled the coat off his head. "Turn your back to the wind," he said.

Kate moved to the other side of her small mound. Kneeling down to shelter the flame from the wind, she struck a match. This time the flame held. The leaves caught fire.

Carefully Kate added small branches, then larger ones. As they, too, caught fire, she sat back, filled with relief.

Anders crawled next to the fire, lay down, and huddled close. Even as Kate watched, he seemed to grow warmer.

When the fire burned steadily, she took long grass and rubbed down Wildfire. Like Anders, Kate couldn't help but hug the horse. Then she went to the carefully packed baskets of food.

As she opened the sandwiches, the bread fell apart. When she tried to pick up a cookie, it broke into mush.

Kate felt sick. "Our food!" she wailed. "It's soaking wet!"

"Forget the food!" Anders growled.

"But what are we going to do?" asked Kate. "We lost all our cookies and sandwiches for the next two days!"

"Forget it!" said Anders again. "We made it with our lives."

As the fire reached upward, Kate spread the wet clothes around it, then went searching for more branches.

This time she needed to go deeper into the trees. Oak grew here and jack pine freshly green with spring. Yet Kate found it difficult to find dry branches.

The farther she walked, the more uneasy she felt. *Bears*, she thought. *There are bears in these woods.* Only two nights ago Anders had wondered if bears had spooked the horses.

Now as Kate searched for wood, a squirrel chattered as though scolding her. A tree grew in a strange shape, and Kate stopped in her tracks. Then, directly in front of her, a bird flew up. Kate jumped, and her heart pounded.

It's only a partridge, she told herself. But it took a long time before her heart stopped thumping.

With each delay in not finding wood, Kate felt more uneasy. If she didn't get back soon, the fire would go out. But she couldn't find windfalls—branches on the ground—of a size she could carry.

She was almost ready to give up when she noticed a jack pine with its sharply pointed needles. On the lower part of the tree, the bare sticks left by dead branches stuck out from the trunk.

Even with Kate's short height, the dead branches were within reach. Best of all, they were dry.

Breaking off one stick, then another, Kate gathered an armload. Turning away from the tree, she started back to Anders.

Just then the nearby bushes seemed to sway in the wind.

But there's no wind here, thought Kate. She was too far into the woods.

She stared at the bushes. Still leafless from winter, the thick, brown branches reached up, almost as high as her head.

Was that a movement? Kate thought so. In that moment she remembered Papa. *He told us to stay together.*

It was too late now. Here she was, all alone.

Again the bushes swayed, this time so suddenly that Kate had no doubt about it. *There's something there, all right.*

In the next instant a large shape moved closer to the branches. Kate gasped.

Whatever it was, it moved again. Through the lighter brown of the bushes, it looked black.

Kate dropped the sticks she'd gathered. Step by step, she edged away, walking backward. Maybe if she was quiet enough, the bear would not see her. Maybe she could escape.

The next instant Kate backed into a tree, slamming into the bark.

"Owww!" she cried out in surprise. And then, "Anders!"

But her brother was too far away. He could not possibly hear.

10

More Trouble

*K*ate clapped a hand over her mouth. Something large was coming this way, moving fast. Had it heard her cry for help?

Moving around the tree, Kate started to run. As she turned to look back, the animal walked out of the bushes.

Kate stared. On its large black side, the animal had a few white blotches. Slowly it raised its head and mooed.

A cow!

Kate started to laugh. On farms without barbed-wire fences, cattle often wandered into the woods. Often it was difficult for owners to find them.

"C'mon, bossy," Kate said. Walking forward slowly, she kept talking.

The cow mooed again. Kate petted her neck, then walked away. The cow seemed eager to follow.

After picking up the wood she had dropped, Kate started back to Anders. As if she and Kate were longtime friends, the cow plodded behind, her bell jangling.

As they came out of the woods, Anders sat cross-legged, with hands stretched out to the fire. When he asked, "Are you Mary with her little lamb?" he seemed like his old self.

Kate grinned. "There's no fleece as white as snow." It felt good to see her brother back to normal.

"Hasn't been milked for a while," he said. "She looks mighty uncomfortable. Think we better help her out."

Using the bucket from the wagon, he knelt down next to the cow and started milking. He offered Kate the warm frothy milk, and she drank deeply. She couldn't remember when something tasted so good.

Anders milked some for himself, then set the bucket in a shallow part of the stream. The cold water lapped against the sides of the pail, cooling the milk.

For a time Anders warmed himself by the fire. When Lutfisk grew tired of sitting next to him, he found a stick and brought it to Kate.

"He wants to play," Anders said. "Give it a toss, and he'll fetch it."

Kate threw the stick as far as she could.

Lutfisk raced off. A minute later he was back to drop the stick at her feet. Several times more he brought it to Kate.

"Want to see something else?" Anders asked. "Take the shovel and leave it somewhere. I'm training Lutfisk to bring me tools."

Kate took the shovel from the wagon and showed it to the dog. While Anders held him, Kate hid the shovel in the dry, brown grass on the other side of the road.

"Go get it!" Anders commanded.

Like a streak of lightning, the dog tore across the road. Finding the shovel, he picked up the handle in his teeth. As he started toward Anders, the end of the handle dragged in the dirt.

Lutfisk dropped the shovel. He nosed along the handle, then picked it up. This time both ends of the shovel stayed off the ground.

"Did you see that?" Anders asked proudly. "He's figured out how to balance the weight in his mouth!"

"Pretty smart dog," Kate admitted.

As the fire died down, Kate tied a rope around the cow's neck and fastened the rope to the back of the wagon.

Anders brought buckets of water from the creek. After drowning the top layer of ashes, he pushed them aside with the shovel. He soaked the hot coals underneath, then held his hand about two inches above the wet pile.

"I still feel heat!" he exclaimed.

Taking several more trips, Anders poured on water until the coals and ashes felt cold to his touch.

When Kate and Anders returned to the wagon, they helped Lutfisk up to the high spring seat. Sitting between them, the dog faced the road, almost seeming human.

Anders clucked to Wildfire. "Tennessee Flats, here we come!" The wagon rolled ahead, and the cow plodded behind.

Anders looked at the sun. Already it was well on its way toward the middle of the sky. "Lost too much time," he grumbled. "If everything goes all right, we'll be in good shape. If not—"

As they continued up the slope in the road beyond Sand Creek, Kate glanced back. Just looking at the swirling water scared her. What if she'd had to break bad news to Papa? What if she'd had to tell him, "Anders drowned in the creek"?

Kate tried not to think about it. Yet Anders also turned for a last glimpse. Kate saw the expression on his face.

Then, as she glanced beyond the swollen water, her eye caught a sudden movement. What was it?

Kate stared in that direction. Whatever it was seemed to fade into a tree. Was someone following them? She couldn't be sure.

Soon the road evened out into two deep ruts stretching far ahead. Kate sneaked another look at her brother. His thatch of blond hair went this way and that, and a streak of mud crossed his nose. But right now he seemed more special than usual.

I'll be nicer to him, Kate told herself, not realizing how hard that promise would be to keep.

At the first farmhouse they spotted they left the cow with the grateful owners.

"Do you think the river will still be frozen?" Kate asked as they continued on their way.

"Maybe." Anders shrugged, as though not wanting to borrow trouble. "Depends."

"What do you mean, *depends*? If the creek is running, will the river be running too?"

"Nope, doesn't have to be. Cricks can stay open all winter."

For a time they rode without speaking. Here and there a pool of water stood, but most of yesterday's rain had disappeared.

"What's it like when the river thaws?" Kate asked.

"Some years it just gets soft, like mush. Other years it goes out with a roar."

"And this year?" asked Kate.

"It's been warm," he said. "Warm weather melts the snow. Lots of rain makes it worse. All that water runs into the rivers upstream."

Kate moved restlessly, thinking about the heavy rain of the day before.

"Those rivers feed into the St. Croix," Anders went on. "The St. Croix gets higher and higher. As the water rises, it loosens the ice along the banks."

"And then?" Kate prodded.

"I've never seen it, but Papa says the current pushes the ice. It grinds and rumbles like thunder, and all of a sudden it goes out."

Kate's hands clenched. "And there's no place to get across."

"No place at all." Anders flicked the reins. Again he glanced at the sun, as though counting the minutes.

Before long, Kate pulled off the sweater Mama had knitted for her. It felt good to have such an unusually warm day in March. Yet Kate longed for food. "I'm hungry," she said.

"So am I. How would you like one of Mama's great big meals right now? Topped off with hot apple pie?"

"How do you think Mama is doing?" Kate asked.

"She'll be all right," Anders said quickly. He kept his gaze on the road as if he didn't want to talk about it.

But Kate wanted to know more. "Do you remember when Lars was born?"

"A little. I was only three and a half. I remember Tina more."

More Trouble

"What was it like?"

"When Tina was born? It was October. I was seven, almost eight."

"I mean, what happened?"

"Lars and I were the only ones home. Papa had taken a load of potatoes to Grantsburg. Tina came earlier than Papa and Mama expected."

Anders' voice softened. Only recently had he begun talking about his first mother. When he did, he always sounded—Kate wasn't sure she could describe it. Wistful, maybe? Sad at something that was gone forever?

"What did you do?"

"I ran to the nearest neighbor, the people who lived where Erik does now. I ran the whole way. When I got there, I couldn't breathe enough to tell them what was wrong. But Mrs. Sandquist took one look and knew. She grabbed her coat and a basket of things. By the time she came out of the house, Mr. Sandquist had the horses ready. I rode back with them."

"And when you got home?"

Anders laughed. "When we drove up in the yard, Lars came running out. 'Baby here!' he said. He looked real proud that he was the only one around to tell about it."

Anders pushed back his hair. "When we went inside, we heard a mighty squall. Mighty big for someone as small as Tina. Mama had taken care of everything."

"All by herself?"

"All by herself."

"She was all right?"

Anders nodded. "Mama was—" He paused, as if searching for words. "Well, you know how *your* Mama is."

"And yours," Kate answered softly, remembering what Mama had told him.

A tinge of red crept into Anders' cheeks, as though he remembered too. But he asked, "You know how your mama always tries to be strong?"

Kate giggled. "Yah," she drawled. "And how she brushes the tears away, as if it's wrong to let us see them."

"You betcha."

When they came to a steep hill, Anders slowed Wildfire. A narrow stream tumbled down next to the road. More water streamed over a bank of red earth. "Good clay for chinking logs," said Anders.

At the bottom of the hill he stopped the wagon. Walking back, he found the spring and called to Kate. "C'mon! Fill up on water!"

Cupping her hands, Kate caught the icy water, washed her face, and then drank. Her hunger didn't go away, but she felt better.

They continued on and soon saw a large log house ahead of them. "Must be Berglunds'," Anders said.

As they drove closer, they found it was a two-family house. According to Papa, Berglund and his family lived in one end, and Petersons in the other. Each end had its own kitchen with a chimney and a cellar underneath.

The large home sat at an angle on the edge of the hill. Nearby were two barns, one for each family. The haylofts were at ground level, instead of one story up. Alongside the barns, the hill dropped away.

Stopping Wildfire, Anders looped her lead rope around a rail. "Let's ask Berglunds for lunch."

"You can work for your meal," Kate teased. "The way you did at Johnson's."

As it turned out, no one answered their knock in either end of the house. Kate and Anders started down the hill, looking for someone. They found that cows lived in the lower level of each barn.

"When they get thirsty, they just stroll down to the river," Anders said.

In the side of the hill they discovered a cellar for storing cream, but no one was there. When they returned to the farmhouse, they climbed into the wagon, and took the trail to Tennessee Flats.

"According to Papa, we're almost there," Anders said.

"And we're ahead of time!" Kate could hardly believe her own

More Trouble

words. "All we have to do is cross the ice, climb the hill, and wait for sundown."

As they passed into a flat field, Lutfisk ran off. Wildfire pricked her ears and moved more quickly.

From the high wagon seat, Kate looked west toward where the river should be. Beyond trees still bare of leaves, she caught a frightening glimpse.

A cold knot tightened her stomach. Quickly she glanced at Anders. Judging by the expression on his face, he, too, guessed the worst.

A moment later they came to a better view. Ahead of them stretched the blue waters of the St. Croix. The ice they needed for crossing the river was gone!

11

The Wild River

*W*ithout a word Anders urged Wildfire across the field to the landing known as Tennessee Flats. A worried frown lined his face.

As soon as they stopped, Kate dropped to the ground. Anders followed.

Around them lay great slabs of ice, thrown every which way, as though by a giant hand. Up and down the St. Croix, on both the Wisconsin and Minnesota sides, ice lined the shore.

Some of the great chunks stood on end, like jagged peaks pointing to the sky. Others lay almost flat, slanting only slightly.

Kate climbed onto one of those pieces. Stepping from one slab of ice to the next, she and Anders worked their way to the water.

"Has the ice just gone out?" Kate asked.

"Probably within the last day. Maybe even last night. Looks like we just missed crossing over."

The river was wide here—at least six or seven hundred feet across. The current was swift and strong with occasional chunks of ice floating downstream.

Kate stared at the deep blue water. As far as she could see in either direction, tall trees lined the hillsides.

"What a wild river!" she exclaimed. Yet she felt its beauty too.

Anders pointed at an opening in the trees across the river and downstream. "See that trail going off in the woods? That must be the landing. But the stone that marks it is covered by water."

To Kate it seemed as if her heart were being squeezed. If Ben came to the top of that hill, they wouldn't be able to see him. Nor would he be able to see them. Though the trees were still leafless from winter, their trunks and branches blocked the view.

Standing there, Kate felt the cold rising from the ice. She felt the wind across the water. Then, looking at the strong current, she felt hopeless.

"And this is supposed to be an easy crossing?"

"Yup," answered Anders. "It's wider here, but more shallow. In summer, I mean."

Kate sighed. "*Whatever* are we going to do?"

Anders shrugged, hunching his shoulders against the wind. "No ferries running yet. Little bit cold for swimming."

But the chill inside Kate came from more than ice. With all her heart she wanted to reach Ben before it was too late.

Like something burned into her mind, she remembered his words: "If you're there to meet me, I'll know you want to see me. If you're not, I'll go away and never trouble you again."

Anders still gazed across the river. "Wish I could have been here before loggers took out the big pine. Till then, this land didn't change in all the centuries the Chippewa Indians have been here."

Next to the crossing, Kate climbed off the ice. Here the ground eased down to the St. Croix with a gentle slope. Now in high water, the river bottom vanished almost immediately.

Going around the ice, Kate walked along the shore. *So I told Mama I'd help Anders figure out what to do*, she thought. Now the idea seemed ridiculous. Before they had left, Papa had prayed for courage, wisdom, and protection. They certainly needed that courage now.

The crossing was located at a bend in the river. Just upstream, stone piers anchored a boom of large logs linked together by chains. Once the river drive started, the boom would keep logs from piling up on shore.

Anders caught up to Kate. "I know one thing. We can't fight this current. We have to find a way to work with it."

"But how?" she asked. "Sand Creek was bad enough." Not by the biggest stretch of her imagination could she think of a way to work with the wild river.

She looked up at the sky. Judging by the sun, it had to be at least twelve o'clock. "Papa said we'd be in trouble. We sure are!"

Anders turned away from the river and started walking around. All of the snow was gone here, the ground dry. But farther back, under bushes and trees, the ground was soggy with long grass and wet leaves.

"What are you looking for?" Kate asked.

"People who use a crossing a lot sometimes leave a canoe or a boat. Maybe we can find one."

Anders and Kate headed in opposite directions. Starting upstream, Kate stopped at every clump of bushes. When she turned around and walked back, she noticed something she'd missed before. From the other direction it had seemed to be a log with branches and dead leaves over it.

This time Kate walked closer. Leaning down, she found the branches loose. When she pulled them away, she discovered a flat-bottomed rowboat. The boat lay upside down and was dirty and wet from being out all winter.

"Anders!" Kate shouted.

When she showed him her find, he looked excited. Together they tipped the boat over. The seams looked tight and the boat safe enough to use.

"That'll do it!" exclaimed Anders. "But there are no oars."

Again they searched, but this time without success. Even with oars, the trip across the swollen stream would be dangerous. They couldn't possibly navigate the river without them.

Then Kate remembered something. "You know, Anders, once Michael Reilly told me how he poled across a river."

"And who's Michael Reilly?" asked Anders.

"A boy I know."

"A boy you know," mimicked Anders. "Was this boy by any chance a friend?"

Kate felt a warm blush seep to the roots of her hair. Yes, of course, this boy was a friend when she lived in Minneapolis. Everyone in school knew that Michael was sweet on Kate. But she wouldn't tell Anders that.

"Michael said—"

Anders interrupted. "And Michael said—" His voice sounded high and sweet. "What, my dear sister, did Michael say?"

Kate flipped her long black braid over her shoulder. "If you will let me tell you," she said stiffly.

But Anders grinned. "You know, you might have the right idea—poling across, I mean. It's harder than oars, especially if I can't touch bottom. I've done it before, but not when the water ran this high."

Leaving the rowboat, he returned to the wagon. There he pulled out an ax and walked toward the trees farther up the shore.

As Kate trailed after him, her mind was far away. *Funny. I've almost forgotten about Michael. Maybe I'll go back to Minneapolis some time. Maybe I'll see him again.*

Kate knew that train fare would be an obstacle. Just the same, she didn't want to give up that hope.

Then her thoughts drifted to Erik. More than once he'd been a real friend. Kate liked talking to him and liked the kind of person he was. *I wonder who I'll marry when I grow up.*

Anders soon found a dead branch that was the size he needed. Using the ax, he shaped a pole about eight feet long and two inches thick.

When he returned to the crossing, he unhitched Wildfire from the wagon. Slipping on her halter, he led her to a patch of meadow grass and tied her lead rope to a stake. Then he and Kate dragged the rowboat down to the river crossing.

Lutfisk leaped into the front of the boat. With his tongue hanging out, he seemed to laugh at his master.

"All right, all right," Anders said. "You get to go along."

Lutfisk flopped on his belly between the first and second seats.

When Kate climbed into the boat, she reached down and slipped her fingers into the river. Quickly she pulled them out. Even close to shore, the water sent a cold tingle up her arm.

"You're sure we can make it across?" she asked. The rowboat seemed smaller all the time, and the river wider and deeper. Both of them were good swimmers, but Kate knew they wouldn't last long in the icy water.

As Anders gazed across the river, he seemed just as uneasy. "Current's mighty strong out there. It's deep, even here where it should be shallow."

"What if we get out in the middle, and you can't touch bottom with the pole?" Kate asked.

"That's what bothers me. The current will take us wherever it wants to go."

"Anders," Kate said slowly, as an idea came to her. "I just remembered something else."

She spoke quickly before Anders could tease her again. "You know, that story I heard about poling across the river? First Michael went upstream, along the shore, where he could touch bottom with the pole."

Anders grinned, as though he already guessed what she'd say. "Then he shoved out into the current, and it carried him downstream. Yup, you've got it, Kate."

As Anders pushed off from shore, the boat grated on gravel. When he stepped in, it rocked beneath his weight.

Bracing his feet squarely, Anders stood up. Pushing with the pole, he sent the boat upstream. Kate faced the bow and watched for rocks.

At first they followed the shoreline where it was more shallow. There the water lapped gently against the sides of the boat. Sunlight danced across the ripples on the water. But a few feet farther out, the current ran deep and strong.

Before long, Anders pulled off his jacket. Each time he used the pole, his muscles rippled beneath his cotton shirt.

Soon he found a rhythm, and they started making good time.

As they came into a small bay in the river, Kate saw animals playing on the ice.

With short legs and long bodies, they had black velvet-like paws and dark brown fur. Their thick muscular tails tapered down to a tip.

Kate turned back to Anders. "Are they otters?" she whispered and reached down to hold Lutfisk quiet. Kate had heard about otters, but had never seen them.

Anders grinned and nodded. Digging the pole into the river bottom, he held the boat from slipping downstream.

The otters had found a huge slab of ice next to the river. As Kate and Anders watched, one of the otters took three or four leaps and jumped. With forelegs back, it slid ten or twelve feet on its belly. Across the ice and down the muddy bank it went, then into the water.

Soon another otter followed the first. Already they had made a slide in the mud with a six-inch-wide groove.

Were they fishing or playing? Kate wasn't sure. The otters swam with heads high, well out of the water, and their backs slightly exposed.

Before long, a large otter turned toward the boat and hissed and snorted. Kate and Anders remained still. When the otter seemed satisfied that they weren't a threat, it went back to the others.

As Kate watched the animals play, all the discouragements of the day fell away. Then Anders started poling again. Soon they left the bay behind and continued up the swollen river.

"Hang on now," he said at last. "It's a mighty wobbly boat. And you lie still, Lutfisk."

With a big shove, Anders pushed away from shore. As the current caught the flat-bottomed boat, Kate clutched the sides.

Each time Anders dipped the pole, they moved farther out into the river. When he could no longer touch bottom, he sat down. Faster and faster they moved with the current sending them downstream.

Just then Kate heard the hooting of an owl. She turned her head to listen. From far away the lonely cry came.

For some reason the call made Kate uneasy. "Anders, is that an owl?"

Without thinking, she twisted around. The boat rocked with her sudden movement.

"Kate!" Anders shouted.

Kate's heart flip-flopped as water splashed over the side of the boat. It rocked again, and she hung on with all her strength.

Then, still quivering, the little boat settled once more into the current.

Kate no longer heard the call, but this time she faced ahead instead of turning. "Was it an owl?"

"Yup," answered her brother. "A barred owl. Or a mighty good imitation."

"In broad daylight?" Kate asked. "Are you sure it's an owl?" She remembered Erik on the way to the maple-syrup making. "Have you ever heard an owl during the day?"

"Yah sure. Once when Erik and I were out in the woods, he started calling like a crow."

Anders laughed. "An owl got mad and kept answering back. I walked till I was almost up to him. He had brownish-gray bars right across his breast. Saw him perched on a branch, as big as you please. When I got too close, he flew away. Have you ever seen one of those big ones fly between trees?"

Kate shook her head.

"Their wings are so wide, I can't figure out how they miss the branches."

As a large chunk of ice floated near, Anders used the pole to push it away. Then Kate heard a faraway sound. What was it? A human voice? She wasn't sure.

This time she turned slowly to avoid rocking the boat. Looking back, she scanned the shore on the Wisconsin side of the river. Someone was there, standing on a slab of ice.

"Anders! It's Joe! He's trying to tell us something!"

As Anders started to look around, the current caught the flat-bottomed boat and thrust it into rapids. The boat moved faster and faster.

"We're in trouble," Anders said suddenly, his voice tense.

Kate clutched the sides of the boat. Then she saw what he meant.

The high water was bad enough. The rapids swirling around them were even worse. But now, huge logs were coming downstream.

"The river drive has started!" said Anders.

Kate's hands tightened with fear. What if one of the logs crashed into them?

In the next instant the little boat hit an eddy and spun.

12

Another Warning

"Don't move," Anders warned Kate. "Stay, Lutfisk," he ordered when the dog started to stand up.

The boat leaned to one side, spun again, and straightened.

Kate drew a deep breath, but they weren't out of danger yet. Only two feet away a huge log bore down upon them.

"Hang on," said Anders. "No matter what happens, don't let go of the boat." Grasping his long pole, he pushed against the log until it floated past them.

A moment later another log threatened them. Again Anders pushed it off. But a third log struck them broadside.

As the small boat rocked, water sloshed into the bottom. Filled with panic, Kate clung to the sides until her knuckles turned white. Then the boat moved with the log and was not damaged.

Anders reached out with his pole. With a mighty thrust, he shoved the huge log away.

As it slid past them, Kate straightened her shoulders. Yet fear still washed over her, as cold as the water around them.

Anders lowered the pole into the river but could not touch bottom. Twice more the logs came too fast, thudding against the boat. Each time it shuddered with the impact. Each time Anders pushed the logs aside.

When Kate finally dared look toward shore, the current had carried them downstream. "Joe wants us to come back," she told Anders.

Her brother groaned. "You're sure?"

As Kate watched, Joe raised his arm and motioned for them to come his way.

"Can't think of anything I want to do less," Anders grumbled. "But it must be something important."

He dipped the pole into the river. Though it didn't grab water like an oar, the pole turned the boat just enough. The current took them toward the Wisconsin shore.

When at last the pole touched bottom, Anders braced his feet and stood up. They'd gone beyond the landing at Tennessee Flats, but Joe kept up with them along the riverbank.

As they came to an island, Anders eased the boat into a quiet channel. Ahead of them, a sandstone cliff rose from the water. Anders landed the boat where the bank was still low.

Joe caught the bow. "Your father asked me to find you," he said to Anders. "After you left, another letter came from Bernhard."

Joe looked at Kate. "Your mother's brother?"

"Ben," she said, as she climbed out of the boat.

"Ben," repeated Joe. "In his letter he said, 'After I wrote, I met a man from your area. He told me that if the ice went out, no one could cross at Tennessee Flats.' "

Anders laughed. "Well, at least he's got *that* right!"

As the boys pulled the boat farther up the bank, Joe kept talking. "Ben said, 'If you want to see me, I'll be at the Rush City ferry landing instead.' "

"The ferry!" Anders looked as if he couldn't believe the bad news. "Lot of good that will do!" He pushed his blond hair out of his eyes. "The ferry's not running yet. Because it's held by cables, a log could smash a hole right through its side."

"I know," answered Joe. "But Ben will be on the Minnesota side at sundown today."

"*Today!*" Kate exclaimed. The sun was past the midpoint. It beat down upon them, giving unusual warmth for this time of the year. Was it one o'clock? Two o'clock?

Kate wasn't sure, but she did know one thing. "We haven't got much time!"

Anders groaned. "Let me tell you the rest. Ben also said, 'If you're not there, I'll believe you don't want to see me. I'll go away and never bother you again.' "

Joe's black eyes danced. "Yah sure, you betcha."

Kate giggled, and Anders grinned. Yet before long he looked back at the main channel of the river. By now, logs floated past in a steady stream, filling the water from the Wisconsin to the Minnesota side.

"Worst of all, I'm hungry," said Anders. "We left our food in Sand Creek."

"I'll get some for you," Joe answered. He pulled a coil of flexible wire from his pocket. "I'll set a snare."

At the thought of food, Kate felt famished again. Yet she also felt grateful that Joe had reached them in time.

"If we'd gone up the hill, we would have missed you," she said. "How did you find us?"

"I followed your tracks. It wasn't hard. You make big ones." He grinned. "Not you, Kate. Anders and Wildfire."

The two boys picked up the boat. Carrying it between them, they walked back to the landing at Tennessee Flats.

"I don't know the way to the Rush City ferry," Anders said. "How far is it?"

Joe thought for a moment. "On the road, maybe seventeen, eighteen miles."

Kate gasped. "That's farther than from home to Grantsburg."

"There's no road that goes straight through," Joe said. "If you take the wagon, you'll have a long trip around. I'll show you a shorter way."

When Wildfire saw them coming, she tossed her head and whinnied. The boys returned the rowboat to its place near the landing. Then Joe picked up a stick and drew a map in the sand.

"There's an old Indian trail starting here at Tennessee Flats.

It goes across this field, through a swamp, and up over that hill."

He pointed, then lengthened the line. "Here's where you cross Wood River."

"We don't have any choice?" Kate felt nervous just thinking about it.

"There's no bridge except at Grantsburg," Anders reminded her. "If we go back to town, it'll be an extra ten or eleven miles. We don't have enough time."

Kate sighed. The Wood River was narrower than the St. Croix. Yet if farmers opened the dam and let water out of Big Wood Lake, Wood River would run deep and swift. There'd also be logs coming down.

Again Joe drew a line. "After you cross Wood River, keep going this way. At Fish Lake School, there's a path through the woods. It angles south to Steven Powell's farm on the St. Croix. From there keep on till you get to the ferry landing."

Kate studied the map. It looked like one long, almost straight line running roughly parallel with the St. Croix River.

Kate took the bucket to get water from the river for Wildfire. On the way back, she saw the two boys talking. When Anders looked her way, he suddenly stopped.

It made Kate feel uncomfortable. Yet it wasn't hard to guess what he and Joe were saying. Once she and Anders reached the ferry landing, they'd have to cross the St. Croix again. With the log drive started, that seemed even more impossible.

Anders left the halter under Wildfire's bridle and tied the lead rope around his waist. Coiling the long reins, he tied up the slack.

"The trail's not wide enough for a wagon," he told Kate. "So don't bring anything you can leave behind."

They left their coats in the wagon, and took only their sweaters. Anders put the match tin in his shirt pocket and buckled a hatchet inside a holder on his belt. After jumping onto Wildfire's back, he helped Kate up behind him.

As Anders lifted the reins, Joe stood back from the horse.

"There's someone in the woods," he warned. "Someone who doesn't belong there, I mean."

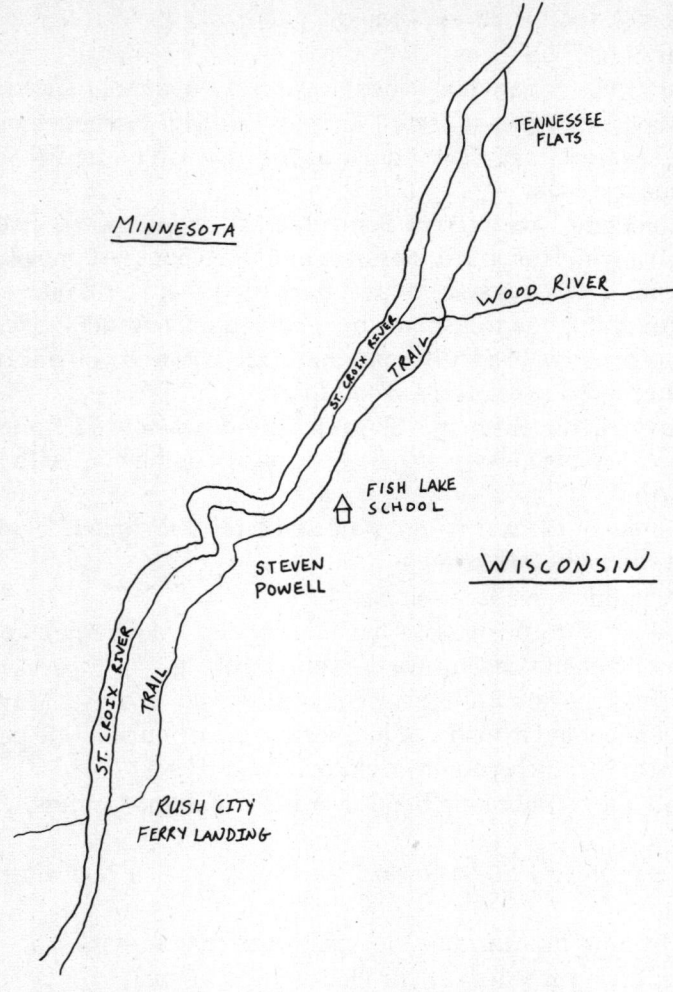

Though ready to flick the reins, Anders stopped. His hands seemed frozen in midair.

"It's a man with big feet, big boots," Joe went on. "He followed you. He walked all around the place where you built a fire."

"And the place where I found the cow?" Kate felt uneasy, remembering that she'd been alone.

Joe nodded. "Then he started coming this way."

"After us?" Kate barely breathed.

"After you for a while." Joe's black eyes no longer danced.

"Maybe that's what I saw," Kate said slowly. "Someone on a horse seemed to slip behind a tree. But I wasn't sure if I was imagining things."

"Sometimes he walked. Sometimes he rode a horse. Every once in a while he pulled his horse into the woods. At one place the ground was marked up, as if he waited there for a bit."

"You think he's still somewhere behind us?" Anders asked.

Joe shook his head. "Not anymore. He followed you a ways, then headed down toward Wood River."

He pointed at the map. "He's not behind you now. He's ahead of you." Tossing away the stick, he rubbed out the map with his moccasin.

In spite of the warm sun, Kate suddenly felt chilled. "So we might run right into him."

Joe nodded, his face solemn.

Kate tried to push aside her uneasiness. "Maybe he's gone by now." Yet she knew it was wishful thinking.

"Or maybe he's waiting for you, Kate!" said Anders. "Maybe he'll hide behind a bush and pounce on you when you ride past! Maybe he'll snatch you off, right behind my back!"

Kate flipped her long braid over her shoulder. "Anders, you are mean!"

Her brother winked toward Joe. But the other boy did not smile.

"Listen to my warning," he said. "The man is evil."

Anders' grin faded. "Evil? How do you know?"

"When I was in Grantsburg, I heard there's been a couple of men hanging around town—men that people don't know. Both are tall, but not fat. One of them has a small scar on the center of his chin."

Kate's fingers clenched. She looked at her brother's back and wished she knew what he was thinking. Was Anders also remembering the scar on Ben's chin?

"Do you know which of the men was following us?" Anders asked.

Joe shrugged. "I saw only one of them, and it was almost dark. He was watching people along the street, staring at them like—"

Joe paused as though words failed him.

"Like his eyes were cold," Kate said.

Joe nodded, but Anders laughed. "So we have an evil man with cold eyes!"

In spite of his teasing, Kate remembered how she felt when she saw the stranger. "Joe, can you go with us?" she asked quickly.

He nodded. "I'll come with you till I hear a partridge drumming. Then I'll get food and catch up again."

"If you're off somewhere, is there some way we can signal you? If we need help, I mean?"

"Call me," he said. "Call me with the hooting of an owl."

13

Fight for Life

*K*ate stared at Joe. That night in the woods Erik had insisted that what they'd heard wasn't a real owl. Only a short time ago, when they were out on the river, she'd heard the hooting again.

"Joe?" asked Kate. "Do you practice calling like an owl?"

When he grinned, Kate had her answer. "Will you show us how?" she asked.

In answer he gave the call of a barred owl. *Whoo, whoo, whoo, whoo—whoo, whoo, whoo, whoo-ah!*

It gave Kate a strange feeling. Joe stood directly in front of her, yet the hooting sounded as real as what she'd heard in the woods.

"Want to try it?" Joe asked. "The call of an owl is the Chippewa word for owl. We say, *goo-coo-ka-oo*."

Kate listened closely. Sure enough, when she used the Chippewa words Joe told her, it sounded like the hooting she'd heard. He'd added only a few words to imitate a barred owl.

Several times Kate tried the call, and finally Joe said, "That's it. I'll hoot like a barred owl three times to tell you where I am. You call back, and we'll find each other."

"And if there's danger?" Kate asked.

"I'll change the call with the *whoo-ah!* fourth, instead of at the end. You'll know it's not a real owl."

Anders flicked the reins, and Wildfire started across the field with Kate riding behind Anders. Joe ran alongside, and Lutfisk followed him.

When they reached the swamp, Joe ran ahead. The narrow path took the high spots through marshy areas, then brought them up a steep hill. When they came out on a ridge, Joe left them to hunt for food.

Anders turned to Kate. "If we spot the timber swindler, we'll sneak away so he doesn't see us. We'll head for Grantsburg and Big Gust." His voice sounded confident, as though he could handle anything.

"You're mighty sure of yourself," Kate said.

"Yup. If we find the swindler, we won't *let* him hurt us."

"But Joe says he's big. And remember? The man we saw near Wood Lake was big. Tall, I mean."

"Tall doesn't always mean strong." Anders flexed his muscles. "'Course with me, it does."

Kate did not smile. She knew that with each step Wildfire took, they were riding into danger.

As they followed the old Indian trail, the woods grew close. Jack pine with sharply pointed needles reached out, brushing against Kate's arms and legs. More than once she jumped before she realized it was only a branch.

"I'm hungry," Anders said after a while. "Really hungry."

"My stomach's growling," Kate answered.

"You don't have to tell me. I can hear it."

By now the skin on Kate's face felt tight and drawn, as though sunburned. She rubbed her nose, and it hurt.

For a time they rode along the ridge. After several turns in the trail, Kate felt uneasy. Joe hadn't said anything about these turns. Had he shown them just the general direction they should take?

Finally Anders pulled up Wildfire. "Do you think we're headed the right way?"

Kate knew her brother well enough to guess that he was trying to hide his worry. She remembered Joe's map. "We should be getting close to Wood River."

As she spoke, both of them glanced up at the sky. A stand of jack pine made it impossible to see the sun. Without the sun they could not tell either time or direction. Except for the thin, packed-down line of the trail ahead, there was no break in the trees.

"Mighty lonely out here," Anders said lightly.

"Mighty creepy, you mean." The pine and oak closed in around Kate, giving her the feeling of a nighttime woods.

Her brother clucked to Wildfire, and the mare stepped out.

"Anders," Kate said, as she tried to take her mind off the eerie woods. "What do you think is happening to Mama?"

When he didn't answer, Kate asked again, "What if she's having the baby right at this moment? What if she's having it, and we don't even know?"

Anders shrugged, and Kate wished she could see his eyes. She felt sure he cared, more than he would say.

"Do you think she's all right?"

"I think she's all right." But his voice lacked his usual confidence.

Kate looked around. *I don't like these woods,* she thought again. There was something about the way the trees closed in. She couldn't explain it. It was something she felt.

Silly! She tried to laugh at herself, but then she wondered: Was it really the forest that bothered her, or something more? Maybe Joe was right—that an evil man walked in these woods.

"Where's Lutfisk?" Kate asked, when she realized she hadn't seen him for some time.

"He always comes back," Anders told her. "He'll find us."

A moment later Kate heard a strange sound. It reminded her of the night near Wood Lake. She poked Anders in the back.

Her brother pulled up Wildfire. As the mare came to a halt, Kate heard the noise more clearly. It was sawing, all right, and close at hand.

Anders slipped down from Wildfire and tied her lead rope

to a tree. Quietly Kate followed her brother.

With each step they took, the sawing grew more distinct. Then as Kate listened, it stopped.

Careful to avoid any branch that would snap, they came at last to an opening in the trees. A large pile of logs stood on the banks of what had to be the Wood River.

Without making a sound, they crept forward. Then Anders put a warning hand on Kate's arm. His lips shaped a word: Wait.

Wait for what? Kate wanted to see the timber swindler, to know who he was.

Anders' frown held her back. When she stopped, he headed for the clearing. Each time he came to another tree, he stood behind it, looking ahead. Then, step by step, he moved on.

When Anders reached the end of the large pile of logs, he looked around and motioned for Kate to come. As she caught up to him, he pointed to a battered black hat on top of the logs.

On the ground lay sawdust and thin slices of wood—pieces of wood newly sawed from the end of the logs. The timber swindler had to be nearby.

Kate's hands knotted into fists. "Where is he?" she whispered. In the stillness her words seemed loud to her ears.

Anders stepped forward into the sawdust. Picking up a small slice of wood with a brand on it, he slipped it inside his shirt.

Then Kate noticed his tracks. In the soft earth near the riverbank, as well as in the sawdust, her brother's boot prints showed clearly.

Kate pointed down. Scuffling his feet, Anders tried to hide his tracks. In that moment Kate heard the sharp crack of someone stepping on a dry branch.

"Anders!" Kate warned hoarsely.

Her brother turned his head toward the sound, and both of them listened. Whoever it was seemed to think he was all alone in the woods.

"The swindler is coming back!" Kate whispered.

Anders bounded away from the pile of logs. Kate followed him into a tangle of underbrush. For a moment they knelt down behind a clump of bushes.

The bare, leafless branches offered little shelter, but from here Kate could see the timber swindler. Tall and fairly slender, he walked to the pile of logs with quick, sure movements. As he started sawing, he stood with his back toward them.

"I want to see his face," Anders said in a low voice. "Let's go around on the other side."

"You mean, let's get out of here," whispered Kate. "It would be much smarter to leave."

Before they could slip into the woods, a dog barked from somewhere off in the trees.

"Lutfisk!" whispered Anders.

The swindler raised his head, listened, and dropped his saw. As he picked up his branding hammer, he looked at the ground.

Anders groaned. "He sees my tracks."

A moment later, Lutfisk barked again. This time he sounded closer.

"He'll give us away," Kate said.

Crouching almost double, Anders crept deeper into the woods, followed by Kate. Moving from tree to tree, they circled the clearing. When they found the trail, they started running.

By the time they came to Wildfire, Kate was out of breath. Anders untied the mare's rope and jumped on her back. Reaching down, he pulled Kate up behind him, then urged Wildfire ahead.

At a turn in the trail, Lutfisk found them. Kate glanced back. No one followed behind.

"We got away," she whispered, still afraid to speak aloud.

"Not yet," Anders warned.

Their path wound around the place where the swindler worked. Knowing that he would pick up any sound, Anders kept Wildfire to a walk. Before long, the trail brought them to another part of the Wood River.

Again Kate looked around. She couldn't push aside her worry that the man would follow. So far the road was empty.

Then Wildfire started down the steep hill. Kate and Anders leaned back to help the mare keep her footing. The trail behind them slipped out of sight.

The Wood River twisted and turned between large trees as it found its way to the St. Croix. Swollen by rain and melting snow, the usually narrow river flowed beyond its banks.

Anders studied the swiftly moving water. "An old-timer would drop a tree for a bridge," he told Kate. "But we don't have the time or the saw. You'll have to go over on Wildfire's back."

Filled with dread, Kate gazed at the cold, dark water. Lately she'd ridden the mare often, but taking her across a flooded river was another matter.

"What about you?" she asked. "Wildfire can carry both of us."

"Don't want to take a chance on our weight. She'll probably have to swim for it."

"So what are you going to do?"

Anders offered his lopsided grin. "Me? I'm riding that log."

He tipped his head toward the bank. About five feet above the waterline, two small slender trees kept an old log from rolling into the river.

"Are you serious?" Kate asked.

"Yup. Used to practice on Rice Lake. If I ever work on a river drive, I'll have to know how."

"You'll have to know how, all right. The water will be mighty cold if you fall!"

"You haven't seen log drivers compete against one another. They can stand and run on a log all day." Anders pulled off his boots and tied them inside his sweater.

"Give me yours," he said to Kate.

She stepped back. "If you get dunked, you'll lose 'em."

"No, I won't. But they *will* get wet when *you* ride across."

Kate found that hard to believe. Surely she'd stay drier on Wildfire than he would standing on a log.

"Hurry," said Anders as he rolled up his pant legs. "The swindler might catch up any minute. And we've got to find Ben."

Though still unwilling, Kate yanked off her boots and stockings and tied them inside her sweater.

Going over to the log, Anders worked it free from the trees. Then he knotted both his sweater and Kate's around his neck.

Fight for Life

Returning to Wildfire, he took hold of the bridle. With Kate on the mare's back, Anders led the horse to the water. Wildfire snorted and stepped away.

Anders tugged at her bridle. The mare started to rear. Kate slid back and almost fell off.

Her brother spoke sharply, and Wildfire settled down, but her eyes rolled with fear. Anders waited a minute, then let go of the bridle.

Kate tightened the reins. The mare moved restlessly, as though sensing Kate's panic.

"If she starts to swim, grab her mane and slide back on her," Anders said as he started toward the log. "If you lean forward you'll push her head down. You have to keep her nose out of water."

Trying to act brave, Kate patted the mare's neck. "It's all right, girl. You haven't got a wagon this time."

Wildfire turned her ears to the sound of Kate's voice, but stood her place. With butterflies churning her stomach, Kate clucked to the mare.

"Dig in your heels," called Anders softly from near the log. "You have to let her know who's boss."

Again Kate urged Wildfire ahead, but the mare refused to obey.

"She'll come when I shove out," said Anders. "If I float downstream, try to take her straight across."

Anders rolled the log the rest of the way down the bank. When it tumbled into the water, he jumped on.

The log rocked, then spun, and Anders nearly lost his balance. With waving arms he faced into the spin. His feet moved quickly, as though he were running in place.

By the time the log slowed its spinning, Anders was halfway across the river. He looked toward Kate and grinned, then called to Lutfisk.

The dog jumped into the water and paddled toward Anders. But Wildfire stayed on the bank, still afraid to go on.

Kate gritted her teeth. *I can do anything my brother can do,* she told herself. Again she dug in her heels. But the mare did not move.

Anders whistled. Immediately the mare responded. As she plunged into the river, the icy water touched Kate's bare feet.

"Yowie!" she cried out, in spite of her best intentions.

Anders grinned. In the next instant, the log beneath his feet rolled in the opposite direction. His arms thrashed the air. Then he turned into the spin and ran in place.

Wildfire whinnied, and Kate clucked to her. "Go to Anders." The river reached Kate's knees, and she flinched against the cold.

Then the water came level with the mare's back, and Kate realized that Wildfire was swimming. Clutching her mane, Kate slid back on the horse.

As the water crept through her clothes, panic washed through Kate. For the first time she wondered if she could hang on.

"Anders!" she called. No longer did she care if she kept up to him. No longer did it matter what he thought. She wanted only to live.

But Anders had landed downstream on the far bank. As though from far away, Kate heard his call, "C'mon, Wildfire." Again he whistled.

Then the current caught Kate, sweeping her off the mare's back. In water over her head, Kate clung to the mane, frozen by a terror colder than the river.

14

Which Way Now?

A moment later Wildfire touched bottom and stood up. As the mare climbed onto the bank, Kate staggered with her to solid ground.

When Anders reached them, he took hold of the bridle. "Good girl!" he said. "I'm proud of you."

Surprised by the unusual praise, Kate turned toward Anders. But he wasn't talking to her.

The mare nudged the boy's shoulder, as though agreeing with him. When she shook herself, beads of water flew off her back in every direction.

The air that seemed warm before the river crossing left Kate shaking. "I need a fire," she said.

As Anders pulled on his boots, he glanced across the river. "I don't dare make one." He gave Kate both sweaters, but told her, "Take only a minute. The swindler probably heard our noise."

Behind a clump of bushes, Kate wrung out her skirt. With hands fumbling with cold, she shrugged into her sweater. Her long stockings proved even more difficult. When she tried to pull them on, they clung to her wet skin.

She struggled with her boots next. Wondering if she'd ever be warm again, she put her brother's sweater over her own.

"Hurry up!" Anders called softly.

When Kate returned to him, Anders was keeping watch, looking back across the river.

"Have you seen anything?" she asked through chattering teeth.

Her brother shook his head. "But the swindler will come. If he followed us before with no reason—"

"No reason?" Kate asked. "We saw him at Wood Lake, don't forget! Remember what you said? 'If we see the timber swindler, we'll just sneak away and get Big Gust!' "

Anders only laughed. "That's what we'll do, all right."

"But what will the swindler do if he finds *us*?" Kate asked.

Anders shrugged, but his eyes were more serious than usual. "Probably hide us somewhere to make sure we don't tell anyone what he's doing. At least not till he's collected the money from the sawmill."

Kate trembled. The chill she felt came from more than cold water.

With a bound Anders leaped onto Wildfire. Reaching down a hand, he pulled Kate up behind him, then flicked the reins.

"Did the swindler have a horse?" Kate asked as they started out.

"Yup. Standing off to one side. A good looking bay with long slender legs. Bet she can run fast."

For a time they rode at a steady pace. As the air struck Kate's wet hair and skirt, she shivered till she thought she'd fall off. Yet she couldn't ask Anders to stop.

When they neared a bend in the road, Kate looked back.

"Anders!" she exclaimed, her voice tense.

A man had ridden up behind them. Though still some distance away, he was riding hard, closing the gap.

As Anders twisted around, Kate pointed.

The man's black hat hid his face, but she had no doubt about the bay horse. Its long legs reached out, seeming to fly over the dirt road.

"Hold on!" exclaimed Anders, and Kate grabbed him around the middle. He dug in his heels and slapped the reins at the same time. Wildfire bolted forward.

The pounding gallop tore at Kate's insides. Just as she felt she could handle it no longer, Anders slowed the mare and turned his head.

"We have to get away from the road. If we stay here, it's just a test of who runs fastest."

Kate didn't like that idea one bit. Wildfire had been traveling hard much of the day. A fresh horse would have the advantage.

"Help me find a place," Anders said. "We've got to hide."

About fifteen yards farther on, Kate pointed to a gap in the underbrush along the side of the road. Anders turned Wildfire into the bushes.

The opening was barely wide enough for a horse to pass through. As soon as jack pine screened them from view, Kate and Anders slid down.

Quickly he snapped on the mare's lead rope. "Take Wildfire in as far as you can. I'll get rid of the hoof prints."

Grabbing a pine branch from the ground, Anders headed back to the road.

As Kate hurried the mare deeper into the woods, Lutfisk caught up. He was wet and covered with sand, and his long tongue hung out.

When Anders found them again, he'd been running hard. "I went back as far as I dared," he said when he caught his breath. "The swindler will figure out that we left the road. But if he follows from where our tracks leave off, he'll enter the woods at a different place."

Anders took the lead rope from Kate. "Be quiet," he warned. "The swindler can't be far behind."

Before long, distant hoofbeats sounded along the road. Anders stopped and put his hand across Wildfire's muzzle.

"Get Lutfisk," he whispered to Kate.

Quickly Kate knelt down. As she tried to keep the dog quiet, the hoofbeats moved nearer. Closer and closer the horse came.

Kate's hands tightened. What if Lutfisk barked? Or Wildfire whinnied?

Soon the horse came even with the trees where they stood. The moment seemed to last forever.

Then the hoofbeats passed beyond them and faded away.

Kate sat back. For a few minutes, at least, they were safe. But her heart still pounded.

As they started out again through the woods, Anders walked at a rapid pace, leading Wildfire. Lutfisk darted in and out of the trees.

Ducking beneath low-hanging branches, Anders picked his way between the jack pine and oak. Often Kate needed to take running steps to keep up with his longer stride.

The faster Anders moved, the more afraid Kate became. What if she lost sight of him? All she could think about was the man on the road. When would he turn and come back?

By the time they'd gone some distance, Kate's side ached with hurrying. Whenever the pines allowed a view of the sky, she looked up. *It's a good thing Anders knows where we're going.* She felt more and more confused.

Sometimes they seemed to head south, other times west, and occasionally, even a bit north. But Kate staggered on, following her tall brother.

When he finally slowed his headlong pace, she whispered, "How will Joe find us?"

"No problem," said Anders. "Joe can track anybody or anything."

"But if he can find us, so can the swindler."

"Depends on how good a tracker he is. He might be fooled by the brush marks. Joe won't be. He'll just follow the marks into the trees."

"I wish Joe would catch up," Kate said.

Anders hurried around any soft ground where they might leave footprints. At last they came to a spring and a clearing where it was safe to build a fire.

There Anders stopped and let the reins trail. Wildfire nosed the ground for grass.

"Take a minute," Anders said in a quiet voice, and his kindness surprised Kate.

Feeling grateful for a chance to rest, she dropped down on a log. During their race through the woods, she'd grown warmer. But now when they stopped, she trembled again.

Quickly her brother collected dry leaves and small branches. In a sheltered spot he started a fire with one of their two remaining matches. Gradually he added the driest wood he could find in the hope that smoke wouldn't betray them.

Unbraiding her long hair, Kate shook it out, then crept closer to the small fire. Lutfisk perked his ears and tipped his head from side to side.

"You crazy dog," she said, petting him in spite of his wetness. While they faced endless trouble, Lutfisk looked as if he were having the time of his life.

As Kate grew warmer, her shivering finally stopped. Yet worry felt like a weight on her back.

"Anders?" she asked, as he sat down next to her. Kate spoke softly to make sure she wouldn't be heard. "If Ben is the timber swindler—"

She paused, afraid to go on. Still it was something she had to know.

"If Ben is the swindler, he needs to reach the St. Croix ahead of us, doesn't he?"

"'Fraid so, Kate." Her brother's voice was little more than a whisper.

"I keep thinking about Mama. I think about the way she looks at that picture."

"The one of her family?"

Kate nodded. "If we find Ben, how will we know if we can trust him?"

Anders shrugged. "We don't know that he's the swindler."

"I'm scared about taking Ben home to Mama," Kate answered. "How will she feel if he's still lying and stealing?"

"Don't worry your head about it," Anders said.

"But I do." Kate looked up into his eyes. "How can Mama forgive Ben when she might lose so much? She's taking a big chance about whether he's honest."

When Anders didn't reply, Kate kept thinking about it. Then suddenly, as though a candle were lit, she felt sure of something. *Mama forgives Ben because Jesus forgave her!*

The idea startled Kate. Through his death on the cross, Jesus had provided a way for anyone who felt sorry and asked forgiveness to be forgiven. By inviting Ben home, Mama was offering that kind of forgiveness.

It made Kate feel proud of her mother. At the same time, she didn't want Mama hurt even more.

"Anders," Kate said quietly. "Wouldn't it be awful to have your brother betray you?"

Anders grinned. "Or your sister."

"Anders, I'm serious. Wouldn't it be terrible? Someone from your own family, and you couldn't trust him?"

"Well, you know how it is," Anders said lightly. "Everybody has a sister they can't trust."

Kate stared at him. "What do I have to do to get you to understand? I'm really scared! All you do is make a joke of it."

Anders looked her straight in the eye. For once no laughter played around his face. "Kate, there's one thing I promise you. Even though I tease you, you can trust me."

Without warning, tears blurred Kate's vision. Impatiently she brushed them away. Yet even that reminded her of Mama.

"Thanks, Anders," Kate said, her voice softer than it needed to be.

Anders looked down at his feet, as though her tears made him nervous. Something inside Kate trembled and broke.

Strange, she thought. *I'm not mad at Anders anymore. I want to trust him, like Mama wants to trust Ben.*

Is that what forgiveness is? Going beyond the bad times? Accepting a brother just the way he is?

"Thanks," Kate said again. She felt amazed that her brother seemed to understand.

Anders grinned. "Think nothing of it. Every now and then I have to remind you what a fine fellow I am."

But Kate wasn't fooled. She knew that he really cared about

what happened to Mama and Ben. He even seemed to care about what happened to her.

"We have to get moving," Anders said after a moment. "Or we'll never find Mama's little brother."

Kate was starting to warm up, but she knew they couldn't wait long enough for her skirt to dry. Quickly she pulled back her hair and braided it again.

Anders bent a piece of birchbark into a container. Bringing water from the spring, he put out the fire.

Kate walked to an opening in the trees. Between the branches of an oak, she found the sun. "Something isn't right," she said.

Then she knew what it was. "We're going the wrong way."

Anders stared at her. "You're sure?"

Kate nodded. She felt as though she were staring into a bottomless pit.

Coming to where she stood, Anders studied the sky and groaned. "We got turned around. Probably when we were moving so fast."

"We've been going back to Wood River, haven't we?" asked Kate.

"'Fraid so." Anders sounded sick. "And the sun's getting lower all the time."

15

Caught Between!

*W*ith a look of panic in his eyes, Anders led Wildfire to a nearby stump. Kate climbed onto the mare's back. Using the lead rope, Anders hurried ahead of his horse.

Faster and faster they moved. Whenever they reached an open place in the trees, Anders looked up. Whenever he looked up, he increased his pace. But the worried look didn't leave his eyes. Kate knew he wasn't really sure where he was going.

Ducking low-hanging branches, Kate tightened nervous fingers in Wildfire's mane.

"What if Ben leaves before we get there?" she asked. The thought haunted her. "He'll go away, thinking we don't care."

Anders glanced back as if he'd heard her. Yet he didn't answer. Even his eyes looked discouraged.

"Anders?" Kate asked.

When her brother still ignored her, Kate raised her voice. "Anders!"

This time he turned to her. "Shhhhh!"

Kate reached forward and tugged the lead rope. Her brother had to stop.

"Anders," she said. "We'll never make it."

"I know. It's impossible." For the first time Anders seemed to give up hope. "We've tried everything!"

"No, we haven't," Kate answered. "Before we left, Papa prayed for us. He asked God to give us wisdom—to help us know what we needed to do. But *we* haven't asked God for help."

She remembered her panic-filled prayer when Anders disappeared in Sand Creek. "We haven't asked God together, I mean."

Anders looked at her, and Kate saw the struggle in his face. Then he said, "Well, at home Papa always prays. So I guess I should try."

He looked uncomfortable, as though hoping Kate wouldn't make a smart remark. She felt too surprised to think of one. Instead, she bowed her head.

For a moment Anders stood without speaking, as if wondering what to ask. "We give up, God," he said finally. "We don't know what to do."

Again he paused, then prayed, "Will you show us where we are? And Jesus, if Ben is honest, help us reach him in time."

"Ah-men," Kate said.

When she opened her eyes, both she and Anders looked toward the sun. Here they could see it plainly, and it rested only a short distance above the treetops.

"So what do we do now?" Anders asked.

"I don't know," Kate answered. "But I know that God will help us." With all her heart she believed He would show them what to do.

Once more Anders started out. He changed direction slightly, then hurried on, leading the mare.

A few minutes later the trees thinned. Anders looked both ways, then walked out from the thick undergrowth.

"A road!" Kate exclaimed.

Anders grinned.

"If you hadn't changed direction—"

"I know," he said, his eyes serious. "I would have missed it."

It wasn't much of a road, but it was empty, at least for now.

"It has to go somewhere," Anders said, and swung up on Wildfire, ahead of Kate.

Once on the road, Anders slapped the reins. The black horse leaped forward. Anders dug in his heels, and Wildfire broke into a canter.

Several times Anders looked back over his shoulder. At last he slowed Wildfire to a trot. A short distance ahead of them a building appeared.

"Fish Lake School!" Kate exclaimed.

"Yah sure, you betcha!" Anders seemed awed by suddenly knowing where they were. "Now watch for the shortcut to the river."

Across from the school they found a hard-packed line of dirt into the woods. Wildfire trotted onto the narrow path willingly, as if there were water ahead.

The path led them west, then angled south. In about a mile, Kate saw blue water ahead. Logs from upstream filled the channel, but Kate breathed a sigh of relief. At least they'd come back to the St. Croix River.

"Not so fast," growled Anders. "We still have six or seven miles to the ferry. And somehow we have to cross over to Minnesota."

The tall trees on the other side of the St. Croix cast long shadows on the water. The wild river looked even more dangerous than before.

"How much time do we have?" Kate asked.

Anders shook his head. "Not much," he said. "Not much at all." As he spoke, the sun touched the top of the trees.

Anders turned Wildfire south to follow the path along the riverbank. With each bit of ground they covered, the shadows on the water lengthened.

The channel was narrower here than at Tennessee Flats. As far upstream as Kate could see, logs rode the strong current.

They had gone more than a mile when they came to a barn and a large frame house set back from the river. "Must be Powells'," Anders said.

Nearby were other buildings, and close to the water a sawmill. Along the bank next to the mill, a rowboat waited, ready for use. But Anders did not stop. With logs coming down the river, they could not use the boat.

"What are we going to do?" Kate asked. The faith she'd felt when praying already seemed far away, long ago.

Anders only shrugged.

Soon after passing the farm buildings, they came to a bend in the river. Massive logs filled the water, piled one on top of another. Some stood on end, others at crazy angles. More logs, riding the current from upstream, slammed against those already there.

Kate's stomach tightened. Crossing the wild river had been difficult enough before. Now it seemed one hundred times more impossible.

But Anders reined in Wildfire. He sat there, looking across the river. "Mighty big log jam," he said slowly.

"Hey, Anders, let's go," answered Kate. "We can't waste time."

Instead, her brother slid off the horse and walked closer to the river. When he turned back, a wide grin lit his face.

"Take a look," he said. "Take a *good* look!"

As Kate urged Wildfire forward, she felt awestruck by what she saw. Close now, she could tell how big the logs really were.

"Some of them are over thirty feet long!" exclaimed Anders. Flipped every which way, they looked like giant toothpicks.

Then Kate guessed what Anders wanted her to see. At the bend, the logs were jam-packed against the shore. "It's a bridge!" she exclaimed. "Let's go!"

The minute she spoke, Kate felt afraid. She'd heard stories about log jams—plenty of stories. Soon the men who drove the logs downstream would catch up. They'd work hard to break the jam apart. Yet even experienced men slipped off logs now and then. Every year men lost their lives that way.

Here, too, ice lined the shore. As far as she could tell, logs were jammed all the way to the Minnesota shore.

"I'm going across," Anders said.

Kate remembered Sand Creek. "If you make one wrong move—"

"I know, I know." Anders wasn't looking at her. He stared at the river, as though trying to find a path over the logs.

In that moment the sun dropped behind the trees on the opposite shore. Soon the logs that were hard enough to cross in daylight would be even more treacherous with darkness.

Quickly Anders removed Wildfire's bridle, snapped the lead rope on her halter, and led her away from the river. On the other side of some bushes, he staked her rope in a patch of grass.

Kate discovered a hollow log, and Anders pushed the bridle inside. Then they returned to the river.

"Keep an eye on Wildfire, will you?" Anders asked. "You can go to Powells'. I'll be back as soon as I find Ben."

Instead, Kate followed him down to the water. "I'm going with you."

"Aw, Kate, you've never walked on logs. It's too dangerous for a girl."

"Dangerous, you call it?" Kate lifted her head and flipped her braid over her shoulder. "Remember what Papa said? That we should stay together, no matter what?"

Anders groaned. "He didn't mean your crossing a river on logs, and you know it."

"Well, I'm not—" Kate stopped midsentence. For a moment she listened. "Was that Wildfire?"

Anders bounded onto a slab of ice. He stared back in the direction from which they'd come.

"You're right," he said, his voice low. "You're coming with me."

"What did you hear?" she whispered.

"Nothing. That's what bothers me." Anders looked uneasy. "It's quiet. Too quiet."

He turned to the river. For a moment he studied the logs again, as though seeking a path. Then he jumped off the slab of ice onto a log. It held firm.

Looking back at Kate, Anders spoke quietly. "Go exactly where I go."

With one foot he pushed down on the next log, testing it. When that log stayed in place, he hurried forward.

Kate jumped onto the first log. As she landed, she slipped. Her heart leaped into her throat. Just in time she caught herself.

Step by step Kate placed her feet carefully and moved ahead. Each time Anders went on, she followed. But then she looked down.

Water showed between the logs, looking black and cold. *What if I slip again? What if my foot drops into a hole? Worse still, what if I fall through?*

Kate froze. The terror of fighting her way out from under the logs overwhelmed her. She could not move.

"Hurry up, Kate," called Anders. "We'll soon lose our light."

Kate didn't have to be told. How much time did they have? Already the sky was gold.

"I'll watch Wildfire," she said, and the ice in her knees seemed to melt. "I'll make sure she's all right."

But Anders had already climbed to a higher log. As he looked over her head toward the Wisconsin bank, he stiffened.

"Kate," he said, his voice urgent. "There's a man coming out of the trees. He's headed this way."

Once again Kate felt overwhelmed by panic. "Can you see who it is?" Soon the darkness of night would fill the woods. Could there be anything worse than being alone with the timber swindler?

Anders shook his head. "C'mon, Kate," Anders said. "We can't take a chance on who it is."

Testing the next log, he pushed down. Again he hurried on, and Kate followed. How long would it take for the man to catch up?

As they worked their way toward the Minnesota shore, Kate looked back. Along the Wisconsin bank she saw a shadow. A shadow that separated itself from a tree, a shadow dark enough to be a man walking toward the logs.

Was it the swindler? Kate wasn't sure. She knew only that danger lay ahead. Even more danger pursued them, following from behind.

16

The Black Hat

*F*or what seemed an eternity, Kate followed Anders across the river. As if desperate to escape the shadowy figure, he bounded over the logs.

Several times Kate looked down into what could be a watery grave. Once her foot caught in a hollow. She tumbled forward, but bounced back up without injury.

A short time later, a log trembled beneath her. As it turned, she jumped to safety.

At last Anders reached the end of the jam. A narrow band of water stretched between the last log and the shore.

Anders jumped across the gap easily, but Kate was shorter. Could she make the leap?

Carefully she walked back a few logs. There she crouched and took a running jump. By just a few inches, she landed on Minnesota soil.

Without wasting a moment, Anders headed into the trees growing close to shore. Soon he found a narrow path that ran parallel with the river. Faster and faster he moved.

Is he hurrying toward Ben or from the swindler? Kate wondered. She had to run to keep up with her brother's long stride.

When they reached an opening in the trees, the large gold ball that was the sun rested just above the horizon. Anders ran on.

Finally he stopped long enough for Kate to catch her breath. "What if Ben's gone when we get there?" she asked. At that moment she couldn't think of anything worse than coming all this way and missing him.

Without answering, Anders glanced back, as though wondering if he were being followed. In the western sky, orange and red had joined the gold.

"It's sundown," Kate said. With the words she felt sick all over. "We can't possibly reach the landing in time."

"Maybe Ben will wait." Anders started running again.

Kate ran, too, and for a time she kept up. But then her head started throbbing, and her throat felt dry. Her breath rose in great gasps, and she had to slow down. Even in those few minutes the sky had changed.

"Go ahead," Kate told Anders when forced to a walk. "I'll catch up."

Her brother shook his head. "We promised Papa we'd stay together."

"That's impossible!" Kate panted still. "You're so much taller. You run faster without me."

Like a song half recalled, she thought of Papa's words. What had he told them? How did that verse go? Be strong? Don't be discouraged?

Then Kate remembered. *Do not be afraid, neither be thou dismayed: for the Lord thy God is with thee whithersoever thou goest.*

The words gave Kate strength. Even here God was with her. Drawing a long deep breath, she again hurried on.

She was stumbling, but keeping up, when a dirt trail crossed their path. The trail led down a slight hill, past some jack pine to the river.

Kate stopped and looked toward the west. In that moment the sun slipped below the horizon.

Kate turned toward the St. Croix, but Anders kept on.

"That's not the ferry landing," he said. "The landing has cables across the river."

Stretching out his long legs, Anders headed downstream. For a short time Kate followed.

Then she stopped. She wasn't sure why. She only knew there was something inside that told her to wait.

Or was it Someone? She wasn't sure. Was God trying to tell her something?

"C'mon!" Anders called.

Instead, Kate motioned to him, then started back the way they'd come. When she reached the trail that crossed their path, she ran toward the river. Rounding the jack pine, she looked down the slope to the water. A man stood on the bank.

Was it Ben? If so, he had the wrong place. In the dusk that follows the setting of the sun, Kate slowed her steps, and walked forward for a better look.

"What are you doing, Kate?" Anders called. He was catching up, but sounded impatient.

Kate motioned to him to follow.

Even from this distance, the man looked young and very tall. With slumped shoulders and back turned to them, he gazed across the river.

As Anders caught up, Kate pointed. "Do you think it's Ben?" For some reason she felt sure it was.

Together they hurried toward the man. A battered suitcase lay on the ground, as well as a bedroll. Tucked under one arm, he held a very long horn. Whoever he was, he seemed lost in thought.

As Kate and Anders drew closer, the man leaned down. He picked up his suitcase and bedroll and turned to go.

Kate stepped into his path. "Are you Bernhard?" she asked.

The young man faced her. "Yah, Bernhard Lindblom. Ben." He dropped his baggage to the ground.

As Kate gazed into Ben's face, she seemed to be looking up and up. She'd grown used to her brother's height, but Ben stood even taller—probably three or four inches over six feet.

Kate started to laugh. "You're Mama's *little* brother?"

Ben seemed to enjoy the joke. "Yah, Bernhard Lindblom, littlest brother of Ingrid," he said with his Swedish accent. His English was surprisingly good.

"I'm Kate," she answered. "Katherine O'Connell. Ingrid's daughter."

Ben offered his hand solemnly. "It is good to meet my sister's daughter."

Kate shook his hand just as solemnly. "I'm glad to meet you." Yet she felt surprised that he was not a boy but a man.

She turned. "This is my stepbrother, Anders."

"I'm glad you're still here," Anders told Ben as the two shook hands. "We almost didn't make it in time."

"Yah?" Ben's grin faded. "I would have gone away."

"We know," Kate said. "But we're here, and we want you to come home with us."

Ben looked around, as though searching for his sister. "Ingrid? She feels the same way?"

"Yah," Kate answered. "I mean, yes. She's expecting a baby, or she would have come herself."

"A baby?" Ben's smile returned.

"Any time," Kate told him. "Maybe she's born by now."

"*She?*" Anders wouldn't let it pass. "*He,* you mean."

"*She,*" Kate said, in spite of Ben's presence.

Anders broke into Swedish, and Kate wasn't sure what her brother said. But Ben roared with laughter.

"You speak Swedish?" Ben asked Kate.

She shook her head. "Just a little bit. Not like Anders."

"I don't speak good English," Ben said. "I am embarr—"

"Embarrassed," Kate said.

"Embarrassed," Ben repeated. "But I speak English for you."

Kate felt moved. Already she liked this tall Swede. "How do you know such good English?"

"I work in America—" He paused, counting. "Six months I work. No greenhorn. I learn."

Kate grinned. Because immigrants sometimes didn't know what was going on, unkind people described them as greenhorns. Ben was learning, all right.

"We better get going," Anders said.

He reached for Ben's battered suitcase. "If the logs are still jammed up, we can cross the river. If they aren't, I don't know how we're going to get home."

As Ben took up his bedroll, Kate looked at his horn. It was made of wood wrapped with thin, narrow strips of birchbark. The pipe was about five feet long and had a slight bell shape on the end.

"What is it?" Kate asked.

"A *lur*," Ben told her, and the word sounded like *lure*. He seemed to think that explained everything.

"Want me to carry it?" Kate offered.

"*Tack*," answered Ben, and Kate knew it was the Swedish word for thanks. "I will carry," Ben added.

He held the long horn carefully, as though making sure he wouldn't bump it against something. It reminded Kate of how she felt about her reed organ.

As Anders started up the rise, Ben leaned down to pick up something Kate hadn't seen before. On his head he placed a black hat.

Kate's heart lurched. When she recovered enough to glance at Anders, she found her brother staring.

Filled with misery, Kate looked at Ben. He could have followed them. All he needed was a few minutes. The minutes when they ran ahead, then doubled back.

"Is something wrong?" Ben asked, and Kate shook her head.

Anders cleared his throat, but Kate was afraid to meet his gaze.

Anders cleared his throat again, and Kate knew he was telling her to watch.

The next instant one side of the suitcase Anders held suddenly opened. Its contents spilled out on the ground.

"Oh, I'm sorry!" exclaimed Anders. Quickly he knelt down to pick up the contents. "Forgive me, please."

But Kate knew her brother well enough to guess how he really felt. What was he doing, looking over Ben's belongings?

When he finished packing the suitcase, Anders took the bedroll instead. Walking rapidly, he led Kate and Ben up the slope near the river.

As they hurried west into the almost dark sky, they reached a place with better light. Anders missed a step, and the bedroll popped open. A neatly rolled blanket fell to the ground, along with a pair of long underwear.

Now how did Anders do that? Kate wondered. This time she had no doubt in her mind. Her brother wanted to check everything that Ben carried.

Without a word, Ben stooped down, picked up his underwear and rolled up the blanket. As he straightened up, the last bit of light reached his face.

For the first time Kate really saw Ben's blue eyes. For the first time she saw the scar on his chin.

Suddenly afraid, Kate swallowed hard. *Oh, Ben!* she almost cried out. *I want to believe you aren't the timber swindler!* Yet she couldn't push aside Joe's words. According to him, one of the strangers had a scar on his chin.

Kate glanced toward Anders and saw her brother's expression. He looked as if his eyes were glued on Ben's chin.

In the growing darkness Anders turned north and led them upstream at a rapid pace. When they reached the log jam, they found torches lit along the river.

"The log drivers are here," Anders explained. His eyes lacked the trust with which he'd first met Ben.

"Log drivers?" Ben asked, clearly not understanding.

"Men who take the logs downstream," Anders explained. He switched into rapid Swedish.

Ben nodded, but answered in broken English. "In Sweden we send logs downriver."

Out in the river several men had ridden logs from upstream. Wearing boots with sharp spikes in the sole and heel, each of them held a long pole called a pike. Its point tapered down into a two-inch thread that looked like a screw.

Using their pikes, the men grabbed hold of the logs to move them. When they wanted to unhook the pole, they gave it a half-turn backward.

Now the men moved quickly across the river, working to break up the jam. When Anders stepped onto a log close to shore, a man bounded over to stop him. "It's very dangerous," he warned.

"I know," said Anders. "But we need to get back across the river."

The driver shook his head. "If the logs let go, you'll be swept under and carried downstream. A lot of men drown that way."

"But we really need to get home," said Anders.

"Sorry," the man said. "But you can't cross now."

17

Moonlit Terror

*K*ate stepped forward. "My mother's going to have a baby. We need to get home. Can you help us?"

The log driver pushed back his battered hat and scratched his head. "Well, little lady, I don't know. She's having a baby, you say?"

Kate nodded. "Any time now."

"And you want to get home? In case she needs you?"

Again Kate nodded.

"Wait here," the man said. Turning, he ran across the logs, moving as easily as if he were on a smooth field. After talking with two other drivers, he brought them back.

"We're going to take you over," the first man said. "Once this drive gets going again, you won't get across for days. But go exactly where I show you."

Taking Kate's hand, he led her onto the logs. The torches on both sides of the river lit their way.

Whenever they came to a log standing straight up in the air, the man showed Kate an easier way around. Step by step he took her across the river.

Kate's brother and Ben came next. Behind them, the two men

followed closely in case Anders or Ben needed help.

Near the Wisconsin bank, a log moved beneath Kate's feet. She gasped and leaped quickly to the next log. Beyond that, she jumped onto shore.

"Thank you!" she called out, looking back to the driver who had helped her.

As Ben and Anders reached shore safely, the man tipped his battered hat. "Got a family myself," he said.

Then he and the other men were gone, bounding back over the logs. When they reached the middle of the river, they used their pike poles to push and pry apart the tightly jammed logs.

A minute later the logs that caused the jam broke loose. "Here we go!" called one of the men. The drivers jumped to safer positions.

Close by, a log spun beneath a driver's feet. Running in place, the man kept up with the rolling log, the way Anders had done at Wood River.

In the next instant the huge mass became a floating island. Free to move with the current, the logs swept out of the bend and down the river.

Anders started away from the water, and Ben and Kate followed. Just before they reached the trees, she looked back. A large boat was coming downstream. A square building in its center looked like a small house.

"What's that?" Kate asked.

"A wannigan. The cook-house shanty," explained Anders. He looked at Ben. "Think we ought to swim out and ask for a meal?"

"Yah, sure," said Ben. He set down his suitcase and *lur* as though meaning business.

Just talking about food made Kate's stomach growl. Ben turned to her. "You hungry?"

"We left our food in a creek," she explained. "Early this morning." It seemed days ago.

Opening his suitcase, Ben pulled out an apple. "Take," he said. "Enjoy."

Kate held the apple to her lips, ready to bite into it. Already she relished the taste in her mouth.

But Ben looked at Anders and shrugged. "Sorry. No more."

For just an instant Kate hesitated. She longed to bite into the apple, to devour every piece. Instead, she held it out to Ben. "Aren't you hungry?"

"I am hungry," Ben said. "But you are littlest." He winked sideways at Anders.

"I don't want to take your last apple," answered Kate.

"I do," Anders said. Reaching quickly, he grabbed it. But then he pulled out his knife and divided the apple three ways.

When they started off again, Kate chewed her share slowly, savoring every bite.

One minute she liked Ben and looked forward to bringing him home. The next minute she wondered, *Can I trust him?*

She couldn't get Joe's words about a scar out of her mind. Her mixed-up feelings made her uneasy.

As they left the river and the torches behind, the night grew darker. Anders headed for his horse.

In the blackness before the moon rose, Kate strained her eyes. Yet she saw no shadow, no large body, no hint of swishing tail. And she heard no welcoming whinny.

"Where's Wildfire?" asked Anders, his voice tense.

"Wildfire?" Ben wanted to know.

"My horse," Anders said shortly. "I left her here."

Kate tried to push aside her panic. "Maybe we've got the wrong place. Maybe in the dark—"

"Nope!" Her brother's voice was filled with anger. "We've got the right place."

Anders stomped around the grassy area. He peered into the surrounding bushes for any sign of what had happened.

"Maybe she pulled up her stake," Kate said, still trying to offer hope.

Anders stopped his pacing. Nervously he pounded one fist into the palm of his other hand. "It's bad enough when the swindler steals logs from the farmers. Now he's taken my horse!"

Kate and Anders and Ben searched farther out, beyond the circle of grass. Finally they had to give up.

Whoever stole the mare had left her bridle. Anders took it

from the hollow log and wrapped the long reins around his waist.

"Well, there's nothing to do but start home," he said. "It's going to be a long, long walk."

They stopped at Powells' large farmhouse, but no one knew the whereabouts of the black mare. Kate saw the pain in her brother's eyes and knew he worried about Wildfire getting hurt.

When Mrs. Powell offered supper, Anders shook his head. "Thanks," he said. "But we can't wait for you to make it. We have to keep searching."

Quickly Mrs. Powell sliced bread and cut cheese for them. Kate and the boys returned outside. In spite of her worry about Wildfire, Kate had all she could do to not swallow the food whole.

Anders moved away from the door to a lighted window. There he stood with his back to the house. As Ben drew close, the soft glow of a kerosene lamp fell on his face.

Clever, thought Kate. While Anders talked, she, too, watched Ben's face.

"We need to go on," Anders said. His voice lacked confidence, as though he trusted Ben less all the time. "Let's keep looking for Wildfire as we go. But be quiet."

Anders held a finger to his lips to be sure Ben understood. "There's a timber swindler around here somewhere. We want to find him, but not have him find us."

"Timber swindler?" Ben asked.

"A man who steals logs from the farmers who cut them. It's the same as stealing money—money the farmers really need."

Seldom, if ever, had Kate heard Anders so resentful. He switched into Swedish, as if wanting to make sure Ben understood.

Soon Ben nodded, but said only, "That's bad." The expression on his face did not change.

Ben picked up his suitcase and tucked his long horn under his arm. As they started back on the path to Fish Lake School, Kate fell in line behind her brother. Ben followed her.

Still feeling uneasy, Kate turned to Ben. "Are you used to

walking in the woods?" She spoke softly in case the swindler was nearby.

"Yah, we have woods." Ben's *w*'s sounded like *v*'s. "We have woods, mountains where I come from. The mountains I miss."

He lifted his horn. "That's where I use my *lur*. It is a long distance between farms. Down one mountain, up next. We talk with this."

"Talk with your horn?" Kate asked. "What do you mean?"

"I play a tune. I say, 'I'm missing a cow. Do you know where my cow is?' Someone calls back. They say, 'Yah, your cow has wandered over to my farm. I'll bring it to you.' Or they say, 'No, I don't know where your cow is.' "

"Do you have all kinds of messages?"

Ben grinned. "Yah. I say, 'Work is done. Come for party.' "

Kate smiled. "A good signal," she said.

Just then she smelled something. Standing still, she sniffed. What was it? She sniffed again, then knew.

"Anders," she whispered. "Someone's cooking meat. Do you think it's Joe?"

Anders lifted his head. "You're right! Food, food, here we come!" For a moment at least he seemed to have pushed aside his anger.

But Kate hung back. "How do you know it isn't the timber swindler?"

Anders groaned. "We don't."

"Remember what you said," Kate warned. "If the swindler stops us from talking to Big Gust, he'll get away with stealing all those logs. Just like he probably stole your horse."

Setting down the bedroll, Anders leaned against a tree. He pushed back his blond hair, as though needing to think.

In that moment a light shone through the leafless branches of a tall oak. As Kate watched, the moon rose into view. Though it wouldn't be full for another five or six days, she felt grateful for every bit of light it offered.

Still holding his horn and suitcase, Ben stood straight, alert, ready to move on a moment's notice. With watchful eyes he strained forward, listening to Kate's every word.

"How far to Grantsburg?" he asked.

Kate saw her brother's arm muscles tense. To Grantsburg? How did Ben know they were going that way?

"Have you been this way before?" Kate asked Ben.

He shrugged, as though he didn't know what she was saying.

Kate wouldn't let it pass. "How do you know we're headed for Grantsburg?"

Ben looked away, avoiding her eyes. "I came in on a train," he said finally. "I stayed at Grantsburg hotel. In the morning—"

Ben stopped, as though embarrassed to tell them.

Kate glanced toward Anders. Their gaze met. *He has to be the one Joe was talking about,* Kate thought. *How long was Ben in town?*

"In the morning I start to find my sister Ingrid," Ben said, as if he heard Kate's thoughts.

Suddenly he looked straight into Kate's eyes. "I couldn't— how you say it—work up courage?"

Kate nodded.

"I couldn't work up courage to go to the farm. I was afraid Ingrid—" Ben stopped, unable to go on.

Kate looked away. *You're so nice, Ben,* she wanted to say. Was he telling the truth? With every part of her being she wanted to believe him. She wanted to tell him, *Mama forgives you. Everything is all right.* But she couldn't speak the words.

Instead, she felt scared that she might bring home a liar and a thief. Scared that Mama would be hurt even more.

Just then Anders looked at Ben, as though wishing he could see inside the Swede's heart.

Anders is wondering too. Desperately Kate tried to recall the times she'd seen the swindler. When she did remember, she tried to push the thought away. Ben would be the same height, the same build. And there was also the black hat.

As if she'd asked Anders only minutes before, Kate recalled her words: "Can you think of anything more awful than having a brother betray you?"

A fear as cold as the ice along the river swept through her.

Anders stood up straight. "We better go."

In that moment all the times Anders had teased her fell away. All the times he had called her dumb girl no longer mattered. Instead Kate realized, *I can trust him!*

Always she had tried to keep ahead of Anders, to look better than he did. *Maybe it's more important for each of us to do whatever we do best!*

"Why don't you lead?" Anders asked her. He moved quickly, taking the place between Kate and Ben.

She started out, not liking this position any better. Yet she knew why Anders had given it to her. This way he could see what happened to her.

They had gone only a short distance when Kate heard a sound in the bushes. The next moment something dark rushed into the path. In spite of herself, Kate cried out.

Then the animal jumped up, yipping with delight.

"Lutfisk!" Laughing at her fear, Kate dropped to her knees. The dog's wet hair smelled and felt full of dirt. But Kate had never been so glad to see him.

She scratched behind his ears. Then he bounded from her to Anders.

"Your dog?" Ben asked.

"Yup!" said Anders proudly.

Lutfisk padded over to Ben, sniffed his pant legs, then backed away. Ben reached out and let the dog smell his hand.

As they hurried on, the scent of cooking meat deepened. Kate stalked forward, the hunger within her growing. She faced the moon now, and it helped her see between the trees.

Then she heard a series of hoots. The *whoo-ah!* came fourth, instead of last.

"It's Joe!" Kate whispered to Anders, hoping Ben wouldn't hear. "Did you hear that? Something's wrong."

Kate cupped her hands around her mouth and returned the warning.

When she heard no reply, she trudged on, moving as quietly as possible. Often she stopped to listen and heard no unusual sound.

But fear clutched her heart. *The swindler,* she thought. *Who is he? Where is he? Ahead or behind?*

Even with Anders walking between them, Ben was something unknown. Whose side was he on?

Moments later, Kate walked around a large jack pine. A shadow slid into the path in front of her. A shadow that had to be a person.

18

Close Call

Kate jumped, and the shadow moved. In the darkness of the woods she could not see the person's face.

"Be very quiet," whispered Joe. "The man I told you about was here."

"Someone stole Wildfire," said Anders. The anger was back in his voice.

"I know," Joe answered. Without a sound, he moved away, and Kate and the others followed.

As the aroma of cooking food grew stronger, Joe stopped. "I snared a couple of partridges. But the smoke and the meat might bring the man to us."

When they came into a clearing, Kate saw a small fire built in a hollowed-out place in the sand. Two forked branches stood upright, holding a third limb above the red coals. On that branch hung two roasted partridges.

Sitting close to the fire, Kate waited for her share of meat.

"It's a bit early for partridge," Joe said. "Sorry it took me longer than I thought."

"How'd you catch it?" Kate asked.

"I listened until I heard one of them drumming with its

wings. I crept up to the log he used and set my snare."

He moved quickly to give Kate and Anders a piece. But when he came to Ben, Joe paused. In the light of the fire he stared, as if seeing the scar on Ben's chin for the first time.

Only when Kate started eating did she realize how famished she was. Anders and Ben looked just as hungry. On the other side of the fire, they wolfed down the food.

While they ate, Joe stood watch around the outer rim of the clearing. One moment he looked into the trees. The next he glanced toward Ben. "Hurry," he whispered as he turned from the trees. "Every minute is danger."

"How far are we from Grantsburg?" Anders asked in a low voice.

Joe moved closer. "Eight, maybe nine miles. We stay on this side of Wood River to get back."

Kate breathed deep with relief. At least she wouldn't have to cross the ice-cold water again.

As Ben finished eating, he grinned. Kate tried to return the smile, but couldn't.

Why, he's my uncle! she thought. The idea came as a surprise, especially since Ben was only five years older than she. Even so, Kate didn't like walking through the night without knowing which side he was on.

Anders devoured his last bite and stood up. "Let's find the swindler. I'm willing to bet he has Wildfire."

"He does," Joe said in a whisper. "I came upon his tracks when I followed yours to the wild river. He led your horse away."

"He followed us right to the St. Croix?" Kate asked.

Joe knelt close to the fire. "He probably wasn't far behind. But his tracks didn't always go right behind yours."

"What do you mean?" asked Anders.

"Right after you crossed the Wood River, he followed close, along the road." Joe spoke slowly, as though choosing his words carefully. "But later on—"

He paused as though unwilling to say what he thought.

Anders prodded him. "Later on?"

Joe glanced quickly at Ben, then away. "Sometimes his tracks were in the woods, as though he stayed behind the cover of trees. Other times the tracks were off to one side of yours. It's as if he guessed where you were going and went straight there instead of following you."

"Are you saying he might have reached the St. Croix before we did?" Anders sounded tense. From across the fire his worried gaze met Kate's.

Kate looked from Anders to Ben. Her very tall uncle was listening to every word.

I'm scared, Kate thought. Again she felt divided. She had to know whether she could trust Ben. Yet she felt afraid to find out.

"How can we find the swindler without him finding us?" Kate asked.

She spoke quickly in English, hoping Ben wouldn't understand. "Anders thinks the swindler wants to stop us from talking about what he's doing."

"Anders is right," Ben answered unexpectedly.

Kate felt as if a fist squeezed her heart. Not only had Ben understood every word, he again seemed to know more than he should.

"Why do you say that?" she asked.

"When we were watching the—" Ben paused, as though searching for the word.

"The men driving logs?" prodded Kate.

"After that. The boat. You call it—" Again Ben stopped.

"A wannigan." Anders supplied the word. "A cook shanty."

"Yah, then. Man near a dark tree."

"A dark tree?" Kate felt puzzled. "Do you mean in the shadows?"

Ben nodded. "A man—how you say it?" He stood up, touched his head and held his hand out at the same height.

"As tall as you," Kate guessed.

Ben patted his flat stomach.

"Thin," Kate said out of her practice in using sign language with Tina.

Ben nodded.

Kate's nervous fingers clenched and unclenched. *Ben, you*

could be describing yourself! In that instant she felt tired all over. Tired of running, walking, worrying. Tired of crossing rivers, trying to find Ben. Tired, most of all, of wondering if he were the timber swindler.

"The man stood in the shadows, watching us?" Anders asked.

"I thought he was a—" Ben paused, then came up with a word. "A log man. But now I know he was watching you."

"What happened to him?" Anders sounded like a dog pouncing on a bone. "Do you remember anything else?"

"His hat. Black. Old." Taking off his own hat, he tapped it.

"And then?" asked Anders.

"I looked back," Ben said. "He was gone."

Anders glanced at Kate, and his mouth widened in a lopsided grin. "Just think, Kate, the swindler was probably close by all the time—just a few feet away when we looked for Wildfire! Just behind a tree when you led us through the woods!"

Trying to pretend his teasing didn't matter, Kate flipped her long braid over her shoulder. Yet she trembled, thinking how close the swindler might have been.

Ben looked solemn as he agreed with Anders. "Yah, it might be so. He looked mean." In the dying embers a shadow darkened Ben's face.

Kate glanced over her shoulder. The night sky was black now, even in the west. Like tall soldiers, the jack pine and oak surrounded the clearing, keeping watch. Yet Kate felt unable to shake the idea that a man might be standing behind a tree.

"Wherever he is, he's got my horse," Anders growled. "I want her back. And I want her back unhurt."

Moving quickly, Joe put out the fire. As the last red coal disappeared, Kate strained to see.

Far above, thousands of stars twinkled brightly. Here, where the moon shone, the ground was almost as light as day. Other places were gray, and still others completely black. The swindler could be anywhere in these unfamiliar woods.

As Kate's eyes adjusted to the darkness, she saw Anders sling Ben's bedroll onto his shoulder. Ben took up his suitcase and *lur*.

"I'll go first," Joe said.

Kate went next and behind her, Ben, then Anders. As Joe led them into the woods, Kate followed with swift, sure steps. She knew she could trust Joe's leading.

They had walked for some time when he stopped. In an opening between the trees Joe turned his head to listen.

Then Kate heard it—the sound of running water. Was Joe taking a path along the Wood River? Or a trail known only to him?

Once more he started out, and the others stayed in line. But now Kate wondered about something else. Even if they found the swindler, they had to have proof. Anders still carried the slice of wood inside his shirt. Would that be enough?

"Where's Lutfisk?" she whispered when they stopped to rest.

Anders shrugged. "I don't know. But he'll find us. I'm more worried about Wildfire."

"If Lutfisk runs into the swindler—"

"He'll bark." Anders didn't like the idea any more than Kate.

"If he'd just find the swindler, then come tell us where he is—"

But the idea seemed ridiculous, even to Kate. How could Lutfisk know he needed to be quiet? It seemed impossible. Yet the dog had so often done the right thing that sometimes he seemed human.

Before long, Joe stopped again, this time at a spring. Kate drank deeply, welcoming the coldness. Again and again each of them drank.

As they walked on, Kate again followed Joe. He moved swiftly, even in the dark, always seeming sure where he stepped.

The woods are his friend, Kate thought suddenly. In the year since moving to northwest Wisconsin she'd become comfortable with the daytime forest. But it still frightened her at night.

I think of them as my enemy, Kate realized. *Will I ever know the woods the way Joe does? Will the wilderness ever seem like my friend?*

As they continued on, the night grew colder. Kate shivered, longing for the warm coat left in the wagon. Ben opened his suitcase and gave her a sweater that hung down past her knees.

Farther on, Joe stopped again. "I'll look around," he whispered as the others drew close.

He pointed down a path that looked dim in the moonlight. "Keep going. I'll find you again." A moment later he disappeared into the night.

Kate shivered, but this time it wasn't the cold. She wished she could follow Joe. Instead, she walked on, leading the others with hands extended to feel any branch she could not see.

As they entered a stand of pines, the trees blotted out the moon. Kate shuffled her feet to feel the trail. But fear walked beside her. She tried to push that fear away, to remember her desire to make the woods her friend. Yet the darkness surrounded her, feeling as real as a person.

What if I walk right into the swindler? On that narrow trail through the pines there'd be no warning.

Kate looked back and saw only two shapes—Ben and Anders—but she felt no better. The swindler could be anywhere, just a few feet away. Around the next bush. Beyond the next tree.

In this great forest, how could they possibly find Wildfire? How could they stop the swindler so he wouldn't keep robbing the farmers? Now that they'd found Ben, Kate felt eager to return to Windy Hill Farm.

It helped her just to think about home. Then Kate remembered Mama. *What's happening to her? Maybe I have a new little sister by now.*

As clearly as if she were seeing it, Kate remembered Papa standing next to the wagon praying for her and Anders before they left.

In the next instant Kate stopped. When Ben tried to walk past her, she held out her arm. Here the pines crowded close, making it even harder to see. As Kate listened, she thought she heard running water again. Yet the night pressed in around her.

Crouching down, Kate felt the ground. On her knees she inched her way forward. Five feet beyond where she stopped, the ground fell away. Her hands reached out into air.

19

One Step Forward

*K*ate's heart pounded. On her knees she moved back. "Stop!" she warned Ben.

Anders came alongside. "What's wrong?" he asked.

"I don't know." In her fright Kate's whisper sounded loud. "There's no ground left." She waited, wondering again if she heard running water.

Anders dropped to his knees and crawled forward. A few feet farther on, he lit their one remaining match.

As it flickered and went out, Kate heard Anders breathe deep. "What is it?" she whispered.

"A steep bank." His voice sounded tense, even afraid.

"A bank?" she asked.

"Cut away by high water. You almost walked into Wood River."

Crawling slowly, Kate inched back in the direction from which they'd come. When she stood up, her knees felt weak. Only a few more steps, and she'd have fallen into the rushing water. No one needed to tell her that in the dark she wouldn't have been found.

"Protection," Kate said softly. "Papa prayed for protection."

For a moment she stood there, shaken and yet moved by what had happened.

No longer did the night seem dark. No longer did the woods feel heavy with evil. Instead, Kate felt cared for by God himself.

"Well, I know one thing," Anders growled. His voice sounded worried. "If we don't all work together, nothing's going to turn out right."

"I walk in woods often," Ben said. "I will go first."

As he took the lead, his tall strong body swung through the woods as if he lived there every day. Yet it felt strange having him lead when Kate didn't know if she could trust him.

Before long, they came to the fork in the trail that Kate had missed in the dark. Soon after they started on the new path, an owl hooted. The *whoo-ah!* came fourth, instead of last.

"It's Joe's warning," Kate whispered to Anders.

When the call came again, fear knotted Kate's insides. "The swindler must be near. But where is he?"

Before long, the trail widened. Far above, the lopsided moon shone brightly, bringing a white light in the midst of darkness. Lutfisk rushed into the opening between trees.

The dog waited to have his ears scratched, then bounded away, as though wanting to show them something. Once he returned to see if they followed him. Then he disappeared again.

Not even Anders could keep up with him. It was too dangerous to call or whistle the dog back.

They had walked for some time when suddenly Anders stopped. In the stillness of the night Kate heard a whinny.

"That's Wildfire!" Anders exclaimed.

As they hurried toward the sound, the mare whinnied again. Anders left the trail. Ben and Kate followed him between clusters of young white pine. With long bluish-green needles, the thick branches grew close to the ground.

From the bottom of a hill, a light shone between the trees. A large clearing formed a semicircle, bordering the waters of Wood River.

On the near side of the clearing, two horses stood with lead ropes tied to a branch. One horse was darker than the other, and Kate felt sure it was Wildfire.

Anders hid Ben's bedroll, then crept silently down the hill. As Kate and Ben trailed behind, the carpet of pine needles deadened the sound of their steps. In the quiet they heard someone sawing wood.

Partway to the horses, Anders looked back and motioned for them to stop. Kate and Ben slid into a cluster of pines. Standing in the darkness, they looked out between the close-growing branches.

In the center of the clearing, near a great pile of logs, a farm lantern sat on the ground. Its glow fell on a man sawing the end of a log. He was big—at least as tall as Ben—and there was no doubt about the strength in his arms. The brim of a black hat hid his face.

As silent as a shadow, Anders slipped from tree to tree. When he reached the horses, he kept Wildfire between himself and the man.

While he untied the mare's rope, Anders stood close, seeming to talk in her ear. But when he started to lead her away, the other horse whinnied.

Anders stopped short.

The swindler jerked upright. Staring at the horses, he seemed to listen.

Anders stood motionless.

After a few minutes, the thief went back to work. Yet Kate could see what Anders could not. As the man drew the saw back and forth, he watched the horses.

Without making a sound, Anders led Wildfire away from the tree. When the mare's shadow separated from the other horse, the swindler put down his saw. With surprising speed, he crept toward Anders, like a hunter stalking its prey.

Suddenly Anders turned and saw the man gaining on him. With a bound Anders leaped toward his horse.

He had one leg over Wildfire's back when the swindler caught up. Grabbing Anders by the other leg, the man yanked him off and pushed him to the ground.

Anders dropped the lead rope. "Go, Wildfire!" he shouted.

The mare crashed through the trees, her head tilted to one side to hold the rope away from her feet. When she reached the trail, Wildfire galloped into the darkness.

With a quick movement, Ben slid his suitcase and horn beneath a low branch. Then he left Kate and the cluster of pines.

In the same moment Anders reached out and grabbed the swindler's boot. As the man tumbled to the ground, his hat fell off. Down the hill he and Anders rolled, struggling the entire way.

When they landed in the clearing, the swindler pinned Anders face down. With his greater weight and strength, he caught and held the boy's arms.

In the moonlight that shone between the trees Kate saw the swindler's face for the first time. Deep furrows lined his forehead and cheeks. Beneath bushy eyebrows, his eyes seemed cold and hard, dark with evil.

As she recognized him, Kate shivered. She had seen him before, no doubt about it. The swindler was the staring stranger!

Just then the man spotted Ben and yanked Anders to his feet. "Come any closer, and I'll hurt him!" the swindler threatened. He locked Anders in a vise-like grip.

Anders groaned and Ben froze. Then Anders kicked. His foot reached the man's leg. The swindler jumped back, but did not lose his hold. Instead, he pushed Anders toward the pile of logs.

Near the far end of the logs, the man shoved Anders to the ground and started tying him. Every few seconds the swindler glanced toward Ben.

Mama's brother stood not more than twenty feet away from the thief. As Kate moved slightly to see around Ben, her eye caught a movement in the trees beyond Anders. Who was it? Friend or enemy?

A moment later Joe stepped out from a pine on the far side of the clearing. He stood partway up the hill and behind the swindler's back.

Kate breathed deep with relief. She'd known Joe only a short time, but felt sure he would help Anders. If it came to that, she could trust Joe with her life.

But Ben? He had hurried forward to rescue Anders, then stopped, as if for her brother's safety. Even so, he and the swindler could be partners.

With every part of her being, Kate wanted to rush down into the clearing. Yet Anders had said, "If we don't work together, nothing will turn out right."

As Kate watched, Joe looked at Ben and pointed. Ben nodded slightly.

Joe motioned with his hands, as though telling Ben to walk toward the swindler, then up the hill. Barely moving his head, Ben nodded again.

Joe held up his hand, as if saying, "Wait."

Quickly Kate stepped out from the trees that sheltered her. For an instant she stood there, then slipped back within the branches.

Yet Joe had seen her. Gazing directly at the pines where Kate hid, he crossed his wrists, then pointed at Anders.

Kate caught the message. She was supposed to untie her brother. But how?

The swindler glanced toward Ben, and the tall Swede stood without moving. Behind the swindler's back, Joe knelt down. He seemed to stretch something between two trees. Then he disappeared.

As the swindler tied Anders' feet, Kate left her hiding place. Running from tree to tree, she circled around to the side of the clearing where she'd seen Joe. Silently she crept up behind the pile of logs and waited.

A few minutes later the swindler spoke to Ben. From the sound of the man's voice, Kate knew he had moved away from Anders. When she crawled around the logs, she was close to Anders, yet could see the swindler and Ben at the other end. Her uncle waited near the lantern, alert and ready for action. Without taking his gaze off Ben, the swindler picked up a gunnysack. Moving swiftly, he filled the sack with sawed ends of wood.

Staying within the shadow of the logs, Kate knelt down next

to her brother. One rope held his hands behind his back. Another rope bound his feet. A rag across his mouth kept him from speaking.

Kate worked at the rope on her brother's wrists. The knots were tightly tied, and her fingers felt clumsy with haste. Moments seemed like years before the rope slipped free.

The knot around his ankles proved even more difficult, but Kate finally loosened it. She looked at the trees behind her, then crept back, away from Anders.

From nearby came the hooting of an owl. It was Joe!

Suddenly Ben took one step forward into the light. The swindler leaped into the gap between Anders and Ben.

"Don't come any closer," the man warned again. His threat sounded ugly and unafraid.

"I don't need to," Ben said.

As he and the swindler faced each other, they seemed evenly matched. Both were tall—well over six feet, and almost the same weight. Both were solidly built.

Yet Kate saw something in Ben's eyes that she missed in the other man—a confidence, a sureness, as though Ben had no doubt that he was in the right.

In that instant Kate knew she could trust Ben. For the first time she believed in him with her whole heart.

He stood just out of reach of the swindler's long arms. When the man lunged toward him, Ben backed away, then started running.

20

New Beginning

$\mathcal{U}$p the hill Ben went, as quickly as his long legs could carry him. The swindler followed.

Anders ripped the loosened rope from his ankles and jumped up. He and Kate scrambled after Ben and the swindler.

Darting this way and that, Ben chose a twisting path between the trees. As he passed between two big pines, he slowed down a bit, as though growing tired. The man behind him picked up speed.

A moment later, Ben seemed to jump over something. In the darkness beneath the trees, the swindler followed in hot pursuit. Suddenly he pitched forward onto his face.

Joe dove from a pine tree and landed on the man's legs.

Turning quickly, Ben dropped onto the swindler's back. The man struggled, trying to throw him off. But Ben grabbed the swindler's arms, pinning them down.

"Your thieving is over, mister!" Anders exclaimed as he caught up.

The swindler had tripped on the wire Joe had stretched between trees. The big man turned his head and glared at Anders and Kate. "If you weren't around, I would have gotten away with it!"

Kate trembled and felt glad that Joe and Ben held the thief. Close up, the lines in his face seemed deeper, his eyes even more frightening.

Kate ran down to the clearing and brought back the ropes the man used to bind Anders. The three boys worked together, tying the swindler securely.

By the time they finished, a wide grin lit Anders' face. Joe and Ben clapped each other on the back, and Kate felt relieved in more ways than one. Without a doubt Ben had proved his innocence.

Yet Kate also felt puzzled. "Where's Lutfisk?" she asked. "He usually doesn't miss out on anything."

Anders whistled shrilly. A few minutes later Lutfisk padded out of the darkness. In his mouth the dog held a handle for what looked like a small sledgehammer. The heavy end dragged on the ground.

Lutfisk dropped it and sniffed along the handle. When he picked it up again, he held the handle close to the hammer and the weight balanced. Reaching Anders, the dog laid the tool at his feet.

"A stamp hammer!" Anders exclaimed. "Lutfisk must have found it someplace!"

Behind the dog came Wildfire. Anders ran toward the mare and caught her halter. With a hand on each side of her head, he looked into Wildfire's eyes. Holding out the lantern, he searched her chest and belly and legs for cuts and other injuries. Then he lifted her hooves.

Finally he patted her neck, as though unable to believe the mare was all right. Wildfire rubbed her forehead on Anders' chest.

Anders unwrapped the reins from around his waist, and slipped the bridle over Wildfire's halter. He leaped onto the mare, then helped Kate up. "How far to Grantsburg?" he asked Joe.

"Four or five miles," Joe told him. "I'll help Ben keep an eye on the swindler."

As Kate and Anders followed the winding trail to town, Lutfisk ran behind. By the time they came to the village, the first streaks of dawn lit the sky. When they reached the fire hall where Big Gust lived, they pounded on the door till they woke him.

"We've got the swindler!" Anders told the marshall.

Big Gust took one look at them, pulled on his coat, and headed toward the street. "Let's get Charlie Saunders."

Kate and Anders followed Big Gust to the red-brick house connected with the county jail. Soon the sleepy-looking sheriff opened the door.

"Got some evidence for you," Anders said, as he gave Charlie the stamp hammer and slice of wood. Quickly he told the story, ending with, "Right now Ben and Joe are holding the swindler."

The sheriff grabbed his hat, and they hurried to his livery stable. Charlie found a horse for Kate, as well as a fresh mount for Anders. They left Wildfire in the stable and saddled three extra horses. Then Anders and Kate led the men back to the others.

Along the Wood River, Big Gust and the sheriff took the timber swindler into custody. After the sheriff collected more evidence, everyone rode to Grantsburg.

As Joe started to leave, Kate turned to him. "How did you know?" she asked quietly so that Ben wouldn't hear. "How did you know that you could trust him?"

"I didn't," Joe answered. "I just knew that if you got Anders untied, we'd be at least two against two."

His dark eyes sparkled with fun. "Of course, we'd have your help, too."

Kate laughed, but then grew serious. "Thanks for everything, Joe," she said softly. "We couldn't have done it without you."

Moments later, Ben reached out and grasped Joe's hand, for now he knew the story. "I would have gone away," he said. "No sister. No Kate. No Anders."

Joe grinned. "I'll see all of you again soon." Then he was gone, running as swiftly as a deer into the new day.

Within an hour Kate and Anders finished talking with the sheriff. After a big breakfast, they came outside to find that one of Charlie's friends had brought their wagon from Tennessee Flats. Anders and Ben hitched up Wildfire, and the boys and

Kate sat together on the high spring seat. As they started home, Lutfisk ran alongside.

On their way to Windy Hill Farm, Anders stopped to string a new piece of wire where he'd left a single strand. Then they hurried on, as fast as the muddy roads would allow them.

Kate felt as if she'd never been so tired, and now and then she dozed off. Even so, the trip home seemed the longest she could remember. As the wagon wheels turned round and round, she wondered what was happening to Mama.

Anders broke into her thoughts. "Pretty soon we go back to school."

"It'll be fun seeing our friends again," Kate said.

"Yup," answered her brother. "Spring term starts April 8th. Unless, of course, we have to solve another mystery first."

He turned to Mama's brother. "Hey, Ben, why don't you go too?"

"Me?" asked Ben. "To school?"

"Sure thing." Anders grinned. "Lots of older boys go. We have a pretty schoolteacher. Just your age, in fact. You can sit in the back row with me."

When Ben grinned, Anders put out his hand. "Shake on it!"

The closer they came to home, the more impatient Kate grew. "How do you think Mama's doing?" she asked more than once. "Do you suppose the baby's been born?"

Ben looked excited, too, but when they reached the house, he held back. "You go first," he said.

"You come with us," Kate answered.

Ben shook his head. As though uncertain about everything, he spoke in Swedish.

Anders translated for Kate. "He says, 'Find out if your mama *really* wants to see me.' He wants to wait outside."

When Kate entered the kitchen, kettles of hot water stood on the cookstove. Tina grabbed her around the waist and hugged her.

"Mama?" Kate asked. "Did she have her baby?"

But Tina wouldn't tell her. Nor would Lars. He just sat at the kitchen table, grinning from ear to ear. Then Kate saw Erik.

"Your mother's here?" Kate asked him, and he nodded.

"The baby's born?"

Erik shrugged, as though he didn't know, but Kate caught the look in his eyes. "Your father wants to tell you," he said.

"Is Mama all right?" Kate asked.

Erik smiled and said, "Yes."

Then Papa came to the door between the dining room and kitchen. "You are home!" he exclaimed. "Come, come!"

His face shone as he led Kate and Anders through the dining room toward the bedroom. Erik's mother opened the door.

Mama lay on the bed, her golden-blond hair curling around her face. The quilt was pulled high, but in the crook of her arm she held a tiny bundle.

Kate stepped forward. "Mama, are you all right?"

Mama smiled, and the glow in her eyes gave Kate the answer she wanted.

"And the baby?" asked Kate as Anders hung back.

"The baby is fine," Mama told them. "A healthy little one, I am glad to say." She turned the bundle in her arms for Kate and Anders to see.

Still Anders stayed back, as though embarrassed to come too close. But Kate leaned down for a better look.

The baby's body was tightly wrapped in a flannel blanket. Only the little face and shoulders and one small fist showed above the blanket.

The tiny eyes were closed in sleep, and thick blond hair covered the baby's head. But the face—

"It's all red!" Kate exclaimed, then wished she hadn't said it.

"Yah," said Mama, not seeming to mind. "That's the way of babies when they're born."

She turned the baby again so that Anders could see. For a long moment he stared down at the little one.

"It's really a nice boy," he said finally.

"A boy?" Kate asked. "This baby is a boy?"

"Yah, sure," answered Anders. "Can't you see his big shoulders?"

Kate stepped back, away from the bed. A rush of disappointment swept through her.

But her mother's gaze held her. "Yah," Mama said. "We have a healthy, wonderful little boy. We are grateful to God."

Kate heard the words, yet deep inside she hurt. After all these months of waiting, a boy. She swallowed against the lump in her throat.

Turning, she started toward the door, but Mama's voice called her. "Kate," she said.

Kate stopped, but did not look back.

Then Papa stood beside her. With a gentle hand he cupped Kate's chin and lifted it until she looked at him. "Mama and I want you to be the first to hold the baby."

"The first?"

"The first of all the children," he said. "Before Anders, and Lars, and Tina."

Taking her hand, Papa led Kate to the rocking chair. Carefully he picked up the tiny bundle and placed it in Kate's arms.

For a moment she wanted to give the baby back to Mama. To say, "Keep him, he's yours. Keep this little boy. I wanted a sister."

But then she looked down. Pulling aside the blanket, she gazed at the thick blond hair. It was like the down of a little chick, lying flat as she smoothed it, then springing back up.

With a nervous hand Kate opened the blanket more. Thin little legs and tiny feet, each with five toes. She counted, then looked at the hands. They were balled in fists, but each with five slender fingers.

As Kate touched one of the hands, the baby opened his eyes and looked up. He moved his head, as though trying to focus on her face.

It's like a miracle, Kate thought. *A miracle!* Her disappointment fell away.

Then she remembered the others around her. She remembered Ben, waiting to know if he was wanted.

"Your brother's here," Kate said softly to Mama. "He wants to know if you really want to see him."

"Of course," Mama said without hesitation. "Of course, I

want to see my brother. Where is he?"

When Ben came in, Kate and Anders and Papa left. It seemed like hours but was only twenty minutes before Ben returned to the kitchen.

"She wants all of you," he said.

"All of us?" Kate asked.

Ben pointed to each of them. "You and Tina. Lars and Papa. Anders too. Even me." His voice was quiet, as though hardly believing his own words.

One by one, they followed Papa back into the bedroom. Mama looked around the circle.

"Papa and I want to tell you what we decided. We want to name the baby after someone special."

Papa cleared his throat. "His name is Bernhard Carl."

Ben gasped. "Bernhard?"

Mama smiled. "After you," she said. "We'll shorten it to Bernie or Hardy when we call both of you for supper."

"For supper?" asked Ben. "You want me to stay?"

"We want you to stay," Papa said. "Yah sure, Mama and I want you to stay as long as you want."

As though unable to take it all in, Ben bit his lip, then brushed a hand across his eyes.

Mama really cares that much about Ben? thought Kate. She felt awed by the wonder of it all. *Mama cares that way, even when he hurt her so much?*

Then Mama seemed to notice Kate's silence. "Is that all right?" she asked.

Deep inside, Kate felt a glow in her heart. In her spirit the wonder grew. "It's all right," she said softly. But she meant much more.

Acknowledgments

Now and then a reader asks me, "When you write a novel, what is real?" By that they mean, "What is truth, and what is fiction?"

Perhaps the easiest way to answer is to tell you about the book you've just read.

On September 15, 1929, a fifteen-year-old girl left West Plains, Missouri. She drove a farm wagon and a horse-and-mule team. Five weeks and three days later that girl, whose name is now Gladys Peterson, reached her family's new home in northwest Wisconsin.

For most of those hundreds of miles, Gladys was alone except for a younger brother named Ellis. Ellis turned eleven during the five-week trip. Yet he and Gladys camped along the way for all but the last two nights. They overcame a number of hardships.

When I talked to Gladys, I asked, "What went wrong on your trip?"

She told me about a day when they were out in the middle of nowhere. Suddenly she looked down, and saw the iron rim coming off their wagon wheel.

To solve her problem, Gladys clipped one strand from the barbed-wire fence along the road. She unwound that wire from the other and wrapped it around the wagon wheel. The wire held the wheel together until she could reach a blacksmith!

During that long-ago trip Gladys kept a journal. I'm grateful that she shared her adventures with me. I'm thankful, too, for my young friend Shannon Benge who reminded me that when I write fiction I mix a little bit of truth with a big amount of imagination.

A number of people helped me with specific details needed for this story: Alice Biederman, Gene Blomberg and Mary Hedlund-Blomberg, Bob Gustafson, Tim Pfaff, Mildred Hedlund, Jim Hoefler, Eunice Kanne, Marita Karlish, Randy Klawitter, Floyd Lang, Lyman Lang, Jane Manders, Tom and Merle Powell, Roy and Grace Soderbeck, and Bill Young.

Others contributed to the overall content of the book and gave valuable time and suggestions while reading the final manuscript: Diane Brask, Frank and Ferne Holmes, Walter and Ella Johnson, Mary Kaliska, Bill and Alice Soderbeck, and Lolita Taylor.

Charette Barta, Ron Klug, Penelope Stokes, Terry White, Doris Holmlund, and the entire Bethany team gave editorial assistance. Still others helped in unseen and quiet ways. To each of them, and especially to Betty Coleman, Elaine Roub, and Darlene and Stan Marczak, I give my heartfelt gratitude. I am indebted also to the Grantsburg, Wisconsin, Public Library and to each of its librarians.

Each time I finish a book, I wonder what I can say about the great number of ways in which my husband Roy encourages me in this work I love. With this novel I especially cherish the laughter we shared while talking about the adventures of Kate and Anders. I hope you will enjoy that kind of fun while reading this story.

THE
HIDDEN MESSAGE

Adventures of the Northwoods

1. *The Disappearing Stranger*
2. *The Hidden Message*
3. *The Creeping Shadows*
4. *The Vanishing Footprints*
5. *Trouble at Wild River*
6. *The Mysterious Hideaway*
7. *Grandpa's Stolen Treasure*
8. *The Runaway Clown*
9. *Mystery of the Missing Map*
10. *Disaster on Windy Hill*

THE HIDDEN MESSAGE

Lois Walfrid Johnson

BETHANY HOUSE PUBLISHERS
MINNEAPOLIS, MINNESOTA 55438

Big Gust Anderson, Mabel Ahlstrom, Harry Blue, Trader Carlson, Rev. Pickle, Charlie Saunders, and Peter Schyttner lived in the Grantsburg/Trade Lake area in the early 1900s. All other characters in this book are fictitious. Any resemblance to persons living or dead is coincidental.

Copyright © 1990
Lois Walfrid Johnson
All Rights Reserved

Published by Bethany House Publishers
A Ministry of Bethany Fellowship, Inc.
6820 Auto Club Road, Minneapolis, Minnesota 55438

Printed in the United States of America

Library of Congress Cataloging-in-Publication Data

Johnson, Lois Walfrid.
   The hidden message / Lois W. Johnson.
     p. cm. — (The Adventures of the northwoods ; bk. 2)
   Summary: When their father leaves to earn money away from home. Kate and Anders assume more responsibility at the farm and uncover a mystery.

   [1. Swedish Americans—Fiction. 2. Mystery and detective stories. 4. Christian life—Fiction.]
I. Title. II. Series: Johnson, Lois Walfrid. Adventures of the northwoods ; bk. 2.
PZ7.J63255Hi   1990
[Fic]—dc20   89–78390
ISBN 1–55661–101–3   CIP
                                                                                  AC

To Jessica Lee,
Daniel Jeffrey,
and Nathaniel Kevin,
because I love you.

LOIS WALFRID JOHNSON is the bestselling author of more than twenty books. These include *You're Worth More Than You Think!* and other Gold Medallion winners in the LET'S-TALK-ABOUT-IT STORIES FOR KIDS series about making choices. Novels in the ADVENTURES OF THE NORTHWOODS series have received awards from Excellence in Media, the Wisconsin State Historical Society, and the Council for Wisconsin Writers.

Lois has a great interest in historical mystery novels, as you may be able to tell! She and her husband, Roy, are the parents of a blended family and live in rural Wisconsin.

Contents

1. Kate Listens In 9
2. The New Boy 14
3. Danger!... 19
4. Fight for Life 25
5. Sounds in the Night 32
6. Wildfire 39
7. Trader Carlson's Store 47
8. Shadows on the Wall.............................. 55
9. Escape! 62
10. Down in the Cellar 69
11. Bad News.. 75
12. Up the Pine Tree 79
13. The Hiding Place 84
14. The Mysterious Message 91
15. Big Trouble 96
16. Winter Search 104
17. December Storm....................................111
18. Whistle in the Dark 118
19. The Flickering Candle.............................124
20. Big Gust Anderson 130
21. Christmas Morning 136
Acknowledgments 143

1

Kate Listens In

In the darkness of a November night Katherine O'Connell woke suddenly. For a moment she lay without moving, wondering if something were wrong.

A sliver of moonlight slanted across the upstairs bedroom she shared with her sister Tina. The little girl still breathed evenly, her sleep peaceful. Kate slid farther beneath the quilt, trying to put aside her uneasiness.

Since moving to northwest Wisconsin, Kate had lost sleep more than once. Sometimes it was only a rooster that wakened her. Other times a screech owl shattered the peaceful woods around Windy Hill Farm. Then there was the night when Kate watched from the storeroom window and spied the disappearing stranger.

Now twelve-year-old Kate had no reason to stand watch, or so she thought. Closing her eyes, she tried to go back to sleep.

A moment later a murmur of voices brought Kate upright. Sliding out of bed, she reached for her robe and tiptoed across the cold wooden floor. Slowly, quietly, she turned the knob and opened the door just enough to slip through.

Still tiptoeing, Kate started down the stairs, keeping to the side of steps that squeaked. Mama and Papa's bedroom was on the first floor next to the dining room. Tonight, though, the voices came from the front room just beneath Kate and Tina's bedroom.

Four steps from the bottom, hidden by the wall between the stairs and the front room, Kate sat down. Pushing back her long hair, she leaned forward to listen.

"We need seed money for next year's crops." Papa Nordstrom's voice was low.

Money! thought Kate, disliking even the word. Kate's Irish father, Daddy O'Connell, had died in a construction accident. In the year that followed, Mama and Kate struggled to earn enough money for food and rent. Then Mama married Papa Nordstrom, and she and Kate moved from Minneapolis to Windy Hill Farm.

"He needs help with his three children," Mama had told her. "As we work together, I'll grow to love him."

Kate knew that had happened. Papa Nordstrom and Mama, Anders, Lars, Tina, and Kate had become a family.

But Kate hadn't expected to be the only one in the family and in her school who didn't speak Swedish. She hadn't expected to have to earn the respect of Anders, the new brother her age.

Now Papa Nordstrom spoke again. "Wages in the lumber camps are good this year."

For a moment there was silence. As she thought about his words, Kate felt an emptiness in her stomach. "I'm just getting to know you!" she wanted to cry out.

Papa Nordstrom's voice sounded sad. "I'd be gone two or three months during the worst part of winter."

Kate moved down another step, but couldn't hear Mama's answer.

"Yah" came Papa's Swedish yes. "Anders will help, and Lars, and Kate." His voice was gruff, the way it sounded when he cared deeply about something. "But I don't want to leave you."

"Can you think of any other way?" Mama asked softly.

For a time, Kate heard only the ticking clock. Then Mama spoke again. "If there isn't any other way, we'll do it. We'll handle it because we have to."

"But with the baby coming—" Papa said.

A baby coming? In her excitement Kate leaned farther forward, trying to hear more. Suddenly she tumbled down the remaining steps.

As she fell into the doorway of the front room, Papa Nordstrom jumped up. "Kate! Are you all right?"

Mama jumped up too, but her voice was stern. "I've told you, Kate, you aren't supposed to listen to other people's conversation."

"But, Mama, is it true you're going to have a baby?"

Mama's smile softened the sternness in her face. Standing up, she reached out and pulled Kate to her in a hug.

Mama was tall for a woman, and Kate short for her age. Kate also knew her own eyes were a deeper blue than Mama's. Yet now, as Kate looked up, Mama's eyes were shining.

"The baby will be born in the spring," Mama answered. "You're the first one to know."

The next morning at breakfast Mama and Papa Nordstrom told the other children the good news about the baby. But Anders and Lars and Tina also heard the sad news that Papa would go away to work in a lumber camp that winter.

"When you were at school yesterday, I butchered the pig," Papa told twelve-year-old Anders.

Anders nodded, his face solemn below his shock of blond hair. Like his father, his shoulders were muscular from farm work. But Papa had brown hair and a neatly trimmed moustache and beard.

Papa went on. "With this weather the pig should stay frozen. It's on the cookstove in the summer kitchen. The meat saw is there for you to cut off pieces when you need them."

Anders pushed his hair out of his eyes and nodded again. When days grew too warm for a fire in the house, the family cooked meals in the summer kitchen. In winter the small building wasn't heated.

As Papa turned to Lars, the nine-year-old looked just as serious as Anders.

"Lars, you and Anders split the wood and carry it in the way you always do. Take good care of the cows."

A tuft of hair stood up at the back of Lars's red head. Papa reached out, smoothed it down, and smiled. Lars blinked, then blinked again, as though holding back tears.

As five-year-old Tina slipped down from her chair, Papa set her on his lap. Tina's white-blond hair was pulled back in pigtails, and her blue eyes widened as Papa talked. "My little one, when the others are in school, you can help Mama all day long."

Then Papa looked at Kate and smiled gently. In that moment she remembered how he had helped her become part of his family. "Papa, I've been thinking. If I stopped taking organ lessons, could you stay home?" Even as Kate spoke, the words brought a pain within her. For years she'd wanted to take lessons and had only just begun.

Papa shook his head. "Playing the organ means too much to you, Kate. And even if you stopped, the money wouldn't be enough."

Then Kate saw the tears in Papa's eyes.

"Kate, my newest daughter, God will hold you with His special love."

Kate blinked as her own tears welled up. Surprised that he hadn't told her what work to do, she swallowed hard.

Clearing his throat, Papa turned back to the rest of the family. "If I bring a team of work horses, I'll earn more money. I'll take Dolly and Florie and get back sooner. You can put Wildfire to good use now, Anders."

As Papa mentioned the horse, Anders sat taller, pride shining in his face. But as he looked his father in the eyes, there was more. "We'll be all right, Papa. I'll take care of everything. Kate and Lars will help."

"All of you must be responsible," Papa continued. "Keep your head on your shoulders. Don't make Mama worry. Take good care of her and each other."

After praying for each one of them, Papa went out to the barn and harnessed the horses. Kate knew that when they came home from school, he'd be gone. A lonely ache crept into her heart.

It wasn't hard to remember what it was like after her first father, Daddy O'Connell, died. The rooms that Kate and Mama rented seemed silent and empty. Before, their lives had been filled with laughter. When Daddy came home from work, he often swung Kate off the floor with a big hug. Sometimes he danced around the kitchen, doing an Irish jig.

Now Kate wondered, *Will it feel just as empty with Papa Nordstrom gone?*

As Kate, Anders, and Lars started down the trail to Spirit Lake School, Kate turned to her oldest brother. "What will we do without Papa?"

"We'll make it," answered Anders. "We have to."

But Kate saw his eyes, and guessed how Anders felt. "I'll miss Papa," she said. She swallowed, quickly wiping away the tears that welled up.

Then she thought of all the things that could happen on a northwoods farm in 1906. *What if something goes wrong?*

2

The New Boy

During the mile hike through the woods, Anders and Lars were strangely quiet. Anders led the way, his long legs stretching out. Lars followed, his freckled face and blue eyes solemn.

Scuffling her feet in the carpet of fallen leaves, Kate kept up with them. The November air was brisk, and she buttoned her wool coat against the cold.

Leaving Windy Hill Farm and Rice Lake behind, they walked along a ridge where the land fell sharply away on both sides. Soon they reached the steep hill overlooking Spirit Lake School.

At the bottom of the hill a creek flowed between them and the schoolhouse. Swollen by fall rains, the creek ran high between its banks. Lars jumped onto the log spanning the water.

Anders followed, moving so quickly that he seemed to run across. On the other side, he glanced up the hill toward school.

Instantly Anders stopped. "He's back."

"Who's back?" asked Kate as she stepped onto the log. Even now, after all the crossings she'd made, she felt almost as scared as on her first day at Spirit Lake School. The cold dark water rushed beneath her feet.

When Anders didn't answer, Kate asked again. "Who's back?"

"Stretch." Anders sounded as if he didn't like the idea. "Must have finished up harvesting."

As Kate reached the end of the log, she looked up the hill. Standing on the porch of the school was a thin boy with curly blond hair and a grin. To Kate's surprise he seemed even taller than Anders.

"Stretch?" she asked. "Why do you call him that?"

" 'Cause it fits."

"Because he's tall?"

"He's tall, all right," said Anders.

Kate realized he hadn't answered her question. "So that's why you call him Stretch?"

Anders looked grim, but wouldn't tell her more.

Finally Kate asked, "What's his real name? No one calls a baby Stretch."

Anders grinned. "Nope, they don't. They give 'em a name like Johnson or Peterson or Olson."

"What does that have to do with it?"

"Well, there's Big Gust Anderson."

Kate nodded. "The one in Grantsburg." The seven-and-a-half-foot-tall village marshal had helped Anders and Kate solve a mystery.

"And there's Church Barn Anderson and Bingo Anderson."

"Oh, you're teasing!" replied Kate.

Anders threw up his right hand. "I'm dead serious. There's so many Swede names the same that everyone calls 'em something different. There's Plaster Olson, Legs Olson, and Gloomy Gus Olson."

Lars chimed in. "And Dusty Olson and Stonewall Olson."

Kate started to laugh.

"Shoemaker Johnson, Tanner Johnson, Hitch Barn Johnson." Anders paused to draw a breath. "Happy Johnson, Spoon Hook Johnson, and Mule Johnson!"

Lars took up the chant. "Andrew Johnson One, Andrew Johnson Two."

"And Three and Four?" asked Kate.

Anders scratched his head. "I'm not sure. But there used to be a Johnson Number 22! And now we have the Johnson just called Stretch!"

"Do you call him Stretch to his face?"

"Yup," said Anders, heading up the hill toward school.

As the new boy went inside the building, Kate spoke softly. "He looks nice enough from here. What's the real reason you don't like him?"

When Anders didn't answer, Kate turned to Lars.

"He stretches the truth," the younger boy told her.

"What do you mean?"

At Anders' look Lars fell silent, but Kate wouldn't leave it alone.

"He's older than the rest of us," Anders said finally. "And he's *biiiiig* trouble."

Kate laughed. "No one around here is big trouble!"

"Ha!" Anders sounded scornful. "That's what *you* think!"

"Then how come he's in school?" Kate asked. "Most boys stop coming around the end of eighth grade."

Though Kate prodded, Anders refused to say more. Finally she flipped her long black braid over her shoulders. "You're just making things up."

Anders turned to her, his eyes angry. "No, I'm not. And you stay away from him."

This time Kate giggled. "Who is he—the big bad wolf?"

Again Anders would not explain. "You listen to me."

"So?"

"So I know what I'm talking about."

Now Kate was angry. "You think you're boss just 'cause Papa's going away."

"If Papa was here, he'd tell you the same thing!" warned Anders darkly.

When Kate entered the schoolroom, most of the children were already at their desks. Their teacher, Miss Sundquist, stood near the back with the new boy. By comparison, she seemed small, and Kate knew Stretch must be close to six feet tall.

Just then he looked up over the teacher's head. Catching Kate's glance, he dropped one eyelid in a slow wink.

Quickly Kate turned away, embarrassed that she'd been caught watching. Reaching her desk, she put her books inside and took out her slate. As Miss Sundquist walked forward, Kate acted as if her only thought was on the lessons ahead.

But a moment later, Kate glanced over her shoulder. Stretch sat two desks back in the last seat of Kate's row and across the aisle from Anders. Though usually self-confident, Anders looked angry and uncomfortable.

Directly behind Kate was Erik Lundgren. Soon after Kate started Spirit Lake School, he had put her long black braid in his ink well. Like Anders, Erik was tall for his age. But unlike Anders' straight blond hair, Erik's was wavy and brown.

Kate hoped that Erik hadn't seen her look back at Stretch. Sometimes it seemed as if Erik saw everything.

" 'Mornin', Kate," he said now.

" 'Mornin', Erik," she replied in the same tone of voice.

"Ready for more ink on your dress?"

It was a constant battle between them. Whenever he threatened, she never quite knew whether he'd put her hair into his ink well again. Deep inside, she felt sure he hadn't meant to wreck her dress that day last March. Yet when she had swung her head, the end of her long braid had stained her dress with permanent ink.

Kate made a face at Erik and noticed that his hair was newly cut. "Got another bowl haircut?" she asked.

Erik flushed red, and Kate felt ashamed. Almost she wanted to say, "It doesn't really look that way." Almost she said it, but not quite. It might have seemed as though she were giving in to the war of words between them.

Erik and Anders were good friends, and both had strong arms and shoulders from farm work. Like Anders, Erik had a streak of kindness that told Kate he looked out for her, even during his endless teasing. But Erik cared more about his schoolwork than Anders did.

Kate looked across the aisle and smiled at Josie Swenson, the girl Kate knew best at Spirit Lake School. Slowly, gradually, she'd come to think of Josie as a friend.

"Kate, I've got to talk to you," Josie whispered. Her hazel eyes with their long dark lashes looked troubled.

"What's wrong?" asked Kate quickly, knowing it must be serious. What could be more important than a new boy in school?

"Something terrible," answered Josie, her voice low.

Kate leaned toward her. It took a lot to get Josie upset.

"Last night our steer was stolen." Josie looked as if she wanted to cry.

"Your steer?"

"The animal we've been raising for meat. We were going to butcher him any day now."

Josie's family lived on a farm near Spirit Lake School. The woods stretched between their place and Windy Hill, the farm where Kate lived.

"Stolen? You're sure?" Kate asked. She knew that sometimes animals worked their way outside the barbed wire fence. "Your steer didn't just wander away?"

Josie shook her head. "I don't know how Papa knows the difference. He won't talk about it in front of us. But for some reason, he's sure the steer was stolen."

"But nothing ever gets stolen around here." Kate hurt for Josie. "No one locks their doors. Everyone trusts everyone else."

"That's the worst of it." Josie fought back tears. "We never expected someone to steal. No one ever has before."

"Except when the disappearing stranger was around," Kate said.

"But he took small things," Josie replied. "Nothing as important as an animal."

In the morning sunlight the freckles across Josie's nose made her look younger than her twelve years. Yet Kate knew her friend often took care of eight younger brothers and sisters.

"It's your meat for all winter, isn't it?" Kate asked with a growing sense of loss for Josie.

Josie's nod was full of misery. "We don't have any other meat."

Then a gleam of hope entered her eyes. "Maybe you and Anders can solve this mystery too."

Before Kate and Josie could talk more, Miss Sundquist rang the small bell on her desk, asking for quiet. Usually calm and in control, the teacher seemed nervous. "As you see, we have a new boy with us," she announced. "I'm sure that most of you already know him."

Kate glanced back to see a careless grin cross Stretch's face. Again his bold glance met Kate's. Embarrassed, she quickly looked away.

3

Danger!

When Kate reached home that afternoon, Papa was gone. Though he seldom talked unless something needed saying, his absence made the house seem quiet and lonely.

"I wonder how far he traveled yesterday," Kate said as she and Anders and Lars walked to school the next morning. "Do you think Papa was outside all night?"

"Nah," Anders told her. "He probably stopped at someone's house. He'd ask if he could sleep on the floor."

Then Kate thought about the horses and the cold night wind. "What about Dolly and Florie? Would someone put them in their barn?"

Anders shrugged his broad shoulders. "Don't know if they'd have room."

When Anders spoke again, his voice sounded different. "I don't like the way you look at him."

"Look at who?" Kate asked innocently.

"You know. Stop pretending."

"Don't know what you're talking about," insisted Kate.

Anders laughed, and the sound was harsh in the November woods. "I'm talking about Miss Katherine Nordstrom!"

"Katherine O'Connell, you mean!"

"Nordstrom."

"O'Connell." Since Kate's first day at Spirit Lake School, it had been an argument between them.

"And you know I'm talking about Stretch! You should see how you look." Anders crossed his eyes. A silly grin slid across his face.

Then the grin slipped away, and he sounded angry. "I mean it! I don't like the way you look at him!"

Kate felt the hot flush of embarrassment creep into her face. "Dumb boy! You're making up tales!"

"Am I?" asked Anders. "Then how come you're red? How come you're always watching what he does? He's up to no good, I tell you!"

"What do you mean?"

"He's just making eyes at Teacher."

"At Teacher?" Kate's voice was small.

"What do you think?" demanded Anders. "That's the only reason he's here. Last fall when we had an old lady teacher, he sure didn't show up after harvest."

"Miss Sundquist didn't teach last fall?"

"Nope!" said Anders. "She just finished three years of high school at Grantsburg. Started when the other teacher got sick and couldn't come back."

"But she's still older than Stretch," answered Kate. For a moment she hung on to a sliver of hope, wondering if Anders could be mistaken. Yet in the time she'd known him, Anders had seldom been wrong about anything.

Anders laughed. "Not much. Teacher's only a few years older than us."

Kate felt as if someone had punched her. *And I was dumb enough to think Stretch liked me.*

"If you want to like someone, like Erik Lundgren," Anders went on, as though reading her thoughts.

"Erik Lundgren?" scoffed Kate, flipping her long black braid over her shoulder. "Just because he's your friend?"

"Nope, because he's—"

"Responsible?" Kate laughed as she used Papa's word, but gave it a scornful twist.

This time it was Anders' turn to look uncomfortable.

Seeing his face, Kate pressed on. "He's responsible, all right. As Papa would say, 'Erik's got a head on his shoulders!' "

"Yup!" agreed Anders. "He does!"

"Wrecked my school dress last year putting my braid in the ink well."

"He didn't mean it," defended Anders.

"Well, whatever he meant, he wrecked my dress!"

But Anders refused to back down. "He just wanted to tease you."

Kate's laugh sounded even more scornful. "So?"

"So if you want to like someone, like Erik."

Kate stopped in the middle of the path. "I suppose next you're going to tell me I should like him 'cause he goes to our church."

Anders grinned. "Well, for a change you've got it figured out."

Kate stamped her foot. "I haven't got words to describe you!"

Anders acted as if he hadn't heard. "And if you weren't so brainless, you'd know that we choose who we like."

"Who says?" The idea startled Kate.

"Papa. And he's right. It can be a dumb choice or a good one. A stupid oaf like Stretch or someone who's—"

"Responsible," Kate finished for him. "Like Papa says, responsible. Then *you* better choose to like Josie." Kate's voice dripped with sugar.

When Kate saw the spark of anger in Anders' eyes, quickly replaced by his flush of embarrassment, she knew she'd struck home. "And you're just jealous of Stretch," she added for good measure. "Everyone else likes him. Why don't you?"

Wanting the last word, Kate stomped away.

She was still angry when they entered Spirit Lake School. In the cloakroom, she slammed her lunch pail down on a shelf. As she went to her desk, Kate made sure she didn't look toward Stretch.

"I have a warning for all of you," Miss Sundquist told the

class as they started the day. "Spirit Lake looks as if it's frozen, but the springs make it very treacherous. You must not go out on the ice."

After a few more announcements, she led the children in the pledge of allegiance. Then they said the morning prayer in unison: "Give me clean hands, clean words, and clean thoughts. Help me to stand for the hard right against the easy wrong."

Kate repeated the words with the other students. For the first time she wondered about them. *Help me to stand for the hard right against the easy wrong. What does that mean?* But she pushed the thought aside.

Arithmetic was always first, and Kate was never as quick at it as Anders and Erik. This morning she had more trouble than usual trying to concentrate. She kept wondering what was happening two desks back.

When it was time for morning recess, Kate stood up quickly to get her coat. As she went out on the porch of the school, she wrapped a scarf around her neck and pulled on mittens.

Stretch stopped beside her. "She don't know what she's talkin' about," he said softly.

Surprised, Kate looked up. Standing next to him, she felt even shorter than usual. Yet she also felt excited that Stretch wanted to talk with her. "Who doesn't know what?" she asked.

"Teacher. Says the ice ain't safe."

"If she says it, I believe it," Kate answered. "No reason to go down there anyway. Plenty to do on the playground."

"Playground?" Stretch's voice sounded scornful. "That's for babies."

Yet as he and Kate circled the frozen yard, the boys were choosing sides for a game. One of them called out. "Hey, Stretch! Come here!"

Someone else objected. "We get him! Com'on, Stretch! Be on *our* side!"

Taller and older than the other boys, Stretch would help any team win. But he shook his head and kept walking.

Kate followed him to the hill at the edge of the playground. There they stood above the road that passed the school. On the other side were trees, now bare of leaves. Beyond lay the shores of Spirit Lake.

"I tell you, I know I'm right." Stretch gazed toward the expanse of frozen water. "I was down there before school."

"Days have been warm," Kate reminded him.

"Nights have been cold," he answered. "Plenty cold."

In the morning sunlight the ice shone. To Kate it looked inviting. "We can ice skate soon."

"We can skate *now*. Com'on and see."

"Teacher said no," protested Kate.

"She just said that 'cause some school-board member told her."

Stretch started down the hill. At the bottom he looked back. "What're you scared of?"

For a moment Kate stood there, feeling uneasy. But then a new thought came to her. *Maybe it isn't Teacher he likes, after all.* Step by step, Kate edged down the hill. "There's not much time."

"If we hurry, we'll get back," Stretch answered.

Kate still didn't feel right about it, but she pushed her uneasiness aside. *If I don't go, he'll think I'm a sissy.* Besides, it'd be fun walking to the lake with Stretch.

"We don't have to go out on the ice," he told her. "Let's just look." In spite of his lazy manner, Stretch walked quickly.

As Kate kept up, she asked, "Did you hear about Josie's steer?"

"What about it?"

"That it was stolen?"

"That so? Well, a steer's only a steer."

"No, it's not! They fattened him for two years to have him ready for winter." For a moment Kate wondered how Stretch could be so cold and heartless. She still felt bad for her friend. "Josie's got eight brothers and sisters!"

"Why do they think the steer was stolen?" Stretch asked.

Kate felt relieved that he sounded more concerned about the whole thing. Just the same, she could only tell him, "I don't know. Josie's father doesn't say *why*. But he *thinks* it was stolen."

Within a few minutes they reached a spot where the road ran close to the lake. As Stretch slid down the steep bank, Kate followed.

The ice had frozen smooth and clear. Kate looked across the

lake to the morning sun. Yet the sunlight did not warm her. Shivering, she tightened the scarf around her neck and felt glad for her wool coat and mittens.

As she squinted against the light, Kate saw a dog far out on the ice. The brown, black, and white hair seemed familiar. Suddenly Kate recognized him. "That's Lutfisk!"

"*Lute fisk?*" Stretch drawled out the word for the dried cod that Swedes soak in lye and eat at Christmas.

"Anders' dog. When he was a puppy, he got into the lutfisk and gobbled it up before Anders caught him. Must have followed us to school."

"Nice dog," said Stretch.

"Yup," answered Kate, then realized she sounded like Anders. "But he shouldn't be out on the ice. I'll get Anders to call him."

"No need." Stretch sounded helpful. "I'll get the dog for you." He called, but Lutfisk did not respond.

"Come here, Lutfisk!" Kate shouted.

In the crisp morning air the dog turned his head. Yet when Kate called again, Lutfisk did not start toward them.

"He hears me," said Kate. "What's the matter with him?" Stepping onto the ice, she moved closer to the dog.

"Come on, Lutfisk!" she tried once more. The dog lifted his head.

Then she remembered Anders' signal for sending Lutfisk after the cows. Raising her arm high, she motioned to the right. Even so, Lutfisk did not respond.

Kate turned to Stretch, who stood on the nearby shore. "You try."

Stretch's shout seemed to echo in the cold air. There was no doubt that the dog heard. Yet as he started toward them, Lutfisk barked, then stopped.

"Come on, boy!" urged Kate, edging still farther onto the ice.

Stretch called again, but instead of obeying, Lutfisk lowered his head and growled.

In the next instant Kate heard a loud crack. She went cold with fear.

The ice cracked again, louder this time. Quickly Kate stepped back. But her movement made things worse.

Once more the ice cracked. Suddenly it opened beneath her.

4

Fight for Life

As Kate plunged through the opening in the ice, she heard Lutfisk bark. Then she slipped deep beneath the surface of the lake.

Gasping, she choked on a mouthful of water. The cold seized her body, sending pain through her stomach and chest.

"You can swim," she told herself as she felt the shock. "You can swim."

Yet her clothing and shoes were heavy weights, pulling her down. Kate tried to lift her arms, and her coat sleeves filled with water. She stretched down a foot and could not touch bottom.

Panic washed over her, and she fought for air. She kicked, then kicked again. Surfacing, she took a deep breath and cried out, "Help! Help!"

Hair streamed in her eyes, clouding her vision. She heard only the barking of the dog.

Where's Stretch? Frantically, Kate looked toward shore, but saw no one.

The edge of the hole was not far away, and Kate reached for the ice with mittened hands. Her long scarf got in the way. Pulling it from her neck, she let it go, and fought for the edge of the hole.

As she touched the ice, it broke off. Her arms thrashed the water, breaking a wider circle. The weight of her coat pulled her down, below the surface.

Once more the sunlight disappeared, and black water closed around her.

Gasping for breath, Kate kicked, but saw only darkness. She kicked again. *Where's the hole?*

Her legs were numb now, and she wasn't sure if they moved. Her ears pounded. She seemed to spin in the black water.

Filled with panic, Kate fought her way upward. Then her head bumped something. *I'm under ice!* The terror of it overwhelmed her as she struggled to see light. Off to one side—maybe.

Stretching out her arms, she tried to head in that direction. Suddenly she found open water and surfaced. As she gasped for air, her head stopped spinning.

This time she heard a voice.

"Kate! Kate!"

Stretch? The voice seemed far away, but she listened.

"Take off your coat!"

Kate reached for the buttons. But her mittens got in the way. She forgot to kick and started to sink.

"Forget the coat!"

Kate heard the voice, but felt numb. *I'm so cold.*

"This way! Reach out your hands."

My hands? Where are my hands?

"Touch the ice with your mittens!"

Kate stretched out her arms, but wasn't sure if anything happened.

"You're almost there."

Through her panic Kate saw the edge of the hole about a foot away. Yet that foot seemed like a mile.

With her last ounce of strength, Kate reached again. Her mittens touched the edge, but the ice broke away. Again she felt herself sink.

"Com'on, Kate!"

Numbly, Kate kicked, unsure if her legs moved. The ice broke again.

"One more try," called the voice. "Almost got it."

But Kate's legs would no longer move. She lifted her arms, trying to reach out, and knew that she couldn't.

"Help her, God. Help her!"

Even though her mind seemed frozen, Kate heard fear in the voice.

"Try again!" The voice was steadier now, and the sound of panic gone.

This time Kate's mittens clutched the ice, and it did not break.

"Hold them there!" the voice shouted.

Kate's teeth chattered. It took all of her breath to speak. "I can't."

"Let 'em freeze to the ice!"

Kate's shoulders ached, and time stretched out forever. But then she knew the voice was right. Her mittens froze, holding her there.

"Don't move! I'll be right back."

"Don't go!" Kate gasped out.

But no answer came, and Kate knew he was gone. She trembled with fear. *I'm going down!* But the mittens held her.

I'm so tired.

Then the voice was back. Though far away, it sounded familiar. Was it Stretch?

"I've got a branch," the voice said. "See it? Right next to your hands?"

Dimly Kate saw the branch. A long thick one.

"Take one hand out of your mitten. Hang on to the branch. Got it?"

Kate's hand trembled, but her fingers curled around the end of the branch.

"Take your other hand. Hang on. Keep your legs straight. I'll pull you out."

The branch began to move, and Kate clung to it. Yet as her body started to slide, the ice broke away. Once again she found herself slipping farther into the water.

"Don't let go!" the voice warned. "Hang on!"

Her hands numb, Kate wondered if she could. But she still heard the voice cry, "Hang on! I'll try again!"

A second time the ice broke. On the third try, Kate's arms, then her stomach, legs, and feet slid onto the ice.

It held.

Kate felt herself being dragged. Then whoever pulled the branch stopped. Someone slapped her cheeks. From far away, a voice called, "Kate!"

Her eyelids felt weighted, but she opened them.

"You're safe," said the voice.

Kate looked up, expecting to see Stretch. Instead, Erik's face hovered above hers. Even through the fog, Kate saw that his eyes looked scared.

Kate shivered and tried to speak. She wanted to tell him she was sorry for saying he had a bowl haircut. She wanted to apologize for every awful thing she'd ever said. But no words came.

Erik didn't seem to care. "You're all right now, Kate."

She closed her eyes as he went on. "You have to walk. You have to get where it's warm."

"I can't," Kate answered, then felt surprised that her voice worked. Her teeth chattered. "I can't feel my feet."

"I'll help."

Taking her hands, Erik pulled her up. "Hang on to my neck." He raised Kate's arm, and the sleeve crackled in the cold.

Kate looked at it dumbly, wondering what was wrong. But Erik slid under her arm and started walking.

Half pulling, half carrying her, Erik climbed the steep bank near the lake. When Kate slipped, he slid under her arm once again. By the time they reached the road, her long braid had turned to ice. Her body trembled with cold inside her stiff coat.

They started toward school, Erik tugging, Kate staggering. Partway there, Kate saw Anders and Lutfisk running toward them. Her brother's face looked white.

"What happened?" he demanded in a voice Kate had never heard before. "Lutfisk came after me."

Reaching Kate's side, Anders stretched out his hands. By crossing their arms, the boys made a chair to carry Kate.

On the way back to school, Erik explained. "I heard Lutfisk bark."

"You went down to the lake?" Anders asked Kate, his voice

angry. "After Teacher said not to?"

Kate's teeth chattered so hard she could not speak.

"How dumb can you get?" Anders exclaimed. "You could have drowned!"

Tears came to Kate's eyes. She sagged, but Erik held her up.

"Be quiet, Anders!" Erik snapped roughly.

Kate heard something in his voice, something she didn't understand. For now she just felt glad that Anders said no more.

As they came to the schoolyard, Kate saw a horse and buggy. *Why was it there?* It didn't make sense. Yet Kate couldn't think beyond her shivering.

Anders recognized the horse. "Miss Ahlstrom's here!"

In spite of her misery, Kate sensed the warning. "Who's Miss Ahlstrom?" she asked through chattering teeth.

"The superintendent of schools," answered Erik, his voice soothing.

"For the whole county," Anders added grimly. "She visits all the schools. Comes to make sure the teacher's doing everything right."

Kate's shoulders started to shake, both from dread and cold. But Anders went on. "You're in big trouble now!"

As Kate's arms and hands trembled, tears slid down her icy cheeks. Yet she felt too weak to wipe them away.

"Be quiet, Anders!" Erik said again. "Let her be."

Their arms still crossed in a makeshift chair, the boys carried Kate up the steps of the school.

When they walked into the entryway, Miss Sundquist was standing in front of the class. As she looked toward Kate, the teacher stopped midsentence.

Every child looked back.

"Study your lessons," ordered Miss Sundquist, heading toward Kate and the boys.

As Erik and Anders set Kate down, her knees felt weak. She started to slip to the floor, but Erik hung on and kept her from falling.

Instead of the stern words Kate expected, Miss Sundquist spoke softly. "Come here," she said, drawing Kate into the cloakroom. "What happened? You're turning blue."

Moving quickly, the teacher grabbed towels from a high shelf. Taking her own coat from a hook, she put it down on a bench next to Kate. "You must change at once," Miss Sundquist said. Then she went out, shutting the door behind her.

Kate's fingers trembled as she pulled off her icy clothes. The teacher's coat was long, and Kate buttoned it from top to bottom.

When Miss Sundquist returned, she had a pair of wool stockings for Kate's blue-with-cold feet. "We'll dry your dress and coat by the stove," the teacher said as she helped Kate up. "Now come and sit as close to the heat as you can without burning yourself."

As Kate left the cloakroom, every child again turned to stare at her. But Kate was still so cold and miserable she didn't care. Making her way to the wood stove, she huddled close.

It was a long time before Kate stopped shivering.

In front of the class Miss Sundquist was again stern. "I believe you all know how serious this is. Kate is still so weak, I'll talk to her later. Starting tomorrow night, she'll stay after school the rest of this week. Now, can someone tell me why she went down to the lake?"

As the teacher looked around the room, everyone remained silent.

For the first time, Kate saw a lady sitting in a corner near the back. Her large hat had an even larger plume that curled down over the side of her face. In spite of her dread that this must be Miss Ahlstrom, Kate felt surprised by the young woman's beauty.

As Miss Sundquist waited for an answer, Kate saw Stretch in his usual seat, the last in his row. For an instant their gaze met. Then Stretch looked down.

Seeing him there in warm dry clothes, Kate felt angry. *Where did you go when I fell through the ice?*

"Someone must know something," said Miss Sundquist when no one spoke up. "Erik? Anders? What happened?"

Anders looked at Erik.

Erik looked uncomfortable, but he was the one who answered. "I heard Lutfisk barking."

"*Lute fisk?*" asked Miss Sundquist, as though unsure she'd heard the name correctly.

"Anders' dog. Must have followed him to school today. When I first saw Lutfisk, he was out on the ice. Kate was in the water, waving her arms."

"And you, Anders?"

"Lutfisk came and got me, then ran toward the lake. I went after him and saw Erik bringing Kate back to school."

"So, Erik. You rescued Kate from the water? Will you tell us how you did that?"

Quietly Erik described what had happened.

When he finished, tears glistened in Miss Sundquist's eyes. "I believe you all realize that Kate would have drowned if Erik hadn't helped her."

From her place near the stove, Kate watched Erik. He looked down, embarrassed by Miss Sundquist's praise.

But the teacher went on. "Erik, I especially want to thank you for keeping your head. If you hadn't, you also would have gone through the ice. Both of you could have drowned."

The room was silent then, and Kate felt uncomfortable. In that long quiet moment, she looked toward the back of the room.

Throughout the explanation, Stretch hadn't spoken a word. And Erik never mentioned him.

Again Kate felt angry with Stretch, so angry that she wanted to cry out, "Because of you, I could have died!"

5

Sounds in the Night

*S*tretch still avoided Kate's eyes.

By now Kate was warm enough to realize the seriousness of what she'd done. Besides nearly drowning, there was something else.

As she glanced back toward Miss Ahlstrom, Kate remembered what Anders said. "She comes to make sure Teacher's doing everything right." Kate liked Miss Sundquist and didn't want to spoil things for her.

In that moment Miss Ahlstrom stood up and walked forward. When she reached the front of the class, she turned toward where Kate huddled by the wood stove. "Kate, I trust you'll be wise enough not to go out on unsafe ice again."

Kate's cheeks burned with embarrassment.

Miss Ahlstrom went on. "I trust you'll value your life more from now on."

Kate wanted to ask, *What do you mean by that?*

But already the county superintendent had turned back to the rest of the class. "I also trust that all of you have learned a lesson," Miss Ahlstrom said. Then her voice softened. "Erik, I want to thank you for your heroism. It is seldom that a boy your age thinks and acts so quickly."

Miss Ahlstrom turned to the teacher. "Miss Sundquist, I value your fine handling of an emergency situation."

Kate breathed a sigh of relief.

Soon after, Miss Ahlstrom left the school. As her horse and buggy passed outside the window, the wheels creaked on the frozen dirt road.

Most of the day Kate stayed near the stove, warming up and drying her clothes and shoes. More than once she stared at Stretch, daring him to look her in the eye. *Where were you when I needed help?* she thought. Yet she never caught him looking her way.

By the time school was over, Kate's dress was dry, and she put it back on. Her coat was still wet and her shoes soggy. But Josie and Miss Sundquist loaned her their sweaters. Kate wore one on top of the other and carried her coat over her arm.

As she and Anders and Lars started home, Anders spoke up. "Of all the things you could possibly do, that was the stupidest!"

Kate lowered her head and looked at the ground.

"Papa tells us to be responsible, and there you go, out on the ice," Anders went on. "What were you thinking of?"

"I saw Lutfisk," Kate spit out, unable to remain silent. "I was afraid he'd fall through."

"You could have called him. One whistle, and he'd have come off the ice."

"I thought he'd come. He's obeyed me before, and you know it!"

"That's what's hard for me to figure out," Anders said. "Why didn't he now?"

Through the panic of those terrible moments in the water, Kate thought back. Why hadn't Lutfisk come? There was something she needed to remember, something that happened.

Then a picture flashed into her mind. *That's it!* she thought excitedly. Just before the ice broke, she heard Lutfisk growl a warning. Was it because he sensed Kate's danger on the lake? Or was it something else?

Now she felt afraid to ask. *I can't tell Anders I went down there with Stretch. I can't tell him that Stretch said the lake was safe, and I forgot and went out on it.*

Kate dreaded what Anders would say if he found out. Even worse, she still had more to face.

Anders reminded her now. "I hate to think what Mama's going to say when she hears you fell through the ice."

"'Specially when Papa said we're s'posed to help her," added Lars, his eyes solemn.

Kate knew they were right. The empty feeling in her stomach tightened in a knot of fear. Her wet shoes and cold feet added to her misery.

What can I do? she asked herself for the hundredth time. As she wondered what Mama would think, the tightness in her stomach moved into her throat. Kate felt like choking.

In that moment she made up her mind. "I'm not going to tell Mama."

"You're not going to tell her?" Lars looked shocked.

"I won't give her the letter from Teacher."

"But that would be lying!" exclaimed Lars.

Anders also looked disturbed. "You don't have any choice, Kate. You have to tell her."

"Why?" asked Kate boldly.

"Why?" Lars's eyes reminded Kate of a hurt puppy. A hurt, yet also angry puppy. For a moment he seemed to search his mind for an answer. "Because it's honest," he finished with an air of triumph.

"Honesty, fiddlesticks!" Kate flipped her black braid over her shoulder. "It's not that I'm lying to Mama. I just won't tell her. That's different."

"No, it's not," argued Lars, sounding sure of himself.

But when Kate stared back at him with her chin up, he looked away, as though not liking what he saw.

"You can't get by with it," warned Anders.

"Miss Sundquist won't see Mama for a while," answered Kate, her voice resentful. "By the time she does, she'll have forgotten."

"Someone else will tell Mama," said Lars.

"Who?" asked Kate. "Are you a tattletale?" She sounded like a cat ready to pounce.

Quickly Lars shook his head, but again he looked away as though he'd seen a stranger.

"And you?" Kate turned to Anders. "Are *you* a tattletale?"

"Aw, come on, Kate. You know I'm not. But Mama will hear from a neighbor or someone . . ." His voice trailed off.

Kate wondered if she and Anders were thinking the same thing. With winter coming, Mama could be pretty much alone on the farm.

"It might work," Anders said slowly as though not liking the sound of his words.

"It might, but it shouldn't," Lars stated stoutly. "Papa says we should be honest, no matter what it costs."

"Papa says this, and Papa says that!" exclaimed Kate angrily. "You tell on me, and when you do something wrong, I'll tell on you!"

Lars stepped back as though she'd slapped him.

Instantly Kate knew she had hurt him. She'd hurt something that had always been special between them.

The next moment Kate remembered how Lars helped her when she first came to northwest Wisconsin. She knew she should say she was sorry, but the words stuck in her throat.

Then the moment was gone. Without looking back, Lars took off, running to the farmhouse.

"Do you think he'll tell?" Kate asked.

Anders shook his head. "But you've started something." His voice was grim. "Something you're going to be sorry for."

When they reached the house, Kate avoided going into the kitchen as she usually did. Instead, she slipped through the front door and up the steps to her room. Quickly she changed out of the borrowed clothing into her everyday work dress.

"Now what can I do?" she asked herself.

The farmhouse had two stoves that used wood—a cookstove in the kitchen and another for heating in the dining room. In winter the family used both stoves for drying wet clothes. But Kate didn't dare hang her coat near either one of them. Mama would wonder why it was wet.

Spreading it out, Kate pulled the coat over the floor grate that let in heat from the dining room. Then she hurried down the steps into the kitchen.

Lars sat at the table drinking milk and eating oatmeal cookies. Mama stood peeling potatoes for supper.

"I can do that, Mama," Kate offered quickly. "Sit down and rest."

Mama looked grateful. "Thanks, Kate. You're always such a good girl."

Kate smiled, but felt uncomfortable. As she looked beyond Mama, she saw Lars. He held up two fingers making horns behind his head.

Kate turned her back on Lars. Bending over the potatoes, she peeled them as though she didn't have another thought in the world. But she was really figuring out what to tell Mama.

After a time Kate spoke up. "I'll be late every night the rest of the week. I'm going to help Miss Sundquist after school."

Then Kate saw Lars's face. He looked shocked. Behind Mama's back, he stared at Kate and mouthed the words, "Big liar!"

Kate glanced away, but couldn't push her uneasiness aside. It was the first time she could remember telling Mama something that sounded true but wasn't. *I'm not really lying*, Kate told herself. *I'm just not telling why I'll help Teacher.*

"It's nice you want to help," answered Mama. "But what about your schoolwork?"

"I'll do it at night," Kate quickly assured her.

"And your organ practice?"

"At night, Mama," Kate said again.

And I'll knit mittens, too, and a scarf, Kate added to herself. *I'll light a candle and knit them in my room so Mama doesn't find out mine are down in the lake.*

Aloud Kate said, "Don't worry, Mama. I'll get everything done."

All through supper and early evening Kate helped in every way she could. After Mama went to bed, Kate slipped downstairs and hung her coat over a chair to dry. She moved the chair as close to the stove in the dining room as she dared. Nearby she set her still-wet shoes.

The minute she crawled into bed, Kate fell asleep.

Sounds in the Night

In the middle of the night she woke up. For a long moment she lay half awake, half asleep, listening. This time she heard no murmur of voices from the room below. It was something else. Something that seemed like bad dream.

Then Kate guessed what must have wakened her. More than any other sound she knew, it filled her with panic.

Sharp teeth chewing wood in the walls! *Gnaw. Gnaw. Gnaw!*

Kate's fingers tightened into nervous fists. Then she heard the scamper of little feet across the wood floor. *A mouse in my bedroom!*

Clutching the quilt, Kate pulled it over her head. For a long time she lay there, her heart pounding.

"Wake up, Tina!" she whispered. Tina had lived on the farm all her life. Maybe she wouldn't be scared. But the five-year-old slept on, and Kate felt embarrassed to poke the little girl.

After a long time, Kate pushed back the quilt and listened. At first she heard nothing and thought the mouse had gone. Then the gnawing started again.

Kate drew up the quilt so fast that it pulled out at the bottom. *He'll get my feet!*

Kate crept to the bottom of the bed, still hiding beneath the quilt. Leaning over, she struggled to tuck it in. From inside the quilt she couldn't manage. But in the darkness of the room she felt too afraid to stand on the floor and put it back where it belonged.

Finally Kate gave up and lay down again. Curling up in a ball, she made sure both her head and feet were covered.

"What should I do?" she almost cried out. Her terror seemed to grow with every minute. "If I tell Mama, she might ask me to set a trap."

Kate had seen the mousetrap Papa Nordstrom used. A little wooden box, it had a small grate to help a mouse sniff out the cheese inside. To reach that cheese, a mouse went up a ramp and through a hole. When it passed through a second hole, a spring dropped down, and the mouse couldn't escape.

Kate wasn't sure what would be worse—not catching the mouse or catching it. She might have to empty the trap. She'd have to carry the box outside. She'd have to open the lid on top and let the mouse go.

From her hiding place under the quilt, Kate shuddered. In the whole world she could not think of anything worse. What if she had to ask Anders or Lars to empty the trap? They'd know. Lars had been there once when she saw Papa find a mouse. What if Lars guessed how scared she felt?

Kate trembled, thinking about it. *He and Anders would laugh at me. And what else would they do?*

6

Wildfire

At school the next morning Kate heard Anders and Erik talking.

"You're renting the farm next to us?" Anders asked. From the expression on his face, it was the best news he'd heard in a long time. "When will you move?"

"Two days from now," Erik answered. "The house is empty. We want to get in before winter."

Secretly Kate felt glad. Sometimes when she glanced Erik's way, she found him watching her. Now and then she wondered why he seemed so interested in what she did. But whenever Erik had a chance to tease her, he seemed like his old self.

When Miss Sundquist called her to the front, Kate dragged herself to her feet. Her leather shoes felt stiff and uncomfortable from drying next to the wood stove. They also squeaked from being wet.

Slowly Kate walked forward. In the quiet room her shoes sounded loud. *Squeak. Squeak. Squeak.*

Erik was the first to notice. As Kate glanced back, she saw him grin. Then Erik snickered, and the boy across the aisle looked up. By the time Kate reached the front, she heard muffled giggles from around the room.

Kate's cheeks burned hot. Quickly she sat down on the bench near Miss Sundquist's desk. As she read for the teacher, Kate thought of one thing. *What will happen when I walk back?*

The other children seemed to wait for that moment. When Kate stood up, every student looked her direction.

Hoping her shoes wouldn't squeak, Kate kept her knees straight. With her feet flat, she walked stiff-legged.

But then she heard Erik whisper. "Hey, scarecrow! What's the matter with your knees?"

As Kate bent her feet, her shoes creaked ominously. *Squeak. Squeak. Squeak.*

Between each creak came snickers from every corner.

Reaching her desk, Kate sat down quickly, took out a book, and pretended she was reading. Even when Erik poked her, she refused to look up.

Two days later, on Thursday, Erik stayed home from school to help his family move. Late that afternoon Kate and Anders started across the field between their home and Erik's. Mama had packed baskets of food.

As they reached the woods between the two farms, the dusk of the November day settled in. When Anders stopped to light the lantern, Kate felt glad.

The farmhouse Lundgrens rented had two rooms downstairs and a loft overhead. Erik and his older brother John would sleep in the loft. Their younger sister Chrissy had a cot in the kitchen, and Erik's papa and mama a bed in the front room.

John had finished eighth grade and now worked at home with his father. But the next morning Erik and Chrissy met Anders, Kate, and Lars at a fork in the trail. From there they walked to school.

As always, Erik and Anders had a good time. As they went ahead, Kate watched them laugh together. In spite of the way Erik teased about her squeaky shoes, Kate still wanted to talk to him. There were gaps in the story he told Miss Sundquist, gaps only Kate knew about. Yet she didn't want to ask those questions in front of Anders.

Friday marked the last endless day of staying after school. On Saturday morning Kate tucked her books under her arm and set out for her organ lesson. Leaving the house, she started down the wagon track with Lutfisk following.

As she came to the barn, she saw Anders hitching his horse Wildfire to the farm wagon. "Hop in!" he called as he finished. "My turn to do the creamery run. I'll take you partway."

A black mare with a white star and four white socks, Wildfire was long-legged and spirited. She was saddle broke when Anders bought her after the Burnett County Fair. In the time since, he had often hitched the mare to a farm wagon, getting her used to that.

"First time I've taken a passenger," Anders said as Kate climbed into the wagon. "Hold the reins while I untie her."

"You're sure she's ready?" asked Kate, not convinced that she wanted a ride behind a skittish horse. Still, it was a four-mile walk to their church at Four Corners, a settlement south of Trade Lake.

"Yup, she's ready," Anders told her as Kate took the reins. "Just hold her steady while I get in."

Once seated, Anders flicked the reins lightly across Wildfire's back.

As they left the farmyard, Mama called to them. "Be sure to stop at Trader Carlson's, Kate!"

Kate nodded and waved, while Anders urged the horse to move out. The mare turned her ears to the sound of his voice and started down the wagon track to the main road. Lutfisk bounded ahead.

"Wildfire's doing great!" Kate exclaimed.

Anders nodded proudly. "Took a while to get her used to a wagon. But she's steady now."

Just then Anders noticed Lutfisk streaking for the woods. Anders let out a long sharp whistle that pierced the stillness of the November day. Instantly Lutfisk stopped.

Turning, the dog picked up speed as he ran back to Kate and Anders. When Lutfisk reached the wagon, he was panting, and his long tongue hung out.

Kate laughed. "He wags his tail so hard, the back of his body swings with it!"

For a moment she watched Lutfisk follow alongside the wagon. "Wish he'd obey me the way he does you." There was something Kate still wanted to find out, but she had to be careful how she asked. "You know the day I fell through the ice?"

"Yup?" answered Anders.

"When I called, Lutfisk lifted his head and looked my way. Then he barked."

"But he didn't come, you said. That's strange."

"Strange, all right," said Kate. "What's more, he growled."

"Lutfisk growled at *you*?" Anders looked at her in disbelief.

"He hadn't growled at me since my first day on the farm."

"Strange," muttered Anders again. "Really strange." Then he shot a quick look at Kate. "Sure you're telling me everything?"

Suddenly Kate felt uncomfortable. In that instant she guessed what had happened. But she wasn't willing to tell Anders that Stretch stood next to her. *Maybe that's why Lutfisk growled. He doesn't trust Stretch.*

"Will you show me how to whistle through my teeth?" she asked instead.

Anders laughed. "Girls don't whistle that way."

"Why not?"

His blue eyes turned serious. "It isn't ladylike."

Kate wasn't sure if Anders was teasing or not. "If I whistled like you, Lutfisk would always come."

"Maybe. Maybe not."

"He would," said Kate, determined now that Anders teach her. "What do you do? How do you make such a loud sound?"

Anders drew his lips tight and blew. His long sharp whistle pierced the air. Lutfisk pricked up his ears and came close to Anders' side of the wagon.

Kate tried to imitate Anders, but no sound came.

"You're just a bunch of hot air," Anders told her.

Kate ignored him and tried again. But no matter how often she blew, no whistle came.

"See what I mean?" asked Anders. "It's not for girls."

Kate stomped her foot on the floor of the wagon. "Just wait. I'll learn!"

Anders grinned. "Maybe you will at that. You're sure a stubborn little thing."

"Stubborn! Look who's stubborn! You promised Papa you'd help. You're not helping me!"

Anders looked down at Kate, the teasing gone from his eyes. "All right. Maybe you really do need to learn."

Putting both reins in his left hand, he freed up his right. "Watch. Try it this way." Placing his thumb and index finger between his lips, he blew another sharp whistle.

"Show me again," ordered Kate.

Once more Anders put his thumb and index finger between his lips. His whistle sounded strong and clear.

Kate watched closely and tried several times. Still no sound came, only the whoosh of air.

Anders laughed, and Kate felt even more determined. Flipping her long black braid over her shoulder, she blew again. This time a whistle suddenly came.

"I did it!" Kate exclaimed.

For a change Anders looked proud of her. "You must be the first girl in the whole school who whistles that way!"

As they reached the main road, Anders tugged the left rein. Wildfire turned south toward the creamery at Trade Lake.

"Pretty good mare, huh?" Anders asked. As he flicked the reins, Wildfire broke into a trot.

Kate grinned. "Nice looking too."

After a week of staying after school, Kate felt better today. Miss Sundquist had kept her busy sweeping the floor, cleaning shelves, and pounding erasers. It was a relief to be out in the crisp November air.

"Mama hasn't found out," Kate said, as though Anders could read her thoughts.

He did. "You might not be safe yet," he warned. "You still have to get past church tomorrow."

"I'll be all right," answered Kate, her voice confident.

"I mean it," Anders replied. "Someone might talk to Mama."

"Let's not give them the chance. Let's leave the minute church is over."

Anders looked at her strangely. "Kate, what's gotten into you?"

Kate felt the flush of embarrassment. Lifting her chin, she said, "I'm protecting Mama."

"You're protecting your own skin." Anders' voice was grim. "I don't like it. What are you trying to hide? Besides falling through the ice, I mean?"

Instead of meeting his eyes, Kate looked out on the field they were passing. He was hitting too close to what really bothered her.

While working together for a horse and organ, she and Anders had become friends. He had seemed like a real brother. Now for the first time, Kate was hiding something important from him. It made her uneasy, but instead of answering his question she asked, "Have you heard any more about Josie's steer?"

Anders shook his head. "You're trying to get me off track."

But Kate kept on. "What are they going to do?"

Anders shrugged his shoulders. His eyes looked gloomy. "Eleven mouths to feed, and no meat for winter."

"Can her father shoot a deer?"

"Not many around. Used to be a lot of 'em. Settlers lived on the meat they killed. Not anymore."

"How come?" Kate wanted to know.

"They hunted any time of the year, whenever they wished. And Papa says there was heavy logging about twenty-five years ago. Brush grew up really thick afterward."

"So?"

"So deer don't come around anymore. Guess they need more open spaces."

"That's why Josie's worried? Hunting isn't good?"

As Anders nodded, his blond hair fell into his eyes. "Got any ideas?"

Kate shook her head. "Not a one. But Mama won't let them go hungry. She'll send over some of our pig."

Even as she spoke, Kate felt uneasy. What if the thief stole from someone else? What if their own pig disappeared?

"Won't be enough," Anders told her, his voice short. "Josie's got a big family. That animal has to be found soon. Before the thief sells it."

"Or eats it."

Twice they stopped at neighboring farms, picking up more milk cans.

"After I leave these off, I'll go on over," Anders said.

"To Josie's? To see what happened? Or to see Josie?"

Anders grinned. "To see what happened. There's some mighty thick woods near their pasture."

"Could the steer wander away?"

"He could. A lot of 'em do. But there's something bothering Josie. For some reason her father doesn't want to talk about what really happened. I wonder if he's afraid we'd talk too much and tip off the thief."

As they pulled into the Trade Lake Creamery, Anders handed the reins to Kate. "Hold her steady so she doesn't move when I jump down."

Kate grasped the reins. Anders tied the lead rope to a hitching rail, then came back to help Kate down.

"You're going to let me walk the rest of the way?" she asked.

"Yup, won't hurt you a bit." He grinned his lopsided smile. "Usually you walk all four miles." Moving to the back of the wagon, Anders swung down the cans and set them on the creamery platform.

Kate waited until he finished before she said, "You could take me there and still go to Josie's."

Anders shook his head. "Not if I want to get back to help Mama like I promised."

"Sure you can." Before he could object again, Kate climbed back into the wagon.

Anders groaned. "You're a pest! All right, hang on. I'll hurry and make up for it."

As they left the creamery, Anders turned Wildfire south again. They crossed a narrow bridge spanning the Trade River, then reached an open road. Anders flicked the reins, and Wildfire moved out in a trot.

"I'm doing good in my lessons," said Kate.

When she moved to Windy Hill Farm from Minneapolis, Kate thought she was giving up everything, including the organ lessons she wanted. Instead, she now had her own pump organ. To Kate it seemed like a dream come true.

"Still going to be a great organist someday?" asked Anders.

"I'm going to travel around the whole United States, like Jenny Lind."

It seemed a long time since Kate had talked to Papa Nordstrom about the Swedish singer. Now Kate felt afraid to share her dream with Anders. Yet she needed to hope, to speak her dream aloud, and believe it would come true. "I'm going to make people feel good, the way Jenny Lind did when they heard her sing."

"But with an organ instead of a voice," said Anders slyly, and Kate was unaware of the trap he set.

"Yup!" she answered the way Anders would.

"Well then, I guess I'm totin' around the great nightingale of Burnett County."

Suddenly Kate hit his arm, returning his teasing. His hands jerked, and the reins slapped Wildfire's back. Without warning, the mare broke into a gallop.

"Now see what you did!" muttered Anders, pulling hard on the reins.

But Wildfire flattened her ears against her head and tore down the dirt road. "Easy, girl," called Anders. "Easy!"

A large rut loomed ahead of them. Anders pulled on the left rein, and Wildfire swung out. But the right wheel caught in the rut, and the wagon bounced hard.

For a moment Kate thought she'd fall off the seat. The wagon bumped again, then rode it out.

Kate drew a breath of relief, but to her surprise, Anders sounded proud. "Yup! A pretty good horse!"

"Slow down!" she cried as Wildfire again picked up speed. As they flew past trees, the terror within Kate grew. "Stop her!"

7

Trader Carlson's Store

*T*hought you wanted Wildfire to *move*," drawled Anders. Looking away from the road, he grinned down at Kate.

Just then the wagon hit a deep hole.

Kate grabbed hold of the seat and hung on with every ounce of strength. "Stop it!"

Again Anders pulled on the reins. This time Wildfire obeyed. But instead of being frightened, Anders laughed. "Aren't you the one who wanted a ride?"

Before the horse could move again, Kate scrambled down. Once on firm ground, she clutched her music and glared up at Anders. "You better make that horse safe before you take Mama to church tomorrow."

Anders grinned. "She'll be safe all right. I'll just put you where you can't hit my arm."

Kate shook her fist, but Anders laughed. "What a big noise you make for such a little one!"

Drawing herself up, Kate tried to stand as tall as her less than five feet allowed. But her effort was wasted as Anders turned the horse to head back to Josie's farm.

Kate set off at a brisk pace and soon reached the Swedish

settlement called Four Corners. Turning at the crossroads, she came to the church built on the edge of a hill. The road past its doors stretched out like a ribbon, dropping away between trees now bare of leaves.

For a moment Kate stood on the church steps, listening to Mr. Peters play the organ. The chords filled the air, spilling through the closed windows.

Each week Kate looked forward to hearing him play, then playing herself. *Strange,* she thought. *Strange we should move this close to the first hand-pumped organ in the county.*

Sometimes Kate wondered if God planned it all. This past summer she'd often thought about God and even asked for His help. He had seemed real to her. But now He again seemed far away.

Kate knew the change had come this past week. The thought made her uncomfortable, and she pushed it to the back of her mind.

Opening the church door, Kate slipped quietly up the stairs to the balcony. Standing behind Mr. Peters, Kate watched his fingers move across the keyboard, seemingly without effort. His black shoes touched the pedals lightly.

Mr. Peters had come from Sweden to study at Gustavus Adolphus College. When he became choir director and organist at Trade Lake, he married a young woman from the area.

Now came the run Kate hoped for. His left foot lit on the pedals, and his fingers leaped down the scale.

As the music slowed to simple chords, Kate saw Erik. Sitting on the side and near the back of the organ, he pushed a wooden handle up and down. The handle pumped bellows, bringing in air to make the pipes sound.

How come he's here? wondered Kate. Always before, there had been another boy. She didn't like to think how Erik might tease after hearing her play.

When Mr. Peters started another piece, Kate moved forward to look at the music.

Mr. Peters heard her and swung around. "Ah, there you are, Kate. A bit early. How are you today?"

As Kate played the first scale, her fingers felt clumsy. With each scale she got worse. Whenever she thought about Erik, she missed notes.

Finally Mr. Peters stopped her. "You can do better than that, Kate. Start over again."

Kate felt the hot flush of embarrassment reach her face. Once more she tried the scale. It sounded even worse.

When she finished, Mr. Peters slid off the bench. Walking around to the side of the organ, he said, "Why don't you take a rest for a few minutes, Erik? I'll pump for a while."

As soon as Erik disappeared, Mr. Peters spoke softly. "Kate, I want you to think of one person who encourages you to play the organ."

Immediately Kate remembered Papa Nordstrom. Soon after she came to Windy Hill Farm, he encouraged her in her dream to be an organist. Where was Papa now? Was he working in a cold, snowy lumber camp? Kate knew he'd like to be home, hearing her play.

Mr. Peters disappeared then, down next to the handle of the organ. But Kate still heard his voice. "Now play."

This time Kate's fingers felt steady upon the keys. She played every note right.

She barely noticed when Erik came back, and Mr. Peters returned to the organ bench. As Kate played the scales and songs she had practiced, she felt a growing excitement.

"You're doing well," said Mr. Peters at last. "Very well for someone who's taken lessons only a few months."

His praise warmed Kate, and he went on. "You have an ear for music. You hear it in your mind, don't you?"

Kate nodded. "When you play, I try to remember the tune. Doesn't everyone do that?"

"No," he said simply. "You're doing what we call playing by ear. When I give you a new piece, you ask how it's supposed to go. I play it for you. You listen and play the way I do. You don't really learn the notes."

Kate was startled, but realized he was right. To her it was the only way to play.

Beneath his moustache, Mr. Peters' lips parted in a smile. "I'm glad you can hear music. But if you depend on listening to someone else play, you'll stop learning. From now on I won't play a new piece for you."

Kate wasn't sure she liked that idea. "That'd be harder."

"It will. But if you learn to read notes, you'll go a lot further."

He stood up, and Kate knew the lesson was over. She felt disappointed and wished he wouldn't make things more difficult. Up to now, playing the organ had been easy, something she wanted to do and just did.

As she headed for the door leading downstairs, Mr. Peters called to her. "You're very gifted, Kate."

Looking back, Kate saw Erik listening. She hoped he wouldn't remember and tease.

Her teacher's next words surprised her. "Because of that gift, I'm going to expect more from you."

That'll be work! Kate wanted to tell him. Almost she wished she didn't have a gift for music. Almost, but not quite.

When Kate let herself out of the church, the air was still crisp, yet warmed by the sun directly overhead. She seemed to float on that air instead of a dirt road. Passing the buildings at Four Corners, she headed north.

One moment she felt excited. "Mr. Peters thinks I'm gifted!" She spoke aloud, wanting to make the words real. "Maybe I really will be a great organist!"

The next moment she felt scared, guessing about how much she'd have to learn, how hard it might be.

Lost in thought, she kicked a stone along the road, sending it ahead of her. She tried to whistle, practicing what Anders taught her. Sometimes she could do it. Other times she couldn't.

In the midst of a strong, clear whistle, Kate remembered her mother. Mama would go to church tomorrow. She would talk to people. Someone might tell her what really happened.

The whistle died on Kate's lips. The sunshine seemed to hide beneath the clouds.

Soon Kate crossed the bridge over Trade River and turned toward Trader Carlson's large general store. From miles around, Indians brought their furs, exchanging them for traps and other needed items.

When Kate passed through the door, a bell jangled. As her

eyes adjusted to the dimmer light, she saw a large barrel piled high with apples. Glass jars held hard candy. Bolts of cloth lined one wall. Hardware items filled another.

Passing the candy, Kate wished she dared spend a penny. Instead, she walked on toward the back of the store.

Papa had told her to come here for moccasins. When the weather dropped well below zero, Kate could wear them all day over two pairs of homemade stockings. She'd stay warmer in the often chilly schoolhouse.

Up to now, Mama had always traced Kate's foot on a piece of paper, then taken the paper to a store that sold shoes. As a clerk helped Kate, she felt uncertain, wondering which pair to pick.

Just then, the bell at the door jangled. Kate looked toward the front of the store.

Stretch!

For a moment Kate froze, hoping he wouldn't notice her. He hadn't been back to school since the day she fell through the ice. Now Kate wanted to avoid him.

Pretending she didn't see him, she took another pair of moccasins from the clerk. When Kate glanced back up, Stretch stood near a jar of candy. The lid was off.

In that instant, his hand darted out, then back. Looking as though he didn't have a care in the world, he slipped that hand into a pocket.

Kate stared. *Did I see what I think I saw?*

When her clerk left to help someone else, Kate kept watching Stretch. Once more she saw his hand dart forward, then back. This time Kate had no doubt.

But she also remembered Stretch's lazy smile. It had been fun talking with him as they walked down to the lake. To herself Kate started making excuses for Stretch. *He's really not bad, like Anders says.*

Just the same, Kate stayed toward the back of the store, hoping Stretch would leave. The minutes passed slowly. Finally she knew she couldn't wait any longer. Mama expected her home.

Kate picked up the moccasins that fit best, yet gave room for her feet to grow. Walking forward, she paid Trader Carlson. Without looking at Stretch, she hurried from the store.

When Kate reached the road, she walked fast, but her thoughts scurried even faster. Before long, she heard a wagon approaching from behind.

A familiar voice called "Whoa!" to the horses. Then, "Kate!" She looked up into Stretch's lazy smile.

"Want a ride?" he called down.

For a moment Kate stood there, unable to make up her mind. Back in the store she hadn't wanted anything to do with him. Here in the sunlight Stretch seemed harmless, even handsome. And she still had a three-mile walk.

Kate tried to push her uneasiness aside. *Everyone gives rides to everyone else,* she told herself. *That's the country way of doing things.* Besides, she wanted to ask Stretch some questions.

As she climbed into the wagon, Stretch grinned again. Kate remembered why she found him likable. She knew everyone at school felt the same way. Everyone except Anders, Lars, and Erik.

"Where you headed?" Stretch asked.

"Home," Kate answered, hoping for a chance to ask why he left when she needed help. "What're you doing?"

"Goin' home too." Stretch tipped his curly blond head toward the wagon load of long slender tree limbs. "Hauling tamarack for winter. I cut 'em up for firewood. Where's home for you?"

"Windy Hill Farm."

"You part of that family? Your name's O'Connell."

"Yup, and proud of it," said Kate, sounding like Anders. She remembered the day she started Spirit Lake School. Anders had been mean, and she'd gotten even when he introduced her as Katherine Nordstrom. Then it had seemed like a victory to tell Miss Sundquist, "I'm Katherine O'Connell!"

Since then, Kate had grown to love Papa Nordstrom and her new sister and brothers. Every now and then she felt sorry for not using their name. Still, she wanted to remember her Irish daddy.

"O'Connell," repeated Stretch. "That's a strange name."

"Strange, you say? It's Irish. Best name in the world!"

"Irish?" Stretch seemed to muddle it over in his head.

"Yah, sure," said Kate, this time sounding like Papa Nordstrom.

"Well, then," answered Stretch, and somehow the words sounded mean. "You and Harry Blue and Rev. Pickle have something in common."

"What's that?" Kate asked.

"You're the only ones in the whole town of Trade Lake who ain't Scandinavian!"

"So?" asked Kate. "I'm proud of being Irish!"

"Proud, is it?" Stretch gathered both reins in one hand and scratched his head as though thinking hard. "Proud. There oughta be a cure for that."

Kate wasn't sure if he was teasing or being mean. But then as Stretch took the reins in both hands, she saw something.

"How come your hand is blue?"

"Blue?" Stretch looked startled. Looking down, he quickly shifted the reins back and wiped the blue hand on his overalls. But the color didn't wipe off.

"What's it from?" asked Kate.

Stretch's lazy eyes weren't lazy anymore. They'd come alive, like those of a animal trying to run for safety. When he spoke, he seemed to make an effort to sound careless. "Musta worked too hard, sawing down trees." Once more he wiped the hand on his overalls.

He's lying, thought Kate. *Lying through his teeth.*

Suddenly Stretch didn't seem very nice. Suddenly Kate wanted to be far away from wherever he was. Seeing a farmhouse near at hand, she said, "Just let me off here."

Stretch stopped the horses, and Kate jumped down and away from the wheels. She wanted only one thing: that he would leave.

Yet as Stretch clucked the horses, Kate remembered her question and called out. "Where'd you go when I fell through the ice?"

Stretch flicked the reins and did not turn.

"Why didn't you help?" Kate hollered after him. But Stretch seemed not to hear.

As the wagon rolled past Kate, it bumped into a hole. For

one moment the tree limbs bounced up. The next moment they dropped back into place. In that one instant Kate saw several wooden boxes set in the wagon.

When the wagon rumbled beyond a rise, Kate slowly followed Stretch down the road. But her thoughts raced far ahead.

Boxes. Until that jolt they'd been covered by tree limbs. *What is Stretch trying to hide?*

As Kate walked, she turned it over in her mind. Finally she shrugged her shoulders. *Maybe I'm just imagining things.*

8

Shadows on the Wall

When Kate reached home she was still thinking about Stretch. She kept returning to one question: *What's in those boxes?*

She found Lars and Anders hauling water for Saturday night baths. Filling the big washtub the family used for baths took large kettles, heated on top of the wood cookstove.

As Lars built up the fire, he glanced Kate's way, but didn't speak.

"Where's Mama?" Kate asked after a long silence.

"Sleepin'," answered Lars, as untalkative as he'd been all week. "Said you're s'posed to clean the lamps."

On Saturday afternoons it was Kate's job to trim the wicks and wash the glass chimneys of the kerosene lamps. Usually she and Lars spent the time talking. But for five days now Lars had been strangely quiet.

Ever since I said I wouldn't tell Mama about falling through the ice, thought Kate, feeling uncomfortable.

A hidden part deep inside Kate knew Lars was right. Yet she didn't want to admit it—even to herself.

"I'm just sparing Mama," she told Lars now.

But Lars didn't answer, and Kate knew that defending herself didn't take away her uneasiness. She sighed just thinking about it. *I don't even like myself anymore.*

Just then Mama came into the kitchen. In spite of her nap, her large blue eyes looked tired. Her knot of golden blond hair, usually centered on top of her head, had slipped sideways.

"Are you all right, Mama?" Kate asked.

Mama smiled. "I just need more sleep because of the baby."

"Mama never sleeps during the day," Kate told Lars when Mama left again. "What'll we do if she gets sick when Papa's gone?"

Lars remained silent, and Kate talked on. "One more reason not to tell her about the ice. I did the right thing."

Still Lars did not speak. Among his freckles his blue eyes looked troubled. The rest of the afternoon and all through supper Kate had to push her uneasiness away.

As she cleaned up the dishes, Anders took out the big round washtub used for baths. Setting the tub on the kitchen floor, he filled it with steaming water.

"Did you see Josie?" Kate asked when she and Anders were alone in the kitchen.

"Yup. She took me out back of their barn. Did you know they tied the steer there?"

Kate shook her head.

"Found out why her father thinks it was stolen. Had a rope around its neck. A good rope that wasn't frayed and worn. It was cut!"

"Poor Josie!" It was one thing to have a steer wander away and become lost. It was something else to have someone steal an animal.

"Did you know they fed that steer almost two years?" Anders sounded angry. "Planned to butcher it about now." He lowered his voice. "We've just got to find that animal before the thief sells it."

Kate had another thought. "What if the thief butchers it? Could Josie's father still recognize it?"

Anders shook his head. "Nope. That's why we have to keep our eyes open."

"But where do we look?"

Anders shrugged his shoulders, but his voice sounded grim. "Don't know. With the disappearing stranger, we found things around here. A steer would probably be hidden in a building."

"People would get mighty upset if we started snooping around their barns and sheds," answered Kate. "It'd look like we don't trust them."

"What's more, people around here are honest. Who would take something like a steer?" Anders was quiet, thinking about it.

Kate began wiping dishes. After a time she broke the silence. "Saw Stretch today."

Anders looked surprised. "You did? Where?"

"First at Trader Carlson's store. Maybe you're right."

"Sure, I'm right," said Anders with his lopsided grin. "Right about what?"

"When you said not to trust him."

"Wel-l-l-l," drawled Anders. "You finally got it figured out. So what gave you that idea?"

When Kate told him about the jar of candy, Anders laughed. "Yup. You caught him with the goods all right. But lots of boys steal candy."

"Including you?"

"Nope. Not anymore. Not since Papa tanned me."

Kate laughed, but then Anders asked another question. "You said first. What's second?"

"Second?"

"Second time you saw him."

Kate wasn't sure she wanted to tell Anders about that. When she described how Stretch came along, offering a ride, Anders interrupted.

"You took a ride with Stretch? After I told you not to go near him?"

"Everyone gives each other rides!"

"So? That doesn't mean you take 'em. 'Specially if you've got pretty blue eyes, long black hair, and you're a girl named Kate!"

"What's wrong with being a girl named Kate?"

"Nothing!" declared Anders. "But there's plenty wrong with a girl named Kate taking a ride from a boy named Stretch! And don't act dumb! You weren't born yesterday!"

"Oh, fiddlesticks!" Kate turned back to the dishes. But a moment later she forgot her own anger at the tall boy with the curly blond hair. "How come you and Erik and Lars are the only ones who don't like Stretch?"

Anders looked at her as though she had lost her mind. "Like I said, 'Dumb girl!' " He stalked out of the kitchen.

In spite of the way Kate talked to Anders, she had some questions of her own. Questions that nagged away at the back of her mind. *What was in those boxes? And why did Stretch have one blue hand?*

As Kate finished the dishes, Tina came in and climbed into the large round tub. Taking the bar of homemade soap, Kate helped the little girl wash her hair.

As youngest, Tina always had her bath first. Then, one by one, each family member took a turn.

"I'm glad I'm second to use the bath water," said Kate. "Lars always gets so dirty."

Usually Tina talked without stopping, using a combination of Swedish and sign language. Tonight she seemed strangely quiet. Soon she finished her bath and pulled on her robe.

Kate started to towel Tina's white blond hair.

The little girl twisted away. "Me do." Pointing to herself, she took the towel from Kate. Her blue eyes didn't quite meet Kate's gaze.

"Something the matter?" Kate asked. Before Mama's marriage to Papa Nordstrom, Kate had always wanted a little sister. Since moving from Minneapolis to Windy Hill Farm, she had grown to love Tina, even though they spoke two different languages. Mama talked to Tina in Swedish, while Kate spoke to her in English.

Once again the five-year-old pointed to herself. "Want no help." Pointing toward Kate, she added, "Liar."

Kate stepped back, feeling as though she'd been struck on the cheek. "A liar?"

Tina nodded, her blue eyes solemn. "Lars said—" Stopping midsentence, Tina clapped her hand over her mouth.

"Oh ho!" Kate said, as though ready to pounce. "So tattletale Lars has been talking?"

Tina's eyes looked scared. She backed away from Kate and ran from the room.

As the door between the kitchen and dining room slammed in her face, Kate stopped. The little girl would go to Mama. She wouldn't say what was wrong. But she'd sit close to Mama so Kate couldn't talk.

Dumb sister! thought Kate for the first time since Mama married Mr. Nordstrom.

Trying to push aside her angry feelings, Kate added hot water to the tub, undressed, and climbed in. Crossing her legs at the ankles, she slid under the water as far as possible.

Though short for her age, she found it harder all the time to fit into the tub. Yet Kate looked forward to her once-a-week bath. Usually the warm soapy water felt good.

Tonight thoughts of Lars kept coming back. "Tattletale!" Kate muttered aloud. "What if he tells Mama?"

All week Lars had stayed away from Kate. Whenever they walked to and from school, he ran ahead, or poked along behind. It hurt Kate.

On her first cold and muddy ride to Windy Hill Farm, Lars had helped her. And when Anders didn't speak to her during their first walk to school, Lars did.

As Kate washed her long black hair, she thought about it. *Lars has been more than a friend. He's been a brother. That is, until now.*

A knock on the door interrupted her thoughts. "Are you almost done, Kate?" called Mama.

Quickly Kate stepped out of the water. "In a minute!" she answered, pulling on her robe.

As Kate entered the dining room, Mama added wood to the fire. She straightened, and Kate saw that Mama was losing her slim waist.

"Tina says we haven't sung together since Papa left," Mama told Kate. "Will you play for us?"

Kate looked at Tina, and the little girl looked down.

It's not the singing she wants, Kate thought. *She doesn't want to go to bed.*

In the front room Kate sat down at her prized organ and picked out the simple songs she knew how to play. Soon she discovered she was right. Tina sang halfheartedly.

As Lars finished his bath and entered the room in a clean shirt and overalls, Kate saw him look at Tina. The little girl grinned, and Kate wondered, *What's up?*

They were still singing when Anders came in, also in clean clothes, and with his thatch of straight blond hair still wet. By now Kate had played every song she knew and started over again. Feeling uneasy, she stopped, and twirled around on the organ stool.

This time she caught Lars in a long slow wink in Anders' direction.

Kate's thoughts were grim. *They're planning something. All this talk about responsibility. Fiddlesticks!*

For the first time in many months she felt shut out by the other children. Since she and Anders had solved the mystery of the disappearing stranger, Kate had been part of every plan. Now she felt empty with loneliness.

"Time for bed, Tina," Mama said.

Tina stood up, walked over to Kate, and tugged her hand. In that moment Kate felt better. Tina seemed her old self.

Lighting a candle, Kate picked up the holder and led Tina to the hallway. Wavering shadows danced on the walls as they climbed the stairs. As Kate and Tina entered the bedroom they shared, more shadows reached out from the corners. The darkness of the November night seemed to touch them. So did the cold.

Kate shivered and pointed to the bed. "Hop in and I'll sing one more song." It had become their ritual, one that helped the little girl go to sleep.

But in spite of the cold Tina looked around at the shadows and refused to climb into bed. Hugging herself, she hopped up and down on bare feet.

"Get in," said Kate impatiently. "You won't warm up until you do."

"Cold," said Tina, one of the few English words she knew. "Cold!" The word ended in a wail.

"You're right," said Kate, feeling the chill around her. Only a little heat from the wood stove had come through the grate in the floor. "Just a minute. I'll be right back."

Setting the candle holder on a small table, Kate hurried down to the kitchen. There she took one of the flatirons heating on the cookstove. Wrapping it in a cloth, Kate returned to Tina. "Now your feet will be warm."

In the dim light Kate lifted the quilt. As she slid the iron between the flannel sheets used in winter, Kate touched something.

When she jumped, Tina snickered. Yet Kate saw only innocence on the little girl's face.

Unwilling to take a chance, Kate turned the quilt back from the top. Then she saw what she had felt—a small wooden box.

A ribbon tied around the box held a silk flower to the top. Kate recognized the flower from one of Mama's old hats.

"Surprise for you, Tina." Kate held out the box to the little girl.

But Tina put her hands behind her back. "Pretty," she said. "You." She pointed to Kate.

By now Kate was curious. Setting the box on the table, she untied the ribbon, lifted the flower, and opened the lid.

A white sheet of paper filled the top of the box. Moving the candle close, Kate read the carefully printed words.

> Pretty on the outside.
> Like this on the inside.

In the semidarkness Kate squinted, wondering if she'd read correctly. She peered at the words.

Curious, Kate picked up the paper. Seeing what was underneath, she shrieked. "Oh, oh, oh!" She edged back from the box.

Tina giggled, but in her terror Kate barely heard. Again she screamed.

Footsteps pounded up the stairs. Anders, then Lars and Mama, tore into the room.

"What on earth is wrong?" asked Mama.

Kate was trembling now. "Oh, it's awful—so awful!"

9

Escape!

Anders and Lars stood at the door, and Mama started toward the box. Anders moved quickly.

"Just a minute, Mama." He closed the box before she could look inside.

"But what is it?" she asked.

"A dead mouse!" shrieked Kate, starting to cry. Collapsing on a chair, she put her hands over her face and wept into them.

"A dead mouse?" Mama drew herself up to her full height. "Why is there a dead mouse in this box?"

"Oh, I never should have done it!" sobbed Kate.

"Never should have done *what*, young lady?"

Kate bit her lip, but it was too late. Mama demanded an answer.

"I was going to be responsible, so you wouldn't worry." Kate's words ended on a wail, broken by another sob. "I'm sorry, Mama."

"Sorry for *what*? I don't know what you've done."

Kate still trembled from her look at the mouse. "There isn't anything in the whole world, not *anything* I hate more than mice!"

"I understand that," Mama said dryly. "Now tell me what this is all about."

Escape!

Kate drew a deep breath. "I fell through the ice on Spirit Lake." She shivered, just remembering the cold water. Then her fear came back. Fear of the dark water, of that moment when she couldn't find the hole in the ice. Yet even more, Kate felt afraid of what Mama would think.

"You fell through the ice, and didn't *tell* me?" Mama spoke in a jumble of Swedish and English.

Kate stumbled her way through the story.

"But why didn't you tell me before?" Mama asked again.

"I was afraid of what you'd say," Kate answered, her voice small.

"I'd say, 'Thank God! You're all right!' " Mama exclaimed.

But Kate knew she had to go on. Her voice sounded even smaller. "So I told you I was helping Miss Sundquist after school."

"You told me a lie, you mean," said Mama sternly.

Biting her lip to keep from crying again, Kate nodded. "I told you a lie, Mama. I'm sorry."

"You're sorry!" Mama snapped. "You're sorry?" Her voice grew in volume with every word. "You lie to your mama, and you're sorry? That's even worse than disobeying your teacher! Worse than going down to the lake!"

Numbly Kate nodded, her eyes downcast, her toe tracing a pattern on the wood floor.

"Yes, Mama. I know, Mama. I'm sorry, Mama."

Mama sighed, and when she spoke again, her voice was quiet with sadness. "Kate, look at me."

Kate looked up. In the candlelight she saw Mama's eyes glisten with tears.

"I never thought my daughter would lie to me," said Mama softly, each word filled with pain.

Kate looked down, no longer able to meet Mama's eyes.

But Mama went on. "Kate, I forgive you. But you must ask God to forgive you. You will also spend two hours in your room every afternoon for a week. You'll go there as soon as you come home from school."

"Oh, Mama!" cried Kate. "I've already been punished!"

"You've been punished for disobedience." Mama's voice was firm. "This is for lying."

Without another word she turned and walked slowly from the room. Her footsteps sounded heavy on the stairs.

Kate looked at Lars. When his gaze slid sideways, she knew he was the guilty one. "You planned this!" Kate accused.

"He was worried about your character," remarked Anders, a gleam of laughter in his eyes.

"You're just as mean as he is!" stormed Kate. She turned on Tina. "You were in on this too!"

Kate glared at all of them. "I can't bear the sight of you!"

"Aw, com'on, Kate," Anders said. "You know you were wrong."

Without answering, Kate ran from the room and headed down the stairs. Snatching up her coat, she pulled it on over her robe and hurried outside. She wanted to be alone, and she knew the best place. A tucked-away spot in the haymow.

On Monday Kate's week of punishment started. "You must stay in your room for two hours each day," Mama told her. "You can't read or do your schoolwork."

"Not even lessons?"

Mama's face was grim. "You must think about the seriousness of lying."

And that's what Kate did—for the first fifteen minutes. *I really am sorry,* she thought, promising herself she'd never lie again.

Halfheartedly she began knitting mittens to replace the ones she'd lost in the lake. But at the end of an hour and a half she could no longer sit still. Restlessly, Kate moved around from one window to the next.

The room she and Tina shared was on the front end of the house with windows facing two directions. On one side, windows overlooked the porch roof and the wagon track that circled the front and side of the house. Beyond that track lay a plowed field with tall oaks at its edge.

On another side, the room had two more windows. From

one of these, Kate saw the wagon track that forked to the right, dropping down the hill to the shores of Rice Lake. That track led through the woods to Spirit Lake School.

A large pine stood close to the second window on that side. Like spokes of a wheel, the branches grew around the trunk and swayed gently in the wind. The needles looked soft and inviting.

Pushing up the window, Kate inspected the tree. Papa had told her it was called a *white pine*, even though its needles were green. Some of the branches grew past the window, almost touching the house. The nearest branch looked sturdy and easy to reach. The next ones seemed like stair steps, descending down the tree.

Kate bit her lip, thinking about it. For a long time she stood there, looking at the branches, then at the ground.

The base of the huge trunk stood near the kitchen door and Mama's watchful eye. "But I could go down the other side of the tree," Kate told herself as an idea took shape. "No one would see."

She was still arguing with herself when Tina rapped, then poked her white-blond head around the half-open door. "Mama says time up." By now Kate knew enough Swedish to understand.

The second morning of Kate's week of imprisonment dawned unusually warm for November. All day the temperature climbed. At school the children talked about the warm spell, eager for afternoon classes to end.

"Ice is going to melt on the lakes," Anders told Kate on their way home from school.

As she started her two hours of punishment, Kate discovered Anders was right. From her bedroom window, she gazed across Rice Lake. Open water surrounded the ice.

Kate longed for only one thing—to be outside on this beautiful day. For a time she stood at the window closest to the white pine, looking up and down the trunk. Again she checked the size of the branches and the spacing between them.

In Minneapolis she'd been a good tree climber. Now Kate felt eager to be out in the sun.

"I can do it," she told herself, quietly lifting the window closest to the tree. Leaning out, she judged the distance carefully. "I'm sure I can do it."

But Kate knew that she shouldn't. Pulling back inside, she closed the window and sat down on the bed. She stayed there only a minute.

Slowly, quietly, she lifted the window. She reached out for the nearest branch and found it an easy distance away.

Grabbing hold of the limb, Kate climbed onto the windowsill. Stretching down her foot, she felt the next lowest branch. As she stepped onto it, the limb bent under her weight. Carefully Kate worked her way over to the trunk.

Once there, she crawled around to the side away from the house. Branch by branch, Kate let herself down the tree.

Dropping to the ground, she stood behind the large trunk, catching her breath. Seeing no one, she slipped across the grass to the wagon track leading into the woods. Soon the hill dropped sharply away. Kate knew it hid her from view.

Yet even here she was not safe. Anders or Lars could come along. Kate hurried down the trail, wanting only to put distance between herself and the house.

Partway to school, she came to the large oak and the clump of birch that she remembered. Off to her right the trees thinned out. As Kate left the trail, she made her way around heavy underbrush. There she found the big rock she sought.

As she climbed onto it, Kate remembered her first day at Spirit Lake School. She'd seen the disappearing stranger from here. In the time since, she hadn't told anyone about the rock.

"It's my special secret," Kate said to herself now. She felt the rock belonged to her.

Nearby, on the side away from the path, the hill sloped sharply away. Long brown marsh grass and small trees filled the area between her and Rice Lake. Now the trees were bare of leaves, and Kate looked beyond them to the west. The sun shone on the ice and open water.

For a time Kate stood there, glad to be outside. A warm breeze stirred the hair that had slipped out of her braid into her face. But gradually the wind grew cold. Kate turned away, looking for shelter.

Small tree limbs lay on the ground from an oak Papa and Anders had sawed up that fall. Seeing the branches, Kate had an idea.

Then she noticed the sun. In the November afternoon it hovered dangerously close to the horizon. Time to be home!

Walking quickly, Kate headed back to Windy Hill Farm. By the time she entered the yard, she was panting. Moving quietly across the grass, she reached the tree, climbed up, and slipped through the window. Closing it, she sat down to catch her breath.

Moments later, Tina knocked, then pushed open the door.

Kate's time of punishment for that day was over. But Tina had a question, one she asked in her own sign language. As she pointed to Kate, the little girl asked, "Do?" which meant, "What have you been doing up here?"

Kate felt herself flush. She didn't want to lie to her little sister.

But Tina didn't wait for an answer. "Supper," she said. Tugging Kate's hand, she urged her to hurry.

When Kate returned home from school the next afternoon, the weather was still unusually warm. For a few minutes Kate debated about what to do. It wasn't long before she slipped out of her room and down the tree. Once again she headed for the big rock. On the way there she heard a cowbell.

Following the sound, Kate discovered a cow wandering through the woods, nibbling whatever grass she found. Kate recognized her.

"Bessie!" she exclaimed, and the cow raised her head. She belonged to Josie's family.

"What're you doing here?" Kate asked, as if the cow could answer.

Lunging at her, Kate tried to catch the rope around Bessie's neck. Bessie edged away. Kate tried again and succeeded.

As she hung on to the rope, Kate wondered what to do next. "If I leave you here, you'll get lost again," she told the cow. "Hard telling when Josie's family will find you."

But Josie lived on the far side of the woods, beyond Spirit

Lake School. "If I take you home, can I get back in time?"

The cow's brown eyes rolled as she mooed her response.

Kate thought of the steer the family had already lost. Sighing, she tugged at the rope. "You don't give me much choice, old Bess."

As Kate started down the trail, the cow turned in the opposite direction. Kate tugged again, but the cow was stubborn and swung her head back and forth. Her large body seemed to loom above Kate.

For a moment Kate felt afraid. Though people in Minneapolis sometimes kept cows in their backyard, she had seldom been close to them. At the same time, she didn't want the Swenson family to have more trouble.

Stepping as far away from the hooves as she could, Kate pulled on the rope with all her strength. "Come on, Bessie!"

This time the cow moved step-by-slow-step in the direction Kate wanted. But the cow had one pace—her own. Precious minutes ticked away as Bessie poked along, reaching for any grass along the trail.

To Kate it seemed forever before she reached Josie's barnyard. There she found her friend's father.

"Tack! Tack!" he said. The word sounded like the tock of a clock, but Kate knew it was the Swedish "thank you."

Quickly she slipped away. Once out of Mr. Swenson's sight, Kate started running. Already the woods were dim. When she came to Rice Lake and the opening in the trees, Kate saw the last bit of orange sun dip below the horizon.

Reaching the large pine, she tried to catch her breath. Still panting, she scrambled up the tree and slipped through the window.

As Kate's feet touched the bedroom floor, a voice spoke from the shadows. A voice that said, "Kate!"

10

Down in the Cellar

*K*ate spun around.

Tina spoke again from the shadows. "What are you doing?" she asked in Swedish. But Kate recognized the words. She'd often heard them from Anders.

"What are *you* doing, you mean? Spying on me?" Kate replied in English.

As her eyes adjusted to the dim light, Kate saw Tina's hurt look. Though she probably didn't understand the words, Tina seemed to catch the sound. Never before had Kate been so mean to the little girl—not even when discovering the mouse.

Tina's lower lip quivered. She pointed to herself, then to the window and the branch outside. She seemed to ask, "Take me with next time."

In the sign language they'd learned to use, Tina moved her hands and feet as though climbing down the tree. She seemed to believe "I'm big enough."

Angrily, Kate shook her head.

Tina answered in Swedish. "Mama's going to be mad."

Kate recognized those words too. Placing her fingers across Tina's lips, Kate pointed to the door, and shook her head. Then she held up her fist and shook it. "You're not going to tell, are you?"

Tina understood the message. Her lip quivered again, and her eyes filled with tears. Turning her back on Kate, she stalked from the room.

Instantly Kate felt awful. But it was too late. She couldn't bring back the words.

When Kate got home from school the next day, it was again warm and sunny. She was holding the upper branch, ready to step down on the lower one, when she heard a loud knock on the door.

"Kate!" called a voice. It was Tina.

Quickly Kate stepped back inside. She lowered the window as Tina shouted again.

"I'm coming, I'm coming!" Kate called back. "What do you want?" she asked, opening the door.

Tina's white-blond hair wisped around her face and her blue eyes danced. She pointed to Kate, then outside, as if to say, "You get out!"

Down in the kitchen, Mama had a basket of food ready. "Anders tells me that Mrs. Berglund has been sick," she told Kate when she came. "He's hitching up Wildfire. I want you to go along and help in any way needed."

"Who's Mrs. Berglund?" asked Kate, always surprised at the number of people her mother knew.

"She's a widow living alone," explained Mama. "Her son works in St. Paul."

"If I go, does it count for one of my days of punishment?" asked Kate.

"Sorry, but things don't work that way," Mama told her, and Kate wished she hadn't asked.

"We'll see how much you manage to help Mrs. Berglund," Mama went on.

Afraid Mama would change her mind and not let her go, Kate pulled on her coat and hurried out the door.

On the way to the farm, she and Anders talked again about Stretch.

"There's something that bothers me," Kate began. "Last Saturday when I saw him, one of his hands was blue."

"Blue?" Anders was curious. "You're sure? Maybe you were just seeing things."

Remembering how Anders felt about her taking a ride, Kate didn't want to admit she'd seen Stretch's hand close up. "I'm sure," she answered. "And only his right hand. He said he'd been working hard, cutting trees. But that wouldn't make a hand blue, would it?"

"Nope," said Anders. His eyes looked puzzled. "But what would?"

The wagon ride went too fast to Kate's way of thinking.

As they drove into the farmyard, Anders told Kate about Mrs. Berglund. "She's old. Really old. Her son doesn't want her to live here alone. She says, 'It's my home. I'll stay as long as I can!' So she keeps a cow and chickens and a garden."

Mrs. Berglund met them at the door. With white hair and twinkling eyes, she smiled like a young person. The lines around her eyes crinkled as though she laughed often. She made Kate feel completely at home.

"*Tack, tack,*" she said in the Swedish "thank you" as Kate brought in the basket of food. "But you must have some with me."

Soon Mrs. Berglund found the cookies. "Just as I thought. I'm sure these are for you and Anders."

"But Mama says I'm supposed to help you," answered Kate.

"You are," said Mrs. Berglund firmly. "I'm much better today. I'm ready to sit down and talk."

Shuffling across the kitchen, she took three glasses from the cupboard.

"I'll get the milk," offered Kate quickly. Pulling on her coat, she headed toward the door, expecting the milk to be in the well as it was at home.

But Mrs. Berglund stopped her. "This time of year I put it in the cellar."

Going to one side of the kitchen, Mrs. Berglund pointed to a ring in the floor. Kate tugged at the ring, surprised at how easily the trapdoor lifted.

Pulling it back, Kate saw stairs that led down into darkness.

For a moment she hesitated, wondering if there were mice.

"It's on the ledge to your right," directed Mrs. Berglund.

Kate knew she'd have to go down whether she liked it or not. Slowly she stepped onto the stairway.

Mrs. Berglund stopped her. "You better take a candle."

As she waited for the old woman to light one, Kate stared into the semidarkness. Nearby, on both sides of the stairs, she saw earth walls.

Mrs. Berglund handed her the candle, and Kate held it out in front of her. Carefully, she continued down the steps. The wood boards creaked beneath her feet. Something that sounded like a mouse scurried away. Kate's heart pounded into her throat.

She listened until the noise quit, then knew she had to go on. As she reached the dirt floor at the bottom of the steps, Kate felt cooler air. Holding the candle high, she looked around.

The dim light didn't reach far enough into the small room, but she guessed it was built only under the kitchen. Peering into the darkness, Kate saw that one side had a boarded-off section and large bins. The other walls seemed to have a wide ledge about three feet from the ground.

A covered pail stood on the ledge closest to the stairs. It looked as though it held milk, and she picked it up.

Starting toward the steps, Kate felt a sudden breath of cold air. Wondering about it, she turned in the direction from which it came. Without warning, her candle flickered, then blew out.

She gasped. As the blackness closed around her, Kate's terror of mice returned.

For a moment she stood there, wanting to drop the milk and the worthless candle. She wanted only the warm, safe kitchen.

Then she heard Mrs. Berglund's voice. "Kate? Did you find the milk?"

Turning to the voice, Kate saw the patch of daylight at the top of the steps. Taking care not to spill the milk, she took a small step forward. As she felt her way, her ankle bumped into the bottom stair.

Stepping onto it, Kate hurried up into the kitchen. The heat of the cookstove reached out. Sunlight streamed through the windows.

As Kate set the milk on the kitchen table, Anders came in. He looked at her strangely.

Quickly Kate pushed back the strands of hair that fell into her face. Her voice slightly unsteady, she asked Mrs. Berglund, "Should I pour the milk?"

Again Kate caught Anders looking at her.

The old woman seemed to see the same thing. "Kate, how did you get so dirty going down for milk?" she asked.

Anders grinned. "That's just the way she is, Mrs. Berglund." His voice sounded dead serious.

Reaching up, Kate rubbed her cheek. Sure enough, her hand came away gritty.

Going to the basin near the kitchen door, Kate washed her face and hands, then threw the dirty water outside. But her questions didn't disappear with the wash water.

"Mrs. Berglund used to be a church organist," Anders told Kate when she returned to the table.

"You did?" Kate was glad to find someone else who played the organ. "Why did you stop?"

Mrs. Berglund's smile disappeared. She held out her hands. Though they were small, the joints on her fingers were large. Some of the fingers turned in the wrong direction, and both hands bent sideways.

Kate felt embarrassed that she'd asked. "I'm sorry. What is it?"

"Arthritis," Mrs. Berglund said simply. "Don't be embarrassed. Over the years my hands just turned this way."

"But don't you feel bad?" Kate's words tumbled out before she could stop them. "Don't you want to keep playing?"

"Oh yes," answered Mrs. Berglund. "With all my heart I want to play. I want to play for the Lord."

"For the Lord?" Kate asked. She'd never heard of anyone doing that.

"Yah," said Mrs. Berglund, sounding as Swedish as her name. "I like to play hymns that help people think about God."

She smiled, and beneath her blue eyes, her cheeks crinkled. "I used to have a dream. I used to wish for a daughter."

"A daughter?" Kate wanted to know more.

"Or someone I could teach to play the same way."

She fell silent then, and Kate was still. She wished she could say, "I want to play for the Lord." Yet Kate knew it wasn't true, and she could not speak.

Even Anders was quiet.

On the way home Anders once again drove faster than Kate liked.

"Stop it!" Kate exclaimed.

"What's the matter? Are you a scaredy-cat?"

"Of course not!" Kate protested, afraid of what he'd think if she admitted her fear. She hesitated, searching for a reason, and finally said, "It's not good for Wildfire."

Anders hooted. "Wildfire loves it. Just watch."

He slapped the reins. Kate's head jerked back as the mare broke into a gallop.

Filled with panic, she braced her feet and hung on to the wagon seat.

Anders laughed. "You *are* a scaredy-cat!"

"No, I'm not!" she stormed. Yet she clutched the seat until her fingers ached.

Then she saw the turn ahead. "Slow down!" she cried out.

Instead, Anders urged the mare on. Wildfire held true to her name. She ran as swift as a fire licking across dry grass in a high wind.

Kate held her breath, too afraid even to cry out.

11

Bad News

*J*ust before they reached the turn, Anders reined back. As they rounded the corner safely, Kate felt shaken. "I'm telling Mama!"

"So now we have a tattletale," accused Anders. "Who are you to talk?"

"We're not supposed to worry Mama!" Kate cried out.

"And you've already worried her enough!"

For that Kate had no answer, knowing he spoke the truth. Yet she didn't stay quiet long. "Will you teach me how to handle Wildfire?"

"Nope," answered Anders flatly.

"With Papa gone, someone else should know."

Anders sighed. "Kate, you are a pest! I said *no*."

But her mind was made up. All the way home she teased him until he gave in.

When they pulled up outside the Windy Hill barn, Anders climbed down. In the growing dusk he lit a farm lantern. "All right, you win."

His voice sounded as unwilling as his face looked. "Help me unharness her. Watch how it's supposed to be done."

Going first to one side, then the other, Anders unhooked the straps holding Wildfire to the wagon shafts. Together they led the mare into her stall.

There Anders taught Kate to unbuckle the belly strap and pull off the harness. "Don't tangle it. Keep it looped over your arm." Then, "Hang it up." Anders tipped his head toward hooks along the wall.

There Kate met her first problem. She couldn't reach the hooks. Stretching as tall as possible, she threw the harness up until it caught.

Next Anders showed her how to take off the bridle. "Easy on her mouth. Don't hurt her, and she'll like you more."

As he put his hand along Wildfire's big teeth, Kate wondered if she could ever get that close to the mare's mouth. Wildfire let the bit drop out, and Anders took the bridle. Handing Kate the halter, he said, "Slip it over her head."

Kate reached high, but couldn't make it.

"What a shorty!" Anders teased. Just the same, he showed Kate what to do. "See that board in the stall?"

Kate squinted in the dim light. Sure enough, in the wall next to the feed trough, one board stuck out just a bit. Using it as a step, Kate grabbed the edge of the trough and pulled herself up.

Wrapping her arm around a corner pole, she reached forward and slipped the halter over Wildfire's head.

"Give her some oats," Anders ordered next. "Let her get to know you."

By the time they left the barn, Kate felt good about what she'd learned. She felt even better when Anders said, "You're strong, Kate. For a girl, that is. Maybe you'll handle it after all."

From Anders that was rare praise.

The next morning something happened that made them forget even Josie's steer for a time.

As usual, Erik and his sister joined Anders, Kate, and Lars on the way to school. Erik had bad news. "Someone robbed us!" he told them.

Kate stopped in the middle of the trail. "What did they take?"

"All our raspberries, our strawberries, and every single jar of blueberries!" Erik exclaimed, his voice angry.

Something in Kate couldn't believe the bad news. "Your fruit for the whole winter?"

Erik's nod was grim. "We picked and picked!" He kicked a branch from the path as though taking his anger out on the thief.

During the summer Kate and Anders and Lars had also picked wild berries in the woods around their farm. Kate knew the terrible mosquitoes and the bites that itched long afterward. She could still feel the long sharp branches that had torn her clothing and left painful scratches on her arms and legs.

"We even drove the wagon out to the sand barrens," Erik went on. "All of us picked a whole day! We filled every bucket we had with blueberries."

"And canned all of them?"

Erik's sister Chrissy answered. "Everything we didn't eat right away. Every jar is gone!" Her eyes filled with misery. "Mama cried."

"The day you moved, I saw you put jars in the root cellar," said Kate.

Unlike the cellar under Mrs. Berglund's house, Erik's root cellar was similar to the one on the Nordstrom farm. A small dark room built into the side of a hill, it had dirt walls and roof. On both cold and warm days that dirt protected the food.

"Any idea when it happened?" asked Anders.

Erik shrugged. "Don't know. When we moved in, we put some jars in the house. Enough for this week. We put everything else in the root cellar. It doesn't freeze there if we're gone and the fire goes out."

"So no one's been to the cellar for a week?"

Erik shook his head. "Not since we moved in."

Then Kate had another thought. Like other farm families, the Nordstroms brought all they grew in their garden into the root cellar. "What about your potatoes and carrots and squash?"

"They're gone too," said Erik gloomily. "All that hard work weeding and watering! Picking the food and bringing it in. And where can we even look to find it?"

Anders and Kate stared at Erik, knowing the food could be almost any place, even dumped off in the woods.

"There's another thing," said Erik, his voice grim. "What if the thief doesn't take care of the food? If the vegetables froze, they'd be wrecked. Then what good would it do to find 'em?"

Deep inside, Kate hurt for Erik and his family. This time of year every night dropped below freezing. And when it grew really cold, only an hour, even in daytime, could spoil all the food.

"Were there any clues at all?" she asked.

"Just one thing, and we almost missed that. Close to the road there was one broken canning jar. I almost stepped on the glass. Looked like it had blueberries in it."

Kate had never seen Erik so discouraged. But they all knew the worst was ahead. Erik's father couldn't go out to buy fruit and vegetables. Farm families lived on what they grew, then stored.

"What'll we eat this winter?" Erik asked, his voice worried.

Deep inside Kate, a knot formed. As though it was yesterday she recalled the year after Daddy O'Connell died. She remembered what it was like not having enough money for food. What could be more awful than trying to live a whole winter without fruit or vegetables?

"We'll give you some of ours," she answered, knowing Mama wouldn't let anyone go hungry if she could help it.

Erik looked grateful, but a moment later asked, "What if the thief comes to your root cellar? What if he takes *your* food?"

Kate saw the quick look that crossed Anders' face.

"For all we know, he's been there already!" he exclaimed.

"I hope not," said Erik grimly. "I sure hope not."

Anders stopped in the middle of the path. "I'm going home, Kate. Tell Teacher I had to work."

Without another word, Anders broke into a run, heading back toward Windy Hill Farm.

12

Up the Pine Tree

At recess time Anders showed up at school. "So far we're all right," he told Kate and Erik. They were out on the playground where other children couldn't hear. "I found an old padlock and locked the root cellar."

"But what about our pig?" asked Kate, feeling uneasy. Before Papa left, he had butchered and put it in the summer kitchen. There it stayed frozen, and Anders would saw off a piece from time to time for them to eat.

Anders looked just as worried as Kate felt. "Couldn't find another lock. If we take the pig into the house, the meat will thaw out and spoil."

When school ended that afternoon, the unusually warm weather still held. "Last two hours of punishment!" Kate told herself, glad her week was almost over.

After her freedom of the day before, Kate found the idea of staying indoors especially terrible. This time she didn't argue with herself even one second. She closed her bedroom door, went to the window, and pulled it up.

Taking hold of the nearest branch, Kate stepped out, then climbed from limb to limb. Partway down the pine tree, she heard a sound and looked up.

Tina!

Tina, reaching for the closest branch!
Tina, ready to climb out the window!

Terror shot through Kate. Before she could move, Tina clutched the limb and swung out.

But her shorter legs did not reach the branch below as Kate's had done. Tina hung in midair, her feet dangling.

Kate froze, unable to speak or move. Then she knew she must. Somehow she called out. "Hang on, Tina!"

Scrambling back up the tree, she saw the terror in Tina's eyes.

"Hang on!" Kate shouted again. The little girl's feet swung in the air.

As she climbed onto the limb beneath Tina, Kate caught a glimpse of the ground far below. *That's where she'd land.* Kate felt dizzy thinking about it.

Trying not to look at the ground, Kate waited for her head to clear. Then she curled her arm around the branch to which Tina clung. Her feet on the limb below, Kate stood up.

As she edged out on the branch, it bent down beneath her weight. *What if it breaks?*

At the same time Tina started to tremble. Her legs swung wide.

Panic washed over Kate like a wave. *How long can she hang on?*

Just as Kate reached her, Tina shrieked. As she dropped, Kate's free arm went around her.

Kate gasped under Tina's weight. "Don't move," she warned, knowing she couldn't hold the five-year-old long.

Then Kate remembered that Tina didn't understand much English.

For a moment Kate stood there, hanging on with all her strength. She wondered if she'd fall just from the terror of it. Tina would go with her.

Then Kate thought of Erik, and how he talked her out of the icy lake.

"Put your hands up, Tina," said Kate, wanting to motion with her head. She felt afraid to move even that much.

But Tina did not raise her hands.

"Grab the branch again." Kate spoke slowly, trying to keep her voice steady.

Tina trembled, but seemed to understand. While Kate held her, the little girl reached up and clutched the branch.

As some of Tina's weight shifted off Kate's arm, she felt the relief. "Trunk," she said, still hoping Tina understood.

One arm around the little girl, the other clinging to the upper branch, Kate slowly took a step.

Again Tina trembled. Yet she moved her hands, one by one. Kate slid her feet along the lower branch.

It seemed to take forever, but at last they reached the trunk.

As Kate caught her breath, her panic returned. *I don't have a free hand. I can't grab a new branch without letting go of the old one.*

She stood there, wondering how to go on, her fear making it hard to think. But then Kate knew what to do. Leaning toward the little girl, she pushed Tina against the trunk. Slowly she let Tina's body drop. At last the five-year-old sat on the branch on which Kate stood.

Crouching behind Tina, Kate reached out, searching for a limb close enough for the smaller girl.

Tina watched. Each time Kate changed position, Tina put her hands and feet in the place Kate left. At last they reached the lowest branch and dropped to the ground.

"Oh, Tina!" Kate exclaimed, giving her such a tight hug that the younger girl squealed.

As they rested on the grass, Kate began to shake. One picture stayed in her mind. Tina dangling from the tree, ready to fall to the ground below.

Kate reached out to feel that ground, glad that she and Tina sat upon it. In that moment Kate felt glad even for the dead, brown grass of autumn. But her trembling would not stop. She felt overwhelmed with what could have happened.

At last Kate stood up. Afraid she'd change her mind, she headed for the house. As she stalked through the kitchen door, Tina followed.

Mama looked as though she'd just wakened from a nap. "Kate! What are you doing out of your room?"

Before Mama could utter another word, Kate spoke. "Mama, I ask your forgiveness." In her determination to confess, Kate's voice sounded bold.

Mama looked startled. "For lying, Kate?"

"No—I mean, yes." Kate stumbled over the words. She had almost forgotten why she was being punished. "For that too."

She flipped her braid over her shoulder and lifted her head. "I ask forgiveness for climbing down the tree when I was supposed to stay in my room."

Mama opened her mouth to speak. Then, seeming to think better of it, she closed her lips and waited.

Kate swallowed around the lump in her throat. "I ask forgiveness for doing something Tina tried to follow."

Mama turned white. "Tina did *what?*"

"She climbed out the window into the tree."

"And she climbed down the tree by herself?"

"No, Mama. She hung from the tree. She couldn't reach the next branch."

Mama moved to a chair and quickly sat down.

"I'm sorry, Mama," said Kate again. Her lower lip trembled. Tears welled up in her eyes and spilled onto her cheeks. Sobs tore at her body, coming from deep within.

Mama reached out for her. "Oh, Kate!"

There was barely enough room on Mama's lap. For a moment Kate thought, *I'm too old to sit here.*

But Mama smelled like newly baked rolls and apple pie. Her arms felt warm and good. Within their safety, Kate broke down completely. "Oh, Mama, I'm so awful!"

"Yah," Mama said quietly, seeming to agree. Hearing Mama, Kate cried even harder.

Yet Mama stroked Kate's cheek, as though she was thinking. When she spoke, her voice sounded stronger. "Yah, we are all awful, Kate."

Through her sobbing, Kate heard the words. But it took a moment before she really heard them. Then she sniffled and pulled back, looking up.

"*You* are awful, Mama?" Kate couldn't believe she'd heard right.

"Yah, I am awful, Kate." Mama handed her a handkerchief.

"But I don't understand. You always seem perfect."

Up the Pine Tree

Mama shook her head. "In the whole world no one is perfect."

"No one?"

"No one." Mama was certain about that. "But you remember, Kate. God did something for all of us."

As she held Kate in her arms, Mama told the story. The story Kate had heard many times before. Yet it had never seemed so real.

"Because He loves us, God sent His perfect Son to die on the cross. When you do something wrong, you can say you're sorry. You can ask forgiveness. Jesus *will* forgive you."

Kate looked up as though afraid to believe that was true.

Yet Mama went on. "When you ask Him to be your Savior, He takes away your sin. He saves you from it."

Kate thought about that for a moment. "So I wouldn't be awful?"

"The Bible says you become clean. As clean as new snow."

In a place deep inside, Kate found Mama's words hard to believe. The memory of Tina dangling from the tree wouldn't go away. *Tina could have died because of me. How can God forgive something like that?*

Then Mama noticed Tina sitting cross-legged on the floor. As Mama reached out her free arm, Tina came to her.

"She's all right, Kate," Mama said, seeming to read Kate's thoughts.

When Mama spoke to Tina in Swedish, her voice changed. Kate knew Mama must be telling the little girl not to climb the tree again.

After a time, Kate blew her nose and said quietly, "I'll go back to my room."

"If you want to be alone, Kate," Mama answered. "But not for punishment."

"Not for punishment?" Kate felt surprised by the love in Mama's voice.

"I think you've had your punishment, seeing Tina in that tree. Now let God forgive you."

God forgive me? thought Kate. But she was afraid to say it to Mama.

13

The Hiding Place

As Kate looked up, Tina dangled from the tree. Her feet swung wide, searching for a branch. But she found none. Her body trembled. Her hands loosened. She fell through the air, crashing to the ground.

Kate wakened from her nightmare, filled with terror. Reaching out in the darkness, she felt with her hand, searching the bed next to her. At last she found the little girl's arm. Tina slept on.

But Kate's eyes filled with tears. "She's all right!" In her relief Kate spoke aloud, repeating the words over and over.

What if Tina had fallen? The memory of the little girl's danger seemed more real than knowing she was safely asleep in her own bed.

For a long time Kate lay there, her hands still clenched with fear. Then she remembered what Mama said. "Let God forgive you." Instead of pushing away the words, Kate thought about them.

I did such awful things. But even so, you love me, don't you, Jesus? You love me the way I am.

I'm sorry, Jesus. I'm sorry about the wrong things I did. Will you forgive me?

The Hiding Place

In that moment there was something Kate knew deep inside. *Yes! I know you will!*

Often before, Kate had heard about God's love and forgiveness. Now that love and forgiveness seemed real. It seemed as though she had opened an early Christmas present.

For a time Kate lay there, thinking about it. Then she dropped off to sleep. When she woke again, Tina was gone. Morning sunlight streamed through the bedroom window. Kate was glad it was Saturday. More than that, she felt good inside for the first time in many days.

That afternoon, soon after Kate returned from her organ lesson, Lars ran in from the mailbox.

"A letter!" he cried. "It's from Papa!"

Kate, Anders, Lars, and Tina gathered around Mama as she settled herself in her favorite chair. Her eyes shone and a slow smile spread across her face as she opened the letter.

It was written in Swedish, and Kate waited for Mama to translate.

"He's well!" she told the children as she read. "He's lonesome for all of us. He found work in a camp close to the railroad." Mama looked up, her face glowing. "If he can, he'll come home for Christmas!"

Lars and Tina cheered, but Anders asked, "Does he say *when* he'll come?"

Mama shook her head, disappointment clouding her eyes. "And he doesn't say he'll come for sure. He says, '*If* I can come.'"

Anders looked as disappointed as Mama. He would be afraid to hope, and Kate knew why.

"Lots of men don't get home for Christmas," he had told Kate once.

"Even if they really want to come?" she asked.

"It's too far to walk when it's real cold. Often there's no other way."

But Kate felt a glimmer of hope. "If he's close to the railroad—" She stopped, knowing how disappointed everyone would be if Papa didn't come.

But Mama spoke Kate's thoughts. "Maybe he can walk to the

railroad and take a train. Maybe he'll leave Dolly and Florie at the camp and come."

"I wish we knew for sure." Lars's voice was small.

"Yah," Mama answered, and Kate felt surprised how often Mama sounded Swedish these days. When married to Kate's Irish daddy, Mama seldom used the Swedish yes.

Now her eyes brightened. "Let's believe Papa will come. Let's get ready for Christmas as though we expect him. If he doesn't come, we'll have Christmas when he does."

They were still talking about Papa's letter when Erik knocked on the door. After they told him the good news, he and Anders went out to the barn. Kate went into the front room to practice her lesson.

Instead of a pipe organ needing to be hand pumped by someone else, Kate had a reed organ. As she pumped the two pedals up and down, the organ filled with air and her mind filled with questions. She still wanted to ask Erik about the day she fell through the ice.

"He's nice," Kate told herself, trying to push aside her memory of the dark, cold water. "He watches out for me." More than once she'd caught Erik looking at her.

But today he still looked worried. Kate knew he must be thinking about the stolen fruit and vegetables.

She touched the ivory keys and started to play. Mr. Peters had given her Christmas carols to practice. Now she had an idea. She could learn "Silent Night" and surprise Papa.

Kate went over the notes for the right hand until she played them without mistakes. She liked the last line especially: "Sleep in heavenly peace."

As Kate practiced the left-hand chords, the boys came in from the barn. Immediately she stopped playing.

"Hey, we want to hear," said Erik.

"Yah, Kate," Anders joined in. He bowed, extending his right hand with a flourish. "Erik, do you know whose pleasure we have the company of keeping?"

Erik grinned, but shook his head.

Anders dropped his voice, sounding formal and adult. "Mr. Lundgren, may I have the pleasure—the pleasure, mind you.

The Hiding Place

May I have the pleasure of presenting Miss Jenny Lind?"

"You meanie!" Kate blurted out. "I never said I'm Jenny Lind!"

"Excuse me!" Anders cleared his throat.

Throwing back his shoulders, he stood as tall as possible, then lifted his chin. "Correction please!" he announced. "This is *not* Miss Jenny Lind. But listen to the marvelous quality of her notes. She *plays* like Miss Lind *sings*."

As Kate wondered what Erik would think, she felt an embarrassed blush rush into her cheeks. Aloud she sputtered, "Aw, Anders, forget it!"

She stole a quick look in Erik's direction. He was shaking his head at Anders.

Anders paid no attention. Chin still high in the air, he went on. "And one day—one day, mind you, she will travel. She will travel around the world playing the organ."

Kate could stand it no longer. "I hate you, Anders Nordstrom! I hate you!" Spinning on the stool, she turned to the organ and buried her face in her hands.

"Stop it, Anders!" said Erik in a low voice.

But Anders was not to be stopped. "Audiences from one side of the country to another, yea, even from one end of the world to another—"

Suddenly Kate heard a loud thud. Whirling around on the stool, she found the boys wrestling on the floor.

Erik jumped him! Kate guessed, filled with glee. "Get him, Erik!" she called out. "Beat him up!"

But just then Mama stood in the doorway. "What in the world!" she exclaimed. "Fighting in the front room! Stop it!"

Immediately the two boys separated. Erik looked as embarrassed as Kate felt when Anders teased.

"I certainly thought you boys knew better than that!" Mama exclaimed. "If you don't have anything more to do, I want you to clean this room for Christmas."

Behind Mama's back, Anders dropped one eyelid in a long, slow wink at Kate. Kate stuck out her tongue. But Erik turned red under Mama's gaze.

Mama had them take all the furniture into the dining room, then said, "Roll up the carpet."

Even Anders moved faster than usual.

Carrying the carpet outside, the boys hung it over the clothes line. Mama supplied a beater and put Anders to work. Each time he hit the rug, clouds of dust rose in the air.

Erik helped Kate sweep the floor, then put down two or three inches of fresh straw. When Mama went out to the kitchen, Erik whispered to Kate, "I didn't mean to make her mad."

Kate giggled. "I've never seen anyone take down Anders."

Erik grinned. "We're a close match."

"You would have won if Mama hadn't stopped you," said Kate.

"You think so?" The grin reached Erik's eyes. Then he sobered. "Sorry, Kate."

"Sorry?" Kate asked.

"About what Anders said."

For the first time Kate wondered how often Erik teased because Anders urged him on. Then she realized something else. "Anders used you as an excuse."

Erik looked relieved. "Glad you feel that way. I wouldn't want Anders teasing *me* about voice lessons."

"You take *voice* lessons?" asked Kate.

Erik nodded, his face flushed. "In exchange for pumping the organ for Mr. Peters. I've never told anyone else."

"Don't worry. I won't tell Anders," Kate promised.

"You won't tell me what?" asked Anders, coming in.

But Kate wouldn't answer, so Anders went back outside. Quickly she asked the question that had bothered her since the day she fell through the ice. "How did you know I needed help?"

"Saw you leave with Stretch," Erik said shortly.

"So you followed us?"

Erik looked embarrassed. "A ways back."

"Why?" asked Kate, though she knew she would have drowned otherwise.

Erik didn't answer right away. When he did, he said, "'Cause you're just a girl." Then he added, "I don't trust Stretch."

"But you didn't say anything to Teacher. Were you afraid to tell on him?"

"Nope." From the sound of his voice, Kate knew Erik spoke the truth.

"Then why?"

When he spoke, Erik looked embarrassed again. " 'Cause of something Papa says."

"Your papa?"

"Yup. He says, 'Believe in someone 'til they prove you wrong.' "

"So?" Kate wasn't sure what Erik meant.

"So when it comes to Stretch, I always think something bad. I figured he ran away when you needed help. But when I got there, he was already gone. I couldn't prove it."

"And you didn't know 'til I told you?"

"Been wanting to talk to him ever since," answered Erik. "But he hasn't been back to school."

In spite of all that had happened, something in Kate still wanted to defend Stretch. "Why do you always think something bad?"

Erik lowered his voice. "His father cheated my father. Papa couldn't prove it. That's why we had to move to the farm we're on."

When Anders finished pounding the carpet, he and Erik laid it on the clean straw.

Mama supervised. "Just a bit more this way," she said, trying to get it square to the room. At last she was satisfied.

"Now, young men, please move the furniture back." Just then Mama sniffed the air and fled to the kitchen to rescue supper.

The organ was the last piece of furniture to move back. Anders stood on one end and Erik on the other. "Better help him, Kate," Anders teased as he took hold of the handle on his side. "He's not very strong, you know."

As Erik grasped the other handle, he winked at Kate and picked up his end. Coming from the dining room, Anders stumbled and almost fell. The front of the organ tipped, nearly slipping out of his grasp.

Kate ran forward, grabbing below the keyboard. Erik hung

on, and Anders recovered his hold. As he righted his end of the organ, the music rack swung down. A book fell to the floor.

"Put it down!" Anders ordered. He and Erik lowered the organ to the floor. "Whew! That was close."

"Close, all right!" said Kate. "You could have dropped it!" Walking around the organ, she inspected each side. She felt relieved to see it was all right.

As she picked up the book, Kate turned it over. "That's strange!"

"What is?" asked Erik.

"This book. I don't know where it came from."

"It fell when we almost dropped the organ," Erik said.

"But it's not mine."

"Aw, com'on, Kate." Anders sounded impatient. "Who else would it belong to?"

"I mean it!" Kate flipped her black braid over her shoulder, determined that he believe her. "It's *not* my book!"

"Then where would it come from?" As he dropped to the floor to rest, Anders pushed his blond hair from his eyes.

But Kate stood in front of the organ. The music rack still hung down over the keyboard.

Then she noticed something she'd never seen before. Curious, she moved closer. "Hey, look!"

Erik was beside her now, just as interested as Kate. "A secret hiding place!"

14

The Mysterious Message

"A hiding place, all right!" exclaimed Kate as Anders jumped up to look.

Behind the usual position of the music rack was an opening. Leaning closer, Kate saw a space between the front and back of the organ. The space extended the full width, from side to side.

"A big hiding place," said Kate. "Big enough to hold small books. Must be where this one came from."

"Bet the organist always put *her* music away!"

But Kate paid no attention to Anders. The afternoon light had faded, bringing shadows and making it harder to see. Kate lit a candle and brought it to Erik. "Could you hold this for me?"

Once more, Kate bent down, looking inside the hiding place. Erik held the candle close.

Reaching in, Kate felt her way around the left side of the opening. "Nothing here."

She and Erik traded places, and Kate checked the other side. Again she felt the bottom, then the sides of the small space. Just as she was ready to give up, she felt something. "There!" she exclaimed. "On this side. There's something stuck!"

"Where?" Erik asked, leaning down for a better look.

"Maybe it's a hidden message!" said Kate.

Anders hooted. "Girls and their imagination!"

Kate felt uncomfortable, but she leaned closer, her fingers still feeling the way. In the crack between the bottom and side boards, she felt a paper. Just a small piece of paper.

Then she managed to catch it between her thumb and forefinger. Gently she tugged. It was stuck.

Once more Kate tried, slowly, carefully.

This time the paper slipped out of the crack. Kate held it up to the light.

"What's it say?" asked Erik.

Anders moved closer, looking over Kate's shoulder.

The piece of paper was small, but Kate handed it to Erik. After finding the dead mouse, she didn't want to look at another message.

Slowly Erik read the words aloud:

> *on my side;*
> *fear:*
> *an do to me?*

In that moment Kate's usual curiosity returned. "What do you think it means?" she asked as Erik returned the paper to her. "Is someone in trouble?"

"Could be," he answered. "But if there is, there's someone on that person's side."

"What about the word *fear*?" asked Kate. "And what's that word?" She pointed to the third line. "*An*? What does *an* stand for?"

Anders took the message and held it close to the candle. Carefully he studied the small piece of paper.

After a moment he said, "It's torn." He ran his finger along the left side. "We've got only part of it."

Leaning close, Kate saw he was right. She went back to the organ, looking again in the secret space. Slowly she slid her fingers across the crack from which she'd taken the message. Yet she found nothing more.

The Mysterious Message

"Let me try," suggested Erik.

As Kate held up the candle, he, too, felt his way around the hiding place. His hand also came up empty.

But Erik refused to leave it at that. Carefully moving his fingers across the wood, he touched each panel and bit of carving on the front of the organ. Next he checked wherever pieces of wood were joined together. Finally he studied the outside panel along the right side.

"What're you doing?" asked Kate.

"Wondered if I could take off that panel. But I can't find a way to do it without hurting the wood." Erik walked around to the back, still searching. "Other half of the message must be here somewhere!"

Anders joined him. While Kate held the candle, the two searched every crack and crevice of the organ. But they found no further bits of paper. Finally they had to give up.

As Anders and Erik set the organ along the wall, Kate had another idea. "The book! Maybe there's a name in it!" Pouncing on it, she opened the front cover. Nothing was written there.

It seemed to be a hymnbook, but Kate could not read the words. She turned to Anders. "Is it Swedish?"

As he looked it over, he grinned. "Yah, sure."

He sounded like Papa, and suddenly Kate felt lonesome. Papa would know what to do with the message. She wondered what his lumber camp was like, and how he was doing.

Erik scanned the pages. "They're hymns, Kate, ones we sing in church."

That didn't help Kate much. She still didn't understand the Swedish church services. Just the same, she kept paging through the book, hoping for a clue.

When she reached the end without finding any writing, Kate felt disappointed. Slowly she put down the book.

Something bothered her. "What if the person needs help? Someone in trouble might write a note."

For once Anders was serious. "Hoping that whoever bought the organ would find it."

"When did you get the organ?" asked Erik.

"A few months ago," Kate told him.

Erik looked puzzled. "Something seems strange to me. Why didn't you find the hidden space before?"

"Yah, Kate," Anders drawled. "You certainly should notice things better."

Kate was weary of Anders and his teasing. But Erik seemed not to notice. Going back to the organ, he turned up the music rack. When he set it in place, the rack completely hid the empty space behind.

Then Erik grasped the top of the rack and swung it forward. "Bring the candle!"

As Kate held it up, Erik took a better look. Once more he put the rack back in the position to hold music.

"That's why you didn't notice it, Kate. See how the hinges are hidden? Unless you knew what to look for, you'd never see 'em. Whoever built this organ knew what he was doing!"

Kate felt better then, but something still bothered her. "We don't know how long the note's been there. Did someone write it many years ago? Or just before we got the organ?"

"How old is it?" asked Erik.

"The man we bought it from said 1885."

"Well, let's just ask him!" exclaimed Erik.

"I don't know who he is," answered Kate. "When we went to the fair in Grantsburg, I walked along the street where things were sold. That's when I found the organ."

"So you don't know who sold it?"

Kate shook her head. "Never heard his name."

Erik turned to Anders. "What about you? Were you there?"

"Saw him, that's all," Anders said. "Papa took care of it. I took Kate to see Wildfire so she wouldn't know."

Kate still remembered that important day as if it had happened yesterday. She remembered sitting down and playing the organ, right there along the street. It was exciting to learn she could pick out tunes, even though she'd never had lessons. Now she understood that she had played by ear.

But in that moment she forgot about the people milling around her. Only after she bargained with the man for the organ did she realize Papa and Anders stood behind her. They had heard her play.

The Mysterious Message

Erik turned to Anders. "You must know the man. Your papa knows everyone."

Anders shook his blond head. "Nope. Only time I ever saw him."

"How did he look?" Erik persisted.

"Light brown hair . . ." Anders' voice trailed off as he tried to remember.

Kate recalled more. "Light brown hair, blue eyes, tall. A long beard."

"But around here there's at least a hundred Swedes who look like that!" Erik exclaimed.

Kate knew he was right. "There's only one person who knows who the man is. That's Papa."

"And he's a long way off in a lumber camp up north." Anders sounded grim. "We don't even know if he'll get home for Christmas."

The mysterious message bothered Kate. She couldn't explain why. For some reason she felt it was important, something she needed to know.

Long after Erik went home she thought about the word *an*. What did it mean? Was it just part of a word? Because the paper was torn, it seemed a strong possibility.

The word *fear* bothered Kate even more. Many times she'd been afraid—when lost in the woods, when facing something new. Even more often, she'd felt afraid of what others would think. She didn't like the feeling.

More than once she asked Anders, "What if someone really needs help?"

15

Big Trouble

The next morning Kate studied the face of every man who entered church. Yet none of them reminded her of the person who sold the organ.

"I'll keep looking," she promised herself. And she did. Wherever she went, she watched for a tall man with light brown hair, blue eyes, and a beard.

At the same time Kate and Anders and Erik kept on with another search. Who would take food from a root cellar? They felt sure it would be the same person who stole Josie's steer. If so, where could fruit and vegetables be hidden?

Each time Kate went into the woods, she took a different way, looking. Always looking.

The unusually warm weather lasted three more days. In her free time Kate escaped to the big rock. It became her special place when she wanted to be alone, away from Anders and his teasing.

Picking up fallen branches, she propped them close together around the trunk of a large tree close to the rock. On the side toward the trail, she left space for a door. By crawling in on her hands and knees, Kate had a shelter of her own.

One afternoon late in November, it started to rain. Before long, the rain turned to sleet, coating every tree limb with ice.

During the night the weather changed again. Kate awoke to the sound of windows rattling in the wind. The upstairs bedroom felt even colder than usual, and she snuggled deep under the quilts. In the morning a four-inch blanket of snow covered the ground.

With snow came thoughts of Christmas secrets. Whispers and presents. Baking and making the entire house spotless.

From a trip to Trade Lake, Anders brought home dried cod, and Mama started it soaking in a barrel of lye. Whether Kate liked the smell or not, they'd have lutfisk for Christmas!

Often Kate thought about the presents she'd give. Sometimes she put on an extra sweater and slipped off to her cold bedroom to knit without anyone knowing. Early in the fall she'd hidden away warm mittens for Anders and Lars. Now, after finishing mittens to replace the ones she lost, she was knitting a scarf for Mama.

Each day Kate practiced "Silent Night" to play for Papa if he came home. But what about Tina? What would she like?

While the snow was still new on the ground, Erik skied over. As he waited for Anders and Lars, he called to Kate, "Come with us!"

Kate longed to go along, to ski across the open field in front of the farmhouse, to swoop down the big hill nearby. But she had to tell him, "I don't have any skis."

On a Saturday early in December, Erik returned. For the first time since his family's food was stolen, he didn't look worried at the back of his eyes.

When Kate came to the door, Erik told her, "Brought some skis."

"Skis?" Kate stared at him, not understanding what he meant.

"Yup. Skis. You know, things you put on your feet."

Kate led him into the kitchen, still not sure what he meant. Erik looked half embarrassed, half proud.

"Like 'em?" he asked, carefully leaning the skis against the wall.

"They're beautiful!" exclaimed Kate. "Where'd you get them?"

"Made 'em," said Erik, rubbing the wood instead of looking at Kate. "Made 'em for you."

"For me?" Kate felt dumbfounded at such a gift. Gently, as though the skis would break, she reached out and touched the wood. The bottom sides were smooth with sanding and waxing.

"But how did you do it?" she asked, still unable to believe they were hers.

When Erik grinned, his embarrassment disappeared. "Cut two boards from a birch. Soaked the front ends in water. Kept 'em in a vise 'til the ends stayed bent." He pointed to the front tips that curved upward. "Pretty good, huh?"

He made it sound easy, but Kate knew better. "Pretty *great*!" She knew Erik liked to work with wood, but never dreamed he could do something like this.

"Papa always makes our skis," explained Erik. "Just watched how he did it."

"And the straps?" Kate asked.

"Found a broken piece of harness and cut it in half. Slid it through." He pointed to the opening he had carved in each ski to hold the strap in place. "Hardest thing was finding buckles. They're pretty old. I'll keep looking for better ones in case these don't last."

Kate thought they were the most beautiful skis in the world. "I can't believe they're really for me!"

Erik grinned again as though it were nothing. "Take my word for it."

Kate caught the pride in his face.

Then he asked, "Want to try 'em out?"

As Kate got her coat, Anders came in. Seeing the skis, he asked, "Where'd those come from?"

"They're mine," Kate said proudly.

"Yours? You going to sit or stand on 'em?" Anders laughed.

Refusing to answer such a dumb question, Kate flipped her braid over her shoulder, and the three went outside.

Just beyond the back step the snow was packed, and Kate set down her skis. She felt excited about learning to ski. Often she'd thought how easy it looked.

Quickly Kate slid her boot inside the strap of a ski. As she stepped onto the other ski, it slid out from beneath her. Suddenly she sat down hard.

Anders laughed. "That's all right, Kate!"

In spite of the cold air, Kate felt the hot flush of embarrassment creep into her face. Without saying a word, she got up slowly, rubbing herself where she hurt.

On her second attempt Kate planted her right ski on top of the left. Trying to move the ski, she lost her balance and landed in a heap.

Kate blinked, refusing to let the boys see her cry. As they took off, she followed slowly, feeling awkward. When they reached the big hollow beyond the farmhouse, she watched as they swooped down the steep hill. Skiing around on level ground, she met them on the far side. But gradually it grew easier. Whenever she fell, Kate picked herself up, dusted the snow off her coat and long stockings, and kept going.

From that time on, Kate skied after school whenever she had the chance. Day by day she felt more sure of herself. She still felt scared on the big hills, but she tried them. Sometimes she surprised even herself by standing up all the way to the bottom.

On those afternoons dusk always came too soon for Kate. She wanted to ski longer. Yet after the cold air, the farmhouse reached out with welcome warmth and the aroma of freshly baked bread.

During the long winter evenings, Kate practiced, learning to play "Silent Night." Once when she felt curious, she took out the book that had fallen from the organ. Kate couldn't read the Swedish words, but tried one tune after another. Then she understood why Mr. Peters wanted her to learn to read notes.

One song seemed familiar. Playing the notes for the right hand, she thought about the tune and wondered if they sang it at church. For some reason it reminded her of Tina.

Then Kate remembered the summer before when Mama and Papa Nordstrom were gone. The four children had been in the root cellar, scared about the storm, and Tina started to sing.

"What is it?" Kate had asked, not understanding the Swedish words.

"Children of the Heavenly Father," Lars told her.

Now Kate felt glad Tina had gone to the barn with Anders. "I'll learn the song for her Christmas surprise!" Kate promised herself. "She'll be here even if Papa isn't."

———

Day after cold day slipped away. Often when Anders, Kate, and Lars came home from school, one of them asked, "Did you hear from Papa?"

Just as often Mama said no, and "It's probably hard to get mail out." Always she tried to smile. Yet as time went on, Mama looked discouraged.

"A neighbor stopped by," she told Kate and Anders in the third week of December. "Mrs. Berglund is sick again. I made meatballs and bread, and I'll send along Christmas cookies."

With the snow too deep for the farm wagon, Anders backed Wildfire between the shafts of a cutter. Its cushions were upholstered in red, and its body painted black with a red pinstripe. With long runners, the cutter slid over snow-covered roads like a large sled with one seat.

Setting the bowl of meatballs on the floor of the cutter, Kate climbed in. Mama handed her a basket with bread and cookies. "They break easily," she warned.

"I'll take good care of them," Kate promised.

Wildfire pawed the ground, anxious to be off. Anders let her go. Soon they left the driveway behind and headed onto the main road. The late afternoon sun cast long blue shadows on the snow.

As the horse trotted along, the bells on her harness jingled. Anders grinned at Kate. He liked to show off Wildfire's good qualities. "Pretty good mare, huh?"

It was a game between them. She knew he really meant to say, "Mighty terrific animal, don't you think?"

And so Kate answered, "Oh, all right."

"Nice black coat," Anders went on, meaning, "Just like satin."

"Well, if you say so," Kate agreed, her voice lukewarm.

"Good high stepper, even in this snow."

"Yup," Kate answered in the casual voice Anders often used.

Big Trouble

But today Anders had a new line. "Bet we can get there in record time."

"Bet we can, but we shouldn't," answered Kate, feeling uneasy. She knew how much Anders liked speed. "Too many drifts. Look at them spreading out across the road."

They were passing through an area where the woods had been cleared. As the wind crossed the open fields, it snatched the snow, heaping it up. The drifts angled higher toward the ditch, lower toward the center of the road.

"No problem!" declared Anders. "Wildfire can handle 'em." Lifting the reins, he flicked them across the mare's back. Immediately Wildfire jumped ahead.

"Stop it, Anders!" Kate said immediately. "Stop it right now!"

Anders laughed. "See how Wildfire likes it? She's been penned up too much."

For a moment Kate wondered if he was right. But then they hit their first drift. The cutter tilted slightly, higher on the ditch side. A moment later the cutter dropped down into a dip.

The next drift was bigger. The cutter tilted more, then settled back on its runners.

Anders laughed, but Kate clutched the cookies on her lap. "Slow down, Anders Nordstrom!"

In that moment Wildfire tore into the biggest drift yet. New snow sprayed up against her forelegs. Kate slid into Anders.

"We're gonna tip!" she cried.

In the next instant they did. Anders, then Kate, spilled out in the snow.

Kate found herself face down in a drift. "Now see what you've done!" she sputtered, coming up with a face full of snow.

Anders was also covered from head to foot. He struggled to his feet. "Where's Wildfire?"

Already the mare was down the road, the cutter on its side, dragging behind.

Standing up, Kate brushed herself off, then looked for the basket she'd held on her lap. "Mama's cookies!" Somehow they'd landed beneath Kate.

Every beautiful cookie was crushed to crumbs. All but one loaf of bread was flattened.

"Oh, Anders, how could you!" moaned Kate. "All that good food! All that work!"

Then she saw the meatballs. They, too, were in the snow.

Kate scrambled to pick them up, then knew it was hopeless. The gravy had splattered in every direction. Meat and gravy mingled with snow and dirt.

"Mama's going to feel really bad!" cried Kate as she found the bowl in a drift. But Anders was already far down the road after the mare.

When Kate caught up with them, Anders looked grim. The cutter lay on its side. The reins were tangled in a bush alongside the road. Wildfire stood in a drift, her sides still heaving.

"Told you we'd tip," said Kate, and Anders looked even more angry.

He unhitched the mare, then said, "We've got to turn the cutter up." Anders seemed to bite off every word.

He and Kate got on one side and tried to lift together. It took all their strength, but finally the cutter rocked onto its runners.

Then Anders saw the damage. One of the long poles that hitched the cutter to the horse had split in half. "Broke the right shaft when we tipped," he muttered.

Kate felt sick inside. She wanted to say, "It's all your fault!" Instead she asked, "What do we do?"

For the first time since she'd known him, Anders seemed angry with himself. "Only one thing to do," he answered. "Walk."

"Walk?"

"Yup, walk. And we better get started. Nearest house is a ways down the road."

Leading Wildfire, Anders set out. Kate set the bowl in the cutter, picked up the one good loaf of bread, and followed. By the time they reached a farm, her legs and feet felt numb with cold. But Anders wanted to go on.

"How come?" Kate asked. "I'm frozen!"

"I don't want to stop here." His voice was firm.

"Oh, Anders, why not?" Kate complained.

"Stretch lives here."

"Stretch?" The older boy hadn't been back to school. Kate

hadn't seen him since the ride from Trade Lake. "He'll help you."

Anders shook his head. "I don't want to ask him for help."

"Everyone helps everyone else," Kate argued. "That's the country way."

But Anders would have passed the farm if Kate hadn't insisted they stop.

When they knocked on the door of the house, there was no answer. "See? No one's home anyway," Anders told Kate.

"Maybe they're in the barn," she answered, looking around. The road from which they'd walked ran along one side of the farm. Steep hills rose on the other three sides, leaving the house and barn in a hollow.

By now the sun lay low against the western horizon. Kate knew that light would soon be gone.

As she started toward the barn, Anders dragged his feet. When she found no one there, Kate headed for a small shed. Just as she reached for the handle, the door opened.

Stretch stepped out. Under his curly blond hair his face looked startled. Quickly he reached behind, shut the door, then stood in front of it. "Looking for something?" he asked.

16

Winter Search

*S*urprised, Kate dropped back.

But Anders stepped forward. "Looking for help."

As he told Stretch about the cutter, the older boy's gaze slid sideways. "Sorry, can't help you out." His voice sounded smooth.

"Why not?" asked Kate.

"Can't leave right now."

Kate couldn't understand this boy who had once seemed so friendly. "Why not?" she asked again.

For an instant Stretch seemed to think. "Can't leave my mother alone."

"I could stay with her while you help Anders," Kate said quickly.

The next moment she almost cried out. Anders had stepped on her foot.

As he faced the older boy, Anders seemed amazingly polite. "That's all right, Stretch. Thanks anyway." Anders tugged Kate's arm.

As they started for the road, Stretch shouted after them. "Try Berglunds. He'll help you!"

"Sure!" Anders called back, then kept walking.

Kate was fuming. "How come you stepped on my foot?" she asked when she thought Stretch could no longer hear. "Why'd you grab my arm? At least you could have let us warm up in the house."

Anders was even more cautious. He waited until they reached the road before speaking. "I wanted you out of there."

Kate raised her chin. "You think I can't take care of myself?"

Anders grinned. "Well, sometimes I'm not sure."

In spite of the distance between them and Stretch, Anders lowered his voice again. "He's hiding something. Notice how he shut the door?"

Kate nodded. She had noticed all right. Yet she didn't want to believe Stretch might be doing something wrong.

Inside her mittens she flexed her fingers to warm them. She tried to wiggle her toes, but couldn't feel if they moved.

Anders spoke again. "And you know what he said about his mother? Far as I know, Stretch doesn't have a mother. She died three years ago."

The cold went into Kate's heart.

Still leading Wildfire, Kate and Anders walked on. As they came to knee-high drifts, Anders stopped.

"Let's ride bareback."

"I don't know, Anders." Kate wasn't used to horses and hadn't ridden Wildfire, even with a saddle.

But Anders didn't give Kate a chance to protest. Clasping his hands, he gave her a step up. Then he clutched Wildfire's mane and swung up behind Kate.

In spite of the drifts, they made good time. Kate even enjoyed the ride.

When they reached the Berglund house, a tall man with blue eyes opened the door. His light brown hair had touches of white near the ears.

He invited them into the entryway, but wouldn't let them come any farther. A strong smell of onions filled the house.

"We've got real bad flu here." He tipped his head toward the onions cooking on the wood stove to clean the air. "Can't let you in. But how can I help you?"

When Anders explained that Mama had sent food for Mrs. Berglund, Kate held up the one good loaf of bread.

"I'm her son Henry," the man answered. "Home to help her out. Sorry for this trouble on our account. But I'll tell you what to do."

Leaving Kate and Anders to warm up in the entryway, he disappeared. Soon he returned wearing warm clothes. Picking up an axe, he told them, "I know just the right tree."

Going to the woods that grew close to the side of their house, Mr. Berglund chopped down a sapling. As he cut off the branches, he told them, "That oughta do you."

He returned to the house and found a hatchet, then shaped both ends of the sapling. When he finished, he handed Anders a strong pole that looked exactly right for a shaft. "You might need this hatchet to fix things up. Drop it off next time you come our way, all right? And here's a rope to lash this shaft to the old one."

By the time Kate and Anders reached the cutter again, it was dark. The farm lantern hadn't broken, and Kate lit it while Anders replaced the shaft.

Once they headed toward home, Kate huddled under a heavy horse blanket. She couldn't help thinking about Stretch. Finally she broke the silence. "Remember what he said?"

Anders guessed Kate's thoughts. "Yup. Stretch told us, 'He'll help you.' "

"And Mrs. Berglund usually lives alone. So Stretch knew her son was home from St. Paul."

"But that's not unusual." For a change it was Anders who defended Stretch. "Everybody knows what their neighbors are doing."

"Even when there's a woods between them?"

"Yup. They depend on each other."

As they turned onto the road to Windy Hill Farm, the moon came up. The large golden ball washed the snow with light.

Again Kate spoke. "You know, there's something that bothers

me about Henry Berglund. Seems like I know him, but I can't figure out where."

Just as they reached the barn, she remembered. "Oh, Anders! That's *him!*"

"That's who?"

"Mrs. Berglund's son, Henry. He's the man who sold the organ!"

"You're sure?"

"Positive!" exclaimed Kate. "Tall with light brown hair. Blue eyes and a beard. That's him, all right. How stupid I am! If only I'd realized it before. I could have asked if he knew anything about the hidden message!"

"We'll go back the first chance we get," promised Anders.

But the next day something important came up. Erik skied over after school. He and Kate and Anders went outside to talk.

Erik had been thinking about something. "Josie's family lost their steer. We lost our fruit and vegetables. Josie's farm and ours are on two sides of the woods. You're on the third side."

"What are you getting at?" asked Anders.

"None of us live far apart."

Then Anders caught on. "So whoever is stealing might know all about us. At least all about where we live."

A scared feeling tightened Kate's stomach. "I don't like that idea."

But Erik went on. "Been thinking about something else. What does that person do with all the food? Eat it? Sell it to someone?"

"If he does sell it, we've got to find it soon," said Anders grimly.

"Before he gets rid of it?" Kate asked.

Erik nodded. "We've got to catch him with the goods. If we don't, you might be the next person he steals from. How long can you keep watching your pig? When's the thief going to find just the right time to grab it?"

Kate didn't like that idea either.

Then Anders thought of something they hadn't tried. "Let's

spread out, all around our farm. Let's look for anything we can find."

"You mean by skiing?" Kate asked.

Anders nodded. "If we go around the drifts, it won't be too deep. Let's each take a direction."

"You can go toward Josie's," Kate answered.

Anders grinned, but all he said was "Yup!"

Erik agreed. "And unless we find something real soon, we'll talk on the way to school tomorrow."

"So what do we look for?" asked Kate.

"Anything that seems strange," Erik told her. "But don't try catching the thief on your own. Come back and tell us."

"Yah, Kate," said Anders. "Remember now."

They divided the area between them, and each set off alone. At first Kate enjoyed skiing. By now she'd gone often enough to feel comfortable with most hills. The day was warm for December, yet cool enough for good skiing.

As she found nothing out of the ordinary, she skied farther and farther from home. She'd never been this way before and liked seeing new hills and farms. Before long, all the markers she knew were far behind.

Finally Kate realized, *I don't know where I am.*

Then she saw the sun sinking toward the western horizon. It gave a sense of direction that would help her get back. But she had to get home before dark.

"Just up this hill," Kate told herself. If she skied back down, it would give a good start toward home.

Reaching the top, Kate looked beyond to a wide valley. Below her lay a house and barn and smaller buildings. Nestled in a hollow, the farm was surrounded on three sides by hills. On the fourth side a road passed the farm.

Just then a boy who sat tall on the seat of a sleigh drove into the yard. Even from a distance, Kate recognized him. She raised her hand to wave and call out.

But in that moment she felt uneasy. Slipping off her skis, she crouched down and peered out from behind a small pine tree.

The boy began throwing branches off the sleigh. Then he

went into the barn, brought out straw, and added it to the layers already in the sleigh.

As he hurried into the house, Kate crawled forward under the tree, trying to see more. Soon the boy came out, carrying a wooden box. Setting it in the sleigh, he returned to the house. Several times he went back and forth, always with more boxes.

Twice he paused and glanced around as though he felt uneasy. Kate crouched lower. With each box the boy added to the sleigh, her curiosity grew. *What's he doing?* It seemed strange that no one helped him. This time of day his father should be home.

At last the boy covered the boxes with quilts and horse blankets. On top of that he placed the long branches he'd taken from the sleigh. Once more he disappeared into the house.

For a time Kate waited. When he didn't return, she decided, "I'll ski down. I'll see what he's hiding in those boxes."

Then she remembered Erik's words. "Don't try to capture the thief on your own."

"Yah, Kate," Anders had said.

A thief? Kate didn't want to call the boy that. She only knew him as Stretch.

While the shadows lengthened across the snow, Kate stayed on the hill, hoping to see more. When she shivered with cold, she remembered her need to get home before dark.

At least she knew where she was. But now that knowledge worried her.

On the way home, Kate thought about Stretch. Was he the one who stole Josie's steer? What did he have in those boxes? She really didn't know anymore, only that Stretch looked guilty. What was he hiding?

With every question Kate felt more upset. Though Stretch was well liked, Anders and Erik and Lars had drawn back, feeling they couldn't trust him.

"Anders warned me," Kate muttered. "But I didn't listen. How could I be so dumb?" The memory of how she had wanted Stretch to like her embarrassed Kate. She had even defended Stretch to Anders. "What will Anders say if I tell him everything?"

As dread knotted her stomach, Kate argued with herself. "I don't have any proof. I'm just guessing. What if I say something, and Stretch's friends find out?" It wasn't hard to guess what they might do if she told on Stretch. Their singsong chant seemed to ring in Kate's ears: "Tattletale, tattletale!"

But then Kate thought of something even worse. *What if I tell and Stretch finds out? Would he try to get even?*

Suddenly Kate felt afraid. Very afraid. She thought about the mysterious message and the word *fear*. That was how she felt.

"I don't need to do a thing," she decided. "I'll just pretend I didn't see Stretch."

17

December Storm

*A*s the sun slipped behind the far hills, Kate skied into the Windy Hill farmyard. She found Anders in the barn, milking the cows.

"See anything?" she asked before he could ask her.

He shook his head and directed a stream of milk toward one of the cats. "How about you?"

Kate shrugged her shoulders, but didn't look Anders in the face. Leaning her skis against a wall, she dropped down on a mound of straw. The cat settled on the dirt floor to lick the milk off her fur.

After a time Anders asked, "Something wrong?"

"What do you mean?" Kate didn't want to talk. She especially didn't want to tell what she'd seen.

Yet Anders kept on. "You don't act like yourself."

Kate felt surprised that he had noticed. She also felt unwilling to meet his gaze. As the silence lengthened between them, she shivered. "I'm going to the house to warm up."

"Why don't you wait a minute? I'm almost done." Anders hung the pail of milk on a nail, out of reach of the cats.

"I'm cold," she answered, still not looking at him.

His next words sounded totally unlike Anders. "Kate, I know

it must be hard to believe. But I *am* your brother."

"My brother?" Kate laughed, a short brittle laugh that sounded as cold as ice. "Are you really?"

Before she could stop them, tears flooded her eyes and ran down her cheeks. She turned away, not wanting Anders to see her cry, not willing to give him another reason to tease. Everything seemed more than she could bear.

Finally Kate drew a long shuddering breath and looked at Anders. If she didn't know better, she would have thought he seemed embarrassed.

"I mean it, Kate. You can tell me what's wrong."

Kate blew her nose. In that instant she thought of something more than her fear of what Stretch might do. She remembered all the times and ways Anders had helped her. She remembered how good it felt when she and Mama and the Nordstroms became a family, working together.

But if I tell Anders everything, what will he say?

In the next instant there was something Kate was sure of. Something that came out of her talk with Mama the day Tina climbed into the tree. Something that came with receiving God's forgiveness. *Anders might tease. But so what? God loves me the way I am.*

The idea was new for Kate, and it gave her courage to begin talking. At first she stumbled, but then her words came faster. To her surprise it was a relief to tell Anders all that had happened.

When she finished, Anders looked at her hard. "Why didn't you tell me you went down to the lake with Stretch?"

"I was afraid of what you'd say."

"How come you were scared to tell me what you just found out?"

"I thought you'd tease 'cause I stuck up for Stretch."

Anders hooted. "You worry about *that*?" But then he said, "Kate, I won't tease you about important things. All right?"

He stretched out his hand and waited for her to shake on it.

When she did, he winked. Kate knew the old Anders was back.

"But the unimportant things—"

Kate withdrew her hand and hit his shoulder. "I know. *You'll* be the one who decides what's important!"

His eyes gleamed with laughter, and Kate knew she'd read his thoughts. She remembered Papa Nordstrom's words: "You'll have to earn your way with Anders."

When she spoke again, Kate sounded like her brother. "Well, then. You better figure out what to do."

"We have to know for sure," Anders told her. "Is Stretch the thief or isn't he?"

Pushing the shock of blond hair out of his eyes, Anders thought for a moment, then went on. "I'll talk to Erik on the way to school tomorrow. You keep Lars and Chrissy busy. If they said anything, it'd get back to Stretch. Somehow we have to figure out how to tell the right grown-up."

"Without letting anyone know we talked," Kate added.

"But how?" Anders looked worried.

They thought about one idea, then another. At last Kate said, "We have to find a way to get to Big Gust."

Since solving the mystery of the disappearing stranger, she and Anders had not seen the seven-and-a-half-foot village marshal. They seldom traveled the eleven long miles into Grantsburg.

"Can he arrest someone out in the country?" Kate asked.

Anders shrugged. "I don't know. There's the county sheriff, Charlie Saunders. Maybe he'd have to come out."

"Big Gust can tell us what to do."

"If we're right about Stretch, we have to be able to prove it," warned Anders.

Kate sighed. "If only I could have seen what was in those boxes."

"Got any ideas?"

Kate shook her head. "All I know is that Stretch didn't want it to freeze. He covered the boxes with quilts and horse blankets."

"So we're back to one problem—proof."

Kate agreed. "Or it's just our word against his."

Anders looked grim. "And we have to find that proof before he gets rid of what he's hiding."

During the night a wet snow outlined the dark tree branches with white. When Kate, Anders, and Lars walked to school, the pines looked soft, bending beneath the heavy snow. Kate lingered behind, enjoying the beauty of the woods.

At the fork in the trail they met Erik and his sister. Looking at Kate, Anders tipped his head toward Lars and Chrissy.

When Kate caught up with them, Lars seemed surprised. Kate had barely spoken to him since finding the mouse in her bed.

"Last day of school before getting out for Christmas!" Kate forced herself to sound glad. For the first time in her life, she'd given little thought to vacation. Too many other things had happened.

Chrissy's eyes sparkled with plans for the school party that afternoon.

Lars was looking forward to something else. "Christmas Eve's tomorrow night," he said. But then came the question Kate dreaded. "Will Papa be home for Christmas?"

Mama and Kate and Anders no longer asked that question aloud. They asked it only in their hearts.

Yes, he'll be here! Kate wanted to tell Lars. She wished she could make that promise. Instead, she had to say, "I don't know, Lars. I don't know."

Kate ached with the hope that Papa would be home. Her thoughts echoed those of Lars. *Christmas Eve tomorrow night.* She wondered if Papa was somewhere in the cold, walking toward Windy Hill Farm.

In spite of Kate's answer, Lars looked relieved to have her talk to him again. Soon he slipped into his old way of telling her things.

Once Kate glanced over her shoulder. Anders and Erik had dropped back, walking slowly. No doubt Anders was telling him about her discovery. They'd figure out what to do.

But then Kate remembered what Anders said. "We have to be able to prove it. We have to find that proof before Stretch gets rid of it."

Soon after they reached school, the sky grew dark and snow began to fall. By noon that snow blocked out the view of Spirit Lake.

December Storm

Cold air swept through the knotholes in the floor, and Kate felt the temperature drop. Then the wind came up, swirling snow around the corners of the school.

Often Miss Sundquist walked to the windows and stared at the sky. Finally she went out to stand on the porch. When she returned, she closed the door hard against the wind.

"We won't be able to have our Christmas party," she said, and everyone groaned. "Instead, I'm going to let you out early. Go right home. Don't stop to play on the way."

Kate wasn't sure which she wanted more, the party or leaving school early. At the same time, she felt disappointed. The snowstorm would make it even harder to go to Grantsburg and talk to Big Gust.

As everyone hurried out of school, Kate tucked the long ends of her scarf inside the collar of her coat. Then she followed Anders and Erik down to the creek.

The log was slippery from packed snow, and Kate drew back, fearful of the water rushing beneath. But for once Anders didn't tease. Reaching back to grab her hand, he helped Kate across.

Erik led Chrissy, and Lars made it over on his own. As they climbed the path back of the school, the hill sheltered them. When they neared the top, a cold wind caught their clothing. Even so, the woods offered protection.

Then they reached a field filled with the stumps of recently dropped trees. There the wind howled across the wide open area. Strong gusts picked up new snow, sending it toward them in clouds.

Already, the wind had erased the path they'd packed down walking to and from school. Anders took the lead, breaking the way. Lars went next. Erik dragged his feet to make the path easier for the girls. Kate followed Chrissy.

Here the wind struck her full in the face, and Kate's eyes started to water. The driving snow stung her cheeks. It felt like a thousand needles pricking her skin.

Kate stopped. Unwinding her long scarf, she wrapped it over her forehead, nose, and mouth, leaving only her eyes uncovered.

As she started out again, falling snow blocked her view of the others. In that short time they'd walked on.

For a moment Kate felt panic. Then Erik called. "Come on, Kate! Hurry up!"

"I can't see you!" she called back.

"Keep coming toward my voice," he shouted above the wind. "Follow the footprints."

When she caught up, Erik told her, "Now don't drag."

They plodded on, not wasting the energy to speak. Often Kate saw Erik turn, checking to see that she and Chrissy still walked close behind.

When they entered the woods once more, the wind lessened. Kate felt relieved. Most of the rest of the way would take them through woods. Yet even here the deepening snow made every step difficult.

"It'll keep us home," Kate told herself. "We can't go to Big Gust."

As she felt the disappointment, they reached the fork leading to Erik's farm. Kate wished they could all stay together. Yet there'd be no way to tell Erik's parents where he and Chrissy were if they stayed at Windy Hill Farm.

"Whatever happens, keep moving," Erik told Kate. He seemed much older than his thirteen years.

A moment later, he and Chrissy disappeared in the swirling snow. Kate trudged on, staying close behind Lars. Anders kept the lead, breaking trail.

Suddenly Kate heard a startled cry. Running forward, she found Anders rolling in the snow. "What happened?"

Anders spoke through clenched teeth. "Feels like someone stuck me with a knife."

As he tried to stand up, Kate offered a hand. Anders motioned her away. "I can do it!" Yet he lost his balance and fell back to the ground, groaning.

This time Anders let Kate and Lars help him to a sitting position. Pulling off her mitten, Kate reached forward to feel his ankle.

"Don't touch it!" he exclaimed.

"What happened?" Kate asked again.

"Couldn't see the path." Anders gritted his teeth.

Then Kate saw two small logs just off the trail. They lay close together, partly covered by ice and snow. Anders must have slipped off the first icy log, twisting his foot between that and the next.

"What should I do?" Kate wanted to know.

But Lars surprised her by asking Anders, "Can you wiggle your toes?"

Anders winced with the effort, but nodded. Even in the swirling snow, Kate saw the pain in his eyes.

Her stomach felt empty, and she knew what it was: fear all the way through. That day when she fell through the ice, Anders and Erik had carried her most of the way to school. Kate knew she and Lars weren't strong enough for that.

"Can you possibly walk?" she asked Anders.

He shrugged, as though knowing he didn't have any choice.

Again Lars took over. "Gotta fix his boot first."

Again Kate looked at him as if to ask, "Do you know what you're talking about?"

Lars seemed to guess her thoughts. "Papa got hurt in the woods once. He told me what to do."

Anders was wearing Papa's old work boots. Lars knelt in the snow in front of Anders, unlaced the boot on the injured foot, then loosened it. Already the ankle looked swollen.

Anders bit his lip, as though fighting the pain. His eyes were wet with tears.

I've never seen Anders cry before, Kate thought. Once Kate would have teased him. Instead, she felt even more scared.

"Put your arms around our shoulders," she told him. She and Lars pulled Anders to a standing position.

"We'll make it," she said, trying to sound confident. But her words seemed to vanish into the snowy air.

Anders stepped gingerly on his bad foot, putting as much weight as possible on his good one. As he limped along, Kate saw him bite his lip against the pain.

He was so much taller and heavier that Kate soon felt exhausted. *What can we do?* she wondered, feeling desperate. *How can we get him home?*

In the next moment Anders stumbled and fell forward.

18

Whistle in the Dark

*J*ust in time Kate and Lars caught Anders. His face looked gray. Beads of perspiration dotted his upper lip.

"What can we do?" This time Kate spoke aloud. When neither Anders nor Lars answered, the words set up a rhythm in her mind.

Then Kate remembered the shelter she'd built that fall. She'd gone there when she wanted to be alone, away from Anders and Lars and their teasing.

The big rock and the shelter weren't far away. There Anders could be out of the wind while she went for help. Yet a part of Kate held out. *It wouldn't be my secret anymore.*

A gust of wind swept down the path, pushing against them. With it came the pain of all the times and ways Anders had teased her. "And Lars isn't any better," Kate told herself, remembering the mouse in her bed.

Her shoulder ached from the weight of supporting Anders. His breathing sounded labored.

"You're strong," she told Anders. "You can do it."

But Anders stumbled again. Never before had Kate seen him so helpless.

Lars stopped. "He can't get all the way home. Not in this storm."

Kate knew Lars was right. As clearly as if Anders had spoken aloud, she remembered his words: "Kate, I'm your brother."

They stood close to the large oak and the clump of birch marking the way to her shelter. "This way," she said, tipping her head to the left of the path.

In a few minutes, they reached the big rock and the shelter Kate had built. The wet snow of the night before still clung to the branches, filling the cracks.

"Hold Anders," she said to Lars.

Kneeling at the doorway, Kate crawled inside. At once she felt the difference. Out of the wind it was warmer. The snow on the branches offered even more protection.

Half pulling, half dragging, they helped Anders into the shelter. Lars took off his brother's boot and pushed snow under the bad leg, propping it up.

Kate drew off her coat, then a sweater. When she wrapped the sweater around his foot, Anders flinched. Even in the half light, his ankle looked more swollen.

"Make sure he doesn't leave," Kate told Lars as she slipped back into her coat. If Anders started out again, she might not find them.

"Why don't you stay too?" Lars asked.

"Maybe I should," Kate answered, looking at Anders. For the first time since she'd known Anders, he was unable to help her decide.

Then Kate remembered Mama. She would be worried, wondering where they were. As Anders trembled with pain, Kate made up her mind. "Might be an all-night snow."

"I'll go," offered Lars.

"We need Wildfire," said Kate. "You've never hitched her up, have you?" Lars was even shorter than Kate. Once more, she wrapped the long scarf around her face.

"Don't stop," Lars said, echoing Erik's words. "Keep moving no matter what."

Outside the shelter, Kate felt the wind again. Close by, the trees thinned out and a steep bank dropped away to Rice Lake.

Kate turned the opposite direction and headed back to the trail.

Soon after coming to Windy Hill Farm, she had lost her way in the woods. Using the sun, she had headed in one direction. But today there was no sun, only steadily falling snow.

When Kate reached the clump of birch and the tall oak that were her markers, she turned onto the path. Snow hid the trail packed down by their daily walks, but Kate watched for the opening between the trees.

"Where are you, Papa?" she muttered as she plodded on. "Are you out in this too?"

After walking for some time, Kate came to the part of the trail edging Rice Lake. Once again the full force of the wind struck her. She gasped, and bent her head low.

Turning her back to the wind, Kate looked around now and then to keep her bearings. As she trudged on, walking backward, the banks of snow looked inviting—as inviting as a large soft bed.

I'm tired, Kate thought, wanting to lie down.

"Keep moving, no matter what," Erik had said.

I'll just rest for a minute.

"Don't stop," Lars had told her.

Now Kate understood why. She wanted only to sleep.

She faced into the wind, and at last felt a rise beneath her feet. She'd passed the spring along the wagon track without knowing it. Step-by-weary-step, Kate climbed the steep hill near the farmhouse. At the top she saw a faint glow. Mama had a candle in the window!

Kate headed for the light. Pushing open the kitchen door, she stumbled in.

"Kate!" exclaimed Mama. She hugged Kate tight, snowy coat and all.

Tina's blue eyes were wide, but it was Mama who asked, "Where are Anders and Lars?"

As Kate told her, Mama exclaimed, "Oh, Kate! I wish you could stay here. I wish Papa was here to go." Moving quickly to the cookstove, she set a kettle over the firebox to make cocoa.

Kate shed her coat and put on a warm dry sweater. "I wish Papa was here too," she said, her voice as small as she felt. "But

Anders showed me what to do with Wildfire."

She caught the surprise on Mama's face. As quickly as it came, it disappeared.

Kate pulled on her coat once more and headed out to the barn, wondering if she could remember all that Anders had taught her about handling a horse. Holding the bridle, she entered Wildfire's stall.

"Get over, girl," she told the mare. But her voice came out squeaky and small. Wildfire didn't move.

"Get over," Kate said again, sounding as bossy as she could. This time Wildfire moved. Kate pulled herself to the top of the feed trough. There she slipped off the halter and held up the bridle.

Her hands shook as she felt along Wildfire's jawline for the place to open her mouth. Carefully she slipped in the bit.

Next came the harness, belly strap, and breast collar. Kate fumbled as she checked the straps and buckles. Finally she picked up the farm lantern and led Wildfire out of the barn.

As she backed the mare between the shafts of the cutter, Kate held her breath. What if Wildfire decided to bolt? Kate knew she couldn't hold her the way Anders did.

Quickly Kate took the lead rope and tied it to a rail. Still talking to the mare, Kate buckled her in.

It seemed forever before she had everything right. At last she lit the lantern, set it in the cutter, and climbed in. *I'm ready—or I think I am!*

At the house, Mama hurried out, handing up a heavy basket. She'd filled jars with cocoa, wrapping them to stay warm. "I'll be praying for you!" she called out above the wind, then stepped away from the runners.

Reins in one hand, Kate waved and clucked the horse. Then she guessed the worry Mama must feel. Turning back, Kate threw her a kiss.

For just a moment Mama smiled. The concern in her eyes disappeared. Before the snow swallowed her up, Mama blew a kiss back.

Kate felt warm inside. She remembered to shift a rein to the other hand as she thought about her first year of school. She'd been afraid to go off on her own to a big new world.

At first Mama walked with her to the Minneapolis school. Then Mama asked older children to take her. When Kate still felt afraid, Mama started a game. Standing inside a front window, she waved. Kate waved back. Kate blew a kiss, and Mama returned it.

The old signal still worked. Now it meant more. In spite of all that had happened, she had no doubt that Mama loved her.

At the bottom of the steep hill, Kate whistled. Lutfisk bounded up, and Kate was glad she'd learned how to call him. She flicked the reins and Wildfire picked up her pace.

By now the December afternoon had faded into dusk. Along Rice Lake the wind had blown the path clean. In other places the snow lay in deep drifts.

Near the edge of the woods, one of these drifts reached the mare's chest. Wildfire hesitated, and Kate shouted, "Come on, girl. Go on through!"

Snow sprayed up as Wildfire plunged ahead. The cutter tilted, then settled back on its runners. Choking down her fear, Kate cried out, "That-a-girl! Keep it up!"

The mare's ears twitched and turned toward the sound of Kate's voice. "Good girl!"

As they entered the woods, the dusk deepened. Kate's hands tensed. Yet she urged the horse on, trying to keep her on the packed trail now hidden by new snow.

Once Wildfire stepped off the trail and staggered into deep snow. For a moment she stood there, pawing the ground. Finding the path again, she strained against the harness.

When dusk changed to night, Kate pulled on the reins for Wildfire to stop. Grasping the long metal handle, Kate held up the farm lantern. As it swung in the wind, she picked out trees on either side of the trail. None of them seemed familiar.

A gust of wind swooped down. The flame flickered but held.

Setting the lantern by her feet, Kate picked up the reins and flicked them across Wildfire's back A few minutes later Kate stopped again to hold up the lantern. This time she felt even more confused. "Where are we?" she muttered, unable to recognize the trees.

In that moment the lantern flickered and died. The darkness of deep woods closed in around Kate as she realized the awful truth—she hadn't filled the lantern with kerosene!

Yet she had no choice but to keep on. As Wildfire moved ahead, Lutfisk barked. Kate peered into the night. No matter how hard she looked, she couldn't find the tall oak and the clump of birch.

The fear within her growing, Kate called out. "Anders! Lars!" But the wind threw back her voice. No one could possibly hear.

Switching both reins into one hand, Kate pulled off her mitten. With her thumb and finger between her lips, she blew hard. Her shrill whistle pierced the air.

For a moment Kate listened. Lutfisk yipped and ran alongside the cutter. But there came no other sound.

Kate's fear changed to panic. Once more she blew hard. Listening, she wondered if she heard a response.

When she whistled a third time, an answering whistle pierced the night. Lutfisk broke away and disappeared in the darkness.

They're behind me!

Kate whistled still again. When she heard the answer, she felt sure. "I went too far!" she muttered. "I've gone past them!"

The trail was too narrow to turn the cutter. Wildfire plodded on as Kate heard yet another whistle. Then it fell away.

At last the dim outline of trees disappeared from either side of the path. Reaching the field, Kate pulled on the reins. She turned Wildfire, and they reentered the woods.

As they drove through the darkness, Kate whistled often. Finally she heard an answer. Then the clump of white birch loomed out of the darkness.

Stopping Wildfire, Kate jumped down and tied the mare to a tree. Carrying Mama's basket of hot cocoa, Kate headed off the path.

Now she had a new fear. *What if I miss the shelter? I'd fall over the steep bank next to it!*

19

The Flickering Candle

*K*ate stood still. Once again she pulled off her mitten and whistled. From the swirling snow she heard the response—a long, clear answer.

Out of the darkness Lutfisk hurled himself toward Kate. When she reached down to pet him, he jumped up and barked. Then he darted away. A short distance off, he stopped, waiting for Kate to follow.

She reached him, and he darted away again. Each time the dog left her, he stayed close enough for Kate to see.

Before long she heard Lars shout, "Kate, over here!" Lutfisk had brought her to the shelter.

Reaching the door, Kate tumbled inside. After the darkness and snow, the shelter seemed warm and safe.

They warmed up on cocoa; then Kate and Lars helped Anders out of the shelter. His arms once more around their shoulders, the three started out. Soon they reached the cutter safely.

As they helped Anders in, he bumped his leg and moaned. Once settled, he spoke between clenched teeth. "Give Wildfire her head. She'll find her way home."

As Kate flicked the reins, Wildfire leaped out. The going was slow as the mare worked through the drifts. Finally they reached the top of the hill and the farmhouse. This time Mama had three candles in the window.

When they came into the kitchen, Kate saw Anders' face. In the light of the kerosene lamp his lips looked white, his eyes glazed with pain. Mama had a bed of blankets ready for him on the floor near the wood stove.

During the night the wind died down. In the early morning sunlight, the snow glistened—white and beautiful. Kate remembered Mama's words: "When Jesus forgives, you become clean. Clean as new snow."

This morning Kate believed those words. She felt peaceful inside. "Christmas Eve tonight!" she told herself. She dared to hope. "Maybe Papa came home during the storm!"

But then Kate remembered Stretch. She remembered how she and Erik and Anders planned to go to Big Gust. And she remembered how Anders got hurt.

Down in the kitchen, Kate didn't need to ask. Tina and Mama worked quietly. Lars was out milking the cows. Papa hadn't come during the night.

Still lying near the wood stove in the dining room, Anders looked pale. He whispered to Kate. "I don't know if I had a nightmare or if it was real. Go check on the pig."

Outside, the snow had blown against the summer kitchen, heaping it in high drifts. Yet in front of the door, the snow was less than a foot deep. Looking at it, Kate felt afraid.

Quickly she shoveled away enough snow to open the door. Inside, the little house was icy cold. But Kate looked for only one thing.

The top of the cookstove was bare. The pig was gone!

Kate's fear changed to anger. She felt angry at whoever stole Josie's steer. Angry at the person who took raspberries and blueberries and carrots and potatoes from Erik's cellar. Angry at the thief who stole their pig.

Kate wanted to pound her fist on the top of the cookstove. Then she noticed. One round stove lid was missing.

That made Kate even more angry. Without that lid, the stove

was useless. If the family started a fire, the room would fill with smoke.

Hurrying back to the house, Kate told Anders, Mama, and Tina the bad news. "The pig's gone!"

Tina's eyes grew wide, and Mama threw up her hands. "In the midst of that storm, someone came?"

Angrily Anders slammed one fist into another. But when he tried to stand up, he groaned.

Lars came in and found out about the pig. He looked just as upset.

As Mama filled plates with eggs and warm brown bread, Anders whispered to Kate. "We've gotta get to Stretch."

"While we can still prove it!" Kate exclaimed in a low voice. "But how?"

During breakfast Mama had more than the pig on her mind. "Christmas or no Christmas, Anders has to see the doctor in Grantsburg. His ankle is even more swollen this morning. I can't tell if it's sprained or broken. It might need to be set."

"I'll take him, Mama," Kate said quickly.

"You, Kate? No, absolutely not."

"I can do it, Mama."

"Eleven miles? You can't do it alone."

"I'm sure I can, Mama," said Kate, even though she felt nervous about it.

Mama sighed. "Well, I guess you're right. But you'd have to take the sleigh so Anders can lie down."

"Sleigh's too heavy for Wildfire alone," Anders told her. "At least with these drifts."

Kate turned to him, surprised that Anders would object to going to Grantsburg.

Anders went on. "Get Erik. See if he can drive their team of horses."

By the time Lars and Erik returned with Lundgrens' horses, Mama had sandwiches and cocoa ready.

Erik looked grim as he checked out the freezing-cold summer kitchen. "Did you see you're also missing a stove lid?"

He spread heavy blankets in the sleigh for Anders. Inside the blankets, he put bricks Mama had warmed and wrapped in bur-

The Flickering Candle

lap. He and Kate helped Anders in, being as careful as they could. Even so, Anders winced with pain.

As they started out, the sleigh bells jingled bright and clear in the winter air. Yet Erik talked only about the pig. "No footprints in the snow."

"Must have been some," answered Kate. "But the wind covered them." For a moment she thought about it. "Maybe that's why he came last night."

"Pretty smart thief." Erik sounded angry. "We haven't got much time."

Kate knew he was right. "If he cuts up the pig, we won't be able to recognize it."

As they reached the main road, the team picked up speed. Yet the going was slow, and the drifts large.

With each delay Kate grew more impatient. "Even if we get Big Gust, how can we prove the pig is ours?" she asked. And something else bothered her. "I keep thinking about that hidden message. If the organ was Mrs. Berglund's, *and* if she wrote the message, do you think she's still afraid?"

"Could be, living alone," Erik answered.

Anders disagreed, calling out from behind them. "She *wants* to stay on her farm. Even though she lives alone."

Kate wasn't satisfied with that answer. "Then what would make her afraid? We still haven't figured out what *an* means."

"An, an, an." Erik repeated the syllable to himself. "What would *an* do to her?"

For a time they drove in silence. Suddenly Anders shouted, "Man! The word is *man!*"

Erik grinned and looked back. "For someone with a bum ankle, you're doing all right!"

Kate had another thought. "Or it could be *woman*."

"Could be either," Erik agreed as the sleigh plowed into another bank of snow.

Anders moaned. "Can we stop somewhere? Every time we hit a drift, my ankle hurts worse."

"Let's stop at Berglunds' and warm up," suggested Kate. "We need to return their hatchet. And I want to ask about the message."

When they reached the house, Henry Berglund opened the door. Mrs. Berglund was up and around again, and she insisted on feeding them.

"Get me the milk, will you, Kate?" she asked as her son and Erik helped Anders into the house.

Kate lit a candle and pulled up the trapdoor. Step by step she descended into the darkness. This time she cupped her hand around the flame, shielding it from blowing out. Yet as she reached the bottom of the steps, the candle burned steady, the flame straight in the air.

Kate saw the milk on a ledge near the stairs. She picked it up, then set it back down. Why was there a breeze before and not today? Why didn't the candle flicker out?

Holding it out in front of her, Kate looked around. This time she felt determined to see all of the cellar.

The earth basement was small. Kate moved closer to the boarded-off section she'd seen last time. Spotting a door, she opened it. Canning jars and squash filled several shelves.

Nearby were large bins of potatoes and bushel baskets with dirt. Kate knew those baskets probably held carrots stored for winter.

Disappointed, she continued to search. *There must be more.* What would cause a breeze strong enough to blow out a flame?

Circling the room, Kate held her candle high. In the wall opposite the steps leading to the kitchen she discovered another door. On either side, wide ledges were dug into the earth wall.

"Kate!" Mrs. Berglund called down. "Having trouble?"

"Be right there!" Kate shouted back. Moving closer to one of the ledges, she peered into the area lit by the candle. This time she saw something far back on the ledge. Fruit jars. Jars filled with blueberries, raspberries, and strawberries.

Swinging around, Kate looked at the other ledge. A number of bushel baskets stood there. They, too, were set far back, almost out of sight.

Between these ledges was the door she'd seen, and Kate opened it. On the other side, steps led upward. Steps covered at the top by double doors slanted over the opening. "That's it!" Kate exclaimed. If the doors were left open even a little, it would cause a draft.

Closing the inner door, Kate went back to the milk. Just then Mrs. Berglund called again.

"Coming!" Kate shouted, and hurried up the steps.

In the kitchen she quickly glanced around. One window looked out on the slanted boards of the double doors to the cellar. Beyond, the backyard stretched away to nearby woods.

Kate set down the milk near a tall cupboard. She started to turn away, then noticed something. A piece of embroidered cloth hung on the wall.

As she stood on tiptoe to read the words, Kate barely breathed. Filled with excitement, she flipped her long black braid over her shoulder.

This was something Anders and Erik had to see!

20

Big Gust Anderson

"Come, come," called Mrs. Berglund before Kate could get the boys. "You still have a long ride ahead of you."

Leaning against Erik, Anders lowered himself into a chair next to the table.

"Christmas Eve tonight," said Henry Berglund after the prayer. "Bad time for you to get hurt, Anders."

Anders agreed. His face looked white and he winced whenever he had to move his ankle. Yet in spite of his misery, he winked at Kate as though to say, "Get talking!"

Kate didn't waste a minute. "Mrs. Berglund, did you ever have your own organ?"

The old woman smiled. "Yah."

Kate turned to the woman's son. "Did you sell that organ last summer?"

"At the street fair in Grantsburg. When they had the county fair."

As she looked back to Mrs. Berglund, Kate's excitement grew. "I think I have your organ."

"Yah? How does it look?"

When Kate described her organ, Mrs. Berglund nodded. "Yah, that's mine all right."

"Then I have a book you left in it."
"Good. I left it for you."
"For me?"
"I hoped the one who got the organ would use it."
"Oh, I am!" Kate exclaimed, and told her about "Children of the Heavenly Father."

But Kate really wanted to ask about the hidden message. More than once, she and Anders and Erik had searched the organ, trying to find the other half of the paper.

"We found part of a message in a crack," said Kate.

"And what did it say?" Mrs. Berglund's eyes twinkled as though she already knew.

"Do you mind if I write it out?" Kate had spied a bottle of ink and a pen on a nearby shelf.

Taking the pen, Kate dipped it in the ink. When she finished, the words said:

> *On my side;*
> *fear:*
> *an do to me?*

Mrs. Berglund smiled. "It's my favorite verse."
"A Bible verse?"
She nodded. "Psalm 118, verse 6."
"And you put it in my organ? I mean, *your* organ?"
"For many years I had it on the music rack," Mrs. Berglund explained. "I wanted to see it there. When Henry took the organ to town, I put the message inside. It must have slipped down in the crack."

"But what does the rest of it say?" Anders sounded impatient.

Now Kate was enjoying herself. She leaned forward and wrote again. When she sat back, Erik jumped up to read the words aloud:

The Lord *is* on my side;
I will not fear:
What can man do to me?

Anders looked puzzled. "Kate, how did you know?" he asked.

"We should get it for Anders," answered Mrs. Berglund.

Her son went to the corner of the kitchen. Coming back, he held up the piece of embroidered cloth.

But Kate had another question. "Were you afraid?" she asked Mrs. Berglund.

Below Mrs. Berglund's faded blue eyes, her smile was gentle. "Yah, I was often afraid."

"Why?" Kate asked again.

"When I played the organ for other people, I was afraid I'd make mistakes. I was afraid of what people would think."

"Did the verse help?"

"Yah, certainly. I always said it to myself. Before I played, I asked the Lord to help me."

"And He did?" Kate needed to know.

"He always did. He still does when I'm afraid. If I hear a strange noise at night, I say that verse to myself."

"Have you heard strange noises lately?" Kate asked quickly, as she guessed what the answer might be.

"Well, now that you mention it, I heard noises a few nights ago, coming from the back of the house. A wagon track goes through the woods there. But it was dark. I couldn't see anything."

Kate turned to Henry Berglund. "Were you here?"

He shook his head. "I was gone overnight. First I've heard about the noises."

On the way to Grantsburg, Kate told Erik and Anders about the cellar. "Why would there be potatoes in *two* places? And canning jars in *two* places?"

Erik's eyes gleamed.

"And why would there be a draft one day and not another?" Kate continued. "Unless doors were open?"

Erik's grin told Kate they were both thinking the same thing.

Anders spoke up from the back of the sleigh. "You know, Kate, for a girl, you're pretty smart." He sounded surprisingly normal.

For once Kate didn't mind his teasing. But then her fear returned. "If it *is* Stretch, what's he going to think if we're the ones turning him in?"

"Now, that's where you *aren't* smart," said Anders.

"If we don't say something, who will?" asked Erik. "He'll keep stealing the rest of his life."

When they reached Grantsburg, Erik went to find Big Gust. Kate stayed with Anders at the doctor's. It was a bad sprain, not a break. The doctor gave Anders crutches and told him to stay off the ankle.

A short time later, Erik returned with the village marshal. After not seeing the big Swede for a time, Kate again felt surprised at his size.

She knew Big Gust was 7 1/2 feet tall, weighed 360 pounds, and wore size 18 boots.

Beneath his moustache, his smile was enormous. When he stretched down his hand to say hello, Kate saw the kindness in his eyes.

"Sheriff Saunders is gone," Erik explained. "But Big Gust's sister lives out our way, near little Wood Lake. He was just ready to leave and visit her for Christmas."

All of them went out to Erik's sleigh, with Anders limping along on his crutches. As he dragged behind, Big Gust turned back. He bent down and picked Anders up.

"Hey, what are you doing?" Anders looked embarrassed, but the marshal set him in the sleigh as gently as if he were a basket of eggs.

Erik grinned at Kate. For a giant known to pick up two men at one time, Anders offered no problem at all.

Big Gust settled himself on the seat and took up the reins. There was just enough room for Erik and Kate to squeeze in next to him, one on either side.

In spite of the cold, Big Gust's coonskin coat hung open. Underneath, he wore his marshal's uniform, a long blue coat with gold buttons down the front. When the coonskin coat swung back, Kate saw the silver star on his chest.

Yet as they headed out of Grantsburg, Kate had to fight down her fear. *What if Stretch finds out I'm the one who told?*

Driving back over the snowy roads, Big Gust told them stories about his boyhood in Sweden. As he talked, Kate felt better.

Each time she wondered what Stretch would think, she repeated Mrs. Berglund's verse to herself. "The Lord *is* on my side; I will not fear: What can man do to me?"

In spite of what Erik had said about the thefts, Big Gust was in good humor. More than once, he reached inside his large pockets.

Kate had heard he always carried candy for the children of Grantsburg, but she'd never seen it before. Now Big Gust drew peanuts in the shell from one pocket, a bag of Christmas candy from another.

"We'll stop at Berglunds' first," he told them.

When they reached the house, the marshal had to stoop down to get through the door. While Anders warmed up in the kitchen, Kate, Erik, and Big Gust followed Henry Berglund into the cellar. There the tall Swede had to crouch on the dirt floor to avoid bumping the ceiling.

Seeing the extra food, Mr. Berglund shook his head. "Someone must have brought it through the outside door. After I take in the potatoes, I cover that door with snow. This year I haven't gotten around to it."

Erik was excited. "Looks like our canning jars!" The bushel baskets with carrots, potatoes, and squash also seemed to be theirs. "And everything looks all right!" It seemed that nothing had frozen.

Kate had an idea. "Erik, did you say a jar was broken? Can you tell if one is missing?"

"Probably," answered Erik. "Mama told me how many she canned of each kind."

They separated the strawberries, blueberries, and raspberries into three groups and started counting.

"They're all here except one blueberry!" Erik told them.

When they left, Big Gust took the wagon track back of the house through the woods. As they drove, Kate felt uncomfortable, wondering if this was the way Stretch had gone.

Soon Big Gust stopped the sleigh in a pine grove, out of sight of Stretch's house. "You stay here," he said. "I'll go by myself."

Kate felt relieved. She was safe. Stretch wouldn't know she'd told the others about him.

The sun was edging down toward the horizon when Big Gust returned. "I found Stretch," he said. "And I found a pig that might be yours."

"Great!" exclaimed Anders.

But Big Gust's face was grim. "Stretch says the pig belongs to him."

Kate looked at Anders, and Anders looked at Erik. It was Anders who spoke. "That's just what we were afraid of. We can't prove a thing."

Big Gust shook his head. "Then I can't do a thing. Not without proof."

As the marshal sat down on the sleigh, Anders groaned. But Kate and Erik looked at one another. In that moment they remembered something.

"The cookstove!" Kate exclaimed.

In his excitement Erik laughed. "The lid was gone!"

"What're you talking about?" asked Anders.

Erik turned to Big Gust. "Did you happen to turn the pig over?"

The big man shook his head.

"Then we've got proof!" cried Kate.

In low voices, they explained to Big Gust, and he grinned.

Forgetting about what Stretch might think of her, Kate jumped down from the sleigh and hurried toward the house.

21

Christmas Morning

As Kate headed through the pines, Erik and Big Gust followed. Anders limped along on crutches, unable to make much progress through the snow.

Big Gust looked around and went back. With one easy swoop he picked up Anders. Again Anders looked embarrassed. At the same time he seemed grateful for the help.

To the village marshal Anders seemed to weigh nothing at all. Big Gust stretched out his long legs, moving without effort through the deep drifts.

Kate went straight for the small building where she and Anders had found Stretch before. When she pounded on the door, Stretch came out.

He grinned at her, and Kate remembered why she thought he was nice. Yet now that idea made her uncomfortable.

Then Stretch saw Big Gust, Anders, and Erik. The grin disappeared as though a mask slid over the boy's face.

"We want to take another look at the pig," the marshal told Stretch.

It took a moment for Kate's eyes to adjust to the dim light of the shed. Over in one corner was a wooden table. A frozen pig lay upon it, and Kate knew it was theirs.

"It's mine, I tell you," Stretch told Big Gust. "How come you're picking on me?"

The marshal seemed to fill the small shed. "Let's have a better look. What would you say if there was a stove lid frozen to the pig?"

Acting as if he didn't have a care in the world, Stretch walked to the table. Yet Kate saw the side of his face twitch.

Then Big Gust turned the pig over. Frozen to the bottom side was a cookstove lid!

Stretch's eyes flickered. Quickly he turned away, but not before Kate saw him bite his lip.

One moment Kate felt good. They had the proof they needed. The next moment she felt sick. As she glanced at Erik and Anders, Kate guessed they felt the same way.

She almost hated to ask Stretch more. "Your blue hand? Did you break a jar of Erik's blueberries?"

For a long moment Stretch hesitated. Finally he nodded.

"And you carried the jars in boxes and hid them in Berglunds' cellar?" Kate continued.

Stretch looked startled, as though wondering how she knew. Slowly he nodded again.

Anders had his own questions, and he was angry. "Josie's steer? Where is it?"

Stretch's shoulders slumped as he seemed to give up. "I took it where no one knew me. I sold it."

"Why, Stretch?" Big Gust's voice sounded as strong as iron, yet sad.

Stretch's face still seemed a mask, frozen like the pig. When he remained silent, Big Gust asked again. "Why did you do it?"

Kate felt surprised that a man so big could sound so kind.

Stretch must have heard the kindness too. His mask cracked. He looked at Kate, then away. When he spoke, he pushed the words out between his teeth. "I was hungry."

"You were *hungry*?" asked Big Gust. "A boy in northwest Wisconsin is hungry? I can't believe my ears!"

"At first I was hungry." Now Stretch was looking at the dirt floor. "Then I learned I could sell things to buy what I wanted."

"But why?" Kate felt numb, as though she wasn't really hearing Stretch.

Again he looked at Kate, then away. He spoke so quietly she could barely hear. "After Ma died, Pa started drinking. Every year he drank more. This fall he sold the cows. He sold the harvest. All he kept were the two horses."

They went to the house then. Big Gust tried to help Anders, but Anders shook his head.

"Not now!" he exclaimed, looking toward Stretch as though unwilling to be carried in front of him. Yet by the time Anders hobbled through the snow on crutches, he seemed to have difficulty moving another step.

The house was cold, and the supply of wood short, but Erik started a fire. Pulling up chairs, they huddled close.

Stretch told them more. "Pa and I had terrible fights. One night when he fell asleep, I took the money he got from selling everything. I knew he'd drink it up, so I hid it. The next day when I came home from school, Pa was gone. The place I hid the money was empty."

"Where is he now?" asked Big Gust.

Stretch shrugged his shoulders. "I don't know. I haven't seen him for a couple months."

"You've been living here all alone?" Anders asked, his voice low. "And no one knew?"

"Pa always kept to himself," explained Stretch. "Wasn't very neighborly. In winter we're always alone."

"Why didn't you tell us?" Anders asked.

Stretch looked embarrassed. "I didn't want you to know. I was scared of what you'd think of my family."

"So you just dropped out of school?"

Stretch nodded, but he didn't look at Anders.

"And what about Kate?" asked Erik. "How come you left when she fell through the ice?"

Stretch turned to her, his eyes strangely moist. "I'm sorry, Kate. I was so scared that I ran away."

Anger flooded Kate's heart. "I could have drowned!"

Stretch looked as though she had slapped him. In spite of his height, he seemed small as he slumped in his chair.

Watching him, Kate remembered what she'd learned from Mama. She drew a deep breath. Before she could change her mind, she spoke softly. "I forgive you, Stretch."

Big Gust put his large hand on Stretch's shoulder. "You'll need to work and pay back what you stole. We'll have a talk and decide how you can make things up to folks. But for now you come with me. We'll have Christmas first."

Stretch and Big Gust carried the pig to the sleigh. "We'll get your food back soon," the marshal promised Erik.

When Kate last saw Stretch, he was harnessing his horses. He and Big Gust would drive to the home of the tall Swede's sister.

"That's why Lutfisk growled at me, isn't it?" asked Kate, as she and Anders and Erik started out again.

Erik flicked the reins, and the horses moved ahead. "What're you talking about?"

"Remember the day I went through the ice? At first I thought Lutfisk was growling at me. But dogs seem to know which people they can trust, don't they? Lutfisk must have been looking at Stretch."

As they drove on, only the jingling of sleigh bells broke the silence.

Then Kate spoke up. "It's Christmas Eve," she said quietly. "We don't have the tree up."

"We don't even have it cut," said Anders. Usually the Nordstroms chopped down a pine on the afternoon of Christmas Eve. Now, as Anders lay in the back of the sleigh, he looked too tired to care.

The team knew they were headed home and set a brisk pace. When the sleigh hit a drift hard, Anders groaned. "Hey, com'on, Erik! That hurts!"

Erik stopped, helped Anders sit up, and pushed more straw under his bad ankle.

When Erik clucked at the horses, Anders spoke again. "You know, we have our pig. And you'll get your food back, Erik. But even if Stretch works to pay them, what about Josie's family? They're still out of meat for winter."

For a time the three were quiet, thinking about Josie's eight brothers and sisters.

"I know!" Anders exclaimed, sounding the best he had all day. "Let's surprise them! Tomorrow we'll see everyone in church. Let's ask each family if they want to give something to Swensons."

Erik agreed. "We can go around the next day, collecting it all."

"And we can see Josie's new kitten," Kate added.

"A kitten?" asked Anders. Even if it was Josie's, he didn't sound too excited.

"A mother cat died, and Josie's been feeding the baby to keep it alive. The kitten's so little Josie doesn't let it go outside. But every now and then it vanishes."

Erik looked at Kate and grinned. "Maybe there's another mystery to solve."

"Maybe." Kate laughed just thinking about it.

The wind was cold now and bit at their cheeks. Kate drew a scarf around her face. In her mind she saw the Windy Hill farmhouse. Mama would set a candle in the window.

"It says we're waiting for the Christ child," she had told them more than once.

But Kate knew that when Mama lit the candle, she also hoped it would draw Papa home.

"It's Christmas Eve," Kate said again. "Papa hasn't come."

The boys were silent, for there was nothing to say.

The sky was orange with the setting sun when Kate saw a small figure on the road far ahead. Closer and closer they came until she knew it was a man. A man walking with his back toward them.

His shoulders were hunched against the cold. His walk was tired, like someone with sore and bleeding feet. But somehow the man looked familiar.

It was Anders who pulled himself up to see and cried, "Papa!"

At the sound of Anders' voice, the man turned.

In the last glow of the sun, Kate saw it was true. "Papa!" she shouted. Into her cry rushed all the gladness that comes after a long wait.

Erik stopped the horses, and Papa reached into the sleigh to hug Anders. Kate jumped down for her hug, and Papa's arm went around her. His beard and lashes were full of ice, his lips cracked from the cold.

When he climbed onto the sleigh, his legs were stiff, but Papa's eyes shone. He was here with them! Home for Christmas!

And when they drove up to the Windy Hill farmhouse, Mama had four candles in the window.

The next morning Mama, Papa, Anders, Lars, Tina, and Kate got up at four o'clock. The house was cold, and the sky still dark.

When Erik's family came to give them a ride to church, they brought a large pine tree. Erik carried it into the front room, and the boughs reached to the ceiling.

Then all of them climbed into the sleigh for the early morning Christmas service. Lanterns bobbing, sleigh bells jingling, they headed into the frosty air.

Erik's father drove, and Mama sat beside Papa, unwilling to be parted, even during the trip to church. Papa had bundled her in a heavy robe, but Mama reached out and tucked her mittened hand beneath Papa's big glove.

The moon was still high in the sky when the horses started up the hill near Four Corners. Kate turned around and looked back to see a string of lanterns following them.

Off to the left was another road with lanterns bobbing in the night. At the top of the hill, lights came from straight ahead. And from far across the valley on the right shone still more lanterns.

From four directions they came—lanterns moving slowly toward church, small dots of light shining in the early morning darkness, growing larger.

When Kate and her family entered the darkened church, candles blazed from every window. More candles glimmered from the Christmas trees. And a candle seemed to glow in Kate's heart.

After the service, Erik's family came into the Windy Hill farmhouse for Christmas breads, cookies, and cakes. Then it was time for Kate to give Tina and Papa their presents.

As she sat down at the organ, she felt afraid. *What if I make a mistake? What will everyone think?* With all her heart she wanted to play well.

In that moment she remembered the hidden message. *The Lord is on my side; I will not fear.* Like Mrs. Berglund, Kate asked for help.

Her fingers grew steady. She wasn't scared anymore. Her notes sounded sure and strong.

As Kate played "Children of the Heavenly Father," someone moved to stand beside her. Yet when Kate looked up, it wasn't Tina she saw, but Mama. Mama with tears in her eyes.

Kate smiled at Papa and started the carol she had learned for him. "Silent Night, Holy Night. . . . Sleep in heavenly peace."

Then Kate received the biggest surprise of all. On the second verse Erik began to sing. His voice sounded scared at first, then clear and strong.

One after another, the others joined in. Erik's family. Tina. Lars. Mama and Papa. Then finally, Anders.

It was going to be a good Christmas, after all.

Acknowledgments

When I was thirteen years old, someone said to me, "Lois, do you have to ask so many questions?"

At the time I was embarrassed. By now I've discovered that curiosity is a necessary part of being a writer. Those who give answers become my cherished friends.

Among these are Gary and Cris Peterson. They didn't know I'd see in their organ more than a piece of furniture. But they do appreciate curiosity, and so, the organ on the cover is theirs.

Alton Jensen and the Grantsburg Historical Society provided information about countless details. Berdella Johnson shared her family stories and her knowledge of Swedish ways. Alice Biederman offered her gift for music and memories of Big Gust at her family's table. Her husband Leon talked of his experience in making skis. Bertha Iverson told about Spirit Lake School and the lanterns of Christmas morning.

Eunice Kanne gave me her research and wisdom as well as her books, *Pieces of the Past* and *Big Gust: Grantsburg's Legendary Giant*. Walter and Ella Johnson knew about barbed wire fences, boots, and canning jars. Helen Tyberg remembered the cold rides and warm bricks of her childhood. Diane Brask described her experiences with tree climbing, animals, and sprained ankles. Mildred Hedlund told about her relative, Big Gust, and her love for his sister. Randy Klawitter reminded me that a young man can learn to walk in the old ways.

Charette Barta, Ron Klug, Carol Johnson, Jerry Foley, Penny Stokes, and Terry White helped with the manuscript. My husband Roy gave his ideas, his understanding of my curiosity, and his love.

And so, a book is never entirely mine. It belongs to all of you who read and to all of you who know and appreciate the past. I thank you!

THE DISAPPEARING STRANGER

Lois Walfrid Johnson

BETHANY HOUSE PUBLISHERS
MINNEAPOLIS, MINNESOTA 55438

Except for historic characters—Big Gust, Trader Carlson, and A. Hult—the characters in this book are fictitious. Any resemblance to persons living or dead is coincidental.

Copyright © 1990
Lois Walfrid Johnson
All Rights Reserved

Published by Bethany House Publishers
A Ministry of Bethany Fellowship, Inc.
6820 Auto Club Road, Minneapolis, Minnesota 55438

Printed in the United States of America

Library of Congress Cataloging-in-Publication Data

Johnson, Lois Walfrid.
    The disappearing stranger / Lois W. Johnson.
        p. cm. — (The Adventures of the northwoods ; bk. 1)
    Summary: When her mother marries Mr. Nordstrom, Kate moves to a farm in northwest Wisconsin, solves a mystery, and learns to adjust to her new stepfamily.

    [1. Swedish Americans—Fiction. 2. Stepfamilies—Fiction. 3. Mystery and detective stories. 4. Christian life—Fiction.]
    I. Title. II. Series: Johnson, Lois Walfrid. Adventures of the northwoods ; bk. 1.
PZ7.J63255Di   1990
[Fic]—dc20   90–2
ISBN 1–55661–100–5   CIP
                                                                       AC

To Marie Johnson, the Mama in the picture,
and to Mom and Dad Walfrid,
for telling me the way it was.

LOIS WALFRID JOHNSON is the bestselling author of more than twenty books. These include *You're Worth More Than You Think!* and other Gold Medallion winners in the LET'S-TALK-ABOUT-IT STORIES FOR KIDS series about making choices. Novels in the ADVENTURES OF THE NORTHWOODS series have received awards from Excellence in Media, the Wisconsin State Historical Society, and the Council for Wisconsin Writers.

Lois has a great interest in historical mystery novels, as you may be able to tell! She and her husband, Roy, are the parents of a blended family and live in rural Wisconsin.

Preface

Yes, there really was a train called the Blueberry Special. In the early 1900's it chugged its way into northwest Wisconsin, then turned around on the same track.

So, too, was there a man of great strength—a seven-foot, six-inch tall village marshal named Big Gust. Loved by law-abiding citizens, he quickly dealt with troublemakers in the small town of Grantsburg.

Near the shores of Spirit Lake, the one-room country school still stands, though children no longer come there for learnin'. Through the pages of this book you may hear the sound of their laughter.

If you had lived in that time you could have known people like Kate and Anders, Mama and Papa, Lars and Tina. You could have known Lutfisk, their dog, and visited Windy Hill, their farm on the edge of the big woods.

It's not too late. Even now, you can join Kate and Anders in the adventure of *The Disappearing Stranger*.

Adventures of the Northwoods

1. *The Disappearing Stranger*
2. *The Hidden Message*
3. *The Creeping Shadows*
4. *The Vanishing Footprints*
5. *Trouble at Wild River*
6. *The Mysterious Hideaway*
7. *Grandpa's Stolen Treasure*
8. *The Runaway Clown*
9. *Mystery of the Missing Map*
10. *Disaster on Windy Hill*

Contents

1. Kate's Secret Plan 11
2. Sunday Surprise 18
3. Mama's Choice 24
4. The Blueberry Special 30
5. Big Brother 37
6. Trapped! 45
7. Trouble Ahead 52
8. Spirit Lake School 59
9. The Mysterious Stranger 66
10. Bees! 71
11. View From the Bell Tower 77
12. Another Surprise 84
13. The Big Storm 91
14. Discovery! 98
15. Missing! 105
16. County Fair 111
17. Scaredy-cat? 116
18. The Syrup Pail 121
19. Footsteps in the Night 128
20. Race Against Time 134
Acknowledgments 143

1

Kate's Secret Plan

On the way home from school Katherine O'Connell slowed her steps. Around her, the noises of Minneapolis filled the street. A horse trotted past, clip-clopping on the cobblestones. Circling a mound of snow, Kate found a place to stop.

The black hair that escaped her braid curled around her face. In the afternoon sunlight her deep blue eyes sparkled. The air felt warm for a Minnesota winter, but twelve-year-old Kate barely noticed. She had an idea.

Rolling it around in her mind, she considered the idea from this way and that. More than once she had tumbled headlong into a plan, sometimes with surprising results. Yet this one might work.

At last Kate tossed her head. Flipping her long braid over her shoulder, she made up her mind.

Walking quickly, she plunged down the street. The church was only a block away. A year ago she wouldn't have thought of going there for help. But that was before Daddy died.

Even now, Kate felt surprised by her idea. Yet it was a good one. She felt sure of that.

At the bottom of the church steps she paused, suddenly

afraid. From here Kate could barely see the tall steeple reaching to the sky. Across the street a grocery wagon stopped, and a boy climbed down. Lifting a wooden box filled with food, he carried it into a house.

Seeing him there, Kate knew it was time to be home. Mama would wonder where she was.

Turning, Kate hurried up the wide stone steps. As she pulled open the heavy door, she tried to look like the young lady Mama wanted her to be. Somehow Kate always forgot.

Inside, where the sunlight did not reach, the entryway seemed dim and cold. Quickly Kate opened another door.

In the main part of the church, afternoon sunlight brightened the large windows. Pews stretched away to the front. Kate stood there a moment, thinking about Mama. Last night she had cried in the dark again.

When Kate asked, "Are you all right?" Mama sniffled her yes.

"Are you lonesome for Daddy?" Kate asked next.

Mama's answer sounded clearer, as though she'd pulled the quilt away from her head. "Yes, Kate. Go back to sleep."

But Kate had one more question. "Mama, do you ever get lonesome for Sweden?"

At the age of seventeen Mama had come from Sweden by herself. "Sometimes," she answered, her voice soft. "Sometimes."

Mama's words scared Kate. *What if she decides to go back to Sweden? I'd have to leave all my friends—Sarah Livingston and Michael Reilly—*

Often the children teased Michael, saying, "You're sweet on Kate!" Michael always turned red, but he never denied it.

In the darkness of night Kate lay there a long time before going back to sleep, wondering, *What can I do?*

Now Kate started down the side aisle of the church. As she passed the organ, she stopped and looked back. "Do I dare?" she asked herself, then felt surprised she'd spoken aloud.

As she looked around, the church seemed empty.

Moving quickly, Kate turned back to the pipe organ. Again she glanced around. "No one will know," she muttered. Without a sound Kate slid onto the bench.

Kate's Secret Plan

For a long time she'd wanted to sit there, feeling the ivory keys beneath her fingers. For what seemed forever she'd wanted to make the wonderful big sounds the organist played every Sunday. Whenever the sermon seemed long, Kate thought about the sound of the music.

She knew the organ wouldn't work without someone hand pumping the bellows that brought in air. Yet she touched the keys the way the organist did, pretending she knew how to play. *I could be a great organist. I could travel around America putting on concerts. If only I could learn.*

Then from somewhere in the dimly lit corners came a sound. In a second Kate was off the bench, starting down the aisle once more.

At the front of the church, she reached a hallway, then a large door. Kate straightened her shoulders, hoping she looked taller. Before she could change her mind, she raised her hand and knocked.

As the sound echoed in the stillness, Kate wished she hadn't come. In all her twelve years she'd never been so scared. Except when Daddy died, that is.

Maybe Pastor Munson won't be here. Kate felt torn between wanting to see him and fearing what he'd think. Just as she turned to run, the door opened.

"Kate!" exclaimed the pastor. *"God dag!"*

His words sounded like "Good dog," and Kate knew only a few words of Swedish. Because Daddy was Irish and Mama Swedish, Kate spoke English at home. Yet she knew Pastor Munson was saying, "Good day," and managed to squeak out her hello.

Whenever Pastor Munson stood in the front of the church, he looked tall and stern. Now as Kate sat down, he seemed still more frightening.

"What can I do for you?" he asked from his big chair behind the big desk.

Kate's hands tightened, and she found herself bunching her skirt inside nervous fingers. *I wish I'd never come. Where do I begin?*

In the silence someone knocked on the door. "Excuse me,"

said Pastor Munson. "I'll be right back."

As he went into the hallway, Kate looked around for a way of escape. Books lined two walls of the study. On the third wall hung a large calendar. JANUARY, 1906. Nearby, the sun streamed through a window.

Seeing the sunlight, Kate felt better. When Pastor Munson returned, she knew what to say.

This time he smiled as he asked, "Can I help you with something?"

Kate swallowed. "When you preached Sunday—" She stopped, afraid to go on. For a moment she waited, but he waited too.

"Yah?" It was the Swedish yes, and his voice sounded encouraging. Yet Kate's hand shook as she reached up and touched the small locket on a chain around her neck. She thought of Daddy and how he'd given her the locket on her last birthday before he died.

Remembering Daddy gave Kate courage. Her voice steadied. "In church on Sunday you said we could talk to you when we have a problem."

Pastor Munson nodded, and Kate went on. "Well, I have a problem. Or rather, Mama has a problem."

"Yah?" asked Pastor Munson again.

Kate had to go on. "Mama needs a husband."

Pastor Munson cleared his throat. "Oh, indeed?"

Now Kate's words came in a rush. "She's always tired. She works hard sewing dresses for rich ladies. And she's been sick, off and on all fall."

Kate stopped, and Pastor Munson nodded, "Yah." This time the word wasn't a question.

"But I think it's more. Since Daddy died she's been so—"

Pastor Munson finished for her. "Hopeless."

"All of Mama's family lives in Sweden." For a moment Kate was silent, looking at her hands as they twisted in her lap. Then she tried again. "Sometimes when I wake up at night Mama's crying. In the morning she pretends she's all right. But her eyes—"

"Look sad."

Kate's Secret Plan

"Yah," said Kate, surprised she'd used the Swedish yes.

Whenever she heard Mama crying, Kate longed to be a family again. To have Daddy back, telling his funny stories. To sing together and laugh. Even to herself, Kate couldn't quite explain it. But to love each other.

She tried to put the thought away. Daddy couldn't come back, not ever.

Kate felt relieved that Pastor Munson seemed to understand about Mama. Somehow he didn't seem quite so stern. In fact, his eyes looked kind. When he smiled, she knew he wasn't making fun of her, the way boys at school might do.

"What's it been? A year now since your papa died in that construction accident?"

Kate nodded. Daddy had been strong, as though nothing would ever happen to him. He'd been a good carpenter. When he came home from work, he always swung her off the floor with a big hug. Sometimes he danced around the kitchen, doing an Irish jig. Tears came into Kate's eyes just thinking about it.

A slow smile spread across Pastor Munson's face. "I think you're right. Your mama needs a husband."

"You do?"

"Yah, surely. But I have a question. Do you feel ready to have a new papa?"

Suddenly Kate felt afraid. She hadn't thought about that.

"It would change your life, you know. A new papa might have a family of his own."

"Maybe I'd get a sister," Kate answered. "I've always wanted a little sister. But what if I got a *brother*? That would be *awful*." To herself she added, *Unless it was someone like Michael, that is.*

For a moment she sat there, biting her lip and thinking. *Pastor Munson will find a husband from Minneapolis. I can still see my friends. I can learn to play the organ.*

Then she remembered Mama crying at night. More than anything, she wanted Mama happy again.

In that moment Kate made up her mind. Inside, she felt uneasy, as though something wasn't quite right. Yet she pushed the feeling away. When she answered, her voice was clear and strong. "I want Mama to have a new husband."

"Then I'll pray," answered Pastor Munson.

"And you'll help?"

"If I can."

"You won't tell Mama I've been here?"

Pastor Munson shook his head, his face solemn. "It'll be our secret."

"Good." Kate felt relieved. She stood up to go. "It's all settled then."

But Pastor Munson held up his hand. "Just a minute, young lady."

Kate stopped in her flight to the door.

"Before you go, we need to pray about it. We better ask God to help us."

Kate nodded. "I thought you'd be good at that."

"Oh, I am. I've had lots of practice." His dark eyes twinkled. "But since you asked my help, I thought you'd like to pray for me."

"Me? *I* pray for *you*?"

"Yah." The word was soft. Then the room was silent, filled with waiting.

"Me?" Kate asked again. Even when she had felt the most scared, she hadn't thought of anything that awful. "But that's what pastors are paid for."

Pastor Munson's eyes seemed to smile, yet his voice sounded serious. "It's hard being a matchmaker. I think I need God's help."

Slowly Kate sat down again. Slowly she bowed her head. Her thoughts felt like the squirrels racing up and down the tree outside the church. *What do I say?* she wondered in panic. *Me pray for him?*

"Just make it simple," said Pastor Munson as though reading her thoughts.

That made Kate even more uncomfortable. In the silence a clock ticked, and the moment stretched long between them. Kate's ideas refused to come out in order. For a long time she'd been angry at God. Often she'd told him, "If you love me, God, why did you let Daddy die?" For a long time she'd told herself,

"God can't possibly hear my prayer."

But Kate felt desperate. For Mama's sake she needed to try. And Pastor Munson waited.

Kate squeezed her eyes shut and cleared her throat. "Mama needs your help, God," she prayed. "She needs a husband. Help Pastor Munson find one. Ah-men."

As Kate looked up, Pastor Munson opened his eyes. A wide smile lit his face. Standing up, he reached out his hand to shake Kate's. "Thank you. I'll do the best I can."

Somehow Kate felt better. Mumbling a quick thanks, she headed for the door. As she reached the safety of the hallway, she even felt good about what she'd done.

She turned back to Pastor Munson. "I can hardly wait to see what happens!"

2

Sunday Surprise

Outside, Kate ran the entire two blocks to where she and Mama rented rooms on the second floor of a large house. Bounding up the steps, Kate flung open the kitchen door. A man stood just inside—a heavyset man with his back toward Kate.

Even without seeing his face, she knew who it was—the landlord, asking for his rent. A shiver slid down Kate's spine, a shiver not caused by the January cold.

"I won't force you out in the middle of winter," he was saying. He drew himself up to his full height. "After all, I'm a just man. But mark my words, by March 15 for sure."

Stepping around Kate, he headed down the stairs.

Mama stood by the wood cookstove. In the lamplight her hair looked golden. It was drawn up, piled on top of her head. Quiet tears wet her cheeks.

Kate walked into her mother's arms, and Mama hugged her. "It's all right, Kate. It's all right."

But Kate felt sure that it wasn't. Stepping back, she looked up into Mama's face. Kate knew her own eyes were a deeper blue than Mama's. Mama also was tall for a woman, and Kate was short for her age. Now Kate cried out in protest, "I hate him! I hate him!"

Mama's stern voice interrupted. "Stop it, Kate!" She turned to the cookstove and stirred the watery stew. When she spoke again, her voice sounded tired. "He's only asking for what is his. If I could just earn more money, we'd keep up."

Kate stalked out of the kitchen, her hands over her ears. She knew it was true, but didn't want to hear the hopelessness in Mama's words. Sometimes Mama sewed far into the night. Other times it was hard to find work.

"Is there anything else we can sell?" asked Kate, looking around.

Mama followed her into the sitting room, her shoulders slumped with discouragement.

"I'll find more work," Kate said, her voice angry. "I'll drop out of school."

"No!" exclaimed Mama. "You're working enough after school and Saturdays. You need book learning to make your way."

"Dumb old Mr. Mark-My-Words!" Kate muttered, then bit her lip. She didn't want to argue with Mama. They'd talked about all this before. But the pain inside Kate went deep.

For two long weeks she woke up every morning, hoping she'd hear about a husband for Mama. "The rest of January, then February," Kate told her one morning. "Fifteen days in March, and he'll make us leave. Where will we go?"

Mama didn't answer, but a new line creased her forehead.

As Kate waited and wondered, the snowy days stretched out forever. *Maybe Pastor Munson forgot his promise. Maybe it's too big an order, even for God.*

Then one Saturday in the middle of January Mama sold another piece of furniture. Coming home, she said, "Help me, Kate. Let's move my trunk into the dining room."

Kate grabbed hold of the leather handle on one end. Mama took the handle on the opposite side. Together they slid the trunk across the floor of their small sitting room. A curl tumbled onto Mama's forehead, making her look young and helpless.

But Kate knew that Mama was not helpless. Kate knew the story of the wooden trunk and wanted to hear it again. "It came all the way from Sweden?"

"Yah," said Mama. "I had the America fever. All over Sweden

people left. I just had to go to America!"

"And your papa built this trunk?" Kate asked the way she had since she was little.

Mama nodded. "I worked on a farm as a hired girl. I saved everything I earned for a ticket to America. Finally when I was seventeen, my papa—your grandpapa—threw up his hands. 'All right, all right! It's useless trying to keep you here!' He started building the trunk.

"When it was time for me to leave, Mama didn't want to go to the train. She said, 'I just can't manage it.' So Papa and I went. It was the only time I ever saw him cry."

"And when you got to America you worked as a maid?" prodded Kate, the way she always did.

"In a boardinghouse," Mama answered. "I saved my money. I had my picture taken and sent it home to Mama and Papa."

Letting go of the trunk handle, Mama went into the bedroom. She returned with a framed picture. "That's when they had *this* taken."

Mama's finger pointed. "Mama and Papa sitting in the middle. My five sisters and two brothers around them. And that's Sophia—the sister closest in age. She's holding *my* picture."

"So you could still be part of the family," said Kate, hoping Mama would go on.

But for once Mama didn't tell the rest of the story. Putting down the picture, she took the trunk handle again. "Over here," she said, giving a mighty tug. "Next to the kitchen door."

When the trunk was in place, Mama set the picture on its wide, flat top. Then Kate knew why Mama wanted to move the trunk. When she started supper, Mama looked through the doorway at the picture. She looked that way often.

The sadness in Mama's large blue eyes made Kate uneasy. *What if she decides to go back to Sweden?* Kate wondered more than once.

At the same time, there was something about the picture that drew Kate. Deep inside she ached with wanting to be part of a big family. *Will Mama and I ever be really happy again?*

The next morning Kate was still thinking about the picture when she and Mama set out for Sunday services. Inside the church, Mama headed for the pew where she knew Kate liked to sit. From there Kate could watch the organist. Listening to the big sounds, she forgot her worry about Mama. During the sermon she let the songs play over and over in her mind. At last she felt sure she remembered every note.

As the sermon dragged on, Kate thought about Jenny Lind. People called her the Swedish nightingale because of the way she sang. Long before Kate was born, Miss Lind toured the United States, giving concerts and hope.

If I could play the organ, I'd make people feel that way. Even Mama would feel better. She'd laugh the way she used to when Papa sang. As though it were yesterday, Kate remembered Papa's Irish tenor voice.

When Pastor Munson shook their hands after church, he pulled Kate and Mama aside. "Mrs. Munson has a fine chicken today. Will you join us for dinner?"

The pastor and his wife lived next to the church. When Kate and Mama entered the parlor, they discovered someone already there. Pastor Munson introduced him. "This is Carl Nordstrom. He visited our church today."

As Mama and Mr. Nordstrom said their *"God dag's,"* Kate looked quickly at Pastor Munson. His face was as solemn as ever, but a smile tugged at the corners of his mouth. Just in time Kate swallowed a giggle. He hadn't forgotten his promise!

During the meal, Kate looked at Mr. Nordstrom whenever she could. His black suit coat covered wide, strong shoulders, and Kate guessed he must be well over six feet tall. His brown hair and moustache and beard were neatly trimmed. His skin looked like Daddy's from working outside.

Kate liked Mr. Nordstrom. Maybe he'd make a good husband for Mama.

As they ate chicken and mashed potatoes and gravy, Pastor Munson asked Mr. Nordstrom about his family. "Tina is four, Lars almost nine, and Anders twelve," he answered in an accent like Mama's. Now and then he used Swedish words, but his English was good.

A little sister! Kate wanted to know more. *I've always wanted a younger sister. But two brothers? Sarah says that brothers are terrible pests.*

"So, you know my old friend, Rev. Hult?" asked Pastor Munson.

Mr. Nordstrom nodded. "He's my pastor in Trade Lake. He said to give you greetings when I came to Minneapolis."

"Trade Lake?" asked Kate. She knew only grownups were supposed to speak, but she couldn't help it.

"Trade Lake, Wisconsin," answered Mr. Nordstrom. "It's the town closest to my farm. Trader Carlson has a big store there. Indians from miles around bring their furs to him."

"Oh," said Kate, her voice small. "You live in Wisconsin?" Her mind filled with the horror of it. *Wisconsin would be even worse than Sweden! Sarah says Wisconsin is a wilderness.*

Mr. Nordstrom nodded. "Yah, I'm a farmer."

"And your farm is in the big woods of Wisconsin?" Mama asked.

"On the edge of a big woods," said Mr. Nordstrom. "And on the edge of a steep hill. Windy Hill Farm, we call it."

His voice warmed with enthusiasm. "In the west we see sunsets over Rice Lake. South of the house I've cleared a field for corn, and north of the barn I'm clearing another. It's a good place to live."

But Kate wasn't impressed. "Do you have bears?" she asked, the horror within her growing. Flipping her long braid over her shoulder, she leaned forward. "My friend Sarah says there are big bears in Wisconsin."

Mr. Nordstrom smiled. "Yah, we have bears, sometimes five-hundred-pound ones. But they're more afraid of us than we need to be of them."

Kate didn't believe him. "But Sarah says bears are wild and mean and knock down log cabins, and break open bee hives, and—"

"Kate," Mama's voice was soft, but with a warning running through it. It was her reminder that children should be seen and not heard.

By now Kate had changed her mind. She didn't like the idea of Mr. Nordstrom from Wisconsin. She wished he'd go home and stay there.

"Mostly we have big Swedes," Mr. Nordstrom went on. "In

Grantsburg, where the train comes in, the village marshal is seven and a half feet tall and three hundred sixty pounds. He takes good care of any troublemakers!"

"Seven and a half feet?" Kate forgot to be quiet. She couldn't imagine someone that tall. Then she wondered about something else. "What kind of troublemakers do you have in Wisconsin?"

But Mama had questions of her own. "And your wife? How does she like living in the wilderness?"

Suddenly Kate felt scared, wishing Mama wouldn't ask. Now she'd find out.

Quickly Kate looked at Pastor Munson. Once more, a smile played around the corners of his mouth. Kate wished she could run away and hide.

Mr. Nordstrom turned to Mama, his eyes steady. "My wife died eight months ago. She had scarlet fever."

"I'm sorry," said Mama simply. "My husband died too—in a construction accident."

For a moment they looked at each other, Mr. Nordstrom's blue eyes meeting Mama's even bluer ones.

Again Kate felt scared. *This isn't the way it's supposed to be!* She wished Mama wouldn't look so beautiful. *She's supposed to get a husband from Minneapolis. She's supposed to stay right here.*

When it was time to say thanks for the meal, Mr. Nordstrom walked Kate and Mama home. Kate walked fast, wishing they wouldn't talk so much.

She liked seeing the light back in Mama's eyes. She liked hearing Mama laugh again. But she didn't like anything else about Mr. Nordstrom's visit.

That awful, nervous feeling in Kate's stomach wouldn't go away. What if Mama decided to marry Mr. Nordstrom? What if he asked them to move to the wilderness of Wisconsin? Kate couldn't think of anything worse.

3

Mama's Choice

After that, letters came from Wisconsin much too often for Kate's way of thinking. Each time a new one arrived, she felt more afraid. Mama's blue eyes sparkled all the time now. Often she asked, "Is there mail for me?"

One afternoon in February Mr. Nordstrom came to visit. When he left, Mama told Kate that in a month she and Mr. Nordstrom would get married.

"But do you love him?" asked Kate, suddenly forgetting about the rent they couldn't pay and how Mama used to cry during the night. "Do you love him the way you loved Daddy?"

"Not yet," answered Mama calmly. "But I will."

"You *will*?"

"I loved your Daddy very much." Mama's voice was warm with remembering. "He'll always have a special place in my life. Nothing can change that."

"But, Mama—" Kate interrupted.

Mama acted as though she hadn't heard. "Once your daddy and I talked. We talked about what I'd do if something happened to him." Suddenly Mama's eyes filled with tears.

She wiped them away and struggled to speak. "I didn't want to think about it. I didn't want anything to touch our love. But death did."

Mama swallowed, then went on. "On that day your daddy told me—"

"You'd have to go on," Kate finished the sentence. "You'd have to face things, even though you're afraid."

Mama smiled, a gentle smile that reached her eyes. "How did you know?"

In that moment Kate felt very grown up. "Once he said the same thing to me."

Mama opened her arms. Her hug felt good. When she spoke again, her words were muffled in Kate's hair. "I've prayed, and I believe Mr. Nordstrom is God's answer to help us. He's a good man, a kind man, a Christian. He'll take care of us. And I can help him."

"You'd marry him without *love*?" Kate was so startled she moved away from Mama's hug. "The kind of love you had for Daddy?" When she and Pastor Munson prayed, Kate thought Mama would wear a beautiful new dress and her eyes would shine with happiness.

Right now Mama's eyes were shiny with tears, but her voice was strong. "As we work together, I'll grow to love him. God's given me peace."

"God!" Kate wanted to spit out. Just in time she caught herself. She didn't dare tell Mama what she thought about God. Or about Pastor Munson for writing to Wisconsin for a husband. Mama could be stubborn, as stubborn as Kate.

"Aren't you afraid of living in a wilderness?" Kate asked, instead of what she wanted to say. "There'll be all kinds of scary, strange things."

Mama didn't answer, and Kate went on. "I'd like a little sister and a happy family. But two *brothers*? And one of them my age?"

Still Mama was silent.

Kate's voice rose. "I'd have to leave all my friends!"

"Yah," Mama answered, and Kate felt surprised. When Daddy was alive, she always said the English yes.

"Yah," Mama said again. "I'm sorry about that. But instead you'll have a family. And you'll make new friends."

"New friends in a wilderness? Sarah says we'd live in a log cabin. She says it's uncivilized, that wild animals run all over the place. We'd be out in the middle of nowhere!"

"Kate, wait and see," said Mama.

"I can't take organ lessons in a wilderness!"

A shadow crossed Mama's face. She sighed. "I know, Kate. But wait and see. Maybe it won't be as bad as you think."

"Wait and see? This is my *life*!" Kate's voice ended on a wail. She felt angry about the way God answered her prayer. Even more, she felt scared. Scared because Mama had accepted Mr. Nordstrom's offer of marriage. Scared about leaving Sarah and Michael and her other friends. Scared about the way her world was going to change.

Flipping her braid over her shoulder, Kate stood as tall as she could. "If I'd known this would happen, I never would have talked to Pastor Munson about you!"

"You *what*?" Mama's blue eyes were dark with anger. "*You* talked to Pastor Munson about *me*?"

"Oh!" Kate clapped her hand over her mouth. But it was too late.

"Just exactly what did you say, Katherine Marie O'Connell?"

Mama waited until the story came out. When Kate finished, two bright red spots flushed Mama's cheeks. Kate had never seen her so angry.

"Well, if that's the matter of it," Mama said, "I certainly will not see Mr. Carl Nordstrom from Wisconsin again. Never again. If he thinks I'm out looking for a husband—"

As the tears welled up in Mama's eyes, she whirled and stomped into the bedroom. Never before had Kate heard Mama slam a door. The sound echoed through their upstairs rooms.

Kate sank down on the floor and buried her face in her hands. It was just what she wanted. Yet it was so awful hurting Mama, so awful taking the happiness out of her eyes.

Then Kate remembered Mr. Mark-My-Words and the rent they weren't able to pay. March 15 was only a month away.

Kate felt scared again—more scared than she'd ever felt about living in a wilderness.

I can't even dream of a family anymore. Maybe living in Wisconsin wouldn't have been so bad after all.

In the two weeks that followed, Kate saw at least five letters addressed to Mrs. Ingrid O'Connell. Mama didn't answer one of them.

"Good!" Kate told herself. "We won't have to move to Wisconsin!" Yet the idea didn't please her the way it once would. As the days passed with Mama pretending nothing had happened, Kate felt ashamed. She felt even worse when she woke up to Mama crying at night.

Then one Friday evening, Kate heard a knock on the door. Opening it, she found Mr. Nordstrom on the steps. Under a long coonskin coat, he wore his black suit. His moustache and beard were trimmed close to his sun-weathered face.

" 'Evening, Kate," he said, tipping his hat. "I'd like to see your mama."

Kate backed away from the door. "What do you want?" she blurted out. "Train tickets cost money. It must be serious."

A strange look crossed Mr. Nordstrom's face. Kate felt embarrassed at being so forward. Then she remembered her manners. "Mama's here. Please come in."

In the sitting room, Mama put down her sewing and stood up. She did not look pleased. "Good evening, Mr. Nordstrom," she said, her voice stiff and formal. Yet as she hung up his coat, a soft pink flushed her cheeks.

When Mama sat down again, Mr. Nordstrom pulled up a chair opposite her. He looked even more uncomfortable than Mama. Twice he cleared his throat, but no words came.

Kate could hardly wait to hear what they'd say. Yet as she started to sit down, Mama turned to her.

"Thank you, Kate." That was Mama's way of telling her to leave.

Dragging her feet, Kate headed for the bedroom. Once inside, she left the door open a crack, then slid down to the floor, peeking through. Both Mama and Mr. Nordstrom sat exactly where they needed to be for Kate to see.

Mama's face looked frozen, as though she were the one who'd come in from the February night. "You must have had a cold trip, Mr. Nordstrom," she said, her lips without their usual smile. "I have some coffee on the back of the stove. Would you like a cup?"

Soon Mama was back with a plate of cookies, cups, and saucers. The strands of hair that had fallen around her face during supper were now in place.

When Mama and Mr. Nordstrom pulled up chairs at the table, he took a long swallow of coffee, then coughed.

Burned his tongue! thought Kate. She almost felt glad for his discomfort. As he quickly set down his cup, it rattled in the saucer.

Mama offered no sympathy. "You shouldn't have come, Mr. Nordstrom."

"I wanted to, Mrs. O'Connell," he answered, his voice just as stiff as Mama's. As he poured the coffee into his saucer, Kate saw determination in his eyes.

"My daughter was forward," said Mama, her voice soft and embarrassed. "I didn't know what she had done."

Mr. Nordstrom's low, steady voice was harder to hear. Just barely Kate picked out a word now and then. Back and forth he and Mama talked.

Then Mr. Nordstrom's words were clear. "I need a wife. Maybe you need a husband. My children need a mother. Maybe Kate needs a father."

For the first time Mama laughed. "She needs a father all right. One that takes her over his knee!"

Mr. Nordstrom's deep laugh joined Mama's. "And how about you?" he asked gently.

"I was happy before—" Mama stopped, and Kate leaned closer to the door, straining to hear.

"Before your husband died?"

Slowly Mama nodded, but didn't meet Mr. Nordstrom's eyes. Kate wished she knew what Mama really wanted to say.

Mr. Nordstrom seemed to guess. "And you'd like to marry a man you love."

Mama looked up, surprise in her blue eyes. "Yah," she said softly, sounding Swedish again.

Standing suddenly, Mr. Nordstrom strolled over to the window. For a long time he gazed down into the street. Kate knew there was only one thing to see—the gas streetlight. Yet Mr. Nordstrom looked down as though his life depended on it.

Then he seemed to make up his mind. Turning, he walked over to stand in front of Mama. There he waited until she looked into his eyes.

"How we met isn't what's most important," he said. "We can help each other."

He cleared his throat. The words seemed hard for him. "I can't promise that you'll love me. But we were friends before you found out what Kate did. Shall we start over again?"

For a long minute there was no sound in the room. Kate waited, afraid to breathe. Mama looked at Mr. Nordstrom as though thinking about what he'd said. Then she nodded and smiled.

"It's warm for February," said Mr. Nordstrom. "Let's take a walk."

Mama nodded again and stood up. Quickly she moved across the sitting room to the bedroom. Kate scrambled to her feet, but not fast enough. As Mama swung wide the door, it slammed into Kate. Mama didn't seem surprised to find her there.

As Mama and Mr. Nordstrom left for their walk, a scared feeling started in the pit of Kate's stomach. No one needed to tell her. Mama and Mr. Nordstrom would get married. What would it really be like living in a wilderness?

4

The Blueberry Special

"Will Mr. Nordstrom's children like me?" Kate asked Mama as they waited on the platform of the train depot.

That morning, Kate, Mama, and Mr. Nordstrom had boarded a Northern Pacific train and traveled north to Rush City. Now Mama's new husband was buying tickets for another train, the Blueberry Special, which would take them into northwest Wisconsin.

Kate shivered in the March wind, but the coldness was in her heart. "What will his children be like?" she asked Mama for the one hundredth time.

For the one hundredth time Mama answered, "As soon as we get to Grantsburg you'll find out!"

Train tickets were expensive, so Mr. Nordstrom's children had stayed on the farm when he came to marry Mama. One moment Kate felt impatient to meet them. The next moment she dreaded the idea. Her scared feelings wouldn't go away.

Lost in thought, she didn't notice a man hurrying around the corner of the depot. Bumping into Kate, he almost knocked her down.

"Pardon me, miss," he said as she caught herself. But the

apology didn't reach his gray eyes.

Without waiting to see if she was all right, the man hurried off, his shoes clicking on the wooden platform. Kate watched him go. Then a cart piled high with luggage rumbled between them.

On one end of the cart sat Mama's wooden trunk from Sweden. Two men grabbed the leather handles and swung it through the wide door of the baggage car.

The trunk was heavy, Kate knew. When Mama sold everything she could to pay the rent, only a little money was left over. The rest of their possessions she packed in the trunk.

The cold March wind stung Kate's eyes, but it wasn't the wind that brought tears. Somehow the trunk seemed like home, a home that was packed away. Yet Mama couldn't pack away Kate's feelings.

By now Kate knew even more about Wisconsin, and her thoughts spilled out. "Sarah said there're just log cabins in Wisconsin."

Mama laughed. "Mr. Nordstrom lives in a white frame house."

Kate didn't believe her. "In winter the wind blows through the cracks between the logs. In summer bugs crawl in."

Mama laughed again. "Oh, Kate."

"Sarah says there won't be any other people around for miles. Just bears. Lots of bears." Kate felt sure Sarah was right about that too.

But Mama seemed undisturbed. Her cheeks were still flushed, her blue eyes happy. Yesterday she and Mr. Nordstrom had stood before Pastor Munson as he married them.

Mama had asked Kate to stand up with them—to be her maid of honor. Mama's smile was soft as she looked into Mr. Nordstrom's eyes and said, "I do!" Kate knew Mama meant that promise to last forever. Mr. Nordstrom's "I do!" was even stronger.

Kate had tried to put on a smile, but needed to swallow her anger. "I'll never learn to play the organ in a wilderness!" she nearly cried out. Then she thought of her friends. *I might never see Sarah and Michael again.*

When Kate told them goodbye, she felt as if she were going

off to the end of the world. *Maybe I am.* Remembering her new brothers and sister, she wondered, *Will they like me?* Kate felt hollow inside, scared about starting a new life.

"Mama? Will you tell me about Daddy?" Kate's voice sounded small and uncertain.

"Again?" asked Mama.

"Again," answered Kate.

As though guessing how Kate felt about Mr. Nordstrom, Mama sighed. Yet she told the story once more. Kate listened the way she had since she was a little girl.

"Brendan and I met on the day I was going to buy a ticket and go back to Sweden," Mama began. "He lived at the boardinghouse where I worked as a maid."

Mama's eyes grew warm with remembering. "He came from Ireland about the time I came from Sweden. Swedes said to me, 'You're not going to marry an Irishman?' And the Irish told him, 'You're not going to marry a Swede? A good-lookin' lad like you?' Brendan always smiled and told them, 'She's one grand block of a woman.' "

Mama laughed and sounded young again. "So marry we did, and I never was sorry. When you were born, people asked, 'Is she going to speak Irish or Swedish?' Your daddy told them, 'This little colleen? This little girl is American!' And American you are!"

For a moment the silence was long between them. Then without thinking, Kate spoke her mind. "He's so different. Mr. Nordstrom's so different from Daddy."

"Yah," answered Mama, and her chin shot up. "But remember, young lady, different doesn't mean wrong!"

Instantly Kate felt ashamed. *I suppose I should feel grateful.* She remembered their long, hard winter. *I should feel grateful that Mr. Nordstrom wants to take care of us.* Instead, Kate's anger about moving boiled up like the clouds of smoke billowing from the steam engine.

The conductor interrupted her thoughts. "All ah-boooarrrd! All ah-boooarrrd!"

Mr. Nordstrom returned then and helped Mama and Kate up the steps of the passenger car. Near the back was a wood stove, and he led them toward its warmth. Kate dropped into the seat opposite Mr. Nordstrom and Mama.

Sliding over to the window, Kate pulled up the green shade and looked out. Near the track stood the large water tank from which men filled the engine. As Kate watched, the men swung the spout out of the way.

Inside the train, signs lined the wall near the ceiling. A big one proclaimed: WARNING: SPITTING AND SMOKING PROHIBITED. FINES AND IMPRISONMENT FOR VIOLATION. COOPERATION OF ALL PASSENGERS IS REQUESTED IN ORDER TO REDUCE THE SPREAD OF VICIOUS GERMS.

Kate looked around and couldn't see anyone spitting or smoking. But she did see the well-dressed man who had bumped into her. He was hurrying onto the train, his shoes clicking as he came to the back of the car.

Removing his spotless hat, he put it in the overhead rack, then sat down across the aisle. Settling himself, he unfolded a newspaper and started to read.

After a final "All ah-boooarrrrd!" the train groaned and slid into motion. Couplers clanked against each other; then Kate felt the cars even out. Moments later, the engine chugged onto the trestle across the St. Croix River. Looking down, Kate caught her breath. Directly below, as though there was nothing between her and the water, the river's strong current flowed black and free. Great chunks of ice, heaped up by the wind, rested against the Wisconsin side.

Mr. Nordstrom leaned around Mama to see. "Lumberjacks will send logs down soon. From shore to shore the river will be full."

Mama was full of questions, wanting to know everything about the new land in which they'd live. But Kate pretended she didn't care.

"Why did you have to drag us off to Wisconsin?" she wanted to say each time she glanced at Mr. Nordstrom.

But Mama had grown up on a farm and looked forward to living on one again. Today it seemed all the strain of the past year was gone from her face. Her hair looked golden and her eyes sparkled as she asked Mr. Nordstrom, "Why do they call this train the Blueberry Special?"

"Blueberries grow wild along here," he explained, his brown head close to Mama's blond one. "People come from all over to pick them. In just one week of blueberry season, a thousand bushels of berries can be shipped from Grantsburg."

Kate flipped her braid over her shoulder. Unwilling to talk with Mr. Nordstrom, she turned her head and looked out the window. Out of the corner of her eye she saw Mr. Nordstrom look at Mama as though asking a question.

Turning back, Kate saw Mama roll her eyes and shrug her shoulders. Kate pretended she didn't notice. Looking out the window once more, she felt pleased with herself. *I'm making it hard for them.* There was nothing Mama disliked more than when Kate acted sullen.

But Mr. Nordstrom looked calm and untroubled. "Another fifteen minutes and we'll be in Grantsburg," he said, breaking a silence.

As the train clacked along, billows of smoke rolled past and sifted through the closed windows. Soon Kate felt tired and dirty. Still she gazed out the window, her back straight and resentful.

After a time she looked back and saw the man across the aisle lean toward Mr. Nordstrom. "Do you live in Grantsburg?" he asked.

Mr. Nordstrom shook his head. "South of it. Down by Trade Lake," he answered, introducing himself.

"Fred Eberly," the man replied, extending his hand. Parted in the middle, his light brown hair was slicked close to his head. His darker brown handlebar moustache waved out against cheeks that seemed too white.

"New in the area?" asked Mr. Nordstrom.

"I'm a salesman," the other man explained. "Three or four times a year I bring goods in my trunk and take a room at the Antler's Hotel. Merchants look at my samples and order what they want."

While Mr. Nordstrom talked with him, Kate watched Mr. Eberly. In spite of his nice suit and slicked-back hair, the man's gray eyes looked stormy. Suddenly Kate remembered Daddy's warning to stay away from strangers. Without understanding why, she felt uncomfortable.

As the train slowed to a crawl, the conductor walked through the car. "Grantsburg! End of the line!"

The tracks edged along the side of a grist mill and the river. When the engine pulled into the station, excitement clutched Kate's stomach. Standing up, she headed down the aisle, then remembered a bag she'd left under the seat. Turning quickly, she almost crashed into Mr. Eberly.

"Watch it! Watch it!" he warned, his gray eyes cold in the face that seemed too white.

Kate drew back, surprised at the salesman's rudeness after the way he talked with Mr. Nordstrom. Slipping around him, Kate found her bag, then turned and started once more toward the door. Ahead of her, Mr. Eberly dropped his spotless hat on his slicked-back hair. His shoes clicked as he left the train.

Outside, Kate found Mr. Nordstrom looking around eagerly. "I asked them to be here when the train came in," he told Mama and Kate.

Kate knew Mr. Nordstrom meant his children. Whenever he wrote, he told Mama about Anders and Lars and Tina. Anders took care of the farm when Mr. Nordstrom came to Minneapolis.

"I'll look for them," he said now. "Maybe Anders misunderstood where we're supposed to meet."

As he hurried away, Kate and Mama followed him off the platform to the wooden boardwalk leading toward a row of buildings. Looking up and down the street, Kate saw no one that could be Mr. Nordstrom's children.

Turning back toward the train, she watched two men unload the baggage. Then Kate gasped. "Oh, my goodness!" Coming their way was the tallest man she had ever seen.

Gazing at his feet, Kate wondered, *How does he manage to buy big enough shoes?*

Then she noticed his long blue coat with gold buttons down the front and a silver star on his chest. "Is he the village marshal?" she whispered to Mama.

"Don't stare, Kate," Mama whispered back.

But Kate couldn't help herself. She had never seen such long arms and big hands.

Though short for her age, Kate knew her own height made little difference. In comparison with the village marshal, even the trainmen seemed small.

As the man moved closer, Kate tipped back her head to see. His eyes and mouth and nose were enormous. Then the big man smiled and stretched down his hand to say hello.

As Kate put her hand within his, it seemed lost. Yet strangely enough, she did not feel afraid. Instead, she looked up into kind blue eyes.

Kate didn't understand his Swedish, but Mama did. "This is Mr. Gustaf Anderson," she told Kate.

"Big Gust," he corrected, his large mouth breaking into a smile. Turning to Mama he spoke again in Swedish. *"Välkommen!"*

It sounded like *Vel comb in*, and Kate knew he was welcoming Mama, telling her Carl Nordstrom was a lucky man.

While Mama and Big Gust talked, the trainmen finished unloading the baggage car. A drayman pulled his horse and wagon near the platform and loaded a large wooden trunk.

"That's ours!" Kate exclaimed. But Mama and Big Gust were talking.

As Kate watched, Mr. Eberly climbed up and dropped onto the wagon seat. The drayman followed and clucked the horse. Pulling away from the train, he headed down the street next to the boardwalk where Kate stood.

Instantly Kate swung into motion. Forgetting everything else, she started toward the wagon. "That's our trunk!" she called out. "You've got Mama's trunk!" But the driver didn't stop.

Running as fast as she could, Kate left the walk and tore into the street. Just then the horse picked up speed. Too late Kate looked up. Instantly she saw her mistake. In another second the big horse would pound down upon her.

Fear shot through Kate as the drayman yanked back on the reins. Rearing up, the horse whinnied and pawed the air.

Kate froze, unable to move.

5

Big Brother

*F*or a moment the large hooves hung above Kate. She opened her mouth to scream, but no sound came. The next instant she felt strong arms lift her high and swing her out of the way.

The horse whinnied again, then dropped to the ground where moments before Kate had stood. As its hooves struck the earth, Kate shuddered.

Big Gust's large eyes looked concerned. "Little girl?"

"I'm *not* a little girl!" Kate told him. "I'm a big one!" But right now she didn't feel twelve years old. The stiffening in her legs was gone, and she felt weak.

Then she remembered why she tried to stop the horse. "They've got Mama's trunk."

Big Gust turned to the wagon, and Kate pointed. "See the red rose painted on the side?"

The village marshal nodded. "Yah."

"And look at the top."

With the trunk in the wagon, Kate couldn't see the words. But she felt sure that Big Gust could.

She was right. From his seven-foot, six-inch viewpoint, Big Gust read the name. "Ingrid Lindblom."

"That's Mama," explained Kate. "Before she married Daddy."

Big Gust turned to the men in the wagon. "Better take it back," he said.

The drayman's face was red. "I'm sorry. My mistake."

As the drayman turned the wagon, Kate saw Mr. Eberly looking at her. His stormy gray eyes made her uncomfortable again. *He's angry,* she thought. *Why's he mad at me?*

Then Mr. Eberly smiled and lifted his hat toward Big Gust. Kate decided she had imagined things. Yet her uneasiness wouldn't go away.

Turning his wagon, the drayman headed back to the train depot. Kate reached the platform almost as soon as he did. Sure enough, there was another wooden trunk. Except for the rose, it looked just like Mama's.

Mr. Eberly and the drayman climbed down and switched trunks. As they drove off again, Mama turned to Big Gust. "I can't thank you enough," she said, her words a jumble of Swedish and English.

As he left them, Mama pulled Kate over to a bench. Tears spilled onto her cheeks. "Oh, Kate, you're safe!"

The warmth of being loved welled up inside Kate. All the anger she'd felt that morning disappeared. Seeing Mama upset brought a tightness to Kate's throat. She couldn't speak. Not yet.

"Why did you run out in front of the horse?" Mama's voice shook with fright at the thought of the near disaster Kate had had.

Kate swallowed. "The picture," she said finally. "I didn't want them to take your picture."

For a moment Mama looked blank. "The picture?" Then her blue eyes cleared. "The picture of my family?"

Kate nodded. "With your sister holding *your* picture."

Mama sighed. "Kate, you're more important than *any* picture. Besides, it's not in the trunk."

Picking up the carpetbag at her feet, Mama opened it. Inside, carefully wrapped in towels, was the picture Kate tried to save. "I didn't want to take a chance in case the trunk was lost," Mama explained.

Then she sighed. "I think God should have warned me when

you were born." Mama's lips quivered as she tried to smile. "A big thing in a small package you are. Always leaping before you look."

Kate grinned and tossed her long black braid over her shoulder. "I'll try to be more careful," she promised solemnly. "I'll really try."

Only a few people remained on the platform, waiting for rides. As Kate and Mama sat down on the bench, trainmen disconnected the engine from the cars. Soon the engine sat alone on a piece of track above a shallow pit.

Then, using long levers, two men pushed the segment of track in front of the engine. Slowly the track moved, and with it, the engine! Walking in a half circle, the men pushed the track around until the engine faced the direction from which it came.

Mama laughed, and her voice sounded almost normal. "That Blueberry Special is really special!"

It felt good to hear Mama laugh. "Maybe it's going to be all right," said Kate and saw Mama's surprised look. "Maybe living in Wisconsin won't be so bad after all."

Then Mr. Nordstrom was back. "I found them! With the warm weather the roads thawed out. There's been rain for three days."

As Mr. Nordstrom waited, two children caught up. "Anders is with the horses," he explained. "But here are Tina and Lars." With a hand on the shoulder of each child, Mr. Nordstrom drew them forward, looking proud.

Lars bowed to Mama, then stared at Kate. Beneath a warm jacket, he was dressed in his Sunday best. But his knickerbockers had mud on them and his boots were wet, as though he'd just stopped at a pump.

A tuft of hair stood up at the back of his red head. Among his freckles, his blue eyes sparkled with mischief.

Just looking at Lars, Kate thought, *He'll put frogs in my bed.*

Tina's hair was white-blond, and the part crooked. Pulled back tightly, her lopsided pigtails looked as though whoever braided them wasn't used to little girl's hair. Now she tugged on one of those braids, putting the end in her mouth.

Tina curtsied to Mama. Turning to Kate, Tina smiled, and

sunlight seemed to dance from within.

Kate liked the little girl immediately. As though sensing it, Tina reached out a hand and tucked it inside Kate's. "My big sister?" she asked.

"Your big sister," answered Kate. She squeezed Tina's hand and felt a squeeze back.

"There's Anders now," said Mr. Nordstrom.

Coming down the street was a team of work horses and a farm wagon driven by a blond muscular boy. Seeing him, Kate smoothed her dress and wished she didn't look so rumpled. Quickly she pushed back the wisps of hair that escaped her braid.

Pulling the reins, Anders stopped the horses, then jumped down and tied them to a post. Like the other children, he wore his Sunday best. His boots also were wet. But unlike Lars, Anders had long trousers. Kate wondered if he was too tall for the knickerbockers usually worn by boys his age.

As Anders bowed to Mama, his thatch of blond hair fell over his forehead. His wide shoulders stretched the seams of his heavy coat.

When he turned to Kate, she said hello in her most grown-up voice. But then, seeing a streak of mud across his face, she smirked, trying not to laugh.

Anders' gaze met hers. With a quick swipe he wiped his hand across his face. The streak widened. Kate snickered.

Anders drew himself up to his full height. His eyes flashed, and his lips tightened as though holding back what he wanted to say. Without speaking, he turned away.

Each grasping an end, Anders and his father lifted the heavy trunk as though it were empty and set it in the wagon. Tina and Lars scrambled in toward the front, and Kate followed, sitting down on the straw. Mr. Nordstrom helped Mama climb up to the wagon seat, and Anders untied the horses. Without looking at Kate, he took the seat next to Mama.

Mr. Nordstrom flicked the reins, and the big horses headed down the dirt street.

Kate turned to Lars. "How far is it?"

"To the farm? Almost eleven miles, and it's bad."

"Bad? What do you mean?" Kate's stomach had settled down. Now it churned again. "Are there bears?"

"Nahhhh," Lars answered, his voice filled with disgust. "Mud. Mud the whole way."

Soon Kate discovered what he meant. As they left Grantsburg, deep ruts filled the roads. Often the ruts widened into large potholes. Even with straw on the bottom of the wagon, Kate soon felt sore from bouncing around.

Whenever he could, Mr. Nordstrom left the road and drove into a field to avoid the ruts. Yet in most places the forest grew up to the dirt track. Overhanging limbs snatched at the wagon.

As the miles fell away, Kate stared at the back of Anders' blond head. Mama and Mr. Nordstrom asked him questions, and the three laughed together. Kate felt left out.

"How old are you, Tina?" she asked, trying to get the four-year-old to talk.

Tina's eyes widened as she nibbled the end of her braid. When the little girl shrugged her shoulders, Kate turned to Lars.

"Speak Swede," he said.

"Swede? But she spoke English."

"Papa learned her those words," answered Lars, the tuft of red hair sticking up at the back of his head. "That's the only English she knows."

"And you?"

"Learned it at school. If we speak Swede, teacher makes us stay after."

Suddenly Kate could no longer ignore all the scared feelings she'd pushed aside. *I have a sister, and I can't even talk to her?* Once more she turned toward Mama and Mr. Nordstrom and Anders. Their laughter made Kate feel even worse.

"And you, Lars? How old are you?" she asked, unwilling to be left out of everything.

"Eight," answered Lars. When he added nothing else, Kate fell silent, too discouraged to think of more to say.

Glancing up, she saw Anders turn back and look at her. As their gaze met, he looked away. "Dumb boy!" Kate told herself. She felt sorry she'd snickered about the mud on his face, yet angry that Anders paid no attention to her.

For some time they traveled, the sharp wind whipping around them. Then grayness replaced the afternoon sun. As the miles fell behind them, the clouds thickened, and the wind grew even colder. Kate and Tina pulled a heavy horse blanket over their shoulders. Mama joined the girls under the blanket, and Lars crawled onto the seat next to his brother.

With dusk came a cold drizzle. Mile by mile, the roads grew worse. As the dampness seeped through the heavy blanket into her clothing, Kate felt the cold enter her bones.

Once Mama asked, "How much farther?"

Mr. Nordstrom answered, "Four more miles."

Mama pulled Tina onto her lap. Both of them looked as miserable as Kate felt.

Kate shivered, and the coldness would not leave. When her teeth started to chatter, Anders turned around. "Your teeth rattling in your head, Kate?"

Behind Mr. Nordstrom's back, Kate made a face. Anders grinned, but Mr. Nordstrom's look silenced him.

The big work horses leaned forward as mud sucked at their feet and splattered their coats. Often their ears turned toward Mr. Nordstrom's voice. "Com'on, Dolly. Com'on, Florie," he encouraged.

Just then the back right wheel dropped into a deep hole. As the wagon lurched, Mama's trunk slid, crashing against the end of the wagon.

"Get over! Get behind me!" Mr. Nordstrom's voice was urgent.

Quickly Mama and Kate and Tina crawled to the left, putting their weight in the front corner. The horses strained, but the wagon did not budge. As they tilted at a sharp angle, Tina began to cry.

We're going to tip! Kate bit her lip to keep from crying out as Tina had.

Mama hugged Tina close, trying to shush her. Suddenly Kate remembered Mama's carpetbag and reached out, rescuing it before it went over the side.

As Mr. Nordstrom and Anders climbed down, the wagon tipped farther. Reaching the ground, they sank into the mud.

The road seemed bottomless. Anders started toward the back of the wagon. Step by slow step he moved, searching for footing. Once he slipped and nearly went down. As he grabbed on to a wheel, the mud oozed over the top of his boots.

At the back of the wagon, Anders picked up heavy planks. Carrying them forward, he placed them in front of the wheels. Then, the mud sucking his boots with each step, he worked his way to the front of the horses.

Watching him, Kate guessed how Anders had gotten mud on his face. *I wish I could tell him I'm sorry.* Kate felt embarrassed that she'd laughed. But Anders avoided her eyes.

At the end of the wagon, Mr. Nordstrom pushed a pole under the back right wheel. "Ready?" he called out.

Anders grabbed hold of Dolly's bridle. "Ready! Giddyup," he urged the horses. "Com'on, Dolly. Com'on, Florie. Dig in. Giddyup!"

The mares strained forward, heat from their bodies steaming upward. The wagon tilted even more. Frantically Kate clung to the side until her fingers grew numb. There was nothing she wanted less than to be dumped out in the mud.

"Just a minute!" called Mr. Nordstrom. "Lars, you take the horses."

Lars crawled down into mud over his knees and struggled forward. Anders slogged past him to the back of the wagon, still without looking at Kate. There he bent down, his shoulder against the end gate. "Ready!"

Unable to reach Dolly's bridle, Lars took the reins. "Giddyup!" he called out, sounding like his big brother. "Com'on, Dolly! Com'on, Florie!"

Mr. Nordstrom leaned down on the pole, giving it his entire weight. Anders pushed against the wagon. Harnesses creaked as the horses strained forward. This time the wagon lurched out of the hole.

When the horses reached firmer ground, Lars stopped them. Anders dropped the mud-covered planks into the back of the wagon. Breaking off a branch at the side of the road, he tried to wipe the mud off his clothes. Even his blond hair had mud in it.

In the dusk Kate watched him scowl. Once he looked her

way, then glanced away. As Anders climbed onto the wagon seat, Kate did not laugh.

Soon the grayness of day merged with the blackness of night. To Kate, used to the gas streetlights of Minneapolis, the darkness seemed to settle in around them. Mr. Nordstrom gave the horses their head, and they kept moving.

It seemed that hours passed before the rain stopped. As the clouds scattered and the moon broke free, they left the road for a wagon track. The stars came out and the wind quickened, whispering in the trees around them.

When Dolly and Florie started up a long hill, they picked up speed. Mr. Nordstrom turned toward Mama. "We're almost home."

Then, out of the darkness rose the shape of buildings on both sides of the track. Mr. Nordstrom stopped the horses and lit a lantern. It *was* a white frame house after all. Yet by now Kate felt too cold and tired to care.

Inside, the fire in the wood stove had gone out. The house seemed as damp as the outside. To Kate, it was one more misery on top of the long awful day.

I don't want to live here! Kate wished she could shout it out. *I want the gas streetlights of Minneapolis. I want our warm little rooms. I want busy, cobblestone streets. I want my friends.*

Even Mama seemed quiet, no longer the glowing bride of yesterday. Kate didn't want to look at her. *If only we could go back to Minneapolis. I wonder what terrible things will happen tomorrow?*

6

Trapped!

*C*ock-a-doodle-doooo!

Kate rolled over, not sure where she was. Through the haze of half-sleep, she remembered yesterday. *Maybe coming to Windy Hill Farm was a nightmare. Maybe it was a nightmare that Mama married Mr. Nordstrom.*

But the rooster crowed again. Cock-a-doodle-doooo! Kate couldn't ignore him. The farm was real all right.

In the bed next to her, Tina stirred, opened her eyes, and smiled. In that moment Kate's feelings changed. *Maybe it won't be so bad after all.* She felt warm with the friendliness of the little girl.

My sister, Kate told herself as Tina closed her eyes and rolled over. Each time Kate repeated those words the relationship seemed more real and more special. Yet she couldn't understand Tina's Swedish.

Quietly Kate slipped out of bed. The room she and Tina shared was on the end of the house and had windows facing two directions. On one side the windows overlooked the porch and the wagon track that circled the front and side of the house. Beyond that track lay the furrows of a plowed field. Farther away, tall trees stood at the edge of a steep hill. Three bee hives stood near the trees.

Outside a window on the other side of the room grew a large pine. The long branches with their soft, green needles reached out to the house, almost touching it. From the other window on that side Kate saw the wagon track fork off to the right and the edge of the hill.

From this height, Kate looked across the wide expanse of what she knew must be Rice Lake. On this March morning the lake was still frozen. On its far side, hills and valleys stretched off to the horizon.

Then, as Kate stood at the window, she felt a small hand within hers. Tina tugged, and Kate guessed the little girl wanted to show her around.

They dressed quickly, and the four-year-old led Kate into the hallway. The night before, Kate had been too tired to notice the other rooms on this floor—a storeroom and the bedroom Lars and Anders shared. Already, both boys were gone.

At the bottom of the stairs Kate saw a door leading outside. But Tina turned to the right and took Kate through the front room into the dining room. There one door opened into a bedroom, another door into the kitchen.

They found Mama searching the pantry. Seeing Tina and Kate, Mama looked relieved. After saying good morning to both girls, she spoke to Tina in Swedish. Kate guessed Mama needed help in finding things. Just the same, Kate felt left out again.

Slipping through the kitchen door, she wandered outside. Nearby stood a pump, and beyond that a summer kitchen. From Mama, Kate knew that when the weather grew hot, farm families cooked and ate in these little buildings. That kept the bigger house cool for sleeping.

The rain of the night before was gone and the air sweet with the smell of spring. Kate crossed the dirt road to a building set on the edge of the hill. Going inside, she found it had large bins for storing the summer's harvest.

Beyond the granary, chickens ran around a hen house, scratching the ground. As Kate walked among them, they scattered. Then she came to the log barn.

The closest door stood open to the morning sunlight. Inside, log beams stretched across the ceiling. As her eyes adjusted to the dimmer light, Kate saw a dog bringing cows through another door.

"Woof!" it barked, nipping heels to move the cows along. As Kate watched, each cow entered a stall as though knowing where she belonged. The dog turned to face Kate. "Woof!" it barked again, more sharply.

Kate stiffened. The dog moved closer, and Kate's muscles tightened.

Just then Anders dropped down a ladder at the far end of the barn. Dressed in overalls, he held a pitchfork in one hand. Putting it down, he came forward.

"Lutfisk!" Anders called. The dog ran to him. "Good dog. Sit."

Immediately Lutfisk sat, and Anders knelt down to scratch behind the dog's ears. The dog's hair was brown with black and white markings. As he petted the dog, Anders' eyes filled with pride. "You don't have to be afraid of him."

"I'm not!" said Kate, though she felt relieved that Anders was there.

"Oh?" he drawled. A slow grin lit his face. "Could have fooled me."

"I'm *not* afraid!" Kate said again. Coming forward slowly, she reached out, gingerly patting the dog's back. "What did you call him?"

"Lutfisk," answered Anders. "You know, *lute fisk*." He said the word slowly.

"Oh," answered Kate. "I know what you mean." She hated the smell of the dried cod that Swedes soaked in lye and ate at Christmas.

"Good stuff, huh?" Anders asked, his voice enthusiastic.

Kate held her nose. "Yah. Good stuff."

Anders still petted the dog. "Got him for Christmas a couple years back. He got into the lutefisk and gobbled it up before I found him."

Turning to the dog, Anders lifted his right arm, and pointed at the door. "Go get Bess." Lutfisk headed outside.

"One cow missing," explained Anders.

"And Lutfisk will find her?"

"Yup. He brings 'em all in. I trained him myself."

Anders spoke good English, and Kate knew he'd learned it at school. She felt relieved that he seemed to have forgotten yesterday. Instead, he looked eager to show her around.

"Want to see Rosie?"

"Rosie?" asked Kate.

"My pig," Anders told her.

"Yours?"

"Papa's fattening another one for the family." Anders led Kate to a pen at the end of the barn. "Got her as a runt 'cause Papa knew she'd die otherwise. See how she's growing? I'm fattening her up for the Burnett County Fair."

"The fair? How come?"

Anders' look told Kate he certainly thought she was a dumb girl. Just the same he explained. "To get a blue ribbon. If I get first, I'll get a better price. If I get enough money selling her, I'll buy a heifer."

"A heifer?"

Anders rolled his eyes, and Kate knew she'd asked another dumb question. "A female calf. Then I'll fatten her up. If I'm lucky and have some extra money, I'll trade the heifer for a filly."

"A filly?"

"Yup. My very own horse."

Anders went back to the cows, pulled up a three-legged stool, and started milking. As milk streamed into the pail, Kate's gaze shifted to Lutfisk. He'd brought in the last cow and seemed satisfied that his work was done. Dropping on the dirt floor behind Anders, he rested his head on his paws. His brown eyes turned toward Kate.

She didn't see Anders' grin until too late. Moving his hands slightly, he directed a stream of milk to hit her face.

Kate sputtered. "Hey! What're you doin'?"

Anders laughed. This time the milk reached her eye. Kate squeezed her eyes shut and wiped them with her fists.

Anders hooted. "Open your mouth!"

Opening her eyes instead, Kate saw his shoulders shake with laughter. "Open your mouth yourself!" she spit out. "And put your foot in it!"

Dodging, she missed the next stream of milk and headed for the door. "Stupid boy!" she flung back. *I'll show him!* Heading into the bright sunlight, Kate felt determined. *If he doesn't want me around, I sure don't want to be there!*

Kate's anger stayed with her as she continued exploring. Beyond the barn was a pasture, the grass still soft and wet from melting snow and three days of rain. Large tree stumps, some four and five feet across, dotted the field.

On the far side of the pasture, the woods began again, and Kate started toward them. As she moved closer, she saw a tree with branches low enough for climbing.

Maybe it'd be a good hiding place when I don't want to talk to that stupid Anders. Kate's scared, lost feeling was back again.

Heading for the tree, she walked quickly. Partway across the field, Kate stopped. What was that? Close to the tree, on the edge of the woods, the bushes moved. Still leafless from winter, the bare branches shook as though something touched them.

Is it the wind? It can't be. There's not even a slight breeze.

Then Kate noticed something else. In a hollow of the tree, where a large branch met the trunk, something glittered in the sun. Again she started out, her curiosity mounting.

But the next moment she stopped in her tracks. Something stood behind the leafless bushes—something black. Something as tall as a man standing up.

"A bear!" In her panic Kate spoke aloud. Her stomach tightened. "Sarah said there'd be bears!"

As she tried to decide what to do, Kate heard a snort behind her. She whirled. "Oh, no!"

A short distance away, a large animal pawed the wet ground. Clods of grass spit out behind his hoof. As he lowered his head, the sunlight glinted on long horns.

Kate stifled a scream. Once again Sarah had warned her. Kate knew what the animal was. "A bull!"

Tossing his head, the bull tugged at the chain between the ring in his nose and a stake in the ground. His dark eyes rolled.

Kate's stomach churned. *Why didn't I see him?* More than once her temper had tumbled her into a mess, but this was the worst.

Fear filled her, blocking out the ability to think. *What can I do?*

Spinning around, Kate started to run toward the tree at the other side of the pasture. Midway she stopped, remembering the black shape in the bushes. "Trapped!" In her terror she spoke aloud. "Trapped between a bull and a bear!"

Turning back again, Kate faced the bull. His feet firmly planted on the soft ground, he swung his head from side to side. His long tongue reached out to lick his nostrils. Straining at his chain, he put himself between Kate and the barn.

Slowly, step by step, she started to circle the bull. His large eyes rolled as if he were watching every movement. His thick neck seemed as strong as an oak, his horns pointed and sharp.

Kate felt the bull's anger. As he pulled at the stake, the whites of his eyes widened.

Lifting his head once more, the bull let out a low guttural rumble. A shudder ran through Kate.

Again he tugged at the chain, tossing his huge head from side to side. Suddenly, with a mighty swing, the bull yanked the stake from the ground.

For a moment he stood there, eyeing Kate. Seeming to sense his freedom, he tossed his head once more. The chain and the stake swung wide.

Then the bull turned from Kate. His tail almost straight up in the air, he plunged away, running across the field.

Kate breathed deeply, relief flowing through every part of her body. But as she headed toward the barn, she saw the bull circling back.

Once again he faced her. Eyeing Kate, he stamped a back leg.

Kate stared, unable to move. "Help!" she wanted to scream. But no sound came. Her feet felt rooted to the ground. *I can't run!* Panic washed through her.

The bull took another step. Kate tried her feet. To her surprise, she could lift them. Slowly, step by step, she edged back.

The bull followed. With each step Kate took away, the bull moved closer. He bellowed, and the sound echoed in the hillsides.

Kate stopped, afraid to move or breathe. Once more the bull

pawed the ground. Clods of grass flew over his back. Dirt spit out, spraying a wide area behind the terrible hoof. Kate trembled. *God, what should I do?*

In the next instant her frantic thoughts became a prayer, her prayer a whisper. "Help me, God!" she pleaded. "Help!"

The moment stretched long as Kate stood there, every muscle tense. *It's hopeless. I'll never get away.*

Then she heard a voice behind her. "Stand still, Kate. Don't move."

Without turning her head, Kate knew it was Anders. With all her heart she wanted to run in his direction. Yet as she stepped back toward the sound of his voice, the bull took another step toward her.

"Did you hear me?" said Anders, his voice low but commanding. "Don't move."

Kate's knees began to shake, but she stood her ground.

"Stay there," said Anders, his voice closer. "Keep still."

Kate longed to turn around. Instead, she stared straight ahead. The bull rolled his eyes, and Kate could not stop trembling.

Then she felt, rather than saw, Anders close behind her. "When I say *run!* you must run," he said, still in a low, steady voice. "Don't look back. Just go. Get Papa. He's in the barn."

Kate wondered if her legs would carry her. In a moment she found out.

"Go!" commanded Anders.

Kate went, her feet flying across the soggy ground. Once she slipped and nearly fell. Catching herself, she ran on.

When she reached the edge of the field, she looked back. Anders had moved ahead, putting his tall body between the bull and Kate. In his outstretched hands was a pitchfork.

Kate headed for the barn. By the time she found Anders' father, she was out of breath. Unable to speak, she pointed to the field. Mr. Nordstrom started off in a run.

7

Trouble Ahead

As Kate watched from a distance, Mr. Nordstrom took the pitchfork from Anders. Step by step, they chased the angry animal toward the barn. Each time the bull pawed the ground, Kate's knees felt weak.

At last Anders and his father managed to shut him into a stout pen. Holding back the tears she didn't want Anders to see, Kate headed for the house.

Mama met her at the door. "Kate, what's wrong?"

When Kate told her about the bull, Mama's face turned white. "Oh, Kate! Another animal! You promised you'd be careful!"

"I know, Mama. I'm sorry."

"Sorry! That's not enough if you get killed!" Mama sounded stern. "You've got to take care of yourself." But then her voice broke. "Don't you know how important you are to me?"

Kate swallowed around the lump in her throat. "Am I, Mama?" she asked, her voice so quiet it could barely be heard. "Am I really?"

Mama's eyes widened with surprise. "Don't you know that, Kate?"

For a moment Mama stood looking at her as though searching Kate's face.

Unable to meet Mama's eyes, Kate looked down and traced an imaginary pattern with her toe.

"Oh," said Mama as if deep in thought. For a moment she was silent.

Still studying the kitchen floor, Kate tried to smile. But Mama knew her too well. "Kate, are you wondering if I have enough love to go around?"

Startled, Kate looked up. "How did you know?" she wanted to ask. Instead she glanced away.

"Look at me, Kate," said Mama in her I-mean-business voice. Gently she reached out and cupped Kate's chin in her hand. "Look at me and remember this. When I have a new husband and three new children, it doesn't mean I love you less. It means my love grows bigger to take in all of you."

"Cross your heart and hope to die?"

"Not hope to die, Kate," Mama answered gently. "I believe I'm needed around here. But I *am* telling the truth."

Mama smiled. "I'm asking the Lord for special guardian angels around you. But you've got to help them out!"

Kate laughed then, and her scared, lost feeling fell away. For the first time since Mama's wedding, Kate felt warm inside. But the fear didn't leave Mama's eyes.

Minutes later, Anders soaped and rinsed his hands in the basin just inside the kitchen door. Catching sight of Kate, he muttered under his breath, "Dumb girl!" Then he combed his blond hair, pretending he didn't see her.

But Kate heard. Worst of all, she knew he was right. She felt stupid all the way through.

She also knew she should thank Anders. He'd risked his life to save her. Yet the words wouldn't come. Instead she said, "You should have told me not to go there."

"You should have been *smart* enough to not go there," he answered.

Kate's temper flared. Suddenly she wanted to hurt him. She wanted to call him the meanest name she could think of. Something that said he was awkward and without manners, even though that wasn't true.

Then she knew what it could be—a name Sarah had taught

her. Kate lowered her voice so Mama wouldn't hear. "If you weren't such a country bumpkin, you'd have warned me."

Anders looked as if Kate slapped him. The red crept up into his face. "Next time—"

He stopped, and Kate knew Anders was very angry.

"Next time," he went on, "I'll leave you there. I'll let that ol' bull—"

Just then his father came into the kitchen, and Kate never heard what Anders would do.

After breakfast, Mr. Nordstrom took a worn Bible down from the shelf. "God *is* our refuge and strength," he read from Psalm forty-six. "A very present help in trouble. Therefore will not we fear. . . ."

The words sank deep inside Kate, touching an empty spot she always tried to push aside. At the same time she felt uncomfortable.

"The Lord of hosts *is* with us; the God of Jacob *is* our refuge—"

Wondering what Anders thought, Kate glanced his way.

Anders surprised her. He seemed to be listening.

As Kate moved restlessly in her chair, Mr. Nordstrom read on. "Be still, and know that I *am* God—"

"Be still?" Kate thought. Outwardly she stopped wiggling. Inside she squirmed.

Then Mr. Nordstrom prayed. "We thank Thee, Heavenly Father. We thank Thee for watching over Kate and Anders. We thank Thee that this is our first morning as a new family."

In that moment the tears Kate had held back welled up and spilled over. Quickly she wiped her cheeks, hoping Anders had not seen.

Mr. Nordstrom cleared his throat, then went on. "Help us, Father, to grow together as a family."

As he said, "Ah-men," Mama joined him. Quietly she stretched out her hand and covered Mr. Nordstrom's. When she smiled, the fear disappeared from her eyes.

But later that day, as Kate thought more about the bull, she wondered if God really did help her. Probably Anders just happened to come along when he did.

About suppertime it started raining again and continued all night. The following day was Sunday, and Mr. Nordstrom said the roads were too muddy to go to church. After breakfast he led them in prayer and singing. The family sang well together, but Kate wished she had an organ and could play the hymns.

When Monday morning dawned, fog hid the lake below the hill. In the silence the gray-white world seemed eerie.

Kate felt scared about starting a new school, scared about meeting the other children. *What if they don't like me? What if they all act like Anders?* She knew there was no way to get out of it, but felt more uneasy all the time. *I wish I didn't have to go.*

That morning Kate spent extra time in front of the mirror. More than once she'd been glad that Mama was a seamstress for wealthy ladies. Often they gave her leftover material. Sometimes Mama figured out a way to use two colors together and have enough for a dress.

The light blue dress Kate put on now was her favorite. As she stood before the mirror, tying her long sash, she knew she looked her best. At the same time her deep blue eyes looked scared.

Catching up the locket from Daddy, she clasped it around her neck, then went down to breakfast. There Kate discovered she and Anders and Lars would take a trail through the woods to school.

"It's shorter than walking around on the road," Mr. Nordstrom told Kate. "No one's logged there lately, so it won't have deep ruts. But where there's mud, be careful. It's as slippery as ice."

When it was time to go, Mama handed Kate her slate and a syrup pail. With a metal handle and tight-fitting lid, the pail protected her lunch from all kinds of weather.

Anders led the way outside. Without looking at Kate, he stalked off on the wagon track leading down the hill past the lake. Red-headed Lars followed, the tuft of hair standing up at the back of his head. Kate fell in behind.

His long legs stretching out, Anders set a brisk pace. With her shorter legs, Kate found it hard to keep up. Each time they came to a mudhole, she edged around it, trying to stay clean.

Sheltered by the woods, patches of snow still covered the ground. In the gray-white fog, pine trees seemed black, and tangled bushes formed hedges. All around Kate, leafless branches closed in as though unwilling to give up land for the track.

She shivered, glad for the warm coat she wore. "How far is it?" she asked the back of Anders' head.

When he didn't answer, Kate raised her voice, trying again. It was Lars who told her. "About a mile."

Before long, the track became a trail, then a path. Here and there other paths led off the main one. Soon Kate lost her sense of direction. She felt glad that Anders led them, even if his broad shoulders looked stiff and unyielding. He was still angry, Kate knew. Always his blond head faced forward as though he wanted to ignore her.

They had walked for some time when Kate heard a school bell ring. As she quickened her steps, Lars turned his freckled face toward Kate. "That's the first bell. We've got another half hour."

Soon after, they came to a high ridge where the land fell sharply away on either side of the path. Small ice-covered pools filled the hollows far below. After following the ridge for a while, Anders stopped.

Lars pointed down through trees still bare of leaves. "That's it."

At the bottom of the hill a schoolhouse stood on a rise near the windswept ice of a lake. Kate felt confused. "Is that the lake near our house?"

Lars shook his head, and his red hair fell over his eyes. "That's Spirit Lake. We live on Rice Lake. We've come through the woods between."

Without a word, Anders set off again, and Kate and Lars followed him down the hill.

At the bottom, a creek flowed between them and the schoolhouse. Swollen by rain and melting snow, the creek ran high between its banks. Kate stopped, knowing she couldn't jump across.

Then she saw the log spanning the water. Anders bounded

ahead, moving so fast he seemed to run across. Lars followed, balancing as if not giving it a thought.

Kate swallowed, but the empty feeling in her stomach didn't go away. *I can't show 'em I'm scared*, she thought. *They'll laugh at me.*

Carefully she set one foot on the end of the log. Then she looked down. The swollen creek rushed beneath her. Kate felt cold with fear.

"Come on," said Anders, speaking for the first time that morning.

Kate set down her other foot. But when she tried to pick up the first one, she couldn't move. Her foot seemed frozen to the log.

"Hurry up!" prodded Anders.

Kate felt like an ice statue. "I can't," she said finally, her words just a whisper.

Anders sounded impatient. "Come on, scaredy-cat! Won't hurt you. Just walk across."

"I can't," said Kate again. The water seemed closer now, rushing even faster. Yet somehow she felt higher above it.

"You better come or a country bumpkin will have to help you," Anders called out.

Kate felt the heat move up into her face and knew she was blushing. "I'm sorry," she said softly, still not taking her eyes away from the water.

"*Sorry!*" Anders exclaimed, but Kate was afraid to raise her eyes to his face. "Sorry, the city girl says. That's not enough." His voice changed, sounding self-important and loud. "The preacher says that when you say mean things, you're supposed to ask forgiveness."

Kate's head shot up. "Forgiveness, my foot!" Catching the grin on Anders' face, she nearly lost her balance.

"Well," drawled Anders, his voice back to normal. "I guess I'll have to help you out again."

When he jumped on the log it shook, and Kate nearly tipped off. Tucking her slate under her other arm, she gave Anders her free hand. As they started up the muddy bank on the opposite side, he let go.

Kate's feet slid from beneath her, and she fell forward on her hands and knees. Her slate and syrup pail dropped in the mud. "Oh, no!" she cried.

"Oh, no!" drawled Anders, echoing her voice.

Carefully Kate picked herself up. Her hands were brown with mud, and her long stockings looked the same. "Oh, ick!"

Taking out her handkerchief, Kate wiped her hands and knees. At least her dress and coat didn't look too bad. Gingerly she picked up the dirty lunch pail and slate.

Sliding back down the bank, Anders stretched out his hand. Once more Kate grabbed hold. As he stepped onto the dead brown grass at the top, Anders let go again.

Without warning the soft ground gave way beneath Kate, and she sat down hard. Cold mud oozed through her stockings and dress.

Helplessly she looked up, wondering if Anders had tricked her. Then she saw Lars grin and knew the answer. Anger filled her. Scrambling up, she nearly fell again.

Once on solid ground Kate stomped her feet. As she faced Anders, she exploded. "You let go on purpose!"

"Me? *I* let go on purpose? How could a country bumpkin think of a thing like that?" Anders grinned at his brother. "Lars, do you think I'd ever do something like that?"

Lars snickered, and Kate's anger grew. "You—You—" she sputtered, unable to find words terrible enough. "You're both just awful!" she stormed. "You planned this!"

Pulling up long dead grass, she tried to wipe herself off. Yet as she twisted around to look at her skirt, she felt sick. Mud covered most of her back side.

"I want to go home," she said, trying to keep her voice steady.

"You can't," answered Anders so quickly that Kate knew he meant business. "You can't walk that far when you're wet. Your clothes will ice up."

His voice softened. "Come on."

Slowly Kate followed. There was nothing she wanted less than to pass through the door of that school.

8

Spirit Lake School

*A*s Kate entered the schoolhouse, she felt the warmth of the potbelly stove reach out to her. Rows of desks, connected one to another, stretched away to the front. Above the blackboard hung a picture of George Washington and another of Abraham Lincoln.

Seeing Kate at the door, a young-looking teacher came to meet her.

"This is Miss Sundquist," introduced Anders, his voice polite. "Katherine Nordstrom."

"Katherine *Nordstrom*?" The name jolted Kate. "I'm Katherine O'Connell!" Anders was the last person on earth she'd expect to call her *Nordstrom*.

The teacher looked at her, then at Anders. "Which is it?"

Anders shrugged and waited, watching Kate.

Kate drew a deep breath. "I'm an O'Connell," she said boldly, even though Mama had asked her to use Nordstrom.

Anders stood there watching, his blue eyes filled with laughter.

Then Kate guessed he was waiting to see if she'd tell on him. Behind her back, she clenched her fist and turned partway for Anders to see.

Anders snickered.

Miss Sundquist turned to him. "Something funny, Anders? I don't think so. Katherine looks wet and cold." Turning back to Kate, she asked, "What happened?" Concern filled her voice.

Below his thatch of blond hair, Anders' face turned solemn. Standing quietly, he stayed within earshot, as though daring Kate to put the blame on him. When she didn't, he drifted off.

Miss Sundquist led Kate to the small cloakroom. Along two outside walls were shelves for lunch pails. On the other walls hooks held coats and sweaters. "You can hang your coat here," said the teacher. "Let it dry before trying to get out the mud. But why don't you wash up at the pump? I have some towels."

Outside, Kate felt the brisk March air even more. As she dabbed mud off her long stockings, the water from the pump felt like ice. Twisting around, she tried to scrub the back of her dress. The brownish gray spot widened.

Her long sash dripped mud. Taking it off, Kate rinsed it under the pump, squeezed out the water, and retied the bow in back.

Inside once more, she felt chilled all through. For a time Kate stood with her back to the wood stove, watching the other children watch her. Gradually she grew warmer, but her stockings stayed wet and soggy. They'd take a long time to dry.

When Miss Sundquist assigned a desk, Kate sat down quickly, hoping to hide the spot on her dress.

A moment later, the teacher asked the children to stand for the pledge of allegiance. Slowly Kate slid out of her desk. Behind her, someone snickered.

"Psssst!"

Kate whirled around.

"Psssst!" The boy directly behind Kate hissed again, trying to get Anders' attention. Anders grinned at him, then tipped his head toward Kate.

Quickly Kate turned back, facing the front. It was no secret the boys were talking about her. As she sat down again, she had one thought. *What are they planning to do?*

To make matters worse, a cold wind swept through a knothole in the floor near Kate's desk. In the next hour her wet legs and feet felt icy, then numb. She shivered, biting her lips to keep her teeth from chattering. With all her heart she didn't want to stand up and get her coat.

Trying to forget her misery, Kate looked around. The strange girls made her lonesome for Sarah Livingston, so lonesome that she ached inside.

Across the aisle two girls shared a double desk. The closest one looked about Kate's age. With light brown hair and hazel eyes, she had clear skin with a dusting of freckles across her nose. When Miss Sundquist called on the girl, Kate learned her name was Josie Swenson.

Maybe I can get to know her at recess, Kate thought.

Later on, though, when she happened to look up, she caught Josie and her friend staring. They were looking at the dress Kate had proudly put on that morning.

"It's store-bought," she heard the other girl whisper. Josie nodded, then looked away.

For the first time, Kate noticed the dresses worn by the other girls. Her own looked too nice.

"Mama sewed this dress," she wanted to shout out. "I'm just like you!" But Kate knew it wasn't true. She was different.

Then she remembered something else. Quietly she took hold of the heart-shaped locket Daddy had given her and slipped the chain inside her dress. Even so, as the other girls looked her way, Kate knew it was too late. They had already noticed her jewelry.

Once again Kate felt lonesome for Sarah. "I'd like to be friends!" she wanted to tell the girls around her. Instead, she felt set apart.

"In this whole school I'm the only one with black hair," Kate muttered to herself. Her misery mounted. "I'm the only girl with one braid instead of two! I'm the only person with an Irish name!"

For a moment Kate thought about it. Then she flipped her braid over her shoulder. *And I'm going to stay that way! I'll show 'em!*

Yet before long Kate's small bit of confidence melted away. Up and down the rows one child, then another, looked her direction, then snickered. Whenever Kate heard them she wondered, *Why are they laughing at me?*

Opening a book, she pretended to read. Anders walked past and snatched the book out of her hands. His hoarse whisper reached up and down the aisle. "You're not reading, Katherine Nordstrom."

With an exaggerated bow, he turned the book right side up. Erik, the boy behind Kate, laughed softly.

Then Miss Sundquist called on Kate to recite.

Kate groaned. "Do I have to?" she wanted to ask. All she could think about was the muddy spot on her dress.

Miss Sundquist called again. "Katherine, come here, please."

Slowly Kate tried to stand up. She couldn't move.

Across the room a girl snickered. One child after another joined her.

Again Kate tried to stand. Yet she felt bound to her seat. She tried to twist around, but couldn't. Then she knew what was wrong. Erik had tied her sash to the desk back of her! Kate's cheeks felt warm with embarrassment as she tried to struggle free.

"Erik Lundgren, untie Kate!" ordered Miss Sundquist.

As Erik set Kate free, every child turned to watch. Slowly Kate stood up, and the children covered their mouths with their hands, hiding their laughter.

Slowly Kate walked forward, plagued by one thought: *Everyone in this whole school is watching.*

When morning recess arrived, Kate eagerly headed for the cloakroom. Yet, once outside, she faced another nightmare. In class Miss Sundquist expected the children to speak English. If they didn't, they had to stay after school. Yet when the teacher couldn't hear them, the children spoke the Swedish they weren't allowed to use during school.

At first Kate struggled, trying to understand what they said. Finally she gave up and added another misery to her list. *I'm the only one in this whole school who doesn't know Swedish!*

Dragging her feet, Kate left the play area and sat down on the porch at the front of the school. "At least Mama loves me!" she told herself, clinging to that one hope.

Around her, the other children shouted and played, but

Kate's thoughts were far away. *I wonder what Sarah's doing now—and Michael. I want to go back to Minneapolis.*

Somehow the morning passed. During lunch hour Kate couldn't get the tight-fitting lid off her syrup pail. Watching closely, she saw Josie ask the teacher for a table knife. Sliding it under the narrow edge, Josie lifted the lid in three or four places until it popped up.

Kate borrowed the knife, but still couldn't open her pail. Finally she turned to Josie. "Will you help me?"

As she showed Kate what to do, Josie smiled shyly.

"Where do you live?" Kate asked quickly, not wanting to miss an opportunity. By the time lunch hour ended, Josie seemed less afraid to be friends.

That afternoon the snickering started again. Miss Sundquist seemed as tired of it as Kate. Searching for the ringleaders, she called out, "Anders!" then "Lars!"

The two boys stood up.

"Go to the cloakroom until you stop laughing."

Lars looked scared, as though he wasn't used to this kind of punishment. Anders was a different matter. As he left his desk, he winked at Erik. Anders didn't seem to have a care in the world.

As Lars and Anders reached the cloakroom, Miss Sundquist spoke again. "Don't come back until you're through laughing!"

After that, the day went better for Kate. Finally it ended. Picking up her books, she grabbed her coat and lunch pail. Once outside, she stood for a moment on the porch, watching children scatter in all directions.

Then, rounding the corner of the school, Kate looked for Anders and Lars. No one was there.

Circling the building, Kate searched. With each step she felt more upset. Finally an awful thought dawned on her. *They're hiding from me! They're pretending they aren't here. They want to see how scared I get.*

Drawing a deep breath, she tried to look calm. *Trouble is, I am scared.*

Just thinking about finding her way through the woods filled Kate with panic. *What will I do?*

For a moment longer she stood there, then made up her mind. "Dumb boys! I'll fool 'em!" she muttered.

Certain that Anders and Lars watched from behind a bush, Kate set out. *I'm not going to let 'em laugh at me!*

Coming to the creek, she slid down the bank, but managed to stay on her feet. The icy water roared beneath the log as Kate put her foot upon it. Swallowing hard, she took one step, then a second, and a third.

To her surprise the crossing didn't seem nearly as bad as that morning. Now she had a greater fear—finding her way through the woods. As Kate reached the end of the log, she leaped onto solid ground.

"I'll show those boys," she said aloud, working up her courage. Straightening her shoulders, she tossed her head and flipped her shiny black braid.

With confident steps, she set off on the path. "I'll make it on my own," she muttered, wanting to look around to see where Anders and Lars hid. "Dumb boys!"

But at the top of the hill Kate faced a choice. The path led three different ways.

For a long minute she stood there, wondering what to do. The bright sunlight that had replaced the morning fog made everything look different.

Maybe I should go back. Half turning, Kate glanced down the hill, then noticed something.

When she looked toward the school, the trees appeared as they had that morning. Choosing the center path, Kate turned around to check herself. "I've got it!"

Starting out once more, she set a good pace and kept to it. "Dumb boys!" she said again. "I don't need 'em." Her confidence was growing.

For a time Kate followed a long ridge that dipped to lower ground. Then she came to a Y-shaped fork, one she hadn't noticed that morning. Turning around, she looked back. This time the trees didn't offer a clue.

The ground was firmer here with no footprints to follow. Kate stopped and looked around again, puzzled about what to do. Finally, she took the trail veering to the right.

The woods were more open now, and March winds had dried the ground. Kate's feet scuffled the brown leaves left by winter. But before long, the path grew faint.

Kate turned back, planning to retrace her steps. But as she looked down she could not believe her eyes. *It's gone! The path's disappeared!*

Her scared feelings returned. *How did I get here? Where am I?*

Then Kate heard the rustling of leaves. "Anders! Lars!" she called out. A squirrel scampered away.

"Anders! Lars!" she shouted again. No longer did she care if they laughed at her. "Come on out! The joke's over!"

Kate listened, then called until hoarse. No one shouted an answer. No one popped out of the bushes laughing.

Finally the terrible truth struck her. *They aren't here! They aren't hiding from me!*

Deep inside, Kate trembled. Around and around, one thought whirled in her mind: *I'm lost in these awful woods!*

9

The Mysterious Stranger

Filled with panic, Kate broke into a run. Branches reached out and whipped her face. Thorns snatched at her coat and legs.

Looking for openings between trees and bushes, Kate tumbled through. Several times she circled large clumps of growth. Finally she had to stop. She could not move ahead through the tangled brush.

Making herself stand still, she took a long, deep breath, but her panic would not go away. *Bears. Bears live in that brush.*

Behind Kate, a branch cracked, and she spun around. In that moment she remembered everything she'd ever heard about bears. "Wisconsin is a wilderness," Sarah had said. "It's filled with bears."

"Yah, we have bears," Mr. Nordstrom told Kate and Mama. "Sometimes five-hundred-pound ones."

It didn't matter that he also said, "They're more afraid of us than we need to be of them." Kate remembered only his words, "Yah, we have bears." Her stomach churning, she tried to push aside fear. But then she had another terrible thought: *What if it gets dark before I find my way?*

Like waves on a beach, panic washed over Kate, and she began to sob. "I'm scared, God!" she cried out. "Really scared." The fear in her voice echoed back.

She tried again. "This is even worse than the bull, God. Maybe you did help me then."

She found it hard to believe that the God who answered her prayers the wrong way could ever do something good. Yet she felt desperate. "If you get me out of this, God, I'll—"

Kate stopped, trying to think of a promise to trick God into helping her. Finally she had it. "If you help me, God, I'll believe you can take care of me. I'll even believe you do good things!"

For a moment Kate stood there, surrounded by silence. She wondered if she'd hear a voice telling her what to do. Now that she'd asked God for help, she felt even more scared. *Maybe God doesn't care what happens to me. Maybe He'll get even for the mean things I've thought about Him.*

Then Kate forgot the maybes. Above the sound of her heartbeat she sensed the stillness of the woods.

Something within Kate broke. She felt strange—still, the way the woods seemed now. For the first time in many months she felt quiet, even peaceful. It helped her remember the words Mr. Nordstrom read. "Be still, and know that I *am* God."

A light breeze touched Kate's face, drying her tears. She drew a deep breath, and her scared feeling slipped away. She felt surprised it was gone.

Then she remembered something else—something Daddy had said. "You have to face things, Kate, even though you're afraid. You have to walk straight ahead."

He'd spoken those words whenever she was afraid. Afraid of starting school. Afraid of trying something she really needed to learn. *Walk straight ahead? But how?*

Kate had heard stories about people lost in the woods. Often they walked in circles, never finding their way out. *Maybe that's what I've been doing.* Her panic started to come back, but so did her father's words. "Walk straight ahead."

How? In the stillness the word seemed to echo back.

Then Kate noticed the sun. Slowly she started out. Carefully, she picked her way around the thickets. This time she used the sun as a guide and headed in one direction.

The minutes stretched long, but at last Kate came to a path. She had no idea where it went, and whether she was going toward school or away. She just felt glad for something to follow. The path had to go somewhere.

After walking a time, Kate saw that off to the left the trees seemed thinner. Perhaps she'd be able to see something from there. Yet she felt afraid to leave the path, knowing she might not find it again.

Carefully Kate looked around. A tall oak behind her. A cluster of birch on her left. Slowly she turned, memorizing the way the trees stood. Then, counting her steps, she moved off the path.

Soon the heavy brush ended. Spying a large rock, Kate climbed onto it. Nearby, the steep hill fell away. Tall marsh grass and small trees broke through the remaining snow. Beyond was the windswept ice of a lake. It seemed familiar.

For a moment Kate thought about it, trying to jog her memory. Then suddenly it struck her. *It's Rice Lake! I know where I am!* She also felt sure she could find Windy Hill Farm. If she kept the lake on her left, she'd be home!

Taking one last look, Kate felt eager to be off. Then she heard the crack of a branch.

Kate stiffened. *Are there bears, after all?*

A second branch cracked. Then came the sound of something shuffling through the dry, dead leaves on the ground. As Kate stood there, the sound moved closer. Closer. Closer.

Kate turned, facing the direction of the sound. As she stood on the rock, she peered over a fallen oak, the dead leaves still clinging to the branches.

Along the path a man came into sight. *Whew! It wasn't a bear.*

Kate opened her mouth to call out, but something told her to be quiet. Then she saw the man's face and was glad.

Under an old hat his curly black hair hung to his shoulders. His long black beard was just as curly and looked as if it hadn't been combed for weeks. He carried a small wooden box and a shovel.

The stranger stopped and looked around. Quickly Kate knelt down behind the fallen oak.

A moment later, she heard the sound of digging. Slowly, quietly, she stood up and peered over the branches.

The man had set the box on the ground. In a small open space away from trees and bushes, he was digging a hole, his back toward Kate. His wrinkled black coat had a long tear on one sleeve.

As Kate watched, the man widened the hole and dug deeper. After a time he set his spade in the dirt and looked around. Her heart thumping, Kate ducked down. When she heard shoveling again, she stood up.

The box was gone, and the man was shoveling dirt back into the hole. Every now and then he stepped on the dirt, stomping it down to pack it. Finally he stood back, seeming to mark the hole between the clump of birch and the large oak.

Again he looked around, but this time at the ground. Breaking off brown clumps of grass left by the melting snow, he carried them to the hole. There he scattered the long strands over the dirt.

Next he collected wet, fallen leaves from under a bush and spread them over the grass. Once more he stood back, looking at his work.

Picking up his tools, the stranger set out. At a muddy spot, he stepped to one side of the path, then kept on toward Windy Hill Farm.

When Kate felt sure the stranger was gone, she retraced her steps to the path. For a moment she stood there, marking the spot between the clump of birch and the large oak. If she hadn't seen the box, she never would have guessed it was there.

Kneeling down, Kate pushed aside the leaves and dried grass. As she uncovered the place the man had dug, she found prints in the dirt. There was something different about them—different from other shoes or boots.

How can I dig up the box? One try in the firmly packed earth, and she knew it was hopeless. She'd have to come back with a shovel. *I'll get Anders. He won't be afraid.*

Quickly Kate covered the spaded earth with the dry grass

and leaves. Satisfied that she'd hidden the spot well, she headed down the path.

At last Kate came to the logging trail, then the wagon track that curved around the bottom of the hill near the Windy Hill farmhouse. When she saw the spring between the road and Rice Lake, she knew she was almost home.

Heavy beams, built around the spring like a large wood box, caught and held the water. Kneeling down, Kate slipped her hands into the wetness. The cold shock went all the way up her arms. But it felt good, too, and she leaned over, lapping water onto her face. Then, cupping her hands, she began to drink.

Finally she rocked back on her heels. For a long moment she sat there, gazing across Rice Lake to the hills beyond.

Her fear of being lost in the woods was gone. But now Kate felt afraid about the stranger she'd seen. *Who is he? What's in the box he buried?* Deep in thought, she didn't hear the step behind her. Instead, Kate felt a tap on her shoulder.

She jumped. Her heart pounded into her throat. *Had that awful looking man come back?*

10

Bees!

*S*pringing to her feet, Kate stepped on the hem of her dress. As she whirled around, she barely heard the rip.

Anders stood there, laughter in his blue eyes. Kate's panic changed to anger. "What are *you* doing here?"

A slow grin lit his face. Reaching down, he plucked a stem of marsh grass that rose above the remaining snow. "All right that I'm here, city girl?" he asked as he began chewing the grass. "It's where I live."

Kate stomped her foot. "I know it's where you live! But what do you mean sneaking up on me like that?"

"Coming to look for you," he drawled. "Just in case you can't find your way home."

"I did just fine," Kate answered, her voice resentful. Yet she felt the blood flooding into her face. "Where were you, anyway?"

"Teacher said not to come back until we stopped laughing. Lars and I couldn't stop laughing." Anders looked as though he was heading off into laughter again. Then he winked. "So we snuck out under the shelves in the cloakroom and came home."

Kate started to smile, almost joining Anders in his laughter. Then she remembered how she felt, hemmed in on every side by bushes, lost and alone. She swallowed around the lump in her throat.

Anders' grin disappeared, and his eyes looked serious. "Forgot you might not remember your way."

"Of course I knew my way!" exclaimed Kate, hoping he wouldn't guess how scared she'd been. "Just took my time walking home."

"You're lying," Anders said calmly. "You still look scared."

Kate straightened her shoulders, trying to make herself look taller. "That's ridiculous!" she replied in her most grown-up voice. "Like I said, I had a good walk."

"Well, just checking to make sure the bears didn't get you."

Suddenly Anders leaned forward, plucked a twig off the sleeve of her coat, and handed it to her. "Got off the path, didn't you? You better wash that scratch on your cheek." Taking out a handkerchief, he dipped it in the spring and leaned forward.

Quickly Kate stepped back, out of reach. "I don't want your help!"

Anders shrugged. "All right by me. But when you wash up, why don't you get the dirt off your face?"

"The dirt?"

"Yup. The ring around the edge of your face."

Once again Kate felt the red creeping up. "Oh, you—you—" she sputtered. Turning, she stomped off toward the house.

Anders' voice followed her. "What's the matter, city girl?" Then he changed to a singsong chant. "Scare-dy-caaat, scare-dy-caaat!"

Without warning, tears welled up in Kate's eyes. She quickened her pace, keeping her back toward Anders so he wouldn't see. *Will I ever feel I belong? Will I ever feel part of this family?*

She was halfway up the steep hill when she remembered. She hadn't told Anders about the mysterious stranger. "Well, I'm not telling him now!" she muttered to herself. "He'd say, 'You're making it up 'cause you're scared!' "

His teasing rang in her ears. *"Scaredy-cat!" he calls me! Well, I had good reason to be afraid. But how can I prove it to him?*

Farther on, Kate met Lutfisk. She hadn't been near the dog

since seeing him in the barn. Today he seemed friendly, and Kate felt relieved. Kneeling, she stroked his black, brown, and white back. When he turned his head to lick her hand, she felt better. *At least one person in this family likes me!*

At the top of the hill, Mr. Nordstrom stood near the beehives, wearing a hat and veil. Aiming his smoker at the entrance of a hive, he pushed the bellows. A cloud of smoke rolled out.

Kate walked closer, and Mr. Nordstrom called to her. "Want to see?"

Thinking about how she disliked his marriage to Mama, Kate started to shake her head. Then she remembered Anders. *I'll show him I'm not a scaredy-cat!*

"Sure," she called to Mr. Nordstrom.

She still felt shy with Mama's new husband. Compared to Daddy, Mr. Nordstrom was quiet and seldom talked unless something needed saying. Yet Kate felt curious about the bees. More than that, she wanted to prove she wasn't a scaredy-cat.

"Ask your mama for some overalls and a straw hat. Tell her there's an old thin curtain in the bottom drawer in the pantry. You can use that for a veil."

Soon Kate was back. The overalls were too big, and Mama insisted that she tie string around her ankles so the bees couldn't crawl inside. On her head Kate wore a straw hat with the curtain draped around to protect her face and neck. It felt hot and clumsy, but she could see.

"Just move slow and quiet," Mr. Nordstrom told her as he took the cover off a hive.

Within the wooden box Mr. Nordstrom called a hive body were a number of frames. "Come closer," he said as she hesitated. "A sunny day like this is a good time to look."

Hundreds of bees crawled across the top of the frames, their wiggling bodies humming. Some of them flew up, heading toward Mr. Nordstrom and Kate. "Stand still," he warned. "Then they won't bother you."

As the bees buzzed around Kate's head, she flinched, wanting to run. "Can they get through my veil?" she asked, fear tightening her muscles.

Mr. Nordstrom laughed. "They seem to get through everything. But you'll be all right. Just stay quiet."

Pushing the bellows, he sent a cloud of smoke toward Kate. The bees left her, and Mr. Nordstrom turned back to the hive.

"What are you looking for?" asked Kate.

"I'm checking on the queen. This time of year she should be laying eggs."

Mr. Nordstrom pulled a frame from the center of the hive body. "See how the bees build honeycomb? All the hexagon-shaped holes? They put eggs and pollen and nectar in them." Mr. Nordstrom tipped the frame toward the sun. "Look close. There's a white line you can barely see. Like a tiny piece of thread."

Kate squinted.

"See it?"

She nodded, her interest growing.

"That's an egg," said Mr. Nordstrom, replacing the frame and picking up another. "Eggs grow into larvae." He pointed to what looked like small white worms. "Larvae grow into bees."

A strange excitement filled Kate—the excitement of knowing she could stand there in spite of her fear of being stung. *I hope Anders sees me.* Aloud she asked, "How do bees know how to do everything?"

"They have different jobs. One hive is like a whole community working together."

"All of 'em?"

Mr. Nordstrom shook his head. "Not all of them. The drones don't work. In fall, when worker bees start worrying about their food supply, they push drones out of the hive."

Kate giggled. "It's like a family. Sometimes they don't like each other."

Mr. Nordstrom looked up quickly. Replacing the cover, he moved a short distance from the hive and took off his hat and veil. "Kate, are you finding it hard to live here?"

Kate glanced away, unwilling to meet his gaze. She didn't want to answer, but Mr. Nordstrom asked again. "It's different for you, isn't it?"

Slowly Kate nodded and began pulling off the old straw hat. Suddenly all the awful feelings of the day washed over her. Falling in the mud. Being new in school. Everyone laughing. And then, getting lost in the woods because of dumb Anders. Kate was afraid to look at Mr. Nordstrom—afraid she'd cry.

"It's hard to get used to changes, isn't it?" he asked.

Surprise caught Kate off guard. Her words were out before she could stop them. "How did you know?"

Mr. Nordstrom's quiet smile reached his blue eyes. "Whether we're children or grownups, it's difficult for all of us. When we have to face new things, I mean."

He cleared his throat. "I wish for your sake your papa hadn't died—just like I wish my Anna hadn't died. But it happened to both of them. And we can't go back by just wishing."

Kate swallowed, knowing he was right, but unable to speak. Always Mr. Nordstrom seemed so quiet, as though nothing really bothered him.

"Look ahead, Kate," he said, surprising her again. "You have to go on."

"How?" she asked, the word exploding from within. It hung between them in the quiet air. Kate wished it was that simple. Inside, there was a little hollow place where her heart used to be. "How?" she asked again. She needed to know.

But Mr. Nordstrom had another question. "What means a lot to you, Kate? I know you want a real family." He grinned. "Not every day. At least, not when Anders is mean."

"How did you know?" Kate's words gave her away.

"I know Anders. He'll get over it. But at least some of the time you want a happy family. Your mama told me so. What else is important to you?"

Kate was afraid to tell him. No one had asked that question before. She hadn't told anyone, not even Mama. Yet somehow she felt she could trust Mr. Nordstrom.

"I want to play the organ," she answered finally, her voice small. But then the strength of her wish welled up, and her words tumbled out. "I want to travel around the United States, giving concerts like Jenny Lind."

"The Swedish nightingale?"

Kate nodded. "But instead of singing, I want to be an organist." Kate stopped. The words were out. She couldn't call them

back, and she felt scared. What if Mr. Nordstrom laughed?
But he didn't.

"You could learn from Mr. Peters," he said.

"Mr. Peters?"

"The organist at our church."

"You have an organ?"

"Yah, sure. The first hand-pumped organ in the county."

"You do? Here in the wilderness?"

Mr. Nordstrom's grin reached his eyes, reminding Kate of Anders. "Well, it's not quite the end of the world."

After a moment he spoke again. "You'd have to have something to practice on. Are you willing to work to buy an organ?"

Kate gasped. "Oh yes! But it's so much money."

"Yah. But let's think. How can you earn the money?"

"I don't know," Kate answered slowly. It seemed impossible. Yet deep inside, she felt hope for the first time. The hope that maybe, just maybe—

"I'll think about it," she said, and Mr. Nordstrom smiled.

He picked up his smoker, and they started back to the house. "You'll be all right, Kate. You'll earn your way with Anders."

Outside the kitchen door he spoke once more. "And when you feel ready, I'd be honored to have you call me Papa."

11

View From the Bell Tower

During supper Kate listened to the other children call Mr. Nordstrom Papa. Since his marriage to Mama, Kate had avoided calling him by name. But that night, in the room and bed that she shared with Tina, she thought about what Mr. Nordstrom said.

Only Daddy will ever really seem like a father to me.

Yet as she lay quietly in the darkness, she thought of something. *Daddy's been dead for a year and a half now. Is it the name that matters? Or how much he loved me?*

When Mr. Nordstrom talked to me today, it was almost like hearing Daddy say, "Walk straight ahead, Kate. You have to face things, even though you're afraid."

Long ago Kate had tucked away those words in her heart. She wanted to remember Daddy saying them. She wanted to remember how it felt when he came home from work and gave her a big hug. How his eyes twinkled when he laughed, and how he sang funny songs that always made her feel better. She wanted to hold those memories of Daddy so they wouldn't slip away.

Strange, though, how more than anything he told her, she remembered him saying, "Look ahead, Kate, not back. Walk straight ahead." He had spoken those words more than once as if he knew she'd need to remember them.

But what did they mean now? Kate still felt scared about the way God answered her prayer for a husband for Mama. She still wanted to go to school with Sarah Livingston and Michael Reilly. Was that looking back?

When Tina fell asleep, Kate practiced saying *Papa* the way the other children did. She tried to fit Mr. Nordstrom's face with the name. Maybe sometime she could say Papa to him. But not yet.

Soon after, Kate drifted off to sleep. Toward morning she dreamed about bees. In her dream she stood near the hives. As she watched, honey started to flow out of the top. Spilling over the sides, the runaway honey became golden rivers along the ground.

Kate scrambled for jars. "Where are they?" she cried out. But not even Mama knew where to get enough jars.

"That's it!" Kate told herself as she woke up.

During breakfast she talked to Mr. Nordstrom. "Do you ever get extra honey?"

"Sometimes. In a good year. You look as though you have an idea."

Filled with excitement, Kate nodded. "If I help with the bees—"

Anders interrupted. "You want to be a *beekeeper*?"

Kate nodded, and shock registered in Anders' eyes. "Bees sting, you know."

"I know," answered Kate, her voice soft. "Are you afraid of them?"

"Of course not!" said Anders, his voice louder than it needed to be.

Looking up from her oatmeal, Kate caught the grin playing around Mr. Nordstrom's mouth. She tried not to smile as she asked, "What do you think?"

"Let's work together. I'll do the lifting and show you what to do. If we get a good crop—more than our family needs—you can take the extra jars to Grantsburg and sell them at the county fair."

"Great!" answered Kate. For the first time she dared to believe she might really get an organ.

As breakfast ended, Mama asked her to put away the milk. By now Kate knew what to do. Going outside, she set the pail of milk on the wooden platform surrounding the pump. As Kate opened a hinged trapdoor in the platform, she saw heavy timbers lining the walls of the well.

In the center of the well a pipe went up into the pump. Nearby hung a rope with a hook on the end. Lying down on her stomach, Kate grabbed the rope. Attaching the hook to the handle of the pail, she lowered the milk. Down next to the water it stayed cool, even in summer.

Just then Anders came up behind her. "Let's go," he said. "Time for school."

As Kate pushed herself up, the sleeve of her coat caught on a sliver of wood. Afraid it would tear, she lowered herself to free the material.

Anders hooted, then spoke in the quavery voice of an older woman. "In all my life—my wh-o-o-ole life—I never seen such a child for getting in trouble."

"Stop it!" said Kate, embarrassed again. Frantically she pulled at the wool thread wrapped around the splinter.

"But, child, how do you manage? One problem after another."

Then the thread came free, and Kate jumped up. A minute later she and Anders and Lars left for school.

This time Kate took no chances about having to find her way home. She noticed every step, every fork in the trail. Yet this morning Anders seemed different.

Maybe he'll be nice for a change. Kate was afraid to hope. Just the same, she decided to test it out. When Lars ran ahead out of earshot, she asked, "Do you know what I saw yesterday?" Soon she told Anders about the man digging down a box in the woods.

Anders looked puzzled. "Long curly hair, you say? And curly beard? Black?"

Kate nodded.

"Can't think of anyone around here who looks like that."

"But I saw him. I know I did!" answered Kate, afraid Anders wouldn't believe her.

"Can you remember anything else?"

"A black handlebar moustache," Kate answered. "Couldn't see his eyes very well, but I think they were blue." For a moment she thought. "No, maybe gray."

"Old clothes?"

Kate nodded. "Black. And dirty."

"Weren't you scared?"

For an instant Kate thought of lying, of saying, "Of course not!" the way Anders had at breakfast. But she wanted to be friends. She decided to risk it, and nodded, still afraid of what he'd say.

Anders was mean all right. "Well, it's good to know you're still a girl."

Kate almost hit him, but then caught the grin in his eyes— and the respect.

"Where's the box? Where's it buried?" Anders asked.

Lars was still ahead of them when they came to the cluster of birch and the big oak. Kate knelt down, swept the leaves and grass away, and showed Anders the spot. Anders' low whistle was all the thanks she needed.

"See the boot prints?" she asked. "They're crisscrossed from stamping, so it's hard to tell. But there's one clear print."

Anders knelt down for a closer look.

"There's something different about it," said Kate. "Is it a boot? Or a shoe? See the heel? The heavy outer line?"

"You're right," answered Anders. "And look at the toe. Almost as if there's an iron plate or something."

Then in the distance they heard the first bell ring.

"Have to go," said Anders. "I'm already in trouble with the teacher."

Quickly he replaced the leaves and grass. "Let's dig up the box after school. Maybe it's buried treasure. Maybe there'd be a reward, and I could buy a horse."

"Or an organ," answered Kate, then wished she could bite her tongue.

"An *organ*? Who wants an organ?"

"I do!" said Kate, sorry she'd let her secret slip out.

"But you can't ride an organ!"

"You're not supposed to, silly! You're supposed to play it!"

Anders began walking fast. As Kate hurried alongside, she caught his look. "Dumb girl!" it seemed to say. Right now, that's how Kate felt. *I wish I hadn't told him.*

As they entered school, Kate looked around and saw that the plain dress she wore today was more like those of the other girls. Yet her relief didn't last long. Soon after she sat down, she felt a slight tug on her braid.

Swinging around, she faced Erik Lundgren, the boy sitting behind her. Lifting his hands as if in surrender, his eyes widened with innocence.

"Stop it!" Kate said, so angry that she spoke aloud.

"I didn't do a thing!" he answered just as loud.

"Yes, you did! You stuck my braid in your inkwell." Kate was right. Pulling her long braid forward, she saw the end. Already the drying ink stiffened the hair.

Twisting her head, she pulled at her dress, trying to see the shoulders. Sure enough, splatters from the braid covered the material.

"Kate, what's the problem?" Miss Sundquist asked.

If I tell her, the boys will be even meaner. Kate ducked her head.

The boys snickered, but Anders gave them a look, and they stopped. As everyone went back to work, Kate felt grateful. She used a precious piece of paper to pass Anders a note.

Three people away from Kate, Miss Sundquist intercepted it. "Kate, this is a serious offense. I expect you to stay in for noon hour."

When lunch time came, the other children ate quickly, then hurried outside. For the first time in her life Kate felt glad to stay indoors. *At least I won't have another hour of trying to understand Swedish!*

Then she heard a ball bounce on the roof. "Anti-Over!" someone called. Kate knew the children must have chosen teams, lining up on opposite sides of the school building.

"Anti-Over!" came the call again. Kate was good at the game and wished she could join them. She reached the window in time to see Lars come around the schoolhouse and tag Anders.

That's strange. Anders is faster. He should have gotten away.

Anders wound up as if for a mighty toss. The ball sailed through the air. "Anti-Over!" he shouted.

Kate hurried to a window on the opposite side of the building. There the team waited, but no ball came over the roof. *Where'd it go?* But she didn't have time to find out.

"Kate!" called Miss Sundquist from her desk. Usually she went outside with the children. Today she remained at her desk, her half-eaten lunch in front of her.

"Yes, ma'am?"

"When I ask you to stay in, I expect you to stay in your seat."

Slowly Kate walked over and sat down. Picking up her book, she pretended to read. Then she heard the door open.

"Miss Sundquist?" asked Anders from the entryway.

"Yes, Anders?"

"The ball's caught in the bell tower. May I go up and get it?"

Miss Sundquist sighed. "All right. But be careful."

"Yes, ma'am. I will, ma'am."

As Kate waited, the sound of a ladder scraped the edge of the roof. Through a window she watched Anders' feet climbing the rungs. A minute later the ball rolled off the roof, landing outside a window. Anders scrambled down the ladder, and Kate went back to her reading.

Not long after, the game moved away from the school. Soon Kate wondered about the quiet. It seemed all the children had gone to the far end of the ball field.

"Kate, will you ring the bell, please?" asked Miss Sundquist.

Standing up, Kate felt grateful for the chance to move around. Going into the entryway, she grabbed the long rope that led to the bell and pulled.

Nothing happened. Kate tugged harder. Still no sound.

"What's the matter, Kate? Aren't you strong enough?"

"I'm fine, Miss Sundquist. I'll get it." This time Kate jumped high in the air, letting the whole weight of her body pull the rope.

But nothing happened. *That dumb Anders. It's one of his tricks.*

Coming out in the entryway, Miss Sundquist tried the rope. No sound came. "Go and call the children, Kate," she said.

Pulling on her coat, Kate went out, glad for the time outside. She was right. The children were all on the other side of the ball field.

When she reached them, Kate said, "Come on in."

A little girl looked at her, turned her hands palm up, then shrugged her shoulders.

Kate pointed to the school. "Miss Sundquist."

The little girl shrugged once more. Kate tried an older child, but couldn't understand the Swedish response.

Again Kate struggled to explain. Then an older boy laughed, and Kate caught on. Everyone was just pretending they didn't know what she said.

Quickly Kate turned away, not wanting them to see the hurt she felt. As she swung around, she bumped into Anders.

He'd been running, Kate could tell. His breath came in long gasps. Seeing him there, she felt angry all the way through. Knotting her fists, Kate beat them against his chest. "I hate you!" she stormed. "I hate you, hate you, hate you!"

For once Anders didn't fight back. Grabbing her hands, he stopped her. "Go on in," he whispered in English. "I'll tell you after school."

Turning to the children, Anders spoke in Swedish, and they obeyed him. Walking slowly, they started toward the schoolhouse.

12

Another Surprise

*W*ill the day ever be over? Kate felt impatient to talk with Anders. Minute by slow minute the afternoon dragged by.

As soon as Miss Sundquist let them go, Kate and Anders and Lars crossed the creek and started up the hill.

Anders poked along until Lars grew restless. "Beat you home!" Lars said, and Kate felt glad to see him run ahead.

"What was that all about?" she demanded.

"The school bell?" Anders grinned. "Well, it started out as a game. I threw the ball into the tower so I'd have an excuse to go up. Thought it was about time we had a longer lunch hour."

Kate laughed. "You managed that all right."

"Yup. There's a pulley hooked to the bell. I just took the rope out of the groove."

Then Anders' face grew serious. "Something else happened."

Though they seemed to be alone in the woods, he lowered his voice. "Turn around," he commanded.

They stood at the top of the steep hill behind the school, and Kate looked back.

"What do you see?" asked Anders.

"A good view of the school."

"Right. And what do you think you'd see if you were up in the bell tower?"

Kate thought for a moment. "A good view of this hill?"

"A *great* view of this hill," answered Anders. "And do you know who I saw on top of this hill?"

Kate couldn't guess.

"Your mysterious stranger!"

"Really? How do you know?"

"Baggy, dirty clothes. Curly black hair and beard. Handlebar moustache. Sound like him?"

Kate nodded, excitement bubbling up. "Sounds exactly like him."

"I tore up the hill as fast as I could," said Anders. "By the time I got here, he was gone. So I started down the path. I ran all the way back to where he buried the box. When I got there, nothing had changed. The leaves looked the way we left them."

"And the man?"

"I don't know. Maybe he heard me coming. Maybe he stepped back in the woods—" Anders didn't finish the sentence.

Kate said it for him. "Stepped back to hide. Maybe he's watching us now." She shivered.

Anders shook his head. "I don't think so. He heard me coming. He probably waited to see me leave. By now, he's probably gone."

"And the box?"

"Let's go look," Anders said, his face grim.

Before long, Kate and Anders came to the clump of birch and the big oak. A heaped up pile of dirt and an empty hole marked the place where the box had been.

"It's gone!" Kate groaned. "The stranger didn't even bother to fill the hole!"

"Maybe he thought people would figure an animal did it. Does look kind of like a badger hole." Anders picked up a stick and poked it deep in the dirt. "Nothing here, all right."

Kate grabbed his sleeve. "Yes, there is." She pointed down at the soft dirt. "Look!"

Anders saw what she meant. "You're right! He's taken a branch and scratched out every print!"

Kate felt uneasy. "Sure acts as if he has a lot to hide. We better be careful."

Anders nodded, his blue eyes dark with thought.

After that, the week dragged by. On Saturday morning, as the sun peeked over the horizon, it wakened Kate. With relief she remembered she didn't have to go to school.

It felt good lying beneath the soft patchwork quilt. Stretching her arms high above her head, she looked over at Tina. The little girl was still sleeping. Her heart-shaped face looked soft and unprotected. Her white-blond hair spread out on the pillow.

They still weren't able to talk much together. During the week Kate had learned more Swedish and Tina more English. Yet after wanting a little sister for so long, it made Kate feel good just sharing a room with her. Tina seemed to like it too.

Trying to shut out the sun, Kate pulled the quilt over her head. She was almost asleep again when she heard what sounded like thunder. Boom! Boom! Boom!

Strange. How can it be thundering with the sun out?

Once again Kate heard the booms. This time her eyes flew open. "Gunshots!" she cried out.

Throwing back the covers, Kate leaped out of bed. "Sarah said it would be like this. She said it'd be wild in Wisconsin!"

Running back to the bed, she shook Tina's shoulder. "Wake up! Something's wrong!"

Boom! Boom! Boom!

Tina rolled over, and Kate shook her again. "There's a fight outside. We have to hide!"

Boom! Boom! The noise sounded closer. "Tina, how can you sleep through this?" Kate was desperate.

Tina opened one eye, then the other. As if in slow motion, she sat up, put her feet on the floor, then stood. Acting as though she had all the time in the world, she walked to the window near the big pine.

"Tina, have you lost your brains?" Kate felt frantic.

Tina motioned to her. "Look!" she seemed to be saying. Pushing up the window, she leaned out and pointed.

Through an opening between the branches, Kate saw the wagon track that passed the kitchen, granary, and chicken coop.

The back of the house blocked a full view, but Kate could see part of the pasture near the barn. This morning no cows grazed there.

Again, Tina pointed that way. Just then, another explosion rattled the windows. Boom! Boom! Two stumps flew high in the air.

Kate slid to the floor. "Will I ever get used to this place?" she asked, holding her head in her hands. She felt dumb, stupid, absolutely ridiculous. "What if Anders finds out?"

In that moment she remembered the little girl. "Tina, don't tell, will you?" Tina stood beside Kate, her face solemn, a question in her blue eyes. "You mustn't tell Anders or Lars," Kate repeated.

Then she remembered Tina didn't understand English. Putting her finger to her lips, Kate whispered, "Shhhhh! Shhhhh!" Next she pointed to herself, then outside.

This time Tina grinned. Pointing outside, then at Kate, she shook her head. They shared a secret now.

Kneeling on the floor beside Kate, Tina hugged her. Relief flooded Kate, and her arms went around her new sister.

As they dressed, Kate heard more booms, but they seemed farther away. When she and Tina went down, the rest of the family was at the breakfast table. Seeing the girls, Mama got their bacon and eggs from the warming oven of the cookstove.

Kate was full of questions. "What are you doing?" she asked Mr. Nordstrom.

"I've been using the field for pasture," he explained. "I want to get it ready for planting. So I drill a hole in each stump as deep as I can in the root system. Then I put in as many sticks of dynamite as I need."

"Why do the stumps keep blowing up, one after another?"

"I light a fuse in one stump, then go on to the next," he told her. "I have to move quickly, away from the one I've lit, so I don't get caught too close to the explosion."

When everyone finished eating, Mr. Nordstrom took down his big Bible. Together they read and prayed as they had every morning all week. Kate was beginning to like hearing the verses, but if someone had asked, she wouldn't have admitted it for anything.

Mr. Nordstrom pushed back his chair. "I want to make sure all the dynamite's exploded. Then I need help picking up. All of you except Ingrid." He smiled at Mama, and she smiled back, her eyes soft.

"Com'on, Kate," said Anders, his blue eyes teasing. "I'll show you how to get dirty."

Kate wrinkled her nose at him, remembering the first day of school.

She soon found Anders was right. Picking up blown-apart stumps was dirty work. Everyone pitched in, dragging the stumps to piles at different places around the field. Sometimes the pieces of wood were too big for Kate. Anders and his father took those, or left them to be blown apart again.

As the sun climbed higher, streaks of sweat started to mix with the dirt on Kate's body. Then she discovered all kinds of muscles she didn't know she had. Soon all she could think about was a soaking bath in the big washtub.

Yet all of them kept at it, even Tina. The piles of wood at different places around the pasture grew steadily higher. As Kate worked, she gradually moved to a far corner of the field, away from the house and barn, but next to the wagon track. From there the track wound through the trees to the dirt road leading to Grantsburg.

The sun was nearly overhead when she came to a stump that wasn't as shattered as the rest. A large portion still lay buried in the ground. Bending down to pick up a loose piece, Kate caught a glint of color. Bright red, it seemed.

Dropping to her knees, she began feeling around in the sandy soil. Brushing aside the dirt that spit up in the explosion, she uncovered what looked like red glass. Digging farther, she saw more red glass—one bead, then another. A moment later she pulled out a necklace.

"Hey, look!" she called, holding up her find. The glass glinted in the sunlight.

Tina was beside her immediately, her eyes shining through the dirt on her face.

Mr. Nordstrom looked puzzled. "Strange," he said. "What's a necklace doing under a stump?"

"Maybe there was a hollow place," answered Anders, his face just as dirty as Tina's. His blond hair looked gray. "Maybe there's more."

Lars was already down on his knees. "Where'd you find it?"

Kate showed them, and everyone began digging in the loose dirt around the stump.

Lars was the first to find another necklace, then Tina found one. All together they unearthed five necklaces—each of brightly colored glass.

"Where'd they come from?" asked Kate.

"I don't know." Mr. Nordstrom's eyes looked thoughtful. "We aren't far from Trader Carlson's. When he buys buckskin and furs from Indians, he trades them traps and food and things like this."

"But why would the necklaces be *here*?" asked Kate, the strangeness of it bothering her.

Lars's red hair was down in his face and his eyes were serious. "I seen them camp near here."

"Just the same, you've got something, Kate," said Mr. Nordstrom. "They always take their belongings with when they leave."

"And why would they hide *necklaces*?" asked Anders. One by one, he put the strings of beads across the palm of his hand, letting them hang down. The glass sparkled in the sunlight.

"Oh!" Kate gasped.

"What's wrong?" asked Lars.

Kate closed her mouth, trying to hide her surprise. "Oh, nothing." But something nagged at the back of her mind. Something she needed to remember.

Mr. Nordstrom's eyes looked thoughtful again. "Let's stop and eat. We'll show the beads to your mama and see if we can find the owner."

As they crossed the field, Kate dragged behind, trying to figure out what bothered her.

Anders dropped back to walk with her. "What is it?" he asked, his voice low so Tina wouldn't hear.

Kate turned to him. "If only I could remember." For a time she thought hard. "It's something to do with the sunlight. When you held up those beads . . ." Kate's voice trailed away. Walking on in silence, she racked her brain. "What is it about the sunlight?"

As they neared the farmhouse, something clicked in Kate's mind. "Remember a week ago?" she asked. "Last Saturday? My first day here?"

Anders grinned. Even through the dirt on his face, his blue eyes danced. "It's not hard to forget. The bull chased you."

For once Kate didn't bristle. "And I got so scared I forgot why I started across the field. Why I didn't see the bull."

Anders' grin faded, and his eyes grew serious.

Kate went on. "When I came out of the barn, I looked across to the trees on the other side of this pasture. I thought I saw something move. Then I figured I must be wrong. When I looked again, I saw a good climbing tree straight ahead. In the hollow where a branch goes out from the trunk, something glittered."

"Something like a necklace?"

Kate nodded, her eyes wide. "And something else. Something black. Something as tall as a man standing up. I thought it was a bear but. . . . What do you think?"

13

The Big Storm

"Do I think it was a bear?" asked Anders. "I doubt it. But maybe—" Leaving the thought unfinished, he fell silent. Kate tried, but couldn't get him to tell what he thought.

As soon as they finished eating lunch, Kate and Anders hurried to the tree on the far side of the pasture. Anders pulled himself up to the lower branches and the hollow Kate remembered. But she wasn't surprised by what they found.

"It's empty!" Anders called down, as disappointed as Kate.

From that time on, both of them kept their eyes open for anything that seemed unusual. Wherever they went, they looked for the stranger. Yet one day followed the next without another glimpse of him. Mr. Nordstrom put the glass beads in a box and asked around, trying to find the owner.

The blustery days of March turned into April showers and then May flowers. Kate became better acquainted with some of girls at school. One of these was Josie Swenson.

Gradually Kate started to believe that Josie might become a real friend—a special friend, like Sarah Livingston.

Anders' pig grew, and the bees prospered. Mr. Nordstrom checked the hives often, and Kate helped him. By early May, when the maples budded, she knew how to direct smoke at the entrance and top, then quietly open a hive.

As the bees buzzed upward and their humming increased to a roar, Mr. Nordstrom stood nearby, watching to see if she could handle it. It took all of Kate's courage to stand still.

Then the bees swarmed around her, crawling up and down her overalls. "I'm not a scaredy-cat!" she told herself, remembering how Anders teased. "I'm not a scaredy-cat!"

When the bees lit on her arms and shoulders, it was even worse. Trying to push aside her fear of being stung, Kate took a deep breath, then let it out slowly. *I'll show Anders*! she thought, as she had many times before. Pushing the bellows of the smoker, she directed a cloud of smoke over her arms and legs.

"Good for you!" said Mr. Nordstrom, interrupting her thoughts. "See the pollen the bees are bringing in?"

As Kate watched, bees lit on the board in front of the hive entrance. Each carried lumps of pollen—tiny golden nuggets—in what Mr. Nordstrom said were baskets on their rear legs.

"Other worker bees put pollen in the honeycomb," he explained. "Here, I'll show you."

As he told Kate what to do, she lifted a frame from the center of the hive body.

"See how the bees pack away pollen?" he asked. "Look! There's the queen!"

A bee with a longer, larger body than the others moved across the frame. Immediately worker bees turned in her direction, clustering around.

"They always protect the queen," Mr. Nordstrom said. "If she died when there are no eggs in the hive, the other bees would gradually die out."

When Kate replaced the frame, Mr. Nordstrom showed her how to close the hive. "If this keeps on, we'll have a good year."

"With extra honey?" she asked.

A grin lit Mr. Nordstrom's sun-weathered face. "Yah, sure. If nothing goes wrong. Still want to buy an organ?"

Kate's heart jumped, glad he hadn't forgotten. "Yes, I want to buy an organ!" she exclaimed, thinking of all the songs she'd like to play. "Will there be enough money?"

Mr. Nordstrom shook his head. "But it'll be a start. You can put whatever money you earn in a jar, and add more when you can."

Walking to the house, Kate took off the straw hat and the thin curtain she used for a veil. "Maybe I can think up more ways to earn money," she said, pushing aside the hair that fell around her face. Getting an organ seemed even more of a possibility.

During the weeks that followed, Kate and Anders often talked about the mysterious stranger. "Why do we see him just once in a while?" asked Anders one morning the first week in June. "Why does he keep disappearing?"

Kate shook her head. They were out in the little house called a summer kitchen. Along one wall was the wood cookstove the family used during hot weather. Along another wall was a tall cupboard for storing dishes and pans. A shorter cupboard had a metal sink and pans for washing dishes. Anders sat on a bench near the third wall, leaning on the table.

Usually Kate liked it here. Today not even a whisper of breeze came through the open windows. The cookstove was still hot from breakfast, and Kate used it for ironing clothes. When one sadiron grew cool, she set it down on the stove. Detaching the handle, she reattached it to another, already heated iron. Licking her finger, she touched the bottom of the iron. It sizzled, and she knew it was hot enough.

"They're sure named right," she said. "Sadirons—makes me sad to use 'em." Running the iron across a piece of white cloth, she tested the heat before touching Tina's Sunday dress.

But Anders wanted to talk about the stranger. "Why doesn't anyone around here know him?" he asked, a frown creasing his tanned forehead.

"The stranger? No one knows him?"

"I asked Papa," said Anders. "He's never seen anyone who looks like what I said."

"Not anyone at all?"

"Nope, and Papa knows *everybody*. He warned me to be careful. To stay away from strangers and tell him if I see the man again."

"Did you tell him why you wondered?"

Anders nodded, his blue eyes puzzled. "Can you remember anything else?"

Kate shook her head, and the sweat on her forehead dripped into her eyes. As she thought about it, she finished ironing Tina's dress.

In the heat of June, that March day—her first day at Spirit Lake School—seemed far away. Recalling the woods and being lost in them, Kate felt a twinge of fear. Every so often the memory of her panic returned. Always she pushed that memory away, trying not to think about it. In the same way, she pushed aside the memory of her promise to God.

Now as Kate thought about standing on the large rock, watching the mysterious stranger, she recalled something. "He had a strange walk!" she exclaimed, setting down the iron to think about it.

"Strange?"

"As though his walk didn't fit his clothes."

Anders hooted. "Awww, Kate!"

Kate felt she had to defend herself. "I mean it!"

"His walk didn't fit his clothes?" Anders' blue eyes gleamed as though he wanted to laugh again. "Any other big clues?"

Kate bristled. "Maybe. Maybe not!"

"Hey, stop it! Don't be so pigheaded."

"Pigheaded, am I?" Kate was hot and tired, even though it was ten o'clock in the morning. "Big and fat like your old sow?"

Anders straightened his face. "Nah," he drawled. "Your eyes are prettier!"

Quickly Kate turned away, wondering if her face was as red as it felt.

"Come on, Kate. Don't be mad," pleaded Anders. "Do you remember anything else?"

Kate picked up another sadiron. "Wouldn't tell you if I did."

Anders shoulders slumped. He pushed back his chair and stood up. "Well!"

Kate felt as discouraged as he looked. She and Anders were taking care of the farm. Early that morning Mama and Mr. Nordstrom had driven off to Grantsburg for a new plow coming in on the Blueberry Special. It was a big day when someone went into town, and when they left Mama's eyes sparkled with excitement.

"Be sure you watch Lars and Tina," she reminded Kate before she left. "Take good care of them."

Now all Kate could think about was the heat. "Whew!" she said as Anders tapped the screen door to chase away the flies on the outside.

"Whew for sure," he answered. "It's hot!"

As the morning went on, the humidity grew steadily worse. Kate gave up on ironing. Yet when she moved away from the cookstove, the heat still felt as though it rose in waves from the ground.

The weather affected even Tina. Usually good-natured, the four-year-old was restless and out of sorts. Finally Kate found the Sears Roebuck catalogue. "If you promise to be very careful you can look at it."

By noon the air felt too heavy to breathe. In midafternoon clouds gathered along the horizon.

As the faraway rumbles of thunder moved closer, Kate sought out Anders in the barn. "Anders? What do you do if there's a real bad storm?"

For once Anders didn't call her scaredy-cat. Instead, he went outside and looked at the sky. In the southwest lightning shattered the blackness. Thunder rumbled. Around Kate and Anders not a leaf moved.

As they watched, the clouds grew larger. "Where are Tina and Lars?" he asked.

"In the house looking at the wish book."

"Let's not say anything yet," he answered. "No use scaring 'em. But I'll get the cows in."

He whistled between his teeth, and Lutfisk bounded around the corner of the barn. Anders raised his right arm high and pointed in the direction of the pasture. "Go get 'em," he ordered, and Lutfisk took off.

"The cows will know it's early and won't want to come. I better help him."

As he started to follow Lutfisk, Kate stopped Anders with

her question. "Where do you go if it's really bad?" she asked again.

"The root cellar, Papa said once. But don't worry. We've never had to use it. Just keep an eye on Tina and Lars."

Kate returned to the house but kept looking out the windows. Finally she went back outside. As she stood on the edge of the steep hill, she had a good view across Rice Lake. The sky looked angry. A large fan-shaped cloud gathered in the southwest.

Moment by moment, the rumble of thunder moved closer. With it Kate's tension grew. Faraway lightning flashed pink in the dark clouds.

She wished Anders would come.

Then she remembered Mama and Mr. Nordstrom. *Where are they? Still in Grantsburg? Or on the way home?* In that moment she recalled every story she'd heard about wagons and buggies struck by lightning.

Trying to push those thoughts aside, Kate hurried back to the house. Yet her worry wouldn't go away. *What if they get caught out in the open? What if they can't get to shelter?*

Up until now she'd often worried about Mama. Often she'd thought, *What would I do without her*? Now it felt strange having someone else to be scared about. It surprised Kate to realize she cared about what happened to Mr. Nordstrom.

The next time Kate went outside to look at the sky, Tina followed. Once more the sky had changed. The clouds were no longer black, but green. Like water in a kettle, they seemed to boil. The air felt still and heavy.

"Tina, go to the root cellar," Kate ordered, running for the house. "Lars! Come on!"

The root cellar was a small room dug into the side of the hill between the summer kitchen and the barn. As Lars caught up to Tina, he ran ahead and pulled open the door. Inside was a short passageway, then a second door leading into a dark, hole-like room. Shelves for storing food lined three walls. Under them, bushel baskets waited for a new crop of potatoes.

Now before harvest the shelves were almost empty, and Kate stacked baskets to make room to sit down. Tina and Lars dropped to the dirt floor, while Kate hurried back outside.

Mama's picture! Running to the house, she snatched it up, then rushed back to the root cellar. Carefully she set the picture on a top shelf. Then, as soon as she caught her breath, she returned outside.

"Where's Anders?" she worried aloud.

Lars followed her. "Should I look for him?"

"You better wait here," said Kate. "He's getting the cows. I'm sure he'll come."

The lightning seemed closer now, the clouds greener. Then Kate heard Lutfisk bark. "Anders must be on the other side of the barn."

It seemed forever before he came out on Kate's side. A sudden gust of wind caught the barn door, swinging it back to crash against the building. Anders grabbed it, flung it shut, and dropped the bar that held the door in place.

Trees bent low before the wind. Nearby, a branch broke off and sailed through the air. "We're here!" shouted Kate, but the wind brought the words back to her.

Anders headed for the house, and Kate called again. "Over here!"

This time Anders heard and changed direction. Bending low, he struggled against the wind, Lutfisk tagging behind.

Lars headed back into the cellar, and Kate followed. Just as Anders reached the outer door, a mighty thud shook the earth. Anders tumbled into the passageway.

"Take the dog!" Pushing Lutfisk in, Anders grabbed the outer door. The wind flung it back, but with a mighty heave, Anders managed to close it, then the inner door.

Still short of breath from running, he dropped to the dirt floor.

"What was that?" asked Kate.

"The crash? Probably a tree," he answered.

In the darkness Tina started to cry.

14

Discovery!

"I want Mama," whimpered Tina from the blackness of the cellar. By now Kate knew enough Swedish to understand.

"I do too," she answered. In the dark she felt Tina's hand reaching out for hers. Pulling the little girl onto her lap, Kate gave her a hug.

"I wish Papa was here," said Lars, his voice small and scared.

"I wish *both* of them were here," Anders chimed in. Always Anders acted so sure of himself, as if he didn't need anyone. But not now.

Me too. Kate felt afraid to say it aloud. She wondered if Mama and Papa were safe. Had they found shelter somewhere? More than that, Kate wished all of them were together. The idea surprised her.

Then she realized something else. Before this, when alone, she'd practiced calling Mr. Nordstrom *Papa*. But never before had she called him Papa in her thoughts.

When did Anders and Lars and Tina start calling Mama by that name? Somewhere along the way it just happened. *Is that what Mama meant when she said, "As Mr. Nordstrom and I help each other, we'll grow to love one another"?*

Now a movement in the darkness startled Kate. "What's that?"

"It's me," said Anders. "Should be some candles somewhere." For a time he searched the shelves, feeling his way. Finally he had to give up.

Just then another thud shook the earth. "That was close," said Anders. "Must be the big oak back of the house."

Now and then the wind whistled through a crack in the outer door. As the rain beat against it, Kate felt scared again. "Where do you think they are?" she asked.

"Mama and Papa? They're inside somewhere." But Anders' voice lacked its usual confidence. "Papa's good about weather," he went on, as though talking himself into believing they were all right. "Being a farmer, he has to be. He notices things."

As they waited, the darkness seemed to close in around Kate. Her scared feelings changed to panic. Then she remembered another day, three months before—the day she was lost in the woods.

She had cried out to God, making a promise. "If you help me, I'll believe you can take care of me. I'll even believe you do good things!"

But now Kate felt ashamed. *The minute I was safe, I forgot about you, God. I figured I did it on my own.*

For a time the cellar was quiet except for the dog's panting. Still hugging Tina with one arm, Kate reached out with her other hand. Feeling the hair on the dog's back, she moved her hand forward and scratched behind his ears. When Lutfisk turned his head to lick her hand, Kate was surprised. Always Lutfisk had been Anders' dog.

The minutes stretched long in the quiet cellar. *I'm your bad-weather friend, God. When I'm scared, I ask for help. When I'm all right, I forget about you. How would I feel if Sarah was my friend only when she needed help?*

Tina moved in her arms, and Kate wondered if the darkness bothered Tina as much as the storm. When the little girl drew a long shuddering breath, Kate began to hum, low and soft. Long ago, Daddy had sung whenever she was scared. Now Kate hummed a lullaby she'd learned from him.

Then she had a terrible thought. *What if Anders laughs?* In the middle of the song she stopped.

A moment later Tina started singing. In a clear, high voice she sang words Kate didn't understand.

"What's she singing?" Kate asked softly.

From the darkness Lars spoke just as quietly. "A Swede song, 'Children of the Heavenly Father.'"

Anders remained silent, but Tina kept singing. Strangely enough, Kate felt better, even though she didn't understand the words. She felt the change in the musty cellar.

Then as suddenly as it started, the rain stopped beating at the outer door. In the darkness Kate heard Anders crawl toward the entrance. "It's moved on. The storm's passed."

One by one they left the shelter—Lars, Tina, then Kate. Outside, she looked around, shocked by what she saw.

A short distance from the root cellar a huge oak lay on the ground, leaving a gaping hollow where the roots had been. The long trunk stretched across the yard, its sprawling branches barely missing the house.

Anders walked over and stood beside the tree. In spite of his height, the upended roots towered above him. Slowly he turned, looking toward the house, the barn, the granary, and the summer kitchen. Here and there, shingles had blown off, but all the buildings stood.

As if in a dream, Anders moved to the front of the house. The others followed. There they found three more uprooted trees. Once again the branches reached out, stretching long across the grass. Yet they had fallen away from the house.

For the first time since Kate had known Anders, he looked visibly shaken. Watching him, her scared feeling returned and with it a gnawing at the pit of her stomach. When Tina took her hand, Kate felt glad she could hang on to something.

For a long moment the children stood there. All around lay large and small branches, tossed about by the wind. Leaves littered the grass.

Kate looked beyond the house to the woods. Even at this distance she could see the wind's path through the trees. "I can't believe it! How could the house stand through all this?"

"Even the windows didn't break!" said Anders, speaking for the first time since they left the cellar.

Then Kate saw the beehives. Standing at the edge of the hill, they'd caught the full force of the wind. Toppled over, the hive bodies lay on their sides.

"Our honey!" Kate exclaimed, running forward.

As she moved closer, the bees swarmed upward, buzzing angrily. Quickly she stepped back.

Usually the hive bodies held the frames apart, giving the bees room to move between. Now, the frames spilled out on the ground, crushing and holding the bees.

"All our work for nothing!" groaned Kate, feeling sick.

"What do you mean?" asked Anders, coming to stand beside her.

"A queen usually stays in the center of a hive. The frames are so squashed together the queen in each hive might be dead. No wonder the bees are mad!"

"They're mad all right. Look at 'em!" Anders edged back.

Just then a spatter of raindrops touched Kate's face. She looked at the sky. "I have to get 'em back."

"Back? Back together?"

"See that cloud? It's going to rain again. Soon it'll be dark."

"Kate, those bees are *mad*."

"Wouldn't you be, too, if your house was blown apart?"

"You're going to fix 'em? You're crazy!"

Kate's chin shot up. "And you, Anders Nordstrom, are going to help me."

"You are crazy! I'm not getting near those bees!"

"If we don't get the hives together, we might lose the whole honey crop."

"So? Do it yourself then."

"I can't. They're too heavy."

Anders started to walk away.

Kate shouted after him. "Anders, it's the beginning of June! The most important time of the year!"

"For what?" Anders shouted back, his voice defiant.

"For building up the hives—so there're lots of bees for making honey."

"So?" he asked again.

"So you won't have honey on your bread all year. So Mama won't have honey for baking. And if we don't have honey to sell, I'll never get an organ!" Kate's voice ended in a wail.

Anders groaned, but he turned back. "All right, all right. What do I do?"

"Find your papa's hat and veil."

Quickly Kate put on the old pair of overalls, and she and Anders tied string around their ankles. When Kate put on gloves and draped the curtain around her straw hat, Anders laughed at the way she looked.

But he didn't laugh long. As soon as Kate had the smoker working, they moved quietly toward the first hive. The bees rose around Kate, and she blew smoke at them. When they quieted a bit, she took the bottom board and set it on the log platform that held the hive off the ground. Then she told Anders, "All right, help me lift."

With Anders carrying most of the weight, they set a hive body on the bottom board. Kate spaced out the frames. Then they set a second and a third box on top of the first. As quickly as she could, Kate replaced the cover and went on to the next hive.

Once she glanced at Anders. His whole body looked stiff, as though waiting for a thousand stings. Even his eyes seemed scared. Yet instead of running, he stood there.

Together they finished the second hive. As Kate moved toward the third, she saw something shiny between the logs of the platform. Getting down on her knees, she took a closer look, reached in, and pulled something out.

"Kate, hurry up!"

"Just a minute!" A square piece of copper lay in Kate's glove. As she turned it over, several bees settled on her arm. A stinger went through her sleeve, and Kate jumped.

"Com'on, Kate, let's get outta here!"

Kate stuffed the copper piece in a pocket of her overalls and picked up the smoker. As she pushed the bellows, clouds of smoke billowed over the bees and frames still on the ground. Yet the angry bees didn't let her alone. This time a stinger reached her shoulder.

Kate flinched and tried to hold down her panic. All she wanted was to get out of there. As quickly as they could, she and Anders put the third hive together.

"We did it!" she exclaimed on the way to the house. As soon as she could, she'd get mud on her stings.

Walking quickly but not running, Anders hurried away from the bees. At a safe distance he stopped and pulled off his veil. "What did you find back there?"

Pulling the curtain from her hat, Kate took the copper piece from her pocket. As Anders turned it over, he gave a long, amazed whistle. "Kate, look at this!"

Thunder rumbled, and Kate knew that rain would return. But Anders didn't seem to care. In the fading light of the day he turned over a piece of copper about four inches square and a quarter of an inch thick. "Look, Kate!" he exclaimed again.

Leaning closer, she saw the letters stamped on one side. "S-v-e-r-i-g-e," she spelled out. "Sweden?"

"Yup!" exclaimed Anders. "It's a genuine stamp of the crown of Sweden. It must be very old."

"And valuable?"

Anders nodded. "Probably. At least to the owner." His eyes gleamed. "Maybe he'd give a reward."

"A big one?"

Anders shrugged. "Who knows? It sure is worth *something*!"

"Enough to buy an organ?"

Anders shook his head. "Nope. Enough to buy a horse."

"An organ."

"A horse."

Kate felt the flush of anger move up into her cheeks. Her long black braid flipped around her shoulders. "An organ."

"A horse," he said firmly.

Kate stomped her foot. "I found it. An organ."

"You wouldn't have found it if I hadn't helped you."

Now Kate was really angry. "You— You—" she sputtered.

"A horse."

Then Kate caught the teasing in his blue eyes. She sighed. "You are *mean*."

Anders grinned. "Yah, sure." He sounded like Papa.

For the first time all day Kate laughed. Anders joined her, and Kate laughed again. All the tension she'd felt as she watched the storm build up drained out of her. Kate wondered if Anders sensed the relief she felt.

Then she remembered. "Mama and Papa? Do you think they're all right?"

As Anders nodded, Kate realized it was the first time she'd called Mr. Nordstrom *Papa* outloud. *Will Anders notice? I don't want to be teased.* If he did, Anders didn't say anything.

"Do you *really* think they're all right?" Kate asked again, now when Tina and Lars couldn't hear.

For once Anders looked solemn. "Yup," he answered. "I can't explain it. Sometimes when Papa leaves me in charge I think, 'Can I do it?' I wonder if I can do even little things. But now—" He broke off, unwilling or unable to say what he was feeling.

In a moment he spoke again as though to reassure Kate. "It'll take longer because of the storm."

Kate looked around. The huge oaks lay on the ground, their roots high in the air. It would take days to clean up the leaves and broken branches. But somehow she felt better.

Anders grinned, as though he couldn't stay serious too long. "Well then, you better get supper ready."

Kate imitated his tone. "Well then, you better get the cows milked."

Then she remembered the copper piece Anders still held in his hand. "What should we do with it?"

"We better hide it."

"But where? It's so strange, all the things happening around here. Where would it be safe?"

Anders looked thoughtful. "Maybe we should set a trap."

15

Missing!

"A trap?" asked Kate.

"Let's use the copper piece to find out who put it there. Maybe it's the man we saw in the woods."

"Good idea!"

"Glad you like it," Anders drawled. "It's your job to put the piece back."

"Mine?" Kate remembered how angry the bees had been. The stings on her arm and shoulder itched and burned. She knew they'd get worse.

"Yup. Since you like bees so much. And let's keep a lookout tonight. Your bedroom has the best view of the hives, but I can see them too."

They agreed that Kate would watch the first half of the night, Anders the second.

"We should have a signal," Kate said.

"If you need me, rap on the wall between the bedrooms." As they reached the house, Anders knocked on the siding. "A long, steady rap to say, 'Your turn. Take over.' I'll rap back the same way so you know I'm awake."

"What if I need help?"

"One long rap. Wait a second or two. Two short ones. Keep repeating it 'til I hear."

A moment later, Tina tugged at Kate's hand. Kate knew the little girl was hungry. Going into the summer kitchen, she lit the kerosene lamp, glad for the glow it shed in the growing darkness.

Gathering kindling, Kate started a fire in the cookstove. Then, slipping back outside, she pushed the copper piece into the hollow space beneath the third hive. By the time Anders finished milking, Kate had soup and hot biscuits ready.

During supper it rained again, but the fury of the earlier wind was gone. When Tina grew sleepy, Kate led her into the house and tucked her into bed. Taking a quilt and pillow, Kate sat down by the window, leaning against the sill to watch.

A gentle breeze touched her there. As the clouds blew away, the moon came up, and Kate felt grateful. If Mama and Papa were trying to get home, the light would help them.

From here Kate had a clear view of the wagon track as it passed the side of the house and curved around the front. Near the beehives, rainwater filled a deep rut. The water shimmered in the moonlight.

Roads must be awful again. Kate remembered their trip from Grantsburg in the March mud. *Will they get through? Where are they?*

As Kate watched, the shadows of bushes near the hives wavered in the breeze. Now and then the moon went under a cloud, then reappeared, seeming brighter than ever. Once the bushes moved more than usual, and Kate sat up. *What's that?*

Crouching by the window, she almost stood up to rap for Anders' help. Then an animal moved away from the bushes. A black animal with a white stripe down its back. Kate relaxed, once more leaning against the window. Only three months before, she would have hidden under the quilt until the skunk passed. By now she'd seen them often and knew she was far enough away.

As Kate watched, the skunk waddled across the pasture. From inside the house Lutfisk woofed. *Would he be just as good a watchdog if a man came to the hive?*

Kate's eyelids grew heavy. The events of the day seemed to march like a parade in front of her. Down in the root cellar they had seemed like a family with all the children together.

Kate yawned. As a shadow darker than night moved toward the hive, she rubbed her eyes. Lutfisk barked again, but Kate barely heard. Putting her head on the windowsill, she fell into an exhausted sleep.

Morning sunlight wakened Kate. She was still sitting by the window, fully dressed. *What am I doing here?*

Then she saw the uprooted trees sprawled around the house and remembered the storm. When she recalled the copper piece, she jerked upright. *Did anything happen when I was asleep?*

In the double bed Tina sprawled spread-eagle, sound asleep. Slipping quietly out of the room, Kate went downstairs. The first floor was as empty as she feared. Mama and Papa weren't home.

"The roads are muddy," Kate told herself firmly. Yet she knew they were long overdue, and her stomach muscles tightened.

In the summer kitchen, she started a fire in the cookstove, then went to the well. Lifting the trapdoor, she lay down on the platform and tugged at the rope. Hand over hand she pulled up the pail of milk. As she tried to stand up, her dress caught on the sliver of wood. Carefully she freed herself, then hurried back to make breakfast.

First Lars, then Tina found her there. Kate was almost ready with pancakes when Anders came in from milking, his broad shoulders slumped.

As he dropped into a chair, Anders looked more tired than Kate had ever seen him. But Kate guessed that something else bothered him. Even with muddy roads, Mama and Papa should have been home. If it weren't for Lars and Tina, she would have asked, "Are you *sure* they're all right?" Instead, Kate swallowed her questions.

Breakfast was even quieter than last night's supper. For the first time since Kate had known him, Anders pushed pancakes around on his plate.

When they finished eating, Anders stood up and took the big Bible down from the shelf. Looking uncomfortable, he glanced at Kate as though hoping she wouldn't make a smart remark. Kate stared, so surprised that she couldn't think of one.

Anders turned to the psalm Papa had read on Kate's first day at the farm. "God *is* our refuge and strength, a very present help in trouble."

His voice grew stronger. "Therefore will not we fear. . . ."

When he finished, Anders closed the Bible. Looking even more uncomfortable, he bowed his head and closed his eyes.

As Kate stared, she caught Tina watching her. Kate bowed her head and peeked when Tina wasn't looking.

When Anders prayed, his words came in a rush. "Jesus, wherever Mama and Papa are, we ask you to take care of them. We ask that you bring them home safely. Ah-men."

Still not looking at Kate, Anders pushed back from the table, his chair scraping on the wood floor. As he stood up, he straightened his broad shoulders as though taking on the world.

A moment later Kate heard the sound—a wagon coming up the hill. Running outside, she saw Dolly and Florie come around the barn. "They're here!" Kate shouted. "They're home!"

Papa stopped the horses and jumped down. As Mama reached the ground, she turned to Kate. When Kate felt Mama's arms go around her, the tears she'd been holding back spilled over.

Mama let her cry. As Kate's sobs quieted, she stood back. Mama held Kate at arms' length, looking into her eyes. Mama's cheeks also were wet with tears.

At last Kate looked at Mr. Nordstrom. He was trying to hug everyone at once—Anders, Lars, and Tina. His long arms almost went around all of them.

As Kate watched, she wanted to tell him how glad she was that he was safe, how good it was to have him home. But suddenly she felt shy before this man she now called Papa in her thoughts.

She hung back, and her tongue felt tied to the roof of her mouth. When Mr. Nordstrom turned to her, holding open his arms, Kate turned away.

Only then did Mr. Nordstrom notice the uprooted trees. "Looks like we've got some work cut out for us, Anders."

Anders grinned. "Well, it's wood for winter." The relief that

Papa was home shone in his eyes.

The Blueberry Special had been delayed, Mama and Papa told them. It was late afternoon before trainmen unloaded the new plow. By then the sky was dark and green. Papa put the horses in a livery stable, and he and Mama went to the Antler's Hotel to wait. At six o'clock the storm hit Grantsburg.

"North of here it's really bad," said Papa. "Probably was a cyclone. Fallen trees blocked the road in several places."

"Coming home it was too dark to see," said Mama. "But there must be a number of houses and barns destroyed."

It was late afternoon before Kate had time to check for the copper piece. Putting on her overalls, gloves, and veil, she crossed the muddy wagon track. Kneeling down on the back side of the third hive, away from the entrance, she reached into the hollow.

Her glove came up empty.

Did I push it back farther than I thought? She tried to ignore a sick feeling. Pulling off her glove, she felt with her hand.

Still finding nothing, she squinted under the platform. Unable to see the copper piece, she stretched out on her stomach, her fingers feeling back as far as she could reach.

A bee buzzed up and circled her head, humming angrily. More bees followed, and Kate puffed smoke in their direction. When several lit on her shoulders and arms, she aimed the smoker toward herself. But the bees were still upset from the day before. Finally, Kate gave up and headed for the house.

Near the wagon track, she met Anders, and had to tell him. "It's gone! The copper piece is missing!"

"Gone! But you watched last night. You didn't see the stranger, did you?"

Kate was embarrassed to tell him. "I fell asleep."

For once Anders didn't tease her. "Well, to tell the truth, so did I. That's why I didn't hear whether you rapped for me."

"I missed our big chance," moaned Kate, her shoulders slumping. "Up 'til now, everything's been hidden away from the house. This was close enough to watch."

Together they started back across the wagon track. Horseshoe prints and the wheels of the returning wagon marked the mud. Yet as they walked to the other side, Kate noticed something. "Anders! Look at this!"

Near the edge of the track Kate knelt down. In spite of the wagon and horses, there was one clear print. "That's it!"

"That's what?" asked Anders.

"The print we saw in the woods. From a boot or shoe. The print left by the mysterious stranger!"

"Aha!" Anders knelt down for a better look. "Yup! Same funny outline. The heavy outer line around the heel."

"Around the toe too," said Kate. "Maybe it's the iron plate you talked about."

Then Kate thought of something that troubled her. "Anders? That day with the dynamite? When I wondered if I'd seen a bear?"

Anders stood up, and Kate stood with him. "You didn't really think that, did you?" she asked.

She was looking into his eyes now, and Kate knew he wouldn't lie to her. "Did you think it was the stranger instead?"

Slowly Anders nodded. "I didn't want to scare you. It's always been safe living out here. No one has ever bothered us."

Kate felt scared all right. "And he's coming closer to the house." A tingle ran down her spine.

Anders started across the grass. "Something still bothers me. We know the stranger's around here some place. But why's he here just now and then? Why does he come around, then disappear?"

16

County Fair

*T*wo days later, Lars ran all the way from the mailbox. "It's here!" he shouted, bringing in the June 8th *Journal of Burnett County*. The family gathered around to read the first newspaper report of the storm.

A week later, the paper included a more complete description of injuries and damage in the area. Not until the June 22nd issue did the *Journal* print pictures and the full story.

Passing north of Windy Hill Farm, the cyclone had left a wide swath of destruction on either side of its path. Miraculously no one was killed.

Since the day of the storm, something had changed inside Kate. Whenever she was with Mr. Nordstrom, she still avoided speaking to him by name. In her thoughts it was a different matter. While she continued to call her Irish father *Daddy*, she increasingly thought of Mr. Nordstrom as *Papa*.

During the weeks that followed, she and Anders did not catch even a hint that the stranger might be somewhere about. Yet both of them kept thinking about the man and his mysterious appearances. Whenever Kate noticed soft earth, she looked for the strange boot print. "What is it that made that print different?" she asked Anders more than once.

Then, on another warm day when Tina was looking through the Sears Roebuck catalogue, Kate thought of something.

"Tina, let me see the wish book for a minute, all right?" Taking the catalogue, Kate turned to the section on men's shoes. Tina grew restless as Kate read the description of one shoe after another. At last she found what she was looking for.

Clutching the catalogue, Kate sought out Anders. "Look!" she exclaimed, her excitement spilling over. "Read this!"

MEN'S MINING SHOE, $1.50. At an additional cost we have fitted this shoe with a heavy iron toeplate, and also encircled the heel with a heavy iron plate, thereby making it practically indestructible.

Anders whooped. "That's it, all right! The kind of shoe that'd make the print we saw!" Then his excitement dimmed. "But there's no mining around here. Who would wear a miner's shoe?"

When they asked Papa Nordstrom about it, he agreed. "You're right. Years ago there was talk of a copper mine in Trade Lake. But it didn't work out. Can't think of anyone who'd wear that kind of shoe."

Much as they wanted to know more, Kate and Anders could not find further clues.

As summer slipped by, Anders brushed his pig each morning, getting it ready for the county fair. Rosie had fattened up nicely, and Anders had high hopes of winning a blue ribbon.

On a hot day in August Papa Nordstrom decided how much honey the bees needed for winter. He and Kate removed the rest of the honey from the hives. It was hard work taking off the top boxes called supers and brushing the bees off the frames.

Using a knife heated in hot water, Mama removed the layer of wax that capped the combs. Then Papa put the frames in an extractor, and spun out the honey. Kate and Mama poured it into jars and pails.

"Do we have enough?" Kate asked.

"Enough for what?" Papa answered, as though he didn't remember what she meant.

"You know." Then she caught his grin. "We do, don't we?"

County Fair 113

"Yah, enough to sell some," he promised. "Not enough for an organ, but a start."

"Great!" Kate exclaimed. The bee stings she'd received didn't seem important anymore.

At last the Saturday of the Burnett County Fair arrived. Anders blocked off the back part of the farm wagon. Papa helped him get the squealing pig inside.

In the middle part of the wagon Papa and Anders set wooden boxes packed with jars of honey for the street fair. People from miles around would bring whatever they wanted to sell.

It was still dark when Papa clucked the horses, and they started down the hill. Mama and Anders were up beside Papa. The rest sat in the wagon bed behind.

Kate watched Mama talk and laugh. *She's different now. Happier, I guess. She even sings around the house, the way she did when Daddy was alive.*

As they turned onto the road for Grantsburg, another thought surprised Kate. *I haven't been lonesome for Sarah and Michael for a long time.*

With the hot winds of summer the road was dry, and the trip went well. When the family reached the Grantsburg fairgrounds, Anders and Papa unloaded the pig while Lars went for a bucket of water. Then Anders washed Rosie and started the careful grooming needed for a blue ribbon.

Around Kate, clusters of people formed. As she listened, men and women who lived far out in the country greeted friends they hadn't seen for a time.

Papa found an empty place along the street and set up sawhorses and boards for a table. Kate covered the boards with a cloth, then set out the honey. Golden and clear in the sunlight, it looked mouth-watering.

Before long, the first buyer came by. As Kate tucked the money away, she felt excited. Soon another woman stopped, put down her money, and set the jar in her market basket. By noon there were only five jars left.

Kate's excitement mounted as she remembered Papa's words: "Every bit helps!" Her little purse was growing fat.

Then a young couple came to the table. *They're not much*

older than me, Kate thought. After asking the price, the husband and wife walked a short distance away to talk.

"It's just what we need," the girl said. "If we're careful, five jars will take us through winter."

Kate could barely hear the man's answer. "For *all* your cooking and bread baking?"

The girl nodded. "I'll use the smallest amount I can."

Her husband sighed. "I don't know what to do. If the storm hadn't wiped out everything, we'd have something to sell too."

"But when we don't have much else to eat . . ."

The young man nodded. "Yah, you're right." He reached deep into his pocket and pulled out a flat leather coin purse. "You get the honey. I'll help you carry it to the wagon."

As they headed back to the table, Kate turned away, pretending she hadn't heard. Swallowing a lump in her throat, she tried to push aside a feeling she used to know well.

Before Mama married Papa Nordstrom, Kate had known that feeling often. It came whenever Kate heard Mama cry at night. It came when Kate wondered if there'd be enough money for food. Always that empty feeling gnawed at the pit of her stomach.

"We'd like all five jars," the girl said in a quiet voice. As she held up two cloth bags, her husband put the money on the table.

"Just a minute," said Kate. "I'll pack 'em so they don't break on your way home." Kneeling down, she collected newspaper from a box they'd used for the honey.

Once again Kate thought about the long winter after Daddy died. Often she'd gone to bed feeling hungry and scared.

I want an organ. With all my heart I want an organ. But deep inside Kate knew the truth. *I don't* have *to have it.*

Then the idea struck her. With one hand Kate gave the young wife some newspaper. With the other, she picked up the money. As she knelt behind the table for more paper, she pulled out her handkerchief. Quickly she put the coins inside and tied a knot.

Holding the handkerchief in her hand, Kate reached for the last jar of honey. Kneeling once more, she set the handkerchief on the lid and wrapped paper around the money and jar. Standing up again, she set the jar in one of the girl's bags.

"Looks like you're all sold out," said the young man.

Kate nodded. "Thanks for your business. Hope you like the honey."

"We will," replied the girl. Each of them picked up a bag. Soon they were lost in the crowd.

The minute they were gone, Kate felt sorry about what she'd done. *How could I have been so stupid? Giving away five jars?*

Then she had an even worse thought. *Maybe they planned that I heard them.*

Like a mouse finding cheese, the awful thought nibbled away in Kate's mind. Finally she pushed the idea from her, refusing to think about it. *No! They were honest.*

Folding up the cloth, Kate took down the boards and set them against a tree. After stacking the boxes, she decided to look around.

Walking slowly, Kate started down the block, stopping now and then to see what people offered for sale. She was almost ready to turn around when she came to a corner. There she stopped, startled by what she saw.

Set back, away from the street and the dust, was an organ. A reed pump organ. Just the kind of organ Kate dreamed about buying!

17

Scaredy-cat?

*A*s Kate stood there, she forgot everything around her. A reed organ! The pipe organ in Minneapolis had to be pumped by someone else. Yet Kate could play this one by herself. She'd just pump the foot pedals up and down.

It's the most wonderful organ in the world! Beautiful carving decorated the high wooden back. On either side of the music rack were small shelves for kerosene lamps. Next to the keyboard were ten stops for changing the sound being played.

Kate moved closer for a better look. The ivory keys looked new, as though they'd never been used.

The owner of the organ walked forward. "Want to try it, young lady?"

Would I! Kate thought. But she felt shy, trying to play in front of someone else.

"Ah, come on," encouraged the man. "Have you had lessons?"

Kate shook her head.

"Why don't you try it anyway?"

Why not? With everyone milling around, maybe no one would notice.

As Kate sat down on the organ stool, her heart leaped into

her throat. Placing her feet on the pedals, she began to pump and heard the soft whoosh of air coming in.

The man reached over and pulled out a few stops. "Now give it a try."

Kate set her fingers on the keyboard, the way she'd seen organists do. The chords sounded mixed up and strange. Moving her fingers around, she listened until the notes blended. Then, using only her right hand, Kate picked out a tune.

Before long she forgot the man standing near the organ, the people passing by on the street. When she felt sure of the melody, she added chords with her left hand, changing the notes until they fit.

Then the special tunes Kate had played in her mind seemed to leap into her fingers. Excitement welled up within her. She couldn't explain it, even to herself. Yet she could play, even though she had never been taught!

At last Kate stopped, not wanting to, but suddenly feeling self-conscious. Standing up, she asked, "How much does it cost?"

"It's a real good organ," he answered. "New in 1885. Solid oak cabinet. Not a nick on it. Everything in perfect—"

"How much?" Kate interrupted.

"I'll sell it to you for twenty dollars. That's a real bargain."

"Fifteen."

"Nineteen."

"Fifteen fifty."

The man shook his head.

"If you have to take it home again—"

"Still have half a day to sell it."

But then Kate remembered. Even if he sold it for sixteen dollars, she didn't have half that much. "I'll talk to my papa," she said in a small voice.

Feeling surprised she had called him that, Kate started away, then turned back. For a long moment she looked at the organ, then started out once more.

This time she almost bumped into Papa Nordstrom. Seeing him there with Anders, Kate felt embarrassed. *Did they hear me play?*

Then she had an even worse thought. *Did they hear me bargain with the man? I don't want Anders to tease me.*

"You're a good organ player, Kate," said Papa gently.

Kate swallowed hard and looked at the ground. He had heard, all right. All of it.

Then she remembered the money. Digging deep in her purse, Kate pulled out the coins she'd earned selling honey. Papa opened his hands, and she dropped the money into them. Once more she felt sorry she'd given five jars away.

At the same time, Anders took money from his pocket and handed it to Papa. A long look passed between them.

Suddenly Kate remembered Anders' pig, Rosie. "What happened? Did you get a ribbon?"

Anders' eyes looked proud. "Sure did. A *blue* ribbon and something even better!"

Kate was curious. "What's that?"

A wide grin split his tanned face. "A man bought her. Gave a really good price!"

Kate felt his excitement. "And you're going to get your horse?"

"Nope. Not yet."

"Then a calf you can raise and sell for a horse?"

Something flickered in Anders' blue eyes, but it passed so quickly Kate thought she imagined it.

"Nope," he said. "But come on. I'll show you a mare I found. It'd be a good one."

Leaving Papa behind, Kate and Anders headed down the street. Soon they came to a place where horses were sold. Anders stopped. "See her? Isn't she a beauty?"

Before Kate stood a black horse tied to a tree. Her coat was shiny, her legs long and slender. The mare tossed her head, and Kate knew she was the spirited kind of horse Anders wanted.

"What's her name?"

When Anders didn't answer, Kate asked again.

"I'd call her Wildfire," he said, his voice low.

"I bet she'd go like wildfire. How much?"

"Little more than I got for the pig."

"Really? Not more than that? How come? She looks like a great horse."

"She is. Except for one thing." Anders walked around to the front of the mare.

As he stood silent and waiting, Kate followed. She looked, then quickly looked away. Across the mare's chest was a deep cut that was still healing.

Kate saw the pain in Anders' eyes. Pain she guessed was for the horse. "What happened?"

"Must have run into a fence. Lot of horses aren't used to barbed wire. Looks like this one ran straight for it "

"What'll happen to her?" Kate asked, afraid to look again.

"If someone takes care of her, making sure the wound doesn't get infected—"

"You could do it!"

A shadow flickered across Anders' face. "Maybe. Maybe not. It's taking a chance. Can't tell for sure if the tendons have been hurt."

"Did you ask Papa?

Anders nodded, but didn't look at Kate. "He thinks the mare will be all right."

"Then why don't you get it?" she prodded.

Anders still watched the horse, and seemed not to hear.

"Take a risk!"

Anders shook his head.

"What are you, a *scaredy-cat*?"

Suddenly Anders turned to Kate, his eyes flashing with anger. Yet, for the first time since Kate had known him, he walked away instead of answering. Kate had to run to catch up.

When they found Papa Nordstrom, Kate waited until Anders moved on to talk with a friend. Then, feeling as though her heart was tearing away from her body, she spoke up. "Why don't you use the money from the honey? Why don't you use it to help Anders buy Wildfire?"

Papa looked surprised. "The mare? But you worked all summer to save for an organ!"

"Yah." Kate seldom used the Swedish yes. But this time it said what she felt. "That horse—" Remembering the wound, she broke off, unable to explain that Wildfire needed Anders, and Anders needed the mare. "Who owns it?" she asked, not knowing what else to say.

"A man just outside Grantsburg," answered Papa. To Kate's disappointment, he changed the subject. "Let's go find Mama. It's time for a picnic. If we hurry, we won't keep her waiting."

Turning away, Papa bumped into another man. "Oh, excuse me!"

As the man lifted his hat, Kate saw his light brown hair, parted down the center. Dressed in a fine suit, he seemed out of place at the fair. He also seemed familiar.

"Don't I know you?" asked Papa, echoing Kate's thoughts.

"Eberly," answered the man, lifting his hat again. "Fred Eberly."

"Yah, sure," said Papa. "The salesman. Met you on the Blueberry Special last spring. Back in town again, I see."

"Right, right," said Eberly, his voice hearty. "Showing the merchants my new line for winter." He smiled, but somehow it didn't reach his eyes.

Kate shivered. For some reason she felt cold. Had a cloud passed over the sun? She glanced up, but the sun still sparkled in the crisp air.

Yet Kate couldn't shake off the feeling. Something bothered her. Was it the man's eyes? Their gray depths seemed stormy, as though he was angry, or mean. Kate couldn't explain it to herself. She only knew she didn't like Mr. Eberly.

Lifting his hat once more, Mr. Eberly moved away and disappeared in the crowd.

18

The Syrup Pail

"We saw Big Gust!" said Tina as all of them climbed into the wagon for the trip home.

"Do you know what he did?" Among his freckles Lars's blue eyes sparkled. "He picked up two troublemakers at the same time!"

Kate was curious. "Picked them up?"

"He held one guy under one arm and another guy under the other. And he carried them off to jail!"

Lars raised his right hand, promising he told the truth. With what she already knew about Big Gust, Kate didn't find it hard to believe. Yet she was silent most of the way home.

Before leaving Grantsburg, she had walked back to see the organ once more. It was gone, and so was the owner. Disappointment ripped through her, turning like a knife, sharp and awful.

Anders was also quiet. Kate wondered if he was thinking about Wildfire.

Most of all, she felt let down. *It was awful telling Papa to use that money for the mare. But what's worse—even though I offered, he didn't do it. Anders doesn't have a horse, and I don't have an organ.*

For Kate the pain went deep. *We both worked hard. Neither of us got what we worked for.* It seemed the whole world had turned dark.

Sunday morning dawned bright and crisp. Kate woke early to see mist rising above Rice Lake. For a moment the mist of tears dimmed her vision. She still felt upset about yesterday.

Trying to leave her discouragement behind, she put on her Sunday dress, then her locket. As she brushed her hair, Kate leaned toward the mirror for a better look at the treasured piece of jewelry.

Whenever she wore the locket, she felt warm inside, remembering Daddy. Kate hoped she would never forget her last birthday before he died. "Oh, Brendan!" Mama had said. "She's too young for such a fine gift."

Daddy had shook his head. His blue eyes danced as he grinned at Kate. "I've had good work this year. I want her to have it."

As though it were yesterday, Kate remembered how she felt when she received the heart-shaped locket. With a small hinge, it opened to a tiny picture of Mama on one side, Daddy on the other.

Thinking about that day, Kate could almost feel Daddy lifting her high in the air. She could almost hear his laughter and his Irish tenor voice singing the songs she loved. "She'll take good care of it," he told Mama. And Kate had. In all this time she had.

After Sunday dinner, Mama and Papa Nordstrom left to check on a sick neighbor. Lars and Tina went along. "If we don't get back, do the chores," Papa told Kate and Anders. "It means they need our help. I might have to go for the doctor."

As Kate cleaned up after the meal, she took the milk to the well. Being careful of her best dress, she lifted the trapdoor and lay down on her stomach to put the milk inside.

The splinter near the opening seemed longer. Carefully, Kate leaned over the jagged edge to reach under the boards covering the well. Hooking the rope onto the pail, she lowered the milk to the waterline.

Just then something nudged her back. Jerking with surprise, Kate scrambled to her knees. A cold nose touched her arm. "Lutfisk!"

The dog edged closer, waiting for Kate to scratch behind his ears. But suddenly she realized something. "My locket! It's gone!"

Feeling sick all over, Kate remembered her sudden jerk. Something had caught on the sharp end of the splinter. Had the locket fallen into the well?

Bending over, she looked down into the dark pit. Black water glimmered back at her. Daddy's gift!

Fear creeping into her heart, Kate sat back on her heels to think. The more she thought about it, the more impossible it became. Where else could the locket be? It had to be in the well!

"She'll take good care of the locket," Daddy had told Mama. "But I haven't! I've lost it!" Kate cried out. "I've lost it!"

"What have you lost?" asked Anders, coming up behind her.

"My locket. My locket from Daddy. It's down in the well! What'll I do?"

Anders knelt at the trapdoor. "You're sure?"

Despair filling her voice, Kate told about Lutfisk. About the splinter and the sudden jerk. "I don't know where else it could be."

"Then let's do something about it."

"Do something? It's *gone!*" Kate wailed.

"Be quiet. Let me think."

"Are you crazy? What will thinking do? It's down the *well!*"

Anders shushed her. "Stop acting like a woman."

"I *am* a woman. Well, almost."

For a long minute Anders knelt there, still looking down in the well. "I think it'll work."

"What will work?" Kate was afraid to hope. "Doesn't the water go way down to China?"

"Just do what I tell you," Anders ordered, his voice impatient. "First of all, take out the milk. Put it in the spring below the hill."

While Kate brought up the milk, Anders disappeared. When he returned, he wore old clothes and carried a ladder and a bucket on a rope. Without another word he tied the rope to the pipe above the platform and started bailing water from the well.

"But that's hopeless," said Kate. "If you take some water out, more will come in."

"Nope." Anders shook his head and kept bailing. "See this pump? Papa and I put it in last summer."

"So?"

"So the pipe going down in the well has a small hole below the frost line. When we pump the handle, water comes up through the pipe. When we stop pumping, the water we don't use drains back out through the hole. That way the pipe doesn't freeze in winter."

"And that's the water I see?"

"Yup! The water that drains out."

Kate wasn't sure she understood, but for two hours she and Anders took turns bailing water. At last the bucket scraped gravel.

"Great!" exclaimed Anders. "We're getting there."

Keeping on, they bailed out as much water as they could. Then the bucket seemed to hit something—something that wasn't the pipe. Anders stopped bailing and peered into the well.

"What is it?" Kate's voice sounded cross. She wanted to find the locket.

"I'm not sure," said Anders slowly. "Looks like a rock. But there wasn't a rock last summer."

They kept bailing, working around whatever it was. Finally Anders set the bucket on the grass next to the pump. Kate helped him lift the ladder through the trapdoor. Slowly they lowered the ladder until they felt the crunch of gravel.

"It's just long enough!" said Kate.

"I know. We had to use it last summer."

It was a tight fit, but Anders slipped through the trapdoor and down the ladder.

"Hey, Kate!" he yelled from the bottom, his voice sounding hollow.

Kate's heart jumped. "Did you find it?"

"Nope, but send down the bucket."

As soon as Anders had the bucket in his hands, he set something inside. "Haul it up!" he called.

Hand over hand Kate pulled up the bucket. "What's so heavy?"

As the bucket reached the light, she saw a syrup pail set inside. On the lid was the rock that held the pail under water. Knotted to the handle of the pail was a strong, thin rope. A rope dyed black.

A moment later, Anders called out again. "I found it!"

Soon he was out of the well, pulling himself back through the trapdoor. From his pocket he pulled Kate's locket and the broken chain.

Quick tears sprang into her eyes. "Anders, I can't believe it!"

"Believe it, believe it," he answered, his voice gruff with the sound that said, "Dumb girl!" But now Kate knew him well enough to recognize his teasing. As he handed her the locket, she felt she was getting buried treasure.

Drying it on her skirt, Kate held the jewelry up to the sun. "It's not even scratched."

"Are there pictures inside?"

With shaky fingers she opened the tiny clasp. On either side Mama and Daddy smiled up at her. Kate nodded, unable to speak.

Anders did it for her. "Good it was watertight."

For a moment neither of them spoke. To Kate it seemed impossible the locket and pictures were all right.

Anders broke the silence. "Well, seems like we've got us another treasure."

Kate looked up, wondering what he meant.

"The syrup pail. That's a strange rope." Going back to the pump, Anders knelt down, peering through the trapdoor. The top of the dark rope was secured to the far edge of the underside of the platform. "No wonder none of us saw it. I wonder how long it's been here?"

Returning to Kate, Anders lifted off the rock and wiped the outside of the pail dry. Then he took out his pocketknife. Prying one side, then another, he lifted the tight-fitting lid. "Take a look at this!"

Carefully they emptied the pail. First came glass beads like the ones they found under the stump.

"Lots of 'em," said Kate. "A jeweled comb . . ."

Coiling her long braid on top of her head, she pushed in the comb and fluttered her eyelashes like a fancy lady.

Anders wrinkled his nose. He was busy with the pail again. "Look!" he said, pulling out a pocketknife with a white bone handle.

Kate felt puzzled. "If someone is stealing, where does all this stuff come from?"

Anders was examining the pail. "Do you see the inside? Coated with candle wax. Even if the can leaked for some reason, the water wouldn't get through."

"Whoever it is—" Kate broke off, not wanting to finish the sentence.

"Is a hard customer. He's been thinking," said Anders.

At the bottom of the pail, Anders made the best find of all. "The copper piece!"

Kate picked it up from his hand. It was the same piece, all right. About four inches square and a quarter of an inch thick. Turning it over, she saw the word *Sverige* and the stamp of the crown of Sweden.

"We'll get a reward for sure!" Anders said.

"If we don't lose it again," Kate replied dryly.

Anders' eyes turned serious. "You're right. Let's pack it up and figure out what to do."

Refilling the syrup pail, they pressed down the lid and began talking in earnest.

"How about hiding it in the house?" asked Kate, thinking that would be safer.

"We never lock the doors. Don't know if we even have keys. Someone could walk in when we're out in the field working. Or in the barn milking the cows."

Back and forth they talked about the best place to hide something. With every idea they had, Anders wasn't satisfied.

"I know!" Kate exclaimed at last. "Look at this pail. What does it remind you of?"

"Our lunch buckets?"

"No, silly! Try again!"

Anders gave up.

"We used jars for the honey we sold, and had only two big tins for honey we kept. So we started filling extra syrup pails!"

Anders caught on. "And they're all in the root cellar! Let's go!"

Taking the pail, they set it on a shelf toward the back of the cellar. Alongside sat several pails of honey.

"Perfect!" said Anders. "If I didn't know it's the third one from the left, I'd never find it without opening every can. It even weighs almost the same."

Kate nodded. "But if you ever *need* to know, there's one clue. See this rust on the handle?" Kate picked up the pail, held it to the light, then set it down again. "It's the only pail with rust."

Carefully, Anders closed both doors of the root cellar.

"It's a real good hiding place," said Kate as she and Anders headed for the summer kitchen.

Just then, on the other side of the wagon track, the bushes moved.

Did someone touch them? For a moment Kate stood there watching. Finally she decided, *It's just the wind.*

Yet for some reason her uneasiness wouldn't go away.

19

Footsteps in the Night

"I'll keep watch the first part of the night," said Anders. It was late, and Mama and Papa had not returned. One of Anders' bedroom windows overlooked the root cellar. "Remember our signal?"

Kate nodded. "When you knock on my wall, I'll take a turn at the storeroom window. But what do we do if the stranger comes?"

"We stay out of sight," said Anders. "We watch from a distance and try to get help."

Kate shivered. "Let's hope he doesn't come back tonight."

Anders agreed. He also decided to let Lutfisk stay outside. "Let's hope he doesn't find a skunk."

Before going to bed, Kate put on her old, dark work dress. Then, taking a needle and thread, she sewed a loop, bringing together the ends of the broken chain. Slipping the locket over her head, she tucked it inside her dress.

For a long time she lay awake. As Kate remembered the stranger in the woods, the terrors of her first day at Spirit Lake School returned. Trying to push those fears aside, she tossed and turned, then finally fell asleep.

Some time after midnight Kate woke to long, solid rapping

on her bedroom wall. Quietly she slipped out of bed and rapped back. Then she tiptoed to the storeroom.

In the dark she circled wooden boxes and bags of seed for next year's planting. When she reached the window, she found the view exactly what she needed. On all sides of the root cellar the yard was open. If the stranger came, Kate would be able to see him. Best of all, the full moon lit the entire area.

Kneeling down by the window, Kate soon lost track of time. A movement in the darkness made her wonder if she dozed. She rubbed her eyes and waited.

There it was again. Across the wagon track, between the granary and the chicken coop, the bushes parted. A shadow separated from the deeper shadow of the bushes. Slowly a dark figure emerged.

Without a sound it glided over the grass, then crossed the dirt track. For a moment it merged with the shadow of the summer kitchen, then moved on. Kate tensed, her heart climbing into her throat.

Silently the dark figure headed toward the root cellar. In the open space where the tree had fallen, the figure moved into the moonlight. The silhouette became a man with a beard, hat, and long hair.

Quickly Kate moved to the wall of Anders' room. Rap, she knocked. Pause. Rap, rap.

Stumbling through the darkness, she headed for the storeroom door. Once she fell over a box. Another time she tripped on a bag of grain, but caught herself. Finally she reached the hall and the door of Anders' room. There she knocked harder. Rap. Pause. Rap, rap.

No response. For a moment she waited, then pounded the signal again.

Turning, Kate slipped down the steps and out the front door. Crossing the porch, she remembered Lutfisk. Where was he? Why didn't he bark?

Running soundlessly on the grass, she hurried to the root cellar. Both doors stood partway open. Through the crack, Kate saw a lantern set on the dirt floor. Now and then the man moved closer to the light. It was the stranger, all right.

As Kate watched, he lifted one syrup pail after another, shaking them as though trying to decide which was his.

I'd better find Anders. Kate started edging backward. *Maybe he's staying out of sight. He'll keep a safe distance.*

Then, from somewhere beyond the barn, a horse whinnied.

"I'll see what's there, then hide," Kate promised herself.

Soundlessly she crept beyond the root cellar. Staying on the grass, she started running, glad for the full moon. As she came around the far side of the barn, she found a team of horses and a wagon filled with crates.

Then Kate's heart did strange flip-flops. Toward the back of the wagon was a big wooden trunk. This time she felt sure it wasn't Mama's but one just like it.

In that moment all of Kate's scared feelings fell away. Only one thought remained. *What's in the trunk?*

As she climbed into the wagon, one of the horses moved slightly. The harness jangled.

Kate froze. Except for the breathing of the horses, the night air was silent. Working her way between the crates, Kate reached the trunk. A padlock hung on the clasp, but it was open!

Slipping the padlock out, Kate lifted the lid of the trunk. Yawning blackness met her. Was it empty? A pang of disappointment shot through her.

Then Kate pushed the lid farther back. Something reflected the light of the full moon. Reaching into the darkness, she felt a syrup pail like the one she and Anders found in the well.

As she picked it up, one of the horses snorted. Again Kate froze, listening. This time she heard a sound. Someone was coming! Was it the stranger?

Quickly she dropped the pail into the trunk, closed the lid, and replaced the padlock. *Where can I hide?* she wondered, filled with panic. No bushes nearby. Around the wagon, the land was clear.

Then Kate spied a large wooden crate, open at the top. Something dark lay at the bottom. Reaching down, she discovered a heavy horse blanket. Tumbling into the crate, she crawled beneath the blanket and pulled it over her head.

A moment later, Kate heard stealthy footsteps on the dirt track. Closer and closer they came. Kate huddled in the crate, scarcely breathing.

Someone climbed into the wagon and edged past the crate where Kate hid. Listening, she heard the lid of the trunk open, then close.

Once more, footsteps approached the crate. Kate's fingers clenched in a nervous ball as she held her breath. The footsteps passed by toward the front of the wagon.

The seat creaked as the person dropped on it and clucked the horses. The wagon started to move, slowly and quietly at first, then picking up speed.

Kate let out her breath. *Have I got myself in a fix!* For a moment longer she lay there, afraid to move. Then, not making a sound, she lifted the horse blanket and looked around.

Far above, bright stars lit the night sky. Under the full moon Kate saw the pine boards of the wooden crate that surrounded her. Straight ahead, in the side of the box facing front, a large knothole offered a place to see.

Kneeling inside the box, Kate pressed her face against the wood and squinted. Through the knothole she saw a man's back, a pulled-down hat, and long hair. It was the stranger, all right!

As he flicked the reins, the horses broke into a trot.

Where're we going? Kate's panic was gone now, but a scared feeling still gnawed at her stomach. Then she felt the wagon make a right turn. They were headed toward Grantsburg.

She wanted to stand up and look around. But what if the stranger looked back? After thinking a moment, Kate decided to memorize the turns.

Yet a wave of hopelessness washed over her. She tried to push away her frightening thoughts, but they kept returning.

Eleven miles to Grantsburg.

Eleven long miles.

Eleven miles filled with trees and bears and screech owls.

Eleven scary miles.

Kate had been to Grantsburg only twice—that day in March and on Saturday for the fair. Even to herself she didn't want to admit how quickly she could become lost. *Where's Anders, anyway? Lot of good our signal did!*

As the horses trotted along the road, Kate had another awful thought. *Did Anders hear my knock? If he didn't, no one will know I'm gone!*

With each passing minute Kate grew more afraid. Panic returned in spite of her efforts to push it aside. Now the crate seemed like a prison. *Maybe I can jump out.*

Then her mind took over. *We're going too fast. I'd get hurt for sure.*

Lying down in the crate, she tried to think. At first her ideas whirled, refusing to come in order. Yet she couldn't go anywhere. She had to figure something out. Gradually she settled down to some hard thinking.

The wagon creaked as the horses moved forward and the miles fell away. Huddled under the horse blanket, Kate felt glad for its warmth. She lay looking up, watching the stars. Her head hurt from trying to work out a plan.

They must have traveled over an hour when Kate felt the wagon turn a corner and stop. Quickly she pulled the blanket over her head. As she listened, the stranger climbed down.

After a moment Kate pushed aside the blanket and peered through the knothole. Only the horses were in sight. For a moment longer she waited, listening. When no sound came, she stood up in the crate.

In the light of the full moon Kate saw trees growing close on both sides of the road. The stranger must have slipped into the woods, but she could not tell in which direction.

As Kate looked around, she saw that the wagon stood near a crossroad. The horses waited just far enough ahead to show her where they'd been and where they were headed.

Are we still on the road to Grantsburg? She didn't know. One tree seemed the same as the next.

Like a squirrel running for cover, Kate's thoughts scurried this way and that. *What should I do? Get out? Hide behind a tree?*

The woods seemed even more frightening than the wagon. *I'd never find my way home. And which way did the stranger go? What if I met him coming back?*

Then she thought of something else. *The road's dry and wagon tracks hard to follow. How will Anders and Papa find me?*

Desperately Kate looked around for something to use—something that marked their trail. Something Anders and Papa would recognize, but the mysterious stranger wouldn't see.

Then she remembered her locket, still tucked inside her

dress. Climbing down from the wagon, she hurried to a bush a short distance after the turn in the road. Reaching up, Kate hung the necklace over a limb. *It's so small. Can Anders and Papa possibly see it?*

Just then a bloodcurdling screech split the night air. As the sound echoed in the stillness, Kate shuddered. Filled with panic, she headed for the wagon.

It did no good to tell herself it was a screech owl. Frantically, she pulled herself up.

As she tumbled into the wagon, Kate heard a branch snap in the woods. *The stranger! He's coming back!*

Desperate, Kate headed for the crate and stepped inside. As she reached for the blanket, she heard another sound, this time from the road. There it was again, soft and low. "Woof! Woof!"

Still standing in the crate, Kate turned in that direction. Near the corner where they'd turned was a low silhouette, dark in the moonlight. *Lutfisk!*

Kate wanted to hug the dog, to get down and follow him home. Yet as she started to climb out of the crate, she heard another branch crack in the woods. The sound was closer and Lutfisk too far away. In another moment the stranger would be here.

I'd never make it to cover! Kate's fear was back again.

Then she knew what to do. "Lutfisk!" she called in a hoarse whisper. The dog started toward her. "Go get Anders!"

The dog stopped. For a moment he waited, and Kate's throat tightened. Then she remembered the command Anders used, telling the dog to get cows. *But will Lutfisk obey ME?*

Raising her arm high, she motioned to the right, using Anders' command. Lutfisk still waited.

Again Kate raised her arm and motioned to the right. In the moonlight Lutfisk cocked his head as though torn about what to do. Then, seeming to make up his mind, he turned back the way he came, heading off at a steady lope.

Once the dog stopped and looked around. Then he disappeared in the darkness.

Kate dropped down in the crate. As she pulled the blanket over her shoulders, she heard footsteps on the dirt road. Quickly she covered her head.

The steps grew closer. Closer. Closer.

20

Race Against Time

*H*uddled under the horse blanket, Kate heard the man climb into the wagon. Once again he worked his way between the crates to the trunk at the back. Dropping something inside, he walked forward again.

"Giddyup!" he told the horses.

For Kate the miles seemed to last forever. The mysterious stranger seemed in no hurry to get wherever he was going. Though she tried hard, Kate could not keep track of the turns.

Whenever the stranger stopped the wagon, she listened until unable to hear footsteps. Then, standing up, she peered into the darkness.

Always one tree looked the same as the next. Always Kate looked for another chance to mark the way; it never came.

With each stop her despair deepened. "Anders, where are you?" She wanted to cry out. Then, "Will Lutfisk get help?" And then, "If I get out of this, will I ever find my locket again?"

In the night sky the moon hung low. A cool breeze sprang up. Shivering and tired, Kate pulled the blanket over her shoulders. As she lay curled in a ball, her panic grew. "I'm scared, God," she prayed. "Really scared."

Then the breeze touched her face, and Kate thought of something she hadn't really believed before. Something important.

"You took care of me that day with the bull, didn't you, God? You helped me when I was lost in the woods and when I was afraid in the cellar.

"When everything changes, and I'm scared of those changes, can I count on you, God? No matter what happens, you're the same, aren't you?"

Deep in her being, Kate knew something more. "When I'm scared, you're my biggest help. If I'd let you, you'd be with me all the time, wouldn't you? Even in this awful wilderness?"

As the breeze changed to a sharp wind, Kate pulled the blanket over her head. Each time her fear came back, she repeated the verse Papa and Anders read: "God *is* our refuge and strength, a very present help in trouble." Before long, she changed the words into a prayer. "God is *my* refuge and strength, *my* help in trouble."

And then, Kate was asleep.

When she wakened, the wagon had stopped. Kate felt confused. *Where am I?* Then she remembered and became wide awake. Fear tightened her stomach. *What happened to Anders? Where's the stranger?*

As she pushed the blanket aside, light shone into the crate. To Kate's surprise she found the sun high in the sky, high enough to be edging toward noon. She felt even more surprised that she could sleep at a time like this.

With the blanket still covering her back, she raised up enough to see through the knothole. The wagon seat was empty. Beyond, the horses stood still, as though tied to a rail.

Then Kate remembered the trunk. She hadn't seen what the stranger put into it, but she had no doubt what was there—syrup pails filled with whatever the stranger had stolen. Kate tried to work it out, knowing the man must have hidden pails along a route and waited with collecting them until he thought it was safe.

Just then she heard voices. "Over here," called a man, and Kate jerked the blanket back over her head. Another man answered, and the two kept talking as they moved closer to the wagon.

"I know one of those voices," Kate told herself. "Who is it?"

Closing her eyes, she concentrated. As hard as she tried, she couldn't figure it out. She couldn't connect the voice with a face.

Then Kate heard someone at the back of the wagon, lifting out the end board. Fear shot through her.

Wood scraped against wood. "One, two, heave!" called the familiar voice. Something heavy dropped onto something else.

Kate followed the sounds in her thoughts. *There goes the trunk. Where's he taking it?*

From the back of the wagon came more scraping. Then the wagon jiggled as someone climbed in and started shoving crates around.

Kate's fingers clenched into nervous fists. *What if they pick up this crate? They'd find me for sure!*

Close beside the crate in which Kate lay motionless, the familiar voice spoke. "That's the last one. All right if I leave your horses here?"

"Move 'em over a bit, out of the way," called the other voice. "I'll take 'em back to the livery later."

"Your horse blanket's here," said the man near Kate. "Want it now?"

"Nah, leave it for the next customer."

As Kate listened, a wagon rolled away. Beside her, footsteps moved forward. Someone clucked the horses, and they backed away from the rail.

Slowly Kate raised up, pressing her face against the knothole. Surprise rippled through her.

Instead of long black hair and a crumpled hat, the driver's short brown hair showed beneath a spotless hat. Instead of a wrinkled black coat with a tear in one sleeve, the man wore a well-pressed suit coat.

Kate felt confused. *What happened to the mysterious stranger?*

She struggled to think. *There's something about this man— something that bothers me. Something I should know.*

As Kate watched through the knothole, the man stopped the

wagon. Jumping down, he tied the horses to a rail and hurried off, still within Kate's line of vision. *His shoulders. There's something about his shoulders.*

A moment later the man stepped onto a wooden platform, and his shoes clicked.

Then Kate knew. She gasped as all the pieces fell into place. In the distance a train whistle blew. Again it sounded, closer this time. Kate heard the hiss of brakes, the squeal of iron on iron. The Blueberry Special!

"They'll turn the engine around," she muttered. "They'll fill it up with water. Maybe they'll need coal. But then they'll leave."

The scared feeling was back in her stomach. "Once the train leaves Grantsburg, that trunk will be gone. All those stolen things lost forever!"

Around Kate, the noise increased. Men called to each other, and Kate felt sure they were turning the engine.

Then the stranger moved out of range of her knothole view. "I'll climb out. I'll run for help."

Pushing back the blanket, she took one last look through the knothole. The stranger was back, looking straight toward the wagon.

Once more Kate crouched down. *What'll I do? The train will leave. He'll get away!*

Her frantic thoughts raced on. *I'll stand up. I'll walk right up to him!*

Even as the thought came, she knew it wouldn't work. *It's my word against his. No one will believe me!*

Then a wagon pulled alongside the one in which Kate huddled. Someone whistled, and Kate recognized it. Anders whistling to Lutfisk!

Relief poured through her. The next second she felt scared again. *How can I warn him? He'll look right at the stranger and not recognize him.*

Then Kate remembered the signal she and Anders had worked out. Rap. Pause. Rap, rap, she knocked against the wooden crate.

Once again she rapped, harder this time. Rap. Pause. Rap, rap. A moment later, Kate heard Anders' voice.

"Kate?" he asked softly from alongside the wagon.

Kate wanted to shout. Instead, she, too, spoke quietly. "Anders? The mysterious stranger is the man standing right in front of you."

"The one with the hat and suit?"

"In a minute he'll get on the train and be gone."

"But this wagon? He'll just leave it?"

"He must have rented it at the livery stable."

"And he took the stuff? How do you know?"

"It's in his trunk." Kate was growing impatient. "You have to get help! If I stand up, he'll see me. He'll know I followed him."

Anders took only a second to decide. "Stay right where you are. I'll get Big Gust."

"You know where he lives?"

"A couple blocks from here. In the fire station."

The silence stretched long, then a wagon creaked from somewhere near the train. Soon they would put the trunk in the baggage car. "Come on, Anders, hurry up!" she wanted to shout.

Through the knothole, she watched trainmen pull up the long spout of the water tank. "All ah-boooooard! All ah-boooooard!" called the conductor.

The neatly dressed man turned his back toward Kate, falling into line with the other passengers.

Standing up in the crate, Kate scrambled out of the wagon, determined to stop him. As she reached the ground, Mama and Papa Nordstrom came down the street.

"Kate!" Mama exclaimed. "We've been looking for you. Anders came to the neighbors and told us you were missing. Where have you been?"

"Mama! Just a minute! We have to stop him!"

"Stop who?" asked Mr. Nordstrom.

"Mr. Eberly! He's a thief!"

"A thief!"

"Anders will tell you!"

Just then Big Gust hurried up. Anders and Lutfisk ran alongside to keep pace with the marshal's long strides.

"A thief, Papa," said Anders. "We've got to stop him!"

Big Gust looked at Mr. Nordstrom. "Are they telling the truth?"

"I don't know," said Papa. "But they've told the truth up 'til now."

Big Gust scratched his head. "It's serious business, stopping someone."

"If you could see inside his trunk—" Kate interrupted.

"His trunk?"

"The big wooden one. The one they're loading right now," she said. "The things he stole are in there, in syrup pails. See how heavy it is?"

As they watched, two men struggled with lifting the trunk onto the train. "Come on, Gust, give us a hand," one of them called.

As Big Gust started over, a leather handle broke. The trunk crashed to the ground. One of the corners split open. Through the opening, Kate saw the shiny metal of a syrup pail.

"Pull it aside, away from the train," ordered Big Gust.

He turned to Kate. "Now, young lady, you'll have to show me the owner of this trunk."

Soon Big Gust had Mr. Eberly off the train. As Mr. Eberly came down the metal steps, his shoes clicked.

"Miner's shoes!" exclaimed Anders in a low voice. "He must have worked in a mine, somewhere away from here."

"In March his face was too white," said Kate. "As if he didn't get much sun. He's the man in the woods, all right. He wore a wig and false beard."

As Kate and Anders moved closer, Big Gust spoke to Mr. Eberly. "The men dropped the trunk. I want you to check that everything's all right."

"Oh, I'm sure it is," answered Mr. Eberly. His voice sounded calm, but his eyes looked nervous.

Big Gust insisted. "Don't want you to have trouble later. Unlock the trunk."

"But I'll miss my train."

"The train will wait, and so will I." Big Gust's voice was firm and as polite as always. Yet as he towered above Mr. Eberly, the marshal's face no longer looked kind.

Slowly Mr. Eberly unlocked the trunk.

"Hmmmmmm. What have we got here?" asked Big Gust, his face innocent. "Maybe you better open one of these pails for me."

Kate hurried forward. "I'll show you which one," she said.

Mr. Eberly turned to her, an angry flush on his face, his gray eyes stormy. "Who are you? This is my business, not yours."

"Well, then," said Big Gust, "no harm in doing what she asks. What do you have in mind, young lady?"

Quickly, before anyone could stop her, Kate unloaded the trunk, setting one syrup pail after another on the ground. Near the bottom, she found what she wanted—the pail with rust on the handle.

"I'll tell you what's in this one," she said. "A copper piece with a stamp of Sweden!"

Suddenly Mr. Eberly bolted. Big Gust barely moved. Reaching out one long arm, he grabbed hold of the back of Eberly's collar. For a moment the village marshal swung the man off the ground. Then, as if in slow motion, Big Gust set Eberly down on the platform.

The smaller man did not move.

Then the marshal called over a drayman with his horses and wagon. Refilling the trunk, Big Gust picked it up and loaded it onto the wagon.

Kate couldn't believe it. "All by himself!"

Anders laughed. Papa turned to Mama, a grin on his face.

Big Gust acted as though nothing out of the ordinary had happened. "I'll take this man to jail and be right back."

Brushing against Kate's skirt for attention, Lutfisk wouldn't be ignored any longer. As she hugged her thanks, he licked Kate's face and woofed.

Then Mama's arms went around her. "I'm *proud* of you, Kate!" she exclaimed, though concern still showed in her face.

When Mr. Nordstrom hugged her too, Kate guessed how afraid he'd been. "Swedes don't hug in public," she wanted to say. Instead, she pulled back and looked into his eyes. "It's awfully good to see you, Papa."

A flash of surprise crossed Mr. Nordstrom's face, then was

gone. "It's awfully good to see *you*, Kate," he echoed, his voice gruff.

When Kate turned to Anders, he looked embarrassed. "Did you rap on my door? I never heard you. I must have just fallen asleep."

Then he told what happened. "Just as I finished milking, Lutfisk found me in the barn. He barked until I followed him to your window. That's how I knew you were gone."

Papa took up the story. "Anders walked as fast as he could to find us at the neighbors. We hitched up the horses."

"Lutfisk ran ahead," Anders told her. "When we came to a crossroads, he took the turn, still sniffing. He sniffed his way over to your locket, where it hung on a branch."

"It reflected the morning sun," Mama added, handing the locket to Kate. "At first we wondered . . ." Her eyes glistened with tears. "Then we decided you hung it there to show us where to go."

Kate nodded. "And the mystery's solved!" Turning to Anders, she explained about Mr. Eberly. "Remember how you wondered why the stranger kept disappearing? He's a salesman who comes to town now and then to show his wares—for spring, summer, fall, and winter! He brought a large trunk, filled with samples."

"And if he decided to sell his samples, he filled it up with whatever he stole!" guessed Anders.

"Remember your trunk, Mama?" Kate asked. "He must have gotten extra greedy. I wonder if he would have taken what he wanted, then sent the trunk back to the depot, saying it wasn't his?"

"So!" said Papa as Big Gust returned. "Let's celebrate!"

"Celebrate?" asked Kate. But no one would let her in on the secret.

When they reached Big Gust's rooms in the fire station, Anders walked over to something big sitting in the middle of the floor. It was covered with a large cloth, which Anders pulled off with a flourish.

There stood the organ Kate had seen at the fair. In the sunlight streaming through a window, the oak wood gleamed gold. Before the keyboard sat an organ stool as though waiting for someone to sit down to play.

"It's for you, Kate," Papa said quietly.

Kate stood there, unable to speak.

"Were the bee stings worth it?" he asked.

Kate nodded, still unable to speak.

"We brought it here on Saturday. Big Gust was going to bring it out today. We wanted to surprise you."

Kate found her voice. "But the money? I wanted Anders to get the mare."

Anders returned her look, but did not speak.

"He figured you needed the organ more," said Papa, his voice soft. "With the money from his pig and the honey you sold, plus what was left over from your mama selling furniture, we had just the amount we needed."

Once Kate would have taken whatever she could get. Now she felt strange receiving such a gift.

"Anders wants a horse?" Big Gust broke in. "Boys your age don't own a horse! You're sure you're old enough?"

Big Gust winked at Papa, then turned back to Anders. "Do you have one picked out?"

Anders told the big Swede about Wildfire. "If she's okay."

"She will be," said Papa. "She'll always have a scar across her chest, but it won't hurt her running. Because of it, she won't cost as much."

Big Gust's smile stretched from one side of his face to the other. "Well, I have just the thing for you, Anders. That is, if you and Kate can agree on what to do. Trader Carlson posted a reward when he lost his copper piece from Sweden. It might be just what you need for that horse."

"What about it, Kate?" asked Papa. "It's up to you."

Anders looked at Kate, a question in his eyes, a question he seemed unable to ask.

As Kate nodded, her excitement spilled over just thinking about all they could do with both an organ and a horse.

Anders leaped into the air, his arms high above his head. "I can't believe it!"

Kate grinned. "Believe it, believe it!" she teased, remembering how Anders rescued her locket from the well.

But she kept another thought to herself. *Maybe the Wisconsin wilderness isn't so bad after all! I wonder what will happen next?*

Acknowledgments

My thanks to the countless individuals who answered my questions and helped shape the lives of Kate and Anders. I'm especially grateful to those who spent long hours telling me the way it was:

Phillip Johnson and Carl Lindell, Sr. talked about the Minneapolis of long ago. From Wade Brask came Anders' dog Lutfisk, the school bell, and the root cellar. The house, barn, and summer kitchen belong to Emma Bergstrom Haight. Arnold Johnson remembered his boyhood in a country school. Helen Tyberg knew what it meant to be both a student and a teacher. John and Gladys Olson recalled the Blueberry Special and salesmen coming to town. Gunhild Kempe talked about growing up on a farm. Mildred Hedlund checked my tales of Big Gust.

Maurice Crownhart and the Grantsburg Centennial Committee provided both pictures and history in *Strolling Through a Century*. Through conversation and her book, *Pieces of the Past*, Eunice Kanne offered her own careful research and a wide variety of details, including Trader Carlson's copper piece.

Walter and Ella Johnson deserve special mention for reading the manuscript, and for sharing ideas about Kate's locket, the well, and the use of dynamite and sadirons.

As we talked together, I came to know all of these people.

They helped me dream about what it was like to be a child in times past.

My gratitude also to Charette Barta, Ron Klug, Jerry Foley, Penelope Stokes, Terry White, and my husband Roy for their work on the manuscript and their ongoing encouragement.

THE CREEPING SHADOWS

THE CREEPING SHADOWS

Lois Walfrid Johnson

BETHANY HOUSE PUBLISHERS
MINNEAPOLIS, MINNESOTA 55438

Except for Rev. Augustus Nelson and Big Gust Anderson, village marshall Grantsburg, Wisconsin, in the early 1900s, the characters in this book are fictitious. Any resemblance to persons living or dead is coincidental.

Copyright © 1990
Lois Walfrid Johnson
All Rights Reserved

Published by Bethany House Publishers
A Ministry of Bethany Fellowship, Inc.
6820 Auto Club Road, Minneapolis, Minnesota 55438

Printed in the United States of America

Library of Congress Cataloging-in-Publication Data

Johnson, Lois Walfrid.
    The creeping shadows / Lois Walfrid Johnson.
       p. cm. — (The Adventures of the northwoods ; bk. 3)
    Summary: Kate plans a birthday party for her stepbrother Anders and gets involved in the mysterious disappearance of items from the Erickson household.

    [1. Swedish Americans—Fiction. 2. Stepfamilies—Fiction. 3. Mystery and detective stories. 4. Christian life—Fiction.]
I. Title. II. Series: Johnson, Lois Walfrid. Adventures of the northwoods ; 3.
PZ7.J63255Cr 1990
[Fic]—dc20   90–49143
ISBN 1–55661–102–1   CIP
                                                                AC

To Walter and Ella Johnson,
friends I can count on,
with thanks
for remembering the way it was.

LOIS WALFRID JOHNSON is the bestselling author of more than twenty books. These include *You're Worth More Than You Think!* and other Gold Medallion winners in the LET'S-TALK-ABOUT-IT STORIES FOR KIDS series about making choices. Novels in the ADVENTURES OF THE NORTHWOODS series have received awards from Excellence in Media, the Wisconsin State Historical Society, and the Council for Wisconsin Writers.

Lois has a great interest in historical mystery novels, as you may be able to tell! She and her husband, Roy, are the parents of a blended family and live in rural Wisconsin.

Contents

1. Trouble Ahead 9
2. Maybelle Pendleton 15
3. Stretch! 21
4. The Unwanted Visitor 29
5. Josie's Secret 35
6. Howls in the Night 43
7. The Search 51
8. City Girl Farmer 55
9. Wildfire! 63
10. Race Against Time 67
11. Kate's Choice 73
12. Out of the Darkness 81
13. Papa's Strange Letter 85
14. The Moving Shadow 91
15. Discovery! 99
16. The Loan Shark Returns 105
17. Frightening News 113
18. Growing Threats 119
19. The Shadows Lengthen 127
20. Lutfisk Meets Calico 133
21. Footsteps Through the Snow 139
22. The Dangerous Chase 147
23. Northern Lights 153
Acknowledgments 159

Adventures of the Northwoods

1. *The Disappearing Stranger*
2. *The Hidden Message*
3. *The Creeping Shadows*
4. *The Vanishing Footprints*
5. *Trouble at Wild River*
6. *The Mysterious Hideaway*
7. *Grandpa's Stolen Treasure*
8. *The Runaway Clown*
9. *Mystery of the Missing Map*
10. *Disaster on Windy Hill*

1

Trouble Ahead

A gust of wind swooped around the corner, caught the barn door, and flung it back on its hinges. As the door banged against the wall, Katherine O'Connell pushed aside the black hair escaping her braid. In the December air her cheeks were red with cold.

A troubled look darkened Kate's deep blue eyes. *Today Papa Nordstrom returns to logging camp,* she thought. *What if something goes wrong when he's gone?* Already there'd been mysterious happenings around Windy Hill Farm.

Pulling off her mittens, Kate reached through the high rail fence to stroke the star on Wildfire's forehead. The mare's smooth coat shone in the early morning sunlight. She moved closer, nuzzling Kate's neck.

Kate laughed. "If you could talk, would you have secrets to tell?"

The mare tossed her head as though saying yes, and Kate laughed again. Picking up a bucket, Kate held it out.

Black and sleek, long-legged with four white socks, Wildfire dipped her head into the oats. But a minute later she lifted her ears and stepped back.

"You don't want oats?" Kate felt puzzled. "What's wrong?"

Still reaching through the fence, she held the bucket higher.

Instead of coming forward, Wildfire edged farther back. Raising her head, the mare turned her ears to listen. The next moment she snorted and struck the ground with her front hoof.

Kate dropped the bucket and jumped away from the fence. "Wildfire, what's wrong?"

Again the mare snorted and struck the ground several times. Her eyes rolled.

Kate's heart thudded. In the months she'd known Wildfire, the mare had never acted like this.

An instant later a howl broke the early morning stillness. Starting low, it rose, dropped, then rose again. In the cold air the sound lingered in the trees.

Kate shivered. A wolf. Across the field, somewhere in the woods. How far away?

Just then Kate heard a shout. She swung around, glad for human company. Her new brother Anders stood on the path leading to the house.

Though twelve years old like Kate, Anders was tall for his age. His wide shoulders stretched the seams of his jacket and blond hair fell over his forehead. Setting his crutches ahead of him, he swung forward.

A few days ago Anders had sprained his ankle. Yet so far crutches hadn't kept him from anything he wanted to do.

Stopping on the snow-covered path, he called again, "Kate! Papa wants you!"

Nine months before, in March 1906, Kate's widowed mother had married Anders' father, Carl Nordstrom. Mama and Kate had moved to Windy Hill Farm in northwest Wisconsin.

As Kate ran to meet Anders, he looked her in the face. "What's the matter? You're scared."

"A wolf, Anders." Kate's voice trembled. "I heard a wolf."

"Don't worry," he said. "It won't hurt you."

Kate didn't believe him. "Did you hear Wildfire whinny?"

"Yup." Anders didn't seem to care. "She'll be your first warning that anything's around. But forget it now. Papa has to leave."

As Kate hurried into the farmhouse, the warmth of the wood cookstove reached out. Yet the kitchen was quiet—too quiet. To

Kate it seemed colder than if she were feeling the December wind.

On Christmas Eve, Papa Nordstrom had returned from the logging camp where he'd worked since November. Only yesterday the family celebrated Christmas together. Was it already time to say goodbye?

A knot of dread tightened Kate's stomach as she joined the family at the table: her new sister, blond five-year-old Tina; her new brother, nine-year-old Lars; Anders; Mama; and Papa Nordstrom.

Mama had trimmed Papa's brown hair, mustache, and beard. Yet his chapped face still showed the bite of walking home in the winter wind. His eyes looked soft, as though he already felt the separation from his family.

"Sven will be here soon," Papa told them, his voice heavy.

Sven would drive into Grantsburg, giving Papa a ride to the train. Kate had known that since yesterday, but now the separation seemed real. And Kate felt something more. An uneasiness swept through her like the wind sighing in a pine tree.

"Do you really have to go?" Her question burst out, though she knew it would do no good to ask.

"We need seed money for spring planting," Papa reminded her.

"But what will we do without you?" The question hung in the air as Kate thought of all the things that could go wrong on a Wisconsin farm. When Papa left in November, she'd asked the same question. She had found out.

Strange things had taken place. She and Anders and their friend Erik had needed to solve a mystery. What might happen now, with Papa gone again, and the long, dark days of January just ahead?

"Kate," Mama said softly, as though warning her not to speak about something that couldn't be changed.

But instead Kate asked, "You came all that way to be here just one day?"

Papa nodded, and for an instant Kate wondered if his eyes were wet.

"I had to know how all of you are," he said, looking around

the table. Reaching out a hand, he placed it on top of Mama's.

"We needed Christmas together," she added. Tall for a woman, with golden blond hair, Mama was expecting a baby in the spring. Under her large apron her usually slim waist was growing.

"Sorry I'll miss your birthday, Anders," said Papa.

Mine, too, thought Kate, but didn't say it aloud. There was something she wanted to know. She remembered the construction accident that killed her Irish father, Daddy O'Connell. "Is it dangerous, working at the logging camp?"

Papa glanced quickly toward Mama, then back at Kate. "Sometimes," he said softly. "But it might also be hard for all of you here without me. We must pray every day for each other. Soon I'll be home again."

Still holding Mama's hand, Papa bowed his head and prayed in Swedish. As she heard their names, Kate guessed he was praying for each member of the family. Yet she couldn't understand Papa's words. Mama had come from Sweden, but Daddy O'Connell had been Irish. They had always spoken English in their home.

A moment later Papa Nordstrom stopped and cleared his throat. He switched into English, as though recalling Kate didn't know what he said. "Heavenly Father," he prayed, his voice deep. "When Kate needs to remember, remind her of thy care for her."

Surprised at Papa's prayer, Kate swallowed. Quickly she brushed away the tear that slid down her cheek.

Then Papa said, "Ah-men."

Kate glanced up to see Anders watching her. But instead of his usual teasing, he looked away.

When sleigh bells jingled in the farmyard, Papa slowly stood up, as though not wanting the time to end. He pulled on his heavy coat and boots, then hugged all of them.

Swinging forward on crutches, Anders followed Papa into the yard. Kate trailed behind, stopping just outside the door.

As he reached the sleigh, Papa looked Anders square in the eyes. "It's been a long time since Mama lived on a farm in winter," he said. "And Kate never has."

Shivering in the cold, Kate strained to hear, but the wind caught his next words and took them away. Papa reached out his hand, resting it on Anders' shoulder. He spoke again, but Kate still could not hear.

The back of Anders' blond head moved as though he were nodding.

Papa brushed a mittened hand across his eyes. *Is he crying?* Kate wondered. At this distance she couldn't be sure. Then Papa's words came clear in the December air. "Take care of Mama and Kate, won't you? And Tina and Lars."

Anders straightened his broad shoulders and stood taller. His father's strong arms wrapped around him. Then Papa climbed onto the sleigh.

Sven flicked the reins, and the horses stepped out. When Papa turned back and waved at Anders, he looked toward the house. Seeing Kate, he waved again.

As the sleigh passed beyond the barn and out of sight, Kate's eyes blurred with tears.

2

Maybelle Pendleton

*K*ate shivered and hurried back into the kitchen. More than once she'd plunged headlong into adventure, sometimes with surprising results. But now Kate watched quietly as her mother turned away from the window. In the silence Mama sniffled once and hurried over to the cookstove.

As Anders dropped into a chair, Mama lifted a stove lid. Pushing in a corncob, she pulled the teakettle over the firebox. But even then she kept her back toward the children.

"Erik's coming soon," Anders said after a time. Erik was Anders' best friend.

Kate barely heard. She was looking at Mama.

"He'll be here *soon*," Anders prodded Kate, even though he, too, watched Mama. "You better get ready."

Her back still turned to them, Mama took the corner of her apron and wiped one eye, then the other. Taking a deep breath, she straightened her shoulders.

When Mama turned their way, her face showed no tears. But her blue eyes held a shadow—a shadow Kate hadn't seen since the time following Daddy O'Connell's death.

Mama cleared her throat. "I'm glad you want to help out, collecting meat for Swensons." Her voice sounded almost normal. "They have a hard time making their money go far enough. I hope they don't lose their farm."

"Josie's got a big family," Anders said gruffly. "Eight brothers and sisters. Nine children is a lot to feed."

"Yah," said Mama. "But I think it's more than that. Mrs. Swenson often seems worried. And she's not the worrying kind."

Josie Swenson was a special friend to both Kate and Anders. Her father had fattened an animal for two years to have meat for this winter. In November the steer was stolen.

Two days before, on the afternoon of Christmas Eve, Kate, Anders, and Erik had solved the mystery of that theft. But they also learned the steer was gone for good.

Reaching for his crutches, Anders stood up. "I'd better get going. Every family I asked promised to help out."

He made it sound as if it weren't important, but Kate saw his eyes. It had been Anders' idea to collect meat and other food from any neighbor who wanted to give. On Christmas Day he'd quietly gone to each of the families in their church.

Kate hurried to put on warmer clothes. By the time Erik drove up with the big Lundgren horses, she was ready.

As Kate went outside, Erik jumped down from the sleigh. "Mornin', Kate," he said, solemn as a judge. A warm cap covered most of his wavy brown hair.

"Mornin', Erik," she answered in the same tone of voice.

It had become a joke between them, a joke started the day Erik put the end of her long braid into his inkwell at Spirit Lake School. Now his eyes danced as he grinned down at her. "Great day for a run!"

Kate agreed. For a moment she forgot that Papa had gone back to the logging camp. Feeling the sunlight warm upon her face, she laughed just thinking about the ride across new snow. It was always fun being with Erik.

Lifting the bundle over the high board sides of the sleigh, Kate and Erik loaded the meat Mama had put aside for Swensons. Kate wrapped burlap around bricks she'd warmed, then climbed up to sit next to Erik. Placing the bricks near her feet, she pulled a heavy robe over her lap and tucked it under her legs. In the cold wind she'd be glad for the warmth.

Throwing his crutches into the back, Anders pulled himself up next to Kate. Erik clucked the horses, and they started down the long track to the main road.

The snow sparkled in the sunlight, and tall trees cast blue-gray shadows. Sleigh bells jingled, bright and clear in the crisp December air.

Kate drew a deep breath. On a morning like this, it was easy to believe that northwest Wisconsin was a good place to live. In Minneapolis, Sarah Livingston and Michael Reilly had been her best friends. Here Kate had learned to depend on Anders, Josie Swenson, and Erik Lundgren. Best of all, Kate had started to feel she belonged.

Yet now when Mama couldn't hear, Kate had a question for Anders. "Will Papa be all right?"

Anders looked as though he were planning a smart remark. Then his eyes turned serious, and Kate remembered he never lied to her.

"I hope so," he told her, his voice less certain than usual. "I sure hope so."

Erik flicked the reins, and the horses picked up speed. "Good idea you had," he told Anders. "About bringing food, I mean."

"*Great* idea!" Anders answered with his lopsided grin. He winked at Kate.

Kate pretended she didn't notice, but Anders wouldn't let her get by with it.

"You like my ideas, don't you, Kate?"

"Yah, sure, big brother."

"Like the time I made the bell not work."

Kate smiled, remembering what he'd done to the bell at Spirit Lake School. That plan had been a good one.

"And your first day of school. Remember, little sister?"

Kate frowned. "Just because I'm short for my age, I'm *not* your little sister!"

"Remember how I helped you cross the log over the creek?"

"Help, all right!" Kate laughed. "You were the biggest help I've ever seen!"

Anders paid no attention. "And remember the time I drove Wildfire too fast?"

"The time!" Kate exclaimed. "The *times*, you mean!" She felt uneasy, wondering what Anders would do next. Hoping to get his mind off trying something else, Kate changed the subject. "We'll get to see Josie's new kitten."

Erik grinned. "Her vanishing kitten, you mean. Maybe you can solve that mystery too." Every now and then Swensons couldn't find Calico, even though Josie never let the kitten outside.

All morning long Erik drove from one farm to the next, collecting food. It was midafternoon when he and Kate and Anders reached the other side of Spirit Lake School. Erik turned the horses off the road into yet another farmyard.

"Who lives here?" Kate asked.

"Maybelle," Anders said, as if he were making a big introduction. "Maybelle Pendleton."

"Pendleton?" Kate asked. "She can't be a Swede."

Anders grinned at Erik. "Only half Swede. The half that's right pretty."

Erik's neck flushed red, but he kept his eyes straight ahead.

Kate looked from one to the other. There was something here she didn't understand. "Who's Maybelle Pendleton? How come I've never heard of her before?"

"She and her folks just came home," Anders said. "Moved away for a while, but wanted to come back to Burnett County."

"But if they just moved here, why aren't we bringing food to *them*?"

"Maybelle's living with her grandaddy and grandmama." Anders drawled out the words, as though explaining to a child. "Her Papa's out looking for work on the railroad."

"How old is she?" asked Kate, thinking she probably knew.

"Twelve, thirteen," Anders told her. "Used to be in our class at Spirit Lake. Too bad we don't have school again until April. That right, Erik?"

As Erik slowed the horses, he ignored Anders. Up until now Kate had been sorry there'd be no school until spring term. In that instant she changed her mind.

"Yup, that's the way it is," Anders went on. "Maybelle's been missing her good friends in Burnett County."

The red moved from Erik's neck into his face. "Aw, go jump, Anders," he growled. "Jump in a lake—a frozen one!"

Stopping the horses, Erik seemed glad for the excuse to swing down and tie them to a rail.

While Anders waited in the sleigh, Kate followed Erik up the path to the house. Ever since she'd known him, Erik had paid special attention to her. But now Kate felt uneasy.

Who is this Maybelle Pendleton? she wondered again. Kate had the feeling she didn't want to know.

3

Stretch!

*T*he farmhouse door opened as though someone had watched for them. No grandparent stood there, but Maybelle herself. Kate didn't have to be told.

"Erik!" the girl cried out, and again Erik flushed red, almost as red as the girl's long braids.

Kate had always liked Lars' hair, and Maybelle's braids were an even deeper color—a red Kate couldn't describe, even to herself. She only knew she had never seen such thick beautiful hair.

"Maybelle, this is—" Erik stumbled over the words. "This is Kate—" He stopped as though trying to remember Kate's last name.

Then he grinned, seeming relieved to come up with it. "Kate O'Connell." His voice sounded too loud. "This is Maybelle Pendleton."

For the first time since Kate had known him, Erik seemed tongue-tied. Already Kate wished she'd never heard of Maybelle Pendleton. When Kate tried to smile, her face felt stiff, and her words sounded stiffer. "Pleased to meet you."

"Glad to see you back, Maybelle," said Erik, no longer stumbling.

"Come in and warm up," Maybelle told them, but she looked only at Erik.

"Oh, we're not cold," Kate answered quickly. "We're going to Josie Swensons'. We're almost there."

"But Anders might be cold." Erik didn't look at Kate. "Bad leg and all. Yup, I'm sure he's cold."

Before Kate had time to move, Erik called out, bringing Anders to the house.

Inside, the air felt warm and more welcoming than Kate liked. Maybelle's mother and grandparents were visiting a neighbor, but Maybelle stirred together cocoa, sugar, and milk. She set the kettle over the hottest part of the cookstove.

Kate dropped into a chair, but her gaze followed Maybelle. As the girl moved around the kitchen, she looked sure of every step, sure of everything she did, sure of herself.

Maybelle was slender and of medium height. Her eyelashes were dark and her eyes a deep brown. But most startling of all was Maybelle's hair. Kate wondered what to call it, even to herself.

As the boys talked with Maybelle, Kate thought about it. Then she remembered. Before marrying Papa Nordstrom, Kate's mother had been a dressmaker in Minneapolis. Once she described a dress the color of Maybelle's hair. A rich reddish brown. Russet. That's what Mama called it. Russet! The color of oak leaves in autumn.

Maybelle laughed then, a soft, tinkly laugh like a spoon against a glass. The boys laughed with her, and Kate realized she hadn't heard what was said. Nor had she spoken since entering the room.

Maybelle didn't seem to mind. As soon as the cocoa was ready, she poured it into a teapot. Returning to the table, she carefully filled Erik's cup. Then she circled the chairs to pour cocoa for Anders and didn't spill a drop.

Yet when Kate lifted her cup, Maybelle reached across the table, pouring quickly. Hot liquid shot over the top of the cup, streaming into Kate's lap.

Kate leaped to her feet, holding out her dress and sputtering.

"Oh, I'm sorry!" Maybelle's voice sounded as sweet as honey dripping from the comb. "Did I hurt you?"

"*Hurt* me? That cocoa's *hot*!" Kate held the front of her skirt away from her body.

"Oh, Kate, forget it!" exclaimed Anders. "Maybelle couldn't help it."

"It was just an accident," Erik chimed in.

But Kate looked up into Maybelle's dark eyes—eyes that didn't look nearly as sorry as the sweet voice sounded. In that instant Kate felt sure Maybelle had spilled the cocoa on purpose.

"An *accident!*" Kate exclaimed, waving the front of her skirt back and forth. "Ha!"

"Stop it, Kate!" said Anders, his voice low.

Kate's temper flared. "*I* stop it? *She* started it!"

Both Anders and Erik looked embarrassed. As Maybelle went to the stove, Anders pinched Kate's elbow. For the first time since she'd known him, he looked shocked at her behavior.

"Kate, mind your manners!" he whispered hoarsely.

Kate flipped her long braid over her shoulder and glared at Anders. Just the same, she sat back and struggled to keep quiet. *Don't they really know what Maybelle's doing?* she wondered.

Maybelle smiled sweetly, looking down her nose as though unable to understand this strange, backward girl. Erik and Anders stared at Kate as if she'd lost her mind.

After that, even the boys were ready to leave. Kate felt glad. She could hardly wait to get out of the house and away from Maybelle. But as they started toward the door, Erik turned back. "Why don't you come with us to Swensons'?"

Maybelle didn't take even a minute to pull on her coat and mittens. As Erik walked and Anders hobbled down the path, Kate knew she hadn't won after all.

When Maybelle reached the sleigh, she jumped up to the place between Erik and Anders. Kate grabbed the heavy robe and threw it onto the straw behind the seat.

Climbing up over the end of the sleigh, Kate circled the food. Her wet skirt slapped against her legs. She'd be cold the rest of the ride, but her misery went deeper.

As Erik started the horses, clouds scudded across the sky. Before long, the clouds darkened and slipped over the sun.

Kate grew even colder. Shivering, she pulled the robe over her head. Even then she heard Maybelle talking to the boys.

The road to Josie's seemed to last forever. Chilled to the bone,

Kate promised herself one thing. She'd get to see Josie's vanishing kitten. Since the mother cat's death, Josie had fed the kitten to keep it alive.

Kate had finally warmed up when she felt the sleigh make a turn. Like a turtle coming out of its shell, Kate poked her head from beneath the robe. Standing up, she looked over the high board sides of the sleigh. The horses had entered Swensons' driveway.

Just then a very tall man came out of the house. He bent his head in order to clear the door.

"Big Gust!" Kate cried, breaking her long silence.

The tallest man in all of Wisconsin, Big Gust stretched up to seven and a half feet. When he straightened, the top of his head reached far above the door. As Grantsburg's village marshall, he had helped Kate and Anders more than once.

Then someone else joined Big Gust on the porch. A thin boy with curly hair. Stretch!

Older than Kate, Anders, and Erik, Stretch had a bad reputation. Usually he grinned and looked as though he owned the whole world. Now the tall blond boy glanced toward the sleigh and drew back, almost behind Big Gust.

The village marshall put his large hand on Stretch's shoulder. He seemed to wait for Kate and Maybelle and the boys.

Kate jumped down from the sleigh. Her wet dress clung to her knees. Underneath her wool coat, the skirt felt clammy.

When Kate first met Stretch at Spirit Lake School, she had liked him. Most of the other children did too. But not Anders. Anders and Erik had never trusted the tall blond boy. Because of them, neither had Lars.

Now Kate dreaded talking with Stretch. When she reached the porch, he appeared even more embarrassed than she felt.

"Hi, Kate," he said, seeming to force himself to speak. His eyes shifted, looking away.

"Hi, Stretch," she answered and wondered what to say next.

Big Gust helped her out. "Stretch and I had a good Christmas together."

Stretch looked up at the giant and grinned. "Yup! Your *little* sister is a great cook!"

"Yah," answered Big Gust with his Swedish accent. "You'll get some flesh on your bones while your father's gone."

His hand still on Stretch's shoulder, the marshall turned to the others. "Mr. Swenson asked Stretch to stay here while he works for them."

"*Here?*" asked Kate, the words spilling out before she thought. "Stretch will stay at *Swensons'*?"

A shadow flickered across Stretch's face. Once again he edged back.

Instantly Kate regretted her words. Big Gust reassuringly slapped Stretch's shoulder.

"Going to turn over a new leaf, this boy is. Going to get his life straightened out and make something of himself."

Stretch grinned. As the shadow left his eyes, Kate remembered why she had first liked Stretch.

Now he seemed to believe the marshall's words could come true. But then the tall boy looked at Anders.

Instead of saying hello, Anders deliberately turned his back.

The shadow returned to Stretch's eyes.

In that instant Kate forgot her wet dress. She even forgot how she felt about the way Maybelle treated her. Instead, Kate wished she could make things right between Stretch and everyone else.

Just then Mr. Swenson came out of the barn, carrying some long poles. Seeing him, the marshall left them. "Promised I'd give Henry a hand."

Anders grinned. "Any hand Big Gust gives will be mighty big. Let's take a look."

Grabbing his crutches from the sleigh, Anders swung off. The others followed.

Across the yard Mr. Swenson and two neighbors stood near a small log building. As Kate and the others watched, one man slid the end of a strong pole under the building. Another man rolled a round log into place. Using the log as a fulcrum, the men pushed down on the pole. Nothing happened.

"What are they doing?" asked Kate.

"Trying to move that building," Erik told her.

"Just a minute," Mr. Swenson called out as Big Gust reached them. "We've got some good help."

Seeing the marshall, the men grinned and stood back.

Big Gust strolled over to the building. Looking as if he used no effort, he pushed down on the pole. That side of the building moved up, a foot off the ground.

Anders laughed. "No trouble at all!"

"Hold it!" Big Gust told the two men.

Taking positions on either side of Gust, the two men held down the pole. The marshall let go. The end of the pole flew up with the men still hanging on. As they dangled in midair, the building crashed to the ground.

Once more Big Gust took his place and pried the building up. As the men came beside him, Gust called the boys. "Come here! Lend a hand!"

Anders swung himself over, then dropped his crutches, and balanced on one foot. Erik and Stretch followed, taking places on the pole beside the men. The five of them held the pole down and the building up. Big Gust slipped a heavy timber for a skid under that side.

As the building settled onto the skid, the giant went around to the other side. Once more Big Gust slid a pole underneath the bottom log. Moving slow and easy, he pushed down and lifted that side. Before long, it too rested on a skid. The building was ready for horses to drag it across the snow.

The hard work done, Big Gust waved goodbye and drove off.

Mr. Swenson turned to Anders and Erik. "Can I help you with something, boys?"

Anders shook his head. "We came to help *you*." Swinging across the yard, Anders led Mr. Swenson to the sleigh.

Everyone followed but Stretch. When Kate glanced back, he stood a short distance away, listening.

"We brought this," Anders said proudly. "It's from all your neighbors." Leaning into the sleigh, he picked up one of the frozen packages of meat, carefully wrapped in newspaper.

"For me?" asked Mr. Swenson, seeming unsure what to say.

"Not just that piece," said Erik. "All this." He pointed to the sleigh, filled with meat and other kinds of food.

"For us? Yah?" Mr. Swenson couldn't seem to believe such great blessing. "For my family? *Tack! Tack!*"

His words sounded like the tock of a clock, but Kate knew it was the Swedish "thank you."

"To make up for the steer that was stolen," said Anders.

Out of the corner of her eye, Kate saw Stretch stiffen. As she turned, he glared at her with angry eyes.

In the next instant Stretch whirled around. With long strides he headed for the barn. When he reached the door, he didn't look back.

4

The Unwanted Visitor

𝒦ate stared at the ground, wishing she didn't have to look at anyone. The silence grew long.

"What's wrong?" asked Maybelle. But no one answered.

"Stretch has his pride," Mr. Swenson told her at last. "But he'll make a good man, that boy. Yah, he'll make a good man."

"Stretch?" Startled, Kate looked up. Much as she wanted things to go better for Stretch, she found it hard to believe he'd become a good man.

"Yah, *Stretch*," said Mr. Swenson, his voice firm. "Yah, certainly," he repeated, making sure Kate understood. "If we believe in him, he'll make a good man. You'll see. And I want the three of you—Anders, Erik, and Kate—to help him."

Ignoring Maybelle's puzzled look, Mr. Swenson turned back to the sleigh. "Now. My family and I say *tack*. It is too much. Too much. We thank you with all our hearts."

If he'd had a suit coat on, he would have bowed, Kate felt sure. Instead, Mr. Swenson went to each of them in turn. When he came to her, Kate's small hand felt lost in his big one. Mr. Swenson shook it heartily.

"Matilda!" he shouted. "Come, Matilda! Meat for winter! Meat from these good boys!" He glanced at Kate. "And this good girl."

Not only Mrs. Swenson, but a line of children tumbled from the house. Smiling shyly, Josie led her eight brothers and sisters.

Kate knew some of the children from school, but it was the first time she'd seen all of them together. Standing in a line, they looked like stair steps, each a bit shorter than the one before.

Beaming with pride, Mr. Swenson introduced them to Kate and Maybelle. "You know Josie."

Josie smiled shyly at Kate but only nodded in Maybelle's direction. In her arms Josie held a small calico kitten.

"Jacob and Joshua, Jonah and Jesse," said Mr. Swenson, as each child stepped forward. "Jethro and James."

Mr. Swenson paused for breath. A little girl was next in line. "And this is Rebecca." With light brown hair, hazel eyes, and freckles across her nose, she looked like a three-year-old Josie.

"Ah, and here is Jennifer," said Mr. Swenson, turning toward his wife and the baby she held.

"You are too kind, bringing all this food!" cried Mrs. Swenson. "It is too much! Too much!" Her eyes shone with gratitude.

Erik and Josie's older brothers helped Mr. Swenson carry the meat to the summer kitchen. Used for cooking during hot weather, the small building was not heated during winter. The meat would stay frozen until spring.

Kate followed Josie into the farmhouse. The main floor looked like two rooms set together in a T. The top part of the T, originally a log home, was now a large sitting and eating area. The later addition, a big kitchen, extended out behind. Along the wall where the two rooms met, a stairway rose to an upper floor of three bedrooms.

Cold from her wet dress, Kate went over to the wood cookstove. Stretching out her fingers, she warmed her hands.

Josie showed her the new kitten. Calico had gray, white, and orange markings and green eyes. As Kate stroked the soft fur, the kitten purred.

Kate scratched her gently between the ears. "This is the vanishing kitten? She looks too happy to disappear."

"Calico likes you!" Josie laughed, handing the kitten to Kate. "But wait a bit. If anything scares her—"

Just then Josie's three-year-old sister came into the kitchen.

"Be kind to the kitty, Becca," Josie told her.

The little girl touched the kitten lightly. "Pretty. Kitty pretty."

Taking one look at Becca, Calico nestled deeper into Kate's arms. Kate stroked the kitten's back until Calico grew quiet.

"Let's have milk and cookies," Josie said, and Kate moved away from the stove. As she sat down, the kitten settled into her lap, purring softly.

A moment later, Maybelle came to the door. Calico lifted her head and looked around. The next instant she leaped to the floor and streaked into the front room.

Kate jumped up and followed, but the kitten was nowhere to be seen. "Where'd she go?" Kate asked Josie. "How can she disappear like that?"

The two of them searched under and behind every piece of furniture in the large open room. They looked around the chimney and large heating stove and beneath the nearby shelves. Kate even checked the branches of the Christmas tree standing near a window. But they found no trace of the kitten.

"See what I mean?" asked Josie. "Every now and then she just vanishes."

Kate found it hard to believe the kitten was really gone. "Can Calico get outside? It's awfully cold, and if she'd couldn't find her way back in . . ."

Josie looked worried. "That's what scares me. But I can't find a hole anywhere. I don't know how she'd get out." She nodded toward the front door that led outside from the sitting room. "See? It's closed."

"Is there anywhere else we can look?" But even as Kate asked, she knew they'd checked every possible place.

Josie led Kate back to the Christmas tree. "I want to show you something." Reaching under the branches, Josie picked up an opened gift, still within its newspaper wrapping. "Look what I got for Christmas!" She held up a long wool scarf. "Mama knitted it for me."

Seeing the deep red scarf, Kate felt happy for her friend. "What a beautiful color!"

Josie stroked the soft wool. "And I got an apple and candy from the party at church. What did you get for Christmas?"

Kate had received both a scarf and mittens, plus a sheet of organ music and an apple. She didn't want to make her friend feel bad. "You'll look really nice in that color," Kate answered quickly, hoping Josie wouldn't ask again.

In that moment Maybelle and the boys came in and joined the search for the kitten. They had no better success.

But Kate didn't want to give up. "If Calico was outside all night, would she freeze to death?" Kate asked.

"Yup," Anders told her. "If she didn't find a warm place. Or a wild animal might get her."

Erik glanced toward Josie. "But the kitten's not outside. All the doors are closed."

Seeing Josie's face, Kate realized her mistake in asking. She tried to comfort her friend. "And the doors were closed when Calico disappeared."

Josie's hazel eyes with long dark lashes still looked worried. "Well, we've got another mystery to solve. Maybe you can figure out this one too."

"The case of the vanishing kitten!" Anders joked.

Yet Kate felt uneasy. She liked Calico and didn't want harm to come to her. "She's just a baby kitten. Where could she possibly go?" Deep inside, Kate wondered, *Is there a little hole somewhere—a hole where Calico gets outside?*

A moment later sleigh bells jingled in the yard. A matched pair of gray horses pulled a new cutter up to the hitching rail.

Through the window Kate saw a man jump down from the small sleigh. Beneath his sealskin cap his hair looked newly trimmed. A thick mustache covered his upper lip. As he tied the grays to the rail, his long raccoon coat swung open to reveal a black suit.

For a moment the man looked around as though liking what he saw. Then he started toward the house.

"Oh no!" muttered Josie. "Leonard Harris. I have to get Papa."

Hurrying into the kitchen, she slipped out the back way.

A moment later the man pounded on the front door.

Drying her hands on her apron, Mrs. Swenson hurried into the room. Pausing a moment, she drew a deep breath, then opened the door. "Hello, Mr. Harris."

"Hello, Mrs. Swenson. And where is your good husband?"

"Soon he'll be here." Mrs. Swenson sounded breathless. "Come in, come in."

Removing his sealskin cap and the long raccoon coat, Mr. Harris handed them to Mrs. Swenson. As he sat down, he looked around, again appearing to like what he saw.

Why does he act as if he owns everything? Kate wondered. In his handsome face, the man's eyes seemed cold.

A moment later Mr. Swenson came in. He offered his hand to the stranger. Yet Mr. Swenson's smile looked stiff. When Kate, Anders, Erik, and Maybelle went into the kitchen, the door closed firmly behind them.

Whatever Mr. Harris needed to say did not take long. Within five minutes Kate saw him stroll to his cutter, a satisfied smile on his face. As his horses left the rail, a large black whip snaked out, snapping above their heads.

Several more minutes passed before the door into the kitchen opened. As Josie came through, Kate heard Mrs. Swenson's stout voice. "Yah, we pray."

Josie's face looked pinched and white, as though she were holding back tears. "That awful Mr. Harris wants to take our farm," she whispered, her voice rising in desperation. "And Papa's afraid he will!"

5

Josie's Secret

"Who is Mr. Harris?" Kate asked Josie.

"A loan shark!" her friend replied. Josie's eyes sparked with anger.

"What's that?" asked Kate.

"A crook," Erik told her. "If someone lends money, he charges interest to pay for the use of that money. But a loan shark charges a really high rate of interest."

"And makes it hard to pay back a loan?" asked Kate.

"Makes it *impossible!*" Erik exclaimed, sounding worried. "People lose their farms."

Kate wondered if Erik was thinking about his own family. A few months before, Lundgrens had been forced to move into the small house near Spirit Lake.

"Does your father have any money at all?" Kate asked Josie.

The other girl shook her head. The anger in Josie's eyes was gone now, replaced by misery. "I don't know what we'll do. If we don't make a big payment on January twenty-fifth, Mr. Harris will take our farm."

"That's less than a month away!" cried Kate. She, too, felt scared and angry.

That night she fell asleep thinking about Josie and her family.

The next morning Kate woke up feeling awful. At first she wondered what had happened. Then she remembered Mr. Harris and his spotless black suit. She remembered how he looked around, as if he already owned everything the Swensons had.

Compared to that, the way Maybelle acted didn't seem important. Yet Erik had always been Kate's special friend. Didn't he feel that way anymore?

Each time Kate thought about it, she hurt inside. In a tiny hidden-away spot, she ached as though she had a bad tooth.

About ten o'clock that morning Erik knocked on the door of the Windy Hill farmhouse. "Let's go skiing," he said, and all of Kate's hurt disappeared.

"You know I can't," grumbled Anders.

"But Kate can." Erik grinned at her. "Let's go."

Kate could hardly wait to get outside. During the months since Erik had made skis for her, she'd become fairly good on them.

Quickly Kate pulled on her warm coat, long scarf, and mittens. The day seemed bright and wonderful. Maybe she'd imagined the way Erik acted toward Maybelle.

"Wait a minute," Anders called as they headed out the door. "I'll ride Wildfire. Let's find out how Josie's doing."

While Erik led the mare out of the barn, Kate slid her boot inside the strap of a ski. Erik had made the straps from old harness and used buckles. On one ski the thin metal was bent out of shape.

Carefully Kate pulled the strap through, trying not to put pressure on the buckle. Then she watched Erik slip a bridle onto Wildfire's head.

The mare looked black and sleek, her socks white and clean. In November Papa had taken their big work horses to logging camp. During these months Wildfire provided their only transportation, except for walking.

Anders planned to ride bareback. Erik rolled a stump over to his friend.

Using Erik's shoulder, one crutch, and his good right foot, Anders lifted himself onto the stump. When Erik brought Wildfire alongside, Anders managed to get on the mare's back. Erik handed up Anders' crutches.

As Wildfire set out, Anders' bad ankle jounced against the horse. Kate saw Anders grit his teeth and guessed he felt pain. But Anders kept going. Wildfire tossed her head and pranced across the yard, her tail flying.

Here on the edge of the steep hill near the farmhouse, Kate gazed across Rice Lake. Beyond the snow-covered hills lay the town of Trade Lake.

Still farther away, four miles from the farmhouse, was the settlement of Four Corners. Each week Kate walked there to take organ lessons. On days like this it seemed entirely possible she would be a great organist, the way she planned.

Erik strapped on his skis and started down the steep track to Spirit Lake School. Kate bent her knees, ready to follow. For a moment she felt a jab of fear. Yet she'd taken this hill more than once. Her hands swinging free, she swooped down the path.

Anders followed, walking Wildfire. At the bottom of the hill, the wind off Rice Lake had blown the track clean. Where it was bare of snow, small stones stuck up from the dirt, catching Kate's skis.

Beyond Rice Lake, they came to woods. When they reached the far side, Erik twisted around. "Let's take a shortcut across this field."

Ahead of her, Erik circled the drifts, finding places where the snow was less deep. Each time he took a hill, Kate skied in his tracks. But then they came to the biggest hill of all.

Standing at the top, Kate looked down, once more afraid. She waited until Erik reached the bottom of the hill, then skied into position. Again she looked down. Long and steep, the hill fell away more sharply than anything Kate had tried.

Erik looked back. "You can do it!" he called.

Kate stood there, trying to build up her nerve. The hill seemed to drop into nothing. Her knees felt weak.

Anders rode up behind her. "What are you, a scaredy-cat?"

That did it. Taking a deep breath, Kate crouched and pushed off.

The wind rushed past her, cold upon her face. Partway down the hill, Kate felt excited. It almost seemed as if she were flying.

Then her right ski slipped too far out. As Kate pulled her foot back, something felt wrong. Arms waving, she fought to keep her balance. In the next instant the ski slid away.

Frantically Kate swung her arms. She felt herself falling forward. She'd go head first down the hill!

Fighting against it, Kate leaned back. For a moment she wobbled and almost went over. Somehow she steadied herself. Holding out her arms for balance, she straightened her right leg and bent her left, crouching down on one ski.

Again Kate wobbled and almost went over. Regaining her balance, she stayed upright until the bottom of the hill. There she sprawled into soft snow.

Emerging from the drift, Kate wiped snow from her eyes. "I did it!" she exclaimed. "I *really* did it!"

But when Erik reached her, he looked concerned. "Are you hurt?"

"Not a great skier like me!"

"You *are* great!" Erik exclaimed. "I don't know how you did it. But are you all right?"

Looking up into Erik's eyes, Kate felt good. He really cared what happened to her. "Yup," she answered.

Erik gave her a hand up. "You're sure?" he asked.

Kate laughed. "Never been better."

"Good show, Kate!" called Anders, riding up on Wildfire. "Greatest show on earth."

Kate brushed the snow off her long stockings. Somehow she'd lost her mittens. Already her hands felt icy cold.

Erik rescued them from a snowdrift, then asked, "What happened?"

"I don't know." Kate bent down to brush off her coat.

Erik found her missing ski against the trunk of a small pine. "Uh-oh, here's the problem. It's that old buckle I had to use. It broke, and the strap fell apart. But I can't fix it here."

"Let's go to Maybelle's and get warm," suggested Anders.

Though her feet were numb with cold, Kate pulled back. "Let's go home instead."

"It's too far," Anders insisted. "And we all need to warm up."

But Erik surprised both of them. Swinging Kate's skis across the mare, he set them on top of Anders' crutches. "I'm going home," Erik said. "I know where I can get a new buckle. Then Kate can ski back."

Maybelle met Kate and Anders at the door and soon had cocoa ready. This time Kate took no chances. She waited, warming up by the cookstove, until Maybelle poured the cocoa. Then Kate sat down at the table.

"What happened?" Maybelle asked.

"Kate was just trying to show off," Anders told her, winking in his sister's direction.

Kate didn't think it was funny. "You know better, Anders Nordstrom!"

"Now, Kate," Maybelle told her, "you don't have to worry when he talks like that. You just get nice and toasty warm."

Maybelle's honey sweet voice made Kate feel sticky all over. Tossing her head, Kate flipped her long black braid over her shoulder.

When at last Erik returned, he held a shiny new buckle in his hand. He gave it to Kate. "I couldn't find a strong enough needle to sew it on."

"Let's go to Josie's," said Anders. "Her father will have what you need."

Instantly Kate grabbed her coat, but Maybelle followed them again. When they got to Swensons', Josie surprised them. She looked like a different person. Even her eyes sparkled.

"Did Calico come back?" Kate asked.

Josie nodded. "But not 'til after dark. I get scared every time she disappears. I'm afraid something will happen to her."

When the boys left to search out Mr. Swenson, Josie, Kate, and Maybelle went into the large room. Becca came from the kitchen.

Looking up at Kate, she held out Calico. "Pretty kitty?"

Kate set the buckle on a low table and took the kitten. Cradling it in her arms, she sat down. As she stroked the soft fur, Calico tucked in her paws, wound her tail around her body, and purred.

Becca picked up the shiny buckle. "Pretty?"

"Pretty," said Kate. "Can you say *buckle*?"

When Becca left, Kate and Josie and Maybelle tried to talk. Yet even to Kate's ears, they sounded stilted and uncomfortable, as though trying to think of something to say.

Strange, Kate thought. *Usually Josie can't talk fast enough.*

Today she seemed to talk around everything Kate wanted to know. Whenever she looked at Maybelle, Josie seemed troubled.

Then Kate remembered. Josie and Maybelle had known each other before Maybelle moved away. Had Josie learned she couldn't trust the other girl?

Erik and Anders returned without finding either Mr. Swenson or a strong needle. When Maybelle joined the boys in the kitchen, Josie whispered in Kate's ear.

"I have to talk to you."

Kate's heart thumped. Only a few months before, Josie had spoken those same words. That time Swensons' steer had been stolen.

"Something else wrong?" asked Kate. The loan shark still weighed heavy on her mind.

But Josie's face seemed to shine. "Yesterday when Big Gust talked to Papa and Mama about Stretch, they asked him to stay here," Josie explained. "After Stretch went outside, I heard Papa say to Mama, 'Matilda, I know we made the right choice. Stretch needs help. But he'll eat big. He'll eat like a man.'

" 'We did the right thing, Henry,' Mama said. 'God will take care of us.'

" 'Yah, he's never let us down,' Papa answered. 'But the steer we raised is gone. And in just one month we must make that big payment.' "

A tear slid down Josie's cheek. "An hour later you and Erik and Anders drove up with the food."

Kate swallowed. Much as they had wanted to help, none of them had any idea what it would mean.

Reaching out, Josie took Kate's hands. "Close your eyes." Josie led Kate across the room. "Promise to keep a secret?" she asked.

Kate nodded.

A moment later Josie put something in Kate's hands. "Open your eyes."

Kate looked down to a small square box.

"It came this morning," Josie explained. "It was supposed to be a Christmas gift, but didn't get here 'til today."

"What is it?" asked Kate.

"If I show you, you mustn't tell anyone." Josie's voice was so low that Kate could barely hear. "Promise?"

"I promise. No one else knows?" asked Kate.

"Just my family. And Stretch, because he was here when it came."

"But what is it?" Kate asked.

"It came from my grandpa in Sweden. Along with this letter."

Josie and Kate sat down on the floor in a place with a good view of the kitchen door.

"I've heard the story since I was a little girl," said Josie. "But I'll read the letter." Unfolding a small piece of paper, she translated the Swedish words for Kate: "Dear Henry—"

"That's Papa," Josie explained, then continued reading:

> "When you were just a boy, I told you the story of this ring. My grandfather—your great-grandfather Joshua—was a hero. One night when out walking, he passed the estate of a wealthy landowner. He saw flames coming from the roof. He woke everyone and got them to safety, master and servants alike.
>
> "As they stood outside, the landowner discovered his youngest daughter missing. Joshua ran back in, passed through the flames, and carried the girl out in his arms.
>
> "The grateful landowner asked, 'What can I give you?'
>
> "Joshua shook his head. 'Anyone would have done the same.'
>
> "But the landowner pulled a ring off his own finger.
>
> " 'You saved my daughter's life,' he said to Joshua. 'This ring is very valuable. Someday you may be in want, and it will save your family.' "

Josie looked up, then went on translating the letter. "Then Grandpa writes":

> "I am an old man. I don't need the ring anymore, but you have many children. Keep the ring if you can, in honor of a brave man, your great-grandfather Joshua. But if you are ever

in need, find an honest man. Sell it, and use the money to help your children."

Josie looked around to be sure no one could hear. Kate's gaze followed hers. Through the kitchen doorway she saw Maybelle laughing with Erik and Anders.

Carefully Josie opened the box. Inside was another smaller box, and she opened that also. On a silk lining rested a gold ring set with many precious stones.

Kate gasped. "Are those diamonds?" When Mama was a dressmaker in Minneapolis Kate had seen diamonds now and then. Some of the fine ladies wore them.

Josie nodded. "And rubies. Papa says all of the stones are very valuable."

The diamonds and rubies caught the light from the window. Seeing their sparkle, Kate almost felt afraid. "What will your father do with the ring?" she asked.

"He plans to find an honest man, sell the ring and make that big payment," Josie answered. "Papa says there might be enough money to pay off the farm and buy machinery and tools. He said, 'Maybe it will even be enough to help other boys like Stretch.'"

"Your papa cares that much about Stretch?" asked Kate.

Again Josie nodded. Her eyes seemed nearly as bright as the diamonds.

Kate reached out and squeezed her friend's hand. "I'm really glad for you, Josie."

"I knew you would be, Kate. That's why I told you. But remember, it's a secret. Papa doesn't want anyone to know something so valuable is here."

"A secret," promised Kate, her voice low. "It's safe with me."

But then Kate looked beyond Josie to the doorway. Maybelle stood there, her eyes wide.

How long had she been listening?

6

Howls in the Night

How much did Maybelle hear? Kate wondered as she brushed her long hair.

Over a week had passed since Kate had seen Josie. The New Year had rolled around with 1906 becoming 1907. Now as Kate got ready for church, questions still whirled in her head. *Was Maybelle listening when Josie talked about that valuable ring?*

Josie didn't trust Maybelle, Kate knew. Neither did she, and with good reason. It'd be a long time before Kate would let Maybelle pour cocoa anywhere near her.

Pulling back her hair, Kate worked it into a single braid. Just as she finished, she heard sleigh bells jingle. Kate glanced through a bedroom window. The Lundgren horses were crossing the field between the two farms.

That week Erik's father had gone to work in a lumber camp. Mr. Lundgren had left his big work horses behind. Kate felt glad. Wildfire could pull only a light cutter by herself, not the heavy sleigh it took for all of them to get to church.

More than that, Kate liked riding with Lundgrens. Hurrying downstairs, she passed through the front and dining rooms into the kitchen. Already the rest of the family had bundled up in winter clothing.

When Anders followed Lars and Tina out the door, Mama held back. "Be sure to tell the children about the party for Anders," she whispered.

Kate nodded. "Thursday morning. Ten o'clock."

As she closed the door behind her, Kate felt the January air nip her cheeks. Strong gusts picked up new snow, driving it in whirlwinds across the yard.

Erik's mother and sister Chrissy sat on straw in the bed of the sleigh. Anders pulled himself onto the seat next to Erik, and Lars started to follow. A knitted cap hid the tuft of red hair usually sticking up at the back of his head. He sneezed and his blue eyes watered in the wind.

"Lars?" called Mama. "Are you catching a cold? You ride back here."

Lars groaned.

"Come on! There's less wind."

Slowly Lars moved down into the straw. Kate knew there was nothing Lars wanted to do less. He'd rather be up front with Erik and Anders.

Kate took Lars' place between the two boys, and Erik flicked the reins. The big work horses headed down the track to the main road.

"Stretch said Mr. Swenson is going to teach him how to be a blacksmith," said Erik.

"Josie's father is a blacksmith?" asked Kate.

"He does that besides farming," Erik told her. "And he's a good blacksmith, Papa says. If Stretch stays with it, he'll learn a trade."

"You mean if he can manage to stay honest," Anders growled.

"Stretch will," said Kate.

Anders shook his head. "It's just his say-so that he's going to go right. Don't forget, Stretch earned his reputation bit by bit."

"That doesn't mean he can't change," defended Kate.

But Anders wasn't convinced. "I don't know why Mr. Swenson asked him to stay there. It's one thing to have Stretch work for him. He doesn't have to live there."

"Yes, he does," Erik broke in. "It's a long walk to his family's farm, especially in winter."

"I still say you can't trust him."

"Mr. Swenson asked us to," answered Kate. "He wants us to help Stretch."

"But how do we know that he's changed?" asked Anders. "What if he really hasn't? He might try to get *us* to do something wrong."

"So we get hurt?" Kate asked. She thought about the way neither Anders nor Erik seemed to realize what Maybelle was doing. "Are you wondering if we'll get hurt 'cause we believe Stretch is all right, even though he isn't?"

"Yup, you got it," said Anders.

"But what if Stretch really does want to change?" Erik shot back. "If we don't believe in him, that's terrible too!"

"So what do we do?" asked Kate. "How do we know the difference?"

For a time they were silent, thinking about it. Around them, heavy frost clung to the pine trees along the road. With each movement of the horses, bells jingled in the cold air.

At last Kate spoke. "I know. We can pray. We can ask God to show us if it's all right to trust Stretch."

Anders looked surprised at her idea. "I don't know—" he started.

But Erik grinned in agreement.

Moments later they reached the church. Anders leaned on his crutches while Erik put the team in a barn. Taking hay from the sleigh, Erik dropped it down in front of the horses.

Kate waited until Anders started talking to a neighbor. "Surprise birthday party," she whispered to Erik. "This Thursday, January tenth. Ten o'clock. Tell all the boys, will you?"

As he covered the horses with blankets, Erik nodded. Kate hurried to the church.

Near the steps groups of people shook hands and talked. "*God dag, God dag,*" they greeted one another. It sounded like "good dog," but Kate knew it was the Swedish hello.

In the entryway, a tall Swede grinned down at Lars, giving permission to ring the bell. Lars' freckled face broke into a smile.

Going to the strong rope that dropped through a hole in the ceiling, he tugged hard. The bell clanged loudly. The rope swung back up, pulling Lars off the ground.

Kate followed Mama and Tina into the main part of the church. There the women and children went to the left, the men and boys to the right. When Mama, Tina, and Kate filed into a pew, Mrs. Lundgren and Chrissy joined them. Nearby sat Josie and Becca, with Mrs. Swenson holding the baby.

Glancing across the aisle to the men's side, Kate stiffened with surprise. A tall thin boy with curly blond hair sat next to Mr. Swenson. *Stretch in church?* It seemed hard to believe. *What's he doing here?*

Seeming to sense Kate's stare, Stretch turned her way. One eyelid dropped in a long, slow wink. Kate jerked her head back. A warm flush crept into her cheeks.

After that she kept her eyes straight ahead, but listened to the organ. In Minneapolis she'd been able to watch the organist. Here he sat in the balcony.

When everyone stood for the first hymn, Kate sneaked a look back. Was Erik up there, pumping the big handle up and down, bringing air into the organ? Kate couldn't tell for sure. But she knew the hand-pumped organ well. It was the one on which she took lessons.

As they sang the first hymn, Kate listened to every note. *I'll be a great organist someday,* she told herself, as she had many times before. For many years she'd admired Jenny Lind, the Swedish nightingale. Kate hoped to travel around the country giving concerts the same way. Instead of singing, Kate would play the organ.

Pastor Nelson wore a black suit with a stiff white collar. When he started preaching, Kate wished she understood his Swedish words. Standing in the big pulpit, he seemed far away. Yet Kate knew he loved young people. Erik had told her so, and Erik knew him well.

Before long Kate's mind drifted. She glanced across the aisle to where Stretch sat with Mr. Swenson. She remembered talking to Anders and Erik. "Help us, God," Kate prayed silently. "Help us know if we can trust Stretch."

Then Kate thought about the hymns they'd sung. She let the songs play over and over in her mind. She wanted to remember every note so she could play them on her own organ.

As soon as the service ended, Kate found Josie. Looking beyond her friend to where Anders stood with a group of boys, Kate lowered her voice. "Birthday party for Anders. Thursday. Ten o'clock. Be sure everyone knows it's a surprise."

"I'll tell all the girls," said Josie.

Kate knew Josie would look forward to the party all week. "Tell 'em to come early so they can hide."

"Is Anders going to be away, so we can sneak in?"

Kate grinned. "As my brother would say, 'Yup!' He doesn't know it yet, but he will be."

Josie laughed, and Kate looked back to the group of boys. Seeing Erik there reminded her. "You know the buckle Erik gave me? I forgot it at your house yesterday. On that low table."

"I'll bring it Thursday," Josie promised.

Then Kate realized something was wrong. Already the sparkle had disappeared from Josie's eyes. She looked worried as she glanced over her shoulder toward the boys. Stretch's blond curly head was there now, too, but turned away.

"How come he's in church?" asked Kate, her voice soft.

"Papa asked him to come. Said he expects it of anyone living with us. And when spring term starts, Papa wants Stretch to go to school."

"To *school*?" Kate found that hard to believe.

"Papa told him he needs more education. That he needs to finish eighth grade."

"Even though Stretch works for him?"

"Papa says that's one of the good things about America. The chance for people to get ahead."

But Kate knew there was still something Josie wasn't saying. "What's the matter?" Kate asked.

Josie dropped her voice to a whisper. "The ring is missing."

Kate's heart thudded into her stomach. "Missing?"

"Nowhere to be found."

"But it was there just before we left."

"I know," sighed Josie. She darted a quick look toward Stretch.

Kate had a different thought. "Your brothers or Becca wouldn't take it, would they?"

"Of course not!" Even the idea upset Josie. "All of them are honest. But that leaves just one person."

"Two," said Kate. "Don't forget Maybelle. Anders says her parents need money. More than usual, I mean."

Josie shook her head. "I don't think she'd take it. But blaming Stretch bothers me even more. When he came to live with us, Papa said we should believe Stretch when he says he wants to make good."

"Your papa told us almost the same thing." As she spoke, Kate remembered her prayer. "Can I tell Erik and Anders about the ring?"

"I asked Papa. He said, 'Yah. Maybe they can find it for us.' But Kate, we have to find it soon. In less than three weeks Papa has to make that big payment. If he can't, we'll lose the farm."

Soon after, Kate's family left for home. During the ride, the wind whipped up. Sitting in front again, Kate spoke softly, telling Erik and Anders about the missing ring.

"It's Stretch," said Anders, his voice low. "He took it."

"Why do you think that?" asked Kate.

"Who else would? All the boys in the family are too young. Besides, they wouldn't steal from their own father."

"But that doesn't mean Stretch would take something," said Kate.

"Doesn't it?" asked Anders. "How do you know?"

"Why can't it be someone who doesn't live in the house?" Again Kate thought of Maybelle.

"Nope," said Anders. "It's Stretch. I'm sure it's Stretch."

All afternoon the wind blew, holding the farmhouse in an icy grip. Even a few feet away from the wood stove, the walls felt drafty and cold.

Darkness fell early. By the time Kate went upstairs, Tina was asleep. Strong gusts swooped around the corners of the house. Windows rattled. In the light of the full moon, pine branches tossed up and down. On the frosted panes, their shadows became pointing fingers.

Blowing out the candle, Kate crawled into the bed she shared with Tina. But the long dark shadows still waved up and down.

Kate closed her eyes, trying to blot out the pointing fingers. In the next moment she heard a howl in the distance.

Clutching the quilts, Kate pulled them over her head. She stuffed fingers into her ears. Even so, the eerie sound reached her. From far away a howl started low, rose and fell, then lingered in the night air.

Kate's muscles tensed. She had never seen wolves, but it wasn't hard to imagine them gathered in a circle, noses pointed at the moon. Another howl followed the first, echoing through the countryside.

Then, as Kate listened, the wolves moved closer.

7

The Search

Somewhere near Windy Hill Farm, a wolf answered.

In the darkness Kate trembled. She wanted to wake Tina and ask, "What should we do?"

Reaching out, Kate poked her. The little girl moved away and slept on.

"Tina!" Kate whispered, but her sister rolled over.

Once again Kate nudged her. This time Tina didn't even wiggle. Her breathing sounded deep and even.

Kate felt silly, wanting help from a five-year-old. Yet Tina had grown up on the farm. She'd know what to do. She might even say, "Oh, Kate, go to sleep!"

Right now that seemed like something Kate wanted to hear. Instead, she lay awake a long time. Each time a wolf howled, she shuddered, feeling more afraid.

When Kate awoke the next morning, the wind had died down. Sunlight streamed through the windows, slanting across the bed.

Monday, Kate thought. *No school!* No school until spring term started on April eighth. One moment Kate felt glad. The next minute she wished she could see Josie and her other friends every day.

Then Kate remembered the wolves. Though the sky was blue and the day bright with sunshine, she felt afraid. She had no idea how long she had listened to the wolves howl.

Trying to push aside the memory, Kate scrambled out of bed, dressed, and went downstairs. When she reached the kitchen, she found Mama sitting at the table.

Usually her mother piled her golden blond hair high on top of her head. This morning it still hung in one braid down her back. It made Mama look young and helpless, but Kate knew better. Though Mama wasn't as strong as most farm women, she wasn't helpless. On the table in front of her lay an open Bible.

Mama saw Kate and smiled. But Kate had seen the lonesome look in her mother's eyes.

When Mama started to get up, Kate noticed the growing bulge under her mother's big apron. Gently Kate pushed her back into the chair. "I'll get it. What do you want?"

Mama lifted her cup, and Kate took the pot from the cookstove. As she poured out the coffee, she saw it wasn't steaming. Lifting the stove lid, she put in small chunks of wood, then set the pot over the firebox.

After breakfast Anders had an idea. "Let's go over and see if we can help Josie."

"I can't ski," said Kate, as she remembered the broken buckle.

"You don't have to. We can ride bareback on Wildfire."

Kate helped Anders with the mare's bridle. She led the horse to a stump, and they both managed to get on. Anders held his crutches in front of him, across Wildfire's mane.

The winter air was crisp and the sky without clouds. As the mare plunged through a drift, snow sprayed up. "Good thing you've got Wildfire," Kate said.

"Yup," Anders agreed. "Would be pretty hard getting along without her. Got any ideas about the ring? Or how we can help Josie's family?"

"Let's start by searching the big room," Kate answered.

Windy Hill Farm, Erik's house, and Swensons' farm were located on the three points of a triangle. Crossing the field, Kate and Anders rode through the woods to Lundgrens' house. From there Erik skied alongside them. Before long they passed Spirit

Lake School and came to Swensons'.

Josie met them at the door. Her eyes looked scared. The house seemed strangely empty with everyone else outside.

When Josie took them into the large open room, Anders asked, "How did your father get mixed up with that old loan shark?"

Josie's hazel eyes sparked with anger. "When Papa first came from Sweden, Mr. Harris was nice to him. He told Papa where there was land and how to get to Burnett County. He said, 'If you ever need money to get started, let me know. I'll help you.' "

"So Mr. Harris isn't from around here?" asked Kate.

Josie shook her head. "When Papa found this farm, he asked Mr. Harris for a loan. Papa was so new to America, he didn't understand that the interest was far too high. Even before we had a big family, he and Mama struggled to make payments."

"Has your father missed payments?" Erik wanted to know.

Again Kate remembered how the Lundgren family had lost their farm.

"Papa got behind when our steer was stolen," Josie told Erik. "He had planned to sell part of the meat. And once he got behind when Mama was sick."

"But he paid later?" Erik asked.

Josie nodded. "Papa wanted to go to logging camp this winter. But there's too much work to leave Mama alone."

"So we *have* to find the ring," said Anders.

"Without it, Papa doesn't have a way to make that big payment." Josie turned to Kate. "And I can't find your buckle."

"That's all right," Kate told her. Without the buckle she couldn't ski, but compared to losing a farm, skiing didn't count. "Let's start hunting for the ring."

Josie showed the boys the two boxes and described the ring. Together they searched the big room.

While Anders and Josie worked as a team, Kate started by peering behind the large heating stove. Erik helped her lift all the wood from the nearby box. Next they searched around the large oak table, and under every chair.

At last they reached the wall next to the kitchen. Shelves stretched between the door and the chimney. The top shelf was above Kate's head and the lowest close to the floor.

Erik stood on a chair and searched behind the few books on the highest shelf. Kate carefully picked up the wooden bowls and tin cups on lower shelves.

When they'd covered every inch of the room, Kate asked, "What about the kitchen?"

"Mama and I looked through everything this morning," Josie said. "And I mean *everything*!"

As Anders dropped down on the floor, he bit his lip as though feeling pain. Kate knew he was growing tired.

"Is there any other place we can look?" Erik asked.

"What about outside?" Kate wanted to know.

"That's hopeless," Josie told her. "What could we find in the hayloft? Or the granary and chicken coop? All of them have a million places to hide something."

"Wait a minute," said Anders. "We've got to use our heads. Who would want the ring most? And where would he hide it?"

A shadow crossed Josie's eyes. "I don't like what you're saying, Anders."

"Well, what about Stretch? What if he has it? What if some night he took off with it?"

"It'd be gone forever." Josie sounded miserable.

But Anders kept on. "Where does Stretch sleep?"

"Upstairs," she told him. "With all the other boys in one big room."

"Where's Stretch now?"

"Out in the blacksmith shop, working with Papa."

Anders grabbed his crutches and lifted himself up. "How about if I look through Stretch's things?"

8

City Girl Farmer

*A*nders started for the door.

"No, Anders. You can't." Josie's hazel eyes were still shadowed, as though filled with pain. But her voice sounded firm. "You aren't going up there."

"Why not?"

"Papa says we're supposed to trust Stretch."

Anders faced her. "Well, it won't hurt to just have one look."

"Yes, it will," said Erik. "It's saying we don't believe he started over."

Just then Josie's mother came in from collecting eggs. "Do you know where Becca is?"

Kate jumped up. "I'll go look. Is she outside?"

"Try the blacksmith shop first. Stretch is good to her. She follows him around to watch what he's doing."

Pulling on her coat, Kate hurried out. She wasn't sure where the shop was, but it wasn't hard to guess. Set closest to the road, the building was off by itself with the door open in spite of the cold.

Becca stood just inside, watching her father and Stretch. Seeing the older girl, she reached up and tucked her hand inside Kate's.

Within a large stone forge a fire burned brightly. Stretch stood nearby, opening and closing the big bellows. With each whoosh of air the fire burned hotter. Even here by the door Kate could feel its heat.

As Kate watched, Mr. Swenson told the blond boy what to do. Stretch took a large tongs and lifted a cherry red piece of iron from the fire. Putting it on the anvil, he picked up a heavy sledge. The shop rang with his measured pounding. Gradually the hot iron took the shape Stretch wanted.

Mr. Swenson nodded his approval. "Good. Good. You've almost got it. Just a little more now."

Just then Stretch glanced up. Seeing Kate, he looked embarrassed, but kept working.

Mr. Swenson glanced toward the door. "Got a good blacksmith here," he told Kate. "He's already got a strong arm."

Stretch kept pounding. When he looked Kate's way again, a glimmer of pride had replaced his embarrassment.

What's it like? Kate wondered. *How does it feel having to make good when you've got a bad reputation?*

A moment later Stretch dropped the hot piece of iron into a bucket. As the cold water sizzled up, Kate took a guess. *It's probably like being new at school. Only worse.* It wasn't hard remembering how it felt to be a stranger, left out and alone.

In that instant Kate made up her mind. She flipped her long black braid over her shoulder. Afraid she'd lose her nerve, she spoke quickly. "Stretch, would you like to come to a birthday party for Anders?"

Stretch looked up, surprise written across his face.

As he glanced toward Josie's father, Kate asked, "Would it be all right, Mr. Swenson? Can Stretch take some time off?"

For a moment Mr. Swenson looked at him, then back at Kate. "Yah, it'd be all right. It might be good for Stretch to have a few hours off." Mr. Swenson winked at the tall boy. "He'll work even harder when he gets back."

Stretch grinned.

"Thursday. Ten o'clock. And it's a secret," Kate told him. "Be sure you come early so you can hide while Anders is gone."

As Stretch returned to his work, Kate left the blacksmith

shop. Starting back to the farmhouse, she thought about her invitation to Stretch. Already she felt scared. Now, when it was too late, Kate felt sure she'd done the wrong thing. Though she wanted to help Stretch, Kate knew Anders would not be pleased.

A half hour later, she and Anders and Erik left Swensons'. On the way home, Kate kept thinking about the party. *What if the others don't accept Stretch? He'll feel even worse.*

When Kate and Anders reached Windy Hill Farm, Mama was coming down with a cold. She looked tired and moved more slowly than usual. Her waist was straight up and down except for the bulge out front.

Three months now, maybe four until the baby comes, thought Kate. *What will it be—a brother or a sister?* With all her heart Kate wanted another sister. But she knew Anders wanted a boy.

That afternoon the supply of wood was low. The box near the cookstove, as well as the one next to the larger heating stove, was nearly empty. Usually Anders and Lars worked together to split wood and bring it in. Today Lars started carrying wood by himself.

Anders sat at the kitchen table, his bad leg stretched across a chair. He glanced up from reading the *Journal of Burnett County*. "Farmers are going to have a meeting on January twenty-second," he said. "They want to get telly-fones out in the country. To every farmer."

"Tell-*eh*-phones," said Kate, correcting Anders. She'd seen telephones in Minneapolis, though she'd never used one. *What would it be like being able to call Josie?*

On his second trip to bring in wood, Lars sneezed. He blew his nose and went back out. Returning with a third load, he dropped it quickly into the wood box. As he covered his nose with his hands, he sneezed again.

Mama looked up from where she kneaded bread. "Are you getting another cold?"

Lars nodded and sneezed at the same time. His blue eyes watered.

Mama sighed. "You can't keep going in and out. Your colds turn into coughs too easily. Kate, will you bring in the wood?"

"There's no more to carry," said Lars. "It needs to be split."

Dragging himself to his feet, Anders reached for his crutches and swung over to the door. Dropping down on a bench, he pulled on Papa's old work boots.

The first boot fit easily on Anders' large foot. As he tried to slip the second boot over his bad ankle, he winced. The ankle was still too swollen.

Anders set down the boot and pulled on the large wool sock he'd been wearing over his other stocking. Picking up his crutches, he hobbled outside.

Soon he returned, looking discouraged and upset. "I can't do it!" he exclaimed.

"Don't be too hard on yourself," said Mama. "I don't know of anyone who splits wood standing on one foot."

"But if I don't split it, who will?" asked Anders. "I hate it when I can't do things—especially things I do well!"

"I'll help," said Kate, even though she wondered if she could. She followed Anders out to the woodpile. Logs of various sizes, sawn into shorter pieces, waited to be split.

Most of those pieces were too heavy for Kate to lift. Choosing the smaller ones, she rolled them over to Anders, and tipped them with the sawn side up. As she stood back, Anders swung the axe, splitting the wood as many times as needed.

Often he needed to sit down on a log and regain his strength. "I can't believe how long this is taking!" he exclaimed once when he staggered on his good foot. That time he leaned against a shed.

"Believe it! Believe it!" teased Kate.

Yet she saw her brother in a new way. *It seems to matter a lot to Anders that he can do whatever he sets out to do.* Tall, with strong muscular arms, he usually had no problem with anything he tried.

As soon as Anders split a pile of wood, Kate carried armloads into the house. Slivers of wood stuck to her mittens. Bits of dirt and sawdust soon covered the front and arms of her coat.

Before long, Kate's shoulders ached. She felt silly with weariness. Coming back outside, she watched Anders. "What's that bird that stands on one foot? A crane?"

Anders grinned, as though guessing how ridiculous he

looked. After that the work seemed to go easier.

The rest of the day dragged by as Kate helped Mama with first one thing, then another. With relief Kate watched the sun slip over the horizon. The short winter afternoon had seemed years long.

When Tina set the supper table, Kate dropped into a chair. As she buttered her potatoes, she saw Mama look hard at Anders.

Kate's gaze followed Mama's. Around the edge of his face Anders seemed pale—almost as pale as on the day he sprained his ankle in the woods. Through her tiredness, Kate felt uneasy.

Mama waited until they finished eating. "Anders, I think I better take a look at your ankle."

"I'm doing fine," he answered quickly.

"You're just pale for no reason?" she asked.

"Really, Mama, I'm fine."

Kate snickered. She knew a Swede could be almost dead and yet say, "I'm fine."

"Yah, maybe so," Mama told Anders. "But maybe not. So let me see."

Anders pushed back his chair and reached down. Slowly he worked off his wool sock. More than once he flinched.

Kate took one look at his ankle and bit her lip to keep from crying out. The ankle was blue and black and purple. Deep marks showed where the sock had pressed into the badly swollen flesh.

Kate could barely stand to look at it. She felt sorry she had snickered.

As Mama checked the ankle, gently feeling it, Anders clenched his teeth. Even Mama's careful touch seemed painful.

Her voice sounded sharp with concern. "Anders, you stood too long today. You have to get your leg up. Keep it raised so the swelling goes down."

Anders grinned weakly, as though trying to hide how he really felt. "Sure, Mama. Soon as I milk the cows." Slowly, carefully, he eased on the sock he usually wore, then reached for the heavier, outside sock.

Mama wasn't going to be put off so easily. "Anders, I want

you to teach Kate how to milk the cows."

"Oh, Mama!" Kate cried out. "I'm a girl. You don't *really* expect me to—"

"Yah, I expect you to milk them." Mama spoke in her no-nonsense voice.

"That's not girls' work," said Kate. "It's for boys!"

"Kate!" Mama's voice was the sharpest Kate had heard in some time. "If you'd grown up in Sweden, you'd know better. In Sweden milking is women's work."

"But, Mama, this is America!"

"It's America, all right! And we all work together! Lars can't do it, and Anders needs help."

Kate sighed loud enough for Mama to hear. Just the same, Kate knew she had no choice. She put on the overalls she wore for beekeeping, then her coat. Anders swung himself through the snow on the beaten-down path to the barn. Longing to escape the work ahead, Kate followed.

Once there, Anders hobbled over to pick up a three-legged stool. "Miss O'Connell, this is your equipment." His voice sounded dead serious. "You must always take good care of this stool."

"Oh, stop it!" Kate snapped.

Anders smirked. "Now I know that you don't take your work seriously, but it's very important that you do."

Kate glared at him, but Anders seemed not to notice.

"Upon you we rely. Without milk we will not have our daily bread."

"Our bread?" Kate laughed.

"Yup," Anders told her, his voice solemn. "Our food. Without you, we will not have milk for our oatmeal."

"That wonderful oatmeal I like so much!" Kate answered.

Anders paid no attention. "Without you we will not have milk for our cheese. We will not have butter for our lutfisk."

"*Lute fisk?*" Kate drawled out the word, wrinkling her nose. She hated the smell of the dried cod that Swedes soaked in lye and ate at Christmas.

Just then Anders' dog brought the last cow into the barn. In winter the animals stayed closer to the barn, but Lutfisk still felt it necessary to nip at their heels.

Seeing the dog, Kate said, "You sure gave him a funny name. Just because he got into the lutfisk!"

Anders whistled, and Lutfisk immediately came to him. Dropping his crutches, Anders knelt down.

The dog had brown and black hair with white and tan markings on his face. Resting one of his paws on Anders' sleeve, Lutfisk gazed up, waiting. Anders scratched behind the dog's ears.

When Lutfisk dropped back to the dirt floor, Anders again took up his role as teacher. Using his crutches, he swung himself over to the cow farthest to the left. She stood next to the high board wall that separated the stall from a walkway.

Patting her wide back, Anders chained the cow to a board in front of her. "This is Clover," he said. "Clover, meet Kate."

The Holstein turned her head as though understanding. In that moment Kate realized how big the animal was. The black blotches on her white side seemed to stretch out forever. Kate was short for her age, but felt even smaller next to Clover.

"First you set the stool on the cow's right side," Anders went on in his solemn voice.

Thinks he can trick me, Kate told herself, remembering how she needed to approach a horse on its left. *Well, I'll fool him!*

Picking up the stool, she set it down on Clover's left. But as Kate walked into the stall, the cow stomped her hind leg.

Kate jumped back, away from the hoof. Once again, she looked up at the big cow. Its black and white side towered above her. Yet, not for anything would Kate let Anders see her fear. *He'll call me scaredy-cat.*

Moving forward, she started to sit down.

In the next instant the cow stepped sideways, pinning Kate against the high wall.

9

Wildfire!

*K*ate beat her hands against the cow's side, then shoved with all her strength. After a very long moment, Clover stepped away. Quickly Kate retreated, far back of the cow's rear hooves.

Anders snorted. "You didn't believe me, did you? And I was trying to help you! Go to the left of horses, to the right of cows."

Her heart in her throat, Kate reached forward and picked up the stool. Carefully she settled herself on Clover's right side.

"Now I'll show you what to do," said Anders, again solemn. Reaching across Kate, he began milking the cow. "Like so."

In that instant the whole thing struck Kate funny. She giggled. "If Sarah Livingston could see me now!"

"Who's Sarah?"

"My best friend in Minneapolis. Before I came here, she told me what it'd be like living in the wilderness. She warned me about the bears and wolves. She said there'd be log houses with the wind blowing through."

"Anyone who makes a good log house knows enough to fill the cracks," Anders said stiffly. "Besides, people are starting to put siding on them. Now pay attention."

But Kate giggled again.

"Look," Anders sounded like a teacher. "First you close one hand, then another. At the same time, you let up or tug down."

Kate's shoulders shook with laughter.

Anders stepped back. "If you think it's so funny, try for yourself!"

"Oh, anyone can milk a cow!" replied Kate.

Picking up the pail, she put it between her knees as she'd seen Anders do. As she reached forward, the pail dropped, rolling onto the dirt floor.

Anders shook his head. "Dirty pail, dirty milk." He took down a second pail from where it hung on a nail in the log beam. "Now keep this one clean."

Carefully Kate put the pail between her knees and turned back to the cow. Just then Clover flicked her tail, swatting Kate in the face. She jumped, and the second pail rolled to the ground.

"Awww, Kate." Anders sounded disgusted. "Even a city girl can do better than that."

Again he took down a pail. "Last one we've got. Now keep it clean."

Kate nodded solemnly, starting to realize milking might not be so easy, after all. Reaching out, she tried to milk the cow. Nothing came.

"Do it again," insisted Anders.

Once more Kate tried. Once more nothing came.

"I said this isn't girls' work!" Kate exclaimed. She was starting to feel sorry for the cow.

Anders groaned. "Stand up!" he said. He dropped onto the stool with his bad leg sprawled out along the side of the cow. "Now keep your eyes open. By this time I could have finished milking every cow."

Kate's temper flared. "By this time *I* could have done the dishes and practiced my organ lessons!"

Once again Anders asked her to sit down. It took several attempts before milk trickled into Kate's pail. Yet gradually she caught on. She even felt excited at what she accomplished. Then she realized milk had flowed down inside her coat sleeves. Her arms were wet.

Going to the pump, Anders washed out the other pails and

sat down near the next cow. Immediately warm milk splashed into Anders' pail.

Lutfisk raised his head.

Moving his hands slightly, Anders aimed a stream of milk toward the dog's mouth.

Lutfisk stretched out his long tongue and licked the milk away. Walking over to a corner, he picked up a sardine can in his teeth. Returning to Anders, the dog set the can on the dirt floor and waited for Anders to fill it.

Before long, Anders had milked four cows to Kate's one. When they finished the milking, Anders looked paler still, even in the light of the lantern.

"Get the oats for Wildfire, will you, Kate?"

"Oats? From where?"

Anders tipped his head toward a walkway. "In that bin. See how it's locked? Make sure you close it the same way. If you don't, Wildfire will lift the cover with her nose."

Kate dipped out the oats and carefully locked the bin. As she held the bucket, Wildfire snuffled her nose into the grain.

"Awful nice horse, huh?" asked Anders.

Kate nodded, hearing the pride in his voice.

"Black shiny coat. White socks and star. Yup. A real pretty mare."

"Teach me to ride her, will you, Anders?" Kate had learned to hitch Wildfire to the cutter, the small sleigh used for only a few people. Twice she'd ridden bareback with Anders, but she'd never taken the mare by herself.

"Nope," said Anders.

"Why not? You taught me how to hitch her up."

"You can't ride her."

"Aw, Anders, come on. If you let me, I'll take some of your turns watching Tina."

But Anders refused. He led Kate out to the large tank for watering animals. Set inside was a stove that heated the water during winter.

The tank heater looked like a U with the sides pushed slightly down. At one end of the U a stovepipe stretched above the water. At the other end was an opening to load wood.

Dropping his crutches, Anders lifted the stove lid and pushed in kindling and small chunks of wood. Then he dropped a lighted splinter down the chute. As Kate watched, the fire caught the wood at the bottom.

"In this weather we have to keep the heater going all night," said Anders.

"Or the water will freeze?" Kate asked.

"Big chunk of ice in the morning."

When the fire burned well, Anders told Kate to load more wood from a nearby pile. Then he returned to the barn for one more look at Wildfire.

Kate followed. "Why can't I ride her?" she asked again. "Give me one good reason."

"You betcha," said Anders. "You don't know how to take care of her."

"You could teach me."

"You have to take mighty good care of a horse. If you don't slow her down after a run, she'll founder."

"Founder?" asked Kate.

"Get sick. You have to rub her down if she gets sweaty. And you have to watch how she eats. If Wildfire ate too many oats, it would affect her circulation. She'd get stiff in her legs."

"Crippled?" asked Kate.

Anders nodded. "Crippled for life. Or she could die." Anders rubbed Wildfire's nose. "Yup. Got to take awful good care of you."

Suddenly Kate felt chilled. She looked around, but the door of the barn was closed against the wind. Even so, as Kate watched Anders with his horse, she felt uneasy. He'd worked hard to get the mare. Wildfire meant a lot to him.

Thinking about it, Kate knew the mare meant a good deal to her too. She tried to push aside the awful thought that came to her mind. *What if something happened to Wildfire?*

10

Race Against Time

I'll take really good care of Wildfire, Kate promised herself. *I'll make sure nothing happens to her.*

Yet Kate's uneasiness wouldn't go away. During the evening she thought more than once about her brother's mare. *What would we do without her?*

How Anders would feel was bad enough. But the only other horses nearby belonged to Lundgrens. In winter their farm was a long cold walk through the woods.

At the same time, Kate longed to ride Wildfire. The next day Kate asked Anders again. Once more he said no.

As the icy winter days passed by, Mama kept a close eye on Lars and his cold. Anders favored his ankle and often propped it up. The bluish purple color faded into yellow and light green. Gradually the swelling went down.

On the January afternoon before Anders' party, Kate walked the long wagon track to the mailbox. When she reached the main road, she found a letter from Papa. Feeling she'd discovered a treasure, she walked fast or ran all the way home.

When Mama saw the letter, she settled herself into her favorite chair. Her eyes shone with happiness. As all of them gathered around, Mama's skillful hands fumbled, awkward in her eagerness to open the letter.

Papa had written in Swedish, and Mama began reading aloud. Tina leaned forward on Mama's knee. Anders and Lars moved closer. But Kate edged back.

I'm trying to learn Swedish, thought Kate. *But everyone else spoke it 'til they started school. Doesn't Mama remember how little I know?*

Kate felt separated from the others. Restlessly she pulled even farther away.

Mama noticed her. "I'm sorry, Kate. I forgot." Returning to the first page, Mama translated Papa's words into English. "Papa says he had a safe trip back. No problems with the weather. Wages are good this year."

As Mama read, her gaze moved quickly across the page. Her words sounded sure and strong. Then she reached the place where she'd gone back to translate.

"Papa talks about his camp. It's up in the heavy timber. Some of the white pine are four feet across. Now and then, even five feet."

As though she were thinking, Mama slowed down. Her gaze darted ahead. When she started translating again, Mama stumbled over the words.

At first Kate thought Mama was in too much of a hurry, wanting every bit of news about Papa. But her mother's gaze seemed to move faster than she spoke. Kate felt uneasy.

What's Mama doing? Kate wondered as she twisted the end of her long braid. *Is she skipping parts of the letter?* There were too many words for the amount Mama translated.

Just then Anders stood up. Looking over Mama's shoulder, he read the letter to himself. Anders could read Swedish as well as English. He'd know what Papa said.

And Kate would do her best to find out.

As she climbed the stairs that evening, Kate thought about Papa's strange letter. Why didn't Mama read all of it aloud?

Though tired from everything that had happened that day, Kate couldn't go to sleep. Turning this way and that, she puffed her pillow and slid deep beneath the warm quilts.

It was no use. Kate's thoughts went round and round. Josie's vanishing kitten, the valuable lost ring, the missing buckle.

Then Kate remembered Papa's letter. The more she thought about it, the more awake she became. What bothered her most was how Mama seemed to skip certain parts.

Anders knows. Whatever is wrong, he knows what it is, Kate thought. Beneath the shock of blond hair, his blue eyes had looked worried. Just like Mama's.

Finally Kate gave up trying to sleep. Her thoughts turned to a piece of Mama's good brown bread. Kate knew how tasty it would be, covered with freshly churned butter.

Pulling on her robe, she tiptoed down the steps, through the front room, and into the dining room. Mama's bedroom was off the dining room. Kate crept even more softly, trying not to wake her mother.

As Kate reached the door to the kitchen, the clock chimed ten times. To her surprise Kate saw Mama sitting at the table. For a moment Kate stood near the doorway, watching her.

Wisps of golden blond hair hung down over Mama's forehead, making her look soft and unprotected. Yet there was something more in her face, something Kate wondered about. *Is Mama afraid?*

Her slim hands held a letter that looked like the one from Papa. Mama's lips moved, as though memorizing every word.

As Kate watched, a tear slid down Mama's cheek onto the page. Carefully Mama blotted it dry.

Then Kate heard someone at the outside door. Quickly Mama pushed her hair into place and wiped the tears from her cheeks.

Kate stepped back, out of sight. Yet she knew by the sound it was Anders, leaning his crutches against the wall. Kate edged farther into the dining room. *Why is he still up?*

"Everything all right?" Mama asked Anders, but her voice quavered.

"Yup! Sheep are snug as a bug in a rug."

Kate wondered if he was trying to sound cheerful for Mama's sake. She heard Anders move over to the cookstove.

"Needs more wood," said Mama, her words ragged as though trying to stay calm.

A stove lid clanked, and Kate knew Anders had lifted it to push in chunks of birch.

"Coffee?" he asked, and Kate didn't need to see. Mama would lift her cup while Anders poured steaming coffee into it.

A chair scraped. Anders must have sat down across from Mama. After a long silence he spoke. "I saw the rest of the letter."

"I thought you did," answered Mama. She lowered her voice, and Kate strained to hear. But she couldn't catch Mama's words.

"Papa will be safe," Anders told her, and Kate wondered if he talked to himself as much as to Mama.

"But he said—" Mama changed into Swedish.

English, Mama, Kate wanted to shout. *English!*

When Anders spoke again, he also used Swedish.

Mama sniffled and blew her nose. The sound frightened Kate even more than the words she didn't understand. Mama never cried except for something really serious.

What are they talking about?

Then edging through Kate's fear came another feeling. Mama and Anders seemed like two friends as they sat there together. For the second time that day Kate felt left out.

One part of her mind wanted to walk in and say, "Tell me too." The other part remembered how much Mama hated eavesdropping. She didn't want Kate listening in when other people talked.

Careful not to make a noise, Kate stayed out of sight. For a long time she listened, but Mama and Anders never returned to speaking English. Only once did Kate recognize a word, and that word was *wolf*. Even the sound of it frightened her.

Soon after, Kate heard one chair, then another, scrape across the kitchen floor. As footsteps neared the doorway where she stood, Kate raced for the stairs. At the top she tumbled into her bedroom, closing the door just as Anders started up.

Panting and out of breath, Kate leaned back against the door. She thought hard. *Whatever is wrong, Mama doesn't want me and Lars and Tina to know. Why? Why did she tell Anders and not me?*

To find out Kate would have to get Mama alone.

The next morning Kate entered the kitchen planning to ask Mama about the letter. But Tina and Lars were already there, helping Mama get ready for the surprise party.

Kate knew Anders wouldn't expect a party. Children seldom had them, and if they did, their friends didn't bring presents. But Mama wanted to celebrate Anders' thirteenth birthday. Kate hoped it would be a great surprise.

They waited with eating until he came down for breakfast.

"Happy Birthday, Anders!" cried Tina, her blue eyes sparkling.

Lars grinned at his brother, and Kate started the singing.

Mama's good wishes were also warm. At the same time, she seemed unprepared for the big day. "Oh, Anders, I need some sugar," she said. "Will you ride to Olsons' for me?"

Behind Anders' back, Kate grinned at Lars. Mama hadn't lied. She needed sugar, all right, but only because the cake was already made and hidden away.

Kate and Mama had worked out a plan to get Anders away from the farm while his friends slipped into the house. No one would walk on the road coming from Olsons'.

So far everything was going perfectly, and Kate knew she should be happy. Yet she couldn't get Josie's family out of her mind. When her friend came today, what would she say about the missing ring?

Slowly Kate stood up, dreading the idea of milking the cows alone. Yesterday morning Lars had been well enough to muck out the barn. Today he was worse again.

Kate trudged outside. *I need to hurry*, she thought. *I want to be ready before anyone comes.*

But nothing went right. When Kate tried to milk Clover, the big cow moved restlessly. Then Kate realized she hadn't fed her.

Setting down the half-filled pail of milk, Kate climbed the ladder to the loft. She gathered armloads of hay and threw it down into the walkway around the large open stall.

Returning to the main floor, she spread the hay in front of the cows.

Clover edged forward. As she chomped her large teeth, her brown eyes rolled at Kate. Kate edged back out of the way.

Clover tossed her head.

"Laughing at me, are you?" asked Kate.

Then Kate found three cats standing on their hind legs, drinking milk out of the pail she'd forgotten. "Scat!" Kate cried, and they did. But they also tipped over the pail. The milk poured out, mixing with the dirt floor to become mud.

With a long *moooooo* Clover turned her head toward Kate. "You *are* laughing at me!" she exclaimed.

Everyone will come by 9:30, she thought. *Josie and Erik might be walking here now.* Quickly Kate dipped out oats for Wildfire, then threw hay into the sheep pen. Usually she talked to the sheep. Today she hurried on, eager to be done.

Once more Kate went back to milking. Each time she filled a pail she poured it into a larger, covered pail. It was going better now, and Kate felt sure she could finish in time. She even felt proud of all she'd learned about taking care of the animals.

If Sarah Livingston could see me now! Kate thought, as she had many times before.

She was milking the last cow when Lutfisk picked up the sardine can between his teeth. Setting it down next to Kate, he woofed.

Moving her hands as Anders did, Kate tried to direct milk into the can. Missing, she tried again. Each time the milk shot outside the can onto the floor. Finally Kate stopped, tipped her pail, and poured milk into the sardine can.

Just then the cow stomped her back leg. Jerking sideways, she hit the bucket. The rest of the milk splashed out on the floor.

Kate jumped to her feet. Losing her balance, she sat down hard.

One moment she felt herself on the dirt floor. The next instant she scrambled up. Yet it was too late. Her boots, coat, overalls, and hands were covered with mud.

Just then Kate heard the barn door open. "Kate?"

Uh-oh! Erik! Frantically Kate looked down. From head to toe she was wet and dirty.

Grabbing a handful of hay, she tried to wipe off the mud. Instead, the hay stuck to her wool coat, adding to the mess.

"Kate?" Erik called again.

Kate ran toward Clover. Brushing past the cow, she slipped into the dark space next to the high board wall. In the dim light Kate hoped the shadows would hide her.

11

Kate's Choice

A moment later Erik found Kate. "How you coming with the milking?"

"Just finishing up." She breathed deeply, trying to catch her breath.

"Your mother says you've been here an awful long time."

"Not so long," Kate told him, trying to keep her voice steady. She didn't want Erik to know how hard it was for her to milk all the cows.

City girl, Anders calls me. Kate hated to admit he was right. At the same time she felt proud she'd learned as much as she had.

"What's the matter?" asked Erik.

Kate swallowed. Not for anything would she tell him about the milk she'd spilled or how she'd fallen on the dirt floor. Nor did she want Erik to see how awful she looked. Kate tried to edge farther into the shadows.

"I'm almost done," she said, wishing he'd leave. More than anything in the world, she wanted to get cleaned up.

"I'll help you finish," Erik offered, moving closer. "Everyone will be here soon."

"No!" Kate burst out. "I'll do it myself!"

Erik stepped back. "Well, you don't have to get mad about it!"

"I'm not! I mean, thank you—I mean, I'll finish up as soon as you leave."

Erik looked hurt. "I just wanted to help."

"You did. I mean, you have. You are."

"I'll take the milk in."

"No!" Kate burst out again. He'd guess how much she'd spilled.

Erik stared at her strangely. This time he moved beyond Clover to the space where Kate hid. For the first time he had a good look at her.

As the corners of his lips turned up, Kate glanced down at her filthy clothes. The shadows weren't enough. They didn't hide the mud that covered her from head to toe.

Erik slapped his hand against the stall and bent over laughing. The sound seemed to echo through the barn.

A hot flush crept up into Kate's neck, then warmed her cheeks. Slowly she walked out of the stall.

In the light from the open door, Erik studied her face. The laughter died on his lips.

"Kate," he said, sounding as if he were trying to be serious, "you've got only a few minutes." But his voice cracked.

Erik took a deep breath, as though trying to straighten his face. "Everyone will be here. Don't you think you ought to get washed up?" In spite of himself, he grinned, then choked.

Kate fled to the house, wondering if she'd ever forget the sound of his laughter.

Reaching the back door, she crept into the kitchen. As she pulled off the boots she wore in the barn, clumps of dirt fell on Mama's clean floor. Kate pushed the boots under a bench. Hanging her mud-spattered coat on a peg, she wanted only one thing: to wash up and change before anyone else saw her.

A basin filled with clean water waited for her. Leaning forward, Kate splashed water onto her face, then gasped. The water was icy cold. Mama must have set it out some time before.

Kate shivered, knowing she had no choice but to use it. She

plunged her hands and arms into the basin. Grabbing the bar of soap, she rubbed at the dirt.

Each time the water touched her skin, Kate flinched. The cold water seemed to smear the dirt around. Finally Kate gave up and wiped off whatever she could on a towel.

Just then she heard a knock on the door. "Mama!" Kate yelped, running through the kitchen. In the doorway to the dining room, she met her mother. "Someone's here!"

As she fled through the front room, a girl giggled from behind a chair. Kate bounded up the stairs.

In her bedroom she pulled off her wet overalls and the dress underneath. Wrapping them in a ball, Kate hid them under her bed. Here, where the sunlight streamed through the windows, she got another look at herself. It was hopeless.

As Kate glanced through a front window, Erik's sister Chrissy came out of the woods. Before long she'd cross the field between the two farms.

Through a window on the side of the house, Kate spied Josie, Stretch, and Maybelle coming up the track from Spirit Lake School. Kate gasped. *What'll I do?*

Then, from the floor grate letting heat into her bedroom, Kate heard low, excited voices. Peering through the grate into the front room, Kate saw more children. They huddled on the floor, trying to be quiet.

Everyone's here! I'll miss the surprise!

Quickly Kate pulled her best dress over her head. Remembering her hair, she dashed to the mirror. Long strands escaped her black braid and hung around her face. Sweeping them back with a brush, Kate picked wisps of hay from the braid.

A muffled giggle drifted up through the grate as someone mentioned Anders' name.

Throwing down the brush, Kate took one more look in the mirror. This time she saw a dark smudge on her forehead. Kate wiped hard, trying to rub the mud away. Frantically she turned toward a window. Anders was coming from the barn!

Heading for the door, Kate tumbled down the stairs. In the front room, she squeezed in beside Josie and tried to melt into the shadows.

Someone laughed.

"Shhhhh! He's here!" Kate warned.

Instantly the giggles stopped.

Then Kate heard Anders talk to Mama in the kitchen. A moment later two crutches thudded across the wood floor of the dining room, coming closer.

As Anders passed into the front room, Erik jumped up. Kate and the others followed. "Surprise! Surprise!"

Anders stepped back, shock written across his face. "Surprise, all right! For sure!"

Turning, he grinned at Mama. "So you needed sugar! You just wanted me out of the house!"

"Happy birthday!" Josie cried, her hazel eyes dancing with fun.

Kate laughed with the others. It was fun seeing Anders so completely fooled. Their plan had worked!

But a moment later Kate's laughter died on her lips. From one of the corners came Maybelle. A sure-of-herself smile curled her lips. Her soft blue dress looked clean and neat and made her brown eyes shine.

Her long beautiful hair no longer hung in braids. It swung about her shoulders. Maybelle had *curls*!

Quickly Kate rubbed her forehead, hoping she'd gotten all the dirt off. At the same time she noticed the strands of hair again hanging around her face.

Maybelle laughed—the soft, tinkly laugh that sounded like a spoon against a glass. She looked up at Erik and smiled. "It was a good surprise, wasn't it, Erik?"

Kate wished she could disappear like Josie's kitten. But then Kate saw Stretch.

As the tall boy with curly blond hair stepped out from a corner, Anders saw him too. For a moment they faced each other and the air seemed to fill with sparks.

"Happy birthday!" Stretch said.

"Thanks," Anders replied. "Thanks for coming." But his voice sounded halfhearted. He turned away—too quickly.

Stretch flushed red. He didn't have to be told. Anders still didn't trust him.

I made things worse, thought Kate, forgetting the way she looked. *I made things worse for Stretch.* It bothered her.

But then Erik moved over and started talking to the tall thin boy. Soon Stretch grinned. His embarrassed flush disappeared.

A moment later Kate saw Josie's face—*really* saw it. Something was very wrong. Josie's hazel eyes no longer danced with fun.

"Did you get more bad news?" Kate asked.

Her friend nodded. "Papa talked to that old loan shark again. Mr. Harris says he won't give us any more time. He says the money has to be paid by January twenty-fifth—or else. That's only two weeks away."

"Do you have any other clues about the ring?" asked Kate. "Anything at all, even if it doesn't seem important?"

Josie thought for a moment. "Just one thing," she said slowly. "Remember the two boxes? One fit inside the other for mailing. Whoever took the ring didn't bother with the boxes."

"Were the lids back on?" asked Kate. "Or the smaller box inside the bigger one?"

Josie shook her head. "Maybe it's not important."

"Well, let's keep thinking about it," said Kate.

Just then Maybelle noticed Kate's reed organ along the wall of the front room. "Is it yours?" Maybelle asked brightly. "I can play for all of you."

"You can?" Kate blurted out.

"Of course," answered Maybelle, sounding as if everyone would be greatly honored. "I play very well."

"Just like she does everything else," said Josie softly, looking at Kate.

But Kate stood frozen to the spot, unable to speak. She knew only that she didn't want Maybelle to touch the keys. Though she couldn't put it into words, Kate knew something very special would be spoiled.

As Maybelle started toward the organ, Kate felt helpless, unable to think what to do.

But Anders hopped over on one foot, standing between Maybelle and the keyboard. "Time for games." He turned to Kate.

"You've got games planned for this party, don't you?"

Quickly Kate put two rows of wooden chairs in the center of the front room. Setting the chairs back to back, she counted to be sure she had one less chair than the number of young people.

"All right, line up for musical chairs," she told them.

They rushed forward and formed a line. Kate sat down at the pump organ and started to play.

Around and around the others walked, circling the chairs. Abruptly Kate stopped playing. Shouting with laughter, everyone scrambled for a seat.

Josie wasn't quick enough and lost out. As she stood aside, a boy pulled a chair out of the circle. Again Kate started playing. Each time she stopped, one more person was short a chair. Finally there was only one chair left for two people. Erik's sister Chrissy won.

As a cheer went up, Kate sensed that someone stood behind her. Before Kate could turn around, Maybelle spoke.

"Kate," she said in the sweet voice that carried throughout the room. "I know you'd like me to help you."

As Kate looked up, everyone seemed to turn her way.

"You missed some of the buttons on the back of your dress," said Maybelle. Reaching out, she started buttoning them.

Kate felt a flush of embarrassment start in her neck and move into her face. She turned her head, trying to see.

Maybelle tossed her curls, as though on the center of a stage. She seemed to enjoy having everyone watch. "I can't imagine how you managed to get hay in your hair." She sighed, a soft little sound, as gentle as a spring breeze.

Finishing the buttons, Maybelle picked a piece of hay from Kate's long black braid. Suddenly Maybelle yanked the braid hard.

Hot tears sprang into Kate's eyes. But when she tried to stand up, Maybelle held the braid firm. "I really want to help you, Kate," she said.

This time Kate did stand up. Jerking her braid out of Maybelle's hands, Kate faced the other girl. She wanted to slap Maybelle's face. She wanted to call her the most terrible name she could think of. A name that described how sly Maybelle was, how underhanded, and how honey smooth.

Then Kate had the name, the most awful one possible. But in that moment she saw Stretch watching.

As he waited, there was something Kate realized. *This is important,* she thought. Without understanding why, she knew. *This is important to Stretch.*

Deep inside, Kate felt afraid.

12

Out of the Darkness

*K*ate tried to push aside her panic. *How can anything I say be important to Stretch?* she wondered.

But Kate had no answer. Standing there with eyes wide open, she prayed. "Help me, God. Help me know what to do."

In the next instant Kate thought of something. *Maybelle's mean. But so what? I've got to show I'm bigger than that.*

Straightening her shoulders, Kate pulled herself up to the tallest her short height allowed. "Thank you, Maybelle," she said, flipping her long braid over her shoulder. To Kate's surprise her voice sounded normal. "Thank you for helping me."

Maybelle's soft white skin flushed pink. Surprise flashed across her face, then was gone.

Kate was glad when the games finished and she could escape into the kitchen. She longed to be away from Maybelle, away from her sugar sweet voice and her curls. Away also from the tension between Stretch and Anders.

Pretty soon they'll all leave, Kate promised herself as she carried the birthday cake into the dining room. *They'll eat and go home.*

As soon as everyone sang "Happy Birthday," Kate cut the cake. In a little while, the children started putting on their coats.

Before long, only Erik, Anders, Maybelle, and Kate remained.

Maybelle turned to Anders. "I hear you have a horse all your own. May I see it?"

"Yup," said Anders, not hesitating a moment. Never had he stopped anyone from admiring his mare.

Taking his crutches, he pulled himself up. Swinging over to the hooks by the kitchen door, he took down his jacket. Erik and Maybelle followed him outside.

Kate longed to go with them. Then she remembered the muddy boots she wore to the barn. *I wouldn't be caught dead in them*, she thought.

A minute later her curiosity overcame her pride. Trying not to touch the mud, Kate sat down on the bench and pulled on the boots. *I'll stay far enough behind so no one notices.*

But her coat was even worse. Kate cringed just putting it on.

When she reached the barn, she found Maybelle stroking the white star on Wildfire's forehead.

"Pretty good horse, huh?" asked Anders.

"She's wonderful!" Maybelle breathed.

"See how sleek her coat is?" he asked, his voice filled with pride.

"I really like Wildfire," answered Maybelle. "I'd like to ride her."

Kate spoke quickly. "Anders doesn't let anyone ride her."

Maybelle swung around. Her stare swept Kate from head to toe, lingering on her coat and overshoes.

Kate felt like a clod of dirt next to a shining piece of jewelry. Just the same she said, "Wildfire's a pretty lively horse."

"Perhaps Anders would like to speak for himself," Maybelle answered. "I'm sure he gives special friends the opportunity to ride."

Turning her back on Erik and Kate, Maybelle gazed up at Anders. "I used to have my own horse, before we moved away." Her deep brown eyes waited for his answer.

Anders looked uncomfortable. "Ah, um—"

Kate wondered if Anders remembered he hadn't allowed *her* to ride the mare. "He doesn't let *anyone*," she broke in.

"I'm sure I'm not just *anyone*." Maybelle's voice dripped with honey, but Kate thought of bees, ready to sting.

"Kate's right," said Anders. "Wildfire's a pretty lively horse."

"But I'm an expert rider," Maybelle persisted, as sure of herself as always.

Watching her, Kate wondered, *How does she do it?* Once more Kate felt like a clod of dirt, a clod stepped on and trampled underfoot.

At the same time she felt uneasy. Again she wondered, *What if something happened to Wildfire?* Kate couldn't explain her dread, even to herself. *Am I getting jumpy with all that's happened around Windy Hill Farm?*

Anders looked uncomfortable. "Well, uh, maybe."

"You know, Anders," said Maybelle, "people usually give me what I want."

Just then Kate saw Erik's face. His eyes widened as though seeing Maybelle for the first time.

But Anders still stumbled around. "Wildfire has a tender mouth—"

Kate stalked off, unwilling to watch Maybelle ride the mare. Hurrying out of the barn, Kate headed for the house, holding back the tears that pushed against her eyes. *He'll let Maybelle ride Wildfire when he won't let me?*

When she reached the kitchen door, Kate realized she didn't want to talk with anyone. Turning back, she hurried to the end of the barn away from the wagon track. In the pasture closest to the woods the sheep called out to her. *Baaaa!*

Slipping through the fence, Kate trudged to the far side of the field. The sheep huddled there, munching the grass that grew up around tree stumps.

Baaaa! they called again.

Kate waited until one of her favorites came to her. In spite of an all brown coat, he had a white triangle on his forehead. She sank her fingers deep into his thick wool.

For a long time she stayed there, close to the trees that grew along the fence line. When Erik and Maybelle left, Kate waited until Anders swung up the path to the house. Then Kate slipped into the barn. Cold and tired, she wanted a place to sort out her feelings.

Inside the barn she climbed the ladder and swung through the hole into the loft. There she settled deep in the hay. A few minutes later, she heard Anders call from below.

"Ka-a-a-ate! Ka-a-a-ate!"

But Kate would not answer. With a bad ankle Anders wouldn't climb the ladder. She waited, staring through a crack between the logs in the wall facing west. Deep red streaks colored the horizon.

Again Anders called, "Ka-a-a-ate! I know you're up there!"

She remained silent, watching the red sky change to gray.

"Kate!"

A moment later the barn door slammed.

It was growing dark by the time Kate pulled herself up and crawled over to the hole in the floor. Long shadows crept across the loft.

She was partway down the ladder when she heard a sound in the deeper shadows of the barn below. Kate stopped and listened.

A cat, she thought. *Or a cow moving. Or maybe it's the sheep.*

Once more Kate started down. She was close to the bottom when she heard another sound. This time it was near at hand, somewhere within the shadows. Was it someone barely breathing?

Kate's heart leaped into her throat. *Should I go back up the ladder?* She waited, listening.

Something was close by. Something or someone. But there in the corner of the barn away from the sun, it was dark. Kate could not see.

Then she heard yet another sound. A slight movement, near at hand. A movement so quiet she wondered if she imagined it.

Filled with panic, Kate whirled. Still she saw no one, only darkness. Only the munching of the animals reached her ears.

But when Kate tried to run, a hand reached out and grabbed her arm.

13

Papa's Strange Letter

Turning, Kate saw a big dark shape. Drawing back her foot, she kicked with all her strength.

"Owwww!" came a moan from the shadows. "Ow, ow, ow!"

"Anders!" Kate cried. "What are you doing here? I thought you left!"

Anders hobbled from the corner, holding his left ankle. "Wow, Kate. You deliver a mean kick!"

"Well, what do you think?" asked Kate. "If you're going to stand in the dark and scare me—"

"Stand in the dark and wait for you, you mean."

"Wait for me?" Kate scoffed. "What for?"

Anders groaned again. Hopping on his good foot, he reached a pile of hay close to a window and dropped down. "Waiting to talk to you."

"We don't have anything to talk about."

"I think we do." His voice was quieter than Kate had ever heard it. He rubbed his bad leg. "Right where I sprained my ankle. Just when it was getting better, I'll have a big bruise!"

"You deserved it, scaring me like that." Kate knew she should thank Anders for standing between Maybelle and the organ. But not now. Kate was still trembling from her fright.

Instead of answering, Anders pulled himself up, grabbed his crutches, and started for the door.

"Anders, where you going?" Kate started after him.

Her brother turned. "To the house. Until you stop acting dumb!"

Kate stopped right where she stood. In the final rays of the setting sun, she saw his blue eyes. He meant it all right, no doubt about that.

Anders' hands tightened on the crutches. "Kate, there's something you have to get straight." His voice was hard as iron, beyond teasing. "When Papa left, he told me I'm supposed to look out for this family."

Kate stared at Anders.

"Mama's having a hard time right now," he said. "We need to take good care of her."

Kate gasped and drew back. As though it happened one moment before, she remembered Mama and Anders together, talking in the kitchen. Again Kate felt left out. "So now you're going to tell me how to act with my own mother? She's *my* mama, you know, not yours!"

Anders looked as if Kate had slapped him. He drew himself up to all of his almost six feet. Flinging open the barn door, he set his crutches ahead of him. Swinging forward on the path, he moved toward the house slowly, as if in pain.

Kate had time only to wonder how much she'd hurt Anders' ankle. Then the wind pushed the door shut with a bang.

In that moment Kate didn't want to face either Anders or Mama. Instead, she lit the farm lantern, got a pail, and started milking the cows. By the time she finished, she was tired, cold, and hungry.

When Kate entered the kitchen, Mama looked up. Kate sat down on the bench near the door and pulled off her boots.

In that instant Kate recalled Anders' words. *Anders says I'm supposed to be nice to Mama. Who does he think I am? Of course, I'll be nice to Mama! She's MY mother!*

Kate still needed to know what was in Papa's strange letter. She hadn't had one moment alone with Mama. Kate felt separated from her, cut off and alone.

That night Kate went to bed wanting only to hide in the dark. Though sharing a room with Tina, Kate felt all alone.

When she heard Tina's deep, even breathing, Kate knew the five-year-old was asleep. In that instant the tears Kate had pushed down all day welled up. Filling her eyes, they spilled onto the pillow. Her feelings poured out like flood waters washing away everything in their path.

At last Kate could cry no longer. As she lay in the darkness she tried to think about the Jesus she had come to love. Right now He seemed far away. Kate couldn't feel His love.

Instead, she listened to the January wind in the tall pine next to the house. Frosted panes of glass rattled, and cold stretched icy fingers across the room. Sliding deep beneath the quilts, Kate covered her head.

A moment later she heard the sounds she dreaded. At first she pushed fingers into her ears, trying not to hear. But the howls came, even through the quilts.

Finally Kate pushed the quilts aside and listened. From far away, off in the distance, the howls started low, rose and fell, lingering in the night air.

Then, from the nearby woods, came the most frightening sound of all. An answering howl.

Kate trembled. What was it Papa had prayed for her? Hurt and cold, lonely and afraid, Kate tried to think back. At last she recalled the words: "Heavenly Father, when Kate needs to remember, remind her of thy care for her."

Kate's thoughts turned into a prayer. "What does that mean, God? How do you care for people like me?"

A moment later Kate drifted off to sleep.

The next morning Kate got up earlier than usual. She had decided what she could ask about Papa's letter. But Kate knew she had to be careful. Mama didn't like it when Kate listened in on other people's conversations. And Mama wouldn't answer questions just to satisfy Kate's endless curiosity. Often Mama told her, "Curious girls and cackling hens always come to no good end."

Kate found her mother alone in the kitchen. "Mama," Kate started out, "when you read Papa's letter, did you skip some of it?"

For a long moment Mama sat without speaking, seeming to debate with herself.

"What scared you?" Kate asked.

Mama lifted her head, as if remembering that a Swede would say "Nothing," no matter how afraid she felt.

But Kate saw Mama's eyes. "Tell me what's wrong," Kate urged.

Mama seemed to make up her mind. "Anders and I talked about it," she answered in a low voice.

Again that strange left-out feeling twisted Kate's insides. Long after going to bed, she'd thought about Mama and Anders together, not telling *her* those parts of the letter. "You talked with him, and you didn't tell me?" Kate sounded as hurt as she felt.

"He's always lived on a farm. I thought he could handle it. And he can. At least it seems he can."

"Then so can I," answered Kate. Her voice sounded strong, but her stomach tightened with wondering.

Mama drew a deep breath. "There are so many things, Kate. Papa's far away, and I can't talk to him. I'm afraid he'll get hurt. That he'll cut himself with an axe or a saw. Or a tree might fall on him."

Kate remembered her question to Papa. "When I asked, 'Is it dangerous?' he said, 'Sometimes.' That's why, isn't it?"

Mama nodded. "He never talks about that. He just plans to do the work and does it. But every now and then the newspaper tells about someone getting hurt."

For a moment Mama was silent, then went on. "In the letter Papa told me something he thought I needed to know."

Once again the fear returned to Mama's face. It reminded Kate of how her mother cried after Daddy O'Connell died. Kate remembered that loneliness well.

Mama cleared her throat. "Papa said a man butchered meat and brought it to the logging camp on a sleigh. Wolves followed the sleigh the whole way. They wanted the meat."

In that instant Kate's left-out feeling disappeared, replaced by fear. In her imagination she saw the wolves following like hungry dogs just behind the sleigh. She saw the horses tossing their heads, rolling their eyes, running to stay ahead of the wolves.

Kate swallowed. "Why did Papa tell you about it?"

"He wanted me to be aware of the danger. He said I must watch the sheep and the calves. Keep them close to the barn. Make sure they're in before dark."

Kate's stomach felt funny just thinking about it.

Again Mama cleared her throat. "Papa didn't know what it'd be like for me to hear about wolves. He knows I grew up on a farm in Sweden. But I lived in the city so long. He didn't know how afraid I'd be, thinking about *him*."

I'm scared too, Kate thought. *So awfully scared.* She seemed to see a low gray shadow creeping along the horizon. The awfulness of it filled her mind.

She reached forward and slid her hand under Mama's. That helped.

Mama's lower lip trembled. Struggling to hold back tears, Mama could not speak. When she did, it was in a whisper. "Oh, Kate, I don't know what's wrong with me. I don't want to be afraid."

Mama blew her nose and cleared her throat. "I guess it's the baby coming and being lonesome for Papa and having Anders hurt and Lars sick. I can't handle everything."

Kate moved her hand to rest on top of Mama's and squeezed hard. "Did Papa say anything more?" Her voice was as quiet as Mama's.

Tears watered her mother's smile. "Yah," she said slowly. "Something he told me to remember." Mama picked up the letter and found the place. "A verse from the Bible. First Peter 5:7: 'Casting all your care upon him, for he careth for you.' "

Mama's laugh was shaky. "Papa always knows what I need. If I throw all my worries on Jesus, I won't be so afraid, will I?"

Mama straightened her shoulders and sat taller in her chair. It was as though she'd taken the promise for herself and started believing it.

Kate wished the promise seemed real to her, too. Somehow

it didn't reach deep inside where she really hurt. Biting her lip, she looked away from Mama's eyes.

But her mother reached out. Tenderly she cupped Kate's chin in her hand. "There's something else wrong, isn't there?"

Kate swallowed around the lump in her throat, afraid to answer.

14

The Moving Shadow

Mama waited until Kate looked into her eyes. Kate knew she had no choice but to answer.

"Sometimes I wonder—" Kate broke off. She didn't know how to say it. Finally she came up with a question. "Does Anders help you more than I do?"

"Why, Kate, why do you think that?"

Kate looked away, afraid to tell Mama all the mixed-up feelings she had.

But Mama wouldn't let it go. "Kate, what's *really* wrong?"

"Sometimes—sometimes I wonder if—" She couldn't finish.

"Do you wonder if I have enough love for all of you?" Mama asked.

Kate nodded, still not looking at Mama.

"You know, Kate, the more children I have, the more I love *you*."

Startled, Kate looked up.

"For a time I had only one child to love—you!" Mama spoke slowly, as though thinking it out. "Now I have three more, plus this little one coming."

Mama patted her growing stomach. "Each of you is a special person, and each of you is very special to me. My love for every one of you gets bigger every day."

Suddenly Kate's eyes felt wet. "Oh, Mama!" The next moment Kate was in her mother's arms. It felt good to be there.

When at last Mama stood up to cook breakfast, she seemed to have new energy and strength. Watching her, Kate knew that Mama would face the day and be all right, even though Papa was far away.

When Anders came in, Kate was busy helping with breakfast. Anders looked at Mama, and Kate saw his relief. It wasn't hard to know that Mama felt better. Across the kitchen table, Anders grinned at Kate and winked.

So he thinks he can just tell me what to do, and I'll do it! thought Kate.

After breakfast, Anders followed her outside into the January sunlight. As they headed toward the barn, the snow crunched beneath their feet, squeaking in the cold.

"Starting the new year right, you know," Anders said.

Kate bristled.

"And as a reward for your excellent behavior—"

"Excellent behavior, all right!" Kate exclaimed.

But Anders paid no attention. "As a reward for your most excellent behavior—" He drew off his cap with a flourish. In spite of his crutches, he bowed. "As a reward I will teach you to ride Wildfire."

"You will? When?"

"Right now."

But Kate drew back, suddenly suspicious. "What's the *real* reason, Anders?"

Her brother held up his hands in mock terror.

"I knew it!" cried Kate. "Did Mama say you had to show me how?"

Anders groaned. "Can't keep *any* secrets!"

In spite of his grin, he still looked unwilling to teach her. Yet when they reached the barn, he handed the mare's bridle to Kate.

"Mama figures that sometime you might need to ride a horse," he explained. "She said, 'What if Kate would ever have to go for help?'"

Kate found the board that stuck out from the others at the

front of the mare's stall and pulled herself up. Gently she put her fingers in the open space between Wildfire's teeth and slipped in the bit.

The saddle was heavy for Kate. Anders hopped on one foot, helping her lift. He showed her how to tighten the belly strap.

Kate led Wildfire outside. There she climbed up on the stump, then onto the horse.

Wildfire pawed the snow, eager to be off. When Kate saw the distance to the ground, she felt a moment of panic.

Anders held the mare's bridle until he explained. "When you want to go left, lay the right rein over her mane. When you want to go right, lay the left rein over. Stay close by where I can see you."

At first the mare walked around near the barn while Anders gave voice commands. "When you want to stop, don't pull back hard. Be gentle on her mouth."

Kate tried it, and Wildfire obeyed.

At last Anders trusted Kate to go farther. "Nudge her sides with your heels," he said.

Wildfire moved into a trot. Kate bounced up and down, fighting the mare's stride.

"Relax!" Anders called out. "Ride with it!"

The mare moved off on the wagon track, eager in the morning sunlight.

By the time Anders called Kate in, she felt more at home on the mare and anxious to try again. Best of all, Anders seemed to be warming up to the idea of her riding his horse.

"Now rub Wildfire down. All over," he told Kate. "And give her some oats. Make sure you close the box and lock it."

Kate did exactly what Anders told her. She didn't want the mare opening the bin by herself.

That night Kate fell asleep thinking about her ride on Wildfire. It seemed more important than ever that the horse be all right.

Tomorrow she'd see Josie in church. She'd find out if Josie knew anything more about the diamond and ruby ring.

As Kate ate breakfast on Sunday morning, Anders came into the kitchen. He looked upset.

"Who's been out to the barn?" he demanded.

Kate knew that if Anders weren't on crutches, he would have stomped across the room. Instead, he hobbled over to the other side of the table. Standing directly in front of Kate, he glared at her.

Startled, Kate looked up to his almost six feet. "To the barn? Not me. I'm about ready to start the milking."

Anders turned to his little sister. "Tina, have you been out?"

Blue eyes wide, Tina shook her head so hard the pigtails flew.

Anders looked back to Kate. "Lars is still sleeping. And Mama hasn't been there. That leaves you, Kate."

"I told you, I haven't been outside this morning."

"Then what about last night? When you fed Wildfire, what did you do with the oats?"

"I shut the bin and locked it, just like you taught me. What's wrong?"

"When I went into the barn, the lid was open."

Kate's stomach tightened. She didn't blame Anders for being upset. "That's bad, isn't it?"

"It's bad, all right! If Wildfire got into the bin, she'd eat herself sick. A horse can founder that way."

"Founder?" This time it was Tina who didn't know what Anders meant.

"Get sick and die. From eating too much."

"Was she in the oats?" Kate asked, feeling scared.

Anders shook his head. "Can't tell for sure. Doesn't look like it. But, Kate—"

"I didn't do it!" she protested. "I locked the bin."

"But who else would leave it open?"

"Not me!" Kate tried to speak calmly. "Anders, you've got to believe me. I took care of Wildfire just like you said."

Anders sighed, but his voice still sounded angry. "Kate, I want to believe you. I really do. But there hasn't been anyone else around."

Kate fell silent, knowing he was right.

Soon after, Erik's family came with their team and sleigh to pick up the Nordstroms for church. At Four Corners, Erik put the horses in the barn and covered each of them with a heavy blanket.

Kate followed Mama and Tina into church. Together they sat down on the women's side.

Mama bowed her head to pray, and Kate knew she should do the same. But just then she looked around. Someone new was sitting with Josie and her mother. Someone with beautiful red hair. *Maybelle!*

All through the hymns Kate felt too upset to even sneak a look back at the organ. But then, just before the sermon, the organist played an introduction for special music. Erik began singing a Swedish folk song, "Children of the Heavenly Father."

Tina's favorite song, Kate thought as she glanced toward the little girl. Erik hadn't told Kate he was singing in church. As far as she knew, he'd never sung there before.

Erik sang the first two verses in English, then in Swedish. Kate stole a look at Mama. Her mother's eyes were wet. One tear slid down her cheek.

Kate reached out and squeezed Mama's hand. Then Erik came to the third verse: "Praise the Lord in joyful numbers: / Your protector never slumbers."

The words reached Kate, deep inside. They reminded her of Papa Nordstrom, but also of Daddy O'Connell. Long ago he had called her "my little colleen"—my little girl. Kate blinked away her tears.

I'll practice even harder, she thought. *I'll play for Erik when he sings in church.*

As soon as the service ended, Kate sought out Josie. Taking one look at her friend's face, Kate forgot everything else. Josie had been crying, too, and Kate felt sure it wasn't because of Erik's singing.

"A letter came from Mr. Harris," Josie said. "He told Papa to find another place to live."

Josie broke down. When Kate hugged her, Josie struggled to speak through tears. "It's bad enough to lose our farm. But how can we move in *January*?"

Again Kate hugged her, not knowing what else to do. Josie

was right. The temperature could easily drop to forty degrees below zero. And January twenty-fifth was less than two weeks away. Where would Swensons go?

At last Josie stopped weeping.

"We'll search your barn," promised Kate. "We'll look in the granary. We'll look *everywhere*! Somehow we'll find that ring! Your family has to have it!"

"Who has to have what?" asked Maybelle, coming up behind Kate.

Kate turned toward the sweet voice. In the light of the window, Maybelle's soft skin and red hair looked more beautiful than ever.

But Maybelle paid no attention to Kate. Instead, she spoke to Josie. "My mother says I can take organ lessons again."

Josie choked.

Maybelle kept on. "If we get an organ at school, I can play for everyone. And I can play for Erik when he sings at church."

Josie looked quickly at Kate, but Kate looked away. She couldn't bear to speak one word. Not even with Josie.

Without looking back, Kate hurried off. Pushing open the heavy church door, she ran down the steps. All the way home she sat between Erik and Anders, filled with misery.

That afternoon Kate moved restlessly from window to window. Near the dining room, the branches of a tall pine reached out to the house. In the winter sunlight its blue-gray shadows stretched long across the snow.

Finally Kate sat down at her reed organ. Starting with her favorite hymns, she began to play. As the music spoke to her, she played on and on. *It doesn't matter what Maybelle says*, Kate finally told herself. *What matters is that I practice and do the best I can.*

A short time later, Mama lit the kerosene lamp. "Better get the milking done, Kate."

Anders' ankle was swollen again, and he sat with his leg stretched across a chair. Mama wanted him to keep it there.

Slowly Kate stood up. Here the kerosene light spread a soft

glow. Near the wood stove, the room felt warm and cozy. But Kate knew from the draft along the walls how cold it would be outside—and how dark.

In the kitchen she pulled overalls over her dress and long stockings. Anders called after her. "Don't forget the water heater, Kate."

Lars followed Kate to the kitchen. The tuft of hair stood up at the back of his red head. "Mama says I'm good enough to help."

Kate grinned. "You're good enough all right."

Under his freckles Lars flushed. "You know what I mean."

"But send him in if he gets chilled," Mama called after Kate.

As Kate opened the outside door, the wind snatched her scarf, blowing the long ends into her face. Winding the scarf around her neck, she hurried to the barn.

Before long, Lars started shivering, and Kate sent him back to the house. Even without his help, the milking went better. Each time Kate filled her bucket, she poured it into a covered pail.

When she finished the cows, she opened the bin of oats. Taking out a scoop, she fed Wildfire. Carefully she closed the cover and locked it. At last she was done.

Picking up one pail and the farm lantern, Kate kicked open the door of the barn. The wind flung it back against the wall. Setting down the lantern and milk, Kate grabbed the door and closed it.

As she twisted the small piece of wood that kept the door shut, Kate glanced toward the side of the log barn. Along the wall it seemed darker than elsewhere. Kate stared, wondering if something was there.

After a long moment, she picked up the lantern. Her boots squeaked on the cold snow as she scurried over to the watering tank.

At the pile of wood she picked up a small chunk. Yet Kate felt strange. Creepy. As if the hair stood up on the back of her neck. As if someone was watching her.

Dropping the wood, Kate listened. *Did I hear something? Did somebody move? Or a boot crunch on the packed snow?*

Kate whirled. Yet she saw nothing beyond the small glow of the lantern. Picking it up, Kate held out the lantern and started back to the pail of milk. As she looked that way, a shadow darker than the others moved against the barn.

Kate's heart leaped into her throat. Her hands trembled. The light of the lantern wavered.

She tried to push away her scared feelings, tried to stop shaking. The few steps to the pail of milk seemed miles long. *Can I leave the pail behind?* she wondered.

Then Kate thought of what Anders would say. *I can't go in without it.* And there were other pails in the barn.

For a long moment Kate stared at the shadows, and they did not move. At last she told herself, *I imagined it. There's nothing there.*

Step by slow step, Kate started toward the milk. She had almost reached the pail when one shadow separated from the rest.

15

Discovery!

The shadow was slender and taller than Kate. Seeming to glide along the side of the barn, it slipped around the corner.

Forgetting the milk, Kate turned and ran. But she felt as if she were living a nightmare. Her legs felt spongy, as though she could not move. The path from the barn to the house took forever.

Tumbling into the kitchen, Kate slammed the door behind her. Leaning back against it, she tried to catch her breath.

Anders looked up from the kitchen table. "A bandit got you, Kate?"

Kate shook her head, her eyes wide. She drew a long, ragged breath.

"Oh, c'mon now. Something must have scared you."

Kate nodded her head up and down, but still could not speak. As she tried to point outside, her hand trembled.

Anders stood up. "Well, I'm sure whatever it was is only in your imagination."

Kate found her voice. "See for yourself!"

"I will." Gathering up his crutches, Anders swung over to the door. Pulling on his coat, he went outside.

Kate followed slowly, wanting only to stay in the kitchen where the kerosene lamp shed a warm, soft glow. The yard was dark and cold.

But Anders called to her. "Where was it?"

"Over there." Kate pointed toward the side of the barn. "Along that wall."

Anders swung off down the path, heading for the lantern Kate had dropped in the snow. He held it high, but its light barely pierced the darkness.

"What'd you see, Kate?"

"A shadow." Again she pointed.

Anders snorted. "Right. A shadow."

But Kate wasn't going to be put off. "A shadow that moved. It slid around the corner of the barn."

Giving Kate the lantern, Anders swung off on crutches again. "If that's so, there should be footprints in the snow."

"You'll find them all right."

As they reached the barn, she held out the lantern. But there, along the log wall, one footprint crisscrossed another, blurring the shapes.

Lutfisk had been there and some small animals, as well as humans. In the place where Kate had seen the shadow, it was impossible to pick one print from another.

"Look around the end," suggested Kate, "Near the wagon track."

There it was no better. "Can't tell a thing," said Anders, shaking his head. "Too many footprints."

"But there *was* someone there!" Kate protested. "I *know*. I'm sure of it!"

"I'm sure you're just seeing things!"

Kate fell silent. She had to admit she did have a big imagination. But the more she thought about the shadow, the more uneasy she felt. The certainty that there had been something real creeping around the barn wouldn't go away.

As Kate pulled on her coat the next morning, Anders came in from outside. His shock of blond hair straggled out from under his cap. "Kate, you let the fire in the tank go out."

In that moment she remembered. She'd started to put in wood, then been scared away. Later, she'd forgotten to go back.

"The tank is a solid hunk of ice," Anders said. "There's not one drop of water for the animals. You're going to have to carry it from the pump. I can't."

Kate groaned, but knew she had no choice. Anders couldn't handle both crutches and a bucket of water.

As she finished watering the cows, Kate stopped near Wildfire's stall. In the sunlight of a nearby window, the mare's coat was brushed smooth. Her black side looked sleek and shiny.

Kate reached up, patting Wildfire's shoulder. As the mare turned to her, Kate stroked the white star in the middle of the black forehead.

When Kate walked around to the mare's other side, she noticed something. Here, too, Wildfire's shoulder looked brushed and smooth. The center of her back seemed just as well groomed. But then the brushing stopped.

On the mare's belly Kate saw the clear line of a cinch strap. There Wildfire's hair lay matted, twisted this way and that. It must have dried wet, without being brushed out.

Kate felt uneasy. She knew she had to tell Anders, but wasn't prepared for what he'd say.

"What did you do, take her out in the middle of the night?" he asked. "After I trusted you to treat her right?"

Kate stared at him. "Are you serious? You know I wouldn't do that."

Anders laughed, but the sound was hard as ice. "You brushed Wildfire, thinking I wouldn't find out. What'd you do, forget the rest? Forget she'd get sick if she's not taken care of?"

Kate felt the hot flush of embarrassment creep into her face. "I promise you. I have not been near your horse since you taught me to ride."

Just then Wildfire sneezed.

"See? I told you!" cried Anders. "She's getting a cold!"

Anders was right. The mare's nose was running.

In spite of being scared, Kate tried to speak quietly. "I didn't do it, Anders. Why would I tell you how she looked if I had taken her out? I could have just brushed her smooth."

"Kate, there hasn't been anyone else around."

"Hasn't there?" Kate's voice was soft, but it had a dangerous edge. "Really now, Anders, hasn't there been anyone else around?"

"What're you talking about?" he asked.

"About last night when you wouldn't believe me."

"Kate, there was nothing there."

"Of course not. By the time you got outside, someone could have easily hidden." Kate picked up a pail and stalked off. Taking a three-legged stool, she sat down and started milking.

Yet the awful feeling that Anders didn't trust her wouldn't go away. Down at the pit of her stomach, Kate felt hurt. *How can I make Anders believe me?* The rest of the morning Kate thought about it, wondering what to do.

Just as often she thought about Mr. Swenson's inheritance. She and Anders needed to get to Josie's and search for the diamond and ruby ring. Time was passing quickly. In just eleven days Swensons would have to move. Yet Anders couldn't possibly go that far on crutches.

The next morning Anders looked even more upset. He and Kate were out in the barn again.

"Wildfire has a cough!" Anders groaned as he checked the mare.

When Anders walked the mare around inside the barn, he noticed something else. "She's limping. She favors one foot."

Turning around from where she milked Clover, Kate watched Anders. She felt scared, so scared she could barely breathe. Her fingers tightened, squeezing harder than she should. Clover stepped sideways.

Kate patted her side. "It's okay, girl. Didn't mean to hurt you."

Standing up, Kate poured the milk into a covered pail and went over to Wildfire.

"See?" said Anders. "She favors her right front foot." He hobbled over to the box that held tools used in the barn. There he found a hoof knife—a straight blade with a curve on the end.

Going back to Wildfire, Anders lifted her front foot and scraped away the mud. Carefully he inspected the hoof.

When he found nothing wrong, Kate left him and fed the sheep. Yet today they offered no comfort.

"Gotta get you over that cold," said Anders to Wildfire.

As though understanding his words, Wildfire coughed. Her nose ran.

"See what I told you?" Again Anders looked worried. "That's what a horse gets if she's ridden hard in cold weather."

Kate started out of the barn, carrying a covered pail of milk in each hand. No matter what she said to Anders, he wouldn't believe her.

As she headed for the house, Anders followed, swinging along on his crutches. "I think I remember everything Papa told me. About taking care of a horse with a cough. About what foundering looks like. But I wish I could make sure."

Kate kept walking. The pails were heavy. Then she had an idea. "Why don't you talk to Mr. Swenson?"

Anders looked thoughtful. "Yup. That's what I should do. But I don't have a way to get there. What we need is one of those newfangled telephones."

Near the house, Kate stopped in the path and swung around. "I could take you."

"*You* take *me*?"

"Pull you on the sled."

The sled was large and used for hauling wood. In spite of his height Anders could easily fit on it. Yet the minute Kate spoke, she wondered if she'd be sorry. A blacksmith had put iron on the bottom of the wooden runners to help the sled glide. Even so, it'd be hard work getting Anders all the way to Swensons.

When they talked to Mama, she said, "Lars can help you, Kate. He's better today."

It was well past lunch before they got started. The weather was mild for January, and the air felt warm on Kate's cheeks. She breathed deeply, grateful to be outdoors.

Lars also looked happy to be out in the sun.

Swinging forward on his crutches, Anders dropped down on the large sled. It had four posts, one at each corner, to hold split wood in place. Settling himself between the posts, Anders angled his crutches across his lap. Kate and Lars took up the rope.

The sled pulled easily on the icy track that passed the barn, then the farmhouse. Often people came this way, taking the shortcut through the woods.

At the top of the hill overlooking Rice Lake there was more snow. There Kate spotted Wildfire's hoof prints on the trail to Spirit Lake School. When Kate pointed them out to Anders, he looked thoughtful but said nothing.

Throwing the rope onto the sled, Kate and Lars gave it a good push. Anders hung on as the sled swooped down the steep track. Kate and Lars followed, then stopped. Near the bottom of the hill, they saw Wildfire's hoofprints again. It looked as if the mare had stopped to drink at the spring.

Soon Kate and Lars caught up to Anders and once again pulled the sled. Farther on, the wind across Rice Lake had blown across the path, sweeping it clean. Patches of dirt and small stones showed through the snow.

For a time they lost Wildfire's hoof prints. Then Anders called out, "Stop!"

Using his crutches, Anders pulled himself up and off the sled. Being careful where he stepped, he studied the ground. At last he pointed down.

"What is it?" asked Kate.

"See the marks in the snow? Something scared Wildfire. She stopped suddenly. Her front feet dug into the dirt."

"Why would she stop right here?" Kate wanted to know.

Anders shrugged. "Maybe a grouse flew up. Or a small animal ran out right in front of her."

He started back to the sled, but Kate had another question. "Could something happen to a horse if it stopped too fast?"

"Too fast?" Anders started to laugh. Then the grin disappeared from his face. Hobbling back, he studied the hoof prints. "You might be right, Kate," he said at last. "I'll check when I get back."

16

The Loan Shark Returns

Maybe Anders will believe me now, thought Kate as they went on. *Maybe he'll find out what's really wrong with Wildfire.* The idea filled her with hope.

Beyond Rice Lake, they entered the woods and soon came to a fork in the trail. In the open area the wind had blown large drifts across the path.

Kate groaned. If she went ahead, she'd be into snow far above her knees. For Lars it would be even worse.

Anders stopped them. "Why don't you go left on the path to Erik's. It's usually not as drifted. If he's home, he'll help you pull the rest of the way."

By the time they reached Lundgrens', it was midafternoon. Erik went on with them, while Lars returned to Windy Hill Farm.

"Let's take the road past school," Erik suggested. "Sleighs have been through, packing a trail."

As they rounded the bend beyond Spirit Lake School, Kate saw Maybelle ahead. Kate slowed her steps, but it was too late. Maybelle waited until they caught up.

"Going to Josie's?" Anders asked.

Maybelle held up a pair of ice skates. "Grandfather gave me these. He told me to ask Mr. Swenson to weld them where they're broken."

When they reached Josie's farm, Maybelle dropped her skates on the packed snow near the blacksmith shop.

"Don't you want to put 'em in the shop?" asked Anders.

"Mr. Swenson will find them," Maybelle said carelessly and followed the others to the house.

Josie met them at the door. "You're just the ones I wanted to see!" Her eyes danced, and Kate wondered what had happened.

Holding Calico in her arms, three-year-old Becca peeked out from behind her big sister. The little girl's light brown hair curled softly around her face. She smiled, and her hazel eyes sparkled like Josie's.

The aroma of baking cookies filled the large kitchen. A number of them were cooling on the table.

"I've got something to tell you," said Josie, a grin from ear to ear. "This morning I found the ring!"

"You *found* it?" Kate couldn't believe the good news. "Where?"

Josie led them into the large open room. She pointed to a chair. "Right there. When I cleaned, it was near one of the legs. So close that I almost missed it."

"That's strange," said Kate. "We looked there. I know we did. How could the ring suddenly appear when it's been missing for two weeks?"

"I don't know," answered Josie. "We can't even guess how long it's been there. All we know is that it's back!"

"Where's the ring now?" asked Anders. "Can we see it?"

Josie shook her head. "Sorry. I wish I could show you. But Papa hid it in a really good place. We watched him put it away and promised we wouldn't tell anyone."

"All of you saw where he put it?" asked Anders. "Even Stretch?"

"Anders!" Kate warned.

But Josie had already heard. "You think he stole it, then put it out again, don't you?"

"Well—"

"Well, nothing!" snapped Josie, sparks in her hazel eyes. "Quit putting the blame on him!"

Anders said no more. Just the same, Kate could see he was thinking. She had to admit the whole thing seemed mighty strange.

It was strange, too, that Maybelle stood so quietly, listening intently to everything they talked about.

But Josie led them back to the kitchen. "Let's have cookies to celebrate finding the ring."

As everyone sat down at the table, Anders looked at Erik, and Erik looked at Anders. Kate recognized it as their old signal. She'd seen them talk that way at Spirit Lake School.

When Josie poured milk, Erik spoke up. "Josie, does your father have any explanation?"

Josie shook her head. "And neither does Mama. They just say, 'It was gone, and now it's back.' "

"But what if it disappears again?" asked Erik, his eyes troubled.

"It won't," replied Josie. "Tomorrow morning Papa will take the ring to Minneapolis. He'll find an honest man and sell it."

"Your father's leaving tomorrow?" Erik looked relieved.

"First thing in the morning," said Josie. "Papa will drive the team to Grantsburg and take the Blueberry Special." The train took passengers to Rush City where they transferred to another train bound for Minneapolis.

"You'll be able to pay that loan shark off?" asked Anders.

"Papa hopes he can pay off the whole farm. Plus buy machinery he needs. And tools." Josie's eyes glowed. "Papa won't know how to act. He and Mama have always struggled to make payments."

Erik knew all about that. "It's hard enough when payments are fair. But yours are way too high."

"Until now," said Kate, trying to comfort Josie. She knew the long hours Mr. Swenson worked.

"Until tomorrow." Josie smiled as she passed the cookies. "Can you imagine what it'll be like to own the farm, free and clear?"

"Hooray!" said Becca, and all of them laughed.

Becca held Josie's kitten up to Kate. "Pretty kitty."

Kate reached out to take Calico. In that instant the kitten leaped from Becca's hands. Like a shot, Calico streaked into the other room. By the time Kate reached the doorway, the kitten had disappeared.

"She's gone again!" Kate exclaimed as Josie and Erik followed her into the large open room. "Where can she be?"

Josie shrugged. "I'd certainly like to know. She has to be somewhere in the house."

"Somewhere in this room, you mean," answered Kate. "Isn't this where she always disappears?"

"Always," answered Josie.

"Let's search again," said Kate, unwilling to let a mystery go unsolved. "Let's look in every corner of the room."

"There are only four corners, Kate," said Anders as he hobbled in from the kitchen. "You look while I talk to Mr. Swenson about Wildfire. Where's your father, Josie?"

"In the barn, I think. That's where Mama and the boys are."

As Anders and Erik left, Maybelle called after them. "Tell Mr. Swenson I left skates for him to fix."

Josie returned to baking cookies. Maybelle dropped into a chair. Her deep brown eyes looked amused that Kate searched so hard.

Starting on one side of the large room, Kate worked her way around it. As before, she peered behind the large heating stove, inside the wood box, and under the large oak table and chairs.

As last she reached the wall next to the kitchen. Between the door and the chimney, shelves stretched from above Kate's head to close to the floor.

Seeming eager to help, Becca pulled a chair away from the large oak table. She dragged it over next to Kate and climbed up. Standing on the chair, Becca put one foot on a shelf, grabbed the edge of the shelf above and pulled herself up. As she reached for the shelf beyond that, Kate stopped her.

"Josie, come see your sister," Kate called into the kitchen.

Josie took Becca down. "Mama says she's much more of a climber than I was. She's like the boys." She turned to Becca.

"Don't do that again. You'll get hurt."

Kate went back to her search, but Becca acted restless. "Out?" she asked Josie.

"You can find Mama," Josie told her and helped the little girl put on her coat and scarf. As Becca started across the yard, Josie watched from a window.

Kate went back to the shelves. From the chair where she sat, Maybelle still looked amused at Kate's search. But then they heard a cry from outside.

"Becca fell!" exclaimed Josie. "Near the shop."

She and Kate grabbed their coats. Outside, they saw Stretch run from the blacksmith shop, pick up Becca, and start toward the house. As Josie and Kate hurried to meet them, Becca wailed.

Awkwardly Stretch patted her back, trying to comfort her.

As Josie reached them, she held out her arms to Becca. The little girl shook her head and clung to Stretch. But she continued to scream.

"Shhhhh," he soothed. "You'll be all right."

Becca's wails changed to long sobbing whimpers.

Coming into the kitchen, Stretch set Becca down on the table. He stepped back, and Kate saw the blood on his shirt. In spite of the cold, he hadn't waited to put on a coat.

Then Kate saw Becca's knee. Her stocking and the long underwear beneath were ripped and stained with blood.

Gently Josie pulled the torn cloth away from the ugly gash. Blood dripped down Becca's leg.

Kate's eyes blurred with tears. The little girl had taken a hard tumble. The wound was deep and still bleeding. Whatever Becca had fallen on must have been sharp.

Josie hurried to the pail of drinking water near the door. Ladling water into a bowl, she wet a clean cloth.

Kate reached forward to grasp Becca's hands. "Josie's going to help you," she said.

Carefully Josie wiped the area around the gash. Becca wailed. Frantically she tried to push Josie away. But Kate held Becca's hands firm.

Quick tears came to Josie's eyes. "Sorry, Becca," she said. "I don't like this either." Taking a clean cloth, she pressed it against the wound.

Becca screamed.

The wail pierced Kate's heart. "It's all right, Becca," she soothed. "You'll feel better soon."

"Just let me fix it," said Josie. The tears spilled over and ran down her cheeks. With her free hand she pushed the hair out of her sister's eyes.

After a minute Josie let up on the cloth. Immediately the bleeding started again.

"You have to hold it longer," said Stretch.

Taking another cloth, Josie pressed it against Becca's knee. Again the three-year-old screamed.

Stretch's arm tightened around her shoulders. "Shush!" he told her. "Yelling isn't going to make it any better."

In the middle of the wail, Becca stopped. She drew a deep shuddering breath. "You mad, Stretch?"

"Nope, I'm not mad. Just want to help you. Like Josie and Kate."

Once more Josie placed a clean cloth against the wound. Becca flinched, and Kate tightened her grip on the little girl's hands. But this time Becca understood they wanted to help.

"What happened?" Kate asked.

"She fell on some skates," Stretch growled. "They're mighty sharp for a little girl."

Josie's eyes widened. "What do you mean?"

"They were lying on the ground outside the shop. You know the part that has clamps for holding the skate on a shoe? That narrow edge?"

Kate glanced toward Maybelle. Lying on its side, that narrow edge would be sharp as a knife.

Josie's eyes flashed with anger. "Who left skates where Becca could fall on them?"

Kate knew. Turning to Maybelle again, she waited.

Maybelle flushed red. Looking away, she avoided Kate's eyes. As Kate stared at her, the silence in the kitchen grew long.

At last Maybelle spoke. "I did," she said slowly. "But why did Becca have to be so clumsy and fall on them?"

Josie gasped. Becca's bottom lip quivered.

Stretch glared at Maybelle. "Big help *you* are."

Maybelle reached for her coat. "Grandpa wants Mr. Swenson to weld the skates," she said stiffly. Without saying she was sorry, she went out the door.

When Becca's knee stopped bleeding, Josie pressed yet another cloth against the wound. Then Kate wrapped the knee with a long strip torn from an old sheet.

By now Becca was sleepy from crying. Taking the little girl in her arms, Josie sat down in the large rocker in a corner of the kitchen. As Josie rocked back and forth, Becca clutched her favorite blanket and looked up at Stretch.

The tall blond boy leaned forward. "Wish I had a little sister like you," he said.

Becca held out her blanket, and Stretch grinned. "Thanks, Becca. But you better keep it for now."

As Josie rocked her, Becca's long lashes rested on her cheek. Drowsily she opened her eyes, then closed them in sleep.

A moment later sleigh bells jingled in the yard. Through the window Kate saw a pair of matched grays pulling a cutter. The horses seemed familiar. So did the man who drove them.

"Uh-oh," she said. "That man is back."

"Mr. Harris?" Josie spoke softly. Trying to not wake Becca, she pushed her foot against the wood floor and turned the chair toward the window. "It's him all right."

As Mr. Harris tied the grays to the rail, he looked around. Below the thick mustache a satisfied smile crossed his face.

"So he thinks it's his already," said Josie. "Well, we'll show *him!*"

"I'll find your parents," said Stretch and hurried out the back way.

Mr. Harris headed toward the house, his step light and quick. Today a cane hung over his arm, but Kate felt sure he didn't need it for walking. His sealskin cap rested at a jaunty angle on his forehead. His long raccoon coat swung open.

A moment later Mr. Harris knocked on the front door.

17

Frightening News

"That awful man!" Trying not to wake Becca, Josie whispered. Yet Kate caught a fighting spirit in her friend's voice.

"I'll get the door," Kate said.

"No, just wait," answered Josie. "Give Mama and Papa more time to get here."

Once more Mr. Harris knocked on the door. His pounding seemed to shake the house.

Kate stood up, but Josie put her hand on Kate's arm, telling her again to wait.

In spite of the noise, Kate grinned. "You're stubborn, aren't you?"

Josie grinned back. "I'm stubborn all right. I've seen what he does to Mama and Papa."

Then in the fading light of the short winter day they saw Mr. Swenson start from the barn. "All right," whispered Josie. "Open the door."

By now it sounded as if Mr. Harris would break through the wood. Kate grasped the handle and yanked the door open.

Caught off balance, Mr. Harris almost fell in. He blinked, then recovered. "I don't believe I know you," he said stiffly. "Tell

Mr. Swenson that Mr. Leonard Harris is here."

Kate swung the door wide, and the man entered. Taking off his long coat, Mr. Harris handed it to Kate, along with his cane and sealskin cap.

Mr. Harris looked around the room, again appearing to like what he saw. Choosing the best chair, he sat down.

A moment later an out-of-breath Mr. Swenson entered the room. Smoothing back her hair, Mrs. Swenson followed.

This time Mr. Swenson did not close the door. From the kitchen Kate and Josie heard every word.

"I came to remind you again about the money," Mr. Harris said. "Your payment is due on January twenty-fifth. I won't wait any longer."

Through the doorway Kate saw Mr. Swenson straighten his shoulders. His large hands clenched and unclenched. "You won't have to. I'll have the money for you."

"You've said that before."

"And I've had the money before."

"But where *is* this money you're talking about? I have to have the full amount. And I don't see it."

"You will. I'm a man of my word."

"And I too," said Mr. Harris. His chest seemed to expand. "In exactly ten days you'll be out of this house. But I'm not a coldhearted man. If you don't want your family in the snow, find another place for them!"

Mr. Swenson drew himself up to his full height. "My family will live here. This is my farm, and it will stay that way."

Mr. Harris laughed. Standing up, he walked close to Josie's father.

Mr. Swenson held his ground. "I have an inheritance." He spoke quietly, but reminded Kate of an oak rooted deep. "Tomorrow I will sell a ring my father gave me. You'll have the money in time. The full amount. I give you my word."

Mr. Harris stepped back. "I don't believe you. Don't forget, you have only ten days." Calling for his coat, he stalked out of the house.

A minute later, Mr. Harris climbed into his cutter. Through the kitchen window, Kate saw his long whip snake out. The grays leaped ahead. Then the growing dusk closed around them.

Slowly Josie stood up with Becca still in her arms. "I'm glad she didn't hear," said Josie, looking down at her sleeping sister. "And I'm glad my brothers were outside."

The Swensons had known other hard times, but Kate had never seen Josie so upset. Tears slid down her white cheeks.

When Kate and Josie went into the other room, Mrs. Swenson stood in front of a window. Her fingers nervously twisted her apron. Staring at the spot where Mr. Harris was last seen, Mrs. Swenson talked to herself.

"What's she saying?" Kate whispered to Josie.

"Her favorite verse. Whenever Mr. Harris comes, Mama gets so worried she repeats it over and over."

Kate strained to hear.

"Casting all your care upon him," Mrs. Swenson muttered, still staring out the window. "Casting all your care upon him, for he careth for you."

"That's Mama's verse!" Kate cried.

Mr. Swenson turned away from the door. He no longer looked the bold man who had stood up to Mr. Harris. "Yah, the Lord cares for us," he said. "Our good Lord had my father send the ring just in time!"

Shortly after, Kate, Erik, and Anders left for home. As they walked, Kate thought of only one thing. *What would Swensons do if they didn't have the ring?*

Soon the three of them passed Spirit Lake School, then the Lundgren house. Erik stayed with them, helping Kate pull Anders on the sled.

By the time they entered the woods between Erik's house and Windy Hill Farm, the moon shone high and clear. Its glow brightened the snow and lit a path through the woods. The trees cast shadows that lengthened with the night.

Kate shivered and wished they were home, warm and cozy around the wood stove. As a sound shattered the night air, Kate jumped.

"It's just an owl," Anders called out from the sled. "Stop acting like a girl."

"I *am* one!" Kate responded. "And proud of it!"

"But he's right, Kate," Erik said, his voice low, as though not wanting to embarrass her in front of Anders. "You don't have to be scared. Listen."

The call came again, and Kate heard it distinctly. *Whoo, whoo, whoo, whoo—whoo, whoo, whoo, whoo-ah!*

Taking a deep breath, Kate tugged on the rope and trudged ahead. Yet every sound tightened her nerves.

Close at hand, a branch cracked, sounding like a pistol shot. Again Kate jumped, and Anders laughed.

"What a scaredy-cat!"

"I am *not*!" Kate answered. "You know I'm not!"

"Don't know nothin'!" Anders told her. "Just watching how you act."

From then on Kate stared straight ahead, barely moving her head. Yet always she watched, her eyes trying to pierce the shadows on either side of the path.

As they moved onto the open field between the two houses, Kate saw a dark shape on the path ahead. Moving quickly, it rushed toward them.

Kate shrieked, but Anders laughed. "See what I mean? You're a scaredy-cat!"

Then Kate saw it was Lutfisk. The dog leaped toward the sled, licked Anders' face, and woofed. Grateful that it wasn't a wild animal, Kate tried to shrug away her fear.

As soon as they reached Windy Hill Farm, Anders headed straight for the barn. Kate and Erik followed him.

Erik lit a lantern, and Anders found the hoof knife he used before. Leading Wildfire to the light, Anders lifted the mare's right front foot. Carefully he scraped away the dirt.

Erik held the lantern close. The outer part of Wildfire's hoof looked like a tough fingernail. Suddenly Anders stopped his cleaning.

"That's it!" he exclaimed.

Leaning forward, Kate saw what looked like a small dark circle near the outer edge of the hoof. As Anders worked with the knife, a sharp little pebble popped out.

"There it is!" Anders looked relieved.

"That's what made Wildfire limp?" Kate asked.

"I think so." Anders let down the mare's foot and patted her shoulder. "Now you're going to feel better, girl."

"How'd you know to look for a stone?" asked Kate.

Anders pushed the blond hair out of his eyes. "Remember that place on the trail? Where you asked if something could happen to a horse if it stopped too fast? I thought something might have jumped out and scared Wildfire. She stopped so suddenly her hooves ground through the snow into the dirt."

"And she picked up a stone?" Kate felt good. For the first time since Anders found the oat bin open, the air seemed clear between them. "Will Wildfire be all right now?" she asked.

"I don't know. We'll have to see." Anders looked Kate straight in the eye. "That's why you need to check a horse's hooves after taking 'em out."

His voice sounded sharp, and Kate's hope vanished like smoke in the wind. Anders still suspected her.

Kate ached with disappointment. "I told you. I didn't take Wildfire out."

"Then who did?"

Kate saw the unbelief in his eyes. *If my own brother doesn't trust me, who will?* she asked herself. It didn't matter that Anders was only a stepbrother. They'd known each other almost nine months.

Kate's disappointment turned to pain. Lifting her head, she tossed her black braid over her shoulder. *Anders will never believe me. Not until I find out who took Wildfire from the barn.*

Then Kate had an idea. *Maybe Stretch would understand how I feel. Maybe he can tell me what to do.*

A few days later Anders sat in the kitchen, a newspaper spread out on the table before him. He read from the January eighteenth *Journal of Burnett County*.

"Look at this!" Anders whistled.

Standing behind him, Kate read over her brother's shoulder. In a bold headline the paper said: BOUNTY PAID FOR WILD ANIMALS BY BURNETT COUNTY IN 1906.

"Bounty? What's a bounty?" Kate asked, forgetting for a moment the unsettled feelings between her and Anders.

"A reward," he told her. "See? Right along the top here." He pointed to small type at the top of four columns.

To Whom Paid was the first column, and under it a list of names. Next came *Amount* and the dollars paid out. Then *Kind of Animal*.

Kate read down the list. "One wolf, two wild cats, one lynx, fourteen wolves." She paused at the awfulness of it. *"Fourteen wolves?"*

"Yup." Anders didn't seem very disturbed. He pointed farther down. "Usually it's not that many. But eight, nine, three. Oh, here's another fourteen."

"Where?" Kate asked, barely able to whisper. "Where were they killed?"

Then she saw the fourth column and picked out the places closest to Windy Hill Farm. "Grantsburg, Wood Lake, Trade Lake."

In that instant Anders looked up at her face. "Do you know why there's a bounty?" he asked.

Kate shook her head.

"Because wild animals kill *our* animals."

But Kate still could not speak.

"What's scaring you?" Anders asked.

When Kate finally answered, her lips felt stiff. "I hear the wolves at night."

Anders grinned, but for once did not tease. Kate wondered if he remembered the promise he had made when Papa said, "Take care of Mama and Kate."

"They won't bother you, Kate. You're safe inside the house."

"But what *will* they bother?" she asked. Deep inside, Kate's scared feeling wouldn't go away.

"Animals that are sick and old," Anders told Kate. "Ones that can't run fast anymore. And wolves bother sheep and calves. They're pretty helpless, you know."

When Anders put away the newspaper, Kate was glad. She didn't want to think about the wolves. "That's why you always get the sheep in before dark."

It wasn't a question. Kate knew the answer.

18

Growing Threats

*E*arly the next morning Erik pounded on the Windy Hill door. "Josie's brother just came to our place," Erik said. "The ring is gone!"

"Missing?" Kate couldn't believe it. "I thought Mr. Swenson sold it right after we were there. Didn't he go to Minneapolis?"

Erik shook his head. "The day he was supposed to go, Josie's youngest brother woke up awfully sick. Mr. Swenson had to go for the doctor and never made it to Minneapolis."

A hard knot formed at the pit of Kate's stomach. "The ring is *really* gone again?"

Erik's blue eyes darkened with anger. "It's *really* gone. Josie wants all of us to come and help them look. This time we're going over the entire farm with a fine-tooth comb."

Erik helped Kate and Anders with chores. While Kate finished up, Erik carried pails of milk into the house. Anders hobbled after him, also carrying a pail and using one crutch.

When Kate entered the kitchen, the boys sat at the table with Mama. Looking Kate's way, everyone stopped talking. The next instant they all spoke at once.

It made Kate uncomfortable. *Are they talking about me?* she wondered. She tried to push her feelings aside.

Soon after, she and Erik and Anders started out, with Anders again on the sled. After a time he walked part of the way, being careful to favor his bad ankle.

When they reached Josie's house, Mr. Swenson sat in the kitchen drinking coffee. His eyes looked bleak, his face lined with worry.

They found Josie in the large open room. "When my brother got better, Papa went to get the ring," she explained. "That's when he discovered it was gone!"

"Could Mr. Harris have come back?" asked Kate. "Could he have stolen the ring?"

"We'd have seen him," said Josie. "We've been here the whole time." Her eyes looked scared. "But this is just what that old loan shark wants! In four days we'll lose the house!"

Four days, thought Kate. *The last time the ring disappeared, it was gone for two weeks. This time it might be gone for good.*

So afraid she could barely think, Kate stared out the window. Only a few days before, Mr. Harris had driven up to that hitching rail. With his handsome cold eyes he looked around as though wanting everything within reach. The idea of that terrible man taking the farm made Kate shiver right down to her toes.

Then she realized something. *This is where Josie's mother stood. She watched that old loan shark. She knew he had the power to take away the farm. She knew he could take even this house— the house where she and Mr. Swenson lived with their nine children.* Again Kate shivered, but not from cold.

Then Kate remembered Mrs. Swenson repeating the verse to herself. When Kate turned back to the room, she no longer felt afraid.

"Did you ask Stretch about the ring?" Anders asked Josie.

"Papa refuses." Josie's eyes were dark with pain. "He says we can trust Stretch."

"But what if you trust him, and he robs you of your farm?" growled Anders.

"Anders, you don't have proof," said Erik. "You're blaming Stretch because of his reputation."

"Right," agreed Anders. "If we trust him, Josie's whole family might get hurt."

"Do you have any clues?" Kate asked Josie.

"Whoever took the ring left the boxes again. They were left open the same way. Do you want to see them?"

Kate picked up the boxes—the small one that held the ring and the slightly larger one for mailing. Going to the window, she held them up.

There in the sunlight she saw something new. "Josie!" Kate cried. "Do you think these are fingerprints?"

One gray smudge marked the larger box. "It's hard to say for sure on this one," Kate replied as Josie looked on. "It might have gotten dirty in the mail. But here's something I didn't see before."

In the light of the window Kate turned the smaller box. "See this fingerprint? It's smudged a bit and isn't clear. But look on the other side of the box. There's another mark just like the first. Both fingerprints are where someone would hold the box to open it."

"You're right, Kate!" Erik sounded excited.

"How big a finger would make that smudge?"

He grinned. "A small one."

Kate felt so relieved that she laughed. "That's what I thought too. All we have to do is figure out who that finger belongs to. Let's look at the hands of everyone we see."

They also decided to search the house, then the other buildings. Josie and Anders went to the granary, while Kate and Erik looked in every part of the barn. After three hours even Kate had to admit they were looking for a needle in a haystack. Finally they had no choice but to give up.

As Erik went to find Josie and Anders, Kate started across the farmyard. There she ran into Stretch. Instead of meeting her gaze, the boy with the blond curly hair looked away.

But Kate remembered her idea and spoke quickly before he could leave. She told Stretch how Anders didn't trust her, then asked, "What should I do?"

"You have to catch whoever's comin' into your barn," Stretch answered promptly.

"But how?" asked Kate, even though she knew he was right.

"Does the rider always come at night?"

Kate nodded. "So far."

"Then hide in your barn," said Stretch. "Wait there 'til you find out who it is. I'd help you if I could, but I gotta stay here."

"Thanks, Stretch," said Kate, feeling better already.

"Be sure you hide where the person won't find you," he warned.

When Kate went to her room that night, she stayed fully dressed. Wrapping herself in a warm blanket, she knelt by the window overlooking the wagon track.

When the house grew quiet, Kate tiptoed downstairs, pulled on her heavy coat, scarf, and mittens, and slipped outside. Hurrying to the barn, she climbed up in the hayloft.

Near the large hole into the main floor of the barn, Kate settled deep in the hay. For a long time she waited with eyes wide open. Fighting down her fear of the dark, she peered through the hole into the floor below.

Gradually Kate grew sleepy. When she wakened, she felt cold all the way through.

What time is it? Kate wondered. She had no idea, but guessed it was very late. She knew only that she had to get warm.

As she quietly opened the kitchen door, the clock chimed four times. Tiptoeing, Kate headed toward the wood cookstove. A voice stopped her.

"What were you doing outside?" Anders asked from the doorway to the dining room.

Kate jumped.

"Been out riding my horse?"

From the middle of the kitchen, Kate faced him. "No," she answered, her voice strong in spite of the scare Anders had given her. "I'm trying to discover who *is* riding Wildfire."

Anders looked as if he didn't believe a word she said. "What're you talking about?"

"Sooner or later the person who took your horse will come back. I'm going to be there."

Anders stared at her. "Maybe you're right," he said slowly. "Don't know why I didn't think of it myself. But I know one thing. I don't want you sitting there alone. I'll go with you."

Grabbing his coat, Anders hobbled out on one crutch. As they crossed the yard to the barn, Kate looked up. In the night sky just before dawn, the stars seemed close enough to touch.

Inside the barn Anders pulled himself up the ladder with his strong arms and one foot. Kate handed up his crutch, then followed. Settling down in the dusty hay, she again peered through the hole into the floor below.

Time dragged on, as each minute seemed to last forever. Yet Kate felt glad for Anders' company. It wasn't as frightening waiting together.

In a crack between the boards of the outside wall, Kate watched streaks of pink edge into the eastern sky. Suddenly she caught her breath.

"Shhhh!" warned Anders. "Someone's coming!"

"I have to sneeze!" Quickly Kate covered her nose and mouth with her hands.

"No, no!" whispered Anders. "Shhhhh!"

From below, the latch of the door jiggled. As someone opened, then closed the door, it squeaked on its hinges. Through the hole into the main floor of the barn, Kate saw a shadow quietly move their way.

Again Kate gasped, trying to hold back her sneeze. The next instant it came. "Achoooo!"

The shadow leaped away, bumping into the stall with a loud thump.

When the door slammed, Anders was already partway down the ladder. Kate tumbled after him as Anders hobbled outside. They each took a different direction around the barn. But whoever the person was had gotten away.

"Aw, Kate, how could you?" complained Anders when they met again near the barn door. "How could you possibly sneeze right then?"

In the first light of dawn Kate saw her brother's face and guessed how upset he felt. "I'm sorry, Anders," she said, her voice low. She felt sick with disappointment. "We were mighty close."

"Close, all right! And now he might not try again—not for a while anyway. We would have caught him right in the act."

Him? Kate wondered. "Who do you think it was?" she asked. But Anders only shrugged.

At least he knows there's SOMEONE, thought Kate. Still it gave her little comfort. She looked away, then down, tracing a pattern in the snow with her foot.

Then she saw it. As the sun edged higher in the sky, Kate saw something dark against the snow. Something close to her foot and closer to the door. Reaching down, she picked it up.

A black button!

"Look, Anders!" She held it out for him to see, then turned it over in her hand. "Four holes for thread to pass through. A raised outer ridge."

A lopsided grin lit her brother's face. "Well, we didn't do so bad after all!"

Kate agreed. Carefully she slipped the button deep inside the pocket of her coat.

All through chores she tried to remember where she'd seen such a button. As soon as they finished milking, she and Anders hurried to Erik's, and the three went on to Josie's. Again Anders rode on the sled, but also walked part way, trying to strengthen his injured ankle.

"Only three more days," said Kate, thinking about Swensons. "Today, tomorrow, and Thursday."

"Not even that," Anders corrected her. "On Thursday Mr. Swenson has to go to Minneapolis and sell the ring. Friday morning he's got to come back on the train."

"And pay for the farm," Kate replied, "before they lose it."

Making the deadline for the payment seemed impossible. Kate glanced at Erik. He looked just as worried as Anders.

When they reached Swensons, Josie and Anders searched the chicken coop while Kate and Erik headed for the blacksmith shop. Both of them felt embarrassed about having to look through the shop.

Stretch didn't make it easier. "You won't find anything here," he said bluntly.

"We believe that, Stretch," answered Erik. "We trust you. But we need to look in case someone slipped in when you weren't here."

Stretch seemed to accept Erik's words. As Kate and Erik searched, the tall blond boy shaped a cherry hot piece of iron on the anvil. Yet he pounded halfheartedly, as if he didn't care about his work.

Finally Stretch dropped the iron into a pail of water. He looked at Erik with a strange expression on his face.

"I ain't got nothin' to keep me here," Stretch burst out, as though finishing something he and Erik had talked about before.

"Nothing? That's not true," Kate protested.

She remembered how sure of himself Stretch had seemed when she first met him at Spirit Lake School. Though he was older than the other children, they liked him. They wanted Stretch on their side for games. With his help they'd win.

But now Stretch looked discouraged. "I got nothin' to keep me here," he said again.

"You have a chance to make good," Erik told him. "Mr. Swenson says you could be one of the best blacksmiths around."

"I could be," Stretch agreed, "and I'd like my own shop someday. Maybe in Grantsburg. But it's no use trying."

"Why?" demanded Kate.

"If people don't trust me, I can't get work," Stretch told her. "Even if I got my own shop, they wouldn't come."

"But Mr. Swenson believes in you," Kate answered.

"Don't make no difference," said Stretch. "Other folks don't. Including your brother Anders."

Kate fell silent, knowing Stretch was right.

In a moment the tall thin boy spoke again. "If folks don't trust me, I'm not sticking around."

"What would you do?" she asked.

"I'd leave."

"You'd go home?" Kate wanted to know. "To your family's farm?"

Stretch shook his head. "Nothin' to keep me there either."

"But your father?" Kate asked, though she knew Stretch's father was gone. "Won't he come back? Sooner or later, I mean?"

Stretch shrugged his shoulders, looking at the ground instead of Kate or Erik.

Then Kate guessed what really bothered Stretch. "You figure

he won't come home, don't you?"

The tall boy nodded, still avoiding their eyes.

Kate wondered how strongly Stretch meant what he said. She didn't wonder long.

"I'd run away," Stretch said quietly. His voice changed, sounding like the hammer he used to pound iron. "I'd leave and never come back!"

19

The Shadows Lengthen

In spite of the heat from the forge, Kate shivered. Stretch meant it all right. "Where would you go?"

"Aw, Stretch," Erik broke in, "stop talking like that. Big Gust and Mr. Swenson believe in you. Kate and I believe in you. We all know you want to make good."

Stretch seemed to grow even taller than his more than six feet. "No, you don't." His voice filled with anger. "You're a goody-goody, likin' the sound of your words. You're just waitin' for me to do somethin' wrong."

"No, we're not," answered Erik. "But we're not dumb either."

Stretch's laugh was scornful.

"You have to give folks time," Erik went on. "Prove they can trust you."

"Prove it?" Stretch scoffed. "I have."

Erik shook his head. "You've started," he said, sounding older than his thirteen years. "You haven't finished."

"Finished! Ha! That's a laugh!" Stretch went back to his work.

"What are you, a quitter?" Erik asked.

But Stretch picked up a new piece of iron. With angry blows he started to pound it into shape. When he refused to speak again, Kate and Erik left. Stretch did not look their way.

Returning to the farmhouse, Kate found Josie, Anders, and Mrs. Swenson in the kitchen. Suddenly the room grew quiet. Then, as everyone looked at Kate, they all started talking at once.

Kate felt uncomfortable, as though reliving her first day at Spirit Lake School. Then she'd been left out, afraid and alone. Now Kate tried to push that feeling aside. She remembered the way they'd kept Anders' party a secret.

My birthday's tomorrow, Kate thought. All week she'd watched Mama. Yet Kate had never sensed that her mother was getting ready. Not once did Kate sniff the aroma of a freshly baked cake. With Papa gone and the new baby coming, Mama seemed to have all she could handle.

In the next moment Kate forgot about her big day. She and Erik had to tell Swensons they once again had found nothing.

Josie looked white and desperate. "Only twenty-four hours left to search," she said. "After that, Papa has to go to Minneapolis."

And after that the loan shark comes, thought Kate.

The next morning Kate woke to her thirteenth birthday. *Will anyone do something special?* she wondered.

At the breakfast table no one wished Kate happy birthday. "Do you remember what day this is?" she asked.

Tina looked at Kate as though she didn't understand. Lars blew his nose. Anders got up to help himself to another piece of toast. And Mama stood at the cookstove. Still fighting a cold, she seemed to not hear.

Someone should remember, thought Kate, trying to ignore her hurt. *Maybe they need a hint.* "It's a nice January day," she said.

"Oh? You think so?" asked Mama.

"Not very cold. Seems like a special day," answered Kate.

But Mama kept stirring whatever was in her kettle.

"Does this seem like a special day to you?" asked Kate, looking around.

Tina shrugged, her eyes wide. Lars coughed into his napkin. Anders heaped butter on his toast.

Finally Kate gave up. *It's bad enough if the others don't re-*

member. But how can my own mother forget? It had been an awful month for Mama, but just the same—

Then Kate remembered. "This is the last day," she said. "The last day for finding Mr. Swenson's ring." When she thought about Swensons losing their farm, her birthday didn't matter at all.

Anders stood up and walked without a crutch. "I'm going over there now," he said. "I've thought of more places to look."

Near the door, he turned back to Kate. "You'll come after chores, won't you? You can walk faster than me anyway. Maybe you'll catch up."

As Kate hurried out to the barn, Anders set off on the trail now broken by horses, sleighs, and people walking. In the barn Kate went to the sheep pen and sank her fingers deep into their heavy coats. *Baaaa!* they welcomed.

When she patted Clover, Kate realized she and the cow had become friends.

Today Kate hurried through the milking, wanting to spend all the time she could at Josie's. As soon as she finished chores, Kate hurried to her room to change clothes. There she brushed out her hair. Unbraided, it fell down her back, thick and shiny. Gathering it together, Kate tied her hair with a ribbon instead of taking time for braids.

As she went outside, the crisp January air felt good on her cheeks. Kate breathed deeply. In the morning sunlight the snow glistened with thousands of diamonds. The walk through the woods seemed special and wonderful, like a gift prepared for her. Yet one thought stayed with her: *If only we could find the ring*.

When Kate reached Josie's, Mrs. Swenson let her in. For a moment Kate stood there, just inside the kitchen. As she hung her coat on a peg by the door, she felt the warmth of the cookstove. Yet something seemed different. The house sounded too quiet for a family of nine children.

Then Mrs. Swenson smiled, and Becca held out a corn-husk doll. Taking Kate's hand, the little girl led her past the stairs leading upward. When they entered the other room, noise exploded around Kate. "Surprise! Surprise!"

Anders jumped up from behind one chair. Erik and Stretch came from behind another. Josie and Maybelle popped out from under the table, while other children seemed to spill into the room.

Then someone began singing "Happy Birthday." Kate stood on the threshold, feeling as if she were going to cry.

"We did it, huh?" Josie laughed. "We really surprised you!"

Kate laughed with her. "You surprised me, all right!"

Josie grinned. "You're so good at solving mysteries, we were afraid you'd figure out this one!"

Kate looked around the room. For the first time she saw a big chocolate birthday cake on the table. In spite of all that had happened, did Mrs. Swenson bake the cake to help Mama?

Then Kate heard a noise in the kitchen. A moment later Mama and Tina, Lars, and Mrs. Lundgren appeared.

"Mama?" Kate asked, unable to believe what she was seeing.

Mama's smile lit even her eyes. "As soon as you left the house, Mrs. Lundgren gave us a ride. We took the longer road around so you wouldn't see."

Reaching out, Mama hugged Kate. "Happy birthday, little colleen."

Kate blinked. Mama hadn't forgotten. She even remembered Daddy O'Connell's special name. So this was what everyone had been planning!

Soon Anders and Erik started the games. Yet as much as she wanted to have fun, Kate couldn't push aside the scared look in Josie's eyes. *How can they have a party for me right now?* Kate wondered. *If they lose the farm, this is the last time we'll be here.*

Whenever Kate looked toward Mrs. Swenson, the kind woman smiled. Yet Kate felt sure the smile covered worry.

After two games Kate said, "Let's spread out and all of us search again. With this many looking, someone might find the ring."

But when they came back together again, no one had found even one clue. Though she tried to smile, Kate could barely eat her cake.

When the party was over, Maybelle was the first to leave. Kate wasn't sorry. At the same time she felt puzzled. More than that, she hated herself for being suspicious.

While eating, Kate had looked at everyone's hands. Maybelle's were small, but so were the hands of some of the other girls. Were any of them small enough to fit the fingerprints on the box? Kate wasn't sure. But she did know one thing. No one had a coat with the kind of button she'd found.

One by one, the partygoers drifted away. As the outside door swung open, Kate saw Lutfisk sitting on the path, waiting for Anders. Then Mrs. Lundgren took Mama and Lars and Tina home. Soon after, Stretch went outside. Through a window Kate saw him splitting wood.

Mrs. Swenson poked her head through the doorway. "Josie, watch Becca while I go out to the barn. She's drawing on a slate in the kitchen."

Looking absentminded, Josie nodded. "Only a few more hours to find the ring," she said to Kate, Anders, and Erik as they sat in the large open room. "If Papa doesn't sell that ring tomorrow, we lose the farm."

Kate's heart felt as if it were being squeezed. "Let's go over everything that happened," she said. "Maybe we can figure out something we've missed."

"I don't understand how that ring could disappear twice," said Erik. "Especially with such a large family."

Josie agreed. "One of my brothers and sisters is always here."

"And so is Stretch!" Anders declared. "Stretch took the ring."

"No, he *didn't!*" said Kate.

"I'm sure he did!" Anders stood up. It seemed strange seeing him without crutches. "How could it be anyone but Stretch?" he demanded, his voice growing louder.

"I believe in him," said Kate.

"So do I," chimed in Erik. "He's trying to make good."

As Erik spoke, Kate realized the strangeness of it all. She still felt the pain of Anders not trusting her. *Is that how Stretch hurts inside? Is that why he says he'll give up?*

Kate wanted to take his side. "Stretch has changed," she said. "Why do you blame him?"

"If someone's going to take something, he has to have a reason," Anders told her.

"Well?" demanded Kate. "What's his reason?"

Anders thought for a moment. "He wants those things."

"Wants a ring he couldn't wear around here?" asked Kate. "What would he do with it?"

"Sell it," Anders answered promptly.

Kate shook her head. "That's not a good enough reason."

"Kate's right," Erik broke in. "You don't have proof."

"Listen," said Anders. "In order to take something, a person has to have the opportunity. So who's had plenty of opportunity? Stretch!"

Just then Kate caught a movement back of Anders. A movement near the door to the kitchen. What was it?

Kate jumped up and ran to the doorway. Poking her head into the kitchen, she looked around. Becca sat there, drawing on the slate.

Turning back, Kate gazed up the stairs. Nothing there either.

"Spooks got you, Kate?" Anders asked.

Kate shrugged and returned to the large open room. Sitting down on the floor, she leaned back against the shelves next to the kitchen door.

But her uneasiness wouldn't go away. She had seen something. A shadow. That shadow had slipped past the door.

20

Lutfisk Meets Calico

As Kate thought about the shadow, Anders went back to his idea.

"A person who takes something needs the opportunity," he said. "The person has to be able to do it."

"Right," drawled Erik. "And we all know Stretch had the opportunity. But that doesn't make him guilty."

"What we have to figure out is who else had the opportunity." Kate was thinking out loud.

"So instead of just blaming Stretch, let's remember who was here when the ring disappeared," said Erik. "And who could have made it reappear."

For a time the room was quiet. Finally Kate broke the silence. "I saw the ring the day after we brought the food."

"How many of us were here that day?" asked Erik.

Kate and Erik looked at each other, then at Anders and Josie. "All of us," Kate answered. "Plus Maybelle."

"And Stretch," said Anders.

Erik turned to Kate. "When did you leave the buckle for your ski?"

"That same day," answered Kate.

"So all of us were here," said Erik.

"Plus Maybelle," added Kate, though she felt strangely uneasy.

"And Stretch," said Anders.

"Now when did the ring show up again?" Erik asked Josie.

"We don't really know," she answered. "We just know when I found it next to that chair leg."

"And when it disappeared again," said Erik.

No one needed to ask the question.

"All of us were here then too!" Anders exclaimed.

"Plus Maybelle." Yet Kate's heart felt heavy. Though she didn't like the other girl, Kate didn't want to believe Maybelle would steal something. Especially from Josie's family.

"And don't forget Stretch," Anders reminded them. "He's been here all the time, like Josie and her brothers and sisters."

Just then Kate wondered if she heard a noise on the stairs. She listened, but no sound came.

"It's Stretch, I tell you!" Anders spoke boldly. "I'm sure he's guilty."

Kate looked at Anders, wondering why he felt so ready to blame the tall thin boy. Maybe if her brother had talked with Stretch the way she and Erik had, Anders wouldn't feel that way.

Just then Kate glanced beyond her brother, and caught a quick movement. Jumping up, she hurried to the window. As she looked out, someone darted around the corner of the house.

Running to the kitchen door, Kate flung it open, tore down the steps, and circled the house. It was too late. Whoever had been there was gone.

Lutfisk still waited outside and followed Kate back to the kitchen door. When she reached the top step, Kate turned to him. "Sit, Lutfisk. Stay."

Lutfisk sat, and Kate felt good about his growing willingness to obey her. But as she opened the door, Josie's kitten bounded out from behind the cookstove.

Suddenly a blur of hair tore up the steps. Brushing past Kate, Lutfisk raced into the kitchen.

Calico hissed and fled into the other room. With a "Woof!" Lutfisk streaked after her. Kate followed the dog.

The kitten leaped into Josie's arms, with Lutfisk only a moment behind. The dog circled Josie, then jumped up. Calico sprang to the floor.

Before Josie could grab her, the kitten tore past Anders. Erik reached down, trying to catch her, but Calico darted between his legs. Erik whirled. In that instant the kitten disappeared.

Lutfisk slid to a halt and cocked his head.

Anders stared at him, then started to laugh. "Lose your victim, old boy?"

His tongue hanging out, Lutfisk seemed to listen. Yet he looked as puzzled as Kate felt.

"Where did Calico go?" she asked.

Even Lutfisk seemed confused. Standing in the middle of the floor, he tipped his head from side to side.

Then he lowered his nose to the floor and sniffed. Passing behind Erik, Lutfisk followed Calico's trail across the room. Near the shelves by the kitchen door, the dog dropped to his belly. For a moment he stayed there, his body tense.

Then, resting his mouth on his front paws, Lutfisk wiggled forward. Close to the wall, he pushed his nose into the narrow space beneath the bottom shelf. "Woof!" he barked.

When Anders called him, Lutfisk refused to leave.

"That's strange," said Kate. "Lutfisk always does what you ask."

"Always," said Anders, a frown creasing his forehead. But instead of going to the dog and forcing him to obey, Anders sat down where he could watch Lutfisk. "I can't figure out what's going on."

Kate also watched the dog. A moment later she jumped up. "Do you see what I see?" Kneeling beside Lutfisk, she took hold of his collar and tried to pull him back.

Lutfisk growled.

Kate wasn't going to be put off. "Get him, will you, Anders?"

As Anders dragged Lutfisk aside, Kate flopped down in the dog's place. For the first time she wondered if the dark space between the bottom shelf and the floor was more than a shadow.

Erik dropped down beside her.

Lying on her stomach, Kate slid her hand into the small space.

Reaching as far as she could, Kate felt along the wall. Her fingers found what she thought she'd seen—a small opening just large enough for a kitten. An opening large enough for an adult hand to slide through.

"Here, kitty!" she called. "Here, Calico. Kitty, kitty, kitty!"

When Calico did not appear, Kate turned back. "You call her, Josie."

"Just a minute," said Anders. "I'll hold Lutfisk."

As Anders pulled the dog farther away, Kate saw one beady eye and a small paw appear in the opening.

Josie took Kate's spot and called several times. Calico would not leave her hiding place. Finally Josie moved back.

"She'll come out when she's hungry," said Erik.

Kate wasn't ready to give up. "Where do you suppose that hole goes?"

"Curious Kate!" Anders hooted. "That's what we'll call you!"

The way Anders sounded, he was back to his old self. Though Kate wouldn't admit it, his teasing almost felt good. *Does he trust me again?* she wondered. It had helped to have Anders there when someone entered the barn. But they still didn't know who that person was.

Kate tossed her head. "Awful Anders, you mean!"

Her brother pushed back his shock of blond hair. His lips parted in a lopsided grin. "Yup, we'll call you curious Kate!"

Ignoring Anders, Kate flopped down on her stomach again. Once more, she reached under the bottom shelf. This time she put her hand, then her arm, inside the hole and felt around. On the other side of the wall was a floor.

Scrunching forward, Kate turned her hand palm up. Wiggling her fingers as far as she could go, she felt a small piece of wood along the inside of the wall. About an inch wide, the wood seemed four or five inches long.

"Aha!"

Still reaching upward, Kate moved her fingers across the wood. In its center she felt the head of a nail. The nail gave Kate an idea. Often a twirling piece of wood held a door shut, providing a lock of sorts.

Moving her fingers to the top of one side, Kate pushed on

the wood. Sure enough, the small piece moved. Again Kate pushed.

Several times she tried. But the piece moved no farther. Feeling puzzled, Kate finally sat back.

"What's there?" asked Erik.

"A piece of wood. It twists on a nail like something to keep a door closed. It moved a little, but it's stuck."

"Let me try," he offered.

Getting down on his stomach, Erik reached inside the hole as Kate had done. Kate stood back, watching. As Erik's arm moved, she knew he was pushing down on the wood. In that instant a shelf in front of Kate quivered.

"Hey! You did something!" she exclaimed.

Erik glanced up. "Did that shelf move, or am I imagining things?"

"It moved all right!" Anders told him. "Maybe the shelves are nailed to a door!"

"Maybe," said Erik. "But if you're right, the door's been closed a long time."

His arm muscles tensed as he pressed again on the small piece of wood. "Here we go!"

Slowly the shelves swung forward into the room.

21

Footsteps Through the Snow

"*It is* a door!" Kate yelped.

While she and Anders took hold of the shelves, Erik gripped the hand hold at the bottom and kept pulling.

Creee-e-e-a-a-k! The door squeaked loudly as though long unused. When it stood open as far as it could go, Erik jumped up. All of them peered into the darkness behind the shelves.

Claws clicked against the wood floor. A ball of fur jumped out. Calico leaped into Josie's arms.

Lutfisk barked. Anders grabbed the dog's collar and held him until he settled down. As Anders let go again, Lutfisk sniffed his way into the yawning hole.

"He's showing us where to go!" exclaimed Josie.

Lighting a candle, Kate set it in a holder and brought the small flame to the entrance. Holding out the candle, she stepped into the darkness.

Anders followed close behind, peering over Kate's shoulder. Erik and Josie crowded in.

"Look at that!" Josie pointed to the huge timbers at either side of the entrance.

"We're going through a log wall," said Anders. "Maybe it was a window, and someone changed it to a door."

Kate saw what he meant. The wall was almost a foot deep, the same width as the doorway leading into the kitchen.

Inside the secret space Kate turned around. The room was narrow, probably three feet wide at most. But it was also long, extending from near the kitchen door, behind the chimney, and over to the logs of the outside wall.

On the side opposite the shelf-door, the wall was built of wide, upright boards. Those boards looked new and unweathered when compared with the logs.

Holding up the candle, Kate looked at the ceiling. Part of it seemed to be the underside of steps leading up. On the side near the kitchen door, the ceiling was only a foot above the floor. Where Kate stood, the ceiling reached above her head. On the far end, it evened out at the height of the second floor. Even a tall man could stand there.

"Well, that explains one mystery!" exclaimed Josie, still holding her kitten out of Lutfisk's reach. "At least we know where Calico's been hiding."

"But there's something we *don't* know," answered Kate. "Where's your papa's ring? And the buckle for my ski?"

Once more Kate held out the candle and gazed up and down the walls. The room seemed empty.

The others looked just as disappointed as Kate felt. It'd be fun having a secret place. There were all kinds of ways they could use it. Yet they hadn't solved the mystery of the missing ring.

Erik felt around the sides of the small room, pressing here and there for a secret panel. Anders checked the wooden floor. Josie held Calico away from the dog. Finally Josie and Erik gave up and left the little room.

Then Kate noticed Lutfisk. After sniffing his way around, he stopped near the entrance. Dropping to his belly, the dog rested his head on his paws.

As Anders left the room, he called Lutfisk. "Here, boy!" But the dog refused to move.

"Lutfisk!" Anders ordered again.

The dog yipped, wiggled forward a few inches on his belly, then stopped.

Still inside the secret room, Kate waited for Lutfisk to obey. "What's the matter with him?"

Anders slapped his leg. "C'mon, boy. You can't get by with that."

Lutfisk snuffled his nose closer to the wall.

Puzzled, Kate kneeled down on the floor next to the dog. Then she saw what she'd missed before. Something bright. Something almost hidden in the darkness. In a crack near the door there was something shiny. The dog's nose pointed right to it!

Tugging Lutfisk's collar, Kate pulled him back just a bit. Sure enough, she was right!

Setting the candle holder on the floor, Kate reached forward and slid her fingers into the narrow crack. Out came a small round object.

"Papa's ring!" shrieked Josie. In the light of the candle the diamonds and rubies sparkled.

Anders grinned at Kate. "Pretty good for a dog, huh?"

Kate grinned back and dug deeper. Next she found the buckle for her ski. Clutching the buckle and ring, she put them on the low table near the shelves.

Josie's eyes glowed. "We can pay for the farm!"

"Just in time!" exclaimed Kate. Relief washed over her like a giant wave. "Tomorrow your father can go to Minneapolis."

"I'll go find him," said Josie, and started for the door. She almost crashed into her mother.

When Mrs. Swenson heard the news, she threw up her hands and rushed out, "Henry! Henry! We can make the payment in time!"

Soon she returned with Mr. Swenson. As Josie told him everything, her father's expression changed from shock, to relief, to joy. Twice he tried to ask questions and could not. Quiet tears wet his roughened cheeks. When at last he could speak, he simply said, "Thanks be to God!"

Erik and Anders showed Mr. Swenson the secret room, then closed the door. In the shadow beneath the bottom shelf, the hole once more disappeared.

"All someone had to do was slide the ring through," Erik

explained. "It lodged in the crack behind."

"This used to be a one-room log house," Mr. Swenson told them. "The people before us added the kitchen. Maybe that's when they made the secret room."

In spite of the celebration, Kate felt uneasy. "We still don't know who did it," she said. "Who pushed the buckle and ring through the hole? And who took the ring out again?"

A moment later, Kate answered her own question. "It can't be Maybelle. She'd never hide the ring here."

"That leaves Stretch," said Anders.

"Nay," said Mr. Swenson, and his wife nodded agreement. "It's not Stretch. But whoever it is had to be able to reach the ring. I hid it high on those shelves."

Then Kate remembered something. "We still have a clue we haven't figured out. The smudges on those boxes. If they're small fingerprints, who made them?"

In that moment Kate noticed the quiet. No longer was Stretch splitting wood outside the window.

Josie jumped up. "Uh-oh! I forgot I'm supposed to watch Becca. Where is she?" Running out, Josie found the three-year-old in the kitchen.

Following Josie into the large room, Becca walked over to the low table. She pointed to the buckle. "Pretty," she said. Then she picked up the ring. "Pretty," she said again.

"That's right," agreed Josie. "It's pretty. Put it back on the table."

But Kate was noticing Becca's fingers. *Small. Small enough for the prints on the boxes? Could it be?*

In that moment Becca held up the ring. The fading sunlight caught the gold, diamonds, and rubies.

"Pretty." Becca closed her chubby fist around the ring and carried it over to the shelves. Dropping to her knees, Becca reached under the bottom shelf and pushed the ring through the hole.

"Did you see *that*?" asked Kate.

Josie had already reached the three-year-old. "Did you do that before?" Josie asked.

Slowly Becca nodded. Her bottom lip quivered.

"I can't believe it!" Josie exclaimed. "All the times we looked for that ring!"

Becca stared at Josie, her eyes bright with tears.

"And you took it, Becca?"

Ducking her head, Becca let out a long wail. She reached out for her mother.

Mrs. Swenson took the little girl in her arms. "Josie's right," she said to Becca. "You mustn't take things that don't belong to you." Mrs. Swenson started toward the kitchen. "Mama needs to have a talk with you. Yah, sure."

As she reached the door, Mrs. Swenson turned back. "Where was Stretch going so fast? I saw him running toward the woods. I called, but he didn't come back."

Erik looked at Anders. "He heard you, Anders." Erik's voice sounded tight with anger.

"He heard you and ran," said Kate. "Ran away!"

"Stretch was here," said Becca in a small voice. "He here when you mad."

Anders stared at the little girl as though suddenly realizing what he'd done.

"Mr. Swenson asked us to help Stretch," Erik went on. "We helped him all right! We accused him of something he didn't do. We helped him give up!"

Anders wiped his hand across his face as though trying to push away what he saw.

Shadows, thought Kate as she glimpsed the pain in her brother's eyes. *Anders accusing Stretch for something he didn't do.*

"I was wrong," said Anders, his voice low and ashamed.

Watching him, Kate wondered about something. *Have I done the same thing with Maybelle? From the moment I met Maybelle, I didn't trust her. Was that wrong? Or am I uneasy for a reason?*

Now Anders struggled to his feet. "What can I do? I've got to tell Stretch I'm sorry."

"Let's all look for him," answered Kate. With all her heart she wanted to make things right for Stretch.

Erik grabbed his coat. "We've got to find him now!"

Kate agreed. "Before he's gone for good!"

"I'll go," said Mr. Swenson. "I'll hitch up the horses."

"If you take the road, we'll look on the paths where you can't drive," said Erik. "Sounds as if Stretch started through the woods."

"You can't run on that ankle," Mrs. Swenson warned Anders as all of them pulled on their coats.

"Kate can't go alone," Anders told her. "It'll soon be dark. She's afraid of the woods at night."

For once Kate didn't argue with him. Though she'd never admitted it to Anders, it was true.

"I'll go as far as I can," said Anders, pulling Papa's old work boots over his woolen socks. "We'll stick together."

As they went out, the winter sun was low in the sky. Long shadows stretched away from the trees and bushes. Erik took the lead, heading into the woods on the path where Mrs. Swenson saw Stretch disappear. Anders followed, with Kate and Josie close behind.

Soon Erik pointed down to footsteps in the snow. "That's him!"

For a time it was easy to follow the tracks. Not many people had come this way. But the boot prints were far apart, as if Stretch were running. Was there any hope of catching him?

To Kate's surprise Anders kept up. As they reached a fork in the trail, Erik stopped. He and Anders studied the snow.

They had come through the woods on a less traveled path. Now they needed to veer left or right. On both of those wider trails the snow was beaten down, crisscrossed by people, horses, and sleighs. An icy crust had formed around many of the prints.

Erik walked six or seven yards in one direction, looking at the snow. Coming back, he tried the other trail. Finally he shook his head. "Too many people."

"We need to split up," said Kate. "Take *both* ways."

Erik nodded. "But you and I are the only ones Stretch will trust, even a little. So one of us better go each way. Maybe he'll talk to us."

Anders looked at Kate. "Let's take the trail to our house. If Stretch goes to his family's farm, he'll head that way."

Erik agreed. "And Josie and I will take the other direction.

There's an old log cabin down that path. If Stretch knows about it, he might head there."

As they started off, Anders set the pace. His long legs stretched out, and Kate had to run to keep up.

"We've got to hurry," Anders called to her. "Stretch had a good head start."

Kate tried to move faster. The path was uneven with boot prints edged with ice.

Farther on, Anders turned back again. "He'll get away for good!" But a moment later, Anders cried out.

As Kate rounded a bend, she found him rolling on the ground.

"Ow, ow, ow!" he moaned, clutching his ankle. "I stepped on it wrong."

Catching up, Kate kneeled down beside him. She felt scared all the way through. How would Anders get home? And how could they ever catch Stretch?

"What should I do?" she asked.

"It feels like I got stabbed." Anders spoke between clenched teeth.

A tight knot formed in Kate's stomach. For a long moment she stared at her brother, feeling helpless. "If only we had one of those newfangled telephones!" she said.

Anders hooted. "Lot of good that'd do out here in the woods."

"I could call and get help. I could call Stretch's farm and see if he's there."

"Kate, talk sense!" Anders said sharply. "You have to keep going."

"Go on?" Kate looked around. The woods seemed eerie in the half-light that lingered before the sun slipped over the horizon.

"You don't have any choice."

"Go all by myself?" Kate stared at the underbrush. Here and there dead brown leaves fluttered in the wind. What animals lurked behind the brush where she couldn't see? "It'll be dark soon," she said.

"Stretch will get away," Anders told her. "He'll leave the area, and we'll never see him again. You're the one who told me how awful that would be!"

Once more Kate gazed at the woods and the long, dark shadows. Her dread of those shadows rushed up, real and frightening. When she spoke again, her voice trembled. "I can't do it, Anders." She stumbled over the words.

22

The Dangerous Chase

"You have to," Anders said firmly. "You have to keep going."

"I can't," said Kate, staring at the darkening woods. "I can't do it alone."

Anders sighed. "You'll be all right. The bogeyman won't get you."

"The bogeyman?" Kate's heart leaped into her throat again. She'd been wondering about the wild animals.

"Well, what is it you're scared of? Stop thinking about yourself."

"I'm not just thinking about myself!"

"Aren't you, scaredy-cat?" His voice goaded Kate, making her more angry than scared.

But then she wondered about Anders. "What will happen to you?"

"I'll make it somehow. Just help me up."

As Kate grasped his arm, Anders struggled to his good foot. "Get me a stick," he said.

When Kate found a stout branch along the path, he told her, "Now get going. You have to catch Stretch."

With one last look at Anders, Kate started off, half running, half walking. The snow on the path was still pitted with prints of all kinds. Wherever the woods opened to the sun, those prints were stiff with ice. The uneven edges made it hard going.

Once Kate looked back. The trees and undergrowth hid Anders from view.

In that instant a bird whirred up in front of her. Kate jerked to a halt, shuddering with surprise. Just an old grouse, she knew. But telling herself that didn't stop her trembling.

All around her, the woods seemed alive. Somewhere behind Kate, something rustled. Then she heard another sound—a scruffy, scuffling sound.

A bear? A bear in the woods?

Kate fled, running until she could no longer breathe and had to slow down. *Sarah Livingston told me there'd be bears.* It made no difference that her friend Sarah lived in Minneapolis, and Kate lived here. Sarah knew.

As Kate caught her breath, she heard the sound again. As though an animal walked on the snow's icy crust. Coming closer and closer.

Filled with panic, Kate turned in the direction of the sound. A short distance away a squirrel scampered across the snow.

Kate felt foolish. Then she remembered. *Bears hibernate in winter. They're sleeping now.*

The woods silent around her, Kate stood there. But she couldn't push away her fear. Again she started out, walking as fast as she could. Soon the sun would edge over the horizon. Soon it would be dark.

She'd come to know the woods during the day. Sometimes the woods even seemed a friend. But at night the animals came out. Were they peering at her with their little beady eyes?

I'm alone, Kate told herself. *What's behind that bush—the one right near the trail?*

I'm all alone in these awful woods. Kate's steps slowed. *But am I?*

"Stop thinking about yourself," Anders had said. Kate knew he was right. She felt ashamed.

Shadows. Some are real. Some I imagine. But there's a real shadow in Stretch's life. Being accused of something he didn't do.

Then Kate remembered Mama's verse: "Casting all your care upon him, for he careth for you." As Kate broke into a run, she started to pray. "Jesus, you cared so much. You even died on the cross. You did something really hard for me. Will you help me do something hard for Stretch?"

Once, far ahead, Kate thought she saw the tall thin boy. Was it Stretch? She called out his name, but no answer came. Then a cramp in her side forced her to a walk.

As Kate reached the top of the hill near the farmhouse, the red-orange sun slipped behind the trees. In the fading light Kate looked across the yard toward the granary and barn. "The sheep!" Kate muttered to herself. "They're still outside!"

As she started toward the pasture, long shadows darkened the sides of buildings. Spying a tall thin shadow along the granary, Kate stopped.

What was it? A tree?

The shadow did not move.

I imagined something, Kate told herself, and hurried on.

As she neared the barn, more shadows darkened the log wall. Kate shivered, remembering the night one of those shadows moved.

Swallowing her fear, she forced herself on. As she drew closer to the barn, a darker shadow separated from the rest. A slender shadow, not much taller than Kate.

The shadow slid sideways, across the log wall. Then it slipped around the corner of the barn closest to the wagon track.

Did I imagine it? For a split second Kate stood there, wondering. She remembered the times Anders and Erik had warned her: "Don't jump into something you can't handle."

Then Kate knew. She hadn't imagined it!

She also felt sure of something else. *I know who the shadow is!*

In that instant, everything fell into place. Starting to run, Kate headed for the end of the barn farthest from the wagon track. Lifting the top rail, she climbed through the fence on that side.

Replacing the pine rail, she ran across the barnyard to the fence on the other side. Once more, she lifted the top rail and slipped through. Reaching the far pasture, she looked around.

On the other end of the barn, near the wagon track, a dark shape pressed close to the wall. Face turned away, back toward Kate, the person leaned out, peering around the far corner.

Kate crept forward slowly, quietly. Just before she reached the end of the barn, the person turned.

"Hi, Maybelle," Kate said quietly, feeling she had known all along.

A surprised look crossed the other girl's face.

Then Kate saw Maybelle's coat. Older than the one she usually wore, this coat had black buttons. Even in the fading light Kate saw a button missing.

"I thought so!" exclaimed Kate. "You're the one who took Wildfire from the barn. You've been riding her at night! Why? Just because you wanted your own way?"

Maybelle's look of surprise faded. She smiled. "I don't know what you're talking about, Kate," she said in the sweet voice Kate had learned not to trust.

"Yes, you do," Kate answered. "You know exactly what I'm talking about. And you're going to talk to Anders!"

"Anders?" Maybelle tossed her head, and her long thick hair swung about her shoulders. "If it comes to that, Anders will believe *me*, not you!"

"It'll come to that," Kate growled. "And he's my brother. He'll believe me!" Reaching deep into her coat pocket, Kate felt the button she'd found.

Maybelle sniffed. Her lips parted, as if to answer. But then she glanced beyond Kate.

"Look!" she exclaimed.

Unwilling to be tricked, Kate refused to turn. She knew that only pasture lay behind her. A pasture surrounded by a fence that enclosed the sheep.

"You can't fool me!" she told Maybelle.

But Maybelle hushed her. "I'm not trying!" For once her voice sounded sharp.

Then Kate saw the fear in the other girl's eyes. "What's the matter?" Kate whispered.

"See along the fence?" asked Maybelle.

Kate whirled, facing the pasture Papa Nordstrom had been

clearing. Tree stumps rose from the snow, dotting the field. Along the far side, the woods grew close to the fence line.

There the sheep huddled, backs to the north wind. Heads down, they grazed on the long dead grass growing up around the stumps.

Just beyond the stumps crept a shadow. A shadow that moved toward the sheep. In the dusk that shadow looked like a large gray dog.

"Lutfisk?" Kate whispered, so afraid she could barely speak. But in the next instant she remembered how Anders trusted his dog with the sheep.

Then Kate knew. "It's a wolf."

Kate had never seen one, yet she knew.

23

Northern Lights

The fear clutching Kate's stomach moved into her throat. Her knees felt weak, as though she couldn't move.

Along the far side of the field, the gray shadow stopped and lifted its head. Then it moved on, once more creeping toward the sheep.

Kate knew she had no choice. In that moment her legs seemed to work. She ran forward and grabbed a loose rail from the top of the fence. Picking it up, she started toward the wolf.

The wolf paused, looked her way.

Kate froze. *What if he comes after me?*

Beyond the wolf, Kate saw something move. Another shadow? More wolves? Kate's breath caught in her throat.

Then one of the sheep bleated. *Baaaa!*

Two other sheep looked up. Kate glanced their way. They still huddled near the fence, clustering together, helpless.

From behind them came another movement.

In that instant Kate felt certain. Two more wolves, maybe three?

Kate's hands tightened on the rail. Step by step she started forward, holding the rail in front of her.

Once more the nearest wolf raised his head. He sniffed, as though catching her scent, and waited. Again Kate's knees felt weak. As she held the rail, her hands trembled.

Then Kate heard quick steps from behind. Someone grabbed the rail from her hands.

Whirling, Kate saw his face. "Stretch!"

The tall boy charged, holding the rail ahead of him.

The wolf closest to the sheep stopped, waited.

Stretch's long legs carried him across the snowy field.

Suddenly the nearest wolf dropped back, slinking away. The other wolves followed. Their gray bodies melted into the darker shadows of the woods.

Kate breathed deeply. She wanted to cry. Then she wanted to laugh. *All this time I've been afraid*, she thought. *Afraid of shadows. Afraid of howls. And the wolves are afraid of US!*

Stretch stayed between the woods and the sheep. Using the rail to guide them, he started the animals back toward Kate.

"You're *here*!" she cried, still feeling she couldn't think. "I was afraid I couldn't catch you."

"You wouldn't have," said Stretch. "I saw Maybelle heading toward your barn. I knew she was the one you're lookin' for. I thought, 'Anders he don't trust me. Why should I care about his horse?' "

"But you came back," said Kate. "Why?"

" 'Cause I knew you'd get the blame."

For a moment Stretch was silent, and Kate thought that was all. But when the tall boy spoke again, his voice was low, as if afraid to tell her.

"Remember the birthday party for Anders?" he asked.

Kate remembered, all right. She also remembered thinking that what she did would be important to Stretch.

"I ain't never seen anyone as mean as Maybelle," he said. "But you weren't mean to her. You acted as if it didn't matter."

"So you came back?" Again Kate felt like crying. "Thanks, Stretch." She wished she knew how to say more.

But then she saw his eyes, and knew she didn't have to. Stretch straightened his shoulders and walked tall.

As they neared the barn, Maybelle started to leave. Kate

broke into a run, circling around to cut her off. Maybelle changed directions, heading toward the rail fence back of the barn. She started to crawl through, then stopped.

Looking beyond Maybelle, Kate saw the path from the farmhouse. Erik ran their way. Not far behind came Anders, one arm around Josie's shoulder, his other hand on the stick Kate had given him. He hopped on one foot.

Erik seemed to know what had happened. Leaping into the pasture, he helped Stretch bring in the sheep. Kate kept Maybelle cornered between herself and Anders.

"I caught her here," Kate said when Anders came up. "She's the one who took Wildfire from the barn."

Maybelle smiled at Anders. "You don't really believe I'd do something like that, do you?"

Anders looked from one girl to the other.

"Maybelle's been riding Wildfire," said Kate.

"Anders, you know she's just talking. Kate makes things up."

"No, she doesn't," said Anders. His voice was quiet, but there was no mistaking the sound of it. "Kate isn't just talking. I believe her."

"It's her word against mine!" Maybelle's voice was no longer sweet.

Anders grinned. "I can trust Kate. She's my sister."

In that moment all of Kate's hurt fell away. Inside, she felt as if she were singing.

"You can't prove a thing," challenged Maybelle.

"I want to show you something," said Kate. Reaching deep inside her coat pocket, she found the button. Slowly she pulled it out.

Maybelle stared, but did not reach out for the button. As she looked toward Anders, she lifted her chin. "I was sure you wouldn't mind if I took Wildfire for a ride."

"I'm sure that I *would*!" Anders snapped. "And you better make sure it never happens again!"

As Maybelle slipped off into the shadows, Stretch and Erik brought the sheep close to the barn. Facing Anders, Stretch pulled himself even taller than usual. He seemed to grow two inches.

Anders spoke before Stretch could. "Thanks for saving our sheep," he said.

Kate had seldom heard her brother so humble.

Anders reached out his hand. "I'm sorry, Stretch. I'm sorry for the way I treated you."

Anger flashed across the older boy's face. Lifting his head, Stretch looked proud. For a moment he seemed to debate with himself. Then slowly, without words, he extended his hand.

Looking straight into each other's eyes, Anders and Stretch shook hands.

It was Josie who broke the tension. "Our farm is safe. Your sheep are all right. And Wildfire will be!" Relief filled Josie's laugh. "But I suppose there'll be another mystery."

"I suppose." Anders grinned at Kate. "Before Papa gets home, do you think?"

"I don't know," she answered. "What else can happen around here?" She looked at Erik.

"Plenty!" he exclaimed. "Until you moved here, we never had one mystery to solve!"

A moment later Mr. Swenson drew up with his horses. As he looked toward Stretch and Anders, a relieved smile came to his face. Giving a wave, he headed for home.

The rest of them went to the Windy Hill farmhouse and sat down to Mama's warm supper.

Later, when Josie, Erik, and Stretch started for home, they came back. "Come outside," Erik told Kate and Anders. "We want to show you something."

Together they walked to the edge of the steep hill. There they could see far around. Erik pointed up.

Kate's gaze followed his hand. In the northern sky, long white shafts of light stretched from the horizon upward. The light pulsed through the darkness, seeming to move and grow.

Kate stood there, filled with wonder. "What is it?" she asked.

"Northern lights," replied Erik softly, and even Anders was quiet.

For a time they watched the glowing beams. Gradually the color changed to pale pink, then blue and light green.

As they started back to the house, Anders, Josie, and Stretch walked ahead, talking. Erik and Kate fell behind.

When Kate looked up, she felt surprised to see Erik watching her.

"Happy birthday, Kate," he said.

"Thanks," she answered, feeling strange. So much had happened since the party, she'd forgotten about her birthday.

But Erik was still watching her. "You're different, Kate," he said, his voice low.

"Different?" She drew back, wondering what he meant. "Awful?" She felt afraid to ask.

"Different from other girls. Better." For a long moment Erik looked at her. "Special. Very special."

Kate smiled, knowing he'd given her one of the nicest presents she could receive.

"Thanks, Erik," she said again. The words weren't half enough, but Erik seemed to understand.

When he and Josie and Stretch started for home once more, Kate and Anders turned toward the Windy Hill farmhouse.

As Kate pushed open the door, the warmth and light of the kitchen reached out, seeming to welcome them. The shadows disappeared, melting away into the night, where they belonged.

Acknowledgments

Often I'm asked, "Lois, where do you get the ideas for your novels?"

I've discovered that ideas are everywhere. Yet I need to recognize which ones are good, which are unimportant, and which will help me shape the story I want to tell.

Countless people—more than I can possibly name—have added to my storehouse of ideas. Among these are the following individuals who gave long hours and detailed information: Shirley Anderson, Goodwin Branstad, Myrtle Carlson, Alwin and Imogene Christopherson, Maurice and Arleth Erickson, Edith Falat, Sarah Harmon, Robert and Jean Hinrichs, Herman and Alma Johnson, Gary and Jane Kaefer, Randy and Renee Klawitter, Henry Peterson, Ida Peterson, Roy and Grace Soderbeck, and Helen Tyberg.

Again I'm grateful to Mildred Hedlund for her help with Big Gust, to Eunice Kanne for her book *Big Gust: Grantsburg's Legendary Giant*, and to all the librarians at the public library in Grantsburg, Wisconsin.

Walter and Ella Johnson and Diane Brask offered their knowledge and love of northwest Wisconsin, as well as their time. My parents, Alvar and Lydia Walfrid, continue to answer my never-ending questions.

Jerry Foley, Penelope Stokes, and Terry White gave valuable

assistance with the manuscript. Charette Barta, Ron Klug, and the entire Bethany team provided editorial wisdom, support, and love.

Many individuals—Betty Coleman, Elaine Roub, and more than I can even guess—have helped in quiet and unseen ways. May their caring for me and you as readers be returned to them many times over.

From the time I begin thinking about a book through its early and final drafts, my husband and I talk about ideas. From his rich experience Roy offers suggestions, encouragement, and practical ways of saying, "Keep on in this work that you love." To him I once more give my heartfelt gratitude.

And finally, special thanks to Daniel Johnson, who reminds all of us that "God cares for *you!*"

THE VANISHING FOOTPRINTS

Adventures of the Northwoods

1. *The Disappearing Stranger*
2. *The Hidden Message*
3. *The Creeping Shadows*
4. *The Vanishing Footprints*
5. *Trouble at Wild River*
6. *The Mysterious Hideaway*
7. *Grandpa's Stolen Treasure*
8. *The Runaway Clown*
9. *Mystery of the Missing Map*

THE VANISHING FOOTPRINTS

Lois Walfrid Johnson

BETHANY HOUSE PUBLISHERS
MINNEAPOLIS, MINNESOTA 55438

Andrew Anderson number 3, Big Gust Anderson, Walfrid Johnson, Reverend Pickle, Charles Saunders, Peter Schyttner, and Oscar Thorssen lived in the Grantsburg/Trade Lake area of northwest Wisconsin in the early 1900s. All other characters are fictitious. Any resemblance to persons living or dead is coincidental.

Cover illustration by Andrea Jorgenson.

Copyright © 1991
Lois Walfrid Johnson
All Rights Reserved

Published by Bethany House Publishers
A Ministry of Bethany Fellowship, Inc.
6820 Auto Club Road, Minneapolis, Minnesota 55438

Printed in the United States of America

Library of Congress Cataloging-in-Publication Data

Johnson, Lois Walfrid.
    The vanishing footprints / Lois W. Johnson.
        p. cm. — (The Adventures of the northwoods ; bk. 4)
    Summary: Kate, Anders, and Erik try to solve the mystery of the stolen creamery checks.

    [1. Swedish Americans—Fiction. 2. Mystery and detective stories. 3. Christian life—Fiction.]
I. Title. II. Series: Johnson, Lois Walfrid. Adventures of the northwoods ; bk. 4.
PZ7.J63255Van 1991
[Fic]—dc20   91–15042
ISBN 1–55661–103–X   CIP
                                                                                  AC

To Daryl, Gail, and Jessica,
because you've discovered
the gift of reading
together.

LOIS WALFRID JOHNSON is the bestselling author of more than twenty books. These include *You're Worth More Than You Think!* and other Gold Medallion winners in the LET'S-TALK-ABOUT-IT STORIES FOR KIDS series about making choices. Novels in the ADVENTURES OF THE NORTHWOODS series have received awards from Excellence in Media, the Wisconsin State Historical Society, and the Council for Wisconsin Writers.

Lois has a great interest in historical mystery novels, as you may be able to tell! She and her husband, Roy, are the parents of a blended family and live in rural Wisconsin.

CONTENTS

1. Danger Ahead! 9
2. Trouble at Trade Lake 16
3. Going Fishing 23
4. Discovery! 30
5. Nighttime Search 37
6. Letter From Sweden 44
7. Accident! 51
8. Two Promises 58
9. The Mysterious Message 64
10. The Vanishing Footprints 72
11. Sounds From the Darkness 77
12. The Secret Room 85
13. More Bad News 91
14. The Butter Tub Disaster 97
15. Sunday Deadline 105
16. Thin Ice! 111
17. Lars's Question 118
18. The Lost Fiddle 123
19. Another Warning 129
20. Snatched From the Fire.........................135
21. Ride Into Fear 141
22. Bone-Chilling Surprises 149
Acknowledgments 157

1

Danger Ahead!

When Katherine O'Connell reached the crossroad, the snowy countryside sparkled with sunlight. Only minutes before, the cloudless sky seemed like Kate's world—warm and wonderful. But now a cold wind crept into her heart. Worry darkened her deep blue eyes.

I'll find Anders, she decided, flipping her long braid over her shoulder. *He'll know what to do.*

Ahead of Kate, the road led past a brickyard, then up a steep hill. On that January day in 1907 her brother and Erik Lundgren were harvesting ice for the Trade Lake Creamery. If Kate found them, maybe she could talk to Anders.

Just then two draft horses appeared at the top of the hill. Their large bodies strained forward into the harness. Huge blocks of ice filled the sleigh behind them.

A tall boy walked alongside, holding the reins. A warm cap covered his brown hair, but Kate recognized him and his horses, Queen and Prince.

"Erik!" she called.

A grin broke across his face. "Hi, Kate!"

As Queen and Prince started down the hill, they picked up speed. The load shifted. Heavy blocks of ice crashed against the front of the sleigh. A brace snapped, and a plank flew off. Ice tumbled onto the heels of the horses.

Queen snorted in terror. Prince leaped ahead.

Erik tugged on the reins. Leaning back, he pulled with all his strength. But the horses yanked him along. Hitting a patch of ice, he slid beside the sleigh.

Kate gasped. If Erik fell, he'd be dragged. The sleigh might even run over him.

In the next instant a rein snapped. Sensing her freedom, Queen tossed her head. A moment later the second rein snapped. Queen and Prince bolted, out of control.

Erik ran after them. But the horses flattened their ears and picked up speed. Without swerving, they headed straight toward Kate.

Her heart pounding, she stared at the runaways. Her feet felt frozen to the ground.

Help! she wanted to cry. But no sound came. Unable to think, she knew only that she'd be trampled.

"Kate!" Erik shouted.

As though from far away, she heard his voice, but panic held her motionless. The horses loomed closer, driven by fear.

"Kate! Get out of the way!"

To her surprise, her legs worked. Leaping out of the road, she tumbled into a mound of snow.

Seconds later, the horses thundered past. With the sleigh swaying behind, they headed for the village of Trade Lake.

"Runaway!" Erik shouted the warning.

As Kate pulled herself from the snow, Erik tore past, calling again. "Runaway!"

But the horses raced down the main street. Near Trader Carlson's store, people fled inside. At the creamery the team rounded the corner, still going full speed. The sleigh swung wide, skidding out, but Queen and Prince kept on. Then the creamery blocked Kate's view.

Stopping at the corner, Erik gazed up the road toward Mission Church. For a long moment he stood there. When he shook his head, Kate knew the horses must be out of sight.

Pulling off a mitten, Kate wiped the snow from her face. Her hand trembled. *Will I ever get used to living here?* she wondered.

Ten months before, her widowed mother had married Anders's father. Kate and Mama had moved from Minneapolis to northwest Wisconsin. There they had become part of the Nordstrom family of Papa, Anders, nine-year-old Lars, and five-year-old Tina. In Kate's new life there always seemed to be something that frightened her.

I don't want to be afraid, she thought now. Ever since she'd been here, things had gone wrong around Windy Hill Farm. In that third week of January, Papa Nordstrom worked far away in a logging camp. In two or three months Mama's baby would be born. And Lars? Off and on for several weeks he'd been sick. And the worst part of winter could still be ahead.

Bending down, Kate brushed snow from her coat and long stockings. *No matter what happens, I want to be*—She thought a moment. Brave seemed a strange word. *Courageous?* That seemed to fit some great hero, not her, Kate O'Connell, newly turned thirteen.

By the time Erik walked back to her, Kate stood as tall as her short height allowed. But her knees felt weak.

"You all right?" he asked, looking scared.

Kate nodded, still too shaken to speak. When at last she found her voice, she asked, "Are *you* all right?" She'd never seen Erik's face so white.

"Yup," he said, flexing his shoulders. "I'll be sore, but I'm fine. It wasn't fun seeing Queen and Prince head your way."

Kate shivered. "I was so scared I couldn't move. Thanks for yelling." Even now her voice trembled.

Erik gazed back up the hill. Blocks of ice lay scattered along the road.

"C'mon," he said at last. "Let's get some hot cocoa. You'll feel better." But he looked as though he needed encouragement himself.

When Kate and Erik reached the Trade Lake Creamery, the buttermaker stood in the doorway. "Your horses, weren't they, Erik? Did you get hurt?"

Erik shook his head.

"That's good. Could have been a bad one." Mr. Bloomquist

was young and short and stocky. As he leaned against the frame building, a friendly smile lit his face. "Better come in and warm up."

"Kate needs to," said Erik. "I'll go after my horses."

"Won't do you a bit of good," said the buttermaker. "By now they're most of the way home."

Erik sighed. "I suppose you're right." He still seemed unable to believe what had happened. "I lost the whole load. It shifted on that hill."

"You shouldn't be using that hill," said the buttermaker. "Usually the men avoid it." Then he seemed to notice Kate's trembling. "Are you hurt?"

Kate shook her head, but her teeth chattered.

"My horses almost ran her down," Erik explained.

"Like I said, you shouldn't be using that hill. Maybe that's what comes from accepting Fenton's bid. The creamery doesn't usually give the job of harvesting ice to a newcomer."

Again Mr. Bloomquist turned toward Kate. "Come in and get warm."

Kate followed Erik and the buttermaker into a large open room. On one side, farmers brought in their milk cans. The buttermaker separated the whole milk and kept the cream. Then the farmers took the skim milk back home with them.

Nearby, in the center of the room, was something that looked like a big wooden barrel resting on its side. Kate knew it must be the butter churn.

Beyond that, a man came through a doorway. Before the door swung shut, Kate noticed a one-foot wall.

"That's the cold room," Erik said, as though he'd guessed Kate's question. "The creamery uses the ice we harvest to cool cream and store butter."

Mr. Bloomquist led them into a smaller room with a large round tank on top of a high brick wall. Opening a door in the wall, Mr. Bloomquist threw in three-foot logs.

Through small holes in another door, Kate saw flickering flames. Pulling off her mittens, she held out her hands to warm them. As she felt the welcome heat, her usual curiosity returned. "What is it?" she asked Erik.

"The tank? A steam boiler. It heats water for the steam engine." He tipped his head toward a shiny bronze cylinder nearby. "Creamery uses steam for all its cleaning and power."

A few minutes later the buttermaker returned to the larger room, closing the door behind him. Erik reached for a glass jar he had set near the boiler. Unscrewing the lid, he offered the contents to Kate. "You first."

Kate's fingers felt warmer, just holding the jar filled with hot liquid. But then she tasted the cocoa. "It's sour!" she exclaimed, making a face.

Erik laughed, as though relieved to find something funny. "Sorry! It's been warming up all day. Now if it was up to Anders, he'd drink it anyway."

For a moment Kate thought about her stepbrother. Before Christmas he'd sprained his ankle. By now he was using that foot again. Yet Kate felt glad he wasn't around when the horses ran away. He might not have been able to escape.

Sitting down on the floor, Kate leaned back against the warm bricks. As her trembling stopped, she noticed small bottles and what looked like test tubes on a nearby desk. "What are those?" she asked.

Erik grinned. "You're feeling better, I can tell. Anders would call you Curious Kate."

"But I really want to know."

"Maybe it's a mystery you'll have to solve."

"Oh, come on. *You* tell me."

Erik laughed, but explained anyway. "When farmers bring in their cans of milk, the buttermaker uses those tubes to take samples. The higher the butterfat, the more we get paid for our cream."

The mention of money triggered a thought and Kate asked, "Did you know the cream checks were stolen last night?"

Erik's eyes no longer teased. "Heard about it when I came to work this morning. First time we ever missed a check."

"We need that money," said Kate, her voice low.

"So do we," answered Erik. "Every farmer does. Mighty hard not to get money we count on."

Kate sighed. That morning she'd walked three miles to pick

up her family's check and buy cloth. The baby Mama expected was getting bigger every day. Even Mama's largest dress stretched tight across her stomach.

And that wasn't all. Soon they'd need flannel to sew little clothes for the baby.

"I went to Gustafson's store," Kate said. "Everyone was talking about the stolen checks. They all said, 'Never before! We've never had such a robbery in northwest Wisconsin!' But it happened."

"The creamery will stop payment on the checks," Erik told her.

"And then what?" Kate wanted to know.

"They'll reissue them."

"What do you mean, *reissue* a check?" asked Kate.

"Write it out again. Trouble is, we have to wait till that happens. And there's something I don't understand. Why would someone steal *checks*? They can't cash 'em around here. If the thief tried, everyone would know who he is."

Standing up, Erik shrugged into his coat. "I have to get back to the lake."

"Can I come with you?" Kate asked. "I want to watch, and maybe I can talk to Anders."

As she pulled on her coat, she heard voices through the door into the larger room.

"I took care of the checks," someone said.

Kate strained to hear, but couldn't catch the quiet answer.

"I could write out new checks tonight." That was the first man speaking again. Then Kate heard only the word *ledger*.

"What's a ledger?" she whispered.

"A record book." Erik was listening too. "For keeping track of the cream farmers bring in."

"I got hold of Sheriff Saunders," the first voice went on. "He'll do everything he can."

"That's Andrew Anderson number 3 talking," Erik whispered.

"Number 3?" asked Kate.

"Because of all the Andrew Andersons. Helps us know which one. Shhh!"

Mr. Anderson's voice sounded heavy with worry. "The thief knew my routine. He knew what night of the month I made out checks and where I put them."

A chair scraped across the floor. As footsteps approached the door between the two rooms, Erik moved quickly through another door leading outside.

Kate followed him. "Who's Andrew Anderson number 3?" she asked when they were safely away from the building.

"You know him. Goes to our church. High forehead, long flowing beard."

As they reached the hill where the ice broke loose, Erik looked around. "Mr. Anderson used to be postmaster. Now he's secretary-treasurer of the creamery." Finding the plank from the sleigh, Erik set it at the side of the road.

"And secretary of the Trade Lake Fire Insurance Company?" For Kate it was all falling into place.

"Yup," Erik said. "Papa says Mr. Anderson is a good man and a careful manager. The creamery and insurance company have done well, mostly because of him."

On the other side of the hill, Kate and Erik left the road.

"You know what's really strange?" Erik continued. "No one even knew that Mr. Anderson had a hiding place for the checks. But the thief found them the one night of the month they were there."

Inside her mittens Kate's fingers clenched, just thinking how Mr. Anderson must feel. With all her heart she wanted to solve the robbery. Yet she knew that someone willing to steal from a creamery might be dangerous.

"If no one knows who took the checks—" Kate stopped, afraid to say what she thought.

But Erik finished for her. "The thief can steal from the creamery again."

2

Trouble at Trade Lake

*K*ate's stomach knotted. "He can steal any time he wants."

"Any time at all," answered Erik.

Kate didn't like that idea. It was bad enough not getting a check today. When *would* they get paid? All the farmers in the area depended on the income from the creamery.

"But you and Anders will get money for harvesting ice," she said.

"Maybe." Erik looked gloomy. "If the creamery can't pay the farmers, how can they pay us?"

Kate and Erik headed across a field partly cleared of trees. Horses and sleighs had packed down a trail to Little Trade Lake.

Erik started walking faster. "I need to hurry. Mr. Fenton's not going to like it that I lost a load of ice."

Soon they passed through a stand of pine trees. Beyond that, deep snow made it difficult to tell where the shore ended and the lake began.

At the center of the bay a patch of cleared ice sparkled in the afternoon sunlight. A sleigh and team of horses waited near a hole of black water.

On the far side of the opening, someone had marked squares

in the ice. A man was using a long saw to cut the squares into blocks.

"It looks like a checkerboard," said Kate. "But it's also like a cake. How do they get out the first piece?"

Erik grinned. "Curious Kate again." Just the same, he told her. "They push the block down and shove it under the ice."

A moment later his grin disappeared. "Well, wish me luck with Mr. Fenton!"

As Kate waited well out of the way, Erik started toward a man holding a long pole. Using the point on the end, the man pushed blocks of ice through a channel of dark water.

LeRoy Fenton, thought Kate. The day before he'd hired Erik and Anders to fill in for men who were sick.

Kate spotted her brother nearby. A shock of blond hair stuck out from beneath a knitted cap. His broad shoulders stretched the seams of his jacket. With boots planted on the edge of the hole, he held out large tongs.

A man wearing a red and black plaid mackinaw stood next to him. "C'mon, c'mon," he said, his gravelly voice impatient.

As Anders reached out over the water, Kate caught her breath. The ice was wet and slippery.

Then she saw a wide band around the toes of her brother's boots. Short roofing nails, poked through the bottom side of the band, gave his feet a grip. Catching a large block of ice, Anders tightened his tongs around it.

The man next to him also held tongs and closed them around the opposite side of the block. Together they pushed the ice deeper into the water. As it bobbed to the surface, they swung it onto the ice, then onto the sleigh.

"That's it," said the man. "All it can hold." He hooked a chain across the back of the sleigh, then waved the driver on.

Anders glanced toward Kate. Flexing his muscles, he grinned.

Show-off! Kate thought. Still, she felt proud of her brother.

When Anders saw Erik, his lopsided grin disappeared. "What's wrong?" he asked.

From near the channel of open water, Mr. Fenton looked up.

Seeing the boys, he called out, "Let's cut the talking and get back to work!"

"Sorry, Mr. Fenton," Erik said, walking over. "But I can't."

Like the man with Anders, Mr. Fenton wore four-buckle boots and a red and black mackinaw. He was of medium height and had a heavyset frame. His arms looked thick and strong.

"Where's your sleigh?" he asked Erik, his long pole still in hand. "We're ready to load."

Erik faced him. "I had a runaway."

"What's the matter, lose control of your horses?"

Erik's chin shot up. "The ice shifted on that steep hill near the creamery."

"And how long have you handled horses?" Mr. Fenton's voice sounded smooth as cream.

Erik straightened, seeming to grow taller. "Since I was nine years old, sir."

"Taking your team too fast, were you?"

A flush of red crept across Erik's face. "No, Mr. Fenton."

Erik's voice still sounded polite, but Kate knew he was angry.

"Queen and Prince started down the hill the way horses always do," Erik said. "A front brace broke. When the plank fell off, blocks of ice hit the horses' heels. They spooked."

By now the man working with Anders had turned toward Erik to listen. The same height and build as Mr. Fenton, the second man had a black beard trimmed close to his face. Mr. Fenton's mustache and hair were the color of sand.

"Well, see what your poor handling has done for us," Mr. Fenton said, as though he hadn't heard Erik. "Without a sleigh to load, we can't take out more ice."

"I know, Mr. Fenton. I'm sorry."

"Sorry! Lot of good that does!"

Erik bit his lip as though trying hard to keep from snapping back. He glared toward Anders, and a look of understanding passed between them.

As Mr. Fenton talked on, Erik again looked him straight in the eye. Finally the man summed up his complaints. "That's what happens when we hire children to work for us."

Erik's flush deepened, yet he managed not to speak.

But Anders stepped forward, directly in front of Mr. Fenton. "You're not being fair!" he exclaimed. "It's your fault the accident happened."

"*My* fault?" Mr. Fenton's eyes looked dangerously cold.

Anders held his ground. "Your fault," he repeated. "For saying we have to use that hill."

"You remember, Anders, that I'm the boss around here." Once again Mr. Fenton's voice sounded smooth.

But the tall blond boy kept on. "Old-timers avoid a steep hill if they can. If we harvested ice on Hidden Lake we wouldn't have to go over that hill."

This time it was Mr. Fenton who flushed red. "Who do you think you are, telling me what to do? You're just a boy."

"A boy who gives you a full day's work," Anders said, and Kate knew he was beyond stopping. "A boy who works just as well as a man."

"A boy who gives me a lot of lip, you mean. I don't have to take that."

The cold January air felt heavy with anger. Anders opened his mouth and just as quickly closed it. An uneasy look flashed across his face.

Be quiet, Anders! Kate wanted to cry out. *What about the money we need?* Would her brother lose the only paying job available to him?

As Anders drew a deep breath, Kate wondered if he remembered. "I'm sorry," he said, the words coming from deep inside.

Mr. Fenton smiled. "I can forget your poor manners if you stop telling me what to do." He reached out to shake Anders's hand as though the matter were settled.

But Anders stood with arms at his side, hands balled in fists. His face looked stony with anger.

Slowly Mr. Fenton dropped his hand. When he spoke again, he sounded as if nothing had happened. "Well, by the time the other sleigh gets back, it'll be dark. We're going to have to call it a day." He looked around at the man sawing blocks of ice. "No work tomorrow," he called.

Kate saw panic on her brother's face. She guessed what he was thinking. No work? No money?

Mr. Fenton glanced toward the man who worked with Anders. "Both Gunnar and I have other work to do. But if the weather holds, be back the day after." His look included Anders and Erik.

Quickly Anders picked up his tongs, hiding whatever relief he felt. He and Erik set off on the trail leading to the road. When they reached Kate, she fell into step behind.

As soon as they entered the grove of trees, Anders spoke. "Of all the—"

"Shhh!" Erik warned in a low voice. "Sound carries. He might hear."

His face straight ahead, Anders stalked the rest of the way through the pines.

They were almost to the Trade Lake Creamery before Kate spoke of the robbery. "What should we do about Mama and the baby?" she asked. "How are we going to buy the things we need?"

Anders didn't seem too concerned. "The creamery will write out new checks. They'll have 'em tomorrow. Or the next day."

"Did they tell you that?" asked Kate.

"No, but they will."

"They didn't tell me either," Kate said. Once Papa had told her that the men who ran the creamery were really wise. Yet she felt uneasy.

Anders turned to Erik. "Fenton didn't even ask if you got hurt."

"I didn't." Erik grinned. "After all, I've been handling horses since I was nine years old." Then his voice softened. "But Kate got a good scare."

"Well, you know about Kate." Anders talked as if she weren't there. "She's a scaredy-cat anyway."

"No, I'm not!" Kate sputtered.

"Kate had good reason to be afraid," Erik said. As they started up the hill toward Mission Church, he told the story.

Anders grew even more angry. "Old-timers use Hidden Lake for harvesting ice," he said.

"Where's that?" asked Kate.

"Back in the woods." Erik pointed to a trail ahead. Leading

off the road to their left, the track wound between swampy land back of the creamery and a cemetery farther up the hill.

"Hidden Lake has a bay close to the creamery," Erik continued. "That's where the men usually harvest ice."

"Until this year," Anders said. "Until LeRoy Fenton came to town in October."

"Who *is* Mr. Fenton, anyway?" Kate asked.

Anders shrugged. "A man who always acts like Mr. Smart. Came from another creamery somewhere. Applied for the buttermaker's job, but Mr. Bloomquist got it."

"So Mr. Fenton works for the buttermaker?" Kate asked.

"Part time," said Anders. "And Fenton got the bid for harvesting ice. Old-timers grumbled, but the job usually goes to the lowest bidder."

Soon they came to Mission Church with its two front doors, one for women to enter, the other for men. Anders turned to Erik. "Doesn't it bother you? Though he's new around here, Fenton acts like he knows everything."

"But isn't he the boss?" asked Kate.

"Yup, and it's all right if he bosses *us* around." Her brother's voice sounded like a growl. "But if Papa was here, Fenton wouldn't get away with what he's doing."

After walking on the road for a time, they cut across a field, then passed into woods.

"Sure miss your horses, Erik," Anders said. Even with shortcuts, it was a long walk to Windy Hill Farm.

"Hope I find 'em when I get home," Erik replied. Like Papa Nordstrom, Erik's father worked in a logging camp, but he had left his team of horses behind.

"When Mr. Fenton makes you work on Little Trade Lake, why do you use that steep hill?" asked Kate. "There's another way where the land is flatter."

Anders snorted. "Yah, sure!"

But Erik explained. "It's flatter and easier. But it's swampy there."

"Like here?" asked Kate.

"No, this is worse," Erik told her. As he spoke, they crossed onto the southwest end of Rice Lake. "There are floating bogs here. The water is much deeper."

Kate still didn't understand. "But it's winter. Isn't Little Trade Lake frozen?"

"Not where it's swampy. Get an early snow, and it keeps the water from freezing. The way in could have been solid ice if we'd known we were going to harvest there."

"You betcha!" said Anders. "We could have stomped down the grass and snow early in winter. It would have frozen hard. Or we could have tramped it down on a cold day. A trail would solid up pretty fast, just like here."

"But LeRoy Fenton didn't do that," explained Erik. "The first horses that tried to go in broke through."

"Through the ice?" asked Kate.

Anders snickered. "Mr. Grouch was driving."

"Mr. *Grouch*?"

"Gunnar Grimm. The man I worked with. Grouch, grouch, grouch all day long. Never talks when I ask him questions."

Kate remembered the other man in a red and black mackinaw. Heavyset and about the same height as Mr. Fenton, Gunnar Grimm lifted the huge blocks of ice with little effort.

"Yup," said Anders. "Mr. Grouch got the team out, but he never should have gone there in the first place. An old-timer wouldn't have. All I know is, I'm going to keep on eye on Mr. LeRoy Fenton."

"And on Hidden Lake?" asked Kate, half teasing.

"And on Hidden Lake," Anders answered. He still sounded angry.

3

Going Fishing

On her way to the barn the next day, Kate stopped in the chicken coop. Eager for their meal of warm mush, the chickens clustered around.

One old rooster, Big Red, tipped his head and cast his beady eyes toward Kate. Watching him, she laughed. "So you think this is your territory!"

As Kate filled the water container, the rooster's long beak darted forward. Just in time Kate jumped aside, avoiding his peck.

"You're a mean one!" she exclaimed. Carefully she edged out the door, making sure she kept her distance.

Soon after lunch, Erik came to the Windy Hill farmhouse.

"What happened to Queen and Prince?" asked Kate when she saw him.

"I found them munching hay, as peaceful as you please. Mama was mighty glad to see me walk in."

Kate remembered her terror of the day before. Even now, thinking about the runaway horses seemed like a nightmare.

"You know what?" Erik sounded as innocent as his face looked. "Maybe we ought to go fishing."

Anders agreed so quickly that Kate guessed the boys were planning to look around.

"We could use some fish for supper," Mama said. Today her golden blond hair fell in ringlets around her face.

Erik winked at Kate. "Better come with. You can bait the hooks."

Kate wrinkled her nose at him. She knew what some of the bait looked like. Worms that Anders and Erik had picked from the rotted wood of a dead tree. She'd do her best to use another kind of bait—small bits of pork rind saved from the last butchering.

Just the same, Kate wanted to go along. So did her younger brother Lars. After watching him fight colds most of the winter, Kate felt relieved to see him well enough to go.

As they put on their skis, Mama poked her head out the door. "Sure your ankle can handle it, Anders?"

"I'll be careful," he told her. It was the first time Anders had tried skiing since spraining his ankle before Christmas. He grinned at Mama. "Kate can bring me back if I don't make it."

Each one carrying something, the four of them skied down the hill near the farmhouse. Anders used a pole when skiing. The rest went without.

"Going to show you my favorite fishing hole," Anders told Kate. He looked like a small boy about to reveal a secret.

But Kate guessed where they were headed. "Hidden Lake?"

At the bottom of the hill, they followed a well-packed trail. Straight ahead through the woods was the school they'd attend when spring term started. Some schools closed just during the worst part of winter. But Spirit Lake School wouldn't reopen until April 8.

As Anders led them onto the ice of Rice Lake, he held out his ski pole. Made of a thin sapling stripped of bark, the pole had a point at the bottom end. The top was broader and easy to hold.

"See that area, Kate?" Anders pointed toward the southeastern bay. "Don't ever ski there."

Kate grinned. "I suppose the bogeyman will get me."

"Worse than that," Anders growled.

"Worse? What could possibly be worse?"

"Kate, my little sister, when Papa left, he told me to take care of you."

Kate giggled at his serious tone. "Oh sure, big brother. Just because you're taller, you can't boss me around. We're the same age."

Anders scowled. "There's a crick coming in on that side. And spring holes."

"Spring holes?" Kate still didn't take him seriously. When it came to teasing, Anders had gotten the best of her more than once.

"Spring holes."

Kate glanced at Erik and Lars. Neither one of them grinned.

"Big round holes," said Anders. "Holes made by springs. The ice never freezes, no matter how cold it gets. There can be a foot or two of snow just resting on top of the water."

Kate squinted her eyes, trying to see. The southeastern bay stretched away, smooth and peaceful in the afternoon sunlight.

"Once when the snow was deep like this, I tried skiing across that part of the lake," Anders went on. "I was going along lickety-split and stretched out my pole." Swinging his pole ahead, he showed her. "The pole dropped down. There was nothing there."

Kate swallowed hard. It wasn't difficult to guess what might have happened.

Avoiding the creek that let out of the southwest end of the lake, they stayed on a packed-down trail through the boggy area.

"Just remember, Kate," said Anders. "If you come through alone, this is the only safe place to cross."

For a time they followed the road to Trade Lake. Then Erik took the lead, breaking trail through a woods. Their wide skis held them up, even in deep snow.

Soon they came to a large open space. Anders and Erik looked around, and so did Kate. On this side of the lake the land sloped gradually down to where water would lie in summer. Across the bay, however, the shore rose to a steep, forested hill and farmland beyond.

Except for animal tracks, the snow was unbroken. With only trees and hills in sight, the place seemed harmless. Why didn't

LeRoy Fenton want men working on Hidden Lake?

Erik put Kate's disappointment into words. "Nothing here to see."

But Anders skied onto the lake. "Well, we told Mama we'd fish. We better get started."

Facing the south shore, he stepped to the left and right, lining himself up with a large tree.

"Looking for something?" Kate asked.

"Yup. My favorite fishing hole."

Taking the ice chisel he carried, Anders cleared off the snow. With a long handle, the chisel had a narrow blade about two inches wide. "I suppose I have to make a hole for you, Kate," he said, and started chopping.

The sound rang out, breaking the stillness. Before long, the chisel splashed down into cold, dark water.

Lars took his turn next, then Erik, all making their own hole. Anders busied himself with a fishing line, then chopped a fourth hole for himself.

"C'mon, Kate, I'll show you how." He handed her a small board with grocery string wrapped around it, then dug into a can. When he held up a soft white worm, Kate stepped back.

Anders laughed. "Won't hurt you a bit, scaredy-cat!"

Erik grinned. "Maybe she'd like some pork rind instead."

Lars had already dropped a line through his hole in the ice. Before long he cried, "I've got something!"

Kate watched his string dip into the water. For a moment Lars let the line go, then jerked it up, setting the hook. As he pulled in the line, he wound it around the small board.

Suddenly the head, then the body and tail of a northern pike appeared through the hole in the ice.

"It's a big one!" cried Kate.

Erik and Anders surrounded the hole, ready to grab if the fish slipped off the hook. But the line held, and Lars swung it to safety, out over the snow. Proudly he held it up.

"Oh, wow!" exclaimed Kate.

Anders clapped his brother on the back. "That's a six- or seven-pounder!"

"It's over two feet long!" exclaimed Erik.

Lars's eyes glowed with excitement. "It's sure the biggest fish I've ever pulled in!"

"Well, let's see if the rest of us can catch up to Lars," Anders said as he let down his line.

Kate reached for a bit of pork rind, then remembered she wasn't going to be a scaredy-cat. Gingerly she poked into the can for a soft white worm. She picked one up so carefully that she dropped it twice.

Looking around, she saw Anders watching her. This time she took better hold of the worm. As she pierced it with her hook, the worm squished.

Kate bit her lip. Quickly she dropped her line through the hole in the ice.

A moment later she felt a tug. "I've caught something!"

"Aw, Kate," drawled Anders. "You can't have something that fast. Ever been fishing before?"

Kate shook her head. Just the same she watched her line, sure that something clung to the other end.

Erik came over to stand beside her. "Let it play with the bait a bit."

Kate loosened her hold, but the line didn't pull down the way it did for Lars. Instead, the string held tight and steady. When she tried to wind it up, the line refused to come.

"Just a minute, Kate." Erik stared into the hole. "Something's wrong."

By now Anders was watching. "Got a really big one?" Handing his line to Lars, he came over.

Pulling off his mitten, Erik felt Kate's line. "She's caught on something."

"In the middle of the lake?" Kate asked.

"Aren't any weeds around here," Anders said. He, too, took hold of the line and pulled gently but firmly. "She's caught all right."

Erik knelt down. Slowly he tugged, being careful not to break the line. But the string held fast.

"Let me try," said Anders. When he pulled again, the string seemed to come free, but Anders could pull it only two or three feet.

From opposite sides of the hole, Anders and Erik tugged once more. Another foot of line came up, dragging something with it.

"A chain!" exclaimed Kate. "It's caught on the links!"

"Well, little sister," Anders said. "For once you're right!"

Reaching into the dark water, Erik grabbed hold of the chain. "Get the ice chisel," he said. "Hurry!"

Quickly Kate slid the long handle through the loop Erik held. Lying across the hole, the handle of the chisel kept the chain from dropping back into the water.

Pulling hand over hand, Anders brought up more of the chain.

"There's something hooked to it!" cried Lars, who had taken in the other fishing lines.

"Yah betcha, old buddy," Anders replied. "Something too big for this hole."

"What is it?" asked Kate.

Anders shrugged. "Whatever it is, we have to make a bigger hole. For that we need the ice chisel. Where's my ski pole?"

As Anders hung on to the chain, Erik slipped the pole through the loop and freed the ice chisel. Then the boys started widening the hole.

When Kate took her turn chopping, she saw something bobbing about two feet beneath the surface. "It's shiny metal," she said.

More than once Kate and the boys stopped to tug on the chain. Each time one of them went back to using the chisel.

At last Anders put it down. "Let's try again."

He and Erik knelt down on either side of what was now a good-sized hole. As Erik pulled the chain, Anders reached out. For a moment nothing happened. Then Erik gave another yank. This time a five-gallon milk can bobbed into view.

When Anders tried to grab it, the can slipped out of his hands. "It's too heavy for a can that size, even if it was full." He leaned back to think about it.

Again Erik yanked hard on the chain. This time a handle appeared above the water. Kate grabbed for it and lifted. But it took Anders's strong arms to swing the can onto the ice.

Chains attached to the handles on either side reached down to the chain on which Kate's line had caught. That chain led down into the dark water.

Once more Erik grabbed the ice-cold links. Hand over hand he pulled until something heavy rose to the surface. With a mighty tug he lifted out a snarl of wire wrapped around a good-sized rock.

"No wonder it's so heavy!" Erik exclaimed.

"Quite a catch!" said Kate.

"For a first-timer, you're not bad!" Anders told her. "But what's a milk can doing down in the lake?"

"Is it watertight?" she asked.

"If the lid's pressed down hard," Erik told her. "Whoever took care of this one made sure."

Two ropes, with ends tied to the handles on either side, crossed the top of the can in an X. The lid looked as secure as someone could make it.

Who would bury a milk can in the icy waters of a lake? What was inside?

4

Discovery!

Kate pulled off her mittens to untie the knots that held the cover of the milk can in place. Ice was forming on the rope. Soon it would freeze solid.

The cold bit into Kate's hands, numbing them. As her fingers stiffened, they grew clumsy. Already a skim of ice coated the top of the can.

"Where's your knife, Anders?" she asked.

Her brother patted his pockets and pulled it out. As Anders cut the rope, Erik yanked off the lid.

Lars reached into the can. "A gunnysack!" He held it up for them to see. A stout string held the sack shut.

Erik helped Lars untie the string. All of them peered inside the sack.

Lars's blue eyes danced. Erik let out a long whistle. Kate felt her heart leap into her throat.

"I thought so!" Anders exclaimed.

It was Kate who took out slips of paper. "Checks from the Trade Lake Cooperative Creamery!"

Anders reached for another handful and read the names aloud. "This one's for Josie's father, Henry Swenson. And here's your father, Erik."

"And Papa?" asked Kate, looking through the checks she held. "Elroy Johnson. Stanley Sundquist. Here it is! Carl Nordstrom."

Lars's grin spread from ear to ear. "It's the loot from the robbery, all right!"

In that moment Kate felt uneasy. Lars's words made their discovery real. With that reality came her awareness of danger. Looking over her shoulder, she asked, "So what do we do?"

Anders returned the money to the gunnysack. Erik retied it, slipped the sack into the can, and replaced the lid. Like Kate, he, too, glanced around.

The hidden lake seemed still and serene, but Anders put their feeling into words. "We're sitting ducks out here. If anyone comes this way, he'll spot us in a second."

"Let's get off the ice," Kate said.

Again they looked around, but this time for a hiding place. On the north end of the bay, tall bent-over grass marked a swampy area. On a second side, the shore rose steeply. Climbing with the milk can and heavy rock would be difficult. But on the south side of the bay, near the place where they skied in, the ground sloped gently upward.

"What about over there?" asked Kate.

"If we could just get rid of this big rock," said Anders. Yet the chain and the wire around the rock were frozen together.

"Can't destroy evidence, anyway," Erik replied.

With Anders carrying the milk can and Erik the rock, they left the ice for the cover of trees.

"Got any ideas?" Anders asked as he set the can down.

"We have to get help," said Kate.

"I know, I know." Anders sounded impatient. "But what do we do with the milk can? If we take it to the creamery, the whole town will see us walking through Trade Lake."

"The whole town—and maybe the thief," said Kate. With each minute she felt more aware of what a dangerous thing they had found.

"So we can't go to the creamery," Lars decided. Surrounded by freckles, his blue eyes looked serious.

"You got it, brother!" Anders replied. "Maybe we should split up—two of us go, two of us stay here."

But Erik glanced at Kate and Lars. "We're sticking together," he said. He sounded as if he wouldn't even consider another idea.

"Where can we hide the can while we go for help?" Kate asked.

Backing off from where they stood, Erik looked along that side of the shore. "There's a brush pile." He pointed. "But we've got a bigger problem."

Kate knew what he meant. "Our tracks in the snow. They'll lead someone right to the milk can."

Then she noticed the light slanting across the slope. Soon the hill would be cold and dark. "We have to decide," she said.

Glancing toward the sun, Anders looked worried. "That brush would do it, so let's cover our tracks."

Leaving the can on the shore, they returned to the fishing holes. Anders and Erik put on their skis and started back to the slope. Lars collected his fish, the lines, and bait, and skied to the place where they'd come in to the lake.

Kate tromped down the snow, hiding the deep round circle left by the bottom of the milk can. There was nothing to do with the large hole in the ice but hope that it would freeze over soon.

Stepping into her skis, Kate picked up the ice chisel and followed Anders and Erik to the shore. Using the two-inch blade, she smoothed out the round mark left by the can.

With Anders carrying the milk can and Erik the rock, they skied close to the pile of brush. Slipping one foot from his ski, Erik stretched out and set down the milk can. Anders handed him the rock, and Erik hid that also. Reaching still farther, Erik pulled branches over the can, the rock, and his boot print.

When all of them joined Lars, dusk was upon them. As Kate looked around, she saw no one. Perhaps the lake was well named, and they were safely hidden.

"We have to decide who to tell," Anders said. "The thief could be most anyone."

Kate felt scared. "Are you saying we could look right at him and not know it?"

"Yup!" Anders offered his lopsided grin. "Now think about

that for a minute! Just think how exciting your life can become."

But Kate didn't like that idea at all. Then she caught the look in Lars's eyes. Always he'd been more tender than Anders. Talking to a thief didn't seem a joke for him either.

"It's not funny, Anders," said Kate, tipping her head toward her younger brother.

"Just letting you know the risks," Anders replied. But he caught Kate's signal. His grin disappeared.

"So what can we do?" asked Erik. "Who do we trust?"

Kate felt at a loss. She trusted Mr. Swenson, Josie's father. But would he be the right person to tell?

"What about Mr. Bloomquist?" asked Lars. In the dusk his freckles stood out on his pale face.

"The buttermaker?" Anders thought about it. "He's new here. I don't know him very well." He looked at Erik. "Do you?"

Erik shook his head. "But we need someone connected with the creamery."

"Let's go to Andrew Anderson number 3," said Anders. "He's secretary-treasurer."

"You trust him?" Kate asked.

"Yah, sure," Anders told her. "With our lives!"

"Anders!" Kate exclaimed. "Stop teasing. It isn't funny!"

For once Anders looked dead serious. "I'm not teasing, Kate. Before Papa left, he told me to take care of you and Mama and Tina.

"And me too?" asked Lars.

"You, too, little brother." Anders winked. "But Kate's the biggest problem. The rest of you I can handle."

Kate sputtered, but Erik laughed. "Don't you worry about it, Anders. I'll help with Kate."

Anders grinned. "Like I said, mighty big problem that it takes two of us."

Before Kate could answer, Anders started back over the ice of Hidden Lake. "Just follow me. I'm your trusty guide through thick and thin. Through the cold of day and peril of night."

In spite of herself, Kate giggled. As she fell into line, she called ahead. "But, Anders, how do you know we can trust Mr. Anderson?"

Anders swung around. "Because Papa trusts him. Papa likes what he stands for. That's why he and Mama named me Anders."

Kate was surprised. She knew only that Anders's mother had died from illness, for Anders seldom spoke about her. Months later Anders's father had married her mother. During the time without one parent, Anders had taken on the responsibilities of an adult.

"Anders? After Andrew?" Kate asked.

"Yup, Anders is Swedish for Andrew. I'm named after the Andrew in the Bible, but also Andrew Anderson number 3. That's why I'm so great!"

In the twilight Kate caught his grin. Knowing they'd soon be surrounded by total darkness, she skied quickly. Lars followed her, and Erik brought up the rear.

After a time Kate called out. "How far, Anders?"

"His farm is north of Hidden Lake."

When they reached Mr. Anderson's house, Anders took off his skis and bounded up the steps. A tall thin man with a long flowing beard opened the door.

"I *do* know him!" Kate murmured under her breath. She remembered times when Mr. Anderson spoke up at church. More than once, he'd helped the congregation make wise decisions.

"Come in, come in," he said now. In the glow of a kerosene lamp, his hair and beard were a salt-and-pepper mixture of gray and white. His lined face looked kind.

As Kate felt the warmth of the wood stove, she realized how cold she had become. In spite of her wool stockings and mittens, her toes and fingers felt numb.

The Andersons were sitting down to supper, and Mrs. Anderson set on more plates. As soon as he said the blessing, Mr. Anderson turned to Anders. "Well, what can I do for you?"

As her brother told the story, Kate watched the older man. The expression in his quiet eyes changed from amazement to relief to joy. Standing up, he clapped Anders on the back. "Well, let's go after it. Let's rescue this milk can from beneath the brush."

In a minute he returned dressed in warm clothing. After lighting a farm lantern, he led them to the barn. Working together, they harnessed the horses.

"We'll get Harry Bloomquist," Mr. Anderson said as they climbed into the sleigh. "He's been working late at the creamery. He'll give an extra hand if we have any trouble."

As they drew up at the Trade Lake Creamery, Kate saw a kerosene lamp glowing through a window. Sitting at his desk, the buttermaker was working on some papers.

"Welcome," he said as they entered the small room with the steam boiler. "To what do I owe this great honor?"

"We've got good news for you, Harry." Mr. Anderson's eyes shone in the lamplight. "These young people found the checks!"

Enjoying every moment, Anders told what had happened. The story sounded even better on the second telling.

We can buy dress material for Mama, Kate thought as she listened to her brother. Maybe they'd even get cloth for baby clothes.

"We chopped a bigger hole and pulled out the can," Anders was saying when Kate heard a noise in the next room—a furtive noise, as if someone moved quietly. Tuning out her brother's voice, she listened.

"Where's the milk can now?" asked the buttermaker.

"Under a pile of brush on the south shore of Hidden Lake," Anders told him.

As Kate heard another sound, she remembered how easily voices carried between the two rooms. Erik, too, seemed to listen. As their gaze met, Kate tipped her head. Erik nodded. Quietly he edged toward the door into the large room.

Kate reached out for Mr. Anderson's farm lantern, picked it up, and followed. Just as Erik turned the doorknob, something crashed in the other room.

No longer cautious, Erik threw open the door. Kate followed with the lantern.

In the middle of the floor a milk can lay on its side. Erik grabbed the lantern from Kate. Its dim glow barely reached into the shadows, yet Erik held it out. Starting around one side of the room, he searched.

From somewhere beyond the large churn, Kate sensed a movement. "Over there!" she cried, pointing into the shadows.

In the light from the lantern two bright eyes shone from the dark.

5

Nighttime Search

Kate stepped back. What animal lurked in the shadows?

But Erik stalked ahead. A large orange cat bounded out. Kate jumped, then felt silly.

The cat streaked past her toward the buttermaker.

"False alarm!" Mr. Bloomquist exclaimed as he came into the room. "Tabby's our best mouser."

"False alarm?" Kate whispered to Erik. "I don't think so. I heard a door close."

"I don't think so either." Erik spoke softly.

The door to the cold room was a few steps beyond where the cat hid. Nearby was another door. Erik flung it open and hurried outside. As Kate followed, Anders and the men caught up.

Erik and Mr. Anderson started around the creamery in one direction. Kate and Anders took another. Mr. Bloomquist checked out the trees behind the building. But no one was found hiding in the dark.

"Whatever it was is gone," said Erik when they came back together.

"*Whoever* it was, you mean," answered Kate. "The noises I heard weren't made by a cat."

"We're all getting a bit jumpy," Mr. Bloomquist said as they returned inside. "Better tell me the rest of the story, Anders."

Anders pushed back his shock of blond hair and spoke quickly. "Then we went for Andrew Anderson," he said.

As Mr. Bloomquist asked one question after another, Kate grew more and more uneasy. "Can't we go to the lake?" she finally asked.

The buttermaker reached for his coat. It took another few minutes to find a farm lantern and light it.

Outside, they climbed into the sleigh. Mr. Anderson took the trail back of the creamery. At Hidden Lake Kate and the boys put on their skis. In the deep snow they could make better time.

Carrying a lantern, Erik led them up the slope. The men trudged behind with the second lantern. More than once, Kate looked over her shoulder, glad that Mr. Anderson was along. What if the person who stole the checks watched from the darkness?

Skiing ahead of Kate, Lars looked tired. Instead of his usual quickness, he had trouble keeping up with the older boys.

As everyone reached the pile of brush, the half moon came out from under the clouds. Kate held the lantern, and Erik and Anders pulled away the branches.

Before long Kate knew something was wrong. "Where's the milk can?" she asked.

Without answering, the boys worked even more quickly. When they had moved every branch without finding anything, they had to give up.

"Are you sure you have the right place?" asked Mr. Bloomquist.

"I'm sure," Anders growled.

Erik looked even more upset. "I *know* this is where I put it!"

"Maybe there's another pile of brush," suggested Mr. Anderson. Leaving them, he walked down to the lake. Kate followed on skis.

Standing on the snow-covered ice, Kate and Mr. Anderson looked back up the slope, searching. The dim light made it difficult to see. Finding nothing else, they returned to the others.

"Are you *sure* this is where you hid the can?" the buttermaker asked again.

Anders's laugh sounded harsh in the cold night air. "This is the place. Are you wondering if we're playing a prank?"

"No, no," Mr. Bloomquist said quickly.

"We didn't plan a wild-goose chase." Erik sounded apologetic, but Kate knew he was angry. "We've been honest with you."

"I believe you," said Andrew Anderson simply. "I know you best, Anders, and I trust you. Someone didn't want us to find that milk can."

"That noise in the creamery," said Kate. "Even a big cat wouldn't tip over a milk can. They're too heavy."

Mr. Anderson nodded. "Good thinking, Kate."

"If that person heard us talking, he got here first," said Erik.

Again Mr. Anderson agreed. "We have to find out who's been here. Let's look around for tracks. And let's work quietly in case the thief is still nearby, listening."

Close to the pile of brush, the snow was too trampled to pick out boot prints. Anders, Mr. Anderson, and Lars used one lantern, while Kate, Erik, and the buttermaker searched with the other.

It was easy to find their ski tracks from the afternoon and also the tracks they'd made coming back. When they spread out in a circle around the pile of brush, Kate discovered boot prints.

Just then Anders called out from the opposite side. "Here's something!" Again boot prints led away into the woods.

"There's two people?" asked Erik. "That's strange."

Lars and Mr. Anderson followed Anders in one direction, while Kate, Erik, and the buttermaker took the other. Kate spotted one boot print, then the next. Of medium size, they were far apart, as though the person either ran or walked fast.

The three had gone for some distance when the lantern sputtered and died. Erik groaned. "It's out of kerosene!"

Mr. Bloomquist sounded just as upset. "I forgot to fill it! I'll go back for the other lantern."

As the buttermaker disappeared into the darkness, Kate spoke softly. "Erik, do you trust him?"

"I don't know," he whispered back. "Maybe it's because he's new at his job. But it's one delay after another. If we'd gone straight to the milk can, we'd have it now!"

Kate sighed. "Every minute we lose—"

"I know. The thief gets farther away."

Kate stared at the ground. "Maybe we can see without the lantern."

They stood in an opening between trees where the light was better. Erik pointed. "There's the next footstep. Let's give it a try."

Watching closely, they started around the west side of the lake. Soon a lacework of branches dimmed what light there was, and they had to stop.

Kate looked up to where the moon hid under the clouds. "I wish it were full."

When the buttermaker returned, he brought the others. The trail Mr. Anderson, Anders, and Lars had followed led off a short distance, then circled back to the hole in the ice. In the lantern light Mr. Anderson looked grim about the time they'd lost.

"If only we had Lutfisk with us," said Anders. "He'd find the thief in a minute." Named after the dried cod that Swedes eat at Christmas, the dog was a good tracker.

By now Lars trembled with cold. "Why don't you go back to the sleigh?" Kate told him. "You could warm up under that heavy horse blanket."

But Lars shook his head. As they set out again, he kept up with the others.

They continued around the side of the lake until the boot prints led up a steep hill. There they left their skis standing in a snowbank and trudged on.

Soon Kate's legs ached from walking through deep snow. When she thought she couldn't take another step, they came to a large clearing. As they started across, the moon broke free of the clouds.

On the other side of the clearing, a large pine looked dark against the night sky. The lower boughs stirred. Was someone behind that tree? Kate couldn't be sure.

Then, next to the pine, bushes moved. Fear leaped into Kate's throat.

Nighttime Search

Reaching out, she touched Erik's arm. "Shhh!" she whispered when he would have spoken. She pointed toward the large pine. "Is someone there?"

"Stay here!" he said in a low voice. Leaping forward, he broke into a run. Anders and the men followed.

After a moment so did Kate, still holding the lantern. Erik wanted her out of harm's way. She wanted to see what happened.

The deep snow slowed them down. Partway across the clearing, Erik stumbled and fell. For a moment he lay there, out of breath. By the time Kate reached him, he was up again, running toward the tree.

He and Kate and Anders reached it together. No one stood on the far side, trying to hide. But there were boot prints in the snow.

As Kate held out the lantern, all of them looked around. Near the bushes, they saw prints that faced the clearing.

"He was watching," said Kate with a shiver. "Watching for us. How long ago?"

Just then the wind stirred the bushes. There was no way to know.

Scouting around, Anders found tracks leading off, away from the pine. Erik took the lantern, and they followed the boot prints to an ice-covered road. There the tracks disappeared.

Again they split into two groups, and each took a direction. With only one lantern it was hard to find a place where someone stepped off the road.

Finally they had to stop searching. No track remained. The footprints had vanished into the night.

Anders groaned. "He got away! We found the money, then lost it!"

To Kate this seemed the biggest blow of all—to be so close and then fail. But Andrew Anderson number 3 encouraged them. "You did your best."

Anders wasn't satisfied with that. "We should have brought the milk can to you. We were afraid the thief would see us carrying it."

"You were right," said the older man. "You could have tipped off the thief. At least we know the checks are still in the area. I'll notify Sheriff Saunders. We'll start our search again."

Walking back through the woods, they picked up their skies, then returned to Mr. Anderson's sleigh. "Climb in," he told them. "I'll give you a ride home."

Lars's face looked pinched and white with cold. As he crawled under a heavy horse blanket, his entire body trembled.

Watching him shiver, Kate felt concerned. Already Lars had been sick too often this winter.

Near the creamery, Mr. Anderson slowed the horses. "With all that's happened, it'd be easy to forget the contest," he told the buttermaker. "We still want you to enter."

What contest? Kate wondered, as Mr. Bloomquist dropped off the sleigh.

Soon they left the road to cross Rice Lake. Kate moved forward to talk to Mr. Anderson. "When will the creamery give out new checks?"

His hands on the reins, Mr. Anderson turned partway. "I don't know," he said.

"You don't *know*?" Anders blurted out.

Mr. Anderson didn't seem offended. "I can't reissue checks until I know what amount they should be."

"The buttermaker keeps a record of that." Erik sounded puzzled. "He writes down how much cream each farmer brings in."

"That's right," said Mr. Anderson. "He puts the information on a daily work sheet, then in a ledger."

"Are you saying—" Erik stopped, as though the idea were too awful to go on.

But Anders jumped in. "Are you saying the thief stole the ledger?"

Mr. Anderson's flowing beard trembled in the wind. "We don't know where it is."

Even in the dim light Kate saw his face. The good man grieved for the farmers.

"What does the ledger look like?" she asked after a moment.

"It's a gray book with green corners. About nine by thirteen inches and two inches thick."

When the horses started up the hill to the Nordstrom farm,

Mr. Anderson spoke again. "There's something I need to tell you young people. From what I've learned about you tonight, you'll keep looking for the stolen checks."

"And the ledger," said Anders.

"But you have to promise me something." In the crisp night air Mr. Anderson's voice sounded deep and strong. "Don't try to catch the thief yourself. Come to me if you see something out of the ordinary."

He looked directly at Anders. "Do you promise?"

"I promise," said Anders solemnly, his voice low.

Mr. Anderson turned toward Erik, then Kate.

"I promise," each of them said.

Mr. Anderson sighed. "I wish you weren't involved in this. But whatever you do, take care of each other. The thief knows who you are. He'll be watching you."

6

Letter From Sweden

As Mr. Anderson drove into the farmyard, Kate saw Mama looking out the window. Kate and Anders climbed down and unloaded the fishing lines and skis, as well as the big northern. Lars stumbled toward the house.

"See you tomorrow," Erik called, as Mr. Anderson continued on to the Lundgren farm. "Let's plan what to do."

When Kate and her brothers entered the kitchen, she saw the worry in Mama's face.

"Where have you been?" Mama asked. A golden curl tumbled onto her forehead. Then Mama saw Lars and forgot everything else. "Come here," she told him gently. "Come next to the stove."

By now the nine-year-old shook so hard he could not unbutton his coat. When Lars let Mama help, Kate guessed how terrible he felt.

"Show her my fish, Kate!" Lars spoke through chattering teeth.

As she held up the northern, Kate felt excited for her brother.

"That's the catch of the season!" said Mama, admiring the big fish. But Lars's lips were blue.

Mama shook her head, as though holding back the words she wanted to say. Was one fish worth having Lars sick?

Anders took out the scale. "Exactly seven pounds!" he told his brother, then measured the fish. "Twenty-nine inches long!"

In the cold night air the northern had frozen. Anders spread newspapers on the table and let the fish thaw enough to clean.

Under the thick dusting of freckles, Lars's skin looked paper white. Though Mama pulled off his boots and wrapped him in warm blankets, he continued to tremble.

Is it my fault? Kate felt uneasy. They'd been gone much longer than expected. *We should have made Lars stay at the creamery.*

"Have you eaten?" Mama wanted to know.

"At Andrew Anderson's," Kate said, and saw Mama's surprise. But instead of asking questions, her mother heated milk.

Even after drinking the warm liquid, Lars continued to shiver.

"I want you sleeping downstairs tonight," Mama told him. "We'll put the cot next to the wood stove in the dining room. You'll be warmer there."

Only after getting Lars settled did Mama sit down. Tall for a woman, she was usually slender. But now, beneath her apron, her rounded stomach looked large. "Tell me everything that happened."

As Anders cleaned the fish, Kate told the story.

"This Mr. Grimm?" asked Mama. "Who is he?"

"You mean Mr. Grouch," said Anders.

But Mama corrected him. "Don't call him by that name. Someday you'll slip and say it to his face."

Mama's blue eyes looked dark with worry. "I don't like this whole thing. Whoever the thief is, he's a dangerous man. You mustn't get mixed up with him."

Kate looked across the table at Anders. How were they going to find the checks if Mama didn't want them searching? And how could they look if Mama said no?

Anders seemed to read Kate's mind. "We don't want to get mixed up with him, Mama. Tomorrow Mr. Anderson will go to Grantsburg and talk to the sheriff. They're in charge. We just want to search for the milk can."

"I don't want either of you looking around." Mama sounded as if her mind was made up. "Anders, you take care of Kate."

Anders kept his face straight. "Sure, Mama. I'll watch out for my little sister. She always does what I say."

Kate choked, but managed to keep her mouth shut.

Mama pushed back her chair. "Papa would know what to do. I wish he were here."

"I do too, Mama," Anders said, his voice quiet.

Kate felt surprised. Since Papa returned to the logging camp, Mama had often had a lonesome look. Even so, she seldom admitted how much she missed Papa.

Pulling herself up, Mama took off her apron. The dress she planned to wear until the baby came already strained at the seams. How could she possibly use that dress another two or three months?

Yet without the creamery check, how could they buy cloth? If Anders got paid, it wouldn't be for a while. And they had no idea when Papa would come home, bringing his earnings with him.

Taking out the large copper wash kettle, Kate set it on the cookstove. Filling a pail at the outside pump, she went back and forth, dumping water into the kettle.

Anders set the washstand near the stove, then put wooden tubs on either side of the wringer. Placing two chairs close together, he set a third wash tub on them. Then he, too, carried in bucket after bucket.

Finally all three tubs were full. Overnight the water would warm up to room temperature.

Taking a bar of soap, Kate rubbed the clothes where they were dirty. By the time she finished, her shoulder muscles ached. But when she tumbled into bed, she lay awake, thinking about the day.

When at last she slept, Kate dreamed about a milk can. In dark waters, it bobbed up and down. She reached out. The can bobbed away. Again Kate reached out. Again the can slipped out of her grasp. Kneeling down, she strained forward. As she grabbed for a handle, she lost her balance and slipped into the icy lake. Still thrashing her arms, Kate woke up.

Tina had pulled all the quilts to her side of the bed. Shivering, Kate yanked them into place, then over her head. It was a long time before she felt warm.

When Kate went down for breakfast, darkness still surrounded the house. Mama had built a good fire in the cookstove. In the large copper kettle sheets and white clothes were boiling. Using a wooden stick, Kate lifted them into the first rinse water.

Working swiftly, Mama shaped bread dough into loaves, then started breakfast. Soon the kitchen filled with the aroma of bacon and eggs and Mama's brown bread.

As Tina slipped into her chair, Anders came in from milking the cows. "No oatmeal this morning," he teased Kate. With the cookstove going all day, they'd have Mama's good soup at noon.

When Lars joined them, he sneezed, and Kate felt scared.

Mama looked up. "Lars, are you coming down with another cold?"

Lars nodded and sneezed at the same time. Quickly he blew his nose. As he turned away from the table, his eyes watered.

"You stay inside today," said Mama. "You've been sick so much we're not going to take any chances."

Kate finished breakfast, then pushed sheets and white clothes through the wringer and into the bluing. As she separated the shirts and tablecloths for starching, Kate watched her mother.

Though the sun had not yet risen, Mama looked as though she'd been up all day. Her pretty face seemed lined with weariness. Before long she disappeared into her bedroom.

"Did she say what's wrong?" Kate asked Anders as he put on layer after layer of work clothes.

"She's probably tired," he answered, as though trying to shrug it off.

But Kate felt uneasy. "Mama never lies down during the morning. What'll we do if *she* gets sick?"

A few minutes later sleigh bells jingled outside the kitchen door. Pulling on her coat, Kate followed Anders into the farmyard. As Queen and Prince came to a stop, Erik jumped down. The morning air felt crisp and cold, but his smile warmed Kate's heart.

"I drew a map of all the lakes in the area," he said.

"So did I!" exclaimed Anders. "I thought, 'Whoever the thief is, he probably can't hide the milk can where he lives. So where would he go? To another lake!' "

"But there're an awful lot of lakes around here," Kate said. Though she'd lived in Burnett County for ten months, she still felt confused at times, trying to sort out the ponds, lakes, and rivers.

Pulling up the collar of his jacket, Erik turned away from the wind. "Lot of people harvesting ice for their farms right now. It'd be easy for someone to drop a milk can in."

"Just one problem," Kate said, wishing she didn't have to tell Erik. "Mama's upset. She doesn't want us looking around."

"Really?" Erik groaned. "But how can we find the thief if we don't look?"

Kate shrugged her shoulders. During the night she had thought it through. More than once she told herself, *But let's search anyway*. Yet she didn't want to disobey Mama.

"Aw, it won't hurt just to take a look," Anders said, as though he'd heard Kate's thoughts.

But Erik shook his head. "We better not." He spoke slowly, and Kate knew he didn't like the idea either.

Climbing onto the sleigh, Erik took up the reins. "Maybe your mother will change her mind." Yet he didn't seem to believe his own words.

Returning to the kitchen, Kate put the first load of clothes into a basket. *Lars*, she thought, as she took the basket outside. She wished she could wash away her scared feelings. Already this winter, a cold had settled in her brother's chest.

And Mama. Often she looked exhausted. Yet Kate suspected Mama's weariness came from more than the baby. Papa was far away, and Mama wanted him safely home.

Snapping the wrinkles from the clothes, Kate moved quickly. But the sheets froze before she could hang them on the line.

As her hands turned red and stiff, her thoughts went on. *The milk can. Where is it now? And where would a thief hide the ledger?*

At lunch time Kate set up a drying rack and hung wool stockings near the cookstove. After freezing in the cold wind, she now felt hot and tired. Yet she needed to use the warm soapy water to wash the kitchen floor and outhouse.

Letter From Sweden

By the time Kate finished scrubbing, the sun slanted westward, and she remembered the mail. Anders and Erik would cut across Rice Lake instead of going past the box.

Kate pulled on her warm clothes and set out on the long walk to the main road and the mail box. To her delight she found two letters—one from Papa, the other from Sweden. *Mama will feel better now,* Kate thought, and walked fast all the way home.

Mama's eyes sparkled as she poured a cup of coffee. Pulling her favorite chair close to a kitchen window, she sat down to enjoy the news.

Usually Mama read Papa's letters to them, but this one was for her eyes alone. "He's well," she said, her soft lips curving in a smile. Folding the letter, she tucked it inside her apron pocket. She'd take it out often to read Papa's words again.

With a warm glow still in her eyes, Mama opened the letter from Sweden. As she read, the color drained from her face. When she reached the end, she dropped the letter to her lap as though wishing she didn't have to touch it.

"Get the picture," Mama said.

Kate felt afraid. She didn't have to ask what picture Mama meant. Hurrying into the dining room, Kate went to the trunk Mama brought from Sweden. On its flat top stood the picture Kate knew well.

Mama's parents sat in the center, surrounded by her five sisters and two brothers. The youngest sister held a framed photograph of Mama.

"So I could still be part of the family," Mama often explained. Soon after coming to America, she'd had the photo taken and sent to her parents.

Now, as always, Mama pointed to each person in the picture. When she came to the smallest boy, she paused. "My little brother, Ben. Only two years of age when I left the old country. A chubby little boy with fat cheeks and happy eyes."

Drawing a long breath, Mama turned the picture over, as though she couldn't bear to see it. Without another word, Mama covered her face with her hands. Her shoulders shook with sobbing, but no sound came.

"Mama, what's wrong?" asked Kate.

Not since Daddy O'Connell died had Kate seen Mama so upset. Her grief seemed even worse because Mama seldom cried in front of anyone.

Kneeling down by the rocking chair, Kate put her arm around her mother's shoulders. "Mama?"

When her mother did not speak, Kate tried again. "Mama?"

Still no answer came, and Kate swallowed around the lump in her throat. "Did someone die?"

Mama shook her head. "Oh, no!" she said at last. "But something terrible has happened."

7

Accident!

*O*nce more Mama broke into sobs.

"Mama, what's so terrible?" Kate felt desperate. Then she heard a sound near the doorway.

Tina stood there, her eyes wide and scared. Behind Tina stood Lars. Mama didn't notice either of them.

"Papa?" asked Lars, his voice a hoarse croak. "Did something happen to Papa?"

His question seemed to reach Mama. "No, Lars. Papa is fine." Mama's voice sounded unsteady. "But my little brother isn't."

Reaching for a handkerchief, Mama wiped her eyes. "My little brother, Ben," she moaned. "He stole money from a shopkeeper and ran away."

With a long shudder she blew her nose. "Six months ago Ben ran away. All that time since, and I did not know."

"How old is he now?" asked Kate.

Mama had to think. "A boy of two when I left the old country." She counted the years. "He's eighteen now. Nineteen this spring."

For a long time Mama sat in her rocking chair, looking out the window. Far across the horizon, the western sky turned gold and red, then gray and black. A log fell in the cookstove, and cold reached into the room.

Kate built up the fire, but Mama still sat in her chair. As though seeing some distant place, she stared into the dark.

When Anders came home from harvesting ice, he looked at Mama, then at Kate. "What's wrong?" he asked.

Kate answered for Mama. "Her little brother stole from a shopkeeper and ran away. No one knows where he is."

Mama drew a deep breath. Her eyes and nose were red with crying.

Aching for Mama's hurt, Kate looked at Anders. *And don't you dare act smart*, she wanted to say. She knew how her brother could tease.

But Anders surprised her. Going over to Mama, he put his big hand on her shoulder. "I'm sorry," he said, his voice gentle.

Mama tried to smile, and Kate knew that the simple words had helped her.

After supper and chores, Anders took out some pieces of old harness. Sitting down at the kitchen table, he riveted the pieces of leather together.

"What're you doing?" asked Kate.

"Making a harness for Lutfisk. If I hitch him to the sled, Tina can ride behind."

Tina looked up from her cornhusk doll. As she crawled onto her brother's lap, her white-blond hair wisped around her face. She started talking in Swedish.

Though Kate couldn't understand the words, she guessed what the little girl said. Tina could hardly wait for a ride behind her brother's dog.

I'll write a letter to Papa, thought Kate. In the dining room, she picked up a wooden pen with a metal point and dipped it into the inkwell.

Dear Papa,

she wrote.

Kate stared at the paper. What could she tell him? How frightened she felt about all that had happened? *I'm thirteen now and shouldn't be afraid anymore.*

For a long time Kate sat there, wondering what to do. *I shouldn't be scared, but I am.* Then she decided what to write:

Accident!

> *Yesterday we went fishing and Lars caught a 7-pound northern. Anders measured it, and it was 29 inches long! We ate most of it for supper tonight, and it tasted good. Mama said it was almost as tasty as lutfisk.*
>
> *I know you have to be gone, but I miss you. This morning Tina got up while it was still dark and crept down to the kitchen. She thought that if she made cookies for you, you'd come home sooner. When Mama found her, Tina had flour all across the floor. She ate at least half a cup of sugar.*
>
> *We are doing fine. We hope you are well.*

We hope you are well? The words sounded stiff, even to Kate. Too often she thought about Daddy O'Connell, and how he died in a construction accident. Often she needed to push aside a fear that something could happen to her new father.

Once more Kate dipped the pen into the ink.

> *I love you, Papa.*
> *Your daughter, Kate*

P.S. *I'm glad you married Mama.*

Blotting the ink, Kate folded the page quickly. Tomorrow she'd take the letter to Trade Lake. She'd look—just look—at cloth for Mama.

The next morning Anders got up earlier than usual. Putting the harness on Lutfisk, the thirteen-year-old hitched the dog to the sled for hauling wood.

One strap of the harness fit across the dog's chest. Two more straps slipped over his back. At first Anders walked alongside, leading Lutfisk until he grew used to the feel of the sled. Then Anders called out, "Haw!" or "Gee!" Soon Lutfisk learned to turn left or right.

"If you use the same commands, you can help me train him," Anders told Kate as he left for work. "I'm too heavy for Lutfisk to pull, but you're light enough. In a few days you can start putting some of your weight on the sled."

When the sun started to warm the bone-chilling air, Kate put on her skies and set off for Trade Lake. Lutfisk trotted alongside, pulling the sled and learning Kate's commands.

On the far side of Rice Lake, she took off the harness and left the sled near a tree. She didn't want to tire the dog by teaching too much at one time.

When she skied on, Lutfisk followed her to the town of Trade Lake. At Gustafson's Mercantile Store, Kate left her skis in a snowbank. As she started up the steps, she nearly bumped into a man in a black and red mackinaw.

Quickly Kate stepped aside. "Good morning, Mr. Grimm," she said.

The man seemed surprised at her greeting, then smiled politely. His eyes looked like the icy water around which he worked.

"Good morning," he answered. "You're Anders's sister, I believe?"

"Katherine O'Connell," she told him, remembering her brother's description—"Grouch, grouch, all day long."

As Mr. Grimm moved on, Kate wondered if he ever smiled. He seemed just as unhappy as his name. Reaching the top step, Kate turned to see what he was doing.

Just then the man looked back. Meeting Kate's eyes, he spun around and walked quickly away.

Trying to push aside her uneasiness, Kate opened Gustafson's door and walked back to the shelves filled with cloth.

When the clerk showed her the material, Kate found only one piece that would be right for Mama. Kate felt the lovely blue cloth. "Not much left."

"Is it for you?" asked the woman.

"For my mother," Kate told her. "She's going to have a baby."

"And needs a new dress." The clerk smiled. "There's still enough. Just barely, but enough. Shall I wrap it up for you?"

Kate longed to buy the cloth and bring it home to Mama. Yet she had only enough money to mail the letter to Papa.

"I'm sorry," Kate said, and felt her cheeks flush. "But I'll have to wait."

As she turned away from the counter, Kate bumped into a redheaded girl. "Maybelle!" she exclaimed.

"Good morning, Katherine." The other girl sounded as formal as a grown-up. Her voice dripped honey.

"Good morning, Maybelle." Kate answered just as sweetly, but her heart thudded. They hadn't talked together since Kate's birthday.

If Maybelle remembered all that happened that afternoon, she gave no hint of it. Slender and of medium height, she had dark brown eyes and red hair.

Not red, russet, Kate told herself, recalling how Mama corrected her. Kate had never seen such beautiful hair.

Today Maybelle wore curls instead of her usual two braids. As she moved to the counter, her gaze fell on the length of blue cloth.

Kate stopped in the aisle, feeling as though she were going to choke. As she watched to see what happened, Maybelle turned to her.

"My mother told me to buy material for a new dress," Maybelle said. "Do you think this color would be nice with my hair?"

No! Kate wanted to cry, though she knew the cloth would look wonderful. Why did Maybelle ask? Kate doubted that the other girl cared to be friends.

Maybelle took the blue cloth and held it up just beneath her chin. "How does it look?" she wanted to know.

Kate debated with herself. If Maybelle didn't buy the material, it might still be there for Mama.

"I know that when I have such clear, good skin I can wear just about anything," said Maybelle. "And of course my eyes are an asset too. But what do *you* think?"

Kate breathed deep. Mama often told her she mustn't lie. But what if Maybelle bought the cloth?

"It looks very nice," Kate finally croaked, hating herself for telling the truth. Without waiting for an answer, she hurried away. She couldn't bear to see Maybelle buy the lovely cloth.

In the part of the store used as a post office, Kate saw Mr. Fenton get his mail from the postmaster. Moving away from the counter, Mr. Fenton tore open an envelope. As he read the letter, he looked shocked, then angry.

Suddenly he glanced up. Seeing Kate, he smiled. As though a mask had dropped, his face smoothed into pleasant lines.

"Just received some good news from home," he said. Stuffing the letter into its envelope, he headed for the door.

Kate left Papa's letter with the postmaster, then followed Mr. Fenton outside. When the man hurried down the steps, Lutfisk barked.

Ignoring the dog, Mr. Fenton started across the road toward the creamery. But Lutfisk ran after him, continuing to bark.

"Lutfisk!" Kate shouted. "Come here!"

The dog stopped, but bared his teeth and growled.

"Be quiet!" ordered Kate, and Lutfisk obeyed. But not before Mr. Fenton disappeared through the creamery door.

Just then a team of horses and a sleigh turned onto the street. A thin boy with curly blond hair walked alongside, holding the reins.

"Hey, Kate!" he called, and she waved.

Kate had first met Stretch at Spirit Lake School. Even taller than Anders, he was older than the other students. Stretch worked for Mr. Swenson, the father of Kate's friend Josie.

As the horses turned onto a path back of the creamery, Stretch called again. "Wait till I unload this, and I can talk."

When Stretch stopped the horses next to the icehouse, Kate found a place to watch. Through open doors, she saw blocks of ice stacked high, with sawdust around the outer edges of the pile. Mr. Grimm stood on top of the ice, waiting for the tall boy to unload.

Stretch set a wooden ramp with one end on the sleigh, the other end on the top layer of ice. Mr. Grimm slid a pair of large tongs down the ramp. A long rope, tied to one handle of the tongs, passed through the loop of the other handle.

As Stretch set the tongs around a huge block of ice, Mr. Grimm tugged the rope. The tongs tightened. Hand over hand, Mr. Grimm pulled the rope. The tongs and ice followed, sliding up the ramp.

The unloading went quickly. Each time a block of ice started up the ramp, Stretch pushed another large piece into place. Then he waited for the tongs to return to him.

The sleigh was almost empty when a chunk split away from the block at the top of the ramp. The tongs loosened, and the

Accident!

ice broke free. As the block slid down the ramp, it picked up speed.

In the next instant it crashed against Stretch, pinning his hand against another block of ice. Stretch cried out in pain.

"Help!" shouted Kate as she ran forward. Climbing onto the sleigh, she leaned into the block of ice. But she couldn't push it aside.

8

Two Promises

"Help!" Kate cried again.

For an instant she stood back. Once again she pushed all her weight into the ice. No matter how hard she tried, the large block would not move.

Stretch groaned. Beads of sweat dotted his forehead.

Then Kate heard a voice behind her. "Get out of the way."

Leaping onto the sleigh, Mr. Grimm tightened tongs around the block of ice. Carefully he pulled it aside, freeing Stretch's hand.

The tall boy dropped to the sleigh. As he cradled his injured hand in his good one, he bit his lip against the pain.

"You need to see a doctor right away," said Mr. Grimm.

"I'll get the buttermaker," Kate said, and slipped away. Soon she returned with Mr. Bloomquist.

Using a clean cloth, the buttermaker wrapped Stretch's hand loosely. Mr. Grimm threw straw into the sleigh to cushion the ride, then covered Stretch with heavy horse blankets.

"I'll take him," said the buttermaker. "Sometimes it's hard to find the doctor. If someone needs me, ask him to wait."

Lifting the reins, Mr. Bloomquist called, "Giddyup!" and urged the horses forward. The team rounded the corner of the creamery and disappeared from sight.

Just then Kate saw Mr. Fenton outside the creamery. With a shrug of his shoulders, he turned away.

Kate trembled. Her knees felt weak, and she sat down on the platform. One moment she felt angry. Didn't Mr. Fenton care about Stretch? He'd been more concerned about his letter than about the accident.

The next moment she wanted to cry, just thinking how Stretch looked. Some of his fingers must have been broken, even crushed. Besides the awful pain now, what would happen to him? Stretch needed strong hands. Josie's father was teaching him to be a blacksmith.

Finally Kate stood up, crossed the street, and put on her skis. Deep in thought, she didn't notice Maybelle until the other girl climbed into a sleigh. But then Kate saw the package under her arm.

The material for Mama's dress! Kate felt sick with disappointment.

As she started home, Lutfisk followed her, jumping up now and then for attention. At Rice Lake Kate again harnessed Lutfisk to the sled. Most of the time he obeyed her commands, and Kate felt good about his progress. But she kept wondering about Mr. Fenton.

What was in the letter he received? Before hiding his feelings, he'd been very upset. *If only I could read that letter*, Kate thought.

By the time she reached Windy Hill Farm, she had decided what she wanted to do. She sought out her mother in the kitchen.

"Mama?" Kate asked as she sat down for cookies and milk.

"Yah, Kate?" Mama's golden blond hair was drawn up, piled on top of her head.

Often Kate felt surprised at how pretty her mother looked. "I've been thinking, Mama."

"Yah?"

"I've been thinking about your little brother Ben."

A flash of pain crossed Mama's face. "I've been thinking too," she said, sitting down next to Kate.

"We can't do anything about Ben," Kate said, stumbling over the words. "I mean, we can pray for him, but we can't do something. Something real, I mean, that we can see."

Mama nodded. "He needs our prayers all right. But what are you trying to say?"

Kate drew a deep breath. She cared so much about this that she was afraid to ask and have Mama say no. Yet she had no choice but to try.

"We can't do anything about Ben," Kate said again. "But we can do something about the person who stole the checks from the creamery."

"Ahhh." Light entered Mama's eyes. "So you're asking me if you can look around even though I already said no."

"Yes, Mama." Kate's voice was small.

Mama stood up, went to the stove, and poured a cup of coffee. When she sat down again, her eyes looked thoughtful. "It would be a way, you say, a way of doing something about Ben. What do you mean?"

"A way of doing something about the kind of thing Ben did," answered Kate softly.

For a time Mama was silent, sipping coffee and staring out the window. "You may be right, Kate," she said at last. "You may be right."

"You mean Anders and I can look around?"

Mama held up her hand. "I have to think about it."

Kate opened her mouth to speak, then closed it again. She couldn't push Mama any further than that.

Just then Lars called.

"Where is he?" Kate asked Mama.

"I moved him into my bedroom," Mama said. "He's starting to cough."

"Oh, Mama!" Kate felt scared. What if the cough developed into pneumonia? Everyone knew there was no good medicine to help.

"I'll sleep on the cot for a while," her mother said. The narrow cot would be uncomfortable for Mama. Yet she could be in the dining room, right next to the bedroom, where she'd hear Lars at night.

So Mama's worried too, Kate thought.

When Kate entered the bedroom, it smelled of onions. Mama had wrapped hot onions in cloth and put them on Lars's chest, hoping to draw out his cough.

Seeing Kate, Lars grinned. But the grin ended in a cough.

"This morning Erik brought over a book," said Kate. "It's named *Call of the Wild*." Books were treasured and passed around from family to family. "Erik said it's about a dog. Want me to read to you?"

Lars nodded. Pulling a chair close to the bed, Kate opened the pages.

> Buck did not read the newspapers, or he would have known that trouble was brewing, not alone for himself, but for every tide-water dog, strong of muscle and with warm, long hair, from Puget Sound to San Diego.

After a time, Kate looked up and saw Lars's eyes closed. She stopped reading, but Lars was listening, not sleeping.

"Kate?" he asked. "Who wrote that book?"

"A new author, Jack London."

"I like Buck," Lars told her. "But he was treated so mean."

Kate continued to read. Each time Lars coughed, she listened. The cough sounded loose in his chest, so she felt relieved. Maybe he'd get over this illness faster than the others. When at last he slept, she slipped away.

Putting on her coat, Kate went outside. She'd left the clothes on the line overnight, hoping they'd dry.

Pulling off her mittens, she worked quickly to take in the sheets. Looped over the line, the cloth had frozen together. As Kate tried to separate the edges, the corners tore off in her hands.

Kate sighed and was more careful with the tablecloths. Yet her fingers were clumsy with cold. In spite of her best efforts, the frozen corners again tore.

Taking the basket into the kitchen, Kate hung the sheets over doors to finish drying, then returned to the clothesline. The long one-piece underwear remained. The arms and legs stood out, like people dancing in the wind.

With the arms stretched above her head and the legs doing

an Irish jig, she found the underwear awkward to hold. Growing more tired and cold by the minute, she carried them to the house one by one. As Kate brought in the last pair, Anders looked up from the table.

Her dragging feet caught the threshold. She stumbled, then grabbed the doorjamb. Not for anything would she fall in front of Anders.

Just the same he snickered. "Doing a dance with the underwear?"

Kate stared at him, her anger as hot as an ember in the cookstove. Anders grinned, as if hoping for a fight. But then Kate saw her mother.

Near the cupboard Mama stood with a mixing bowl, her head bowed, her spoon still. Since learning about Ben, she had seemed broken, ready to weep at a moment's notice.

Without speaking, Kate turned her back on Anders and set the table.

When they finished eating supper, Anders stood up, ready to start the chores.

"Sit down," Mama told him. "Kate and I have been talking."

Anders dropped back into his chair.

"I've been thinking about what Kate said," Mama went on. "I've been thinking about my little brother."

Tears came to Mama's eyes, and she brushed them away, as though afraid to show her feelings. "I don't like to see a life wasted."

Her lips trembled as she struggled to speak. "I'm going to give you permission to look for that milk can. If you find the checks or the ledger, you'll help every farmer around Trade Lake."

"Thanks, Mama," said Anders.

In spite of his quiet voice, his eyes filled with excitement. He glanced toward Kate, seeming to ask, "What did you say to her?"

"Just a minute," said Mama. "I'm not done."

She cleared her throat. "You and Kate and Erik are good at solving mysteries. But this is more than just a game. Any person who steals from hardworking farmers has to be a dangerous criminal."

Kate's stomach tightened. Mama had thought about this all right.

"You must promise me something," Mama went on. "You must watch out for each other. Anders, you take care of Kate."

"I will, Mama." Anders flashed his lopsided grin. "I'll take care of my little sister."

"And I'll take good care of my big brother," promised Kate, her voice dangerously sweet. "He always does what I say."

But Mama refused to be sidetracked. "If you find something, you must tell a grown-up at once. You must ask someone like Andrew Anderson number 3 for help."

"We will, Mama," said Anders. For once his voice sounded serious.

Mama looked at Kate.

"I promise, Mama," she said, and meant it. She had no doubt that this was something Mama had carefully considered.

I got what I wanted—Mama's permission, thought Kate. But then she realized what a dangerous request she had made. There might be serious trouble trying to bring such a man to justice.

Deep inside, Kate felt the beginning of fear.

9

The Mysterious Message

I don't want to be afraid, Kate told herself as she had on the day Erik's horses ran away. More than once since then she'd noticed people who seemed to have courage. Now she wondered, *What does it mean to be brave?*

During the evening the outside temperature fell steadily. When Kate went upstairs, strong gusts swooped around the house. Cold seeped through the walls. As she settled into bed, a loud crack rocked the room.

Kate jumped. Her fingers balled into nervous fists as she waited, listening. What was it? A gunshot? What was wrong outside?

Next to her in the bed, Tina slept blissfully on. Kate pulled the quilts over her head and tried to stop trembling. Still the cold stayed with her, as though lodged in her heart.

Anders calls me a scaredy-cat, she thought. *But I won't be afraid.*

In that instant another loud crack shot through the room. Kate tumbled out of bed. Catching up her robe, she raced down the stairs. Feeling her way through the dark, she tiptoed to the dining room. There she lit a candle.

Nearby, Mama lay on the cot. As Kate held up the candle, her mother stirred in her sleep. Kate tiptoed closer, thinking, *She needs to know what's going on.*

When the floorboard creaked, her mother woke with a start. "Kate?" Her sleepy voice seemed to come from far away.

"I'm sorry, Mama. Sorry to wake you."

Her mother yawned. "Is something wrong?"

"A loud noise, Mama. Two loud noises. They sounded like gunshots."

"A gunshot?" Mama sat up, suddenly alert.

Just then the loud crack sounded again. Kate shivered with fear, but her mother laughed.

"Oh, *that!* It's just the house. When the temperature goes way down, the house cracks as it settles."

Kate felt like a small child, afraid over nothing. "I'm sorry I woke you, Mama," she said stiffly.

But her mother took Kate's hand. "I remember the first time I heard that sound. I didn't know what was happening, and it frightened me." Reaching down to the foot of the cot, Mama took a quilt and gave it to Kate. "Why don't you pull up a chair?"

Wrapping herself in the quilt, Kate settled down. As she felt the heat of the wood stove, her embarrassment slipped away.

"Is there anything else that frightens you?" asked Mama.

Kate hesitated. *Should I tell her I'm scared about Papa?* More than once, she'd seen articles in the newspaper. Usually they started with the words "Man hurt in logging camp." Sometimes they even said "Man killed."

"What's wrong?" asked Mama, and Kate felt it safe to begin. "Could a tree ever fall on Papa?"

"Yah," said Mama. "When lumberjacks cut down the tall pines, the trees sometimes fall the wrong way. And sometimes branches catch in other branches. A tree stays half up and half down. If it falls at a bad time, someone gets hurt."

Kate shivered. "Will Papa be all right?"

"I don't know." Mama was honest. "I hope so."

Kate pulled up her feet, away from the cold floor. "Mama, do you feel scared about Papa?"

"Yah," answered her mother. "Sometimes I'm very scared. I wonder what he's doing—if he's happy, if he's well, if he's been hurt." Mama smiled. "I have a long list. Most of all, I feel scared that he won't come safely home."

Kate clutched the quilt and wrapped herself more tightly. "What do you do? When you're scared, I mean?"

"I pray," said Mama. "I pray for him and all the men. I ask God to help me remember."

"Remember what?" Kate needed to know.

"That no matter what happens, God is with us."

For a long time Kate sat in silence. She felt better just talking about what scared her. "I want to remember too," she said finally.

As Kate crawled back into bed, she heard another loud crack. This time she paid no attention. Her imagination had turned the sounds into gunshots. She didn't want to be tricked again.

I want to know the difference, Kate thought. *I want to know when I need to be afraid, so I'm careful—and when I'm just scared about something that doesn't matter.*

On an afternoon when Anders and Erik had time off, the temperature hovered just above freezing. The boys and Kate skied to Little Trade Lake, then on to Big Trade Lake.

The places where ice had been harvested were easy to spot. Sometimes small pine trees marked the corners of a hole. Other times a tangle of branches warned people away from the thin ice.

Whenever Kate and Anders and Erik discovered such a place, they stood at a safe distance from the edge of the hole. Taking turns, they poked around in the water with a long pole. Always they searched for a milk can just beneath the surface. Yet nothing seemed out of the ordinary.

On their way home, they skied into the settlement of Four Corners. There they found Mr. Peters, Kate's organ teacher and choir director at their church.

"You're just the one I want to see," he said to Kate. "I have something to show you."

As they followed him into the church, he told them more. "I want to start a string band."

"A band for playing at church?" Kate asked.

"Certainly," he said. "But it'll be more than that. I'll ask people from other churches too. We'll play for special events around the area."

"We'll travel?" asked Kate. She liked the idea.

"We'll travel." To Mr. Peters it seemed an accomplished fact. "Would you like to play the organ? You'd have no problem with the music. You're coming along well."

Kate felt a warm flush in her cheeks. She knew Mr. Peters didn't pass out compliments unless he meant them. Yet in that moment an ache replaced her excitement. She dreaded what she had to say. "I don't know if I can take lessons anymore." Kate stumbled over the words.

"Because of the stolen cream checks?" Mr. Peters asked. "Don't worry about paying me right now."

But Kate felt torn in two. "If we get behind in the payments, we might not be able to catch up." More than anything else, she wanted to play the organ.

Mr. Peters brushed her concern aside. "Let's just wait and see what happens."

Then Kate thought of something. "How could we take an organ around?"

"I'll show you." Mr. Peters started up a flight of stairs to the balcony and the pipe organ on which Kate took lessons.

Strange, she thought, as she had many times before. *Strange that I should move this close to the first hand-pumped organ in the county.* Often Erik helped Mr. Peters by pushing a wooden handle up and down. The handle worked a bellows, bringing in air to make the pipes sound.

Now the organist walked over to a suitcase sitting on the floor. Picking it up by the handle, he held it out. "Here you are, Kate, a telescope organ. It weighs only thirty-two pounds."

Setting down the oak case, Mr. Peters opened it. To Kate's amazement an organ folded out, complete with pedals, keyboard, and music rack.

Kate giggled. "I can't believe it!"

"Believe it, believe it!" said Anders. Clearly he enjoyed this almost as much as Kate.

Standing in front of the organ, she tried the keys.

"It's like your organ at home," said Mr. Peters. "When you pump the pedals, the air comes in to make the keys sound."

"And you've got music!" Erik exclaimed. He kneeled down and pushed the pedals with his hands.

Kate started to play.

"So, what about it?" asked Mr. Peters.

Kate felt so excited that she laughed. "Of course I want to do it!"

"Good!" said Mr. Peters. "Take the music along, and you can start practicing."

Then he turned to Erik. "Now, what about you? You have a good singing voice. How about an instrument with which you can sing along?"

Erik looked disappointed. "I'd like to play the guitar, but I can't."

In that moment Kate realized how seldom Erik talked about money. Before moving to the farm next to Windy Hill, his father was cheated out of land he owned. As a result, Erik's family found it especially hard to earn the money they needed.

"Tell you what," said Mr. Peters. "I have a guitar you can start out on. I know you'll take good care of it."

A grin lit Erik's face, but Mr. Peters didn't wait for thanks. "Now, Anders, what about you?"

"Me?" Anders looked startled. When Kate laughed, he flushed red.

"Yah certainly, *you*," answered the musician. "What instrument would you like to play?"

Looking nervous, Anders pushed the blond hair out of his eyes.

To Kate's amazement, he seemed at a loss for words. "I'll think about it," he said at last.

Kate blinked. Was Anders really willing to play an instrument? He never seemed interested in music.

"You let me know," Mr. Peters answered. "If we work hard,

we'll play in Central Park on Fourth of July and Midsummer Day."

When they left the church, Kate felt that she skied on clouds instead of a snowy road. *Maybe I'll really become a great organist,* she thought. *I'll be like Jenny Lind. I'll encourage people with my music. I'll help them feel better.*

"Well, Kate, it's a start," Erik said, and she knew he was happy for her.

But Anders smirked. "Can you see my little sister? Traveling around Burnett County, playing the organ?"

He turned to Erik. "Do you remember whose company we have the pleasure of keeping?"

Erik grinned, and Anders went on. "You may think this is my little sister." With a flourish of his hand he pointed toward Kate. "But this truly is a woman of great musical gifts."

An angry flush warmed Kate's cheeks. "Aw, Anders, be quiet!" Somehow he always made her dream sound ridiculous.

"What?" he asked. "Would you tell me not to speak? Someday—*someday,* mind you, I will travel around the country, yea, around the world. I will travel ahead of you, putting up posters, advertising your coming. 'Miss Katherine O'Connell,' they will say. 'Come to hear this accomplished organist. She plays like Miss Jenny Lind sings.' "

When Erik hid a grin, Kate felt even more angry. "Stop it!" she said to Anders. "Stop it, stop it, stop it!"

But with Anders there was no stopping. "Oh ho! Methinks the lady is angry." His voice turned serious. "Kate, my dear, you must learn how to act when you go on stage."

But Kate stuck out her tongue at him. The moment she did, she felt embarrassed. *I'm thirteen years old! Almost grown-up!* As tears welled into her eyes, she skied off, unwilling to let Anders or Erik see her cry.

But her brother's voice followed her. "I'll tell everyone you're my sister. I'll say, 'I knew her when—' "

Blinking away tears, Kate turned back. "And I'll say, 'I'm not related to you!' "

Once again she took off and was still ahead when they reached the bridge over Trade River. In spite of his longer legs,

Anders skied more slowly, still careful of the ankle he'd sprained.

But Erik called ahead. "Let's stop at the creamery and find out how Stretch is doing."

They found Josie Swenson's father talking to the buttermaker. Mr. Swenson looked upset, and Kate remembered how much he wanted to help Stretch.

"Doc Jonas doesn't like it," Mr. Swenson said. "Two of Stretch's fingers are badly smashed. Doc told me to take Stretch to Minneapolis. We'll go tomorrow and see what another doctor can do."

Mr. Swenson shook his head. "Stretch needs that hand if he's going to be a blacksmith. He can't get a good grip on the sledge without it."

As though it were yesterday, Kate remembered Stretch's dream. He wanted to make good. He'd even said, "I'd like my own shop someday. Maybe in Grantsburg." Would Stretch lose his dream because of one block of ice?

Kate looked down at her own fingers. She knew how much she needed them to play the organ.

"Matilda is going with us," said Mr. Swenson, talking about his wife. "We'll take all of the children except Josie. She'll take care of the animals."

He looked at Kate. "Will you help with the milking and keep her company overnight?"

Kate grinned. "I'd like to. Tell Josie I'll come over tomorrow afternoon. Before dark."

When Mr. Swenson left, Anders asked the buttermaker, "Has anything more come up?

Mr. Bloomquist shook his head. "Not about the stolen money." But Kate had the feeling he wasn't telling everything.

That night Kate jumped out of bed twice, thinking she heard a noise outside her window. Each time, she saw a sleigh pass the house, using the shortcut through the woods to Spirit Lake.

Toward morning Kate decided what to do about a dress for Mama. When she woke again, it was daylight. Tina had slipped out of bed to dress downstairs by the stove. As Kate pulled the quilts off her head, she saw her breath in the frosty air. A draft seeped through the windows and outside walls. Before long, Kate's nose felt icy.

Bounding out of bed, she dressed quickly. Her fingers fumbled in the cold. In her warm dress and wool sweater and stockings, she hurried to a window. As she looked off in the distance, the snow glistened, white and beautiful.

Then Kate looked down, close to the house. In the snowbank on the other side of the track, there seemed to be letters—large letters that spelled words.

Kate's heart pounded as she read the warning:

STOP SNOOPING

10

The Vanishing Footprints

Stop snooping?

In spite of the cold room, Kate stood at the window looking down. Sure enough, in the bank of snow across the track, the letters stood out. She wasn't imagining the words.

Even worse, Kate realized what the message meant. *Someone was here last night. Right outside our house.*

Kate began to shake, whether from cold or fear, she wasn't sure. Yet she felt certain of one thing. Mama didn't need to see this message. Not right now. Not with Papa gone and the baby coming.

Running to the door of her bedroom, Kate called out, "Anders!"

When he didn't answer, she hurried down the stairs. Where was he, anyway? Out in the barn? Then he, too, had seen the message.

She found Anders sitting in the kitchen, calmly eating his breakfast.

As Anders looked at Kate, he seemed to read her face. Stuffing half a piece of bread in his mouth at once, he stood up. "Well, better get to the chores."

Kate pulled on her coat and went outside. Anders followed. Kate headed toward the trail that led through the farm.

"What's wrong?" asked Anders.

"C'mon. I'll show you." Kate marched straight to the bank of snow, then stopped. "What do you see?"

"S-T-O—" Here on the ground Anders needed to step back. "Stop snooping?"

Kate watched him, her eyes wide.

"Oh, Kate, it's a joke!"

"A *joke*?"

"Sure, one of the boys from school. Someone came through last night—" Anders stopped in midsentence. "Last night. After we spent all day looking around." He stepped forward and stared at the letters. "I guess you're right, Kate. It's not a joke."

"But who would do a such a thing?" she asked. "Creeping in here during the middle of night. Standing outside our windows, writing in the snow."

"Pretty awful." Anders looked angry.

Kate felt the same way. "At first it scared me. Now it makes me mad. Who does that person think he is, coming onto our farm and *threatening* us?"

"*He*? We don't know it's a he."

Kate sighed. "No, I guess we don't. But if it's the person who carried the milk can and rock, it has to be someone strong."

"Guess you're right," Anders said, clearly not liking the idea. "It's probably a man." Grinning, he flexed his muscles. "Or a big strong boy."

Once again they studied the letters in the snowbank.

"Whoever it was used a long pole," said Anders. "He stood on the trail and reached over."

"A long pole?" Kate was thinking. "Like the kind used to push ice around?"

"Could be," said Anders, "though I suppose he could use the handle of a rake or shovel." As he stood on the trail, he reached out, judging how far his hand would extend.

"Nope. It would have to be a pole—the kind you're talking

about, the kind used for harvesting ice."

"So maybe it's someone you work with."

"Yup," said Anders. "But it wouldn't have to be. Every family that takes in ice has one of those poles."

Once again Kate stared at the words. This time she saw something she hadn't noticed before. "Look!" she exclaimed, pointing.

On the left side of the message, between the trail on which they stood and the first S, was one boot print.

"Only one," said Anders.

"As though he wanted to leave it there," added Kate.

Anders studied the print. "I think you're right. It doesn't look as though he lost his balance and stepped forward by mistake."

"It's like a signature. Like someone saying, 'This is me. Watch out.'" Kate started shaking again.

"Ah, come on, Scaredy-cat!" Anders said when he saw her tremble. "We're not going to let him get the best of us."

Kate's teeth chattered, but she tightened her fists. Trying to hide her shaking, she leaned down to look at the boot print. Suddenly she noticed something. Her shivering stopped.

"Anders!"

"Ah, the lady made a discovery!"

"Be serious!" said Kate. "It's the footprint we followed through the woods that night."

"Yah, sure, you betcha." Anders shook his head and his blond hair fell into his eyes. "That's the boot print for a four-buckle overshoe. Every man and boy in Burnett County has a pair of boots like that."

Kate felt disappointed. "Well, how about the size?"

Again Anders shook his head. "About medium size. Not real big, not real little. In fact, *my* boots are bigger than his."

Kate grinned. "But you have awfully big feet!" Then she realized something. "At least we know that print isn't yours. Let's look around. Maybe there's more boot prints that size."

They started by searching the trail that passed through the farmyard, then dropped down the steep hill into the woods.

Soon Kate and Anders realized their search was hopeless. Sleighs and horses, using the shortcut to Spirit Lake, had crisscrossed the snow. There was no way to tell what direction the man took.

"Well, there's one thing we *can* do," said Kate. "Let's wipe out the words."

Anders started back to the snowbank. "I want Erik to see them."

"He'll be coming soon to pick you up. But we need to figure out how to get hold of him—when Erik doesn't know we need him, I mean."

Anders snorted. "Stop talking nonsense."

"That's not nonsense. There must be some way we can send messages back and forth."

"Well, we can't signal with a mirror," Anders said. "That'd be all right if there were just a field between us. But there's also a big woods."

Just the same, he had a think-it-through look in his eyes. Kate felt sure his mind was ticking faster than a clock.

A moment later, Lutfisk bounded up. Pulling off his mittens, Anders knelt down to scratch behind the dog's ears. Lutfisk stretched out his long tongue and licked his master's face.

Anders grinned. "I know what we can do! Lutfisk gets the cows when I tell him. Why can't we train him to get Erik?"

"Why not?" Kate liked the idea. "I'll sew a little cloth bag. You can tie it to a rope and put the rope around Lutfisk's neck."

"Yup, that would do it!" Anders looked as excited as Kate felt.

Getting his ski pole, he walked into the bank of snow. "I'm not going to wait for Erik." Carefully he wiped out every letter. "Mama doesn't need something more to worry about."

"But we have to tell Mr. Bloomquist," said Kate.

"Or Andrew Anderson number 3." Anders started for the barn.

For a minute Kate stood there, looking off over Rice Lake. In the morning sunlight the surrounding hills seemed quiet, peaceful, safe.

But then Anders called to her. "C'mere, Kate!"

When she came near to the barn, Anders held up his hand, stopping her. "Look!" He pointed down.

In front of the door the tracks of people and animals mingled. But in the snow just off the path, Kate saw one medium-sized boot print. "It's not yours, is it?" Even as she asked, she knew the answer.

"Like you said, my feet are bigger."

"I don't think he meant for us to see this one," said Kate slowly.

Anders agreed. "If he came in the dark, he probably didn't know he stepped off the path."

Then Kate had an even worse thought. "You know what, Anders? That boot print points right toward the barn, as though someone opened the door and walked in. Whoever wrote the message could still be hiding in there."

Anders scowled. "Thanks a lot! Can't you think of something better to tell me?" Watching where he stepped, he looked for more medium-sized boot prints.

Inside the fence that extended beyond one end of the barn, the cows and sheep had trampled the snow, hiding any possible evidence. Anders and Kate turned away from there, knowing any search was hopeless.

The trail to Spirit Lake passed close to the other end of the barn. Staring at the tracks, Anders shook his head.

Kate saw what he meant. Here, too, sleighs and horses had crisscrossed the snow.

"Well, better get it over with." Anders returned to the side door of the barn. Slowly he pushed it open. In the stillness the door creaked loudly.

Anders waited, as though listening, then peered into the gloomy shadows.

Close at hand, two cows turned their heads to watch. From farther away, Wildfire whinnied her greeting. Beyond that, the sheep softly bleated.

Kate followed Anders inside. In the half light her brother seized a pitchfork and stalked from one end of the barn to the other.

11

Sounds From the Darkness

*T*wo cats leaped out from behind a barrel. Kate jumped. But Anders walked on, searching the shadows.

Still holding the pitchfork, he climbed the ladder to the loft. As he crossed from one end of the haymow to the other, the floorboards creaked. From overhead his footsteps sounded as heavy as a man's.

Finally Anders started throwing hay down through the hole onto the main floor. Kate spread it out for Wildfire and the cows, but she felt uneasy. Someone could easily hide in the great mound of hay in the loft. Without moving all that hay, it would be impossible to find him.

As Anders milked the cows, Kate went to the hen house. Finding the water frozen, she brought warm water from the house. As she fed the chickens, she kept a wary eye on Big Red.

When Tina came in, the rooster looked up from the morsel he pecked. Cocking his head, he cast a beady eye toward Tina, then started toward her.

Backing away, Tina held out her hands to ward him off. But

Kate took no chances. Bounding over, she stood in front of the little girl.

As though to say "Who do you think you are?" the rooster stretched back his long neck. Flapping his wings, he flew upward. As his claw reached out, the sharp spur on his leg tore Kate's skin.

"Owwwww!" she cried, jumping out of reach. "Ow, ow, ow!"

At a safe distance, Kate checked her leg. Her wool stocking was torn as well as her long underwear. Drops of blood left red stains.

When Mama saw Kate's leg, she exclaimed, "That rooster!" Soon after, she told Anders, "I want you to butcher that old chicken. He's too mean and tough for frying, but we'll have a good stew."

As the family finished breakfast, bells jingled in the yard. Kate pulled on her warm coat. "I want to ride with Erik and Anders to Trade Lake," she told Mama. "I'll ski back." Clutching a package, she hurried outside.

Anders loaded their milk cans into the sleigh. Kate put in her skis, then climbed up between Erik and her brother. On the way to town, she and Anders told Erik about the message in the snow.

"And guess what?" said Kate. "Anders is going to train Lutfisk to fetch you!"

Erik grinned. "*Fetch* me?"

"Like he does the cows!" Kate enjoyed the joke. "We'll tie a little cloth bag around his neck. If Lutfisk obeys, we can get hold of you whenever we want."

"Good idea!" Erik said. "Let's start training him after work this afternoon. He won't have trouble learning."

At the creamery Erik and Anders unloaded their milk cans. "Can we talk for a minute?" Anders asked the buttermaker.

Mr. Bloomquist led the three of them from the large room into the small one and closed the door between. As they sat down, Andrew Anderson came in through the door leading directly outside. Anders told the two men about the message and the boot prints.

I don't like it!" exclaimed Mr. Anderson. "Your father's gone, and you folks are alone on the farm."

"Is there anything more we need to know?" asked Anders. "Anything that would help us figure out who the man could be?"

The buttermaker looked at Mr. Anderson. When the older man nodded, Mr. Bloomquist spoke quietly. "Andrew and I didn't want to get you any more involved. But in spite of our good plans, you're in the middle of this. You might as well know we aren't getting our checks from New York."

"What do you mean?" asked Kate.

"Every Wednesday the creameries in this area haul tubs of butter to Grantsburg. We fill up a refrigerated railroad car. It reaches New York in time for the Monday morning market."

"They like our product," said Mr. Anderson. "Burnett County butter always brings a cent above market price. But we aren't getting paid. For three weeks we haven't received a check."

Anders turned to Kate. "Do you understand what that means?"

"I think so. The farmers bring in their milk. The creamery separates it and keeps the cream that makes the butter. The creamery sends the butter to New York. And if New York doesn't pay, the farmers don't get paid. Right?"

"You've got it." The scowl was back on her brother's face.

"It affects all the farmers who bring in cream," said Mr. Anderson. "Which is just about every farmer in the Trade Lake area."

Kate sighed. "It's getting worse all the time, isn't it?"

"But there's something to give us hope." Mr. Anderson squared his shoulders. "The bank gave us a short-term loan to help until checks come from New York. We'll reissue the checks for the farmers."

"Write them out again?" Kate asked. "I thought you couldn't because the ledger was stolen."

"It was. But we still have some daily work sheets. Our good buttermaker used them to record how much cream each farmer brought in. For some strange reason, some are missing. But we'll do what we can."

"You'll add up those amounts?" asked Erik.

Mr. Anderson nodded. "We can't pay the full amount until

we find the ledger. But we'll make out checks for what we know. It'll take time, but we can do it."

Time, thought Kate. *Just what we don't have. Mama needs a new dress now.*

"If all goes well," said Anders.

"If all goes well." Mr. Anderson sighed.

Watching his eyes, Kate wondered, *How long will a bank loan money to a business where everything is going wrong?* The bank had a responsibility to other customers too.

"I have to go to North Branch for a few days," Mr. Anderson continued. "I need a better hiding place for the work sheets."

Anders looked at Kate and grinned. "Well, we know just the place."

Kate laughed. "Why don't you take them over to Swensons' right away, before Mr. Swenson leaves? Tell him Kate and Anders and Erik sent you."

Soon after, Mr. Anderson left by the door leading directly outside. Anders and Erik followed. Through the window, Kate saw them turn the horses toward the ice harvesting on Little Trade Lake.

Using the other door, Kate walked into the main room. Already Mr. Bloomquist was taking milk from a farmer. Stopping in front of the large wooden churn, Kate watched it rotate.

Then she heard low voices. Curious, Kate walked around to the other side of the churn and found Gunnar Grimm and LeRoy Fenton. As she stared at the men, they stopped talking.

Kate's heart pounded. *There're so many doors in this place. How long have they been here?*

She wished she could run from the room. Instead, she walked slowly toward the outside door, trying to pretend it wasn't important that she saw them. As she crossed the street, her mind raced. *Gunnar Grimm. LeRoy Fenton. What did it mean?*

The morning felt warm for January, and Kate welcomed the gentle breeze. At least there was one thing she could do. Clutching the package she'd brought from home, she hurried into Gustafson's store. When the clerk showed her the material she had on hand, Kate's heart sank. There was nothing as nice as that blue cloth.

"Sorry," she said finally. "I just don't see what I want."

"Is it for yourself?" the woman asked.

Kate shook her head. "For my mother."

"Ahhh!" The clerk remembered. "You're Kate O'Connell. Your mother's going to have a baby."

Feeling miserable, Kate nodded. If only she'd been able to buy the material the other day, before Maybelle came in. Now it was too late.

But the clerk folded back a large piece of cloth. "Here it is—under here. Isn't this what you wanted?"

In the dim light of the store the blue cloth seemed alive with color. "It's still here?" Kate couldn't believe it.

The clerk smiled. "Yah."

"But Maybelle was going to buy that piece!"

The clerk looked as though she wanted to laugh. "Maybelle purchased green material instead. She told me, 'If Kate says the color looks wonderful, it must be awful.' "

Kate giggled. "And I was telling the truth!"

She set down the package she'd brought along. As she opened the wrapping, she gazed at the mittens and long scarf inside. Hand knit and warm, they were also beautiful. Mama had knitted them as a Christmas gift, using more expensive red yarn.

As Kate touched the wool, her hand lingered, feeling the softness. She had worn the scarf and mittens only once.

Tempted to change her mind, she spoke quickly. "Can I trade these for the blue cloth?"

"Trade the scarf and mittens? They're lovely," said the clerk. "And they're unusually well made." She seemed to guess how much Mama's gift meant to Kate. "Are you sure you want to give them up?"

For a moment Kate hesitated. "Yes," she said finally. "You make trades, don't you?"

"Yah." The clerk still looked unwilling. "If you're sure. And you can pick out some lace for your mother's dress."

Kate thought quickly. If Mama wanted lace, she could take some from another dress. "Can I get a small piece of flannel instead?"

The woman smiled. "A small piece."

As soon as the clerk wrapped the material, Kate hurried from the store. All the way to Windy Hill Farm she thought about what she'd done. One moment she felt excited. The next moment she remembered the red scarf and mittens.

When Kate reached home, she led Mama to her favorite chair. "Sit down," Kate said. "Close your eyes. Open your hands!" She placed the package on her mother's outstretched palms.

Mama pulled aside the paper wrapping and gasped, "Oh, Kate!" Carefully she stroked the blue material. "How did you buy such lovely cloth?" As she heard the story, tears welled up in her eyes.

Then, from beneath the dress material, Kate pulled the flannel cloth. "For the baby," she said. Seeing Mama's soft smile, Kate felt glad she'd made the trade.

Late that afternoon she skied to Josie's. Kate looked forward to being with her friend. They'd talk half the night together.

Bounding alongside, Lutfisk yipped and jumped in Kate's way. Finally he sniffed some rabbit tracks and bounded off.

As the winter sun set in the west, Kate and Josie brought in Swensons' cows and milked them. By the time they finished, night had settled over the farm.

The main floor of Swensons' log house had two rooms—a sitting and eating area and a large kitchen. Between the two rooms, stairs went up to the second floor.

"Can you imagine all my brothers on that train?" asked Josie as she and Kate ate supper at the kitchen table.

Kate laughed. Her friend had six brothers and two sisters. "Jacob and Joshua, Jonah and Jesse, Jethro and James. And Rebecca and Jennifer."

Finally Kate had gotten them all straight, even remembering their names. But she had to say them in order like a rhyme.

Across the table, Josie leaned forward. "I've got so much to tell you!" With no school until April 8, they didn't get to see each other as often as they liked.

Just then Kate heard something—a strange sound that seemed to come from along the outside wall. "What was that?" she asked, looking toward the large window next to the table.

"What was what?" Josie answered. "I didn't hear anything." Kate went back to eating. A moment later she heard a scratching noise, as though something were dragged along the wall.

Standing up, Kate went to the window and peered out. She saw nothing but the blackness of night.

Slowly Kate sat down. She was positive she'd heard a noise. But the glass pane yawned dark and cold and empty. "Is there some way to cover that window?" she asked.

"Why?" Josie looked as though she thought her friend a bit strange. "There's nothing out there."

"How do you know?"

"I just know," said Josie.

But Kate had lived in Minneapolis. She didn't like having windows without shades pulled at night.

"Stop acting like a city girl," Josie told her. "Out in the country there's never anyone around."

Kate settled back in her chair, unwilling to show her friend how uneasy she felt.

"Now, tell me everything that's happened," said Josie. Her soft skin seemed to glow in the light of the kerosene lamp.

But Kate once more heard the noise. Wanting more light, she said, "I can hardly see to eat. Do you have another lamp?"

Josie laughed. "Anders is right. You *are* a scaredy-cat! And you're supposed to keep *me* company!"

Kate swallowed. Even so, she carried a lamp from the other room into the kitchen. Carefully she set the lamp on the end of the table closest to the window.

Just then the scratching started again, louder this time. "Oh!" said Josie, her hazel eyes widening with fright. "Now I know what you mean."

"Any ideas?" asked Kate, trying to sound calm and unafraid.

Josie shook her head. "It can't be a branch rubbing against the house. There's no tree there."

"Then what *is* it?" asked Kate.

"I don't know," Josie whispered. "What should we do?"

"Maybe we could take a quilt," Kate whispered back. "We could hang it over the window. If there's someone there, he couldn't see us."

"*He*? Who do you think it is?" Josie's eyes looked as round as silver dollars.

"I don't know, but whoever it is couldn't see us."

Josie nodded, too scared to speak.

Kate looked toward the window. "Is there some way I could fasten a quilt at the top?"

But just then a head appeared above the windowsill—a head with beady black eyes.

In terror Kate pushed back her chair. It fell over, crashing against the floor.

12

The Secret Room

"Josie!" Kate cried.

Her friend was already hiding under the kitchen table. "Come down here," Josie whispered, her voice hoarse.

But Kate felt too frightened to move. She stared at the darkened window.

As she watched, the head moved closer, closer. Yes, the eyes were large and beady. Something red waved above them.

Kate clutched the edge of the kitchen table. Now a large yellow beak appeared. The mouth opened and closed. Through the glass Kate heard a hoarse cry. *Cock-a-doodle-doooooo!*

Suddenly Kate started to laugh. She dropped into a chair.

"Are you crazy?" asked Josie from under the table.

Kate held her sides with laughter. "Cock-a-doodle-dooo, all right!"

When Kate could stand up, she flung open the kitchen door. Hurrying around the corner, she grabbed Anders as he and Erik tried to get away.

"You boys!" sputtered Kate. "How can you do such an awful thing? Scaring Josie out of her wits!"

Anders snorted. "Scaring Kate, you mean. Not a bad joke, huh?"

"I'll get even with you!" Kate stormed.

But her brother's hand darted out, thrusting the rooster's head in her face.

Backing away, Kate ran up the steps. When she reached the doorway, she turned. "Well, as long as you're here, you might as well come in. Josie's got cookies."

"What a gracious invitation!" Anders exclaimed. Just the same, he and Erik started for the house.

By the time they reached the kitchen, Josie was out from under the table. Smoothing her hair, she smiled at Anders.

Taking off his cap, he pushed back his thatch of blond hair. A lopsided grin lit his face. Anders had more than one reason for walking this far, Kate felt sure.

She glanced at Erik. *Does he feel the same way about me?*

As her fear disappeared, Kate's normal curiosity returned. "How did you *do* that?" she asked Anders. She recognized Big Red's head. The rooster must have found his way into the stew pot. "How do you make his beak open and close?"

Anders laughed. "Kate, your curiosity is going to get the best of you someday."

Erik explained. "See this muscle in the rooster's neck?" Anders pulled it up and down.

Kate still didn't want to get too close.

After devouring Josie's cookies, Anders told Kate, "I discovered more footprints."

Her eyes widened. "Where?"

"On the one side of the barn we didn't check. You know that back door? I found footsteps leading away."

"And you followed them?"

"Not very far. A short way off they disappeared. Vanished. Blotted out by blowing snow."

When the boys left for home, Josie told Kate to bring a lamp. "I want to show you something."

Josie led her to the secret room they'd discovered a short time before. Kate hadn't seen the room since the day they found it. She felt eager to look around.

Together they opened the door, then stepped inside. The room was narrow, probably three feet wide at most, but also long. On one end, the ceiling was high enough for a man to stand. On the other end, the ceiling went close to the floor.

As Kate set the lamp down, Josie picked up a carefully wrapped package.

"What is it?" asked Kate.

"Before Papa left, Andrew Anderson number 3 came over. He told Papa that you and Anders sent him."

Kate grinned. "We sent him all right."

"Papa said, 'I'm going to Minneapolis today.' They talked about it. Finally they agreed on something. When Papa left, he told me, 'I put some papers in the secret room. They'll be safe there. No one knows we have them.'"

So Mr. Anderson had liked their idea! Kate felt glad. Certainly the hidden room had to be the safest place around. Leaving the package in a corner of the room, Kate and Josie returned to the kitchen.

As they cleaned up supper dishes, Kate heard a sound along the road. "What's that?" she asked, and listened again.

She couldn't decide what she heard. Perhaps a horse coming their way. Yet there was something strange. Was the horse moving slowly, as though the driver didn't want anyone to know?

Kate blew out the nearest kerosene lamp. "Josie, get the other one."

As the second flame flickered out, the girls stood in darkness. "What's wrong?" Josie whispered.

"I think there's a horse coming. But if there is, it's not wearing bells."

"But everyone puts bells on their harness," answered Josie.

"I know," Kate whispered. "Shhh!"

Together they crept into the large open room. Standing well back, they gazed out the window.

The night was too dark for Kate and Josie to see well, but the outline of a horse seemed to pass between the sky and the house.

Kate ducked down. "It's the boys," she whispered as a horse and cutter stopped at the hitching rail. "They've got Wildfire this time. They're coming back to scare us."

As the girls watched, something shadowy moved next to the

horse. Kate heard the clink of harness. "It's Anders and Erik all right. How can we scare *them*?"

Moving away from Kate, Josie crawled forward to one side of the window. Even as she peered out, she edged back. "Kate, it's—"

But Kate interrupted. "How can we get even?"

On her hands and knees, she crawled closer to the other side of the window. Trying to stay out of sight, she stared into the darkness.

"Kate—" Josie started again.

Just then the person turned away from his horse. For a moment his heavyset body seemed outlined against the snow. In that instant Kate felt panic in every part of her being.

She scrambled back from the window. "Josie—" In the darkness Kate's voice trembled.

"I know," answered her friend. "It's not the boys. What can we do?"

As she spoke, a boot squeaked on the snowy path leading to the house.

Kate had only one moment to think. Staying on her hands and knees, she crawled toward the secret room. Finding the latch, she opened the door, and slipped inside. Josie followed close behind.

With no windows, the small room was even darker than the one they left. But Kate closed the door behind them.

"Kate—" said Josie.

Laying a hand on her friend's arm, Kate whispered, "Shhh! There's someone at the outside door."

"I wish we could see," Josie whispered back.

The two girls strained to hear. The door into the house creaked. Next to the floor, Kate felt a rush of cold air. The door closed.

Kate and Josie sat without moving, scarcely breathing. From their hiding place, they heard the scratch of a match.

Kate seemed to see a small, flickering light. Then it disappeared. Had she imagined it?

Again she heard a match being lit. From her place next to the door, she gazed up. Above her head, she saw a dim light. As she watched, the light brightened. Had the intruder lit a kerosene lamp?

In the next moment Kate realized something. *If light can come in, I can see out.* Without making a sound, she stood up.

Moving her fingers toward the splinter of light, Kate found small pieces of wood set into the door. Like narrow slats, they slid beneath her hand. One moved up, another down, leaving a crack wide enough to look through.

Kate moved her face closer to the crack. Someone stood at the dining room table, holding the lamp. A cap covered his hair, and his back was turned toward Kate.

A man of medium height—strong, muscular, and wearing a red and black plaid mackinaw. Who was he? LeRoy Fenton and Gunnar Grimm both had such jackets.

Kate watched each movement. *Look this way!* she wanted to cry.

Instead, the man moved toward the opposite wall. Holding out the lamp, he started around the room, knocking the wall with his free hand. Why was he here?

In that moment Kate remembered the two men listening in the creamery. Was this one of them? Was he trying to find the daily work sheets?

As the man passed to the other side of the wood stove, Kate lost sight of him. From the sound of his movements, she decided that he had started around the end wall.

Where's Lutfisk? Kate wondered. If ever she needed him, it was now! But she heard no bark, no dog somewhere in the woods, chasing rabbits. Not even off in the distance.

Instead, she felt a movement. Close to her feet, Josie quietly shifted her position in the darkness.

Right outside the hidden room, the heavy footsteps moved toward them. Closer and closer the man came. *Why is he searching?* Kate wondered again.

Near at hand he rapped the wall, and Kate had a terrible thought. *Maybe he's looking for me.*

Heart in her throat, she stepped back. Suddenly she felt something beneath her foot.

Josie gasped.

I stepped on her hand! Kate thought.

The man drew closer, still rapping. Would the door sound hollow? What if he discovered the peephole Kate used?

With all her heart, she wanted to look out, to see the face of the man who searched. With all her heart, she knew she could not. If she stepped on Josie again, her friend might cry out.

13

More Bad News

Then the man rapped, directly in front of Kate, but above the slats and below. After what seemed hours, he walked on.

Careful of Josie this time, Kate moved forward. As she peered through the narrow crack, the light moved out of the room.

For a minute Kate waited, wanting to be sure. Finally she knelt down next to Josie. "He's in the kitchen."

Josie breathed deeply, as though she'd held her breath all that time. As they listened to the man move around, neither of the girls spoke.

When Kate once again stood up, she saw a sliver of light near the doorway. Instead of entering the room, the unwelcome visitor started up the stairs. Step by heavy step, he climbed to the second floor.

"What do you think he's looking for?" asked Josie.

"For the papers, don't you think?" At least that's what Kate wanted to believe.

"Mr. Anderson's papers?" Josie sounded disturbed. "But no one knows they're here."

"*Someone* knows he brought them," Kate whispered. "That someone is in this house!"

Just then the heavy footsteps started down the stairs. Kate took her place at the peek hole, trying for a glimpse of the intruder's face.

Yet when the man came into her line of vision, she saw only his back. Setting the lamp on the table, he blew out the flame.

As Kate's eyes adjusted to the darkness, she felt rather than saw the man move to the outside door. When it creaked, she knew it opened. When it creaked again, she believed it closed. But was the intruder inside or out?

Without moving, Kate and Josie waited in the secret room. Her ear close to the slats, Kate heard hooves along the icy road. At first near at hand, they gradually moved off in the distance. Finally the hoofbeats stopped. Only then did the girls come out of their hiding place.

"We should look outside," said Kate. "Maybe the man left footprints."

"Maybe," said Josie. "But you're not going to catch me out in the dark. I'm staying right here."

Kate started for the door, but Josie called her back. "Kate, we're here all alone. There's no one else around."

Kate pulled on her coat.

"What if that awful man left his horse and walked back?" Josie asked. "You wouldn't hear him."

Her hand on the doorknob, Kate stopped. She didn't like the idea of going out in the dark any more than Josie. "I'll look in the morning," Kate said, slowly taking off her coat. "It's not snowing. If there are tracks, they'll still be there."

From that time on they lit no lamps. Instead, they pulled quilts from Josie's bed and spread them out on the floor of the secret room. Long after they crawled between the blankets, they lay awake in the darkness.

"I'm scared," said Josie at last.

"Me too," answered Kate. They had taken off their shoes, but still wore their dresses.

"Do you think he'll come back?" Josie's voice quavered.

"No, I don't think so." Kate wanted to be strong for her friend. Instead, she felt shivers of fear.

The secret room was getting cold. Kate opened the door a

crack to let in heat from the nearby stove. As she tried to settle down, she thought about the night their house made loud cracking sounds.

"What do you do when you're scared?" she had asked.

"I pray," Mama had said. "And I ask God to help me remember."

"Remember what?" Kate wanted to know.

"That no matter what happens, God is with us."

I want to remember too, Kate thought now, as she had on that night. Soon she fell asleep, warm and tucked away as if in a nest, within the secret room.

The next morning Kate woke to the barking of a dog. "Where am I?" she muttered as she opened her eyes. The room was dark with only a sliver of light.

As she came fully awake, she thought back to the evening before. The boys coming to scare them. The man who entered the house, searching for something. The hidden room that sheltered them.

The dog continued barking, as though trying to get their attention. Sometimes he seemed close at hand, other times farther away. But the bark seemed familiar.

"Lutfisk!" Kate exclaimed. "What's he doing here?"

Scrambling out from beneath the quilts, she slipped on her shoes and hurried to a window in the large open room. It was Lutfisk all right. He bounded between Swensons' front door and the hitching rail.

As Kate stepped outside, the dog's bark changed to a joyful yelp. His tail wagging, he raced up the steps onto the porch.

Kate knelt down and hugged the dog. When he licked her face, she drew back and laughed. "Good boy!" she exclaimed, relieved to have him here. "Where were you last night when I needed you?"

Lutfisk barked, a quick, short yip, as though talking to her.

"I suppose you want your ears scratched," said Kate. Lutfisk wiggled and yipped again.

In the bright morning light the snow twinkled, as though

covered with diamonds. In such a world Kate's fear of the night before seemed impossible. Had someone really entered Swensons' house?

Recalling her plan to look for footprints, Kate stood up. Usually the Swenson family used the kitchen door. Maybe the unwelcome visitor made the only tracks to the front door.

Walking to the edge of the porch, Kate looked down. She groaned, feeling sick all the way through. "Why did I wait?"

She found it hard to remember how afraid she'd been. "Why didn't I look right away?" She only blamed herself.

Lutfisk bounded off the steps. Kate tried to catch him, but it was already too late. For some time the dog had run back and forth between the porch and hitching rail. Any human footprints were covered by those of Lutfisk.

Walking up and down the path, Kate searched, but finally had to give up. Not one clear boot print remained.

When Kate left Josie's, she skied to Trade Lake. She found Anders and Erik on their lunch hour, warming up in the creamery.

Just seeing them, Kate felt better. Sitting down in the room with the steam boiler, she spoke in a low voice, telling the boys what had happened last night.

"You never saw the man's face?" Anders asked.

Kate shook her head. "But he looked strong. Medium height, shorter than you. He wore a red and black plaid mackinaw."

Her brother snorted. "You're describing half the men in Burnett County. Did you see his hair?"

Again Kate had to say no. "Covered up by a cap."

Erik scowled. "I don't like it. You and Josie were there alone!"

Anders felt the same way. "What if that man found you? We better tell the buttermaker."

They found Mr. Bloomquist in the large open room, packing butter into sixty-pound tubs. With quick movements, he placed a circle of parchment in the bottom of a tub, then another piece of parchment around the sides.

"We need to talk to you," Anders said.

"Bad news?" the buttermaker asked, his voice low.

Anders nodded.

Mr. Bloomquist glanced around. "Just a minute." Standing up, he walked over to take samples from the milk brought in by two farmers.

"Something's wrong with Mr. Bloomquist," said Kate.

When the short, stocky man returned to them, he filled the tub with butter. Folding the liner across the top, he set the wooden cover in place.

What's the matter? Kate wondered. *He acts as if we aren't here.*

Anders tried to speak, but Mr. Bloomquist looked around, as though saying, "Wait till the farmers are gone."

Taking four tin strips, he nailed the cover in place, then stamped it with the name and address of the creamery. Below that he wrote a shipping number.

By the time the two farmers left, Anders was tapping his foot, clearly tired of waiting. Mr. Bloomquist nailed the last tub shut, then led them into the smaller room. Dropping into his chair, he said, "Now, let's hear what's going on."

Erik and Anders pulled up benches, and Kate told the buttermaker about the nighttime visitor.

Mr. Bloomquist shook his head. "Did Andrew leave the work sheets there?"

"I think so," answered Kate. "We didn't open the package, but Josie's father said Mr. Anderson brought papers."

The buttermaker moved restlessly in his chair. "It's one thing for someone to steal the cream checks. They're small, and the thief might get by, cashing them in different places. But why would he take the ledger? And why would he want the work sheets?"

As though too nervous to sit still, Mr. Bloomquist jumped up and paced the floor. Finally he came to a stop in front of Kate. "As long as he's searched Swensons' house, maybe that's the safest place to leave the papers. At least till Andrew gets back. But how did the man know where to look?"

Kate bit her lip. Should she say something about Leroy Fenton and Gunnar Grimm standing behind the butter churn? Was one of them guilty, or both? Or neither one? Kate couldn't prove a thing, and she might blame an innocent man.

Once more Mr. Bloomquist started pacing. Though a young man, his face looked old with worry. "When I got this job in November, I never dreamed it'd be like this. But there's more."

Striding to the doorway, Mr. Bloomquist looked around the large room, then shut the door. As he sat down, Kate, Anders, and Erik drew close.

Even so, Mr. Bloomquist spoke so low that Kate could barely hear. "Of all the things that have happened, this is the worst!"

14

The Butter Tub Disaster

The buttermaker ran his fingers through his hair. "What a time for Andrew to be gone. I've never needed him more!"

"What's wrong?" Kate found it hard to believe anything could be worse than what had already happened.

"When we finish packing the butter tubs, we set them in the cold room," Mr. Bloomquist explained. "This morning I didn't feel right about the butter packed yesterday. I did something I've never done before. I opened a tub. The butter looked all right, but I tasted it." His voice rose in anger. "It was salty. Too salty to eat!"

Kate looked at Erik, and Erik looked at Anders. No one spoke.

Again Mr. Bloomquist ran his fingers through his hair. "What if I'd sent out those tubs of butter? Who would buy from us again?"

"Has anyone got something against you?" asked Erik. "Like a grudge, I mean?"

Mr. Bloomquist shrugged. "I don't know. I've wondered if

someone's trying to ruin me. But I don't have any enemies. I've been here only since November. Whoever spoiled the butter did it in just a few minutes."

"What do you mean?" Kate asked.

"When I finish churning a batch of butter, I check it for quality. Yesterday I tasted the butter, and it was exactly right. Then Gunnar Grimm called me into this room. When I returned, I filled the tubs."

"You were away from the butter for just a few minutes?" Erik asked.

"Not very long. I took a sample from a farmer too. In that time someone came in, threw in a large amount of salt, and churned it enough to mix it."

"The tubs you just packed—they're good butter?" Erik asked.

"They're good, all right. That's why I closed them up. But every tub packed yesterday had too much salt."

Just then Kate remembered something. "When Mr. Anderson talked about a contest, what did he mean?"

"There's a state buttermaker's contest next week. The creamery board wants me to enter."

"Is there a prize?" Anders asked.

"The largest amount ever offered by the state buttermaker's convention." Picking up a newspaper, Mr. Bloomquist pointed to an article.

Anders whistled. "$1,139.40! That's a lot of money."

"It would be divided among the winners. If I were a winner, it would give our creamery a good name."

"Something you need right now," Erik said. He stood up. "Anders and I need to get back to work."

But Kate had another question. "Was this butter supposed to go to the contest?"

Mr. Bloomquist shook his head. "No, to New York. But if a batch was ruined once, it could happen again. We might not even know for a while."

Kate felt more uneasy all the time. How could she find out what she needed to know?

"Mr. Bloomquist," she said slowly, "Mr. Fenton works for you, doesn't he?"

"Part time, learning the business. He's a good worker, knows what he's doing. Yesterday he was gone, harvesting ice."

Except for a few minutes, thought Kate, remembering again how she'd seen Mr. Fenton near the churn. Soon after, Mr. Grimm must have called the buttermaker into this room. Were the two men working together? Or did someone else spoil the butter?

"What about Mr. Grouch?" Anders asked, as though sensing Kate's thoughts. "I mean, Gunnar Grimm. You trust him?"

The buttermaker drew back, as if offended by the question. "Certainly. He's new around here, but he's trustworthy."

As Anders and Erik headed for the door, the buttermaker called to them. "The man who usually hauls butter to Grantsburg has the flu. Want to take your team tomorrow, Erik? Good money in it for you."

"Sure thing," Erik said. "This is our last day harvesting ice. The men we filled in for are coming back."

When Kate reached home, Mama had cut out her new dress. Her nimble fingers moved swiftly as she pinned the pieces together. "The cloth is beautiful!" Mama told Kate as she opened her arms for a hug.

But Kate saw the worry in Mama's eyes. Lars was still coughing, and coughing hard. Again Kate read to him from *Call of the Wild*.

That evening, while doing chores, Kate told Anders what she'd seen the day before.

"Mr. Grouch?" asked her brother. "And LeRoy Fenton? Somehow those two men keep popping up. I wish I could keep a better eye on them."

On her way to the barn the next morning, Kate read the thermometer. Thirty-four degrees below zero, Fahrenheit. Long before sunup, she and Anders milked the cows. When Erik drove into the yard, he helped Anders load the milk cans into the sleigh.

Erik wore his father's long coonskin coat. A warm cap covered his brown hair. With his forehead, nose, and chin wrapped in a heavy scarf, only his eyes showed.

Just then Lutfisk bounded up. "Erik!" said Anders, pointing to his friend. But the dog faced Erik and barked.

"He doesn't recognize your clothes," Anders said.

Erik pulled off a leather glove and stretched out his hand. "Come here, Lutfisk. It's me—Erik."

Again the dog barked. Anders pointed. "Go to Erik."

Wagging his tail, but still cautious, Lutfisk walked over. Erik let him smell his hand.

"Good dog," said Anders. "Let's try it again."

When he felt satisfied with what Lutfisk was learning, Anders led the others into the kitchen. While Erik warmed up by the cookstove, Kate and Anders pulled on every warm piece of clothing they owned. Anders wore Papa's long fur coat, while Kate put on Anders's sheepskin jacket. It hung down, well past her knees, which was just what she wanted.

Mama watched as they pulled on wool mittens. "If that cold air touches your face more than a minute, your skin will freeze," she warned. "And you're going all the way to Grantsburg?"

"We don't want to worry you, Mama." For once Anders didn't tease. "The man who usually takes the butter is sick."

Mama shook her head. "Do everything you can to be careful."

"We will, Mama," Anders promised.

Kate wrapped a scarf around her face, leaving only slits for her eyes. Carrying bricks warmed in the oven, she went outside.

"*Great* day for a trip!" Erik exclaimed as he followed Kate. Through the scarf covering his mouth, his voice sounded muffled. With all his heavy clothing, he moved slowly, yet he managed to help Kate onto the seat at the front of the sleigh.

Erik set the packed lunch in the back. Mama made sure they wouldn't go hungry. Though wrapped in blankets, the food would be frozen long before they reached Grantsburg.

"It'll get warmer this afternoon," Anders called to Mama, as he left the house. "Might even get up to ten below!"

The boys sat down on either side of Kate, and Erik flicked the reins. Queen and Prince headed out with the bells on their harness jingling.

During their drive to Trade Lake, the eastern sky turned red,

The Butter Tub Disaster

then orange and gold. When they reached the creamery, Kate climbed down to warm up.

Mr. Bloomquist opened a door. LeRoy Fenton and Gunnar Grimm were with him. As the three men rolled out the sixty-pound tubs of butter, Erik and Anders loaded them onto the sleigh. Then all of them came in to warm up at the steam boiler.

"God dag, god dag!" said Anders, as he pulled off his mittens.

Kate glanced sideways at him. Her brother sounded as if he were saying "good dog." But he seldom spoke the Swedish greeting. What was his reason now?

"A good day to go to Grantsburg," Anders continued.

A slow smile eased onto Mr. Fenton's face. He pulled off the cap that covered his sandy-colored hair.

Erik looked even more alert than usual. Kate wondered if he and Anders had planned something?

"You know what I like about this cold?" Anders asked. "I like watching the steam rise from the horses' nostrils. Dragon breath, I call it!"

Kate saw a corner of Mr. Grimm's mouth turn up. She felt surprised. According to Anders, the man always looked as grim as his name.

"But you know what's best of all?" Anders went on. "When it's this cold, I like going to school just to see who didn't make it."

The hint of a smile appeared in Mr. Grimm's eyes. Even as it came, the look disappeared.

Did I imagine it? wondered Kate. *No. I don't think so.*

Anders summed it up. "Yup, a good day to go to Grantsburg, all right!"

"When it's thirty-four below, I just want to go home," Erik said.

"Home? Where's home to you, Mr. Fenton?" Anders asked.

Ah ha! thought Kate. *So that's what this is all about.*

"Home? Why, out east," answered Mr. Fenton smoothly. He stroked his mustache.

"Out east? Where about?" asked Anders quickly, the drawl gone from his voice. "What town?"

Mr. Fenton hesitated. "Philadelphia," he said. "You know, the city of brotherly love."

"Right, right." Anders turned to Mr. Grimm. "And you, Mr. Grouch? I mean—" Anders flushed red to the roots of his blond hair.

"Yes?" Mr. Grimm sounded dangerously calm. Yet the hint of a smile returned to his eyes. "Are you speaking to me?"

Clearing his throat, Anders started again. "Yes, sir, I'm speaking to you, sir. Do you have a family?"

Now he's polite, thought Kate.

"I'm staying with Reverend Pickle," answered Mr. Grimm with his gravelly voice.

"You're new, too?" Kate blurted out. "How come everyone harvesting ice is new at it?"

But no one gave her an answer. Pulling on their heavy coats, Mr. Grimm and Mr. Fenton started out of the room.

"Have to admit I'm relieved to see this butter go," Mr. Bloomquist said to Anders and Erik. "Be sure the tubs don't get banged up. I want them to look good when they reach New York. And get a receipt at the train."

Minutes later, Erik turned his horses toward Grantsburg. Queen and Prince stepped out, pulling the loaded sleigh as though it were no work at all.

Soon the horses left the road and started across a field. During the winter, farmers left their gates open. People cut through fields and woods to take the shortest way to town.

A rein in each hand, Erik talked to Queen and Prince, and their ears turned to the sound of his voice. Seeing how he guided the horses, Kate thought about why she liked Erik. Always he seemed to watch out for her. On her birthday, he had surprised her.

"You're different, Kate," he had said.

"Different?" Kate wasn't sure what he meant. "Awful?" She felt afraid to ask.

"Different from other girls. Better," Erik explained. "Very special."

In the frigid air the memory of his words warmed Kate. It didn't matter that he looked strange bundled against the cold.

The Butter Tub Disaster

Inside the layers of clothing, the warm cap, and the wool scarf was a special friend.

In the early morning sunlight the crust on the snow shimmered like ice. Through the scarf covering her mouth, Kate breathed deep. The problems at home and the creamery dropped away. Almost it seemed as if Kate had imagined them. Almost, but not quite.

Whenever they drove into a woods, she felt warmer, sheltered from the wind. Yet by now the bricks at her feet felt cold. Her toes tingled, then grew numb. Erik stopped the horses and told Kate to get down.

"Get down?" she asked.

"Walk, or you'll freeze. You have to walk to get warm."

Knotting the reins around a post at the front of the sleigh, Erik dropped to the ground. So did Anders.

"Giddyup!" Erik called to Queen and Prince. Avoiding the deep snow on either side, he and Anders and Kate walked in the packed down snow behind the sleigh.

If they came to a hill, Erik climbed onto the sleigh. Taking the reins, he made sure the horses didn't move too fast. Now and then he let Kate ride. Before long, all of them walked once more. Yet by the time they reached Grantsburg, Kate felt the coldest she'd ever been.

At the train depot, a refrigerated car waited on a side track. "No need for ice today," Erik said, as he pulled alongside. Climbing down, he and Anders started transferring the tubs of butter into the railroad car.

Kate carried their lunch into the station. Inside the women's waiting room she set the food basket next to the potbellied stove to let the sandwiches thaw. Pulling off her mittens, she warmed her hands, standing as close to the wood stove as she dared.

Nearby, a woman sat on one of the wooden benches, comforting a crying baby. Another young child clung to his mother as they waited for the train.

Through the large window, Kate watched Anders and Erik shoulder the heavy tubs of butter. The sleigh was almost empty when Erik returned to the railroad car. Picking up a tub he'd set down, he shook it.

Shake a sixty-pound tub? thought Kate. *Why?* She couldn't even lift something that heavy.

As Erik put the tub aside, Anders finished unloading the sleigh. The station agent joined them to count the tubs of butter. Thirteen, fourteen, fifteen.

A moment later Erik picked up the mysterious tub and followed the agent into the depot. As Kate joined the boys in the office, the man made out a receipt.

"Do you have a hammer I can borrow?" Erik asked.

When the agent gave him one, Erik picked up the tub. "C'mon," he said, and Kate and Anders followed him outside.

"Where you going?" asked Kate. The boys couldn't enter the women's waiting room, and she wasn't allowed in the waiting room set aside for men and boys.

On the long platform, Anders pushed open a large sliding door. Erik and Kate followed him into another part of the station, the freight room. As Erik set down the heavy tub, Kate looked around.

In the light from the partly opened door, she saw wooden barrels and boxes of freight. At the moment there was no one there to watch what they were doing.

One by one, Erik pried up the metal strips on the butter tub. As Anders lifted the cover, Kate peered inside.

"Rocks!" she exclaimed. "Why would someone fill a tub with rocks?"

"Shhh!" said Erik, as though wanting to take no chances of anyone hearing them. He lifted out some of the rocks.

Lodged at the bottom of the tub, a gray book stood on end. A gray book with green corners. Was it the stolen ledger?

15

Sunday Deadline

*A*nders whistled softly. "It must be the creamery ledger!"

A grin lit Erik's face as he winked at Kate. Carefully he removed enough rocks to pull out the large book. When he turned the pages, Kate saw neatly written names and amounts.

"We really found it!" Kate exclaimed, keeping her voice low.

Before long they shivered with cold in the unheated freight room. Erik replaced the book and the rocks. Putting on the cover, he nailed down the metal strips and stood up.

"Be right back," he said quietly, lifting the tub to his shoulder. But his eyes looked excited.

Acting as if nothing important were happening, Erik strolled across the platform and over to his sleigh. Setting the tub inside, he covered it with a heavy horse blanket. Then he led Queen and Prince to the livery barn across the tracks.

When Erik returned to the freight room, he joined Kate and Anders just inside the large sliding door.

Anders spoke in a voice too quiet for anyone on the platform to overhear. "We have to find Big Gust." He pushed back his thatch of blond hair.

"Let's wait a few minutes," Erik answered, just above a whisper. "I don't want to take any chances."

Together they watched as other men brought horses and sleighs alongside the refrigerated car.

"They bring butter from a long way around," Erik explained to Kate. "They come from Webster. Falun. Doctor's Lake. West Sweden Creamery used to come here. Now they ship out on Frederic's new Soo Line."

A few minutes later, Anders nudged Kate. "See that man with a small mustache? That's Oscar Thorssen. Kind of a celebrity around here. Took the first prize at the Northern Wisconsin State Fair in 1898."

"For making butter?"

"Yup. When Mr. Thorssen won, he was only twenty-four years old."

"He's got the most butter of all," Erik said. "Twenty-eight tubs."

From the distance Kate heard a train whistle. The Blueberry Special! The whistle sounded again, closer this time and piercing the below-zero air.

Soon the engine puffed around the bend near the Hickerson Mill. Billows of black smoke rose from the large stack. Brakes hissed, releasing steam. Iron squealed on iron, and the engine came to a stop.

Working quickly in the frigid air, trainmen separated the engine from the freight and passenger cars. The engine moved farther on, then backed onto another track.

Stamping her feet in the cold, Kate leaned out of the sliding door to watch. The engine moved onto a section of track above a shallow pit. Using long levers and walking in a half circle, two men turned the track until the engine faced the direction from which it came.

Kate laughed, remembering the first time she'd seen the turntable. "Like Mama says, that Blueberry Special is really special!"

But Anders wasn't listening. He seemed miles away, gazing at the refrigerated car. Finally the men slammed the door shut and coupled that car to the rest of the train. Only then did Anders look away.

"I don't see Big Gust around," he said.

A seven-foot, six-inch-tall Swede, Gust Anderson was the Grantsburg village marshall. Because of his great height, the marshall lived in the fire hall. On more than one occasion he'd helped Kate and Anders.

"I'll keep an eye on the train till it leaves," Erik said.

By the time the Blueberry Special blew its departing whistle, Anders returned, saying, "He's not at the fire hall."

When he asked the station master where to find Big Gust, the man pointed away from the station. "He takes most of his meals at Walfrid Johnson's."

When Kate, Anders, and Erik went outside again, the air seemed warmer. As they set off for the building a short distance away, snow started to fall.

The minute they found themselves alone on the street, Anders exclaimed, "What a funny hiding place for a ledger!"

Erik grinned from ear to ear. "The thief would have sent it to New York!"

"How did you know that tub was different?" asked Kate.

"It weighed just the same," Erik said. "But when I put the tub down, I heard a sound. A rock rolling, I suppose. It was so cold we were moving really fast. I could have missed it."

"Three men helped you load the butter," Kate said. "Mr. Bloomquist. Mr. Fenton. Mr. Grimm. Which one put the ledger in the tub?"

"Not Mr. Bloomquist," said Erik. "He'd hurt himself by doing something like that."

Kate agreed. She'd come to like the buttermaker. "Yesterday he wasn't acting. He was upset."

"So that leaves two of 'em—Grouchy Grimm and LeRoy Fenton," Anders said. "I bet it's Mr. Grimm. Did you see how he sidestepped my questions? That's what he did every time we worked together. What's he got to hide?"

But Kate shook her head. "I think it's LeRoy Fenton." She looked up at Erik. "What do you think?"

As they came to a large frame building, Erik grinned. "I think it could be either one."

Walfrid Johnson had his blacksmith shop on the ground floor.

His family lived on the floor above. Anders led Kate and Erik up the stairs on the outside wall.

A short woman with a warm smile opened the door. "Come in, come in. Get out of the cold."

Several people sat around a large square table in the dining room. Big Gust was one of them. A woman stood next to him, serving food. Though he was sitting down, Gust was as tall as the woman standing beside him.

Seeing Kate and the boys, he called out, "*God dag!*"

When Kate walked closer, he looked down at her. "Little girl? What can I do for you?"

"I'm not a little girl!" Kate told him, flipping her long braid over her shoulder. "Not even if I'm short for my age!"

Big Gust's rumbling laugh came from deep in his chest. "You're right, young woman. Just like I'm not a big man! But what can I do for you and these tall boys with you?" He winked at Anders and Erik.

"We need to talk," Anders said.

The marshall's grin disappeared. "One minute," he said. Pouring his coffee into his saucer, he let it cool. As soon as he finished his meal, he unfolded his long frame and stood up.

Even now, after seeing Big Gust half a dozen times, Kate felt surprised by his height. The size of his large hands and feet fit with his tall frame.

Big Gust shrugged into his blue coat and started down the outside stairs. "It's too cold to talk here," he said. He led them to the fire hall.

There Gust made himself comfortable in an oversized chair. "What's wrong?" he asked with his deep laugh. "Somehow you attract trouble like bees to honey."

As Kate and the boys found chairs, Big Gust leaned forward to listen.

"Not good, not good," he said at last. "The one you really need to see is the sheriff, Charlie Saunders. But he's gone for the day. And you say Andrew Anderson number 3 talked to him?"

Anders nodded. "But Mr. Anderson is in North Branch. He doesn't know what just happened."

Big Gust rubbed his large chin. "Worst of all, this time of year we could have some mighty stormy weather. If we get a bad wind, you won't be able to get to town for help."

The marshall's blue eyes looked thoughtful. "Tell you what to do. If you can't get the sheriff, go to Reverend Pickle."

"The marrying man of Trade Lake?" Erik asked.

Big Gust nodded. "One and the same. Seldom a week goes by that he doesn't have a wedding or funeral. He's getting up in years now, but when he was a young man he was a detective."

"*Reverend Pickle?*" asked Anders.

"Yah, certainly," said the marshall. "Reverend Pickle. If you need help, he'll know what to do."

Before they left, Big Gust reached into his large pockets for peanuts in the shell. "Hold out your hands," he said and filled Kate's hands, then those of Anders and Erik.

As they went out the door, Big Gust offered a warning. "Whoever the thief is, be careful. He sounds like a bad one."

When Anders, Kate, and Erik returned to the train station, they ate their lunch, then climbed back on the sleigh. As Queen and Prince headed out of Grantsburg, new snow swirled around them.

"I've been thinking," Kate said.

"*Thinking?*" asked Anders.

Kate paid no attention. "I think Mr. Grimm is a different person from what he seems to be."

Anders looked ready to poke fun at anything she said, but Erik seemed to listen.

"Good? Bad? How do you mean, *different*?" he asked.

"I don't know." Kate was still wondering about it. "I just believe he's not what he seems."

Anders laughed, but Kate kept on. "Whoever the thief is, why would he send the ledger to New York?"

"Come to think of it, what else could he do?" Erik asked. "With the ground frozen, he can't bury it. It's too big to hide in a milk can."

"What if he had thrown it in a hole in the ice?" asked Kate. "Would it wash up on shore in spring?"

"Whoever the thief is, he's mighty smart," Erik said slowly. "He's got everything figured out."

"There's something else that bothers me," Kate answered. "Don't you think the thief has given us some kind of signal? He sent the ledger to New York, where it's sure to be seen. Doesn't that mean he's ready to leave Trade Lake?"

The grin disappeared from Anders's face. "Gotcha!" he exclaimed. "The ledger would have reached New York by Monday morning. At least that's when they put the tubs on the market."

"And if someone opened that tub—" Kate pulled up her scarf to protect her face against the cold. "Big trouble!"

As they passed through a clean-cut field, gusts of snow whirled around them, filling in the packed-down trail. As Queen and Prince headed into the drifts, snow sprayed up against their forelegs. Steam rose from their nostrils.

Erik let the horses set their own pace. "A ledger in a butter tub is real strange. Whoever found it probably wouldn't waste the time it takes for letters to go back and forth. He might even send a telegram to the Grantsburg train depot."

"The thief knows that," said Kate. "He's been smart about everything else."

"Except for using rocks in a butter tub." Erik grinned. "Now if it were me, I'd have put in some sawdust to deaden the sound."

But Anders no longer joked. "If we've got it figured right, the thief will leave town by Sunday night."

"That means we have only four days to find him," said Kate. "Or we might never find out who he is!"

16

Thin Ice!

"That also means we have only four days to find the milk can," said Erik.

Anders scowled. "Or the thief will take the checks with him when he leaves. If he goes to a city where he's not known, he might be able to cash them."

A rein in each hand, Erik turned the horses onto a trail through the woods. The sheltering trees offered welcome relief from the wind. Even so, Kate's fingers tingled with cold, then grew numb. Before long, all of them climbed down to walk behind the sleigh.

"So what do we do with the ledger?" Kate asked.

"Well, we can't take it to the creamery." Anders felt certain about that. "The thief would just steal it again. Let's wait till Andrew Anderson comes back. We'll ask him."

Together they agreed that Anders would hide the butter tub in the Windy Hill barn.

"There's something we still don't know," said Erik. "Why does someone want to get even with Mr. Bloomquist?"

Some time later they climbed onto the sleigh. Kate huddled under a heavy horse blanket in the back. Her thoughts were as miserable as her cold body. Every grown-up who knew about the robbery had warned them, and with good reason.

When at last they came to the Nordstrom mailbox, Anders called out, "Letter for you, Kate!"

Like a turtle coming from its shell, Kate poked out her head. A letter just for her? Papa's handwriting! He must have written the day he received her letter. In spite of the biting wind, Kate felt warm.

"I'll be over tomorrow," Erik said as he pulled up outside the Nordstrom barn. "We'll look for the milk can again."

"And we'll find it!" Anders exclaimed. Swinging down the butter tub, he started for the barn, then turned back to Erik. "Let Lutfisk follow you home. In the morning, early, I'll try sending him over with a message."

When Kate entered the kitchen, she could no longer feel her feet. Pulling off her boots, she curled up close to the cookstove. As her toes returned to life, they prickled, as though touched by a thousand needles.

With her fingers still awkward from the cold, Kate opened her letter. Papa had written in English, using a bold, strong script.

As Mama, Anders, and Tina clustered around, Kate remembered Lars. "Let's read it where he can hear," she said.

In the bedroom Kate began to read.

Dear Kate,

Thank you for your letter. It was good for a father to hear from his daughter. I miss you very much.

Remember how we talked at Christmas about the big loads of logs the sleighs carry? This week I saw a sleigh carrying 56 giant logs. That's 37,120 board feet of lumber!

You might wonder how only four horses can pull such a load. Last fall men built roads of ice into the woods. For weeks they hauled water to make the road one-foot thick. Then other men cut ruts in the ice. The sleigh runners slide in those ruts. On hills the men lay down straw to slow the sleigh so it doesn't run over the horses.

Kate looked up. "That's why Erik had that accident! There

Thin Ice! 113

should have been straw on that road! Maybe the load of ice wouldn't have shifted."

She returned to reading:

> When I came back after Christmas, I got a new job. Now I'm what is called a water-tank conductor. I work at night and repair the road of ice. In our camp we have two tank sleighs, and I use the smaller one.
>
> Our horses, Dolly and Florie, help me pull barrels of water up a skid to fill the tank on the sleigh. Then I drive up and down the road. Wherever the ice is thin or dirt shows through, I lift long poles to unplug the holes in the tank. Water runs out and fills the bad spots. That water freezes to make the road good again.
>
> To see in the dark I light lard oil torches on the corners of the water tank.

Then Kate came to a blank space. Had the paper been wet, then wiped dry? Glancing ahead, she stopped reading aloud. "This is just for me," she said finally.

Folding the letter, Kate took it to her room where she could be alone. Wrapping herself in a quilt, she huddled on the grate that let in heat from the stove below. Then she reread the last page of the letter.

> When my first wife Anna died, I was very sad. I didn't know God had something good in store for me. You prayed for a father and didn't know it would be me. When I married your mama, you became my new, special daughter.
>
> I can never take the place of your Daddy O'Connell. I want you to remember him and what a fine man he was. At the same time, I feel honored to be your second father.
>
> When you are afraid, remember that you also have a Heavenly Father. He has promised you something: "Fear thou not; for I am with thee: be not dismayed, for I am thy God: I will strengthen thee; yea, I will help thee" Isaiah 41:10.
>
> Even when I cannot be with you, your Heavenly Father is.
>
> With love to my special daughter,
> PAPA

Kate stared at Papa's words. *When you are afraid?* How did

he know? She had tried to make him feel good, instead of telling how scared she really felt.

For a long time she held the letter, thinking about the verse. *Fear thou not; for I am with thee.* Each time Kate repeated the words, she felt better inside, even warm.

Though she hadn't told Papa how she felt, he somehow knew. Kate felt cared for by God himself.

When Kate read Papa's letter again the next morning, she found a small slip of paper that had slipped down inside the envelope. It read:

P.S. I'll start home January 31.

Running downstairs, Kate told Mama, "Papa's coming the 31st! That's today!"

Her mother's quiet smile lit her eyes. "And it's sooner than I expected. Many of the men will work longer."

By noon the thermometer showed eighteen degrees above zero. After the temperature of the day before, the weather felt warm and balmy.

When Erik skied over after lunch, he held out a piece of paper. "Lutfisk did it! I got the message from you!"

Seeming to know they talked about him, the dog jumped up, wanting attention.

Anders grinned with pride. "We'll send him over whenever we need you." Kneeling down, he scratched Lutfisk behind the ears. The dog woofed and licked his master's face.

Kate and the boys decided to search two small lakes they hadn't tried before. With Anders carrying a long pole, they skied across country. Whenever they found a hole in the ice, they felt new hope. Using the pole, Anders or Erik poked around in the water, looking for the milk can.

As they skied toward the second lake, snowflakes drifted lazily to the ground. Soon dark branches were outlined in white. By the time they finished searching, pine trees wore a new robe.

Anders sighed. "Well, we've done our best." He looked cold and discouraged. "That's the last of the lakes close by. Maybe we should start over again."

Erik shook his head. "Not today. The wind's coming up."

"Let's go to Little Trade Lake," Anders said.

Kate felt uneasy. "That's out of the way." It would take time to ski to Windy Hill Farm, and Erik's house was farther yet.

Putting on her skis, Kate started for home. Erik followed, but Anders wasn't ready to give up.

"We have to cross Rice Lake anyway," he said. "Let's look there again."

When they reached the southwestern corner, they followed the trail through the boggy area. As they cut slantwise across the lake, Erik took the lead. Soon he pointed off to the right. "Something's over there! See those markers?"

About fifty feet from shore, four small pine trees stood upright in the snow. A skim of new ice covered what had been a large hole.

Taking off her skis, Kate walked as close to the hole as was safe. New snow dotted the thin ice, making it difficult to see.

Using the long pole, Erik struck the ice and broke it. As Kate peered down into the lake, she thought she saw a glimmer. Was that something just beneath the surface?

"Isn't that a milk can?" she asked.

"Might be." Erik sounded afraid to hope. He and Anders took turns poking around in the water with the long pole. No matter how hard they tried, they couldn't make the pole reach far enough.

Finally Erik skirted the thin ice and headed toward shore. Kate and Anders followed him.

Near a tall oak Erik pulled off his mittens and grabbed a stout branch that extended toward the lake. He pulled himself up onto the limb and crawled out to see better.

For a few seconds he stared into the dark water. "There!" he exclaimed finally. "There's a glimmer of metal in the water. Could be a can!"

Standing on shore, Anders and Kate moved around, trying to see what Erik meant. Soon Anders pointed toward the center of the hole. "Yup! That's it! See that round circle? Look hard. Isn't that a rim?"

Erik edged still farther out on the branch. "It's the bottom of a milk can, all right. Upside down, same as before."

"We found it!" whooped Kate.

"You betcha!" Anders stepped forward for a better look.

"We really did it!" Kate said, moving onto the ice.

Anders stretched out an arm, holding her back. "We haven't done anything yet!"

"So how do we get the can out?" asked Kate.

"That's the problem." Again Anders looked into the cold water. "Before, we had solid ice to stand on. This time we don't."

"The can's lined up with the tree," Erik called down. "Almost exactly in the center of the hole. There's at least ten feet of thin ice on every side."

"How did the thief get it there?" asked Kate.

"Probably threw it." Anders sounded unhappy. "We aren't playing around with an amateur. He's got good aim to land it where he did."

Slowly Erik started edging back along the tree limb. Close to the trunk he stopped and pulled something from a small sharp branch. Tucking it inside his pocket, he dropped to the ground.

When he reached Kate and Anders, Erik held out his find—a small piece of cloth.

"Part red, part black!" exclaimed Kate.

Erik nodded. "See the jagged edges? Looks like it's been torn from a mackinaw."

"So the thief was up that tree before you!"

"I think so." Erik pushed back his cap. "Way I figure it, he threw in the can, then checked to be sure it landed right."

"So all we have to do is look for a red and black mackinaw," Kate said. "That sounds simple enough."

"Except for one thing," Anders told her.

"What's that?"

"An awful lot of men in Burnett County have red and black mackinaws!"

Kate sighed. She knew Anders was right. And the two men they suspected most—Gunnar Grimm and LeRoy Fenton—both had one.

Still the piece of cloth offered a slim clue. "Not every man will have a *torn* mackinaw," Kate said.

Turning back to the hole, she gazed at the round metal rim just beneath the surface of the water. "Isn't there any way we can get the can out?"

"Not with the ice the way it is," Anders told her. "One wrong step, and we'd drop right through."

"Let's go for help," Kate said. "Now before the snow gets worse."

Putting on their skis, Kate, Anders, and Erik set off again, this time for the village of Trade Lake. Erik took the lead, retracing their tracks.

As they crossed Rice Lake, Kate felt the change in the weather. Whirlwinds caught the new snow, spraying it through the air. Like small grains of sand, the snow pelted her face. If this kept up, they wouldn't be able to reach the creamery.

"Erik!" Kate shouted, fighting to speak. "Erik!" she called again.

But the wind took her words, flinging them away. She wasn't even sure if Erik heard.

17

Lars's Question

*B*ending her head against the wind, Kate struggled to keep up with Erik. Near the southwestern shore of the lake their earlier tracks were blurred. Erik kept on, avoiding the creek, and finding the path. As they entered the shelter of woods, the wind stilled.

Kate breathed deep. Yet even here snow had piled up. The woods were dark, the sky gray with falling snow.

When they came out from the trees, the white wind swooped across the open field. Driving snow stung Kate's cheeks. Her eyes watered, but she didn't want to give up. Wrapping her scarf around her face, she skied on.

A few minutes later Erik stopped them. "We can probably reach Trade Lake. But if we go that far, we won't get home. Everyone will wonder what happened to us."

"Mama knows we're smart enough to get out of a storm," Anders said.

"Mama will worry about us," replied Kate. "And Erik's mother will worry about him." Like Papa Nordstrom, Erik's father was away, working at a logging camp.

"If we don't get help now, the hole in the ice will freeze over," Anders said. "The thief can come back, take the can, and leave town."

Anders was right, Kate knew. Yet as she opened her mouth to agree, another gust of wind struck her. She staggered, then caught her breath.

"I'll go for help," Anders said to Kate. "You and Erik ski home. Tell Mama I'm safe."

"No!" Erik objected. "The storm is getting worse all the time. If you lose your way, you could miss the town."

"And what if your bad ankle gives out?" asked Kate. "There'll be no one to help you."

Anders sighed, clearly unwilling to stop.

"Let's stick together," Kate said. "That means going home."

She and Erik turned, starting toward Windy Hill Farm. After a short distance, Kate looked back. Anders stood there, as though trying to make up his mind. In the snow that swirled between them, he started to disappear.

"C'mon, Anders," Kate called into the wind.

But Anders heard. Pushing off, he followed Kate.

On the far side of the woods they once again skied onto Rice Lake. Drawing close to the hole where they'd found the milk can, Erik stopped.

By the time the storm ended, drifts might cover the small pine trees. The hole in the ice would be frozen, and the milk can hidden. Would they be able to find it again?

For a moment they stood there, facing the tall oak. Through the driving snow, Kate stared toward shore.

"One branch reaches out over the water," she said finally. But was that enough? Other trees dotted the shoreline. Would they mistake one of them for the tall oak?

"Pine trees," she said, pointing. "One left of the oak. Several on the right." She tried to remember the distance, to mark the spot in her mind.

Erik nodded, then Anders. Taking the most direct route, they struck out for home. As the wind clutched their clothing, they bent almost double, skiing on.

Soon the early winter darkness blended with the falling snow. Kate lost sight of Erik. Following the tracks of his skis, she caught up. Even Anders hurried now, the cap he usually wore at a jaunty angle pulled low over his forehead.

As they started up the bank along the shore, Anders stumbled. *His ankle*, Kate thought. *What if he hurts it again?* But Anders caught himself. He followed close behind, as though making sure Kate didn't lose her way.

At the top of the hill, the farmhouse faded into the swirling snow. Then Kate saw a glow of light. Mama had placed three candles in the window. Their warmth reached out, across the wind and cold.

Three, thought Kate. *One for Anders. One for me. Is the third candle for Erik?*

Then Kate remembered. January 31. Today Papa started home. Was he out somewhere in this awful storm?

During supper Kate felt bone-tired from skiing, but Mama looked even more weary. All afternoon she had sewed on the new blue dress. With Lars sick, she often missed sleep.

"I'll read to him," Kate told Mama after washing the dishes.

Once again she opened the pages of *Call of the Wild*. Each day she and Lars had followed the adventures of the strong dog, Buck. By now they were almost to the end of the book.

When Kate finished the last chapter, Lars lay with eyes closed, as if too tired to hold them open. Yet Kate knew he wasn't sleeping.

At last he spoke. "Kate?"

His voice was so soft that she leaned forward. "I'm here."

"Kate, did you like reading about Buck?"

"I liked Buck," Kate said carefully, not wanting to spoil the story for him. "He was a special dog—a smart dog, wasn't he?"

Lars nodded. "A *magnificent* dog."

Kate smiled. Lars seemed so small, lying there in bed, that the word seemed bigger than he was.

For a moment Lars was quiet. "That's what he was—a magnificent dog. Even when people were mean to him."

"Did he remind you of Lutfisk?" Kate asked.

"In some ways," said Lars, his eyes still closed. "But I'm glad our dog is different."

After a time Lars spoke again. "'Course we've always been

nice to Lutfisk. We've taken good care of him." His voice sounded drowsy.

Kate sat down on a chair next to the bed, waiting for Lars to fall asleep. Instead he opened his eyes. "I don't like the way the story ends. John Thornton was nice to Buck. He treated him right. I don't like that John Thornton died."

"I'm glad you felt that way," said Kate. "I did too."

"You did?" Lars's blue eyes seemed too bright. "You know what, Kate? When I grow up, I'm going to be a writer."

Kate smiled. "Just like I want to be an organist?"

"Yup. And I'm going to make stories end different."

The last word ended on a cough. As Lars tried to sit up, Kate pushed another pillow behind him. His body shook with coughing.

When he dropped back, Lars looked exhausted, his face flushed. Yet beneath his freckles, he also seemed strangely white.

What would we do without him? Kate wondered. The idea frightened her so much she could scarcely breathe.

"Kate?" Lars said softly. "How come you're different from the way you used to be?"

"Different?" asked Kate. "What do you mean?"

"You're not the same as when you first came here." Again Lars coughed. Pushing himself up, he leaned forward. In between the coughing, his breathing rattled. "My chest hurts," he said when able to speak.

Kate stood up and rubbed his back. Through his nightshirt Kate felt Lars's spine and ribs and his thinness. Then, thinking about his cough, she felt afraid.

When Lars lay back again he kept his eyes open. "You still get into all kinds of trouble," he said.

For a moment a grin lit his face. "Can't figure out how *anyone* can find so many mysteries to solve. But it's like—" He stopped, as though to think about it. "It's like God means something to you."

Then Kate knew what Lars was talking about. She remembered the day last fall when Tina could have been badly hurt because of something Kate did. On that day her whole life had changed.

Now Lars stared at her, his eyes unblinking. "Kate, do you love Jesus?" he asked.

Kate looked him straight in the eyes. "Yes, Lars, I love Jesus." It felt good to tell him, but she wondered, *Why does he want to know?*

In that moment her younger brother seemed very special to her. She reached out and took his hand. "Are you afraid, Lars?"

Lars nodded. A tear slid down his cheek. "I'm scared, Kate." His voice was so soft that she could barely hear. "I'm scared I'm going to die. Would I go to heaven? Am I good enough?"

Kate had never seen her brother so serious. Again she remembered the day she cried out, "Mama, I'm so awful!" Her mother had agreed, saying, "Yah, we are all awful." But then Mama explained that no one is perfect.

"Lars," Kate said, and her voice wavered. "You know how much God loves you. How He sent His Son Jesus to earth as a little baby."

Lars nodded. "And Jesus died for us on the cross."

"When we do wrong things, we can say we're sorry." Kate's voice was stronger now. "If we ask forgiveness, God *does* forgive us."

"Even you, Kate." Lars grinned weakly.

Kate grinned too, but she went on. "And Jesus takes away our sin. He forgets all about it."

For a time Lars was silent, seeming to think. "I believe that," he said finally, his voice little more than a whisper. "So will I go to heaven?"

Quick tears blurred Kate's vision. She could barely speak. "You'll go to heaven, Lars. Jesus will be with you, no matter what happens to you."

Lars closed his eyes. His face looked peaceful, and for a time he did not cough. Yet he held tight to Kate's hand.

18

The Lost Fiddle

For a long time Kate sat next to Lars's bed. When at last he fell asleep, his grip on her hand loosened. Kate fled to her room and cried.

The next morning she was first to enter the kitchen. Crossing the floor, she slipped and fell. When she lit a kerosene lamp, she found the reason.

"Ice?" she muttered. "On the kitchen floor?" Three feet from the cookstove, someone had spilled water. During the night it had frozen.

Quickly Kate started a fire in the stove. Then she discovered a long ridge of snow near the outside door. Taking a broom, she swept it up as though it were sand. Putting down a small rug, she blocked out the narrow crack beneath the door.

More snow lay on the window ledges, sifted in through cracks too small to see. As Kate cleaned up, her mother entered the kitchen.

Mama's face looked set and white. In spite of her growing weight, she moved quickly between the stove and table. But then she burned the oatmeal. Kate knew Mama's thoughts were far away.

As Anders and Kate walked to the barn for chores, the wind

swooped across the hill, striking them full force. Anders reached back and took Kate's hand, as though afraid she'd lose the way. Bent almost double against the wind, they crossed to the barn.

Anders held the door for Kate. When he let go, it crashed shut. For a moment they stood just inside, catching their breath.

Here, away from Mama, Kate could ask what she wanted to know. "Where do you think Papa is?"

Anders shook his head.

So he's worried too.

Kate tried again. "If Papa left camp before the blizzard started, how far would he get?"

"Depends on how deep the snow is and how big the drifts are."

"Are there towns along the way?"

"Not many."

"Houses?" Kate asked, her voice small.

"Some. They're far apart. But Papa's wise," Anders added quickly, as though trying to make her feel better. "He's like most farmers, smart about weather. He probably saw this coming."

"And went inside?"

Anders shrugged his shoulders. Lifting the cover of a bin, he took out oats for Wildfire. The mare's black coat was thick with winter hair. She nuzzled his jacket, but for the first time Kate could remember, Anders didn't talk to his horse.

All day long the wind blew. Kate wandered from room to room, thinking about Papa trying to get home. About the milk can in the lake. And about Lars. What if he needed a doctor?

During the afternoon Mama showed Kate how to cut the flannel cloth. Much as Kate wanted to make a few clothes for the baby, she couldn't keep her mind on it.

Anders looked just as restless as Kate felt. He, too, wandered between windows. Snow, driven against the glass, blocked the view.

In the strange half light Kate sat down at her organ. As she played familiar hymns, Tina came and stood beside her. In her small clear voice, she began to sing.

When Kate looked up, Mama sat nearby, the almost-finished dress forgotten in her lap. Staring at the snow-darkened windows, she bit her lip, then lifted her chin.

A gust of wind rattled the windows. In the nearby bedroom, Lars coughed from deep in his chest.

"It must be pneumonia," whispered Mama.

What'll we do? thought Kate. *What if we have to go for the doctor?*

Mama hurried to the bedroom. "Play some more, will you, Kate?"

When Kate finished the hymns she knew, she practiced the music Mr. Peters gave her. Thinking about the string band seemed the only bright spot in the day.

Late that afternoon Kate and Anders hurried through snow and early darkness to the barn. While Anders started milking, Kate fed the sheep and cows. Even here the wind howled around the corners.

Kate shivered. "I'm scared, Anders."

"About Lars? So am I."

His answer surprised Kate. Six feet tall and muscular from farm work, Anders seldom showed fear about anything.

"A lot of people die from pneumonia," said Kate.

"I know," answered Anders, his voice quiet. "Lars has never been strong. Not since the day he was born. From the time he was little, Mama taught me to watch out for him."

Again Kate felt surprised. Anders seldom mentioned his first mother.

"Lars always gets sick easier than the rest of us," Anders went on. "And he always takes longer to get well."

In the silence the wind shrieked through cracks in the barn. The ache in Kate's stomach tightened in a knot of fear.

"Anders?"

"Yup?"

"Does the wind ever stop?

"Nope. Not till the storm's over."

"I don't like the wind." Kate shivered again. "I don't like looking out and seeing nothing but white."

"That's what Papa said."

"Papa?" asked Kate.

"At Christmas when he left for logging camp. That's what he said."

Kate remembered that day. From outside the farmhouse door, she had watched Papa leave. As he stood near the sleigh, he talked to Anders. Kate strained to hear, but the wind swallowed the words.

Now Anders turned from the cow he was milking. "Papa said, 'It's been a long time since Mama lived on a farm in winter. And Kate never has. They don't know what it's like when the wind blows all day and there's nothing to see but snow.' "

Kate stared at her brother. "Papa said that? He always knows, doesn't he? What else did he say?"

" 'Take care of 'em, Anders. Take care of Mama, and Tina, and Lars.' " Anders grinned. " 'And Kate.' "

"Take care of *me*? Papa knows I can take care of myself."

"Papa knows you need taking care of. Curious Kate—that's you. Always getting into something."

Kate tossed her head, and her long braid swung down her back. She wasn't sure if Anders was teasing or not. She was thirteen now and could take care of herself.

"Better put some wood in the tank heater, Kate."

"Why don't *you* do it?" she answered, tired of his orders. Besides, she hated going out in the dark.

"Sure thing," said Anders, standing up. "If you finish this cow."

Quickly Kate headed for the door. Though she'd learned to milk when Anders sprained his ankle, it still took her longer than she liked.

Outside, she hurried to the woodpile near the large tank for watering animals. A stove set inside the tank heated the water in winter.

The heater looked like a U with the sides pushed slightly down. At one end of the U, a stove pipe stretched above the water. At the other end, a stove lid covered the opening for loading wood. Lifting the lid, Kate dropped in small chunks of oak.

When she returned to the barn, Anders had moved on to

another cow. Taking a stool, Kate sat down to milk the cow next in line.

"Anders, what're you going to do about the string band?"

"Well, I'll join it." He sounded as though he wondered why Kate asked.

"You will?" Kate wished she could see her brother, but a cow stood between them. "What instrument will you play?"

"The fiddle, of course." His matter-of-fact voice made it seem there was no other choice.

"The *fiddle*?" Kate found it hard to believe she'd heard correctly. "That's a hard instrument to play. And you—"

She stopped, knowing she shouldn't go on.

"And me—I'm a country bumpkin. Is that what you're thinking?"

Kate felt a blush go to the roots of her hair. During her first week at Windy Hill Farm, she'd called Anders that name. Since then she'd learned he was anything but.

Yet a fiddle didn't fit with what she knew about him. *Anders? Playing a fiddle? With his big fingers and hands?*

"In fact," he continued, "if I can find it, there's a fiddle around here. Mama used to play."

"Your mother?" Kate asked, feeling more strange all the time. "Papa's first wife?"

Anders nodded.

"You never told me that."

"Lots of things I don't tell you," said Anders. "You don't know *everything* I know."

But Kate remembered last summer and the day of the big storm. It took all her courage to sing in front of Anders. "I thought you didn't like music."

"Well, you're wrong. Before she died, my mama started teaching me how to play. She said I had a good ear for it."

Kate wanted to laugh. But in the next moment she was glad she hadn't.

"I was starting to get good," said Anders. "Then Mama died. At first I played all the time. Then I couldn't stand to touch the fiddle. And I knew it bothered Papa to hear me. It reminded us both of Mama."

For a time Anders was silent. Kate heard only the sound of milk splashing into their pails. Then he stood up and walked around to Kate's side of the cow.

"One day I wrapped the fiddle in a cloth and gave it to Papa. I asked him to put it away for me. And he did."

"So you don't know where it is?" Kate stopped milking.

"All I know is that Papa would put it somewhere safe. Where it wouldn't be too hot or too cold. Where the wood wouldn't crack."

"How do you know?" Kate asked. Then she saw her brother's eyes. In the light of the kerosene lantern they seemed moist.

"When I gave it to Papa, he unwrapped the cloth. He felt the wood as though he wanted to touch something Mama loved. Then he wrapped the fiddle again and put it away."

Kate leaned closer to the quiet voice. "I think we should find that fiddle."

Anders answered slowly. "Kate, I'm scared. What if we find the fiddle, and I can't play it?"

Kate knew what he meant. He wasn't afraid that he couldn't play the notes. It was more than that. Could he play again, remembering his first mother and how it felt to lose her?

Then Kate felt sure of something. "You'll be able to play. It's what your mama would want you to do."

"You really think so?" Anders stared at Kate as though her answer were the most important thing in the world.

"I think so. Pretend you're playing for *her*."

A strange expression crossed his face. Kate wasn't sure what it meant. Was this the Anders who never showed fear or tears?

Turning, he stalked away. With his back toward Kate, he stared out a window. For a long time he stood there, though Kate knew he couldn't see into the storm.

All her life she'd heard people say that men and boys shouldn't cry. Now she wondered, *Is that how Anders feels? That he can't cry, no matter what happens?*

When he returned to milking, Anders seemed his usual self. "I'll play the fiddle again," he said. "Yah sure, you betcha."

19

Another Warning

That night Kate and Anders searched for the lost fiddle. They had almost given up when Kate pulled a chair over to the cupboard in the pantry.

"I can't reach far enough," she called to Anders. "Come do it for me."

Sure enough, the fiddle lay on top of the cupboard, far back against the wall.

Climbing down from the chair, Anders opened the cloth and felt the wood. Without a word, he carried the fiddle into the front room, where he could be alone.

From the kitchen Kate listened, but heard no playing. When at last a note came, it sounded scratchy and out of tune.

Mama raised her eyebrows.

"It was his mother's," Kate explained. From that time on, Mama listened too.

As though Anders struggled to remember the fingering, there came a note, a pause, then another note. Sometimes he plucked the strings. Other times he drew his bow across. Then it sounded as if he was tuning the fiddle.

When Kate woke the next morning, she found herself buried deep beneath the quilts. As she pulled them away from her head, she saw her breath in the cold air.

After breakfast Anders went out to brush the snow off the windows. Yet the white wind still blew, pelting snow as though sand. Before long, the windows again gave only an eerie half light.

"It's Saturday," Kate told Anders when they were alone. "Papa started home Thursday—two days and two nights ago."

"And tomorrow's Sunday," answered her brother, as though unable to talk about Papa. On Sunday the thief would leave town.

That afternoon both Kate and Anders forgot everything except Lars. While Kate read to him, Lars started shaking with a chill. As he coughed, he held his chest.

"Oh, Kate, I hurt," he said when he could speak again. "It's such an awful pain."

Kate pushed another pillow under his back and put on more quilts, but Lars still trembled.

When she glanced up, Anders stood at the door, his eyes scared. Coming close to the bed, he flashed his lopsided grin. "You gotta get well, buddy."

Against the white pillowcase, Lars's hair seemed even redder than usual. His face looked pale, but he grinned for his brother.

Awkwardly Anders patted Lars on the shoulder. "When you're well again, we'll hitch Lutfisk to the sled. You can ride across the hills."

Lars's grin disappeared in a cough. Leaning forward, he coughed several more times. Kate handed him a handkerchief.

When it came away from Lars's mouth, Anders watched. As though unable to handle being there, he bolted from the room.

A short time later, Kate heard Anders tune the fiddle. Gradually the notes sounded clearer, then strong, even beautiful. Lars lay without speaking, but Kate saw his eyes and knew that he listened.

As Anders started a Swedish folk song, Mama came to the doorway. Halfway across the room, she stopped and tilted her head toward the music. The melody seemed to sing.

"It's good to remember," Mama whispered when Anders finished. "We're children of the Heavenly Father." Neither she nor Kate moved.

Early Sunday morning the family gathered near Lars's bed to have church together. When Mama asked Kate to read, she chose the words that Papa sent her: "Fear thou not, for I am with thee; be not dismayed; for I am thy God. . . ."

Glancing up, Kate saw Mama bite her lip. Kate read on: "I will strengthen thee; yea, I will help thee. . . ."

As they bowed their heads, Mama laid a gentle hand on Kate's arm. When they prayed for Lars, Mama moved her hand to his shoulder. "Jesus, in Thy name we ask Thee to heal Lars."

Then, as often before, Mama prayed for Papa. "Lord, we don't know where he is." Mama's voice broke, and she stopped.

Kate opened her eyes. Mama struggled for control.

"We don't know where he is, God," she went on. "But thou knowest. Thou art his Heavenly Father."

Her voice grew stronger. "We ask thee to take care of Papa. We ask thee to keep him warm and safe and bring him home to us soon. In thy name, Jesus, we pray. Ah-men."

When Mama stopped praying, no one spoke. Within the small circle around Lars's bed, it felt warm. Kate knew the warmth was love.

Then her brother's cough broke the silence. Again Kate heard the wind. It seemed to separate them from the rest of the world.

A short time later, Tina grew restless, and Kate led her to the kitchen. "Look!" Kate said to her little sister. "Jack Frost painted the windows last night."

Five-pointed stars filled one pane and snowflakes another. At a window covered with solid frost, Kate asked Tina, "Want to make footprints?"

Tina shrugged, not understanding Kate's English.

Balling her hand into a fist, Kate pressed the side of her little finger against the glass. The heat of her hand melted the frost. Using her thumb and fingers, she added a big toe and four smaller ones. Sure enough, there was a footprint!

Tina giggled, and started making her own prints in the frost.

"C'mon, Anders," called Kate. "We need some *big* feet."

Anders joined them, pressing his large hands against the glass. One after another, he placed footprints, until it seemed a person walked across the window.

Standing back to look, Tina giggled again.

An hour later, Kate lifted her head and listened. After three days of howling wind, the world seemed strangely still. The storm was over!

When Kate and Anders went outside to shovel, the clouds had disappeared. Drifts curled around the corners of the house. As far as they looked, they saw smooth, unbroken snow—snow that glistened in the sunlight.

"We are *buried*!" exclaimed Anders. Every trail and path had blown shut.

As they started toward the barn, Kate saw the relief in her brother's face. He even seemed to walk more quickly.

"You were scared, weren't you?" she asked.

Anders nodded, his blue eyes shading darker. "How do you get a doctor in a howling blizzard? How do you travel for miles when you can hardly get to the barn?"

"Maybe Papa will be able to get through."

"Maybe," said Anders. "I hope so."

They harnessed Wildfire, then hitched her to chains attached to a heavy log. As the mare moved ahead, the log dragged along the ground, smoothing out the snow and packing down the trail.

Soon after lunch, Kate heard the jingle of bells. Erik drove out of the woods and across the field between the two farms. He, too, dragged a log behind the Lundgren team of horses.

Waving at Kate, Erik turned Queen and Prince down the hill toward Rice Lake. Anders followed with Wildfire. When they returned, they had smoothed a trail all the way across Rice Lake.

"When we reached the road, we saw men working," said Anders. "Every few miles people will be out."

Mama looked hopeful. "Maybe Papa will come home."

And if we have to go for the doctor, we can, thought Kate.

When she and Anders were alone, Kate asked about the milk can. "Is it still there?"

"As far as we can tell. No footprints at least. But we can't get to Andrew Anderson's yet. Not till some time after dark when the men finish working on the roads."

Kate sighed. "We're out of time. It's Sunday night."

At dusk the first sleigh passed through the farmyard. The neighbor stopped at the house, asking, "Are you all right, Mrs. Nordstrom?"

Mama nodded her head, and said, "Yes, except for Lars."

Then came the question. "Have you heard from Carl?"

Mama's blue eyes clouded. Her *no* was even more quiet than her *yes*.

When Anders and Kate did the chores, she thought she heard another sleigh. Above the lowing of the cows, she listened, then decided she imagined it.

As they left the barn, the Milky Way lit a path through the sky. When Kate held out the lantern, she thought she saw something. Stopping, she set down her pail of milk.

Anders almost bumped into her. "What's the matter?"

Alongside the track, the wind had packed the snow into a drift. In the middle of the smooth whiteness, Kate saw letters, then words:

KEEP AWAY

Anders snorted. "Keep away? Keep away from what?"

But Kate felt afraid. As she held the lantern high, she saw more writing. Moving the lantern closer, she traced the words, letter by letter:

OR ELSE

"Or else what?" Anders scoffed.

"Keep away or else," read Kate, the fear within her growing. Suddenly she felt angry with Anders. "How can you laugh? Whoever wrote those words came through while we were in the barn. He came through *now*, during the day—"

"The night," Anders interrupted.

"But it's been dark only a short time. And in that time—"

"He came, wrote a message, and left," Anders finished for her.

"*If* he left," answered Kate. She looked over her shoulder to make sure no one stood behind her. Beyond the glow of the lantern, the shadows edged away into night.

Then the wind swept across the top of the bank, blowing new snow in her face. Kate stepped back. "Keep away from what?" she asked.

"From whatever we've been doing."

"I suppose." Kate thought about it for a moment. "Haven't been doing much, sitting in a house while it snowed. But this afternoon where did you go?"

"Across Rice Lake."

"And just before the blizzard, what did we do?"

It wasn't hard to remember. Kate answered her own question. "We found the milk can." Again she glanced over her shoulder. "*Keep away or else*. Or else *what*? What would he do?"

"What would he do?" her brother asked. "I can tell you."

In the light of the lantern Kate saw Anders grin.

"No, don't," she said quickly. "I don't think I want to hear."

"But you asked." His voice changed, sounding low and mysterious. "He'll creep up on you at night. As you walk from the house to the barn, he'll pounce on you!"

"Oh, *Anders!*" Kate clapped her hands over her ears. She refused to hear more. From now on she would dread the walk to the barn even more.

But she wasn't going to let Anders know. Not for anything would she let him know how she felt.

She returned to her pail of milk and picked it up. Flipping her braid over her shoulder, she walked to the farmhouse as though she didn't have a care in the world.

But when she reached the door, she saw the look in her brother's eyes. "After supper," she whispered. "We'll look for tracks after supper."

20

Snatched From the Fire

*F*or the first time in his life Anders helped Kate with supper dishes. Then they shrugged into their coats and went outside.

"Strange!" Anders said. "You're right. Whoever wrote that message had to come while we were in the barn."

Kate's fingers clenched with nervousness. "Maybe it's someone we know well."

"Someone we see every day without guessing he'd try to scare us," Anders said.

Holding out the lantern, Kate started across the yard. "When we were in the barn, I thought I heard something. But there weren't any sleigh bells."

Once again, whoever wrote the message seemed to have used a long pole. With the new covering of snow, it was easy to find the medium-sized boot prints Kate and Anders had seen before. Starting at the snowbank, they followed the prints along the plowed trail that passed the house.

Halfway to the barn, the boot prints suddenly vanished. Kate and Anders stood there, unable to believe what they were seeing.

"How can footsteps disappear in midair?" she asked.

"They can't," her brother answered. "But they have. See these prints beyond? They're entirely different."

Kate stared at them. "Different all right, but almost the same size!"

Holding the lantern close, Kate leaned down. "Look how the right boot turns, just slightly?" A step farther on, she pointed again. "And here the left boot twists a bit!"

Suddenly she laughed. "He stood there changing boots! See? From here on, a new set of prints!"

But in the next instant Kate's laughter died on her lips. "Who *is* this person? He knows we're watching him. He knows we'll try to follow." Tracking the man no longer seemed a game.

Anders took the farm lantern. "Just the same, let's see where his new boots take us."

Step by step they followed the prints to the water tank, then back to the trail. Near the tracks made by the runners of a sleigh, the boot prints vanished.

"Well, he's gone anyway." Kate felt relieved.

But Anders groaned. "We've lost him again! We're no better off than before. Worse, come to think of it."

"Worse?"

"We know how bold he is, coming into our yard again. We know how he plans, even bringing along an extra pair of boots. And he's doing everything he can to scare us off."

Kate shivered. "He's a dangerous man!" Then she remembered. "I didn't load wood in the tank heater." Earlier that winter she'd forgotten, and by morning the water turned into a block of ice.

Hurrying back to the water tank, she opened the lid of the stove. But the fire had gone out.

Kate groaned. Now she had to start all over again. Taking newspaper from the barn, she crumpled and lit it. As the flame caught, she lifted the stove lid.

In the light of the burning newspaper, Kate saw something. Reaching into the narrow pipe for loading wood, she pulled out a small piece of paper.

Then she felt heat on her hand. Quickly she dropped the burning newspaper in the snow.

"What're you doing?" asked Anders, clearly impatient.

As the newspaper turned into black flakes, then burned out, Kate spoke softly. "It's cold here. Let's go in the barn."

Once there she held the piece of white paper close to the lantern. The paper had caught in the pipe for loading wood.

The name of the person to whom the letter was addressed was charred and impossible to read. So, too, was the opening part of the letter. Kate read the remaining message aloud:

> *I opened your mail by accident. I found this check, made out to cash and sent by your old friend from New York. Are you still working with him to cheat people out of money? Are you being dishonest again? I had hoped your time in jail cured you of that weakness.*
>
> *I love you, my brother, but I plead with you. Send back the money while you can. Turn to honest work.*

Kate looked up. "It's signed 'Your sister,' and then the initial O."

Anders grinned. "This explains the missing checks from New York! The thief knows someone who writes the checks to him, instead of the Trade Lake Creamery. Whoever that person is sends the checks to the wrong address."

Kate thought about it. "With the slow mail service, it worked. That is, until his sister opened his mail."

"So all the thief has to do is go to his hometown and pick up his mail. If the checks from New York are made out to "cash," he can cash them anywhere. He'll get a lot more money than from the cream checks."

Slowly Kate folded the letter. "That's what I don't understand. When he'll get those big checks, why steal from the farmers? And why take the ledger?"

Anders shrugged. "I don't know. Maybe he's greedy. Or maybe he has a grudge, like Erik says. But I do know one thing. We have to go for help. Now. Tonight. Before he gets away."

Yet when they returned to the house, Mama was the one who needed help. "Will you stay with Lars for a bit?" she asked Kate. "He's sleeping, and I need to lie down. Anders, will you take care of Tina?"

Kate and Anders looked at each other. They both knew they couldn't leave.

In the bedroom Kate watched her younger brother sleep. She listened to his labored breathing.

Until recently, she'd paid little attention to Lars. Always she and Anders did things together. For the first time Kate wondered, *What was it like before I came? Has Lars been left out, because of me?*

He seldom complained about anything. Often Kate took him for granted, as though he were a younger copy of Anders. Lars's illness forced her to notice him as a person. She liked what she saw.

Now he lay limp, as though his body had no strength left. Beneath the freckles, his skin seemed flushed.

Kate reached over, felt his forehead. It was hot, too hot. Lars was burning up with fever.

A pang of fear shot through Kate—a fear so strong that she trembled. Even this morning, she could push fear to the back of her mind. No longer could she do that.

Will Lars die? The thought filled her with panic.

Going to the washstand, Kate dipped a cloth in cold water. Wringing it out, she placed it on Lars's forehead. Then she wet his face and arms with another cool cloth.

The nine-year-old stirred and opened eyes that were too bright. He seemed dazed, as though wondering where he was.

"Papa!" he cried out. "Papa, I see the horses!"

Kate leaned forward. "Papa isn't here right now."

Lars paid no attention. "Papa! I see the horses. See them down by the lake? They're thirsty. I'm thirsty too."

Hurrying out of the room, Kate called, "Mama!"

In the kitchen, Kate took the dipper and filled a glass with water from the covered pail. Returning to Lars, she held the glass to his lips. After one swallow he pushed it aside.

"Papa, I want to go swimming—"

His words became a mumble Kate couldn't understand. She looked up to see Mama at the door. Behind her stood Anders, and next to him, Tina.

"Papa, the water—" Lars's words were clear again. "It's so cool—"

"He's out of his head," said Mama. "He doesn't know what he's saying." She walked to the washstand and dipped another cloth in the water.

Lars's eyes glazed with fever. As he looked up into Kate's face, his vision seemed to clear.

"Kate?" he asked, his voice weak. "Kate, are you scared?"

"Scared, Lars? What do you mean?"

"Don't be scared, Kate. You don't have to be scared. The angels are all around us."

Quick tears flooded Kate's eyes. *Is he dying?* she wondered. Her knees felt weak, as though they would no longer hold her up.

Then Anders stood beside her. For the second time in two days he took Kate's hand. He seemed to sense she needed it. With his free hand he reached out to his brother.

"Lars," Anders said, his voice gruff. "You're right. We can't see the angels the way you do. But they *are* all around us."

Blinking away the tears in her eyes, Kate looked up at Anders. Somehow he always surprised her.

"Jesus is here too," said Mama, coming to stand on Kate's other side. "Jesus loves you, Lars."

"I know." His voice was weak.

"And we love you." Mama and Kate spoke almost together.

"I know." Lars's voice was weaker yet. He closed his eyes and lay still, his face pale against the pillowcase.

Kate barely breathed. "Is he—"

Mama shook her head. "No." She led them into the kitchen. "You must go for Dr. Jonas."

Kate's heart pounded against her chest. The doctor lived miles away, beyond the village of Trade Lake.

"Tell him it's an emergency," urged Mama. "That Lars is very sick. I hope we're not too late."

Anders met Mama's eyes, but Kate saw her suffering and looked away.

Anders scribbled on a piece of paper. Tucking the message inside the small bag Kate had made, he fastened it to a rope.

Hurrying to the door, he shouted. When Lutfisk came, Anders tied the rope around the dog's neck.

Opening the door again, Anders went out on the step. "Go get Erik!" he said.

Lutfisk barked.

Anders pointed across the field. "Erik!" he commanded.

With another bark, the dog streaked away into the night.

21

Ride Into Fear

*K*ate's fingers fumbled with haste as she pulled on her warmest clothing. When she and Anders were ready to leave, Mama put one hand on Kate's shoulder, the other on Anders's. "God will go with you," she said.

As Anders and Kate hurried outside, she saw the thermometer. "Almost forty below," she told Anders. "It'll be even worse by morning."

In the barn they worked together to harness Wildfire.

"What did you tell Erik?" Kate asked.

"To meet us at the fork in the trail." Anders moved toward the door. "I'll get the cutter."

When Kate brought Wildfire outside, Anders backed the mare between the shafts of the small sleigh. Kate put in heavy blankets, then wrapped her long scarf around her face.

As they settled themselves in the cutter, Anders called out, "Giddyup!" Wildfire pranced across the yard, her black tail swishing. At the bottom of the steep hill, her long legs reached out. She seemed to sense their need to hurry.

When they came to the fork in the trail, Erik jumped into the cutter. Lutfisk was with him and bounded alongside.

"What's wrong?" Erik asked.

"Lars is really sick," said Kate. She felt like crying just talking about it. "We have to go for the doctor."

"What happened?"

"His temperature shot up. He was talking strange—out of his head. Mama's says it's an emergency."

Soon they crossed Rice Lake. As they turned south toward the village of Trade Lake, they found the road packed into a smooth trail. The moon edged above the horizon, orange and round.

Inside her wool mittens Kate wiggled her fingers. Already they tingled with cold. She thrust her hands beneath the heavy blanket.

Fear settled like a knot deep inside. "What if Lars dies?" she asked.

The question hung between them, seeming even colder than the January air. Then Anders flicked the reins and urged Wildfire on. "It'd be pretty awful."

Under the full moon Kate saw the scarf had slipped from her brother's face. A tear shone on his cheek.

It startled Kate. She remembered only once when she'd seen tears in her brother's eyes. Then he'd been badly hurt. Even in these last days with Papa out in the storm, Anders seldom spoke about his worry.

Now he pulled the scarf across his face. Kate wondered if he was trying to hide his feelings.

The creamery was dark when they passed through the center of town. As they crossed Trade River, the mare's hooves thundered on the wooden bridge.

"I sure hope Doc is home," said Anders.

Neither Erik nor Kate answered. For many miles around there was no one else who could help.

When they reached the doctor's house, a kerosene lamp glowed through the window. Throwing the reins into Kate's lap, Anders jumped down. Erik ran for the stable. By the time Doc Jonas hurried out with his black bag, Erik had the horse ready.

With a wave of the hand, the doctor flung himself into the saddle. Digging in his heels, he broke into a gallop.

Anders followed at a slower pace with Wildfire and the cutter.

"Will Doc Jonas get there in time?" Kate asked.

"I don't know." Anders spoke so low that Kate could barely hear. "But we've done our best."

As they passed back through the village of Trade Lake, Wildfire slowed down, as if by habit. Just then Kate caught a faint glow through a creamery window.

"Stop," she said to Anders, close to his ear. "There's someone there."

"I can't stop here," Anders whispered back. "By now he's heard Wildfire."

Rounding the corner by the creamery, they started up the hill. A safe distance away, Anders pulled Wildfire to a halt. Jumping out, he tied the mare's lead rope to a tree.

The three crept back to the creamery. At the window where they'd seen the light, they peered in. The small glow of a flickering candle broke the darkness.

A man wearing a red and black mackinaw leaned over the buttermaker's desk. As he looked through papers, he held each one to the light.

"Who is it?" Kate whispered. With his back turned to them and a cap covering his hair, it was impossible to tell.

Anders shushed Kate and motioned to her and Erik. Careful to walk in soft snow that left no sound, the three edged back from the window.

When far enough away not to be heard, Kate spoke again. "Who is it? Mr. Grimm or Mr. Fenton? From the back they both look the same."

Erik shook his head, and Anders shrugged. "We have to go for help," he said.

Together they agreed that they needed more than one grown-up.

"I'll tell Mr. Bloomquist," Kate said. She knew where he lived.

"He left today for the buttermaker's convention," Erik told her. "At least he was supposed to."

"I'll go for Andrew Anderson," said Anders.

In that moment Kate remembered what Big Gust told them. "Let's ask Reverend Pickle too."

"You get him, Kate," Anders said. "Take Wildfire. You've got the farthest to go."

Kate's stomach tightened. She hadn't handled Wildfire since before Christmas, and then only a few times. Could she remember how?

But Anders took it for granted that she would. Quickly he gave directions to Reverend Pickle's house.

"I'll stay here," said Erik. "If the man leaves before you get back, I'll follow him." Quietly he edged away, back toward the creamery.

Anders and Kate hurried to the cutter. "Remember what you do?" he asked.

Kate nodded. Often she'd watched Anders. Just the same, she wondered if she could manage the spirited horse.

"Don't slow down when you pass the creamery," Anders warned. "Keep going as if you don't see anything." Then he, too, slipped off into the night, heading north to Andrew Anderson's farm.

Kate called "Giddyup!" and Wildfire turned her head, as though hearing Kate's uncertainty. Just the same, the mare obeyed. At the top of Mission Hill Kate turned around, directing Wildfire south, back over the way they'd come.

As she neared the creamery, she saw Erik crouched outside a window. Like a shadow he edged away, dark along the wall.

Kate glanced toward the window. The candle still burned. The man was nowhere in sight.

Where is he? thought Kate. *Did he hear Wildfire coming? Or did he see Erik?* If the man went out a back door, he could creep around the building, catching the boy.

I should warn Erik, Kate told herself and slowed the mare.

Then she remembered her brother's words. "Keep going. Don't stop at the creamery."

Kate flicked the reins. Wildfire's hooves pounded across the bridge.

The full moon rode high, lighting the snow as if it were day. Reverend Pickle's farm bordered on two lakes. "You'll know it," Anders said. "There's an artesian well in his front yard."

An artesian well? Kate knew such a well was one where water

flowed to the surface under its own pressure. But how would it look? She should have asked Anders.

In the next moment Kate forgot her question. As she passed into the woods, the trees cast long shadows.

Kate slid to the center of the seat, as far from the trees as possible. Yet the branches reached out, dark and threatening.

At Four Corners, she turned Wildfire. Here in an area with fewer trees, drifts were again filling the packed-down road. As Wildfire lunged into them, snow sprayed up. More than once the mare slowed her pace, fighting her way through.

Soon the way again led between trees. As Kate turned the mare onto another road, the woods seemed alive. Like pointing fingers, long pine branches reached out. Then an owl screeched, shattering the night air.

Kate trembled. "I can't do it!" she cried out to the darkness. "I'm going back!" The wind caught her words and flung them into her face.

She reined in Wildfire, then remembered Lars. Had the doctor reached him by now? Was Lars still fighting for life?

And where was Papa? Somewhere in this awful cold, struggling through drifts to reach home?

And her brother Anders? Scaredy-cat, he calls me! Usually Kate feared small, imaginary things. Now she faced something real. No doubt the thief would leave the area tonight.

Fighting down panic, Kate clucked to Wildfire, urging her on. A short distance away, she saw a farm with what must be an artesian well. In spite of the cold, water gushed from a pipe, spilling down a slope to create a pathway of ice.

I was so close, thought Kate. *What if I had turned back?*

Leaving Wildfire at a rail, she hurried up the steps and pounded on the door. A moment later a woman with gray hair invited Kate inside.

"Mrs. Pickle?" she asked. "Is Reverend Pickle here? We need his help."

"I'm sorry," the woman answered. "He was called out an hour ago. Is there something I can do?"

Unable to believe such bad news, Kate stared at her. "I came so far. He's really not here?"

Just then a heavyset man passed through the hallway behind the woman. The man wore a red and black mackinaw.

Without thinking, Kate fled from the house. Leaping into the cutter, she flicked the reins across Wildfire's back. The mare headed back over the same road.

When Kate came to her senses, she pulled off a mitten. Quickly she felt her scarf to be sure her ears, nose, and cheeks were covered. If not, they would soon be too numb for her to know. Within a minute she'd suffer frostbite.

Gazing through the narrow slits for her eyes, Kate directed Wildfire. Soon she let the mare find her way home. That way led where Kate wanted to go—through the village of Trade Lake.

Once again trees closed around her, and her fear returned. Who was the man in the hallway? Gunnar Grimm? Too late she remembered him saying that he stayed with Reverend Pickle.

Was he also the man who entered Josie's house? And the man who looked through papers at the creamery? If he slipped out while they talked, he could have reached Pickle's farm before Kate.

Where was that man now? Somewhere behind, coming after her, trying to catch up?

"I'm all alone on this cold dark road," Kate muttered. From behind any tree someone could step out and leap into the cutter.

Kate shivered with fear. Before long, that shivering changed into a trembling that would not stop. But then she felt ashamed. *What am I doing, feeling sorry for myself when Lars might be dying?*

"God will go with you," Mama had said. Her words seemed an echo of Papa's letter.

"Fear thou not, for I am with thee," Kate told herself now, repeating God's promise. "Be not dismayed; for I am thy God."

Over and over she said the words, clinging to them like life itself. "I will strengthen thee; yea, I will help thee."

In that moment God's promise became more real than ever before. Kate felt sure of something. *No matter what happens, God is with me!*

The trees still reached out to clutch her. The road still seemed dark and lonely. But deep inside, Kate felt peaceful, unafraid.

When she reached the village of Trade Lake, she saw no light in the creamery. Nor was there light in any of the houses. Tightening the reins, she stopped Wildfire to give herself time to think.

Since leaving Erik and Anders, Kate had taken it for granted she'd find them again at the creamery. Yet no shadow emerged from between the buildings. Either one of the boys would have stepped out.

What do I do now? Kate wondered.

In that instant a question came to her mind. Where would the thief go when he left the creamery?

Only a desperate man would be out on a night like this. In such bitter cold, people stayed inside. That left the thief free to do whatever he wanted. If he planned to leave the area, he'd go to Rice Lake for the milk can. Erik would follow.

"Giddyup!" said Kate, and Wildfire moved out.

At the southwest corner of Rice Lake, Wildfire left the road, crossed the field, and entered the woods. Partway through the trees, she stopped.

Kate urged Wildfire on, but the mare tossed her head and would not move. "Oh, Anders," Kate grumbled. "You shouldn't have let me take this horse."

She flicked the reins, and the mare took one step forward, then another. Once more she stopped.

"Go ahead, Wildfire," said Kate, trying to sound as though she were boss.

The mare's ears turned to the sound of Kate's voice. Yet the horse would not move.

Climbing down from the cutter, Kate walked forward to take the bridle. In that moment she saw what the mare sensed. Shadows. Shadows moving among the trees.

Kate's heart pounded. Her fingers knotted in fear. Who was it? What was there?

Wildfire lifted her head as though to whinny. Quickly Kate reached up, touched the mare's muzzle and quieted her. When Wildfire stood still, Kate took the bells from the harness, muffling the sound.

"It's all right, girl," she whispered, wishing she could believe her own words. Moving back to the cutter, she pushed the bells under the blanket where they wouldn't jingle.

Returning to the mare, Kate grabbed hold of the bridle. Together they took one step forward, then another.

Off to the right a shadow moved. Kate froze. Who was it? Friend or enemy?

As she stood there, the shadow blended with the trunk of a tree. Like an enemy breathing on the back of her neck, fear again gripped Kate. She tried to push it aside, but couldn't.

Then there was something she knew, *Maybe what counts is doing the right thing, no matter how scared I am.*

Ahead lay Rice Lake and beyond that, Windy Hill Farm. Should she wait or go on?

As she felt the cold, Kate knew she had no choice. If she didn't keep moving, she'd die, standing there in the sub-zero cold.

Slowly she lifted one foot, then another, forcing herself ahead. "Fear thou not, for I am with thee." She repeated the words to herself. Drawing a deep breath, she took a third step.

Suddenly, from out of the darkness, someone stood behind her. Startled, Kate jumped. In the next instant, she felt a hand over her mouth, cutting off her cry.

22

Bone-Chilling Surprises

*G*asping, Kate struggled to free herself. The strong arm held her prisoner.

"Sorry, Kate," said a low voice.

She tried to swing around, but the person would not let her move. "Shhh!" he warned, again speaking softly.

In that instant Kate knew it was Erik. As she sagged with relief, he let her go.

"What do you mean, scaring me like that?" she asked in an angry whisper.

"Be quiet!" he warned again. "The thief is ahead. He built a fire on the ice."

Then Kate saw the flames. Even through the trees and bushes the light shone for some distance.

Taking Wildfire's bridle, Erik led the mare off the path to a sheltered spot. Tying her lead rope to a tree, he threw a horse blanket over her back.

"Where's Anders?" Kate whispered when Erik returned.

He pointed ahead. A short distance off to the right, a shadow left a tree, raised a hand, then stepped back close to the trunk.

"I couldn't get Reverend Pickle," she said.

Erik leaned close. "Andrew Anderson is here. I hope we're

enough." Again he pointed, this time off to the left.

At first Kate couldn't spot Mr. Anderson. Then with the help of the full moon, she saw a tree trunk that looked thicker at the bottom than it should.

Together Kate and Erik crept forward. Close to the shoreline they knelt down behind a bush and peered through its leafless branches. In front of them clumps of bent-over grass marked the boggy end of the lake. There was only one safe place to cross—the trail Anders and Erik had packed down.

From this distance the fire seemed small. Beyond the dancing flames, the branches of the tall oak reached upward.

Then, in the light of the fire, Kate saw a heavyset man in a black and red mackinaw. Holding out his mittened hands, the man warmed himself by the fire. Then he picked up an ice chisel and started chopping.

Kate breathed deep. No wonder Anders and Erik and Mr. Anderson waited, watching from the cover of trees.

In the bitter air, minutes seemed like hours as the man chopped a hole. Twice he stopped to warm himself, then returned to his work. Whenever he turned his back, Kate and Erik stamped their feet, trying to keep from freezing.

Finally the man knelt down next to the hole. Reaching into the water, he pulled out the milk can and set it on the ice. Just as quickly, he pulled off his wet gloves and replaced them with dry ones.

From this distance it looked as if a rope now held the stone, instead of a chain. Taking a tool from his pocket, the man cut the stone free and dropped it back into the water. Shouldering the milk can, he picked up his chisel and started toward them.

Andrew Anderson moved onto the path, then the lake. Anders and Erik followed, and with them, Kate. As they drew close to the man, Kate saw his sandy colored mustache and beard. LeRoy Fenton!

For one instant surprise and fear flickered across his face. Then a mask slid down. "Hello!" he said smoothly, as he came close. "Fancy seeing you here!"

In that moment Kate spotted something. On the underside of the man's raised arm, a tear in his mackinaw.

Bone-Chilling Surprises

Mr. Anderson stepped in front of him. "Just a minute. I have some questions for you."

"Certainly, certainly. Be glad to talk to you any time. But not in this cold. How about tomorrow at the creamery?"

"I want to talk now," said Mr. Anderson.

Instead, LeRoy Fenton started around the older man. Erik and Anders moved quickly. But just then a dark shape appeared on the path, running toward them. When the shape barked, Kate knew it was Lutfisk.

Within three feet of Fenton, the dog stopped and growled deep in his throat.

Mr. Fenton stepped sideways, but Lutfisk moved with him, baring his teeth.

The milk can still on his shoulder, LeRoy Fenton stopped. "Whose dog is this?" he asked, sounding less smooth than usual.

"He's mine," said Anders with pride in his voice.

"Well, call him off," he ordered.

"After you've talked to Mr. Anderson," Anders replied.

In that moment Fenton lifted his head, seeming to listen. Along the trail, boots squeaked on the packed snow. The steps moved closer, closer.

A minute later someone stepped onto the ice. A man in a black and red mackinaw. Kate's heart pounded. Gunnar Grimm! Was she right in believing he was innocent? Or were the two men partners?

Kate glanced at Mr. Anderson. He, too, stood waiting, watching.

Mr. Grimm faced LeRoy Fenton. "Mighty cold night to try leaving town."

The mask on Fenton's face seemed to crack, then break with anger. "What is this, an ice party?"

Mr. Grimm chuckled. "Nope! It's time for explanations. Why don't you tell them how you took the cream checks and ledger?"

"And how you had the New York checks sent to your hometown!" said Anders.

The milk can still on his shoulder, LeRoy Fenton turned to Mr. Anderson. "You know I'm trustworthy. Don't believe a word they say."

"But I do," answered Mr. Anderson.

Suddenly Fenton threw the ice chisel toward the dog. Backing away, he broke into a run. For one instant he glanced toward the wheat-colored grass, then veered from the boggy area. Changing direction, he headed for the southeastern shore.

Lutfisk started after him.

"Stay, Lutfisk!" Anders called.

The dog stopped and looked back, clearly not wanting to obey.

"Stay!" commanded Anders again. Lutfisk sat down on the ice and woofed.

"Stop, Fenton!" shouted Mr. Anderson. Across the end of the lake, the snow stretched out, clean and unbroken under the full moon.

As the distance widened between them, Kate felt sick. "He'll get away!"

"No, he won't," said Erik.

Then she remembered. The spring holes!

Again Mr. Anderson shouted. "Fenton! Stop! Don't go any farther!"

One hand still supporting the milk can, Mr. Fenton looked back. The next instant he wavered. The snow gave way, and the can fell from his shoulder.

"Help!" he cried as he slipped through the ice. His arms flailed in the cold water.

The others started toward him. Using the ice chisel, Anders tested each step before taking it. Erik and the men followed in his footprints.

"Get a blanket, Kate," said Erik. "But watch where you walk." Hurrying to the cutter, Kate pulled out a heavy blanket. By the time she returned, the men had Fenton out of the water and into clothing loaned by the others.

As LeRoy Fenton stood by the fire, he shook with cold. Mr. Anderson put the blanket around his shoulders.

"Are you a detective?" Kate asked Mr. Grimm when she joined them around the fire. "From New York, I bet."

When Mr. Grimm smiled, Kate remembered thinking he wasn't the grouch he seemed.

Bone-Chilling Surprises

"I was trying to solve a robbery in New York," he said. "All my leads pointed here. But I didn't know who the man was. You're the one who tipped me off."

"Me?" asked Kate. "How?"

"By being curious. You asked, 'How come everyone harvesting ice is new at it?' I've been watching Fenton ever since. Tonight I followed your cutter tracks here."

As the men started to lead LeRoy Fenton away, Kate faced him with a question. "Why did you put salt in the butter?"

"I'm a better buttermaker!" he said. "The job should have gone to me!" Then his mouth snapped shut, as though realizing he'd given himself away.

Standing at the fire with Anders and Erik, Kate spoke softly. "Mr. Fenton's the real grouch, not Mr. Grimm."

"Can you imagine?" Erik said. "Making all that trouble because of a grudge? What a way to get even!"

"Maybe he thought he'd still get the job," Anders said as he went for Wildfire.

When her brother returned, Kate climbed into the cutter. "The farmers will get paid!" she exclaimed.

"And the creamery will get its checks from New York," Erik said. He started to laugh. "Curious Kate! It doesn't take a detective to figure that out!"

Anders laughed, too, and Mr. Grimm's words seemed funny even to Kate. But now that the excitement was over, she could think of only one thing. "I wonder what's happened to Lars."

When they reached Windy Hill Farm, Erik told Anders, "I'll put Wildfire in the barn."

When Kate and Anders entered the kitchen, it was quiet. *Too* quiet, Kate thought.

A tall bearded man stood by the cookstove. Was it the doctor?

The man turned. His lips were cracked, his skin reddened by wind and cold. The heavily bearded man seemed a stranger.

Then Kate cried, "Papa!"

He opened his arms, and she walked into them. She felt his bear hug, then heard the emotion in his voice. "Kate! My newest daughter!"

When she stood back, she saw the relief in Anders's face. He tried to speak, but no words came. When he reached out to shake his father's hand, Papa put his arms around him.

Then Mama stood at the door to the dining room.

"Lars?" Kate and Anders asked together.

"He's better," Mama answered softly, her eyes as blue as the new dress she wore. "The doctor says Lars passed the crisis. He'll be all right."

Throwing off their coats, Kate and Anders tiptoed into the bedroom.

Lars lay with his eyes closed, his face pale against the pillow. His red hair was matted, twisted every which way, but his skin no longer seemed flushed with fever.

As they stood there, Lars opened his eyes. A slight smile came to his lips. Then he drifted back to sleep.

Swallowing around the lump in her throat, Kate looked at Anders.

One tear slid down his cheek, then another. When he saw Kate watching, he brushed the tears away, but did not seem ashamed.

Returning to the kitchen, Kate and Anders found Erik there. As they gathered near the warmth of the cookstove, Papa put his arm around Mama's shoulders.

Kate's heart leaped. "You're really home!" she said to Papa. "Now spring will come!"

Anders grinned. "With maple syrup—and logs floating down the rivers."

"And another mystery, I suppose." Erik winked at Kate.

"Maybe we'll find out what happened to Mama's brother," Kate said, then wished she hadn't spoken.

But tonight not even the thought of Ben could destroy Mama's happiness. In the lamplight a golden curl dropped over her forehead. She slipped a hand inside Papa's, and her lips curved in a smile.

As the heat of the stove reached Kate's fingers, another warmth crept into her heart. She looked around, needing to see those she loved. Mama, Papa, Anders. And upstairs in bed, Tina. In the next room, Lars. *My family!* thought Kate.

Then Erik moved closer to the stove. Kate saw the relief in

his eyes. She had another person she could trust. *My special friend!*

Within the warmth of that circle, spring had already entered the room.

Acknowledgments

"Aw, come on now!" you might be thinking if you live in a warm and sunny climate. "Thirty-three and forty degrees below zero?"

Yes, that's right. Now and then—not often, of course—even those of us who live in northwest Wisconsin complain about the weather. Other times we feel almost proud to be survivors. And so, I assure you, the temperatures given in this book were actually recorded in a 1907 issue of the newspaper, *Journal of Burnett County*.

In spite of the hazards or because of them, those who live in this area are a warm and helpful people. I offer my heartfelt thanks to those who described the early Trade Lake area for me: Imogene Erickson, Emma Bergstrom Haight, Robert and Jean Hinrichs, Clare and Dorothy Melin, and Pharis and Kathryn Stower.

Others gave needed information or special help at just the right time: Robert Anderson, Alice and Leon Biederman, Diane Brask, Wade Brask, Alwin and Imogene Christopherson, Betty Coleman, Maurice and Arleth Erickson, Alton Jensen, Dick and Lois Klawitter, Randy and Renee Klawitter, Henry Peterson, Elaine Roub, Helen Tyberg, and my parents, Alvar and Lydia Walfrid.

Walter and Ella Johnson offered unique wisdom in a variety

of ways, including the fine art of bartering, how to harvest and store ice, and the mysterious uses of milk cans and butter tubs.

Mildred Hedlund helped me with Big Gust, as did Eunice Kanne and her book, *Big Gust: Grantsburg's Legendary Giant*. I'm also grateful to J. C. Ryan for his book, *Early Loggers in Minnesota*, the Grantsburg Historical Society, and all the librarians at the Grantsburg Public Library.

Dale Olson, world champion cheesemaker for the Burnett County Dairy, Alpha, Wisconsin, helped me begin my search for information about creameries. A father and son team, John D. Wuethrich and Dallas Wuethrich, of the John Wuethrich Creamery at Greenwood, Wisconsin, showed me the contrast between buttermaking in the early part of the century and the automated, up-to-date methods now used.

Once again, my husband Roy offered ideas, encouragement, and love. Jerry Foley, Penelope Stokes, and Terry White gave suggestions for the manuscript. Charette Barta, Doris Holmlund, Ron Klug, and the entire Bethany team gave valuable editorial assistance.

Finally, I want to give my thanks to you, the readers of this series. Sometimes you read these books by yourself, tucked away in a quiet spot. Other times you read aloud as a family, a community group or classroom. Whichever way you follow Kate and Anders in the Adventures of the Northwoods, you encourage me by saying, "I've read all of 'em. When's the next book coming out?"